The
MX Book
of
New
Sherlock
Holmes
Stories

Part L
The True Sherlock Holmes:
England's Greatest Hero
(1889-1896)

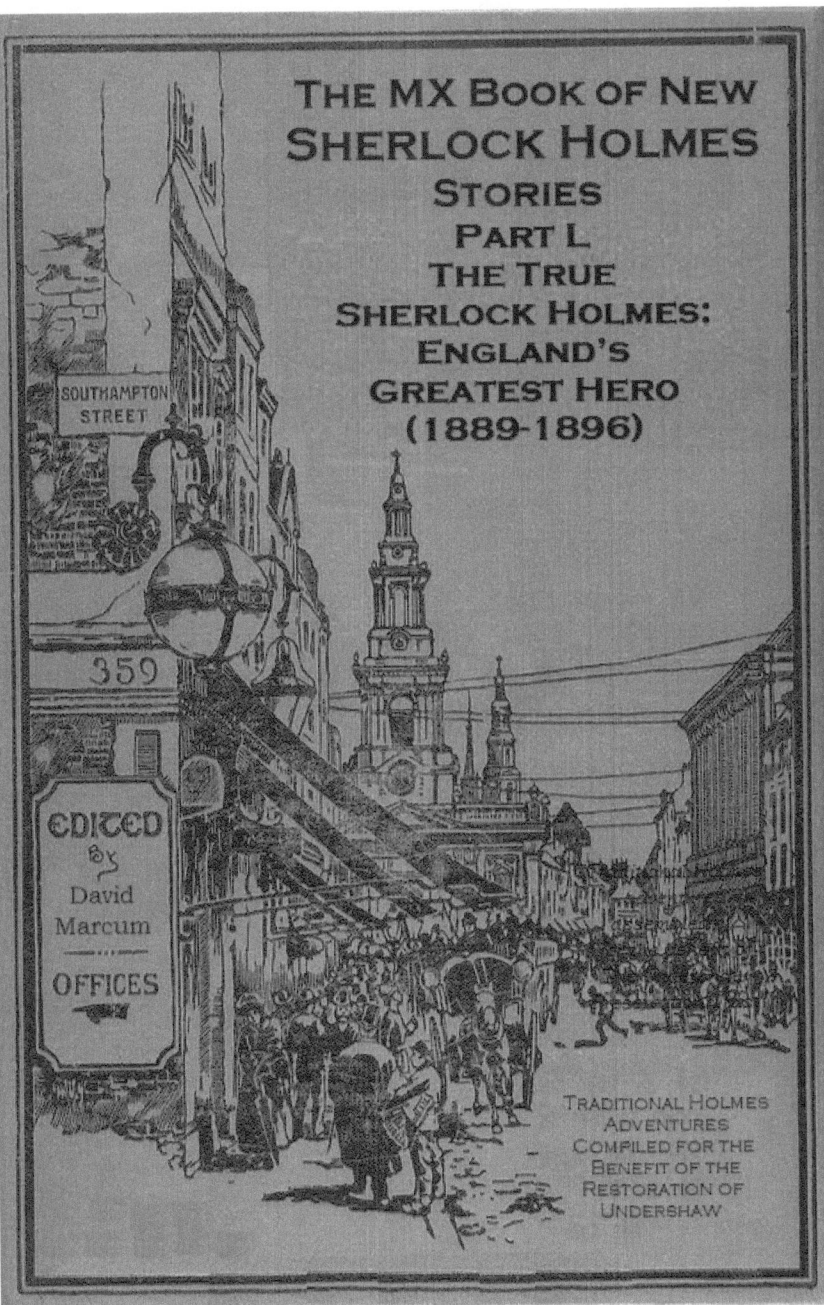

THE MX BOOK OF NEW
SHERLOCK HOLMES
STORIES
PART L
THE TRUE
SHERLOCK HOLMES:
ENGLAND'S
GREATEST HERO
(1889-1896)

SOUTHAMPTON
STREET

359

EDITED
By
David
Marcum

OFFICES

TRADITIONAL HOLMES
ADVENTURES
COMPILED FOR THE
BENEFIT OF THE
RESTORATION OF
UNDERSHAW

ISBN Hardback 978-1-80424-687-0
ISBN Paperback 978-1-80424-688-7
AUK ePub ISBN 978-1-80424-689-4
AUK PDF ISBN 978-1-80424-690-0

Published in the UK by
MX Publishing
335 Princess Park Manor, Royal Drive,
London, N11 3GX
www.mxpublishing.co.uk

David Marcum can be reached at:
thepapersofsherlockholmes@gmail.com

Cover design by Brian Belanger
www.belangerbooks.com and *www.redbubble.com/people/zhahadun*

Internal Illustrations by Sidney Paget

CONTENTS

Forewords

Adventures

(Continued on the next page . . . .)

(Continued on the next page . . . .)

These additional adventures are contained in

(Continued on the next page . . . .)

Part LII – The True Sherlock Holmes:
England's Greatest Hero (1902-1923)

(Continued on the next page . . . .)

The MX Book of New Sherlock Holmes Stories
Parts I – LII (2015-2025) contain the following:

(Continued on the next page . . . .)

PART III: 1896-1929

PART IV – 2016 Annual

(Continued on the next page . . . .)

PART V – Christmas Adventures

(Continued on the next page . . . .)

(Continued on the next page . . . .)

(Continued on the next page . . . .)

(Continued on the next page . . . .)

The Lambeth Poisoner Case – Stephen Gaspar
The Confession of Anna Jarrow – S. F. Bennett
The Adventure of the Disappearing Dictionary – Sonia Fetherston
The Fairy Hills Horror – Geri Schear
A Loathsome and Remarkable Adventure – Marcia Wilson
The Adventure of the Multiple Moriartys – David Friend
The Influence Machine – Mark Mower

Part X – 2018 Annual (1896-1916)

Foreword – Nicholas Meyer
Foreword – Roger Johnson
Foreword – Melissa Farnham
Foreword – Steve Emecz
Foreword – David Marcum
A Man of Twice Exceptions (A Poem) – Derrick Belanger
The Horned God – Kelvin Jones
The Coughing Man – Jim French
The Adventure of Canal Reach – Arthur Hall
A Simple Case of Abduction – Mike Hogan
A Case of Embezzlement – Steven Ehrman
The Adventure of the Vanishing Diplomat – Greg Hatcher
The Adventure of the Perfidious Partner – Jayantika Ganguly
A Brush With Death – Dick Gillman
A Revenge Served Cold – Maurice Barkley
The Case of the Anonymous Client – Paul A. Freeman
Capitol Murder – Daniel D. Victor
The Case of the Dead Detective – Martin Rosenstock
The Musician Who Spoke From the Grave – Peter Coe Verbica
The Adventure of the Future Funeral – Hugh Ashton
The Problem of the Bruised Tongues – Will Murray
The Mystery of the Change of Art – Robert Perret
The Parsimonious Peacekeeper – Thaddeus Tuffentsamer
The Case of the Dirty Hand – G.L. Schulze
The Mystery of the Missing Artefacts – Tim Symonds

Part XI: Some Untold Cases (1880-1891)

Foreword – Lyndsay Faye
Foreword – Roger Johnson
Foreword – Melissa Grigsby
Foreword – Steve Emecz
Foreword – David Marcum
Unrecorded Holmes Cases (*A Sonnet*) – Arlene Mantin Levy and Mark Levy
The Most Repellant Man – Jayantika Ganguly
The Singular Adventure of the Extinguished Wicks – Will Murray
Mrs. Forrester's Complication – Roger Riccard
The Adventure of Vittoria, the Circus Belle – Tracy Revels

(Continued on the next page . . . .)

Part XII: Some Untold Cases (1894-1902)

PART XIII: 2019 Annual (1881-1890)

(Continued on the next page . . . .)

PART XIV: 2019 Annual (1891 -1897)

(Continued on the next page . . . .)

(Continued on the next page . . . .)

The Adventure of the Headless Lady – Tracy J. Revels
Angelus Domini Nuntiavit – Kevin P. Thornton
The Blue Lady of Dunraven – Andrew Bryant
The Adventure of the Ghoulish Grenadier – Josh Anderson and David Friend
The Curse of Barcombe Keep – Brenda Seabrooke
The Affair of the Regressive Man – David Marcum
The Adventure of the Giant's Wife – I.A. Watson
The Adventure of Miss Anna Truegrace – Arthur Hall
The Haunting of Bottomly's Grandmother – Tim Gambrell
The Adventure of the Intrusive Spirit – Shane Simmons
The Paddington Poltergeist – Bob Bishop
The Spectral Pterosaur – Mark Mower
The Weird of Caxton – Kelvin Jones
The Adventure of the Obsessive Ghost – Jayantika Ganguly

Part XVII – Whatever Remains . . . Must Be the Truth (1891-1898)
Foreword – Kareem Abdul-Jabbar
Foreword – Roger Johnson
Foreword – Steve Emecz
Foreword – David Marcum
The Violin Thief (*A Poem*) – Christopher James
The Spectre of Scarborough Castle – Charles Veley and Anna Elliott
The Case for Which the World is Not Yet Prepared – Steven Philip Jones
The Adventure of the Returning Spirit – Arthur Hall
The Adventure of the Bewitched Tenant – Michael Mallory
The Misadventures of the Bonnie Boy – Will Murray
The Adventure of the *Danse Macabre* – Paul D. Gilbert
The Strange Persecution of John Vincent Harden – S. Subramanian
The Dead Quiet Library – Roger Riccard
The Adventure of the Sugar Merchant – Stephen Herczeg
The Adventure of the Undertaker's Fetch – Tracy J. Revels
The Holloway Ghosts – Hugh Ashton
The Diogenes Club Poltergeist – Chris Chan
The Madness of Colonel Warburton – Bert Coules
The Return of the Noble Bachelor – Jane Rubino
The Reappearance of Mr. James Phillimore – David Marcum
The Miracle Worker – Geri Schear
The Hand of Mesmer – Dick Gillman

Part XVIII – Whatever Remains . . . Must Be the Truth (1899-1925)
Foreword – Kareem Abdul-Jabbar
Foreword – Roger Johnson
Foreword – Steve Emecz
Foreword – David Marcum
The Adventure of the Lighthouse on the Moor (*A Poem*) – Christopher James
The Witch of Ellenby – Thomas A. Burns, Jr.

(Continued on the next page . . . .)

Part XIX: 2020 Annual (1882-1890)

(Continued on the next page . . . .)

The Adventure of the Matched Set – Peter Coe Verbica
When the Prince First Dined at the Diogenes Club – Sean M. Wright
The Sweetenbury Safe Affair – Tim Gambrell

Part XX: 2020 Annual (1891-1897)
Foreword – John Lescroart
Foreword – Roger Johnson
Foreword – Lizzy Butler
Foreword – Steve Emecz
Foreword – David Marcum
The Sibling (*A Poem*) – Jacquelynn Morris
Blood and Gunpowder – Thomas A. Burns, Jr.
The Atelier of Death – Harry DeMaio
The Adventure of the Beauty Trap – Tracy Revels
A Case of Unfinished Business – Steven Philip Jones
The Case of the S.S. Bokhara – Mark Mower
The Adventure of the American Opera Singer – Deanna Baran
The Keadby Cross – David Marcum
The Adventure at Dead Man's Hole – Stephen Herczeg
The Elusive Mr. Chester – Arthur Hall
The Adventure of Old Black Duffel – Will Murray
The Blood-Spattered Bridge – Gayle Lange Puhl
The Tomorrow Man – S.F. Bennett
The Sweet Science of Bruising – Kevin P. Thornton
The Mystery of Sherlock Holmes – Christopher Todd
The Elusive Mr. Phillimore – Matthew J. Elliott
The Murders in the Maharajah's Railway Carriage – Charles Veley and Anna Elliott
The Ransomed Miracle – I.A. Watson
The Adventure of the Unkind Turn – Robert Perret
The Perplexing X'ing – Sonia Fetherston
The Case of the Short-Sighted Clown – Susan Knight

Part XXI: 2020 Annual (1898-1923)
Foreword – John Lescroart
Foreword – Roger Johnson
Foreword – Lizzy Butler
Foreword – Steve Emecz
Foreword – David Marcum
The Case of the Missing Rhyme (*A Poem*) – Joseph W. Svec III
The Problem of the St. Francis Parish Robbery – R.K. Radek
The Adventure of the Grand Vizier – Arthur Hall
The Mummy's Curse – DJ Tyrer
The Fractured Freemason of Fitzrovia – David L. Leal
The Bleeding Heart – Paula Hammond
The Secret Admirer – Jayantika Ganguly

(Continued on the next page . . . .)

Part XXII: Some More Untold Cases (1877-1887)

(Continued on the next page . . . .)

Part XXIII: Some More Untold Cases (1888-1894)

Part XXIV: Some More Untold Cases (1895-1903)

(Continued on the next page . . . .)

The Tragedy of Woodman's Lee – Tracy J. Revels
The Murdered Millionaire – Kevin P. Thornton
Another Case of Identity – Thomas A. Burns, Jr.
The Case of Indelible Evidence – Dick Gillman
The Adventure of Parsley and Butter – Jayantika Ganguly
The Adventure of the Nile Traveler – John Davis
The Curious Case of the Crusader's Cross – DJ Tyer
An Act of Faith – Harry DeMaio
The Adventure of the Conk-Singleton Forgery – Arthur Hall
A Simple Matter – Susan Knight
The Hammerford Will Business – David Marcum
The Adventure of Mr. Fairdale Hobbs – Arthur Hall
The Adventure of the Abergavenny Murder – Craig Stephen Copland
The Chinese Puzzle Box – Gayle Lange Puhl
The Adventure of the Refused Knighthood – Craig Stephen Copland
The Case of the Consulting Physician – John Lawrence
The Man from Deptford – John Linwood Grant
The Case of the Impossible Assassin – Paula Hammond

Part XXV: 2021 Annual (1881-1888)
Foreword – Peter Lovesey
Foreword – Roger Johnson
Foreword – Steve Emecz
Foreword – Jacqueline Silver
Foreword – David Marcum
Baskerville Hall (*A Poem*) – Kelvin I. Jones
The Persian Slipper – Brenda Seabrooke
The Adventure of the Doll Maker's Daughter – Matthew White
The Flinders Case – Kevin McCann
The Sunderland Tragedies – David Marcum
The Tin Soldiers – Paul Hiscock
The Shattered Man – MJH Simmonds
The Hungarian Doctor – Denis O. Smith
The Black Hole of Berlin – Robert Stapleton
The Thirteenth Step – Keith Hann
The Missing Murderer – Marcia Wilson
Dial Square – Martin Daley
The Adventure of the Deadly Tradition – Matthew J. Elliott
The Adventure of the Fabricated Vision – Craig Janacek
The Adventure of the Murdered Maharajah – Hugh Ashton
The God of War – Hal Glatzer
The Atkinson Brothers of Trincomalee – Stephen Gaspar

(Continued on the next page . . . .)

(Continued on the next page . . . .)

Part XXVIII: More Christmas Adventures (1869-1888)

(Continued on the next page . . . .)

Part XXIX: More Christmas Adventures (1889-1896)

Part XXX: More Christmas Adventures (1897-1928)

(Continued on the next page . . . .)

The Adventure of the Chained Phantom – J.S. Rowlinson
Santa's Little Elves – Kevin Thornton
The Case of the Holly-Sprig Pudding – Naching T. Kassa
The Canterbury Manifesto – David Marcum
The Case of the Disappearing Beaune – J. Lawrence Matthews
A Price Above Rubies – Jane Rubino
The Intrigue of the Red Christmas – Shane Simmons
The Bitter Gravestones – Chris Chan
The Midnight Mass Murder – Paul Hiscock

Part XXXI: 2022 Annual (1875-1887)
Foreword – Jeffrey Hatcher
Foreword – Roger Johnson
Foreword – Steve Emecz
Foreword – Emma West
Foreword – David Marcum
The Nemesis of Sherlock Holmes (A Poem) – Kelvin I. Jones
The Unsettling Incident of the History Professor's Wife – Sean M. Wright
The Princess Alice Tragedy – John Lawrence
The Adventure of the Amorous Balloonist – I.A. Watson
The Pilkington Case – Kevin Patrick McCann
The Adventure of the Disappointed Lover – Arthur Hall
The Case of the Impressionist Painting – Tim Symonds
The Adventure of the Old Explorer – Tracy J. Revels
Dr. Watson's Dilemma – Susan Knight
The Colonial Exhibition – Hal Glatzer
The Adventure of the Drunken Teetotaler – Thomas A. Burns, Jr.
The Curse of Hollyhock House – Geri Schear
The Sethian Messiah – David Marcum
Dead Man's Hand – Robert Stapleton
The Case of the Wary Maid – Gordon Linzner
The Adventure of the Alexandrian Scroll – David MacGregor
The Case of the Woman at Margate – Terry Golledge
A Question of Innocence – DJ Tyrer
The Grosvenor Square Furniture Van – Terry Golledge
The Adventure of the Veiled Man – Tracy J. Revels
The Disappearance of Dr. Markey – Stephen Herczeg
The Case of the Irish Demonstration – Dan Rowley

Part XXXII: 2022 Annual (1888-1895)
Foreword – Jeffrey Hatcher
Foreword – Roger Johnson
Foreword – Steve Emecz

(Continued on the next page . . . .)

Part XXXIII: 2022 Annual (1896-1919)

(Continued on the next page . . . .)

(Continued on the next page . . . .)

Part XXXVI: "However Improbable . . . ." (1897-1919)

(Continued on the next page . . . .)

(Continued on the next page . . . .)

Part XXXIX: 2023 Annual (1897-1923)

Part XL: Further Untold Cases (1879-1886)

(Continued on the next page . . . .)

Part XLI: Further Untold Cases (1877-1892)

Part XLII: Further Untold Cases (1894-1922)

(Continued on the next page . . . .)

Part XLIII: 2024 Annual (1874-1888)

(Continued on the next page . . . .)

(Continued on the next page . . . .)

Part XLVI: Occupants of the Canonical Realm (1861-1889)

(Continued on the next page . . . .)

Part XLVII: Occupants of the Canonical Realm (1890-1898)

Part XLVIII: Occupants of the Canonical Realm (1899-1924)

(Continued on the next page . . . .)

Part XLIX: The True Mr. Sherlock Holmes –
England's Greatest Hero (1880-1888)

Part L: The True Mr. Sherlock Holmes –
England's Greatest Hero (1889-1996)

(Continued on the next page . . . .)

Part LI: The True Mr. Sherlock Holmes – England's Greatest Hero (1897-1901)

(Continued on the next page . . . .)

Part LII: The True Mr. Sherlock Holmes –
England's Greatest Hero (1902-1923)

A Thousand Cunning Windings
by David Marcum

". . . a thousand cunning windings . . . ." So said Mr. Sherlock Holmes in "The Final Problem" to describe the path he traced when cornering Professor James Moriarty. But that phrase can also apply to over one-thousand brilliant Holmes adventures in *The MX Book of New Sherlock Holmes Stories*, now finishing at fifty-two massive volumes . . . .

K now this from *The Gospel* of The Church of the Traditional Canonical Sherlock Holmes:

"In the beginning was The Canon, and it was good.
But it was not enough."

– *The Book of Holmes*, (Chapter I, Verses 1-2)

And if that isn't clear enough, Verses 3 and 4 continue:

"Verily, verily, I say unto thee: There have
NEVER been enough traditional and
Canonical Holmes adventures.
There NEVER will be."

And as Dickens wrote, *"This must be distinctly understood, or nothing wonderful can come of the story I am going to relate."*

The initial original Canonical (and pitifully few) Sixty Tales were just the merest glimpse into the long lives of Sherlock Holmes and Dr. John H. Watson. Those Canonical adventures served as the main structural fibers of *The Great Holmes Tapestry*, but there were so many empty spaces in between that needed filling in order to reveal a full and vivid image. This is accomplished by way of post-Canonical adventures called *pastiches.*

The Canon relates sixty events across a period from 1874 ("The Gloria Scott") to 1914 ("His Last Bow") – from when Sherlock Holmes was twenty years old to when he was sixty. Forty years. But consider that most of those cases just take a day or so, or sometimes only a few hours. Forty years is approximately 14,600 days, and yet the total on-page narrative of most of the Canonical cases, when tallied, equals around six

1

months – three days here, two here, and approximately one month for *The Hound*. (Even the off-stage events of The Great Hiatus, nearly three years in duration, is just a fraction of forty years.) There is so much more between 1874 and 1914 that is left undescribed – not to mention whatever happened in Holmes and Watson's lives before 1874 and after 1914.

And even though The Canon is the core of The Great Holmes Tapestry, the stories that make up this core were chosen by Watson as representative examples of Holmes's skills – they were not necessarily his greatest triumphs or "best" cases. Watson had thousands of recorded adventures from which to choose when selecting for publication, and he had reasons for what he picked . . . and for what he suppressed. *What about all of those other cases that weren't published in Watson's lifetime?*

That's where the Post-Canonical Chroniclers step in . . . .

"Apart from what you have told me,
can you give me any further
information about the man?"
– Sherlock Holmes
"The Illustrious Client"

In 2015, we knew less about Mr. Sherlock Holmes than we do now, for back then, there were over one-thousand fewer of his adventures that had been revealed to the curious public. Don't misunderstand – there were still quite a few post-Canonical Holmes narratives in 2015, but they were harder to find, *and there were not enough.*

". . . we must hunt for this man's secrets."
– Sherlock Holmes
"The Illustrious Client"

Growing up, I had the very-common experience of discovering and reading The Canon, and re-reading it, and then realizing with crushing disappointment that the ride was seemingly at an end. I was fortunate to discover Holmes in 1975, at age ten, just one year after Nicholas Meyer had ignited the current and still-burning Sherlockian Golden Age with his discovery of the lost manuscript for *The Seven-Per-Cent Solution* (1974). While it was flawed – the implications that Moriarty was not evil, and that the Great Hiatus did not occur, were obviously grafted onto Watson's original manuscript by some later Moriarty heir to posthumously rehabilitate the evil Professor's reputation – this book revealed the basic but staggering truth that Watson's stories *did not have to cross the First Literary Agent's desk to be both accepted and amazing.*

The hunt was on to locate Watson's other missing narratives, filling in all the gaps and spaces between what we know from The Canon. Meyer continued by finding an exponentially better second Watsonian manuscript, *The West End Horror* – and the dam holding back the release of these various historic documents was washed away forever.

> *"But that is not enough, Mr. Holmes."*
> – Lord Bellinger, Prime Minister
> "The Second Stain"

In the following years, I tracked down, collected, read, and chronologicized almost every existing traditional Canonical Holmes adventures – *but there were not enough.* And in the early 2000's, I noticed a disturbance in the Holmesian Force: Several media adaptations that incorrectly placed Holmes in Modern Times began popping up. One in particular gained a lot of traction, painting Holmes as a broken sociopathic murderer. That would be fine if it stopped there, for there have been a lot of insulting works over the years that similarly attacked Holmes – the worst up to that point being Michael Dibdin's *The Last Sherlock Holmes Story* (1978), in which Holmes was presented as a gleeful Jack the Ripper, whose death was arranged by Watson.

> *"We must not lose sight of our main inquiry."*
> – Sherlock Holmes
> "The Naval Treaty"

I was dismayed when aspects of this modernized sociopathic Holmes began creeping into what were supposed to be traditional Canonical adventures, as presented by people who should have known better: In these "traditional" adventures, supposedly Canonical Holmes now had a "mind palace". Watson's wound was psychosomatic. Mrs. Hudson was the widow of a drug dealer. Irene Adler was a dominatrix. Mary Watson was a secret agent assassin. And people were adapting to this – accepting this – as if maybe Holmes had always been a sociopath, or that Watson really wasn't wounded, if one just read The Canon a little more closely. Many said, "It's okay – as long as this attracts new people to Sherlock Holmes, who cares how they get there?" But they were all showing up with the expectation and looking for hints that Irene Adler really was a dominatrix, or that James Moriarty was . . . whatever that was supposed to be.

I became increasingly . . . shall we say *peeved.* And then I became motivated – a fiery motivation that has only increased every day since.

I little dreamed the strange shape
which that campaign was destined to take.
– Dr. John H. Watson
"Charles Augustus Milverton"

One night in early 2015, I had a dream, and it abruptly awakened me. If I'd gone back to sleep, I might have forgotten it, but instead I went ahead and got up, as it was nearly time to arise anyway. And I kept thinking about that very-vivid vision.

I had dreamed that I'd edited a book of new Holmes stories, along the lines of *The Mammoth Book of Sherlock Holmes Stories* (1997), or the many volumes that Martin H. Greenberg co-edited with a number of other people over several decades – new Holmes stories, set in the correct time, indistinguishable from the Canonical tales that originally appeared in *The Strand.*

". . . we must take our own line of action."
– Sherlock Holmes
"The Disappearance of Lady Frances Carfax"

That morning before going to work, I looked around at my Holmes collection – now nearly 5,000 volumes, but somewhat less then – and saw a number of authors represented there that I'd love to invite. Later that morning, I emailed Publisher Extraordinaire Steve Emecz with the idea, and he was willing. (Steve has always been most supportive of various project ideas.) I had no idea that I'd started something that would be a huge part of my life for the next ten years . . . .

That email is on the next page . . . .

David Marcum

to Steve ▾

Steve,

This is the idea I had for a future book. I was literally dreaming about it when I woke up this morning.

I would like to contact a specific list of authors (see below) – who I would pick because they write well and who write the kinds of Holmes stories that I would want to read – and have each one of them pen a Holmes short story.

The volume would be along the lines of all of those anthologies that have come before, such as *The Mammoth Book, Holmes for the Holidays, Murder in Baker Street,* etc. Like *The Mammoth Book,* I would arrange the stories by chronological date, and not by a perceived author importance.

I would be the editor, and I would format it. (As you know, I have strict standards.) I would ask that each story be 5,000-8,000 words in length, much like stories from the Canon. The stories would be traditional and Canonical Holmes only, as narrated by Watson. The characters would be in standard settings, and it would be like when authors were writing *Star Trek* novels, and they were told that they could use the characters, but essentially put them back as they found them when they were done. There would be no weird Alternate Universe or present-day stuff, no Holmes-is-the-Ripper, nothing where Watson is at Holmes's funeral or vice-versa. etc. Essentially nothing that shockingly contradicts what is in the Canon.

I would contact each author personally to explain the project and request a submission. That way other authors who didn't get to play wouldn't necessarily get their feelings hurt, since it would go on behind the scenes and the book would simply appear as a finished product.

Each author would retain the rights to his or her story, for use in a future collection of their own. To avoid the question of who gets what, royalties would go to Undershaw, or some other good cause of your choosing.

Also, it would generate some new Holmes stories that I would get to read, and that would be great!

If eight participated, it would be a pretty good nice book. If more played, so much the better. We could even consider doing two versions, the standard paperback, and possibly a collectible hardcover – that would be your call, of course.

So, what do you think? I think I could put this together fairly easily, once the stories arrived. It would be a lot of fun, and it would be something really cool for MX as well.

I await your thoughts....

David

... and if you can't easily read it, I wrote:

January 22, 2015 9:40 a.m.

Steve,

This is the idea I had for a future book. I was literally dreaming about it when I woke up this morning.

I would like to contact a specific list of authors (see below) – who I would pick because they write well and who write the kinds of Holmes stories that I would want to read – and have each one of them pen a Holmes short story.

The volume would be along the lines of all of those anthologies that have come before, such as The Mammoth Book, Holmes for the Holidays, Murder in Baker Street, *etc. Like* The Mammoth Book, *I would arrange the stories by chronological date, and not by a perceived author importance.*

I would be the editor, and I would format it. (As you know, I have strict standards.) I would ask that each story be 5,000-8,000 words in length, much like stories from the Canon. The stories would be traditional and Canonical Holmes only, as narrated by Watson. The characters would be in standard settings, and it would be like when authors were writing Star Trek novels, and they were told that they could use the characters, but essentially put them back as they found them when they were done. There would be no weird Alternate Universe or present-day stuff, no Holmes-is-the-Ripper, nothing where Watson is at Holmes's funeral or vice-versa. etc. Essentially nothing that shockingly contradicts what is in the Canon.

I would contact each author personally to explain the project and request a submission. That way other authors who didn't get to play wouldn't necessarily get their feelings hurt, since it would go on behind the scenes and the book would simply appear as a finished product.

Each author would retain the rights to his or her story, for use in a future collection of their own. To avoid the question of who gets what, royalties would go to Undershaw, or some other good cause of your choosing.

Also, it would generate some new Holmes stories that I would get to read, and that would be great!

If eight participated, it would be a pretty good nice book. If more played, so much the better. We could even consider doing two versions, the standard paperback, and possibly a collectible hardcover – that would be your call, of course.

So, what do you think? I think I could put this together fairly easily, once the stories arrived. It would be a lot of fun, and it would be something really cool for MX as well.

I await your thoughts . . . .

David

"We must define the situation a little more clearly."
– Sherlock Holmes
"The Red Circle"

When Steve approved, I also emailed a couple of Sherlockian friends, and their opinions were positive. So I started sending out invitations – and I was very clear: The books could have no actual supernatural solutions. There might be some element of *"What was that . . . ?"* at the end of the story – perhaps Watson looks back as they drive away and sees a mythical creature after all – but the crime could not have been caused by the creature. No real vampires or wolfmen or actual Jekyll-Hyde transformations. No aliens or Old Gods or intelligent brain-mutating parasites. Although one naysayer who is bored with The Canon and favors pure Holmes-versus-Actual Supernatural Creatures later sneered at these "Scooby Doo solutions", Holmes stated it exactly right: *"No ghosts need apply."*

Likewise, there could be no anachronistic elements. "Mind palaces" and other such incorrect modern references were forbidden. Technology had to agree with the year in which the story took place – with absolutely no Steampunk. The story itself had to fit into the Holmes and Watson chronology. For instance, close reading of The Canon shows that Watson only had a practice during those years when he was married. Watson's residences when living away from Baker Street – Paddington and Kensington and Queen Anne Street – had to be correct for the period in which the story occurred.

Finally, there could be no aspects of parody. People had been calling Our Heroes things like *Hairlock Combs* and *Fetlock Jones* since the late 1800's. It wasn't funny then, and it isn't funny now.

"We must strike while the iron is hot."
– Sherlock Holmes
"The Cardboard Box"

When I started sending invitations, I was afraid that no one would respond, so I kept widening the net. I went through my entire Holmes collection, looking for pasticheurs and finding ways to contact them. Then, to my amazement, I had the first positive reply – from Lyndsay Faye, who wrote back within a few hours of my initial email, stating: *"I'd be happy to – when do you need it by?"*

Wow – this thing might happen after all.

7

"Well, I think we must wait
for a little more material."
– Sherlock Holmes
"The Red Circle"

I'd been worried that there would be no interest, and I'd also thought that, at best, the final result might be a one-volume paperback of maybe twelve stories – if I was lucky. So I kept sending more invitations, and getting more replies from people saying that they were in. Then . . . the first story arrived, from Luke Benjamen Kuhns, and I first experienced that brand-new thrill – that *addiction* – of receiving new Holmes stories in my inbox.

"Our material is rapidly accumulating."
– Sherlock Holmes
"The Dancing Men"

As 2015 progressed, word spread about this new project, and an increasing number of people wanted to join the party. I began receiving more emails and more stories, and pretty soon it became apparent that this was going to be a really big book. Maybe too big for just one book . . . .

"We will confine ourselves for the present
with your permission to this very
interesting document."
– Sherlock Holmes
The Hound of the Baskervilles

Over several months, Steve Emecz and I worked out book lengths and sizes, and he was receptive when I shared that I thought it would become a two-volume set. And he was still receptive when that grew to three volumes. By late Summer 2015, the set had grown to 63 stories – more tales than in The Canon.

"We need certainly to muster all our resources."
– Sherlock Holmes
"The Five Orange Pips"

From the beginning, the royalties from this project have gone to support the restoration of Undershaw, one of Sir Arthur Conan Doyle's former homes. For a number of years, the site had been in disrepair, and was more recently in danger of being torn down or cut up into private dwellings, disrespecting the historical significance of the place. A movement had helped to save Undershaw, and Steve Emecz and MX

8

Publishing had been part of that, having published several previous volumes whose royalties had also helped the site.

> *"Now, we must make the best use of our time . . . ."*
> – Sherlock Holmes
> "The Speckled Band"

Now the building was saved, having recently been purchased by the nearby Stepping Stones School for special needs children – and Steve suggested that the royalties from the new books go to the school. This only made the project more popular with the contributors.

The three volumes were published in Autumn 2015, and I was very fortunate to be able to travel to England – my second Holmes Pilgrimage – to attend a launch party high on a festive outdoor deck atop one of London's noted skyscrapers – at the location of Steve's then-employer. And then I returned home, and things settled down for a week or so . . . but it wasn't long before I started receiving emails about when to contribute to the *next book* . . . .

> *"Why should you go further in it?*
> *What have you to gain from it?"*
> – Sherlock Holmes
> "The Red Circle"

Next book? Next book! I'd had no plans for anything past the first three books. But receiving new Holmes stories by email *was* an addiction, and people wanted to contribute – both former and new pasticheurs – and others wanted to read further volumes with stories about the True Holmes, and most of all, *there are never enough traditional Canonical Holmes adventures. Never enough.*

> *"We must begin again."*
> – Sherlock Holmes
> "The Disappearance of Lady Frances Carfax"

So I wrote to Steve and explained, and we decided upon one more book – or maybe we decided on one new book per year. (I can't remember exactly.) In any case, I announced it, and more stories arrived, and Part IV, published in Spring 2016, had twenty-one stories. And then came the questions about the *next* volume . . . .

> *"We must begin from a different angle."*
> – Sherlock Holmes
> "The Illustrious Client"

It became apparent that there were so many contributors anxious to reach into Watson's Tin Dispatch Box, and also so many readers who were *starving* for more traditional Canonical adventures, that we could produce a lot more than one book per year – so it was decided to have a Spring *Annual*, and an Autumn themed volume. And 2016's themed Autumn volume was *Christmas Adventures* – 30 stories, (It's still one of the most popular of the series. We did another three-volume Christmas set in 2021.)

> *"We must hustle and put the thing through."*
> – Sherlock Holmes
> "The Three Garridebs"

By then, the pattern was set. I would announce a "Call for Submissions" about six months before publication of a particular set – the *Annuals* in Spring, and themed books in Autumn – such as Christmas, and Untold Cases, and seemingly-supernatural-but-not-really. More and more stories would arrive, necessitating that we eventually grew to six volumes per year – three for the *Annuals*, and three for the themed sets. I was usually reading new stories for the next set while also finishing final edits for the current set, and by the time the current set was published, fresh to the excited reading public, it was far in my rear-view mirror as I edited the new stories.

> *"We will raise as much as we can in money . . . ."*
> – John Ferrier
> *A Study in Scarlet*

In September 2016, the Stepping Stones School at Undershaw held their grand opening, and my deerstalker and I were invited as special guests (representing Holmes and Pasticheurs) because of the books' connection to the school. It was my own Holmes Pilgrimage No. 3. At that time – and since then as well – I was told that while the money raised for the school was substantial and useful – over $135,000 as I write this foreword – the more important aspect of the books' association was that they raised awareness of the school all over the world.

> *"We will have some indication as to*
> *where the document has gone."*
> – Sherlock Holmes
> "The Second Stain"

There were a number of milestones as the books progressed. A set of six volumes, taken from the early anthologies, were published in India by

Jaico. A single volume was translated and sold in Japan. Phil Growick, an initial contributor, had the brilliant idea of taking Holmes stories and assigning them to different artists – each of whom would produce a painting related to that tale, and all for charity. He published four different volumes of *The Art of Sherlock Holmes,* and almost all of the stories in those books were taken directly from *The MX Book of New Sherlock Holmes Stories.* He even had a gallery showing for one set of paintings, and more were planned before COVID shut things like that down. And contributor Sean Wright – who co-wrote (with Michael Hodel) *Enter the Lion* (1979), one of the best post-Canonical adventures way back in the late 1970's, not long after the current Sherlockian Golden Age commenced – suggested a volume of stories from this series that were contributed by members of the BSI – and thus *An Investee's Anthology* was published in 2022.

> "... *he has done a considerable amount of writing lately* ..."
> – Sherlock Holmes
> "The Red-Headed League"

During his lifetime, the late Philip K. Jones compiled an amazing database of post-Canonical stories – approximately 16,000 of them at the time of his passing, not long after the first MX anthology volumes were published. If one disregards the number of parodies and non-traditional non-Canonical stories that he included, then there are approximately 10,000 traditional and Canonical adventures listed – a fairly complete list up to that time. Since then, *The MX Book of New Sherlock Holmes Stories,* with these final four volumes, has 1,063 stories – or approximately ten percent (10%) of the other traditional and Canonical adventures ever written. Additionally, these books have had over 200 contributors world-wide. Some authors wrote a single story, while others have stepped up and contributed dozens – to my everlasting gratitude.

> "*We must each try our own way*
> *and see what comes of it.*"
> – Sherlock Holmes
> "Wisteria Lodge"

I never cease to be amazed at the directions taken by the different contributors. From the common point of the traditional Canon, stories in these books may be comic or tragic. One might find a cozy murder or a strict police procedural murder investigation – or no murder at all. Holmes might investigate a stolen document or jewel – or something that ends up completely crime-free. The setting might be a British city or the countryside, or another country or continent. Holmes's client might be a businessman or a criminal, or a little old lady or Royalty. He might work for a private interest, or as an agent of the Government. The adventure might be a complicated swindle or a ghost story or a spy mission. The tale may be cerebral, or filled with breakneck action. Holmes might progress steadily from one witness to another, or he may be settled in to unlock a mysterious puzzle or code. Holmes might solve the crime from his armchair, or – as he says in *A Study in Scarlet* –"*Now and again a case turns up which is a little more complex. Then I have to bustle about and see things with my own eyes.*"

"I should wish to go further into this matter.
It interests me."
– Professor Presbury
"The Creeping Man"

Another wonderful thing to me that occurred along the way was that these books gave some people their first opportunities to be published authors, and they went on to write more stories – about Holmes, and in other areas too. Some authors used these books as a "prompt" – reminders every six months to write more Holmes stories so that, as these accumulated, they would have enough to be collected into their own books. There have been quite a few volumes of these "children" of the MX anthologies.

"*. . . we will go out together and see what we can do.*"
– Sherlock Holmes
"The Norwood Builder"

One of the best stories of a "child" of these books was the creation and success of Derrick and Brian Belanger's *Belanger Books*. I first "met" Derrick when he reviewed one of my own books, and we became email friends. He was among the very first group of authors that I invited when I had the idea for the anthologies, and his contribution was his first written Holmes adventure. I "met" his brother, Brian, when he took over as MX's cover artist after the untimely passing of the previous artist. (I've since seen them several times on those occasions when I've attended the yearly Sherlock Holmes Birthday Weekend in New York.)

After Derrick had a taste of writing about Holmes, he and Brian had an idea: To form their own publishing company. I had an email from Derrick in August 2015 – a month or so before the first MX anthologies were published – asking me if I'd be involved in their publishing venture, and I've been thrilled to be associated with them ever since. I've edited over two-dozen books for them, and they've published both of my Solar Pons short story collections, with another on the way.

Belanger Books has published many Holmes anthologies since its inception, including several volumes in their anthology series *Sherlock Holmes: A Year of Mystery*. They have themed Holmes collections related to Poe and Lovecraft and H.G. Wells. There are sets devoted to The Early Years and The Denarian Years, and The Great Hiatus and World War I, and the Montague Street days Before Watson. There are Canonical sequels and team-ups with Solar Pons and other Great Detectives and Female Detectives, and stories centered around the Theatre.

I'm thrilled that Belanger Books came into being, and I believe that it was directly because of Derrick's initial involvement in *The MX Book of New Sherlock Holmes Stories*, and the joy he found when writing his first Holmes adventure. More important, I'm also thrilled that Belanger Books has gone on to be one of the two most-respected and important Sherlockian publishers ever – the other being MX Publishing. Both companies work together very closely to support each other's projects and charities, and spread the True Sherlockian Word far and wide. I'm very proud to be associated with both MX Publishing and Belanger Books.

> *"I cannot really see how we can get*
> *much further than our present position."*
> – Sherlock Holmes
> "Silver Blaze

In 2023, one of the MX contributors wrote, asking me what the future plans were for the series. He wanted to keep contributing for as long as the books continued, and he wanted to keep collecting every volume too, but he wondered how many stories that meant he'd need to write over the years, and how much extra bookshelf space he'd require. His email set me to thinking about an end game . . . .

> *"I think that we have gathered all that we can."*
> – Sherlock Holmes
> "The Priory School"

I'd joked before that the books should fittingly go to Part MX – Volume 1,010 for those who don't speak Roman Numeral – but sadly that wasn't realistic. When I started considering, we were then up to forty-two volumes, and I wondered if we could reach fifty – which seemed like a good number upon which to stop. If we had three Spring volumes in 2024, (Parts 43, 44, and 45), and three in the Autumn (Parts 46, 47, and 48), then we could reach fifty with just two volumes in Spring 2025. If the stories kept arriving at the usual rate, we would have over 1,000 of them upon reaching the Spring 2025 volumes. And personally, 2025 would be ten years since the books began in 2015 – a milestone – and personally I would turn sixty – my own milestone.

> *"We must prepare for the worst."*
> – Sherlock Holmes
> "The Disappearance of Lady Frances Carfax"

The same person who had asked me about the books' future warned me that strictly limiting the final set to two volumes might be a mistake, as a lot of people would certainly want to participate at the end, but I was adamant: Fifty was a solid and pleasing number, and I would close the door. But that person – it was Kevin Thornton – was correct: Enthusiasm was high, and we were going to need extra volumes. I didn't want to increase to fifty-one – there's nothing pleasing about that number – but fifty-two felt good. There are fifty-two cards in a deck, and fifty-two weeks in a year – and an ambitious reader could read one volume of this series per week for an entire year. (I highly recommend this as a self-improvement activity, and would like to hear from whomever completes this Noble Quest.)

> *"In over a thousand cases I am not aware that*
> *I have ever used my powers upon the wrong side."*
> – Sherlock Holmes, "The Final Problem"

As I write this foreword to the final volumes, I'm currently finishing the final editing process. As mentioned, I've been thrilled to receive new Holmes stories nearly every day for the last decade, and I'm going to miss that incredibly – although I will now have more free time to read other things, without my spare minutes and hours being devoted to printed-out stories on 8½ x 11-inch paper and with an editing pen in hand. I've also enjoyed being something of a Sherlockian influencer, able to nudge the Sherlockian ship in directions that I wanted it to go . . . .

> *"Then we must take that as our working hypothesis."*
> – Sherlock Holmes
> "The Bruce-Partington Plans"

Not long after I first discovered Holmes in 1975 – before I'd even read all of The Canon – my parents gifted me with William S. Baring-Gould's incredible *Sherlock Holmes of Baker Street* (1962), the amazing biography of Holmes that establishes so many things – his birth date and background, his *other* older brother Sherrinford, his upbringing and schooling, his travels in America as an actor, his relationship with Irene Adler and his son, and the circumstances of his death. (That's right – as a historical figure, he wasn't immortal.) I don't agree with everything Baring-Gould posited, but I concur with much of it, and it was a great jumping off place when constructing my own 1,200-page (and ever-growing) Holmes Chronology.

> *"Well, we will take it as a working hypothesis*
> *for want of a better."*
> – Sherlock Holmes
> "The Man with the Twisted Lip"

As the editor of these fifty-two volumes – and a few dozen more as well for MX and Belanger Books, I've been able to nudge the ship in the direction I believe to be correct, encouraging certain ideas that I hope will become even more established in the reading consciousness as time goes on, in the same way that Baring-Gould's ideas have found popular footing. For instance, whenever the question came up, I encouraged contributors to reinforce the idea that Holmes lived at No. 24 Montague Street (as first discovered by Sherlockian Michael Harrison) before moving to Baker Street. I arranged the stories of each set in chronological order, and in the order to match what I believe is the correct chronology. I firmly aver that Holmes wore a deerstalker, and that he wore it in town and also the country. (Anyone who would shoot *V.R.* into his wall with a hair-trigger pistol would not be concerned by fashion dictates. He would dress as needed in useful clothing to go to work at a moment's notice.) Thus, he wears a deerstalker in these thousand-plus stories.

> *"We must look for consistency."*
> – Sherlock Holmes
> "The Problem of Thor Bridge"

These books helped to further establish that Holmes retired to Hodcombe Farm at Beachy Head on the Sussex Coast. Study of The Canon reveals that Watson had *three* wives – not two, not seven – and these books strengthen that conclusion. There is now much additional evidence, by way of these books, that Nero Wolfe was Holmes's son, and Solar Pons was his nephew. We know a great deal more about The Great Hiatus than what was revealed in "The Empty House", and we also know why Holmes "retired" in 1903, and more about what he was up to in those years leading to World War I and "His Last Bow".

"Their cumulative effect is certainly considerable,
and yet each of them is quite possible in itself."
– Dr. John H. Watson
"The Abbey Grange"

While these books are coming to a close, there are already plans for other similar volumes, although they will not be the size of the MX anthologies, and they will be one-time projects with much-less rigorous editing demands. But one thing will not change: The new books will absolutely stick to what made the original MX volumes so successful: *Firm adherence to the Canonical model.* Holmes will not be substituting for Van Helsing or Doctor Who. He will not be a sociopathic murderer with a "mind palace", and he will not be a joke, or realize halfway through and adventure that he's a character in someone's book, or be covered in tattoos while paying off a prostitute in the doorway of a modern-day Manhattan brownstone. These new books (when they arrive), as well as all fifty-two volumes (and over one-thousand stories) of *The MX Book of New Sherlock Holmes Stories*, hold to a basic premise: They were all generated by a desire for more traditional Canonical adventures – *and there are never enough traditional Canonical Holmes adventures.*

* * * * *

"Of course, I could only
stammer out my thanks."
– The Unhappy John Hector McFarlane
"The Norwood Builder"

As always when one of these collections is finished, I want to thank with all my heart my incredible, patient, brilliant, kind, and beautiful wife of almost thirty-seven years, Rebecca – Every single day I'm more stunned at how lucky I am than the day before! – and our amazing, funny, creative, and wonderful son, and my friend, Dan (with whom I was able to share a multi-week Holmes Pilgrimage No. 4 around England and Scotland in Spring 2024). I love you both, and you are everything to me!

With each new set of the MX anthologies, some things got easier, and there were also new challenges. For several years, the stresses of real life have been much greater on all of us than when this series started. Through all of this, the amazing contributors have pulled truly amazing works from the Tin Dispatch Box. I'm more grateful than I can express to every contributor who has donated both time and royalties to this ongoing project. It's amazing what we've accomplished.

Finally, I cannot express how thankful I am to all of those who keep buying these books and making them the largest and most popular Sherlockian anthology ever.

I'm so glad to have gotten to know so many of you through this process. It's an undeniable fact that Sherlock Holmes authors are the *best* people!

I wish especially thank the following:

- ☐ *Steve Emecz* – From my first association with MX in 2013, I saw that MX (under Steve Emecz's leadership) was *the* fast-rising superstar of the Sherlockian publishing world. Connecting with MX and Steve Emecz was personally an amazing life-changing event for me, as it has been for countless other Sherlockian authors. It has led me to write many more stories, and then to edit books, along with unexpected additional Holmes Pilgrimages to England – none of which might have happened otherwise. By way of my first email with Steve, I've had the chance to make some incredible Sherlockian friends and play in the Holmesian Sandbox in ways that I would have never dreamed possible.

  Through it all, Steve has been one of the most positive and supportive people that I have ever known.

  From the beginning, Steve has let me explore various Sherlockian projects and open up my own personal possibilities in ways that otherwise would have never happened. Thank you, Steve, for every opportunity!

- ☐ *Roger Johnson* – From his immediate support at the time of the first volumes in this series to the present, I can't imagine Roger not being part of these books. His Sherlockian knowledge is exceptional, as is the work that he does to further the cause of The Master. But even more than that, both Roger and his wife, Jean Upton, are simply the finest and best of people, and I'm very lucky to know both of them – even though I don't get to see them nearly as often as I'd like. I look forward to getting back over to the Holmesland sooner rather than later and visiting with them again, but in the meantime, many thanks for being part of this.

- ☐ *Brian Belanger* –I initially became acquainted with Brian when he took over the duties of creating the covers for MX Books, and I found him to be a great collaborator, and wonderfully creative too. I've worked with him on many

17

projects with MX and Belanger Books, which he co-founded with his brother Derrick Belanger, also a good friend. Along with MX Publishing, Derrick and Brian have absolutely locked up the Sherlockian publishing field with a vast amount of amazing material. The old dinosaurs must be trembling to see every new and worthy Sherlockian project, one after another after another, that these two companies create. Luckily MX and Belanger Books work closely with one another, and I'm thrilled to be associated with both of them. Many thanks to Brian for all he does for both publishers, and for all he's done for me personally.

☐ *Bonnie MacBird* – I first met Bonnie in 2013, during my Holmes Pilgrimage No. 1, when I was joining Roger Johnson and Jean Upton for lunch at The Sherlock Holmes Pub, and they brought Bonnie along. I didn't know she was famous then – just that she was a very nice lady. After lunch and an extensive exploration of the Holmes exhibit, Roger guided us on the route taken by Holmes and Watson, as described in "The Empty House", from Cavendish Square to Camden House in Baker Street. Later that evening, Bonnie attended my first book signing at the Sherlock Holmes Hotel in Baker Street. I saw her again in 2015 at the launch party of the MX anthologies, and then several times after that at Sherlockian gatherings in Indiana and New York. In the meantime, we've stayed in touch by email.

During our first meeting, along the way of the "Empty House" walk, she rather shyly stated that she was working on writing a pastiche. I hinted that I'd like to read it, but no such luck – until *Art in the Blood* was published in 2015 and I was able to read it as my book-of-choice while in London for Holmes Pilgrimage No. 2 – the first of her very successful Holmes series from HarperCollins. Bonnie has been an incredible supporter of these books from the very beginning, and I'm thrilled and thankful that she is a part of them for the final volumes.

And finally, last but certainly *not* least, thanks to **Sir Arthur Conan Doyle**: Author, doctor, adventurer, and the Founder of the Sherlockian Feast. Honored, and present in spirit.

As I always note when putting together an anthology of Holmes stories, the effort has been a labor of love. Looking back over ten years, this has never wavered. These adventures are just part of the many tiny threads woven into the ongoing Great Holmes Tapestry, continuing to grow and grow, for there can *never* be enough stories about the man whom Watson described as *"the best and wisest . . . whom I have ever known."*

David Marcum
March 4th, 2025
The 144th Anniversary of
the monumental first day of the
Jefferson Hope Murder Investigation

Questions or comments
may be addressed to David Marcum at
thepapersofsherlockholmes@gmail.com.

Foreword
by Bonnie MacBird

Well, here it is. Bringing it on Holmes, editor and Sherlockian scholar extraordinaire David Marcum presents the final volumes of his magnificent series for MX publishing, which has brought 52 volumes of over 1,000 stories by Holmesian writers from all over the planet – from the famous to the newly fledged, all writing from the heart and from the mind, reflecting our hero: Mr. Sherlock Holmes. This series has taken in more than $134,000 in support of the Undershaw school for special needs children.

You hold in your hands the last of these volumes, representing over ten years of David Marcum's creative life. He's diligently read, edited, championed, and also beautifully added to this astonishing collection of ongoing adventures of our heroes.

All of these works have been traditional, in emulation of that genius storyteller Sir Arthur Conan Doyle, whom we happily acknowledge here as the mastermind. He has enthralled thousands of readers for more than 130 years. His craft seems so effortless (until you try your hand at it), his prose both brisk and evocative, and even "cinematic", although most of it predates cinema. His wit is crisp, his insights subtle, his characters unforgettable.

How wise that he chose as the storytelling "voice" that of the pragmatic, energetic man of action, John Watson, who doesn't waste words on endless scenic detail or overweening innuendo but, by golly, gets cracking on with the story.

And how exquisitely drawn is Sherlock Holmes, with just enough mystery to the man himself to make us insatiably curious! He is acknowledged as the first superhero of popular fiction, but with no supernatural trappings. He seems to work miracles – but its sheer intelligence, knowledge, stamina, reasoning . . . and let's not forget . . . artistry that are his superpowers. He is a scientist, a logician, and an artist who sees what others do not. Of course, there's also a facility with baritsu, boxing, and single stick when needed.

Ah, the aspiration these stories awaken! Could we not be more like Holmes or Watson with practice, with learning? And wouldn't we be a better person if so?

But setting aside inspirational qualities of these stories, we must also acknowledge the absolute crazy fun they provide, and even more so, the comfort. In a world fraught with conflict and violence, with ignorance and prejudice, these stories amuse and entertain as they bring us close to characters who demonstrate what our world needs most – rational, fact-based critical thinking, courage, and friendship. Armed with those, these two men stand side by side to fight evil and win. Always win.

And at the end, we find ourselves fireside, once again at 221b. And so very glad to be there. Thank you, David and MX. And thank you, Sir Arthur.

Bonnie MacBird
Author, *The Sherlock Holmes Adventure Series*
for HarperCollins
February 2025

"Let me recommend this book – one of the most remarkable ever penned."
by Roger Johnson

That, you'll remember, was Sherlock Holmes's opinion of *The Martyrdom of Man* by William Winwood Reade (1838-1875), who was pithily defined by the *Dictionary of National Biography, 1885-1900* as *"traveller, novelist and controversialist"*. The *DNB* noted of the book so remarkably endorsed by Holmes: *"in this work the author does not attempt to conceal his atheistical opinions"*. S.C. Roberts, in the very first issue of *The Sherlock Holmes Journal*, observed that *"Holmes, with his social moodiness, his artistic temperament and his queer intellectual interests, had no doubt re-acted against the conventional beliefs of his squirearchical family and Winwood Reade's book was exactly the work that would catch him on the rebound."*

Reade was an extraordinary man, who led an extraordinary life. The same could be said of Sherlock Holmes, of course, though his life was considerably longer. It was fairly early in their partnership that he urged John Watson to read *The Martyrdom of Man*. If the Good Doctor did so, he probably didn't accept Reade's statement that: *"The soul must be sacrificed; the hope in immortality must die."* And if Holmes's own opinion at the time matched Reade's, we know that it did become more positive. Consider his discourse on the moss rose in the case of "The Naval Treaty":

> *"What a lovely thing a rose is!"*
> *He walked past the couch to the open window, and held up the drooping stalk of a moss-rose, looking down at the dainty blend of crimson and green. It was a new phase of his character to me, for I had never before seen him show any keen interest in natural objects.*
> *"There is nothing in which deduction is so necessary as in religion,"* said he, leaning with his back against the shutters. *"It can be built up as an exact science by the reasoner. Our highest assurance of the goodness of Providence seems to me to rest in the flowers. All other things, our powers our desires, our food, are all really necessary for*

our existence in the first instance. But this rose is an extra. Its smell and its colour are an embellishment of life, not a condition of it. It is only goodness which gives extras, and so I say again that we have much to hope from the flowers."

That has nothing to do with the case in hand – not directly, at any rate. The intention was probably to encourage his client Percy Phelps to a more optimistic attitude, but Holmes's observations are surely sincere, however unexpected. And no one, surely, can doubt the sincerity of his admonition to the tragic Eugenia Ronder:

> *We had risen to go, but there was something in the woman's voice which arrested Holmes's attention. He turned swiftly upon her.*
> *"Your life is not your own," he said. "Keep your hands off it."*
> *"What use is it to anyone?"*
> *"How can you tell? The example of patient suffering is in itself the most precious of all lessons to an impatient world."*

Detective stories didn't begin when Arthur Conan Doyle wrote *A Study in Scarlet*. Among the Baker Street sleuth's predecessors were the Chevalier C. Auguste Dupin, protagonist of three short stories by Edgar Allan Poe, Emile Gaboriau's Monsieur Lecoq of the French Sûreté, Inspector Bucket in *Bleak House* and Sergeant Cuff in *The Moonstone* – creations respectively of Charles Dickens and Wilkie Collins. Their exploits are still read and enjoyed more than a century-and-a-half later. But who now reads, for example, *The Boy Detective, or The Crimes of London* by Edward Ellis, the apparently endless exploits of Deadwood Dick by Edward L. Wheeler, or those of Jack Harkaway by Bracebridge Hemyng?

Even though he ranked the Holmes Saga low among his literary work, Conan Doyle achieved something remarkable: Fifty-six short stories and four novels, of genuine quality. At first, the detective appears to be essentially one-dimensional, but as we and Dr. Watson come to know him better, we realise that this is a character of real depth. It isn't merely the excitement of the crime and the solution that keep us reading and re-reading – there's also the fascination of his personality – and not only his but the admirable Doctor's as well. *

Even before the last remnants of copyright in the Canonical Holmes stories finally expired, there was a considerable output of parody and pastiche. Parody has different aims and different rules, but pastiche requires fidelity to the substance, the style and the spirit of the original, and that fidelity is too often missing – especially since the expiration of the Conan Doyle copyright – and the ability to post pretty much anything online. As they used to say, *"Never mind the quality, feel the width!"*

Fortunately, that does not apply to this book and its predecessors. David Marcum has worked tirelessly with his many authors to ensure that these new tales of Sherlock Holmes and John H. Watson are up to scratch.

And don't forget that none of the contributors will receive any financial reward, as the proceeds from the publication will go to the upkeep of Undershaw, the house that Arthur Conan Doyle had built for himself and his family near Hindhead in Surrey. Since 2016 it has been home to the Undershaw School, providing care and education for children aged eight to nineteen with Autistic Spectrum Disorder and associated learning needs.

Roger Johnson
BSI, ASH
February 2025

---

* Watson has so often and so unjustly been depicted as an idiot, especially on film! That will probably continue, but eventually, I hope, it will only be for comedic purposes.

An Ongoing Legacy
for Sherlock Holmes
by Steve Emecz

Undershaw
Circa 1900

Fifty two is a wonderful number of volumes to complete the world's largest-ever Sherlock Holmes anthology. It's unlikely we will ever see another collection like this, with over twohundred Holmes authors participating. It has taken ten years and a mammoth amount of editing from David Marcum to gift the world more than one-thousand new, traditional stories.

As many have commented – the fifty-six short stories and four novellas that Sir Arthur penned was painfully few for the dedicated fan, and wading through the myriad of pastiches on offer is difficult for those yearning for more Conan Doyle. *The MX Book of New Sherlock Holmes Stories* is a haven for those wanting an extension to The Canon in a very similar voice to ACD.

Whilst the collection draws to a close, our work continues with multiple resulting projects coming from this huge set of stories. We come together on 17th May, 2025 at Undershaw to celebrate in person with David and many of the participating authors – and hopefully many of you online too. We'll raise a glass to Sir Arthur, who would no doubt be proud with what we all together have been able to achieve.

Steve Emecz
February 2025

The Doyle Room at Undershaw
Partially funded through royalties from
The MX Book of New Sherlock Holmes Stories

A Word from Undershaw
by Emma West

Undershaw
September 9, 2016
Grand Opening of the Stepping Stones School
(Now *Undershaw*)
(Photograph courtesy of Roger Johnson)

It is with immense gratitude that I write the final words from Undershaw for this last publication of *The MX Book of New Sherlock Holmes Stories*, a collection compiled in support of Undershaw's restoration.

These stories have not only entertained us, but have also played a vital role in transforming the lives of our students. Thanks to the generosity of MX Publishing, we have been able to maintain this historic building while developing an inspiring learning environment for 102 students with Special Educational Needs and Disabilities.

Our partnership with MX Publishing has enriched our school community, offering opportunities and experiences that may otherwise have been out of reach for many of our students. Undershaw stands as a beacon of creativity, learning, and success – fitting for a place so closely linked to the literary legacy of Sir Arthur Conan Doyle.

As we mark this milestone – 52 volumes in the series – we also look forward to celebrating with "A Soirée with Sherlock Holmes", a special event dedicated to the great detective and his creator. Led by MX

Publishing, the evening will include a wonderful auction, streamed around the globe, with proceeds directly benefiting our students. These funds will support the creation of a cutting-edge media lab, complete with state-of-the-art computers, cameras, editing software, and a green screen, allowing our budding writers to bring their stories to life in print and on the screen.

Undershaw is more than just a historic site – it is a place where storytelling, imagination, and creativity thrive. The legacy of Sherlock Holmes continues to inspire our students, equipping them with skills for the future while fostering a lifelong love of literature. We are incredibly fortunate to be part of this ongoing journey and deeply grateful for our enduring partnership with MX Publishing. Their unwavering support has helped change the lives of countless young people.

Though the final volumes of this incredible collection, the impact of these stories – and the generosity behind them – will live on. The pages may close on this chapter, but the spirit of Sherlock Holmes, and the difference this series has made, will remain. Thanks to the unwavering support of MX Publishing and their community of authors and readers, Undershaw will continue to inspire generations to come, ensuring that the Great Detective's legacy is not only preserved, but carried forward into the future.

With heartfelt thanks and appreciation,

Emma West
Headteacher
February 2025

"Undershaw" Hindhead, Conan Doyle's House.

Editor's *Caveats*

W hen these anthologies first began back in 2015, I noted that the authors were from all over the world – and thus, there would be British spelling and American spelling. As I explained then, I didn't want to take the responsibility of changing American spelling to British and vice-versa. I would undoubtedly miss something, leading to inconsistencies, or I'd change something incorrectly.

Some readers are bothered by this, made nervous and irate when encountering American spelling as written by Watson, and in stories set in England. However, here in America, the versions of The Canon that we read have long-ago has their spelling Americanized, so it isn't quite as shocking for us.

Additionally, I offer my apologies up front for any typographical errors that have slipped through. As a print-on-demand publisher, MX does not have squadrons of editors as some readers believe. The business consists of three part-time people who also have busy lives elsewhere – Steve Emecz, Sharon Emecz, and Timi Emecz – so the editing effort largely falls on the contributors. Some readers and consumers out there in the world are unhappy with this – apparently forgetting about all of those self-produced Holmes stories and volumes from decades ago (typed and Xeroxed) with awkward self-published formatting and loads of errors that are now prized as very expensive collector's items.

I'm personally mortified when errors slip through – ironically, there will probably be errors in these *caveats* – and I apologize now, but without a regiment of professional full-time editors looking over my shoulder, this is as good as it gets. Real life is more important than writing and editing – even in such a good cause as promoting the True and Traditional Canonical Holmes – and only so much time can be spent preparing these books before they're released into the wild. I hope that you can look past any errors, small or huge, and simply enjoy these stories, and appreciate the efforts of everyone involved, and the sincere desire to add to The Great Holmes Tapestry.

And in spite of any errors here, there are more Sherlock Holmes stories in the world than there were before, and that's a good thing.

David Marcum
Editor

Sherlock Holmes (1854-1957) was born in Yorkshire, England, on 6 January, 1854. In the mid-1870's, he moved to 24 Montague Street, London, where he established himself as the world's first Consulting Detective. After meeting Dr. John H. Watson in early 1881, he and Watson moved to rooms at 221b Baker Street, where his reputation as the world's greatest detective grew for several decades. He was presumed to have died battling noted criminal Professor James Moriarty on 4 May, 1891, but he returned to London on 5 April, 1894, resuming his consulting practice in Baker Street. Retiring to the Sussex coast near Beachy Head in October 1903, he continued to be associated in various private and government investigations while giving the impression of being a reclusive apiarist. He was very involved in the events encompassing World War I, and to a lesser degree those of World War II. He passed away peacefully upon the cliffs above his Sussex home on his 103rd birthday, 6 January, 1957.

Dr. John Hamish Watson (1852-1929) was born in Stranraer, Scotland on 7 August, 1852. In 1878, he took his Doctor of Medicine Degree from the University of London, and later joined the army as a surgeon. Wounded at the Battle of Maiwand in Afghanistan (27 July, 1880), he returned to London late that same year. On New Year's Day, 1881, he was introduced to Sherlock Holmes in the chemical laboratory at Barts. Agreeing to share rooms with Holmes in Baker Street, Watson became invaluable to Holmes's consulting detective practice. Watson was married and widowed three times, and from the late 1880's onward, in addition to his participation in Holmes's investigations and his medical practice, he chronicled Holmes's adventures, with the assistance of his literary agent, Sir Arthur Conan Doyle, in a series of popular narratives, most of which were first published in *The Strand* magazine. Watson's later years were spent preparing a vast number of his notes of Holmes's cases for future publication. Following a final important investigation with Holmes, Watson contracted pneumonia and passed away on 24 July, 1929.

Photos of Sherlock Holmes and Dr. John H. Watson courtesy of Roger Johnson

The
MX Book
of
New
Sherlock
Holmes
Stories

Part L
The True Sherlock Holmes:
England's Greatest Hero
(1889-1896)

The Enigmatic Friendship
by Jim Hawkins

In foggy London where mysteries unfold,
Holmes and Watson's story is told.
Sherlock is sharp and often quite terse,
But Watson stays loyal, not willing to curse.
His new friend dear Holmes, whose mind he admires,
And whose logic so often inspires.

Watson, so blade straight, so admirably true,
Ignored all Holmes's faults 'cause down deep he knew
That behind the façade that Holmes always wore,
He valued dear Watson right down to the core.
Their friendship was forged when *the game was afoot*,
So Watson, it seems, found it best to stay put.

The Adventure of the
Twentieth Gun
by Mike Adamson

"It's the wedding, you see."

Inspector Lestrade spoke as if the matter were self-evident, and I had to agree, for I also found the issue almost painfully obvious. I knew the attention Holmes had invested in this question over the last weeks and understood that no other conclusion had emerged to date to rival this one in its simplicity.

We stood in the July sunshine in the busy beauty of St. James's Park. The grand rise of Buckingham Palace, beyond the trees, seemed to emphasise the gravity of our friend's words.

Holmes could only nod with a pent, bitter resignation. "I fear you are correct, Inspector – or should I say Chief Inspector. You must forgive me the habits of a decade."

"It's three decades in the force for me, soon enough," Lestrade replied, and I found myself noticing the silver that had invaded his temples. Lestrade had been a fixture of life, a feature of the landscape, these many years, but in the summer of 1889, I had to remind myself that time marches on and careers advance. He had been a twenty-year man with the Metropolitan Police the day we met.

"The wedding," Holmes repeated, glancing over his shoulder at the great, square-cut fascia of that grandest of all the dwellings in London, the Duke of Buckingham's masterpiece. "And needless to say, there is no question of altering plans one iota."

"How could they?" Lestrade asked, brows raised. "The date is fixed – 27 July. The marriage of Princess Louise of Wales and the Duke of Fife will be the first grand state marriage performed in the chapel of Buckingham Palace. Foreign dignitaries and guests of honour will be coming from all over the Empire and beyond. The Mall will be packed with spectators, twenty-deep for the processions." He scowled and shook his head. "It's a nightmare, and we've exactly eleven days left to do something about it."

"It would be so at the best of times from the standpoint of simple public safety," Holmes agreed, "but under the present circumstances, it is little short of suicide. Does Her Majesty understand the extremity of the situation?"

"I had the ordeal of explaining it to her," Lestrade said with a rueful look, as if the experience had been one he would not wish upon an enemy. "This is an Affair of State. It's been in the planning for over a year, and to change the venue would be of no help. Only cancelling it would head off the likelihood of a tragedy, and that is impossible for entirely political reasons. How would Britain look if we couldn't guarantee the safety of important personages in the very heart of London? Her Majesty has been the target of assassination attempts before and has soldiered on, giving not one inch of ground to any who would try to intimidate her. She has faith in her police, her military, and intelligence services to make things right – to get in the way of any attempt, against her or anyone else." He gave a sad shrug. "The novelty of the present situation was rather wasted on her."

Holmes squinted in frustration. "I imagine the irony was not, however – that a weapon invented in London should threaten the peace and stability of the Empire is a bitter jest worthy of the most-evil of minds."

Almost a month had gone by since our frantic dash up to the Midlands in pursuit of the Maxim machine guns stolen from under the very noses of their creators, * and while the thieves had been run down inside a single day of effort, the army had recovered only nineteen of the twenty guns taken. That boded ill, for a weapon of terrible potential was unaccounted for and, by definition, in criminal hands. Holmes had studied the matter intently for weeks in an effort to deduce the most likely target. We were agreed that the theft of the guns had been staged to facilitate a very singular operation, and amongst all the events unfolding in Britain this summer – sports matches, religious gatherings, concerts, and the like – one stood head and shoulders above them all as a target of ripest opportunity.

Was the objective to extort or to inflict crippling harm to the institutions of this land? To embarrass the British Government was only one aspect. To demonstrate that Her Majesty's Government could not assure the safety of its own capital and people would be to damage the light in which the British Empire was viewed throughout the world. That such mayhem should occur due to a British invention, over which control had simply been lost, was a crowning jeer that would see foreign powers reassessing the respect with which they approached Britain. France, Germany, Russia, the United States all might feel themselves in a strengthened position when it came to bargaining, and there had been speculation that a calamity in the capital – should the missing Maxim Gun put in an appearance during the Royal Wedding, in any shape or form – would encourage the rejection of British rule and begin a cascade of independence movements throughout the world.

Holmes wafted a fly from his face as he stared off at the palace. "I am at present distancing myself from the political ramifications of catastrophe," he said bluntly, "and focusing instead upon the human suffering inherent in this. Mr. Maxim's creation is a military weapon, and while the military itself – in more countries than Britain – hasn't as yet come to any consensus as to the ultimate utility of the automatic weapon, criminals have no such hesitation. It would be a foul day indeed if the machine gun were to be field tested in an orgy of destruction against the public and the Monarchy."

I shook my head. "For what possible reason would anyone do such a thing? To make a political point, perhaps, but it is a black and dishonourable way of doing so. How could anyone who perpetrated such a deed ever lift his head in civilised company again?"

Holmes smiled humourlessly. "In chaos there is profit, Watson. That is a *maxim* to live by, no pun intended. A truly wicked mind might profit in a hundred ways from the breakdown of law and governance that would erupt following such a massacre. Quite apart from the consequences to Britain's global standing, one might expect the police forces to be quickly stretched beyond breaking point by an outpouring of public rage that the authorities had failed to protect them from such rampant criminality in the first place. It would be a failure of the social contract between citizen and state – and the truth is that the state would have been the one to 'fumble the ball', as the saying goes. Lives would be lost wholesale. Property damage would run into the millions of pounds, and this nation would be scarred by the fiasco for a hundred years."

We held silence for a long moment as strollers went by and heard the lilt of brass from the bandstand, where red-coated musicians made their way through "The Blue Danube". Children and their governesses played on the green lawns, and a stall sold ice cream – so many elements of safe, sane normality that I could have wept with frustration and helplessness at the thought of what hung over this city, this civilisation, should our gravest fears prove correct.

"How will they do it?" I asked softly, pencil hovering over my notebook as I fought to find the words to describe what we were exploring. "Who exactly is the target? Important personages, or the general public?"

Holmes heaved a sigh as he gestured to the long stretch of The Mall, running between the palace and Trafalgar Square to the east. "Thousands will pack this avenue. Should some means be found to site the weapon overlooking the processional route, the potential slaughter is beyond imagining. That said, every point of overlook is already known, charted, and marked to be under police exclusion in the twenty-four hours before the event. This much is obvious. The palace security staff render any locality within the palace precincts out of the question. The same goes for the upper levels of St. James's Palace. The top of Admiralty Arch? The top floors of the other buildings lining The Mall? Easily searched and placed out of bounds." He snorted through nostrils flared with frustration. "Perhaps the gun will be mobile, sited in a closed van or wagon. To that end, every vehicle will be stopped and searched, and all the local roads will be closed in advance of the processions. Again, easily done. And our shadowy foes must know this."

Lestrade nodded with a blank, exhausted kind of look. "The ceremony will be in the private chapel. Every conceivable overlook of the venue has been studied. The Commissioner has the assurance that other forces around the country will contribute men on the day – We'll saturate the place with uniforms if we have to. We cannot fathom any way that weapon can possibly be turned on the figures who represent the highest-value targets. And there are simpler ways to take life. A long-range sniper might, perhaps, make a clean kill, but he would have to be a long way off, and the procession will be moving at a trot, not exactly a docile target."

"What about the foreign dignitaries?" I asked. "They must make their way here outside the security cordon of the event itself."

"The King of Greece, the Grand Duke of Hesse, Crown Prince Frederick of Denmark, and many more. They have their own security, bodyguards, all negotiating with the Metropolitan Police so that everything dovetails on the day."

Holmes turned on his heel and shook his head. "Something is wrong. It makes no sense! The Royal Wedding is *too* attractive a target, *too* ripe a plum for the picking. It is too *hard* a target. Therefore, it is a classic case of misdirection."

I swapped glances with Lestrade as the policeman shook his head. "I understand what you're saying, Mr. Holmes, but we can't take that chance."

"Oh, not at all, Lestrade. Mount defences like a castle wall, of course. But every fibre of my being tells me the blow will fall elsewhere."

Now Lestrade swept off his hat and seemed distressed to the point of frustrated anger. "If that's the case, we're back at square one with an entire country, and not a pin to put between a thousand events, any of which would provide a public tragedy and a political death knell."

Holmes grimaced, and the bright day did nothing to dispel his black mood. "It is as it is, Lestrade. And the Royal Wedding, I am almost positive, *cannot* be the target."

Holmes was moody in the hansom, and though I would have liked to return to Paddington and share the summer's afternoon with Mary, I had the strongest intuition he needed my calming influence. Intuition is a strange thing and runs quite counter to Holmes's cool logic, but even he will admit that it is the conflux of countless pieces of information, some from sources too subtle for us to recognise, which creates those flashes of inspiration or epiphany we have come to know so well.

Such a flash was in store for Holmes, but it came from the most unexpected quarter.

When the cab deposited us before the black front door of 221 Baker Street, we found a young boy waiting upon the step. He must have been no more than eleven years of age and wore a school uniform – the blazer, tie, and cap of some regional academy whose colours I didn't recognise. He sat with a schoolbag over his shoulder, watching the busy comings and goings upon our familiar thoroughfare, but when we dismounted the hansom, he bobbed to his feet and snatched off his cap.

"Mr. Holmes, sir? I'm Robert Threadgold, sir. I wrote to you a few days ago about a mystery."

For a moment, I thought Holmes, in his distraction and frustration over the Maxim case, would sweep by the lad without even acknowledging him, but I did him a disservice, for Holmes paused after paying the cabbie and looked down his long nose at the boy. The lad was clean and tidy, hair shaved over his ears, a shine on his shoes, and his wide-eyed, hopeful expression must have found its way through Holmes's granite shell, for my friend crooked a thoughtful expression for a moment.

"Threadgold? I recall the name. You're from – ?"

"Elderbridge, sir, in Hertfordshire. It's about the railway."

"Railway?" I asked with a puzzled look. "Mr. Holmes has a great many problems to consider, young man. Are you sure this matter warrants his attention?"

"I'll say, sir! It always means something when trains are in the wrong place at the wrong time, and that goes double when the line's condemned." He swallowed hard. "I had to part from my school outing to Regent's Park to get to you, gentlemen, and I'll probably cop a thrashing for it."

Holmes gave a shrug and put his key to the lock. "Then let us make your sacrifice worthwhile. Come up, Mr. Threadgold, and tell us all about it."

In moments we were up the stairs and into the old digs, and I felt a pang of homesickness. My life with Mary was everything I could have wanted it to be, but there were times, perhaps in the still of night, when I missed my years at Baker Street.

Hats and jackets went onto a wall rack, and Holmes refrained from tobacco in view of our client's tender years. I found a pitcher of lemonade waiting for us and poured all around.

"Now, Mr. Threadgold," Holmes announced as he sank into his armchair. "Do tell us of your mystery train."

I had the feeling Holmes was using the encounter for some much-needed relief from the affair at hand, indulging the boy more for his own sake than for that of the case, but I saw a flicker of interest develop in his ascetic features all the same. Perhaps there was something to this matter, after all.

"Well, it started a few days ago, gentlemen," the young man said, with all the proper manners his school had taught him. "Elderbridge is a small place, serving the roundabout farms, but it was founded as a home for miners. There's a chalk workings about a mile to the west. It's all closed up now. They finished there, oh, about the time my dad was born. But the village is just over a low hill from the railway, and we can always hear when a train goes through because of the steep turn. They slow right down to take the bend and have to work hard to get through. In Elderbridge, we say we can tell the time by the sound of wheels scrabbling on the rails. But I heard a train three nights ago. It came up from the south after midnight, well after the last service, and it didn't leave the normal way."

"Didn't leave?" Holmes asked, eyes narrowed.

"That's right, sir. I heard it arrive, then I heard it make an easy job of the track. The only easy line is the old spur to the mine. But that's been rusted and overgrown since my dad were a lad."

Holmes sat forward. "A train arrived, and instead of going through on the line northward like regular services, you believe it turned into the old workings?"

"That's right, sir. The next day, I went exploring as soon as school was over, but I found nothing. Just the old rusty track running back into the woods, all the way to a boarded-up tunnel through the next hill to the mine beyond." He squinted in thought. "There were some works done there a few months ago. I remember Dad saying they were repairing the old timbers that close up the tunnel mouth."

"A ghost train," I interjected with a smile. "There are countless ghost trains on the lines of this country."

Holmes managed a flicker of humour. "If we set aside my colleague's jocularity for a moment, we do indeed have a mystery to be answered. For what possible reason might a train surreptitiously return to a worked-out mine in the small hours? And then effectively vanish." He turned a cool eye on the boy. "Are you positive it didn't merely pause at Elderbridge Station, then return the way it had come? It might have done so after you fell asleep."

"I'm positive, sir. I sleep lightly, and I always know when a train goes down the line . . . ." He gave a sheepish smile. "I'm going to be an engineman when I grow up. I know the schedules of our line like the back

50

of my hand, sir. I know every type of locomotive and rolling stock on the network, and I go trainspotting every weekend. My mum says it's the bane of her life, but my dad would have given anything to be a train driver instead of a farmhand."

"I'm sure, I'm sure," Holmes murmured, his mind circling rapidly back to the facts. He rose and rifled through a stack of maps on the dining table. "Elderbridge, in Hertfordshire . . . ." He drew out a sheet and presented it to the lad. "This is your area, yes?"

"Yes, sir! Elderbridge is right . . . *there*! On that tight bend through the hill cutting. The old spur isn't marked, but it's there, all right, about two-hundred yards from Elderbridge Station."

Now Holmes paused for a long moment, eyes seeing into some other space than the one we occupied, and he turned to rifle through stacks of papers on the table. He flung documents right and left until he found the schedule for which he was looking, then flipped pages in an impatient flurry until his gaze settled upon the information he wanted. He stared at it for a long moment, then consulted the map once more, ran his finger down a list on the page before him, and let go a sigh somewhere between relief, satisfaction, and a whole new dread.

"Thank you, Mr. Threadgold. You have provided a very important clue that might just make the difference between life and death. I will take your case of the train where none should be. Indeed, I shall walk you up to the Park and have a word with your schoolmaster as to the valuable service you have done both myself and perhaps a great many others, which will hopefully obviate any administrative reprisals your actions might otherwise have incurred."

He took his jacket from the coatrack, drew on his deerstalker, and showed our guest to the door. "Watson, if you're amenable to an excursion of the utmost importance, you might use the next hour to drop by Paddington, have a word with your dear lady . . . and pack your revolver."

"It's that kind of case?" I asked with a wry look.

"Very much so. I would venture to say it may be one of the most important journeys of our lives."

"If it's so important, shouldn't we be calling in the troops?"

The train made its way north through this July's bright but changeable weather, and we had a first-class compartment to ourselves as the northern suburbs flowed by.

"And tell them what?" Holmes shook his head and steepled his fingers to help marshal his thoughts. "I can only imagine Lestrade's reaction were we to bring to his attention a schoolboy hearing a train in the night and from there deducing a threat to nation and state. He would rightly remind us of how tightly-stretched police resources are in these times and – with some justification – accuse us of clutching at straws with this outlandish notion."

"What exactly was it you saw in those papers that so convinced you?"

"Those papers are the schedules of upcoming events of interest, supplied by Scotland Yard. Conventions, parties, state functions, sporting events, dignitary travel, religious gatherings."

"Yes, you've been puzzling over them for weeks, sorting them into orders of ascending priority as targets of interest for whoever made off with that confounded gun."

"The name of Elderbridge rang a bell. That stretch of track runs between Harlow and Royston, and is a main connection for through traffic to the Midlands and north. Expressly, it is mentioned in the schedules as being on the route of several Royal Specials for the movement of dignitaries in preparation for the wedding. No one of especial importance as yet, but tomorrow – *tomorrow* – Her Majesty is due to take that line to an appearance at Royston Town Hall. Approaching from the south, her train will negotiate that bend and gradient as slowly as any other. Passing, at a crawl, the spur line where some unknown train vanished three nights ago."

"But what does it *mean*?" I exclaimed, at a loss as to what to put down in my notebook.

"Mean?" He sighed, taking out his pipe and tapping it in his fingers. "It could be nothing. The merest pursuit of wild geese." After a long pause, he went on grimly, "Or it could mean an attempt on the life of Queen Victoria."

"Then, surely – ?"

"Would Lestrade commit his resources, send men with us, second men from the Hertfordshire Constabulary? Perhaps. But by the time the official mind has reached consensus on the mere question of assistance, our window of opportunity to act may have closed. Thus, you and I will reconnoitre that line, that tunnel, and find out if some malevolent force lurks in waiting in its dark, silent stretches, or if indeed, young Mr. Threadgold merely dreamt that he heard a train, and no threat exists. If the latter, all well and good. We shall return to London having enjoyed a brief sojourn in the country. But if his ears are as sharp as a lad's ought to be and his instincts as acute as we might hope, then tomorrow might tell a very different story."

He lapsed into silence, and I frowned at the notebook on my knee. Ever since those guns had been stolen, a dark weight seemed to have hung over me, and to give those forebodings shape and form in this way was both a relief in one way and nothing short of horror in another. Part of me

52

hoped very much that Holmes's suspicions were unfounded, yet that would still leave the threat of that terrible weapon out there, unaccounted for and able to pop up anywhere, at any time, and wreak the kind of havoc for which it had never been designed. Better, perhaps, to face the music sooner than later. This hard, uncomfortable thought gave me the starting point for my notes, and I wrote with a will as the train carried us into the countryside.

The train dropped us at Elderbridge Station at twenty minutes to four. The cutting was still flooded with the high summer sun, and in the warmth of the day we walked up and over the low hill to find the village nestled in its arc of trees and fields. We had seen the old spur as we arrived, its red-rusty rails curving into the forest, where trees overhung in dense growth the space that would once have been kept clear for trains to pass through. We had shared a glance filled with meaning, knowing we would walk that way when evening came, and resolved to spend a few convivial hours at the village pub, over cider and the best fare as could be provided.

The village was served by a tall brick establishment known as The Saracen's Head, and we rented a room for the night, sharing since there was but one available, the rest being occupied by seasonal workers come in to harvest the crops. We presented the aspect of mere holiday-makers, a couple of City gents getting a breath of fresh air to blow the metropolis's smoke from our lungs, and we played the part with ease. I engaged the locals in darts as the warm summer evening lingered, and we watched swallows darting through swarms of midges in the pub's yard as the light became golden. Truly, this is the most beautiful time of day at a beautiful time of year, and I was sorry our errand was of such grave import.

Sunset was due around ten minutes past eight, and as the evening thickened, Holmes and I excused ourselves to take a last constitutional, pocketing the door key we had been issued. Indeed, twilight was gathering as the sun went below the hills, and by this point the railway cutting was in blue shadow. We walked over the hillock on the station lane and sat at a bench on the footpath to watch the stars appear. The last train to London was due southward from Royston at 8:27, and we heard it pass through, stopping briefly, its smoke rising over the treetops. As soon as it had departed, the stationmaster would close up. He walked home five minutes later and nodded us a good evening as he went by.

The moment he was out of sight on the path into Elderbridge, we rose and made our way down, by the last glimmers of day's end, into the gloom of the tracks. The side toward the village was the steep cutting. The other side of the tracks, on the outside of the bend, was a solid line of oak woods, with a footpath alongside the railway leading to farms beyond the wood.

We crossed the tracks at a level gravel pad and turned south for the disused line.

The sky was clear and filled with blazing stars, and our eyes adjusted gradually to their cold light. The moon, a couple of days past full, was big and bright in the eastern sky and shone full into the old spur line's course, creating a bright dapple through the trees that enabled us to find our way without much difficulty.

The woods were silent as a tomb. Only the scratchings of mice and voles and the occasional hoot of an owl broke the forest's warm slumber. The smell of the earth filled our noses, and a breeze rustled the treetops.

Holmes went to one knee by the rails and risked a match to inspect them. "Ah," he breathed, and shook out the match at once. "The rust has been abraded at the apex of the rails – young Mr. Threadgold was right. One or more trains have been along this track in the recent past."

I drew my revolver and spun the chambers with that once-heard, never-forgotten metallic sound. "Lead on."

We picked our way carefully through the milky moonlight, making as little noise as the forest creatures themselves, and soon Holmes pointed at the tree debris alongside the tracks. "Light branches were snapped away by the passage of the train. We're definitely on the right track, if you'll pardon the pun."

Perhaps half-an-hour after leaving the main line, we found a cutting before us, where the spur ran back into the rise of a hillside. A hundred yards on, the tall brick-lined entrance to a tunnel was a maw of black shadow where rotting boards lofted in blank denial of entry. Holmes made a soft *shhh* sound to me, and we walked on the rank grass alongside the rails to muffle our footfalls. We passed into the cutting and crept as stealthily as we might towards that wall of rough wood.

And as we did so, I saw what Holmes had obviously hoped we might see. A glimmer of light between the boards reached my wide-open pupils, and I stifled an intake of breath or any exclamation to my friend. Clearly, this tunnel wasn't as deserted as it should be.

Hardly daring to breathe, I followed Holmes. We flattened out against the barrier of great timbers, put our eyes to gaps between the boards, and found lamplight some way into the tunnel, glimmering on the metal and timber of a railway carriage. We heard nothing, but clearly someone was in residence, and Holmes squeezed my shoulder to draw me back.

We retreated along the cutting, and at a safe distance, he whispered in my ear. "Remember, young Threadgold mentioned recent repairs to that barrier? Repairs, my foot! They were modifying the barrier into *doors* – for how else could that train have entered the tunnel, yet the barrier remain intact behind it?"

"What's the play?" I asked in like volume.

"We need to know how the situation in there lies. If we can tell Scotland Yard precisely what they're facing, they can move against these desperate fellows. And I believe I know how we may do so. If they are to move that train from the tunnel once more, they will need to get up steam, which means considerable fire smoke. Unless I am mistaken, the locomotive will be parked directly beneath the tunnel's first ventilation breather, which they must also have uncovered for it to be of utility. And that gives us a way in."

It sounded desperate to me, but Holmes knew what he was doing, and I followed him as he took us back to the beginnings of the slope. There, we entered the trees and carefully climbed the hill. The sounds of the night around us couldn't have been more peaceful, and the sky was a riot of stars, such as one never sees amongst the city's lights. When we paused for a moment's breather, I could appreciate the myriad points in the not-quite-dark bowl of the heavens and the cloudy luminescence of the Milky Way stretching across the sky.

Twenty minutes saw us on the slope above the tunnel, picking our way with care, and we came to a squat brick-and-iron structure that rose bluntly from the earth, some six feet across, and seeming almost like a well, though without crank handles nor weather cover. In a patch of silver moonlight, we saw that an iron grill cover had been swung aside, revealing a shaft plunging into total blackness.

"Holmes," I whispered urgently, "you surely don't intend to go down there!"

"I have little choice," he replied, and I saw him feel down the wall with a questing hand. "Ah, the rungs of the inspection ladder remain. I must trust to them being stout British iron, resistant to the elements." He stripped off jacket and deerstalker, passing them and his revolver into my care, then swung a leg over the well-like parapet and felt for the rungs with a toe. "I shall return at the earliest possibility."

With that, he disappeared down into darkness, and I was left standing in the moonglow, keenly aware of how alone I was. Should he fail to return, it would be up to me to act. Whether I would be any more effective in such a method of entry than Holmes struck me as a ludicrous question – but what choice would I have?

A very distinct one, actually. Not for a moment could I forget that the life of our dear Queen was in the balance, and my first responsibility was to her, not to Holmes. This notion was a torment, and I railed against being faced with it, but if I had cause to think that Holmes had failed in his reconnaissance, my duty was clear enough – to remain at liberty to warn Lestrade by telegram to prevent the Queen's train from taking this line tomorrow. And Holmes must face the consequences of his actions, rash as I now believed them to be. Did we really need to know the strength of those secreted in the tunnel, to move against them?

I was occupied with these anguished thoughts for some time, the minutes seeming like hours as a result, but a scuffle of shoe leather on iron soon heralded Holmes's return, and I gave him a hand over the parapet. "You weren't worried, were you, Watson?" he whispered as he took back his things.

"Not for a minute," I replied, not entirely convincingly. "Was it worth the effort?"

"Eminently." We began to descend the hill once more, and he whispered with less caution. "I descended to the bottom of the shaft, which lies open to the tunnel. A locomotive is directly beneath it, as I predicted. With some minor gymnastics, I was able to get a look into the tunnel, and just a single carriage is in tow. There are lights inside. I heard the muffled voices of men in conversation. Given that it takes just two men to run the locomotive and two to operate a Maxim Gun effectively, we are dealing with a minimum of four. Allow for a couple of guards and someone giving the orders, and we have just a small company to deal with."

"What next?"

"Return to Elderbridge, knock the postmaster from his bed if he has already retired, and send an emergency wire to London. The wheels of their downfall will be placed in motion thereby, and we may rest safely in the knowledge that Scotland Yard will take it from there."

That might have been the plan, but we were barely a hundred yards on our way along the spur to the mainline when a figure moved in the blackness, and we heard the distinct double-double clash of a rifle bolt as a cartridge was injected into the chamber.

"Hold it right there!" came the snarl in the darkness, then we heard a breaking twig off to our other side, followed by the sound of a revolver cocking.

And my blood went ice cold. For this time, just perhaps, Sherlock Holmes had taken the art of daring just a shade too far.

Falling afoul of the game one played was, perhaps, always part of the risk. I took consolation from the fact my dear Mary understood this, but in my heart couldn't help being sorry that I had been unable to avoid placing myself in this jeopardy. The two roughs with the guns had the drop on us, and we could but freeze in place as a lantern was uncovered, and we squinted against the harsh light. We were relieved of our arms and frog-marched back along the line, two guns in our backs at all times.

A knocking at the barrier, clearly in a coded pattern, brought a challenge from within that was answered with a password, and a moment later a heavy bar moved, allowing one of the doors to swing. We were prodded within at gunpoint, and the door closed behind us. We stood in the half-light of lanterns, four hard faces staring at us with undisguised hostility.

"Well, well, well," was the grunt from a scar-faced, bewhiskered giant who seemed to be in charge, "if it isn't the great detective, Sherlock Holmes, the private pig himself." Eyes like gimlets bored into us, and I feared a rain of blows might follow, but the whisky-tainted breath merely resumed with ominous words. "The gaffer *will* be pleased after the trouble he's been put to more'n once by this piece of work." A battered seaman's cap inclined toward the carriage thirty yards deeper in the tunnel. "Lock 'em up, boys. We'll take 'em with us when we're done here, and God have mercy on 'em when they reach journey's end."

With many a shove to the shoulder and enthusiastic prods to the ribs with rifle butts, we were herded along the track to the single carriage at the end nearest the engine, and the leader went up first, via a couple of crates standing below an open side door. It seemed to be a guard's van, as there was no passenger seating, just rough stools, bedrolls, and packs of food and gear. We ascended and found ourselves in the light of oil lamps, under the eyes of equally desperate sorts who sat around a few boards placed on a packing case, playing cards.

None spoke, but it seemed all recognised Holmes's austere features and deerstalker. I began to regret giving a literal description of him in my writings. Had *A Study in Scarlet* not appeared in print two Christmases ago, Holmes might have passed anonymously through this trap. Or not – These men seemed to know him for reasons quite divorced from my humble narrative.

We were prodded towards a baggage compartment at the front end of the carriage, and two of the roughs hauled out what I recognised as ammunition boxes – two of them, containing potentially thousands of rounds to be fed to the dreadful weapon that must also be on this train. There, we were thrust into the gloomy space. At gunpoint, they patted us down. My notebook was removed, as was Holmes's magnifying glass, and they left us in the light of a bracket lamp, with crated supplies on which to rest, and a bucket for our convenience. When the door shut and locked from the outside, Holmes lowered his hands and beckoned me down to a crate.

"Take heart," he whispered. "I know it seems black, but all is not lost, I promise you. In fact, now they have us pinned, they'll be at their least vigilant, which eases the difficulty of what I must accomplish."

"And what's that?" I asked near silently.

"Why, complete the plan as if nothing had occurred. And to that end, I'm afraid I must ask you to remain in their grip, for if the trap is to be sprung, they cannot be allowed to imagine either of us was ever at liberty."

I shook my head in the wan yellow gleam of the lamp. "I'm truly not following. We're locked up in the tunnel. We're disarmed and outnumbered. What can we possibly do to change matters, much less carry through our original intentions?"

In answer, Holmes reached under his cap, from the lining brought a set of picklocks, and gestured at the padlock on the baggage compartment's side freight door. "I can be out in ten minutes, and the breather chimney is directly over the locomotive's funnel – I can climb from there."

"There's no way I could follow," I returned glumly.

"No need. Indeed, it is vital you should not. I need you to remain here and maintain the illusion that I also am present."

At my curious expression, he drew together materials from among the stores – a sack, a package, straw from the floor – and removed his jacket. He arranged the sack upon a crate, placed the package on top, stuffed the arms of his jacket with straw, wrapped the garment around the sack, then placed his deerstalker atop the whole, and had a scarecrow-like facsimile of himself. Before I could remark that it would fool no one, he gestured at the lamp.

"Turn the wick as low as it will go. If they look in to check on us, they will see you and me sitting together and, indeed, will have heard your voice engaging me in desultory converse during the evening."

"While you will be far away," I added, half-wondering what he was letting me in for.

"I'll be back," he added with the reassuring flash of a smile. "Fear not. I must be present and correct in the morning when they will doubtless inspect us, and we must remain right here until the last possible second. *Then* we'll scurry like foxes before the hounds."

They had left me my fob watch, and observing the time crawl around the dial by the feeble glow of the oil lamp on the compartment wall was my only diversion. I timed Holmes at six minutes until he had the padlock open, then we shook hands with an affirmation of good luck – I choose not to think of it as a goodbye – before I lowered the lamp wick, took my place on the packing case next to the dummy, and watched Holmes move the chain and lock with exaggerated care so as to prevent their metallic clink giving us away. Then he applied his shoulder to the stout handle of the sliding door and eased it along a fraction of an inch at a time, until he had a gap wide enough to pass through sideways. He nodded his assurances to me, then slipped through, perched on the outside of the carriage, and exerted his considerable strength to return the door to its closed position. The lock was low enough to be obscured by the gear piled in the chamber, so I did not need to refit the chain for appearances.

I heard only the faintest scuffle from outside to inform me that Holmes was negotiating the side of the car around to the cold, silent engine. The footplate was, of course, unmanned, so he was in no danger from that moment forth. He needed only to scale the top of the boiler, make his way forward, climb precariously atop the smoke-stack, then reach up, seize the lowest rungs of the service ladder in the breather chimney, and he was on his way to the outside world.

Time: I calculated in my head as I imagined him swarming up that ladder. If he fell, it was all over, and we were both more-than-likely dead. But if his wiry strength took him upward until he could get a foot to a rung, we were in with a chance – as were Her Majesty's life and the stability and peace of England, Britain, and her Empire. I heard nothing, not the slightest murmur to suggest a mishap, and when two minutes had elapsed, I breathed easier. I gave him one more minute to feel his way to the top of the shaft in the black shadows, then he would ease over into the clear starlight and dappled glow of the moon through the trees. His pupils would have expanded like a cat's, and the night would be amply bright enough for him to navigate back down the hill.

We had taken twenty minutes to scale the hill, thirty to find our way from the main line to the tunnel, and I assumed he would go with greater caution than ever. The guards were probably lulled by having already caught the interlopers – they wouldn't be expecting anyone else – but Holmes couldn't risk capture a second time. In my head, I allowed him thirty minutes, speaking softly as if answering his comments, just enough to make it seem we were both yet captives. But by half-past-ten, I was willing to place him back at the main line.

Along to the crossing, up the slope of the station laneway, over the crest, and into the village: Ten minutes more, maybe fifteen. Then what was his plan? To knock the postmaster from his bed and convince him to send a telegram to the emergency operator in London, who would send it on to Scotland Yard for Lestrade's attention, at the highest priority. Holmes was perfectly capable of operating a telegraph himself if he had to. How long? A few minutes of waffling and explanations to obtain cooperation, then draft a quick message and see it on its way. By eleven, I could imagine him fretting, smoking anything he could beg or borrow while he waited on acknowledgement – he couldn't wait too long, for he must, I now saw, return to this pit of vipers if the charade were to hold.

And if it were to hold, I must also do my part. At five-past-eleven by my watch, the door behind me unlocked with a loud *clack* and lamplight spilt in. I half-turned on the crate to cast a sullen eye at the silhouetted thug who stared in at us in the gloom. "Just keep it like that," he grunted. "No trouble out of the pair of you, or maybe the gaffer'll get damaged goods." A moment more, and the door thudded shut, the key turned in the lock, and I breathed a sigh of relief.

Time remained uppermost in my mind, and I studied my watch again. Five minutes for the message to be resent to Scotland Yard from the London receiving station. Lestrade or any other senior detective on duty would be informed, and hopefully he would reply at once with some brief sign that all was in hand. More time would be taken up as it was retransmitted to the local line. Not until at least quarter-past-eleven could I see Holmes being able to take his leave of the postmaster, and very possibly of the village bobby by this point. Ten minutes down the hill and across the tracks, twenty to thirty for a stealthy creep through the shadowed woodland to avoid any further guard patrols, then up the hill to the breather chimney, down the rungs . . . drop with the greatest care onto the locomotive's upper casing, creep along to the cab, down to the footplate, onto the side of the carriage, along to the side door . . . .

I heard that door begin to stealthily slide just after midnight, and couldn't have been more overjoyed than to see Holmes's dirty face appear in the yellow gloom. Now I was sure the plan would work – whatever the plan actually was, from this point forth.

We spent the night in fair discomfort, for there were no creature amenities. I was an old soldier and could make do, but I wasn't obliged to like it. We rested sitting on the floor, backs to the wall, and sleep didn't come easily, though I trusted Holmes's whispered assurance that we could safely leave matters in other hands. The simple fact was I didn't have the athleticism to follow Holmes's lead in escape. We were once again locked inside the baggage compartment – Holmes had reset the padlock to conceal the fact that it had ever been open – and the train remained in the tunnel, some distance from the main line. We were under guard and had been informed explicitly that whoever was behind this wicked business would be taking up his ire with Holmes at his earliest convenience.

"Who do you think it is?" I whispered at one point, and Holmes's reply was almost laconic.

"Who do we know bold enough to scheme the assassination of the Queen? To court the chaos that would follow? Republican sentiment would spring to the fore, seeking to abolish the Monarchy, and the outpouring of public grief would overboil in violence, riots, and lawlessness. In such chaos, rich profits can be reaped by those positioned to do so. It takes remarkable audacity and a despicable ruthlessness of the sort we have encountered on a number of occasions over the years. At this point, I must favour the shadowy Professor Moriarty, with whom we brushed last December. He would indeed have a score to settle, given the escapades of his I have foiled."

"We must make a clean break when the time comes," I added almost silently. "His mercies will be terrible to behold."

"I am not eager to find myself in his power," Holmes replied, a murmur in the darkness. "Follow my lead when matters begin to unfold. I doubt we will need to go far. Just a few yards, in fact."

I glanced at his profile in the gloom and wondered quite what he meant, but was reassured that he had a plan, and settled myself to pass the dark hours in whatever rest I could manage.

In mid-July, the sun returns at around four a.m., with a pink twilight for half-an-hour beforehand. In the tunnel, we would know nothing of the beauties of daybreak, and I expected our captors to be in no hurry to greet the morn. Her Majesty's Special wasn't due to pass Elderbridge until twenty-minutes-to-ten, and we had that long to spend in nerve-wracked waiting.

Sure enough, I heard the roughs moving around seven o'clock, voices from the engine's cab, and the scrape and rattle of coal being shovelled. Firing up the engine from cold would take at least two hours for the firebox to heat through all parts of the machine. There was much coming-and-going in the carriage, and we smelt bacon frying, likely over some camp stove contraption. A kettle boiled shrilly, and my mouth watered at the thought of food. We were unlikely to receive anything, and sure enough we were offered only a beaker of water each when the inner door was unlocked and opened around eight.

Holmes nodded to me when we were locked in once more. "They'll wait for the last moment, then open the tunnel doors and back along the spur to the main line. The Maxim is almost certainly set up in this carriage's rear connecting door and will rake the Royal Special as it goes slowly by the spur. We must be ready to move on the instant if we are to see this day through."

"Count on it," I replied, working and limbering my joints after their uncomfortable night.

My nerves were stretched wickedly as the hour for action approached, and we sensed that the locomotive was up to temperature. We heard the reciprocating valves chuffing softly as the great machine idled. At last, Holmes steepled his fingers in an almost meditative concentration before

61

he turned to the padlock and dealt with it, more quickly this morning given his familiarity with it.

"If they come in now, we may be undone," he murmured. "I'm banking on them having too much to occupy them to be concerned about us. After all – " The padlock opened with a sharp click. "We're safely locked up, aren't we?"

I smiled and flexed my hands, hoping I might get the chance to strike a righteous blow or two in the process. In the hours since we were taken prisoner the previous night, I had had more than my fill of being helpless.

At last, we heard voices calling between the carriage and the engine, and our world gave a shudder as the locomotive went into reverse gear and wheels clawed for purchase on the rails. "This is it," Holmes breathed, concentrating. He set an eye to the surround of the sliding door and watched for daylight as the train backed out of the tunnel. "Stand ready, Watson. Time?"

I clicked open my watch. "Nine-thirty, on the nose."

The engine was little more than idling, backing the carriage along the track at walking pace. They were being supremely cautious, attracting as little attention as possible. We eased along the spur as the moments went by, and with five minutes to the scheduled time of passage for Her Majesty's transport, we felt the brakes take hold.

Holmes waited with the sliding door's stout handle in his grasp, ready to put his shoulder to it when the moment came, and I could only wait in an agony of suspense, my watch open in my hand. "Nine-thirty-nine," I breathed. A locomotive whistle shrilled some way off, and my blood turned to ice. "She's here – Dear God! – *She's here!*"

"Wait . . ." Holmes hissed. *"Wait!"*

The seconds raced by, and we heard the sound of a locomotive working hard on the steep bend, then nothing for long moments until our world was shattered by the terrible tearing thunder of the Maxim. Like a whole firing platoon crashing into action, the weapon poured forth shot at an unspeakable rate, and we heard the jingle of spent shell casings piling up beside the weapon.

"Now!" Holmes shoved the door, and I realised he was using the sound of the Maxim to cover our escape. He stooped, set a hand to the floor, and pivoted over to drop beside the carriage. I repeated the action, then followed him forward, dropping into a crawl to pass the hot, aromatic engine. Under the noise of the clamouring machine gun, the engine driver and fireman on the footplate had no idea we crept by their nest. Indeed, their attention would be almost anywhere other than upon us, and we rose unobserved and ran to the front of the engine, where Holmes slapped the platform above the buffers. "Up, Watson! Quick!"

We scaled the ironworks until we stood upon the very bows of the locomotive, and Holmes had us flatten out against the great forward boiler hatch. I followed his example in slipping my fingers into my ears – in anticipation of *what*, I could not imagine.

The Maxim fell silent after unloading what must have been many hundreds of rounds, and I wondered why the Royal Special had taken so long to go by the spur. Even at slow pace, it should have been well through the trap in twenty seconds . . . .

When it came, it was as if the world ended. Not one but *two* machine guns opened up, and the sound of their demolition of the train was both spectacular and awful. My nostrils filled with the smell of broken timber as shards and splinters filled the air, and the iron of the locomotive was assailed as if by a swarm of angry bees – a boiler-shop clangouring as ammunition tore through the ruined carriage and was stopped by plate steel.

Rounds overshot and ricochets tumbled through the branches all about with terrible screeches and whines. Holmes and I had taken cover in the only safe place, the absolute far end of the train with all the engine's metal between us and the guns, and I wondered what kind of shambles the Maxims had made of the very place we had spent the night.

I didn't have long to wait, for the fusillade ended as abruptly as it had begun. All we heard for long moments was an angry escape of steam from the damaged engine. Then a shout from afar brought a smile to Holmes's lips, and we dropped down to the track bed. Figures moved through a haze of cordite smoke in the rays of the morning sun, and we saw red-coated soldiers fanning out around what little remained of the train.

The carriage had been reduced to matchwood, and I grimly realised that our captors were somewhere amongst the smoking, collapsing wreckage. The guns had left them no chance, the sheer weight of fire defeating what cover the timbers had offered. Likewise, the engine crew had succumbed to the sparking rebound of rounds, and I scowled sadly as I half-glimpsed their bodies on the footplate. This was a terrible morning's work, and I grieved that I should have lived to see such a thing.

"Mr. Holmes!" called a familiar voice, and the figure of Inspector Lestrade emerged from the morning light as the redcoats passed us along, and we found another train parked across the end of the spur.

As we joined Lestrade, I took in the ruin the criminals had made of it, the way the weight of shot had smashed and torn away the very timbers of the first carriage's construction. But it was not a passenger carriage, and where holes gaped, bright metal showed.

Lestrade nodded proudly. "Thank you for your warning and suggestions. It was a rush job, Mr. Holmes, but the railway workshops got it lashed up overnight. Sheet steel all down the left-hand side, firing slots fore and aft, and Mr. Maxim was happy to let us have two of his guns and experienced men to operate them."

Holmes nodded grimly and stood with fists on hips to view the catastrophic damage to both trains. "History might just record this as the first action ever fought by fully automatic weapons. Both Mr. Maxim and the army have their field test, of the most graphic possible sort. It is inevitable that military technology should embrace ever more terrible kinds of destruction, and I shudder to imagine what form wars to come may take."

Lestrade shook his head, offering small cigars, which we accepted with thanks. "I doubt it, myself, Mr. Holmes. We've just seen how awful these things really are, and I'm sure that when we report what we've seen, the War Office will think twice about acquiring something so wicked. I have to wonder why an inventive genius like Hiram Maxim would think of something so evil, and I'm absolutely confident it'll never be used in warfare." He smiled with a nod as he finished. "Mark my words, Mr. Holmes, Dr. Watson. It'll never happen."

I think there must have been many at the time who felt as Lestrade did, and I wanted to believe it myself. Surely the rules of warfare would forbid such an escalation of its horrors. But I had the uneasy suspicion that such notions were merely hope whispering to the conscious mind, and the years since have gone a long way to confirming my feeling as pragmatism, not cynicism. Artillery has grown ever heavier, battleships ever mightier, and the machine gun is here to stay.

But on that summer's day in 1889, we could congratulate ourselves on averting a wicked plan. There would be no attempt on Her Majesty's life. The Monarchy would continue undaunted, the Royal Wedding would take place as planned – and the missing Maxim was restored to its rightful hands – namely the Royal Army's embryonic, experimental machine gun unit.

We boarded the Special and moved up to Elderbridge Station, where points were adjusted and we diverted into the village's goods siding, there to wait until eleven o'clock, when a train came up from the south – a magnificent, mirror-polished black locomotive with the bold number "5" in red upon her forward hatch. The train went through without pausing, and we glimpsed the opulent Royal carriages in which our beloved Queen travelled. The redcoats had formed up on Elderbridge Station platform in review order to present a salute, answered by a shrill blast of the express's whistle. For an old army fellow, it was rather a moving moment, and I couldn't help raising a hand in salute also, though none noticed and only I enjoyed the sentiment.

A crew would come up to deal with the wreckage on the spur line and reseal the tunnel. For now, with the rogue Maxim manhandled along to the train and loaded aboard by brawny soldiers, we had a clear line to run back down to the metropolis. With our luggage sent down from The Saracen's Head, Lestrade invited us into a carriage for tea and smokes with the detachment's officer, and we passed an hour companionably enough, during which the inspector informed us that Professor Moriarty had taken another considerable step towards being considered not simply the chief enemy of the public good, but perhaps the most wanted criminal who had ever drawn breath. The War Office was chagrined to have employed his intellectual brilliance in years gone by on training exercises, and well-appreciated the magnitude of the foe the nation faced.

Holmes had given his undertaking to make Moriarty and the threat he represented the core of his work from that moment forth, and the foiling of this latest outrage was simply a further chapter in the unfolding of that tale. I could hardly credit the coolness with which Holmes entertained the fact he was wanted so badly by so terrible a man. They were the irresistible force and the immovable object. Moriarty was the dark to Holmes's light – not that Holmes would have entertained so poetic a metaphor – and they would war until something gave. I prayed silently that when the catastrophic day came, I would not be left grieving.

Holmes was never one for accolades and honour, but, just occasionally, he accepted the odd token of gratitude. He had a few items in his possession expressing such thanks from those he had served, but this time the honour took a different form. I cajoled him into considering this case an exercise in close protection – that he had been both security consultant and bodyguard. That seemed to mollify his caustic side, such that when Princess Louise of Wales and the Duke of Fife tied the knot in the chapel at Buckingham Palace, there were three additional guests in the outermost circle.

Anonymous in our finest attire among a sea of guests, including kings and maharajas, generals, admirals, and politicians of every stripe, Holmes, Lestrade, and I watched in respectful silence as vows were exchanged and new affiliations of blood created. I had never imagined I would set foot in the palace, let alone be present at a ceremony of national note, and I was quietly touched that Her Majesty valued so highly the gallantry of our actions on her behalf.

I couldn't think of a better rebuttal to the ambitions of our Professor of Evil than this moment, but when the reception was done with and guests streamed from the palace, Holmes wore a pensive look as we boarded a hansom for home.

"What is it?" I asked.

"It would be a mistake to think that Moriarty is any more than irritated by these events. He likely considers it a minor setback. If he cannot launch anarchy today, he will find another means."

"This threat will never be over, will it?" I murmured, feeling abruptly very down.

"All things find their level, my friend," Holmes replied philosophically. "But the great task of my life would seem to be ensuring that the outcome, however it arrives, does not, under any circumstances, leave that man at liberty, or perhaps even alive. I swear this, even at cost of my own life."

I glanced at his narrow profile and could only nod with a small, brave smile, for I knew Sherlock Holmes gave that assurance with every fibre of his being.

NOTE

* For more information about the theft of Maxim's machine guns, see "Such Profitable Treason" in *The MX Book of New Sherlock Holmes Stories – Part XLVI: Occupants of the Canonical Realm (1861-1889)*

Antoinette's Apparition
by P. C. Shumway

"Listen to this, John," said my wife, as she read from *The Daily Telegraph*'s society column. "'*Lady Okehurst of Vauxhall Manor will present the Marie Antoinette diamond necklace at a dinner party this afternoon.*'"

It was a raw, damp day in April. Mary and I were reading the papers by the fire after breakfast, as was our custom on Saturday mornings. I looked up from the latest edition of *Sporting Life*.

"As I recall from my history lessons in primary school, the necklace was destroyed. If memory serves me, it was an elaborate arrangement of diamonds which King Louis XV of France had commissioned during the previous century. He died before the purchase was made."

"I thought King Louis XVI bought it for Queen Antoinette."

"He offered to buy it, but she refused the lavish gift. A scandal ensued shortly thereafter involving Cardinal de Rohan and a woman impersonating the Queen who tricked the Cardinal into borrowing enormous sums of money to buy the tawdry thing. I can't remember the woman's name, but it's believed she took the necklace and had it broken apart and sold in pieces on the black market here in London. Although Marie Antionette never wore the monstrosity, the public believed she was involved in the extravagance, and it led to her disfavor and demise."

Mary shook her head at my lack of appreciation for historical drama and gaudy jewelry. She looked back down at her paper.

"It says here that nineteen of the diamonds, nine of which are quite large, including the magnificent pear-shaped queen diamond, were recovered after years of searching by generations of Hornsby and Pussett Jewelers. The diamonds have been set in a new necklace and sold to the Right Honourable Lord William Okehurst of Surrey. He recently promised the exquisite necklace to the baroness on the occasion of their wedding anniversary. Lady Okehurst is showing the jewelry in its first public appearance to a small group of high society at Vauxhall Manor at noon today."

Mary set her paper on her lap and looked over at me. "How very exciting. Can you imagine wearing a piece of history?"

"I imagine there are rumors of the stones being cursed by Marie Antoinette's ghost and the necklace leading to ruin for whomever possesses it."

"You're incorrigible," Mary said, raising the paper to her eyes and rereading the article in case one of the diamonds had escaped her attention. I thought no more of the matter.

Later that afternoon, when we were about to have our tea, there was a ring at the front door. I answered the bell, since we had been without a housekeeper for the past week. The woman, without giving notice, ran off with an American tourist she met outside Buckingham Palace. I opened the door, and to my surprise there stood Mr. Sherlock Holmes, grinning like a schoolboy at an ice cream social.

"Good afternoon, Doctor," said he. "Still without a housekeeper, I see."

Holmes stepped into the hall and I closed the door. I hadn't seen my friend in several days. I supposed my unpolished boots and state of the room supplied him with deductive fodder about my staff situation. He was in an excited state and had a gleam in his eye that told me he was on a case.

"If you aren't too fatigued from last night's medical call, perhaps you would join me in a little adventure."

I admit I was feeling tired and enjoying the lazy comforts of domestic life that afternoon. However, the thrill of the chase which accompanies Holmes's cases stirred my attention. I was at a loss about how he deduced I had a late-night call. My expression must have asked for an explanation.

"You are a creature of habit, Watson. Whenever you return from a medical visit, you put your hat on a peg, place your Gladstone bag on the top shelf of the hall cabinet, and hang your coat – unless it is very late and you are exhausted, in which case your hat still finds a peg, but you invariably drop the Gladstone on the floor and toss your coat over the back of the nearest chair."

As usual, his deduction was obvious once it was explained.

"So, what do you say? It's a pressing matter. I have a cab waiting outside and a police inspector scratching his head."

"Never too tired for an adventure," I replied as I grabbed my coat off the chair and stuck my head in the parlor to let Mary know I was throwing in my lot with Holmes. Mary, as always, was happy to see me join my friend in one of his cases. I took my hat from the rack and followed Holmes out the door.

We climbed into the waiting hansom cab and headed south and east. We were travelling towards the Palace before I realized I hadn't asked Holmes where we were headed or what the case was about.

He looked at me and said, "The so-called Marie Antoinette necklace has vanished."

Apparently, Holmes shared my dislike of the moniker.

"Mary read an article in the paper this morning about Lady Okehurst's presentation of the necklace to the public today at a dinner."

"We are headed for Vauxhall Manor now. Athelney Jones' telegram didn't provide any details, other than it was a stumper."

I remembered the portly Lambeth inspector from our case involving the Agra treasure two years prior. The pompous Athelney Jones disapproved of Holmes's methods. I was therefore surprised my friend had been summoned. Only a baffling puzzle could incite the inspector to ask for assistance.

We passed the Palace Gardens, Victoria Station, and Westminster, crossed over the Thames, and navigated under the Vauxhall Station tracks. A few minutes later, we came to Vauxhall Manor. The villa comprised a three-story brick house built in the Jacobean style, surrounded by exquisite gardens, and encompassed by a high stone wall topped with brick and mortar. We drove up to the west wall's double iron gate, which appeared to be the main entrance. A footman stepped up to our cab and opened the door. We paid off the driver before being taken up a short pathway leading to the front doors of the Manor. Jones was standing on the front steps talking to the Vauxhall police sergeant and one of his constables. The two uniformed men left to inspect the grounds as the fat inspector turned to greet us. His overcoat and coat were unbuttoned. It appeared he had put on two stone in as many years.

"Mr. Holmes the theorist and Doctor Watson," Jones said. "The commissioner insisted I elicit your cooperation. I recall you were of some little help in apprehending Jonathan Small in that Sholto affair a couple of years ago, but you will need more than wild theories to solve this mystery. There is some real hocus-pocus at play here."

I was put off by the arrogance of Athelney Jones. Holmes, however, seemed unaffected.

"We are at your service, Inspector. Pray, give us the details of the case thus far."

Jones placed his thumbs under his braces and pulled his shoulders back.

"The Baron and his valet are presently at his estate in Leicestershire. Lady Okehurst hosted a dinner at noon to display her famed Marie Antoinette necklace, but when the safe was opened, the necklace was gone."

"Perhaps you could begin with a description of the household and when the necklace was last seen."

"The Right Honourable Lord Okehurst keeps a full staff," the overweight inspector said, as he produced a notepad from his coat pocket and looked at it. "A butler, a head housekeeper, a valet, a ladies' maid, a groundskeeper, three housemaids, a cook, a kitchen maid, two stable boys, and a footman – whom you've seen. I have spoken briefly with each of them. The groundskeeper and the two grooms were in their small cottage next to the stables all morning. Lady Okehurst instructed them to keep out of sight during her gala. Also living at the Manor is the Baron's sixteen-year-old nephew, the Honourable Edmund Okehurst."

"The jewelers Hornsby and Pussett delivered the necklace at ten o'clock this morning under armed guard. The baroness put the jewels in the safe herself. Several maids, the butler, and the housekeeper witnessed the proceedings. The safe is one of those fancy Herring-Hall parlour safes with a Pillard combination lock. You see, I'm a bit of an expert on safes. As you can imagine, when one has been in the official force for as many years as I have . . . ."

Jones let his statement of experience trail off into our imaginations as he pulled upon his braces in a show of authority before continuing.

"Lord and Lady Okehurst are the only people who know the combination. Inside the safe are two shelves, and a security drawer with a lock to which there are only two keys. The baron keeps one key on his chain and the baroness keeps the other key in her bedchamber nightstand drawer. By ten-fifteen, the jewel-case with the necklace was locked in the security drawer and the safe door was closed. The safe is in the dining hall, and was in full view by the staff. It was opened at noon by Lady Okehurst, only to find the necklace had vanished. It's simply impossible. The housekeeper thinks the ghost of Marie Antoinette has reclaimed her diamonds."

"Along with the jewel-case?" Holmes asked impishly.

"Apparently so," replied the humourless inspector. "Lady Okehurst is waiting for us in the dining hall. Perhaps you would care to examine the safe and speak with her."

"By all means. I would also like to interview the guests and the staff."

"The dinner guests were dismissed since the necklace must have been taken before they arrived. I can provide you with a list of attendees."

"They were released without a search?" I asked.

"I couldn't bloody-well search His Grace the Archbishop of Canterbury or the Duke of Wellington now, could I?"

"I suppose not," I admitted.

The inspector pulled upon his braces again.

"None of the guests could have opened the safe and taken the necklace in a room full of other guests, the baroness, and the staff all milling around. The safe is in full view of anyone in the dining hall, as you will see. This way, gentlemen."

Jones led us through the prominent front doors and into the marble-floored entrance hall. The foyer was twice the size of our Baker Street sitting room and furnished with polished cherry tables and wall cabinets. The butler collected our overcoats and hats. "Thank you, Mr. Bernard," said the inspector as he directed us past a double stairway, through a wide hallway, and into the dining hall. It was a massive open room with a high ceiling and crystal chandeliers. Tall, latticed windows faced the gardens. Six large round tables were set around the room. The tables were covered with the finest white linen and polished cutlery. A crystal vase of fresh-cut flowers was set in the center of each table. At the far end of the room stood the marble-topped parlour safe. An arrangement of flowers adorned the top of the safe. As the inspector had noted, it was in full view.

A maid was gathering plates and cutlery from one table. She wore a white apron over her black dress and a white cap atop of her long black hair. Athelney Jones addressed her.

"Excuse me, Miss – ?"

"Julia Thatcher, sir."

"That's right. Julia," Jones said, as he produced a notebook from his coat and glanced at it. "Please stop what you're doing, Miss Thatcher. I gave instructions nothing be disturbed in this room until we finish our investigation."

"Yes, sir. Sorry, sir."

"Thatcher?" Holmes remarked. "Not Bernard? You aren't related to the butler?"

"No, sir," replied Julia, as she looked at her feet.

Athelney Jones gave Holmes a side glance, then said to the young maid, "Let the staff know we will be interviewing each of you again."

"Yes, sir," said the girl, as she set the dishes on the table, curtsied, and scrambled out of the room. "Thank you, sir."

Lady Okehurst and her personal maid sat at the table nearest to the safe. The baroness was visibly upset and was waving off a cup of tea when we approached her.

"My Lady," Jones said, "these gentlemen are here to assist with the investigation. May I present Mr. Sherlock Holmes and Dr. Watson?"

The baroness did not offer her hand, so we merely bowed slightly in greeting.

"May we be permitted a seat at your table, Lady Okehurst?" Holmes asked. "We need to discuss the events of this afternoon."

Lady Okehurst waved her hand, as if dismissing a servant. She was an attractive woman nearing forty-five years of age. She had dark hazel eyes, carefully braided light brown hair, and was wearing a dark blue dress with a low neckline in preparation to donning the necklace.

"Perhaps," Holmes said, "your Ladyship could recount the events leading to the disappearance of the diamonds."

The baroness sighed. "If I must." She paused with a look of bored dissatisfaction, as she was displeased about recalling her embarrassing experience to a private detective.

"As I have already related to the official police, the jewelers arrived at ten o'clock with the necklace. It was in a locked strongbox and carried by a Hornsby and Pussett guard. Mr. Victor Pussett unlocked and opened the box himself. From the strongbox, he produced a mahogany jewel-case perhaps eight inches in length and four or five inches in width. He opened the jewel-case and handed it to me."

The baroness paused at the memory of Queen Antoinette's diamond necklace snuggled in blue velvet.

"The necklace is exquisite, gentlemen. The diamonds are of the finest quality, and set in a silver-and-gold chain."

She paused again to collect her thoughts.

"The necklace must be recovered at any cost."

"Don't worry, my Lady," Jones said. "I will sort out this mystery."

"Please continue, Madam," Holmes said. "What did you do after viewing the necklace?"

"I closed the jewel-case, turned, and walked over to the safe. I handed the case to Bernard."

"The butler, Mr. Pierre Bernard," the inspector said, looking at his notebook.

"Bernard was standing just to the left of the safe. I dialed the combination, raised the handle, opened the safe, withdrew my key from my sleeve, then unlocked and opened the drawer. Bernard handed over the case and I opened it once again to show the necklace to Alice here, who was standing to the right of the safe. The new housemaid, Julia, sneaked a peek over Alice's shoulder."

The baroness smiled slightly at the thought of a lowly maid trying to get a glimpse of the stunning necklace.

"I closed the jewel-case and placed it in the drawer, which I immediately locked. I stepped aside and Bernard closed the safe door, lowered the handle, and turned the dial to lock the safe."

"I assume his back was to you at that point?" Holmes asked.

"Yes of course. Alice can confirm that the necklace was placed in the safe and it was locked. There is no question of that."

"It happened just as m'Lady describes," Alice said.

Alice was a wisp of a girl, about twenty-five years old, with plain features, short brown hair, and a pale complexion.

Holmes looked at the ladies' maid and asked, "What happened next?"

"As soon as the safe was closed, Mr. Pussett asked to be dismissed. Then he and the guard took the strongbox and left."

"Who else was in the room at the time?"

Alice wrinkled her nose in thought and looked at her mistress as she replied.

"The other maids were in and out of the room setting the tables for dinner. I think Mrs. Ellsworth was in the room then, straightening the table linen and giving orders."

"She's the housekeeper," Jones offered, looking at his notes.

"Mrs. Ellsworth runs a tight ship," Lady Okehurst said, "as I expect of her."

"Was your nephew Master Edmund in attendance?" Holmes asked.

"Heavens, no! Edmund has no interest in social affairs, unless there are young eligible ladies present."

"Pray, continue."

"I left the dining hall to rest and dress for dinner. I returned an hour later to greet the arriving guests. At noon, when all the guests were seated, I opened the safe. I unlocked the drawer with my key, opened it, and discovered the jewel-case containing the necklace was no longer there. It had simply vanished."

"When I spoke with the staff," Jones interjected, "they said at least one of them was in the room the entire time."

Holmes turned to the baroness and asked if she would be so kind as to open the safe for us. We all stood, and she walked over to the safe and dialed the combination, raised the handle, and swung open the door. There were documents stacked on the two shelves. She then took the key from her sleeve and opened the security drawer. It contained a checkbook, a stack of ten-pound notes, a pearl necklace, a set of pearl earrings, two pairs of diamond cufflinks, and several gemstone broaches. She stepped aside and Holmes discreetly looked around the documents on the shelves, the contents of the drawer, and examined the lock on the drawer before closing it.

"Thank you, Madam."

Lady Okehurst locked the drawer. When she was about to close the safe door, Holmes stepped over and said, "Permit me, my Lady." The baroness stepped aside. With his back to us, Holmes swung the door closed, lowered the handle, and turned the dial.

The baroness returned the key to her sleeve and rolled her eyes at the inspector.

"Are we quite finished?"

"Yes, of course," Jones replied. "Thank you for your time, my Lady."

Holmes turned around after closing the safe and faced the baroness.

"Just one more question, if I may. Do you have any suspicions?"

Lady Okehurst glared at him and said, "Certainly not."

The baroness turned and walked out of the room, with Alice following in her wake.

"Maybe they are all in it together," I suggested, once Lady Okehurst and Alice were out of earshot.

"Don't think for a minute, Doctor, that I haven't already thought of that," Jones said with more bluster than I thought necessary. Then the inspector seemed to be lost in thought for a minute, as if he was trying on the idea and making it his own.

Holmes slowly shook his head.

"It is a possibility, Watson, although the baroness seems to be truly upset. I suspect if she were to stage a robbery, she would have done so without embarrassing herself in the company of high society. And why not take the other jewels?" Holmes turned to the inspector. "I assume the necklace is insured?"

"I haven't had the opportunity to ask the Baron yet. Perhaps the butler will know." The inspector waddled out of the room and returned with Mr. Bernard in tow.

Pierre Bernard, dressed neatly in black tails, stood erect at attention. He was perhaps fifty years in age, with balding black hair peppered with gray. I noticed Holmes studying the butler's shoes. Jones introduced us and waved his hand towards the chair.

"Please have a seat, Mr. Bernard."

"Thank you, sir"

"You are of French descent, are you not?"

The butler sat with his back straight on the edge of the chair vacated by his mistress.

"Yes sir, I immigrated to England when I was twenty-four."

Jones turned to a fresh page in his notebook. "Is the necklace insured?"

"I do not know, sir."

"How long have you been in service to Lord and Lady Okehurst?"

"Five years and two months, sir."

The inspector scribbled in his notebook and asked him to again recount the events of the afternoon. His account of the delivery of the necklace and the placement of the jewel-case in the safe matched that of Lady Okehurst.

"Do you perchance know the combination of the safe?" the inspector asked.

"Certainly not, sir."

"What did you do after the safe was closed and your mistress left the room?" Holmes asked.

"I noticed two of the tables weren't set properly, so I made some adjustments. The tables must be equally distributed with adequate space for the guests."

"Who else was in the room at the time?"

"As I recall, Mrs. Ellsworth ordered the new housemaid, Julia, who had the impertinence to spy a glance of the necklace, to fetch the cutlery and naperies from the kitchen. Julia hurried off, and Mrs. Ellsworth busied herself with the flower arrangements. There was no one else in the room at the time."

"Did you discuss anything with Mrs. Ellsworth?" Jones asked. "Perhaps you talked about the necklace?"

The butler raised his chin slightly.

"Mrs. Ellsworth and I do not engage in idle chat."

"Did either of you leave the room from the time the necklace arrived until it was discovered missing?" Holmes asked.

"At some point there was a loud crash heard from the kitchen. Mrs. Ellsworth muttered, 'What now?' and marched off in that direction. A minute later, she returned and said something under her breath about incompetence."

"You were alone in the room during that time?" the inspector asked.

The butler looked down his nose at the fat inspector and said, "Yes, I was alone for a minute before Mrs. Ellsworth returned from the kitchen."

"When she returned, you stepped outside to smoke a cigarette," stated Holmes.

Bernard's eyes opened wide. Holmes smiled and said, "A small bit of soil adheres to the heel of your left shoe, and the tobacco stains on your fingers are evident."

The butler was mortified that his appearance was less than immaculate. "Yes, sir," he admitted. "I stepped outside before the festivities began."

"I presume you left the house through the servant's entrance?" asked Holmes.

"Yes, of course," Bernard said. "It is on the side of the house which leads down to the north gate."

"Is the gate locked?"

"I would assume so, sir. It is always kept locked. There is a bell pull which runs underground from the gate to the house to announce deliveries. The gate was unlocked briefly for the bread delivery this morning and once for the butcher. There are two keys to the gate. One key is kept on the wall just inside the service door entrance, and Mr. Brown, the groundskeeper, has charge of the second key."

Inspector Jones shook his head at Holmes.

"You will never make it far, my boy, if you keep wandering off track. Mr. Bernard couldn't steal the necklace if he was out of the room."

"However," I said, "if he was out of doors, that means Mrs. Ellsworth was alone in the room."

"I see what you are getting at, Doctor," Jones admitted, as he rubbed his double chin.

"Are there other gates in the villa's wall?" Holmes asked Bernard.

"Just the main gate on the west wall where you entered."

"Did you see anyone when you were in the garden?"

"No, sir. I saw no one. When I returned, Mrs. Ellsworth was showing Julia the proper way to fold a napkin. Rosa and Audrey, our other housemaids, came in from the kitchen with the washed cutlery and began setting the tables. I left the dining room to attend the front door. For the next hour I was busy greeting the guests."

"Where were you when the safe was opened?"

"I was standing by the hallway leading to the foyer so to be of service to Lady Okehurst while keeping a watchful eye on the front doors."

"That will be all for now, Bernard," said Holmes. "Please locate Mrs. Ellsworth and send her in."

"Yes, sir."

The butler left us and headed for the servants' quarters.

A few moments later, Mrs. Ellsworth stepped into the room and curtsied.

"Mr. Bernard said you wanted to talk with me again?"

"Yes, Madam," said Jones. "Please have a seat. We are establishing the whereabouts of everyone from ten o'clock until noon."

The housekeeper sat down in the chair vacated by the butler. She was a stout woman in her early sixties with her grey hair tied in a bun. She wore a black dress with a silver chain around her neck, suspending half-moon spectacles on her bosom. As she talked, she darted ferret-like glances around the room. Her account of securing the necklace in the safe was the same as told by Lady Okehurst and the butler. Jones asked what she did after Lady Okehurst retired to her rooms.

"I was arranging flowers when we heard a loud crash from the kitchen. I left Mr. Bernard and went into the kitchen to find that our new girl, Julia, had dropped a tray of silverware on the floor. Of all days! I instructed her and Audrey to rewash the cutlery and was about to return to the dining hall when Julia asked two or three foolish questions. I don't think that girl has a brain in her head! When I returned to the hall, Mr.

Bernard was straightening the chairs at one of the tables. A little later he snuck off to smoke one of those horrible cigarettes of his."

"How long were you in the kitchen?" asked Holmes.

"Only a minute, sir."

"And how long were you alone in the dining hall after the butler left?" asked the inspector.

"Three or four minutes, I suppose. I was just finishing the flower arrangement on the parlour safe when Master Edmund came in from the direction of the drawing room. He said 'Whoever heard of flowers on a safe?' The young master went into the kitchen and came back out eating a scone and dropping crumbs on the floor. He said I was needed in the kitchen, so I went back in to see what was taking so long with the plates and napkins."

Athelney Jones scribbled in his notebook.

"So Master Edmund was alone in the room. How long were you in the kitchen?"

"Only a few minutes, sir. When I returned to the dining room with Julia and the napkins, Master Edmund was just leaving. He said something about making himself scarce before all the fun started. Julia apologized for dropping the tray. I had to show the silly girl how to fold and place the napkins. It was about then that Mr. Bernard returned from the garden. A few minutes later Audrey and Rosa came in with the cutlery and tea plates."

"Does Master Edmund know the combination to the safe?" asked Holmes.

"I don't think so sir, but not for lack of trying. It isn't proper for me to say, but I caught him last week fiddling with the combination. You know how boys are. I think he was just curious."

"Thank you, Mrs. Ellsworth," said Holmes. "How do you yourself account for the disappearance of the necklace?"

"It's really not my place to say, sir."

Jones leaned back and crossed his arms. He knew where the conversation was heading. The housekeeper took a deep breath to steady her resolve.

"Well, it seems to me sir, there are supernatural powers involved."

"Supernatural powers?" I asked.

"Those jewels are cursed, sir. They brought ruin to Queen Antoinette. She was beheaded, you know."

"Yes, we know, Madam," said Jones.

Just then, the young nephew walked into the room, heading for the kitchen. Jones stood and said, "Master Edmund, would you permit a word with us?"

Mrs. Ellsworth lowered her voice and leaned in.

"I think the ghost of Queen Antoinette took the necklace. No one except the mistress could open the safe. The necklace couldn't have just disappeared on its own."

"You have a point there," Holmes stated. "Would you be so kind as to have the three housemaids, the butler, and Lady Okehurst join us here in one-half hour?"

"Yes, sir," she said as we all stood. "Thank you, sir." She curtsied again and left us.

The young man smiled as he walked over.

"Have you questioned Antoinette's apparition yet?" he asked impishly.

"Not yet, my Lord," said the inspector without a smile. "We were told you have some experience with this safe."

"That old woman should mind her own business," he said, looking in the direction of the servant's quarters.

"Any luck with the combination?" asked Holmes.

The young man turned and looked at my friend. "And who the devil are you?"

"This is Mr. Sherlock Holmes, sir," said the inspector.

"The detective? How grand. No luck with the safe. I played with the combination lock a couple of times last week when I thought no one was looking, but I didn't get anywhere with it. I wasn't trying to steal anything."

"I assume you were trying to get a peek at the will," Holmes stated. "I noticed it was amongst the papers on the top shelf."

"I am next in line for the title. I wanted to make sure of my inheritance."

"Naturally," Holmes said.

"If you have no further questions, I'll take my leave." Without waiting for a reply, the young man turned on his heel and walked into the kitchen. He emerged a few seconds later with another scone.

"Good luck catching your phantom," he said, smiling, as he walked out of the dining hall.

"I'll be the laughing stock of the force now," Jones said. "I suppose you want me to hire a medium to contact Marie Antoinette's ghost."

"There is no need, Inspector," "Holmes stated. "The case is solved."

"Solved!"

"Yes. I just need to confirm my theory."

"Mr. Sherlock Holmes and his *theories*! And just how are you going to check your theory?"

"By going for a stroll in the garden and then observing Julia's left ear."

Jones frowned. "You are a funny one, Mr. Holmes."

"If you would round up the Vauxhall policemen who are wandering around the premises and have them here in a half-hour, I will expose the criminals. Come, Watson, let us enjoy these beautiful gardens."

I followed Holmes down the corridor towards the servant's quarters. We reached the service entrance and stepped outside.

"Criminals?" I said. "You mean there is more than one?"

"Obviously, my good fellow. Look here – these are Bernard's footsteps. Let's see where they lead."

We followed the butler's footprints through the garden and down towards the north gate. Holmes stopped at the planters along the way and played with the dirt around the plants. When we reached the gate, he reached down and picked up a cigarette stub.

"Just as I suspected. Here is what's left of Bernard's cigarette."

Holmes tried the gate, but it was locked. He peered through the iron bars of the gate at the ground on the other side.

"I'm afraid we may not recover the necklace, Watson. If we cannot deliver the jewels, we can at least deliver some justice."

"Are you saying the butler stole the necklace? But how? The safe and drawer were locked. He was alone with the safe for only a minute. No safe cracker could open that safe in that amount of time."

"I will reveal all, Watson. You know my proclivity for the dramatic. Let us return to the dining hall."

We made our way back to the hall and met Athelney Jones. He introduced to us Sergeant Johnson and Constable Davies, who worked in the Vauxhall district. The sergeant was a big burly man of forty years, and I placed the lean constable in his late twenties. Mrs. Ellsworth entered with Bernard and the three housemaids. Holmes asked them to have a seat at the tables. Holmes whispered something to the inspector and the two uniformed men. The officers walked over to the table where Bernard sat and stood at the ready. As the housemaid Julia walked past, Holmes asked her if he could have a look at her earrings. The girl blushed slightly as she pulled back her long black hair. Holmes said he was thinking of buying similar earrings for his wife.

Lady Okehurst and her maid entered the room and Holmes asked them to have a seat at the table nearest the safe. Holmes stood beside the safe and said, "Thank you all for coming. As you are aware, the diamond necklace was placed in this safe shortly after ten o'clock and when the safe was opened at noon it was gone. The solution to the mystery isn't ethereal.

The ghost of Marie Antoinette didn't take back her diamonds. Simply stated, Mr. Bernard opened the safe and stole the necklace."

The butler started to stand in protest, but the two uniformed men stepped in and placed their hands on his shoulders.

"Your daughter Julia created a diversion by dropping the tray of silverware in the kitchen, which drew Mrs. Ellsworth away long enough for you to open the safe and take the necklace. The shape of Julia's ears shows her bloodline quite distinctly. You kept your relationship a secret to protect your daughter in case you were caught."

"Leave my daughter out of this!" Bernard cried. "You expect us to believe that I cracked that safe, picked the lock on the drawer, removed the jewels, relocked the drawer, and closed the safe in one minute?"

"He has a point, Mr. Holmes," said Jones. "No one can open that safe that quickly. Even if he knew the combination, it would surely take too long to – "

Holmes reached over, lifted the handle of the safe, and swung open the door.

Everyone in the room gasped.

"The safe was never locked, Inspector," Holmes stated. "After the necklace was secured in the safe's drawer, Bernard closed the safe door and lowered the handle. As he stood in front of the safe with his back concealing his exact movements, he most likely moved his arm as if he was turning the dial as I did, but he left the dial on the last number of the combination. The safe isn't locked until the tumbler is turned. All he had to do was to unlatch the door using the handle and swing it open, as I have demonstrated. He had taken a mold of the baroness's key at an earlier date, and, with his duplicate key, unlocked the drawer and took the jewel-case. He quickly relocked the drawer, closed the safe, and turned the dial. It took less than a minute to complete the task."

The solution to the mystery was so simple it was humbling.

"And where is my necklace now?" Lady Okehurst asked.

We all turned to the butler.

"I'm not saying another word."

"It's in the hands of another of Bernard's accomplices," stated Holmes. "After stealing the necklace, Bernard walked down to the north gate and passed the jewel-case through the bars to a confederate. Watson and I will attempt to track the accomplice, but I hold little hope. The man most likely boarded a train at Vauxhall Station and is now miles from here. To be sure, Watson and I will follow his tracks to see where they lead."

"Take Officer Davies with you, Mr. Holmes," ordered the inspector.

We took our leave of Lady Okehurst, retrieved our hats and overcoats from the foyer, and walked out the front doors and through the front gate. Dusk was upon us. As we walked past the police wagon parked in front of the Manor, Holmes reached over and removed one of the side lanterns. We made our way along the wall to the north gate. Holmes lit the lantern and held it to the ground. He walked around the path and studied the footprints. Since it had rained the night before, the impressions were distinctive.

"There are two men," Holmes remarked. "A tall lanky fellow, and a short man who walks with a slight limp."

We followed the prints down the path to a side street and turned left, heading west towards the train tracks. Holmes paused and looked around.

"Just as I thought. They didn't risk hiring a cabbie who might later identify them. Apparently, they walked to Vauxhall Station. Let's keep following their tracks to be sure."

The footprints were often barely visible as we walked down the street. Then their prints vanished altogether. We crossed two more streets and came to the walkway leading left to the station. Holmes dropped to his knees and, holding the lantern above his head, bent over, putting his nose close to the ground. Then he sprang up, stepped to his left, and dropped to his knees again. He repeated this exercise several more times. It reminded me of a cat in a grassy field pouncing upon an elusive mouse.

Holmes stood up and rubbed his chin. "This is an unexpected development. The footprints continue west. Apparently, our quarry did not board a train. You see, Watson, I'm not infallible. It appears they headed for the Thames."

We followed the trail of invisible footprints under the railway overpass towards the river. Once we left the road, the prints reappeared on the muddy ground and turned left upon the embankment. We headed upstream along the river for a short distance towards Lack's Dock, then turned right and walked down to the water's edge. Several small wooden wharves jutted out into the river. Upon the longest of the piers, there stood an old man with a scruffy white beard. He wore an old dark-blue pea jacket and a weather-beaten grey cloth cap. He stood next to a small skiff and was talking to himself as he coiled a length of rope. Holmes interrupted the man's one-sided discussion and asked him if he had seen two men, one tall and one short.

"Aye," said the old salt. "They was in a hurry, they was. The tall feller paced up and down the boards for over an hour. The short feller sat on me bench, took off his shoe, and rubbed his foot. Holes in his stocking, there was. But Ah wouldn't call them *men*. They was wee shy of twenty."

"Did they have a small box with them?" I asked.

81

"Ah didn't see no box, but the tall feller was carrying a cloth bag. Said they was 'couriers'. Ah asked him what was in the bag, and he said it was none of me business and none of his own. 'We're professionals,' the feller said. 'We mind our customer's privacy, and don't look in packages or ask questions. Do we Alfie?' The little feller told him to shut up. Ah told them they could be breaking the law. The feller said, 'If we don't know what we carry, then we can't be committin' no crime. Can we, Alfie?' The little feller told him he talks too much. 'We don't always courier bags,' the tall feller said. 'Sometimes we just deliver notes. Nothing illegal about that, now is there?'"

"The tall feller walked up to the edge of the wharf again, looked upstream, and walked back laughing to himself. 'One time we delivered a coffin,' he said. 'Remember that Alfie?' 'Shut up, Max,' said the little feller as he put his shoe back on. The tall one laughed and said, 'It was heavy, but we didn't look inside. If ya don't know, ya don't know. Us professionals don't ask questions. We just courier from one place to another, we does. No harm in that now is there? It isn't illegal.' Ah said it might be."

"He walked to the end of the wharf again, looked upstream, and walked back swinging the bag. 'We got ourselves another job tonight,' he said. 'We gotta deliver a dog. Nothing wrong with that, is there?' Ah said it depends on where you're taking the dog, It best not be headed for the pit, ah said. Ah told him ah don't go in for those fights. Then the feller got his britches in a knot and said it was none of me business! A few minutes later, a steam launch ferried up to the end of the wharf."

"How long ago was that?" Holmes asked.

"Not long. Everyone's in a hurry today. She didn't tie off. Dark feller on the starboard gunwale shouted something in French, and the tall feller threw him the bag. Boat went downriver on full steam. The two courier fellers took off on foot heading north along the shore."

Holmes fished a coin from his pocket.

"Can you describe the boat?"

"She's a bonny launch. Crimson with two white lines. Dark-blue funnel. *Mona* painted on the stern in silver and gold."

"Thank you, my good man." Holmes handed him the half-crown and turned to Davies.

"Make your way back to the Manor with all haste and inform Inspector Jones of our progress. Ask him to telegraph the authorities downstream to apprehend the steam launch *Mona*. They'll have a tough time spotting her in this darkness. Watson and I will keep on the trail of the two confederates."

82

The officer saluted and ran off in the direction from which we came. We followed the shoreline until we picked up the trail of footprints leading back over the embankment and north along the river. Holmes looked up at the cloudy black sky as he waited for me to catch up.

"I'm afraid with this moonless night, the *Mona* may get to the Channel."

"You think they're headed for the Continent?"

"If they pass Gravesend, the diamonds will be back on French soil by morning."

We followed the footprints of the two couriers until they made the road. I couldn't see any prints on the cobblestones, yet Holmes, holding the lantern over his head and with his knees bent, occasionally let out a cry as we scurried along. I was fatigued from a brief night's sleep the previous and my bad leg throbbed, but I kept walking at Holmes's quick pace until we reached Pinchin Lane. I recalled it was at Mr. Sherman's house on Pinchin Lane that Holmes sent me nearly two years ago to fetch Toby, a gangly, good-natured dog, to track down Jonathan Small in the Agra treasure affair. I could still see in my mind that lop-eared mutt loping along with his nose to the ground and his tail wagging in the air as he followed a trail of creosote left by Small's aborigine accomplice. As we approached the house at No 3, we became aware something was amiss. A badger ran down the pavement and a falcon perched above the open door. There was a trail of blood drops from the door leading up the lane. We could hear dogs barking from within.

We stepped into the shop and found old Mr. Sherman sitting upon the floor, amongst overturned crates, holding his battered head with both hands. He was bleeding from his nose and mouth. I applied my handkerchief to his split lip and pinched the bridge of his nose. After a minute, the bleeding slowed, and he explained what had happened.

"Two young men came asking for Toby," he said, looking at Holmes. "They said you were on a case and sent them to borrow the dog."

It was apparent that their customer had read my story in *Lippincott's* and knew he could acquire a dog with a mere mention of my friend's name. I was distraught. I never dreamed my writing would be abused in such a fashion.

"I didn't like the looks of those boys," continued Sherman, "but I fetched Toby from the back room. Old Toby didn't like the looks of the two rogues either, and he started growling and baring his teeth. The taller one took a muzzle that was hanging on the wall and tossed it to me. He said, 'Muzzle the beast.' I told him Toby never wore a muzzle in his life. That's when the shorter boy stepped forward and punched me hard. I didn't see it coming. My old knees gave out and I hit the floor. Toby pulled the leash out of my hands and attacked the boy. I didn't know the dog had it in him. Toby sunk his teeth in the boy's arm and wouldn't let go. I stood up and took a swing at the taller boy, but he was too fast and I found myself beat to the ground again. I'm too old for fisticuffs. I was dazed and couldn't get my legs under me. It was a blur of fangs and blood. And fur. I heard Toby yelp in pain as I passed out. When I came to my senses, the boys and Toby were gone."

Mr. Sherman's nose stopped bleeding. I helped him up so he could sit on a crate.

"I'll be fine. Go after them. Take my stick. It's by the door."

Without a word, Holmes spun around, grabbed the hickory walking stick, and tossed it to me. I followed him out the door. Holmes picked up the lantern we had left outside, and we followed the trail of blood which led up the lane. It was all I could do to keep up with Holmes. The fatigue I had earlier was replaced by anger and purpose, but there was no ignoring the pain in my leg from my old army injury. In a matter of some minutes, we caught up to the men. They were dragging and kicking poor Toby. Holmes walked up to the taller man and said, "That's no way to treat an animal."

"Mind your own business," said the young scoundrel. Holmes calmly set the lantern on the ground and stepped up to the man and hit him hard with a flurry of punches. The rogue fell to the ground, letting go of the leash. Just as the shorter man came to his comrade's defense, I struck him over the head with the hardy stick. He collapsed to the ground. They knew they were outmatched and didn't get up. Holmes knelt beside Toby and reached for the muzzle.

"I wouldn't do that, Mister," said the taller man, spitting blood.

"He doesn't look so fierce to me," Holmes said as he removed the muzzle. Toby leaped on my companion, knocked him on his back, and licked his face. Holmes laughed and said, "Yes, yes, I'm glad to see you too."

"I've never known you to throw the first punch, Holmes," I said, as we were in a carriage heading back towards Kensington. We were fortunate to hire a passing four-wheeler and returned Toby to Sherman's. The old naturalist thanked us and shed tears of joy as he took Toby in his arms. We then delivered the two couriers, bleeding and proclaiming their innocence, to Athelney Jones at Vauxhall Manor. The next day, we learned the steamer *Mona* was spotted passing by Gravesend with a full steam on. However, the police didn't have a steamer stoked in time to catch her. A steam launch was also seen some distance away by a night-watchman on the Thames Haven Pier, but the boat soon vanished into the dark waters of the channel.

The French authorities were alerted, and lookouts were stationed at all the ports. Throughout the following days, searches were made at every wharf along the French coast. The boat was never found, and Lady Okehurst never recovered her necklace. It was surmised by the authorities that the *Mona's* boiler exceeded her limits and exploded while crossing the channel. More than one penny newspaper professed the ghost of Marie Antoinette had reclaimed her diamonds.

The Adventure of the Intrepid Follower

by Arthur Hall

I was bound for home one early summer morning when it occurred to me that it had been some time since I had seen my friend, the consulting detective, Mr. Sherlock Holmes.

Considering that I had spent a sleepless night attending Mrs. Agatha Burnett, a patient of long standing, I felt remarkably refreshed as I saw that I was within walking distance of Baker Street. After a moment's consideration, I altered my direction so that I might pass near my former lodgings.

Before approaching the door, I was pleased to see that the sitting room curtains had been opened, suggesting that Holmes had risen from his bed earlier than was usual for him and was probably breakfasting. I was admitted almost at once by Mrs. Hudson, Holmes's landlady, who greeted me with affection and much enthusiasm. I promised not to leave before seeing her again and took the stairs, reflecting on the enduring familiarity of this place that had once been my home.

"Come in, Watson."

I was bidden to enter when I had hardly reached the landing. That he would have recognised from of old my tread upon the stair didn't surprise me, for this was among the least of Holmes's exceptional powers. I opened the door and entered, unprepared to find that he was not alone.

The lady who sat in the basket chair I would have judged to be at about thirty years of age, resplendent in a green costume that set off the rich auburn shade of her hair which she had pinned beneath her bonnet. I felt slightly embarrassed because of my intrusion, but she smiled and Holmes called to me again.

"Good morning. Do come and meet Mrs. Maria Blackwell, who has placed a most interesting problem before me."

I returned the greeting to include them both, hung up my hat and coat, and seated myself in the armchair that I had used so often in the past, as he indicated.

"I have explained to the lady how you have been of such great assistance in many of my past enquiries," he continued, "and she had barely begun to tell of her experiences when I heard you conversing with Mrs. Hudson as you entered."

"I will be in your debt, as well as that of Mr. Holmes, if you can throw any light upon this puzzling circumstance," Mrs. Blackwell said with a hint of anxiety, "for neither my husband nor myself can see any sense in it."

"Please tell us then," said I, "what it is that has caused your distress."

"Pray be precise as to details," Holmes said before she could begin. "Leave nothing out, since it is often the small things that prove to be vital."

"Very well, sir." She paused briefly, I supposed to collect her thoughts. "It is our custom to frequent Simpson's Dining Rooms, in the Strand, for luncheon several times every week. We have found it to be an excellent establishment. Do you know it?"

"We have had dinner there, on occasion," my friend confirmed.

"For about the last three weeks, we have been made uncomfortable by the presence of a gentleman who always occupies a table near ours, noticeably so, and is quite obviously listening to our conversation. This may seem a trivial complaint, sirs, but my husband is sometimes of an aggressive disposition resulting from his experiences in India, where he twice narrowly escaped attacks by murderous tribesmen and suffered considerable wounds. I feared for the action he might take."

This I could understand from my observations after Maiwand and other occasions. Many of my comrades who fared badly had been left with a violent streak added to their dispositions.

"Very little that I am consulted about is trivial, Mrs. Blackwell," Holmes assured her, "although it may at first seem so. Tell me: Did your husband at any time seek a confrontation upon recognising the unwelcome interest from this intrepid fellow?"

"He did indeed." I saw the quick flash of her green eyes as she remembered. "When he became aware that we were being observed as we ate, Edwin strode to the man's table and furiously demanded he explain himself. The reply was delivered with outrage and protestations. We were told that we were imagining things, that the man had never been so insulted in his life. He denied all accusations and stormed out of the restaurant. I was surprised by my husband's restraint, for I fully expected him to follow."

"But this situation continued, or you wouldn't be here," Holmes mused. "Had your observer any physical peculiarities with which he might be identified?"

She nodded. "The incident has indeed been repeated. Edwin seemed excessively worried, but did nothing more. He remarked to me that he noticed that this man's eyebrows were joined as a continual line across his forehead, rather than being individual as is normal. Is that the sort of feature you meant, Mr. Holmes?"

"Doubtless it will prove to be useful. Kindly enlighten us as to what occurred on subsequent occasions."

"Edwin was determined that we shouldn't be influenced by this event to change our venue, and suggested that we should ignore this man and continue as usual. We have done so several times since then, and this man has always ensured that he dines in close proximity to ourselves, but has said nothing more."

"Has no other incident occurred? I cannot help but form the impression that something has brought this to a head."

"There was one curious variation." She paused, possibly thinking that what had occurred would be irrelevant. "My husband has dined alone or with a friend at Simpson's on three occasions since then. He noticed each time that the man who watches us entered the restaurant and then immediately retreated before he could be offered a table. After that, his scrutiny of us when together has resumed."

"Most interesting." Holmes raised his eyes to look at her. "Have either you or your husband noticed this troublesome fellow at any time other than at Simpson's? For example, as you walked in the streets of London, or near your home?"

She shook her head. "Not at all. We live in Mayfair, and I am sure we would have become quickly aware had he followed."

At that, my friend placed his chin atop his steepled fingers and the room fell silent. The window was closed, but still faint sounds filtered up from Baker Street. The clatter of horses' hooves, a loud shout of reprimand that could have been from a constable, and snatches of excited conversation from passers-by reached our ears before Holmes's expression changed suddenly.

"Mrs. Blackwell, I perceive that there is something which you have neglected to include in your narrative. It is obvious that you and your husband enjoy a life of adequate financial means, since otherwise your frequent visits to Simpson's wouldn't be affordable, but it strikes me that this man has made no threats and his actions are apparently without purpose." He leaned forward in his chair. "Is there perhaps some special reason why you couldn't alter your luncheon appointments to a different restaurant, and is there no reason known to you or your husband why you should have been observed in this way?"

She stared us in silence, visibly wrestling with some unmentioned disclosure.

"I have no reason for my suspicion," she said at last, "except that Edwin will only speak of his work in the vaguest terms. There is some secrecy here, and I have wondered if this sequence of events could be connected with some aspect of his employment. To enquire of him would be useless, since the slightest reference is met with polite evasion."

"Then you have you no indication at all as to his employment?"

She shook her head, but then seemed to recollect something.

"There was a morning, months ago, when I took a cab to visit an old school friend. The route was through Whitehall, and I thought I saw Edwin with another man enter one of the buildings. I have never been sure though – it was no more than a fleeting glimpse."

"Thank you," said Holmes. "That may have a bearing on the matter. To conclude, I am concerned as to the reason for this unwelcome scrutiny. Could it be that its reason is to extort a sum of money from you or your husband?"

"That is doubtful." She smiled. "We are only moderately well-off, barely able to afford the upkeep of our accommodation in Mayfair. Some of our neighbours' capital must greatly exceed ours. If profit were the object, then surely one of them would be more likely victims."

"So it would seem. I think that is all I need from you, Mrs. Blackwell, except to ask when and at what time you and your husband intend to take luncheon at Simpson's next."

"We have a reservation there at mid-day, tomorrow."

"Excellent." He rose from his chair and I put down my notebook and did likewise. "Then you will not be surprised to see Doctor Watson and myself dining not far away. I beg that you make no sign of recognition, and that you ask your husband to ignore us also. We will see what can be learned then."

"I did not inform Edwin that I intended to consult you, Mr. Holmes," she said with slight embarrassment. "I felt I had to do something, but was unsure how he would respond."

"Then he will not in any way impede our enquiry. When you have given Doctor Watson your address and any further relevant details, he will conduct you out and procure a cab. Good day to you, Madam."

I returned to the sitting room in less than five minutes, to find Holmes scribbling on a telegram form.

"To Lestrade, perhaps?" I ventured. "To enquire whether Mrs. Blackwell's hot-tempered husband is known to Scotland Yard?"

He glanced up at me with an appalled expression. "Why ever should I wish to do that? I am sending a message to Mycroft, to establish whether Edwin Blackwell works for him or in some capacity elsewhere in Whitehall."

"Do you believe that your brother would disclose that information?"

"That is doubtful, but I'm depending on the way he replies as an indication. A stroll to the nearest Post Office is in order I think, if you would care to accompany me."

I was glad to stay for luncheon on our return, for by now I was famished. In her uncanny way, Mrs. Hudson had anticipated my presence and served a welcome dish of thick beef stew. Although I welcomed this brief return to my old life, I felt I had been drawn into Holmes's life unintentionally. A chance visit had turned into my participation in an adventure, reminiscent of those we had shared many times before.

After our meal, Holmes and I fell into a conversation that lasted for well over an hour. Presently I gained the impression that he was detaining me with the intention of sharing whatever information might be forthcoming by way of Mycroft's answer.

I saw the telegraph boy from the window, as he arrived in the late afternoon. Mrs. Hudson had barely left after delivering the message into Holmes's hands before he tore open the envelope and gave a cry of triumph.

"Ha! I knew it. My brother is this vague only when he wishes to conceal something. Mr. Edwin Blackwell, our client's husband, is one of Mycroft's minions."

"Then that is the reason for the unwelcome attention he receives at Simpson's," I replied confidently.

"I think not, although that is the reason Mr. Blackwell didn't alter the venue for his wife and himself. There is some significance in being at that place at that time. Still, we will not go into that, since it is Mycroft's business and, I am convinced, unconnected with our enquiry."

I attempted to define an alternative reason for the situation, unsuccessfully. "Then I fail to see – "

"Think back. Did not Mrs. Blackwell mention that this mysterious observer realised that Mr. Blackwell was dining alone or with a friend on more than one occasion?"

"I believe so."

"And didn't the watcher then retreat and leave the restaurant?"

"That is how Mrs. Blackwell described the incident, doubtless from her husband's revelations."

Holmes sank into his armchair. "Then what conclusion can be drawn from that?"

"It appears," I said after a moment, "that this man sought to hear the conversation only when Mrs. Blackwell was present."

"Bravo, Watson! It isn't Mister Edwin Blackwell who is under observation, though it at first seemed most likely. It is our client herself!"

"But why? From our conversation with her, I gleaned nothing unusual, or anything that could explain this."

"Nor did I, as yet. We may, however, learn much during luncheon tomorrow. Now, I have taken up quite enough of your time today. Forgive my selfishness, and be sure to meet me at Simpson's at mid-day tomorrow."

With that dismissal I left him. As I hailed a cab, I wondered how difficult it would be to arrange for a *locum* at such short notice.

As it happened, I was fortunate. The newly qualified Doctor Ollis was kind enough to take on my duties for the few days that I estimated Holmes would need to conclude his enquiries.

After familiarising my temporary replacement with the intricacies of my practice, I procured a passing hansom. I arrived at Simpson's a little early, but Holmes was already waiting. We hesitated until our client arrived with her husband, a tall florid man whose eyes were never still, before allowing ourselves to be shown to a table for which we expressed a preference. This was situated near to that of Mr. and Mrs. Blackwell, as was but one other, and I saw a look of satisfaction cross Holmes's face as that was occupied by an unaccompanied man shortly afterwards.

"That is Mrs. Blackwell's tormentor?" I quietly asked him.

"Undoubtedly."

I turned closer. "Do you know him?"

"I know *of* him."

"Who is he?"

"His name is Erasmus Snead. Lestrade once considered him as one of the perpetrators of a minor fraud scandal, but lack of evidence prevented his arrest. However, I suspect a different connection here."

I observed Mr. Snead as I enjoyed my roast beef. He was a small man, partially bald and thin-faced. From his stillness and the inclination of his head as he ate, it certainly appeared that he was paying much attention to the conversation between our client and her husband.

As for Holmes, he ate with unusual relish, even enjoying dessert. As we drank our coffee, I reflected that this probably meant that he was close to defining this man's purpose.

"I trust you have enjoyed your meal," my friend said after both the Blackwells and Mr. Snead had departed.

"Very much so. I am curious, though, as to what other connection you suspect Mr. Snead has with this affair."

"I am wondering how he gained the ability that he must have, if his intentions are as I surmise. I suggest you leave here for Baker Street and wait for my arrival, for I have a call to make before I return. No – put your money away. I will settle the bill."

And so it transpired. We engaged separate cabs outside Simpson's and I was conveyed to my former lodgings. After a short conversation, during which I assured Mrs. Hudson that I needed no further sustenance, I repaired to my armchair of old and promptly fell asleep. The sounds of

Holmes ascending the stairs woke me, and from my pocket watch I discovered that almost two hours had passed.

"Halloa, Watson!" he exclaimed cheerily as he entered.

"Evidently you have confirmed whatever suspicions you had of Mr. Snead."

"Indeed." He hung up his coat and lowered his thin body into the other armchair. "I now know something of him, but the reasons for his attentions to our client elude me."

"Where have you been, then?"

"You will recall that I have sought information before from Miss Gloriana Roland, the once-celebrated stage actress who is currently playing a supporting role at the Lyceum."

I nodded. "You have mentioned her on occasion."

"Quite. Sadly, her career is no longer as successful as it once was, but she remains an oracle of all and everyone in the theatrical world."

"You have enquired of her about Mr. Snead?" I ventured.

"As soon as I laid eyes upon him, I recalled that I had encountered his name somewhere before. Miss Roland explained that he was once a professional mimic, whose act knew popularity in many London playhouses. He was known as 'The Great Minah', obviously named after the Indian bird that has the ability to reproduce human voices and other sounds. Apparently he left the theatrical world under a cloud, since he was found to be helping himself to the contents of the pockets of his fellow performers while they were on stage in costume. A pity, she said, but he subsequently degenerated to petty crime and disappeared into the underworld."

"Which is likely how he came to the attention of Inspector Lestrade. So, his intention seems to be to overhear Mrs. Blackwell's voice until he is able to imitate it."

"Excellent, Watson. My conclusion exactly."

"But what can his purpose be?"

Holmes shrugged. "The first possibility that presents itself is of course profit or gain. I recall that Mrs. Blackwell stated that she and her husband have only moderate assets, yet this remains the most likely reason for some sort of impersonation. I will know more after a visit to Somerset House tomorrow and, unless you are otherwise engaged, I may be able to satisfy your curiosity then."

I stopped in Baker Street for luncheon the following day. Mrs. Hudson was unmistakably pleased to, as she put it, "see us together like old times", and I soon discovered that her culinary skills hadn't diminished.

Our meal completed, Holmes and I resumed our discussion of the previous afternoon.

"If our supposition is true," I began, "then what can be the purpose of it? Why would this man Snead go to such lengths to attain the ability to imitate Mrs. Blackwell's voice?"

Holmes sat back in his chair, his hawk-like features set in a serious expression.

"He must do this in a situation where our client isn't required to be seen, only heard."

"Her face obscured perhaps. Or masked? No, that is ridiculous."

"Of course! Once more you have solved it, Watson. Have I not said many times that it is you who should be the detective, and not I?"

"What can you mean? It was no more than a passing thought, instantly discarded."

His grey eyes twinkled. "No, not a mask, but a *veil!* A widow would wear such."

"But Mrs. Blackwell is not a widow."

"Perhaps it is intended that she should become one. It isn't a likelihood that I am prepared to ignore." He rose and put on his coat. "No, you will not need to accompany me. I am going to see Mycroft, but will not be long, if you care to wait."

He was as good as his word. Little more than an hour had passed, and much of the mid-day edition of *The Standard* was still unread, when I heard a hansom come to rest and peered from the window to see him alight. Soon we were seated, and he took up his clay pipe as I waited eagerly for his explanation.

Through a cloud of fragrant smoke, I fancied I saw relief in his expression.

"My brother wasn't pleased to see me," he said then. "I interrupted him in something that he clearly considered important, but when I confided the reason for my visit he became quite amiable."

"You warned him of the possible danger to Mr. Edwin Blackwell," I ventured.

"Quite so, but as it turned out I need hardly have troubled myself. Mycroft, in that most intuitive way of his, had already decided that Mr. Blackwell is overdue for promotion and should take up a post in the colonies. He gave me to understand that Mr. Blackwell and his wife will sail from Tilbury on the *Glenmaddock* this evening."

"They will have almost no time to prepare for their departure."

"That apparently isn't at all unusual. When it is considered that an emergency situation exists, as it does in the West Indies at the moment, remedial action is often swift."

"So, we have lost our client?" I said as he blew smoke rings at the ceiling.

"A small thing, when we remember that the safety of both she and her husband is now assured. Mycroft was about to arrange for their house to be cleared and their goods sent on, but I asked him to delay this for a day or two. I want to preserve the impression that it is still occupied, now that Mr. Snead has had sufficient time to perfect his impersonation. What do you say to assisting me in watching the place, until he makes an appearance?"

"I am at your disposal, of course."

"Capital! From my morning visit to Somerset House, to verify my suspicions as to what is at the root of all this, I learned much. Tonight will find us in Mayfair. If my theory has merit, then Snead, or whoever is with him in this, must visit Mrs. Blackwell's home, either to make her a widow by disposing of her husband and thereby making their scheme credible, or to ensure that she is elsewhere when their impersonation is due to take place." He paused to knock out his pipe. "You will stay to dinner, won't you?"

As it transpired, our vigil that night was uneventful. Holmes used his pick-lock to enter the house and light some of the lamps to indicate occupancy while I took up station beneath a large spreading beech nearby, but all to no avail. I returned home, and the next morning rose late – still a little weary – and returned to Baker Street, where I discovered that Holmes had already departed sometime before. The coffee pot, which had contained the extent of Holmes's breakfast, was stone cold to the touch.

He reappeared not more than a half-hour before luncheon, and I saw at once that his enquiries, whatever they were, had been successful. His first words confirmed this by their tone.

"I'm glad to see that Mrs. Hudson has been looking after you. The crumbs adhering to your waistcoat and the warm but empty coffee pot make that clear. I now must tell you all that I know, and that this episode was with the objective of gain after all, but I'll wager that neither Mrs. Blackwell or her husband are aware of their increased prosperity." He sniffed the air. "Ah, roast chicken, I think."

The meal was delicious, but taken almost in silence. The air of impatience surrounding Holmes was almost tangible. We finished our coffee more quickly than is our custom.

"I spent the morning with Mr. Saddler, of Duffield, Rowe, and Sons," he explained afterwards, "who, you will remember from your notes, are the Blackwell's solicitors. He knew nothing of their emigration, but was quite confused when I informed him of Mr. Blackwell's intended demise.

He was more bewildered still by notification from Portugal of a considerable and unexpected inheritance for Mrs. Blackwell, although he proved most helpful when I revealed my intentions."

"So, we now have the purpose of all this."

"Indeed, a message has informed Mr. Saddler that he can expect a visit from 'Mrs. Blackwell' – actually our adversary, disguised and claiming to be our widowed client. Knowledge of the inheritance has evidently not reached the Blackwells as yet."

"You believe that Mr. Snead could carry out this impersonation successfully, even convincing someone who is acquainted with Mrs. Blackwell?"

"I do. The message told of the sender's intent to call upon Mr. Saddler at five o'clock this evening to collect the bank draft. This didn't sit well with the solicitor, since it isn't the customary way to secure an appointment. I managed to convince him that it would be prudent to issue a false document, or one dated for next week."

I heard a hansom or carriage pass down Baker Street at a frantic pace, and anticipated my friend's next remark. It wasn't long in coming.

"I suggest we arrive outside the office of Duffield, Rowe, and Sons well before five, in order to find a place of concealment."

"Why do we not simply confront Mr. Snead as he emerges from the building?"

"He is a mere tool in this affair. My enquiries have revealed quite another player in this drama."

"Who is that, pray?"

"The answer to that question you will observe for yourself later, because Mr. Snead will lead us to him."

He would say nothing more. I saw that he was enjoying the suspense, and knew from of old that I would receive nothing further until he was ready to impart it. Presently, I attempted to continue with my reading that his arrival had interrupted, but Holmes was restless. He stood up abruptly and took up his violin. A mournful dirge soon filled the room, and I was glad to make the excuse of informing Mrs. Hudson that we would require a late dinner since I had again been invited to stay. Fortunately, silence returned after a short while.

Our hansom deposited us in Paddington before four-thirty. The office of Duffield, Rowe, and Sons was situated near the corner of a small square. Holmes knew of its features from his earlier visit, and had no hesitation in guiding me to the colonnade of broad pillars surrounding the public baths opposite. They provided adequate concealment, and we began a short and silent wait while a dwindling crowd circulated among the nearby shops.

At exactly five o'clock, a hansom, pulled by a fine black mare, came to rest near the centre of the square. It was quickly dismissed and a solitary black-clad figure was revealed, apparently searching the surroundings uncertainly. It made off in the direction of the solicitor's office, and I heard Holmes's snort of contempt.

"His appearance will be convincing to some, but to a student of humanity, it is an obvious falsehood."

"How so?" I enquired. "Had I not known otherwise, I wouldn't have doubted that we are observing a woman."

"Look at the movement. He has neglected to adopt the graceful walk that Mrs. Blackwell exhibits. A crude attempt."

We exchanged no more words until the figure emerged, a short while later. He immediately set off with us in pursuit. Mr. Snead, for it was certainly he, took no precautions to ensure he had no followers, procuring a passing cab and announcing his destination quite audibly as Paddington Station. After an anxious few moments, another hansom discharged its fare not far away, and we boarded it immediately. A single glance at Holmes told me that, like a hunter, he was full of the thrill of the chase.

It wasn't far, and at journey's end, we dismissed our cab and saw that Mr. Snead had done so also. I had expected him to either take a train or meet his accomplice here, but he did neither. No more than five minutes had passed before another hansom appeared, to collect our quarry unbidden.

Holmes was unperturbed, since cabs were plentiful in the vicinity of the station. We were soon in pursuit once more with our driver, on the promise of an extra half-sovereign, taking care that we remained undetected. We were eventually led to Soho, to a dismal back-street called Blacksmith's Walk, where Mr. Snead alighted and Holmes instructed our driver to continue to the next corner.

"I saw his destination," Holmes explained when our conveyance had left us. "He was at the door of the fourth house from the end of the street. It is here, I think, that we will meet Mr. Snead's accomplice."

We approached the house and Holmes rapped upon the door with his stick. There was no response, nor could we hear any movement from inside. We stepped back to look up at the building and saw soiled and tattered curtains drawn across every window.

"Had we not witnessed Mr. Snead's entry, I would have thought the place abandoned," I said.

"Doubtless that is what we are intended to believe." Holmes bent to lift the cover and peer through the letter-box. "There is no one within sight, at least."

"Perhaps he has escaped by means of a rear exit."

"That is one possibility. Another is that he may be hiding in there

96

until we leave."

With that, he produced his picklock and quickly swung the door open.

"Go carefully, Watson. Have your weapon ready."

He entered quietly, his heavy walking cane at the ready, and I followed with my service revolver drawn. We found ourselves in a dingy parlour, full of dust and the smell of long neglect. A door led into a larger sitting room, with a battered table beneath the single window and a tall-backed armchair facing it.

We approached it silently from both sides. That it was occupied we knew, since an arm dangled from one side. I believe that Holmes was about to speak to Mr. Snead, but suddenly he was still. The man glared at us with empty eyes, his coat and shirt thick with drying blood. A long knife protruded from his throat.

"His murderer cannot be far away," Holmes said then. "He had insufficient time to withdraw the blade before we disturbed him."

"But why was he killed? I would have thought him essential to the success of this crime."

He shook his head. "No longer. He has outlived his usefulness. This isn't a surprising act, from one who has already demonstrated an extraordinary degree of ruthlessness."

"I believe you know who is behind this."

"Indeed, I do. My enquiries at Somerset House and with Mr. Saddler were most enlightening. He assisted us considerably by agreeing to my suggestion that he treat Mr. Snead as if he were genuine."

I looked around the room. An open door, revealing a staircase leading to the upper floor, seemed a likely hiding place if our quarry had remained in the house. I was about to point this out to Holmes when a shadow detached itself from the gloom of the darkened kitchen ahead of us.

A tall man, quite elderly and with an unkempt beard, stood framed in the doorway. His clothes, I saw, were creased and a little dusty. He held a revolver, aimed at Holmes who stood between us.

"It is quite unnecessary to search further, gentlemen," he said in a hoarse voice.

"Good evening, Mr. Henry Pilcher," my friend responded.

"You know me then?" In the fading light I could make out the man's craggy features, and that his eyes were hard and wild.

"Of course. It wasn't difficult to identify the man who set Mr. Snead to impersonate Mrs. Blackwell."

"That man was a fool, but I was determined that he wouldn't prove to be an expensive one."

"And so you killed him. It is likely that you will face the hangman for that."

97

"About that we will see. You can know nothing more about me."

"Much to the contrary, Mr. Pilcher. I have learned that you are the half-brother of Mrs. Blackwell, although she is unaware that her father was married during his years in Portugal before bigamously wedding her mother. I know little ff the part he played in the Vila Real silver mine scandal, other than that he left his profits to be equally divided between your English half-sister and yourself. I confess to being astounded at the extent of your greed, and at the measures you were prepared to take to gain possession of her share in addition to your own. That she and her husband are alive today is so only because your plans were anticipated."

"How you learned these things sir, I cannot imagine." It was now too dark to see, but the scowl was in his voice. "But I will tell you that I couldn't stand by and see a woman I had never set eyes upon take half of the sum I need to save my life. When I left Portugal, it was to escape massive gambling debts. I knew that the men I owed were criminals, and wouldn't hesitate to take my life as an example to others who sought to cheat them. The entire sum of my inheritance would ensure that I could settle my obligations after returning to Portugal, and still have sufficient means to live the remainder of my life in some comfort. What were the lives of an unknown, unlawful half-sister and her husband to me, compared to that? I would do it again. The need to survive is strong in me."

"That is quite apparent," Holmes agreed. "But now you must face justice instead. What do you propose to do now?"

"That should be obvious to you." A sinister note had entered his voice. "You cannot be allowed to frustrate my plans. To conceal your bodies will be a problem it is true, but – "

He brought his pistol up to fire at Holmes's head, but in that instant my friend stepped out of my line of fire as I expected, revealing to our adversary that I was armed. I fired twice before Mr. Pilcher could carry out his threat, and he crumpled to the floor without a sound.

"Thank you, Watson. I knew you would be ready."

"We have enacted this routine before now."

"Indeed. I suggest we touch nothing, but procure a hansom to Scotland Yard, where we will explain ourselves fully."

From then on the matter was swiftly concluded by Scotland Yard, and the inheritance transferred to its rightful recipient. We heard nothing more until a few months later, when a letter bearing a Jamaican postmark arrived for Holmes.

He never allowed me to see it, but related its contents as being the heartfelt thanks of Mrs. Blackwell and her husband. Holmes mentioned also that he did not immediately recollect the lady, but recalled the case after some reflection.

This didn't surprise me, for it was always his custom to forget his clients as soon as his enquiries were successfully concluded. He smiled wistfully, and I knew he would never mention the matter again.

Eyes of Wood, Judging
by Marcia Wilson

Part I: In the Beginning

The first meeting between Galvin, Gentleman Wayfarer, and the Chapel of the Virgo Fortis (known coarsely as the Virgo's Fortress) set the precedent for their future meetings. Fate is capricious and indulgent, but not without humour. The little wandering tradesman is now a well-known guest of the old house of worship. Harry the Sithcundman would call him a stormy petrel, for his arrival always coincides with a "house-cleaning" and Harry dislikes outsiders. We may respect Harry's choice of words, for an old chairman has the right to comment on many things.

We shall begin with Brother Jerome.

He was a friar of the humblest orders, just barely within the lowest Third. If a fourth rank existed, he would have happily consigned. It was on the beneficence of his authorities that he maintained the ancient Chapel, which had been "created" – if such a word is not overly-broad – the day a minor lord granted to the Crown a small plot of slub in a crater of earth and surly stream in service to the All Saints. Hindsight is always clearer than foresight, and the common opinion held that the gift was a nice way of shrugging off the responsibility of owning property undesired by even the most credulous of realtors. King John may have felt some offense at the pittance as he had long resented his father's nickname – "Lackland". Not to be outdone, he soon piled another beneficence upon the beleaguered virgate: The condition of a house of worship to be staffed only by those without influence of the Crown. Bitter at the ruint hopes of employing this miserable mire to their own profit, the aspirators abandoned schemes of acquisition, and King John's reputation as a giant in vengeance if not height remained unsullied.

Thus were its origins, and thus did it remain through four complete rebuildings. The Saint came after the second, politely just ahead of her fall from canonical grace in the sixteenth century. In another city she might have been carted off, burnt for firewood, or left to crumble . . . but one rarely tells an Englishman his business without an aching ear to show for it, and the inattentive governors worked in her favour. Her original Peter and Paul were smashed during the discomfiture of Henry VIII. The Apostles drifted away one by one, down to even Barnabas. Only the Virgo

100

Fortis remained in a dark nook in the private audience room, unable to comfort her dispersing company, friend to only the insects that crept in the silent dark.

It was in this darkness she survived, as would a spark of hope in the bleak of Ash Wednesday. The calendars on paper and the events clocked by the sun and moon rolled on, and she remained at rest, a fly frozen in amber from a previous Time *in petto*. At long last, the history of London turned the complete clock, and it was again safe and fashionable to bestow her mantle in public.

Currently, the Chapel was in tradition with her previous architectural incarnations: An arthritic claptrap assembled one room at a time by the politically neutral and extravagantly miserly, forever hosting scandals by housing the soulless contemptible such as usurer, highwayman, and pacifist. It had come to asymmetrical magnificence in the days of the Great Fire, and hereafter became vital in its ability to unite her bitterest foes – for what can be better than an enemy to which all can agree to share? The Chapel reigned supreme as a gritty eyesore and a bone of contention for all spiritual experts heard to lament that the Fire had not travelled just one street further – a slight exaggeration to be sure, but we may allow the grouchers their brievance. His Mysterious Ways had yet to respond to the authorities' repeated petition in the tradition of the Beckett Solution.

Year after year the Chapel lumbered, holding itself in order thanks in part to the inexplicable devotions of her caretakers – of which currently was Harry, a yonderly oldster who condescended a bed and food as wages for dusting, sweeping, and mopping. The Virgo malingered alone in the lightless backstreet of its borough, her cheerful poverty ensuring little damage, but much pity from kings and wastrels alike. The legal coda remained a steadfast nightmare.

Upon the declining quarter-of-the-century, the Authorities were on the verge of requesting its annual prayer meeting in favour of the Beckett Solution when an antinome arrived with a new perspective.

He was an odd youth, not even a stripling fifty against the Greybeard Board, and fresh from a grueling journey to the Holy Land – her epiphanies still shone in his periwinkle eyes. Despite his demeanor, which was embarrassing in its optimism and wholecloth faith in – of all things! – Man! – he spoke clearly and simply. He had been a policeman before his Journey, so owned the required level of faith in humanity's gift in demonstrating its failures, while showing the right sympathy for those who wished to rise above their comrades.

They listened to his modest proposal to repair the Chapel and re-stock her with proper Saints, using Holy Images rescued in his sojourns. They asked him only once if he really believed his budget was acceptable, and agreed to cover the promissories for the first of many painful renovations. The iron strikes when it is hot, and no one would let it cool. Many a priest walks with God – few can count fourteen Saints as companions of the road! It would continue to be called a Chapel, and the build should remain sacred . . . but not a strict Church, per se. It would in truth be a museum of sorts, perfect for the discreet storage of still-holy-if-outdated objects! To be staffed by a holy man free from profane motives! What a nice solution! *Morceaux de musée!*

Thus it happened that Brother Jerome and the Chapel (speaking through the personage of Harry, Sithcundman charman) settled with each other. The Friar borrowed the backs of many a bewildered porter and occasional old mate. The Virgo Fortis' house was emptied to a wooden skeleton – An empty shell! A shawp! Roofers clad the top with a crazy-quilt of donated slates. With the top somewhat London-proof, the frère restored the innards and hauled in a train of crates dressed in exotic stamps. These great coffers of olivewood and pine were taken up the narrow stairs with much sweat and muffled oath-making. Many splinters found satisfaction in the flesh of the carriers as, one by one, they were placed in the nook under the sloping east roof. A comfortable, quiet cave overlooking a private wooden rail where the brave could peep over and stare at the Virgo Fortis, moved to the fine old altar below. This nook had been built long for discreet observance such as spies outside of the faith. Now it was put to a more Christianly purpose, and about time!

What strange newcomers to emerge from the coffers! They smelt of strange lands and showed toil. the planks were scraped and scratched, gouged, ground-in with unrecognisable soils and grit. In some places a bullet-hole stared back at the shocked labourers. The Large Eyed Saints had arrived. The workers could retire, and the long-suffering Harry was left to sweep, dust, and mop in peaceful sinecure.

It is now that we point out that years have passed and all is one economic package. It remains as it ever was – a bewildering success just beneath the paper-thin edge of ignobility. Broth and bread are passed out weekly in the kitchen, a Blab School sits in the back, and the local tradesmen know where to go when they need to take on a pert young apprentice or a lass of work. Best of all, in trade for living in the city of London, the Chapel offers respite for all mourners. Be they of no faith or too many, the bereaved will not be turned back and comfort of a very immaterial sort is doled out, with far larger proportions than two chopins of soup and a bannock!

Our story only starts here, the way a fairytale must begin with the announcement of a kingdom, a castle, and its king. It does not truly begin

102

until long after Jerome welcomed into the Chapel's fold a remarkable Wanderer . . . .

It was late, and the altar candles were low. Brother Jerome had to oil the feet of the Virgo Fortis by their flickers. She was in better shape than her Large Eyed spiritual army up the balcony, for her character was good English Yew, hard as iron and polished to a glow. Her form was a comely woman in rich robes with a handsome black beard upon her soft face, milk-white arms bound to her cross with real hempen rope. Her wooden robes depended in an imaginary breeze, exposing slippered toes upon the pedestal. At the base crouched her servant, a cheerfully grinning dwarf with a reback. He had a pack upon his back and a mutchkin cap upon his brown wooden head and his burled hands posed to ready up a tune for his mistress. Brother Jerome had the habit of talking to this stalwart fellow in his absent moments and the parishioners were eternally startled at walking in on their conversations.

Rain patted down the old window glass, rinsing off another weary layer of soot for the next day. Despite the damp, the air was cozily scented with Sister Sarai's kitchen as a pot of cinnamon-milk steamed with a cinnamon-stick for tomorrow's pudding. Harry was sweeping the narthex with Axar, who was new to the flock and had come barefoot, wearing only his late father's shirt with coins sewn in the seams. A note was wrapped around his neck tied with packing string: An unsigned reminder that Father Ambrosius had promised Axar a bed.

Jerome knew Ambrosius, and daily paid his predecessor a gentle "How-do" before the graveyard gate. A sweet soul, Ambrosius had been too holy a man to tackle the profane work of reports. Luckily, Harry remembered a conversation in which Axar was discussed, and he could vouchsafe the noughty child's future had been set aside by the lovely old priest. He needed more opportunities than most, and this was attested with his withered right hand and twisted spine.

This was well for Harry, for Ambrosius had typically forgotten to write anything about him in his ledgers. In the absence of a disclaimer the Chapel made room for one more bed among the orphans. Harry put aside his usual annoyance of children to teach the lad the secrets of his Trade – After all, as he grudgingly admitted to the Friar, one of these days he might fall ill, and then who would be here to protect the Chapel from its dirty-footed visitors? Jerome was so astonished at this admonition that he found no fault with the logic. As well as he might!

Harry was a simplistic man and Jerome liked him very much. The old fellow could barely stand, but stood firm for his art. For him work was all-important, and he wouldn't take meals or rest in his tiny room upon his tinier bed without his duty finished. It was a good example he set for Axar. Someday the boy might grow enough to replace him in the sinecure – should Harry ever get absent-minded enough to die.

Jerome heard the dull clap and jow of the main's wooden bell. Someone's disagreement with that sticky front door betwixt narthex and outside. A wet breeze rolled across the floor and across the frère's sandaled toes. The humble man put down his mineral-oil cloth and went to see.

Harry had been all day upon that troublesome spot that guarded the narthex doors from the wastrels. They could be found there on cold nights huddled for warmth, and Old Harry considered it his duty to shoo them out without troubling the friar about it. It was an aggravation how their muck and dust could gather from the crack between the double doors and the stone plate of floor. His gnarled hands moved patiently in a scything stroke, its ash grip worn into the shape of his palms from years of work. Harry had replaced the brush many times, and eventually the pole would wear down, but for now all was in working order, nice and neat, the straws tight and tidy. They caught the grime and obeyed his command.

Axar waited patiently with the dust pan, his strong good hand clamped tight upon the wooden bar. He was a handsome little lad, with curly black hair and snapping sloe eyes and the beginnings of a stout chin. There was nothing he could do about his jimpy good looks, but Harry was determined the child should rise above this disadvantage and become an accomplished man of work!

"Here now Master Axar," he would say, "hold that strong good hand to the job. Your left won't suffer for work." And he would wait until the boy won a proper grip for his dust pan and brush. "Good enough, good enough." High praise indeed! "Hand upon the tools, howk up the dust! There's a lad! If the palm can't work, the back of the hand must catch up! Palm or hardle, palm or hardle! No dallying, no dallying, no drumbling for you in this world!"

Their patient scartling paused upon the foyer: An unseen hand rocked the iron knob and the elderly narthex doors creaked open. It was a smart little fellow hobbling awkwardly into the Chapel with a crutch wedged into his left arm. He was clad clean and patched with sky-blue scraps of cloth at the hems, cuffs, elbows, and knees. Worn shoes boasted cowhide and wood block engraved with flowers. A cerulean-trimmed soldier's pack dandled off one shoulder, warping his stride and adding to the weight upon his crutch.

A sky-coloured cloth tied about his neck and a shirt off the matching bolt peeped from beneath that worn black frock coat. Banding the brimless hat was a jaunty moult off the kingfisher. His black hair untidily fell across one eye in the manner of labourers in want of barbers, and his wide eyes were round and black as night.

"Ah, hello." The stranger grinned brightly through a powerful squint and paid the compliment of a half-salute to the forehead. A brown bird's wings fluttered on the hardle of his slatternly bare hand – a godless tattoo. "I'm here for Brother Jerome."

"He serves this Chapel." Harry answered stoutly. "And you must not know him, or you'd come at a more civil time."

"Ah, but I was told to come straight over," grinned the Infernal, "No matter the hour. Which I did, as soon as I caught up my tools.

"But I forget my manners. Galvin. Galvin Dooley the Younger, of the Dooleys." This was said proudly, with strut of the chest. "Ah. Coffee-sellers, horses, tack repairs, carving, and smatters. Can't afford the shoemaker? Our cobblers will see you smart. Do some metalworking when it doesn't cut into the local businesses. That'd be rude, you know. Heard you was needin' woodwork copied for the Guilds."

"I know nothing of that."

"A-ha. You made it, Galvin."

Harry turned, offended at the warmth within the frère's voice, but face matched tongue. Brother Jerome was happy to see this lowly scroil of a guest.

"But it is late and you are tired, I am sure."

Confound the Friar! Harry held back, his trusty broom a sceptre of disapproval lowered between the corruptible Axar and the troublesome Outsider as poor Jerome indulged his woefully higher spirit, which settled so poorly upon this coarse plane! Here he was, clasping his hand with the shackaback's own, dirty paw – with a tattoo, the heathen! And letting him come in for work and not arrive by the Tradesman's Entrance? (For even chapels have these useful passages for the un-Christian and unbaptised). This was disaster! He stepped backwards, guiding Axar further from contagion.

"Harry, I shall show Galvin our guest-room. He will be copying the sill-carvings before they decay further."

Harry seethed like Sister Sarai's milk as the Friar led the houseless one off to a rude cupboard with a wall-bed. The door clicked shut and the Chapel resumed normal affairs – just the walls, the Saints, and Sister Sarai downstairs.

The man of God's eyes crinkled in a smile upon the old Sithcundman. "I believe you may not approve, Harry. The sills are rotting out and beetley. We need proper replacements. I cannot shame the Chapel."

Well, it was true the Chapel shouldn't be embarrassed, and Father Ambrosius himself had been very fond of making things "modern" for the newcomers to this planet. Harry had little patience for what the old priest called "*aggiornamento*", but that was official and learned Church stuff, not something that befitted his thankfully low status.

However, it must be said that keeping up-to-date (As if History could spoil like milk!) was one thing. This – granting a stranger a place to sleep with a real door, was another! It was an insult, giving him privacy! Who knew what he was hiding in his pack as they spoke? Harry had a real door on his bedroom too – but he'd earned that right, fair and square, sweeping and dusting for years before asking for a bit of board between himself and the hall-draughts.

Harry spat into a linen square and stuffed it hastily within his pocket. "Cain't expect much from them," he said importantly. "They don't know honesty at all." He chuckled without warning. "Don't you worry none, Friar. I'll keep watch. I'm an expert on liars."

"And he is a liar?"

"He's one o' them, ain't he? Not respectable, not honest like us."

"He is one of the forgotten folk."

"An' they be forgotten, sometimes, for a reason, yea?"

And with that nugget of observation, Harry swept Axar and his broom down the hall together, his long, long crippled strides stepping carefully over (but never upon) the lines of plank and stone.

Brother Jerome slowly wended back up the stairs to the old balcony housing the Large Eyed Saints.

In mental silence the man stood, simply resting in his sandals, regarding the quiet pantheon with their backs to the sloped roof and wall. The cool dot of Holy Water upon his brow offered clarity of thought.

The Saints were emotionally carved, each representing the butt of a foreign tree painted in strange, shimmering hues with much gold. Their skins were shaded by the natural property of the woods into browns and honeys. Large, wide eyes stared in eternal awe upon the world *God* had wrought. Lean hands clasped prayers upon shapeless breasts beneath robes limp over the vital bag of bones. Some owned ocellated wings, for in the older days they knew the terror of angels. There bore the axe or sword-marks of martyrdom. Many were twice-martyred: A sharp edge notched here. A bullet-hole there. Splintering craters upon a serene black cheek, and upon the rosemary robes of a Mother Mary licked the scorch of extinct fire. There was a being recognised as Anthony. His parents huddled as Lilliputians, praying beneath the protective wings of his Egyptian cloak.

Anthony, champion of all threatened with erasure, stood before the world bravely and beautifully, his ligneous countenance terrible to challenge. There were times when the friar suspected Anthony had

106

adopted the cause of the forgotten little Virgo Fortis. His great, wooden head had an air about him that said, "Forget if you wish, but I shall not."

Jerome wandered with his eyeballs: Fearless Paul, green eyes (so unusual for a sculpture) snapped with life. The Benjamite's left hand raised up against invisible terrors, guiding Gentle Peter at the steerage as their cracked little boat sailed through the ruinous seas of Man. Michael brandished his levin. Raphael stood upon Tobit's fish and leaned forward with a hooked pole, his ashwood well-bucket a new replacement for the lost original as his blue-green robes eternally fought the yellow blister of strange, moist-loving fungus.

There was a Black Sarah, and Deborah, for who else could be this tall woman with her back against a carved palm? John in the wilderness hunched with a locust, shaggy in raw pelts. He wore the scapegoats, it was whispered, so that others may not. Another man with a face full of kindly tragedy and a dog at his side was probably Heraclitus, declared an "honorary Saint" with Socrates (who might be the man with that suspicious-looking cup painted black on the inside). Jerome hoped he was, for though he was not official, his support of the Lapsi appealed to the friar's doctrine of charity to all.

There were three others. Like the theoretical Heraclitus, their origins were so far back in time, the identifying symbols were still in flux. They might be one Holy person. They might be another.

But they were *Holy*. It exuded from the pores of their perfumed woods, eternally balming the atmosphere with the scent of time itself. Before them, as if by vet, Anthony stood out, his splintery stare upon the forgotten Virgo Fortis below the balcony with all the countenance of a brother who seeks to protect a beloved little sister.

Jerome's introduction to this learned company is important. His family's inheritance had come unexpected, and since a policeman may not also be a gentleman of means, PC Lytle's devotion to the Home Office was erased with the lawyer's knock upon his dormitory. Like John the Baptist, he decided the wild places might ease the strain of all that godless wealth. He pointed his toes to the Holy Lands with neither plan nor compass, just a driven urge to be away. Eventually he got there, and eventually he returned, and it was on his way back home that he found his calling, collected his Churchly name of *Jerome*, and blundered through one last *bona fide* wilderness, dry and whispery with endless winds from the northern mountains.

There dozed in the center of this dry land a small stone ruin, scalped of room and stoved east wall. Facing that gap were the Large Eyed Saints, long abandoned by wars, famine, plague, and other appropriate weapons of Death. Some still tottered upright. Others rested face-down in the shifting dust. All waited the inevitable as reverently as the living martyrs they represented. Patient Raphael tottered sadly over a filling well, the suffocated water-table sending a ruinous seep of yellow mould through the earth to the blue-robed Mary and suckling Christ. It was quiet here, a hostel for the small brown birds in nesting-season, but even they were gone, winging to fertile lands closer to the sea. Jerome was the only soul in that Chapel still clad in flesh, though he sensed many others about him without.

He made camp in a corner politely away from the praying Saints, and the sun turned the firmament over to the stars. The yellow mould glowed quietly in the night, and its illumination made an irregular-spotted trail of foot-steps from the well to the vulnerable Hallows.

Jerome found this ominous. Another deadly seep was marching here. An army with the colours of his own country. The soldiers would see firewood and souvenirs, not a gentle hermitage with the only drinkable well for days' march.

His sun-bleached head bowed, and he joined the wooden Saints in prayer.

A philosophical or sensible man may have let the Chapel's guardians, with their unknown and therefore circumspect flavor of Christianity, return to Nature. Jerome had never claimed possession of either quality. He was a poet of pragmatism, and his patron was known as the irascible old fellow who snaps like a badger upon the meat of truth. The Saints were about to be released from Purgatory.

Luckily for Jerome there was a village nearby, mobile and tented. It was governed by a calligrapher of rare quality. He had many beautiful daughters and strong sons and was eternally plagued by suitors who loved to remind him his only wealth was in his children, not his commissions in gold ink.

That good son of Ishmael had little patience for those who would insult his worldly meagerness by offering to take a child "off his hands". Raising his equity was a natural solution to both problems – a rich man need only be pestered by problems he cannot purchase away. It was simple for Jerome to pay for his services in Libyan Glass and bright cloth – meaningless to Chieftain Basil.

They made a merry rescue party under a lean desert moon, these children of the one God. Much later in a distant sea-port, Jerome received an excellent letter from Chieftain Basil to inform him the empty temple had been the cause of rage by a foreign nobleman with a reputation for loving precious relics. So deep was his love, he had invented a new way of collection: Taking home what attracted his magpie eye, and then possibly remembering to send thanks when the original owners gently reminded him he had forgotten to ask permission.

The spoils of war were writ. Jerome smiled in the stinking confines of his little cabin. He had rescued the Saints. With the remainder of his inheritance he had a purpose. Jerome remembered an old relic of his days on foot-patrol: The Chapel of the Virgo Fortis, crucified by antiquated deed of property to existence. Many a copper walked by with a quicker step and lighter whistle upon their lips when her shadow touched their sticks! Jerome had no such fear. He'd often tipped his helmet to its front as a pleasant neighbor. He was not a stranger to its innards on holiday. A chapel forced to exist, lacking in all but one saint. And he had rescued an Observance of Saints without a house. The two were destined for partnership!

Jerome was thinking all these things now, and his gaze wandered to his personal favorite, the Black Sarah. She had suffered the most, but there was something unquenchable about her strength of character, which was less yewen and more juniper. She was very old, and in the manner of some very old folk, snapped with vigour.

"It is a strange evening," the frère said. "I am not sure what I should think."

The Black Sarah continued to smile with her small mouth. She was unblinkingly tranquil, for the eyes of wood are wood, and conjure only what the audience wishes to see. Jerome wished he could repair the bullet-wound in her cheek, but she strongly disapproved of cosmetics.

"I promised to keep this Chapel open for all in need," he tried again. "And a dishonest man inside a Church is clearly in need. I was a policeman once. I wonder if I should be one again." He took a long, slow breath from the depths of his breast.

This was a poignant speech, but though he listened hard, the man of God did not hear anything. That was the nature of a Hallow. It spoke to you in its own time, in its own terms – if it even spoke at all! Hallows were not, as his predecessor Ambrosious liked to say, "obligated". It was up to the low petitioner to discern the meanings. Best to err on the side of Compassion.

Part II: A Robbery of Note

Galvin emerged early with a yespen of felt-soft paper and charcoal sticks. As the children watched (and Harry swept), the tinker gently pasted a length of paper to one of the church's murky sills with flour paste. The little brown bird tattoo bobbed against his skin, inked wings attempting flight. He stroked a charcoal over the paper and like ghosts from a fog, the old shapes emerged: A dragon growing out of a plant! A bush of flame before a Judge! Four stone tablets, two shattered upon the earth!

"That oughter do. A good clear imprint is all they need."

"It costs you time."

"Time's what the living got, though they never know how much." With that wisdom, Galvin set to work on new sections.

Thus began an unlikely resort between the Chapel and the Great Unwashed – or in the case of this particular exception, the Tinkers, for their cleanliness puzzled the Londoners. The watching orphans began a more voluntary approach of soap, sparing Sister Sarai the aggravation she preferred to devote to their penmanship. Harry sniffed and snorted and foretold gloom, but it was rare when he had to sweep after the man. This didn't allow Axar the luxury of getting closer to the Intruder than he must.

Galvin was a cheerful oddity. He knocked the frozen dirt off his shoes before stepping inside and scrubbed the soles of his patchwork shoes on the mat. If it wasn't always perfect when he left, it was at least no worse than before. Harry didn't forgive this breach of manners, for he was chary of anyone stealing his work. He wanted conversation with the scoundrel, but his curiosity burnt with suspicion and counselled silence. This might be a Chapel, but it wasn't in a part of London where one would be so arrogant as to ask questions.

Not directly, that is.

"How is it he is paid to make these rubbings?" Old Harry asked after another long visit. "Where does he go with them?"

"He is only delivering the images to the wood-wrights." Brother Jerome shrugged. "They will take the papers and carve what they see. It is simple."

"But he gets a shilling a paper!"

"It is well worth the work."

Old Harry had doubts about that.

The Virgo Fortress would have been lively enough with one guest, but the next day she had a second, one long-known to the Chapel and its Sithcundman.

If Galvin was clean-cut, Inspector Lestrade was sober. If Galvin hunkered over with his trade and his crutch, Lestrade strained upwards with his fine walking-stick, in the off-chance he might finally grow taller than the people around him. If Galvin was forever cheerful, the policeman was official and stern as a Roundhead. Galvin played with his charcoal-sticks, his cigarette-tips, and a seashell tied around his neck to keep his hands out of mischief. Lestrade carried a pet pocket watch and constantly stroked its gleaming head with his gloved fingers, which he never took off in a sniffing commentary to the state of the Chapel.

"I'm looking for a man," the little policeman announced in a Sunday-strict voice. "A Tinker by name of Galvin. He works with horses on occasion. Odd-jobs, small tasks and small wages."

"That could still be a lot of people," replied Harry. "We haven't any horses now. Our Chapel is full of souls looking for smatters. They come and go, and we pay in bread."

Lestrade rocked back and forth on the heels of his shiny shoes. The half-coach hat in his grey-gloved hand was beginning to show signs of worry as the fingers moved back and forth over the brim. "He wears a lot of bright blue."

"I may have seen someone of that description."

"If you see him, I'd appreciate you telling him to leave word of his usual address. We have questions."

"The Yard, eh?" Galvin chuckled. "Never takes 'em long." He was rubbing over a scene of loaves and fishes, a detailing that crept over the sill and outside the lip of an old window. Since it was a rare, fine day (dry) the Shackaback was out in it and perched on a step-ladder to chase the fine work. The unknown carver had loved the cross-hatch of scales and fins. Galvin would be spending most of his day on less than a foot of work. Because the window had to be kept open for the task, the court was treated to the pellucid strains of the children's choir under the sister's baton.

Harry was out too, for bright days meant he could sweep dust instead of mud. It also allowed him the means to spy on the Invader to his peaceful home. Lastly, he was a mannerly fellow and it was only fair to give the scoundrel space for running away at the news the police were looking for him. Tepefaction, it ought to be said, was an awkward social art for the old fellow.

Since the affairs of the Natural World weren't quick enough for him, Harry had decided to prod things along – Axar's malleable soul needed separation from this rascal.

"Aren't you worried?" the Sithcundman sniffed.

"Oh, they always want to know where we are in case we see anything. But me?" A shrug. "Nothing to see. Other than that robbery in High Street."

"What robbery?"

"What robbery? Lord save us! The *robbery*! High Street! Hansen's Silver-smithy!" The picaroon stopped to frog-eye the other's ignorance. "The old gander surprised 'em sure, for the bobbies found the door wide open an' the rats fleeing with fistfuls of trinkets in their clutches. There he was, him lyin' across the floor with his head knocked in by the stone table."

"Hansen's?" Old Harry repeated. "That is a common name, I am sure."

Galvin gulped a bit for air, and finally swam up for speech. "Hansen's – got everyone upset! Good and solid silver, and maybe even a murder too!"

Harry shrugged with his broom and played the air with the weary English gesture that meant, "Well, that's a pity," for the Sithcundman of Dust was above such affairs. "I beg your English pardon – '*maybe*'?"

"There's no tellin' yet. Hansen's been hooverin' between life and death. If he lives, 'tis prison for someone. But if he finishes dyin', it's murder and the dance."

"Well, why don't they talk to the servants? Shouldn't they know something?"

"Heh, what servants? He paid a woman to clean, but she never stayed. Always went home at night. Nobody else was there. That whole shop, he didn't trust nobody but his ownself, for all the good it did him."

Harry gulped for air and looked frantically to Axar, who was chasing ants. The Sithcundman overlooked that small sin in favour of remaining innocent of his ears. "You know a lot." (That was not a compliment.)

"Oh, there's lots I know!" (It was taken as such.)

The men fell silent. Only the soft swish-swish of Harry's broom over the sun-warmed tiles could be heard, and the scrape-scrape of Axar's little trowel as he dug grime from between the cracks, pretending the fleeing ants were the people of Britain before the Black Death. (His education was a little eccentric.)

Without warning the little tramp sighed. "I am sorry. This ain't the sort of talk to have by a house of God."

"Friar Jerome says we are all children of God," Harry reminded him with the tart side of the tongue. "And children can be bad or good." He made sure Axar was listening.

Galvin sighed again and set down his paper. He pulled out his tobacco-pouch and rolled a darning-needle cigarette. He offered the first smoke to the old guardian, who refused just as politely.

The shackaback finished his assembly and leaned back. In a few breaths, his contribution was adding to the mundungus off the factory-stacks of the borough.

"Us'd take a bit of our business to Mr. Hansen. He booked fair, he did. When it came to th'ore that came out o' the ground, he'd take the silver and let us have the lead. We use a lot o' the lead, you know. Almost

112

as much as we does the scrap iron." Galvin chuckled. "We'd meet up at th'scrap's market just off of Coventry, and he'd speak to us like we was anybody else. I s'pose it was because we weren't concerned with his silver, anymo' than he was for our lead and crumbs o'metal.

"Ever'body's upset about old Hansen. I can't say I know much about it, othern' what I read in the papers. It ain't on my rails. I keep to my smatterings. Things worth money are worth killing for." The little man plucked up his ball and tossed it one-handed into the air. "It looks bad for whoever did this." The little rambler shuddered. "Cain't take a life back once it's gone. Aye, a deep dwale it is. The longer he sleeps, the worse his chance. The borough holds its breath! Waitin' to see who he put in his will, as he didn't hold faith with any heirs."

"Ah, well. That's his choice." Harry relaxed enough to sermonise. "Inheirt'nces and property . . . all that's no favour to thems who gets it." He thrust his broom into a dried-up crust of street mud and sent it skirling into the opposite wall. To Axar's delight, the projectile burst upon impact, giving him fresh material with which to create graves for his fallen representatives of humanity.

"Aye to that! I pity them who wishes to find heirs. If the rumours are true, they – "

"Excuse me, Mr. Harry," one of the little orphans had poked his head out of the door. "Is it safe to give dead flies to the hens?"

"Oh, Llew! The questions you ask!" Harry wrung his hands upon his broom. "No, it is not! What if they're poisoned?"

"Then can I leave 'em for the rat-traps?"

"Nothing will kill a rat so easy!" Harry despaired of youth. "Why is it you of all people wish to know how to work better?"

"We've got comp'ny coming, Mr. Harry!" Llew yelped. "Impo'tant people!"

"There is no one more important than He whose House this is!" Harry's sentence was worth a month of sermons, but the eloquence failed his audience.

"Sherlock Holmes is comin'!" hopped the little scoundrel.

Axar gasped and dropped his trowel.

Harry clutched his broom. "What nonsense, Llew!"

"Well, I dunno! But he's comin', and the Sister's fixin' up a tea tray an' all!"

A tea tray! For someone who never set foot in this Chapel? Such extravagance! It was one thing to offer spiritual shelter to the needy, but to slice bread and plate butter for a stranger? The world had turned into a Dutch map – warped and sideways! Harry frantically cast his eye for the impressionable Axar, but the lad seemed not to have noticed. In the short-

113

minded ways of children, he was thinking more of the exotic visitor than the disgrace of generosity.

In his concerns, the old Sithcundman forgot himself and his duties. He stamped across the sweep into the Chapel where Axar's mates were lapping like so much sea-water at the hems of the Frère's robes.

"That would be Mr. Sherlock Holmes," Jerome was smiling to a question.

"Is he the smartest man in London?" asked a waif.

"I can only say he is very smart indeed."

"Smarter than you, even?"

"He's had a good education, and he never stops learning. He told me so himself."

But the song of schooling fell on tone-deaf ears.

"He's still in school!"

"Of course! Life is learning!"

"We can't stay in school all our lives," Llew scoffed. "We've got honest work to do, same as anyone."

"There's differn't kinds of school, you scamp." Galvin had come up from behind and gently rapped his work-smeared knuckles on the bony young skull. "Work isn't the same all the time. You keep your eyes open and your mouth shut, you'd be surprised how much you learn."

The lad stopped howling, but rubbed his head with a confused scowl. "Is education the same as having business sense?"

"Here, who taught you those long words?"

"Me da, Garesthissoul."

"That's the right ideer."

But Harry had no patience for this chatter, which was too much like barking of foxes in the hedgerow. "Friar Jerome, sir! What is happening?"

Jerome lifted his arms, and the foxes hushed.

"Friends are coming to look at our carvings before we start repairs." From one to another, his beautiful smile caressed like sunshine. "It would be a pity to miss seeing them, would it not? Before you know it, they shall be deconsecrated and taken out."

"Taken where?" asked a young impling – a yellow-haired, yellow-skinned little wastrel who made her coin selling scraps to the dustmen.

"That's none of your concerns," Harry said straight to Axar, and with the business end of his broom brushed the child out of the room and into the corridor where, he swore, a layer of dust had collected against the wainscoting.

"Children!" the Friar lectured the rest, "It is time to eat. Wash yourselves well. Mr. Holmes and Dr. Watson will be having tea, and then tour the Chapel."

"If they're here to see that," asked a leader in mischief, "why don't they do it first?"

"Because gentlemen know their manners. It is rude to go straight to business."

Axar endured the loss of gossip with a pout, and the pout remained staunch as his strong hand was filled with a fresh rag and a miserly drop of oil. The unjust nature of his situation, which was to toil away as his classmates gobbled news, rankled. No oil could balm his sentence! Sad were his responsibilities and honour, for he did owe the venerable old Sithcundman his education, and this was part of learning the trade of a Gentleman of Chores. As his master rubbed against the top of the wainscot, the child knelt and did the same with the bottom.

A soft sound from below had the old sweeper's attention. "What is it now, Axar."

"Look!" Axar held up his rag. In a few strokes the clean cloth was clabbered with a thick black paste. "But it looked clean! It held so much dirt and still looked clean!"

"Ah." Harry smiled at his pupil's advancement. "You've got it, my Axar. That is the nature of dust. It is invisible by itself, like a flake of snow. But it exists, Axar. It matters. All of those little bits of dust with it, we wouldn't see at all without the rag and oil. "That is why what we do is so important. It is not our job to see what others do not, but to know beyond a doubt that clean is clean."

"I didn't know it was so tricky."

"Dust is like sin upon a person. Never assume a person is nice because he looks it. The world is filt up with men and women who look and act like any of us, even though they ain't. No, they ain't. They're people of dust, Axar. Walking lumps of sin and mud, and it'll take more than our rags to clean 'em off. That's the work of the Anointing One, and His oils, and that alone."

Part III: The Arrival of Sherlock Holmes

Axar's impressionable eyes and ears missed the introduction of Sherlock Holmes. Harry would witness the invasion, and with a will the old charman dug grime out of the teeth of the carved angels holding up the Autograph Book in the foyer. Galvin noticed.

"You don't look as though you're glad of the guest. We're talking Sherlock Holmes, sir. He ain't the Earl o' Cork!" * Galvin was struggling to balance his day's labours in his crutchless arm before heading out. Old Harry was out of temper – the vagabond should be going out the back, not the Holy front doors!

"I don't approve," Old Harry snapped. The poor thick-headed perambulant didn't realize this ire was a chance to see he wasn't on the list of approved guests either! Such pitiful ignorance! "Solving cases for money. Shame!" (Harder scrubbing.) "I've never once been around when . . . *celebrities* . . . came by to bother the Friar!"

"Never?" Galvin pondered this as he looped a heavy bag over his shoulder, and finally shrugged. "T'each his own, and that's the truth, but I must leave for my evening drop, and cannot see him m'self."

Old Harry resolved not to be spared this indignity. The unfairness of life remained a constant. However, came the hopeful thought, perhaps Sherlock Holmes was just a figment of the papers. Such creatures did exist: All false-fronts and cosmetics, when in truth they were hollow, empty beasts.

The Sithcundman was dismayed to see the vanity of the press was true. Sherlock Holmes was a tall man. He swept in, dipped his stick-thin fingers into the font, and blessed himself at the small Hallow at guard. His brow was tall. His hairline was tall upon his head as he slipped off his hat. The lofty peak of a nose tethered his cloud-pale eyes above the thin rivulet of a mouth. Like the stout stone that singularly held up the mountain rested his chin, a handsome thing that aimed upward to the plaster medallions into the ceiling.

"Now, look at this, Watson!" the invader exclaimed, the tip of his walking stick high. "Truly excellent examples of the art. Early Regency for certain. It has the style of Houdon."

"Perhaps," said the other man who followed his steps. He didn't bless himself with the font, but gave a half-wary nod of respect to it and its wooden keeper – much like a warrior ought to greet a noble opponent. "It is hard to see the fine details that would let us be certain."

This aide-de-camp to General Holmes was flat-shouldered and walked with a limp he tried to ignore or overcome, like the soldiers who came to Chapel on the best holidays. Harry glared hard at the man's shoes, but there was no flaw in the polish, no niddling lassitude. Like Holmes, he pulled off his hat and peered up. A military-clipped moustache sat at-rest, the same sable as his thick hair. A handkerchief peeped from within his sleeve – Halloa! What is this? *Both* sleeves! How queer! Tucked so skillfully back, they were almost impossible to be seen. None could fool old Harry, though! His eyes could find the smallest mote of dust, the tiniest misplacement. Sharp and glittering did his crafty old eyes look upon the two, and he couldn't gauge which deserved the closest glare.

"Houdon's work is as distinct as a Rembrandt," that Holmes was saying.

"Yes, and like Rembrandt, he had students." Watson tipped his neck backwards-up to stare at the ceiling – which was growing a cobweb in the corner until Harry's ladder could return from repairs! "There is a reason why most Rembrandts are just out of gaze in the museums, Holmes. The authentication of many pieces are in dispute."

"It is illogical to draw a sneering line between master and teacher if the mastery is so close," Holmes laughed.

"Should a student be a master for his ability to mimic the master?"

"Better to ask if the master has bettered the world, wouldn't you think? From there the question of a student's individual value is pointless. But as for Houdon's pupils, not even Charles Byrne could view this close-up!" Holmes's stick thrust up to a smug plaster of the sun, whom, it was whispered, resembled a certain prime minister judged poorly by history. "Ah, but we are here for the oaken arts, are we not?" Holmes swept downward, his tall gaze skiing from peaks to bottom, head and stick and mercury gaze and all, to pin a shocked Harry. The Sithcundman felt as if he were bathed in black fog, staring into the dangerous lamps of a speeding omnibus!

"You must be Harry," the demon was saying. "The frère said you held sinecure for the Chapel. Allow me to introduce myself. My name is Sherlock Holmes, and this is Dr. Watson." Both men smiled and gave that brief, painless nod of the head that stands for warmth amongst the English.

"Ay, there was word you were comin'," Harry managed to say. His poor broom groaned under his grip. "I clean here." That suddenly didn't seem like such a braggadocious thing.

"A good thing," cried Holmes. "We shall be certain to come to you with any questions. Now, Watson, I believe we were promised tea?"

Harry was left blinking in a vacuum, but that didn't soothe against the pounding of his heart. Wickedness glittered in those grey eyes, wickedness indeed! Harry knew a Bible-man at first blink, and he was far and away from it. He found his handkerchief and applied it to his brow with a deep breath. When his heart calmed, he plucked up his instrument of war and began a new battle.

Sherlock Holmes accepted his lip-worn cup with the manners of a lord. The brew smoked pleasantly in the chill. The friar's rooms were luxurious only to book-worms and paperlice. In the corners rested a colony of moths, starving with the silent dignity that behooved their station until the money-spiders Jerome was hiding from Harry found them out. "Well, Brother Jerome. You were a policeman in your youth." Mr. Holmes curled the tea in its white bowl with scarce-darker fingers. "You avoided the scandals of the seventies by being elsewhere."

"Ah, if 'elsewhere' means the tamer lands of Galilee! Oh, it was tamer, make no bones! For all the crime I witnessed abroad, I cannot say it held a candle to what I'd seen when I wore the blue." He laughed at himself and put his head against the wall. "The Met was about to dismiss me anyway – Coming into money made my post complicated. So, I left to find myself."

"One might say you found more than your ownself in the journey."

"Too true. The Large Eyed Saints are a wonder, and I am heartened at their future within these walls. The Virgo Fortis was lonely too long."

"Your note was interesting, but not informative. You found something that requires discretion."

Jerome produced a coin on a chain. It was no larger than a holiday three-penny, and stamped with a lively little hare. "I believe this is from part of the silver lost in the High Street robbery."

"It is the personal sign of Hansen's."

"You fear someone in your Chapel has a connection with this crime."

"It is possible."

Holmes lowered his deadly gaze to the geegaw. Watson angled his head to better see all three participants: The friar, the detective, and the silver hare.

"It is no secret I only maintain the Chapel and keep to the charities of my status. Those who don't love her will not be pleased that we might . . . just possibly might . . . be harboring a fugitive."

"Is this not the traditional refuge?" Dr. Watson asked.

"Of course, but a refugee must declare his intentions! Here we may have a refugee under false pretense. It would complicate matters to a kickshaw! I am aware that many a chequered past has come here. It is not my place to have them check their sins at the door. But murder is murder, and I should not like to think that stain would come here without an explanation. Inspector Lestrade has already been by."

"His job is to be proven wrong more often than not." Holmes scoffed. "Just as it is mine to find the truth of the matter, no matter what garb it wears."

Dr. Watson cleared his throat. "Are there no other clues?"

"Ah, none that I can think of. I try to watch, but this Chapel is surprisingly large."

"Let us use what information is at hand. Has this sort of thing happened before?"

118

"I couldn't say, outside of my own observance. My poor predecessor was going blind, and his records are what you may imagine."

"You have a small school of lads and lasses, ten each."

"Yes. Though needs must say it is now twenty-one lads. We have a new pupil here. He arrived only a day after the robbery. Perhaps I ought to let an eleventh lassie in to balance." He wondered at the look passed from Holmes to Watson, and how the doctor returned the courtesy. They were masters of silent speech, these men, comfortable in wordless spaces.

On the other side of the door, Harry's hand-bones creaked over his broom-handle.

"Ah, wait. There is one other beneath the rooves . . . I hired a tinker to make rubbings off the carvings to be replaced. Clever fellow. I knew him before I took off my helmet."

"Questioning him might be informative." Holmes mused, unaware that Harry was nodding as vigorously as his stiff neck could allow. "The next time he shows, send me a wire or a bright boy."

A bright boy? But Axar was the brightest lamp in all the Chapel! Harry's heart lurched inside his brittle chest. He held that organ in with his breath and slowly stepped away, his fear for Axar placing wings upon his weary old feet.

Part IV: A New Development?

"That is a stout little lad."

Harry wanted to puff up in pride and bristle at the same time, for while he knew this was only true, it would do no good to feed and water a child's vanities. "Two good ears an' eyes, that's certain, for he rarely needs twice-telling, and watches the dust."

"An admirable trait." Mr. Holmes clapped his hand into his palm. "A man who listens well goes far."

Axar glanced from side to side, looking for the "man". The lad wondered if his confusion would improve with exposure, or perhaps said causes of confusion would run their course, much as an ill East Wind or a wintry freeze. Old Harry had kept him hopping since coming downstairs, cleaning this and polishing that, and dusting here, sweeping there. The downstairs had never looked better!

Harry had even knocked upon the kitchen door, greatly bold, to see if Sister Sarai needed help cleaning the kitchen. That good cook had dismissed him with a verbal box to the ears and a threat with her meaty paws, for this was her realm! To infer that she wasn't within full capacity in her own land! What nerve!

119

His senses restored, Harry packed himself and his apprentice to the farthest parts unknown from the nun, which was high in the attic-rooms where the spiders could be entrusted to produce a tithe. It was here Sherlock Holmes had found them, and Harry looked most displeased to Axar's confused eyes.

Why? All the child could see was a trade in words adults enjoyed – *Boring!* With a nod of his head Mr. Holmes turned and left, with Dr. Watson in tow. Axar hadn't even noticed his presence!

Mr. Holmes was a very large presence indeed.

Poor Harry! Just as he lowered the oil lamps for trimming, the narthex doors creaked. If it wasn't Inspector Lestrade again, just as the investigators descended from the heights!

"Ah, there you are." Mr. Lestrade sniffed with a degree of self-importance and rocked back and forth on the balls of his feet. "Admiring the carvings, no doubt."

"They are historically important." Holmes agreed lazily. "I see your work at the river has been fruitless – and wet! Would you join us for an early supper?"

"Thank you." Lestrade stamped his toes and grimaced. "But what makes you think my day has been fruitless?"

"I notice you aren't disagreeing with me." Holmes laughed. "Very well. You are chilled to the bone, Friend Lestrade. Allow me another examination of this moulding here, and then we shall discuss the particulars of our professions with the good Jerome's excellent pekoe."

"Oh, very well."

Holmes tilted perilously over the edge of the scalloped rail to frown at a dark pool of carving – something like a green man, or green dragon, and a large tree fruited with human heads sprouting from his mouth.

"Don't kill yourself, man!" Lestrade leaned to the side and, to the horror of Old Harry, pressed the forbidden switch. A white-hot sun flooded the atmosphere from the darkest corners of the ceiling, illuminating every particle, every mote of dust! Before this Old Harry staggered back, he and Axar overcome with multiple sneezes.

"Modern lights!" Watson crowed.

"Ah, yes. Limited in its use thanks to some folk who believe it unholy." Lestrade sighed.

"Those lights are only for need!" Harry reproached from behind a snowy handkerchief. Behind him, Axar gave one final " *'ter-choo!'* "

"My apologies." Lestrade drawled, for the "daylight" was stingy indeed. "Mr. Holmes, have you a good gander?"

"I have and thank you. Come, Watson. Lestrade needs a hot drink."

"I shall follow you both," the doctor answered. He brought up the rear, but paused to look very thoughtfully at the puzzled dustmen.

Part V: The Council of the Treen

"And now that we are all here," Holmes began, "we may await Watson's verdict. It was good of you to come so quickly, Lestrade."

"Has anyone noticed your disguise?" Watson smiled under his mustache, brown eyes halfway inside a brown study. Holmes looked at him side-ways, but said nothing.

"No." Lestrade was curt enough to be rude, his well-known symptom of a contused temper. He tugged off his gloves, and the henna'd bird flexed its wings with his fingers. "They'll see me because they must see a policeman, but they never notice the likes of Galvin unless they're watching his hands and what the hands are doing." He shook his head, violently.

"I've been watching this place, as you know," The little fellow helped Jerome pass the platter of bread. "When I'm not looking for contacts on the waterfront! Any news, yea or nay, will still be more than what I had yesterday." He jerked a thumb to his former brother of the blue.

"If I may, gentlemen?" Dr. Watson unexpectedly broke into the conversation. His trim military face had been faraway with some opaque thinking. Now he was sharp and focused. "I saw something that may be of use."

"Of course, Watson." Holmes urged.

Dr. Watson was a man who took light matters merrily, and serious matters gravely. He rinsed his throat with a sip of tea and began in a quiet voice:

"I am positive Axar is the same child I saw in Hansen's silver shop – in '80."

Sherlock Holmes's brows floated to the ceiling and Lestrade, who knew better, had been drinking tea. He strangled to keep it from soiling his shirt-front. Frère Jerome fell back with his eyes round.

"It was some years ago, Watson. Can you be this certain before the courts?"

"Without a doubt! I was about to go India, and a stout silver watch is a better investment than the gold watch one keeps for civilian affairs and dinners . . . ." Here the doctor pulled the silver copulae through his fingers. "I wished a chain identical to the style of my watch. Morgan Hansen fashioned my family's silver, you see, and his nephew, J. James Hansen, had inherited.

121

"He assured me he could easily match his uncle's work." Watson tipped the bottom of the chain over and spread a silver fob upon his palm: A tiny hare leaped across the centre.

Lestrade examined it closely. "Beautiful work!"

"I thought so too. There was a small child in the corner of the shop, hidden under the table-clothes and doing his best to be invisible, even as his ears drank our conversations. I had a feeling he didn't have permission to be in the room of business, so I returned his courtesy and pretended I did not see him."

"One of your many talents, Watson, which are easy to praise and difficult to duplicate."

"I believe he was enamored of my new uniform. It was very smart with polished buttons." Watson chuckled a moment before his cognac coloured eyes slid back to the past. They watched him read aloud the past as it scrolled past his memory. "The child wasn't well, gentleman. I can vouch for his features, which have scarce changed, and I am aware of how the Court may question me. Can I swear there are no siblings? Are there no cousins? I cannot say, but the curvature of the spine and how his right hand draws to his chest . . . That could not, in my belief as a medical professional, be replicated lightly. He would be about the proper size, ten years grown. I believe his growth is not as healthy as it should be. One might easily mistake him for one of the urchins off the fag-end." This cut was finished with a sharp jerk of the head in the direction of the potteries.

"How did you learn of this boy in the here-and-now?" Jerome was baffled.

"The first newspaper reports to announce the robbery and attack at the silver shop were in that evening. I knew there might be more news upon the morrow, and paid a knocker-up to bring me the first edition. She was good as her word and, as I had hoped, there were more details in the pages."

"As they ought." Holmes sniffed. "*The Daily Grammatic* costs enough."

"They are competing with *The Daily Graphic*." To the others Watson clarified: "*The Grammatic* apes *The Graphic* in all ways, and they hired a veritable army of skilled artists to wander about the entire isle to crayon up a library of 'authentic illustrations' for future news stories."

"Much to the amusement of London." Holmes had discarded his empty teacup for a cigarette. "They paid admirable wages to walk all over British Creation and practically the entire city of London in the hopes one will be appropriately maudlin or sentimental to pair up a future three-inch column of tragedy."

Lestrade, who felt a record of images a fine idea, cleared his throat and spoke into his teacup to the man of God: "They refused to share their archive of engravings with Mr. Holmes."

"Ah."

"They had done a beautiful lithograph of the street with Hansen's, and so they included it to fit the story of the crime. The details were small, but one can clearly see the face of that child from inside the window, peeping out like a Punch at a fair."

"And when we were finally able to speak to the artist for the paper, he remembered taking the job because upon the flash, Hansen himself 'rared up' from the back and yanked the boy away from the window." Holmes blew a stream of smoke to the ceiling. "He later penned an apologetic sort of letter to the paper, explaining that privacy was his *modus operandi* with the sensitive nature of his clients."

Lestrade's peaty eyes narrowed, which was an unfortunate side-effect of his being deep in thought. He meant no ill, but his moments of rumination were unfailingly alarming to the uninitiated. To Holmes's amusement, he tried to touch the top of the ceiling with his eyeballs. "Horse-gills! Anyone with the sense given the goose knows not to cause trouble with an artist. That just ensured they'd remember the encounter! So – a robbery with malice that we know will lead to a murder charge – Hansen will never wake again – and an un-accounted-for child that is now in this church!"

The little man leaned back in his small chair, balancing his teacup and saucer on his fingertips. "So much of this doesn't make sense! As soon as I got your note about the coin, I made inquiries of Hansen's neighbors. As discreetly as can be, considering that street!" Lestrade again rolled his eyes as well as a tumbler before a critical audience. "Even you would find it poor pickings, Mr. Holmes. After quite a lot of cups of tea and boiled coffee and beer and cider and wine and Welsh whisky (which actually exists, by the by), the locals warmed up enough to admit that there was a crippled-up little boy that lived in Hansen's shop, but no one talked about him because Hansen wouldn't tolerate it. They were clear that it was in their best interests to keep him at arm's-length, since his customers declined in quality with Morgan's passing."

"Declined, did he?"

"Morgan may have turned the shop over to his nephew, but that nephew's reputation was not . . . good enough for the old clientele."

"Ah. A common-enough story."

"It was by accident I learned of Old Harry, and how he'd been dismissed without warning to wash up here."

Holmes laughed. "And you call this unhelpful? You are a detective, Lestrade! Shouldn't the peculiar lack of information be helpful?"

Lestrade's lungs released a plaintive bagpipe-dirge that sent the money-spiders running.

"Perhaps we can solve this riddle backwards." Holmes addressed the room. "Hansen's confidential work inspired enemies. He once had noble clients. Discretion is the word. We may accept he had reasons for hiding the boy. But as to how he arrived here? Frère, what can you tell us?"

"He came to us the very day following the robbery – *Ahem*, late, that is. It was almost ten o'clock."

"Tell us what you saw, sir. Not what you know happened."

The man in brown smiled ruefully as Lestrade snorted.

"I was transferring the candlelight in the alcoves. There is precious little to be heard within. I did not hear the doors open or shut. Simply the knock upon the frame as Harry let me know there was a boy to see Father Ambrosius.

"He was small for his age, his spine cruelly twisted. It made me wonder if he was one of those poor sweeps. His right arm was drawn close to his chest, the way a man will do when he has an injury, and he was barefoot against the cold. It was not remarkable that he was wearing a man's shirt, for children in these poor boroughs will often do that. The shirt was tucked up under his bad hand, keeping the hems from dragging the floor.

"When the boy saw me, he pointed with his good hand to his neck, around which was tied a grimy note."

Jerome produced this note in question, and Sherlock Holmes plucked it up.

"Where is the string?" he demanded. "The note was tied with string, was it not?"

Jerome blanched and dove back into the drawer. "We had to cut it. The knot was too deep, and too close to the child's neck."

The string was produced with an embarrassed smile traded with Lestrade. "*Protect the knot!*" had been the mantra of their elders in the Force, and the importance of string was rarely over-appreciated when it came to crime.

Holmes examined this poor length of cotton twine, bending, twisting, holding it up to the light and even smelling it.

"A two-handed knot, and the loops are perfectly even. He could have hardly tied it for himself. Thankfully, this has not been washed."

"It was clean – miraculous, considering the rest of the lad."

Holmes layered the evidence upon his leg and took up the note:

Dear Father Ambrosius,

You once offered bed and board for my son in the event of my passing. If you are reading this, my time has come. Please take care of Axar with my blessings. He has money to give you.

Regards,

A.H.

"And a more wretchedly contrived thing I've rarely read." Lestrade complained.

"We may agree there are more believable examples in the world." Holmes laughed. "Dear me! The inept writer wants us to believe he is a doting father. A poor forger, with an unusually powerful right hand and arthritis. See how cramped the *T*'s are, and the *I*'s are almost horizontal."

"Axar's shirt contained money sewn in the hem. I gave him new clothes. He settled into our life easily enough. It was only two days later that I found this coin on the floor near the Large Eyed Saints. I picked it up and made no word of it, but I noticed Axar sweeping mightily there with his eyes cast side to side for days after."

Lestrade said it with no pleasure. "He's connected to the crime in some way."

"I know. But I do not understand the entire matter."

"An excellent point. Understanding is precisely what is needed." Holmes examined the paper a moment more. "Did you keep the shirt?"

"Absolutely." Jerome exclaimed.

"Excellent!" Holmes beamed.

"Sister Sarai washed it."

"Ah." The beam dropped.

"It was lousy." The churchman scolded gently and produced a folded-up garment from the same drawer hiding the note.

"The same hand wrote the note and sewed the money into the shirt." Sherlock Holmes spread the cloth over the desk and stretched it flat so that the bottom would be a single straight line. The others crowded close to see. "See the thread here, and here? Again, a severe slant. It mimics the slope of handwriting."

"Hastily done." Lestrade sniffed. "Very clumsy."

"You have seen many a secretive pocket in your line of work, Lestrade . . . as have you when you were a policeman, Friar. How would one normally hide money in their clothing?"

"Well, with a great deal more care than this!" Lestrade waved his hand.

"Watson is an upstanding sort and unlikely to know the particulars of such deception. Would you mind explaining?"

"I'll try. Doctor, old coppers like Jerome and me know to look for incriminating things, but not everyone has pockets. A clever needle and thread will make small pockets of any thin, strong cloth they can find. The money, or letters, secret correspondence, whatever it is they'll be hiding, is sewn up tight and then that packet is sewn inside."

"And I've hardly ever seen any sewing inside the bottom hem." Jerome added. "Too risky."

"Risky, did you say?" Watson repeated.

"Aye, yes. If the seam bursts, your money would fall in the street. Clever thieves – Remember the Cauldwater Gang, Geoffrey? – were good at finding people with caches there, and even better at slicing open the coat-hems, taking out the packets, and walking away before the victims even knew it!"

"Money in the bottom hem will make a shirt hang stiff. Someone would be bound to notice." Lestrade frowned. "This is peculiar, Mr. Holmes. The shirt is fine linen, a gentleman's choice. What would a raggedy child be doing with it?"

"This was sewn up with no consideration. The money was jammed into the hem and sewn up – a shabby trick you'd expect from a penny dreadful or cheap sensationalist novel."

"Your Harry's the key, Jerome." Lestrade smiled. "But I know his type. The more he's pressed, the more he'll muzzle. He must be brought to confession."

"We must watch him." Jerome rose. "Harry has lied with good intentions, but he has still lied to God."

Ever happy to join a hunt, Holmes followed. Watson lingered with his hand on the door-jamb, blocking Lestrade's path enough to get the little man's attention.

"Lestrade, if I may," Watson cleared his throat with a smile. "What does this Welsh whisky taste like?"

Lestrade thought about it as they followed their leaders.

"Expensive," he said at last. "The old sweep said it was three-and-six a bottle, and I believe him."

Watson whistled his admiration. "A twenty-year Scottish malt is five! What did your wife say to you when you came home with those fumes?"

"Who says I'd go home after that? Holmes may call me an idiot at times, Doctor, but that doesn't mean I'm anybody's fool."

126

Watson chuckled softly, but again his eyes were elsewhere. Lestrade asked if something was on his mind.

"Oh." Watson shook himself. "I don't know. I'm still thinking."

Sherlock Holmes wished to see the Large Eyed Saints again, this time with a guide. The visitors held back with an awkward respect as Friar Jerome lit extra lamps, transforming the room from grotto to softly-illuminated cavern. Shadows leaned up against the sloped walls, and wooden fingers, lean as mantis, glowed as they clasped their objects of office.

"Here is where I found the coin." Jerome nodded to a puddle of blackness. "It was directly under the robe of Saint Anthony."

Sherlock Holmes stepped closer and examined the darkness, rose lightly to his feet, and peered up with new curiosity at the terrible calm of the saint. "A remarkable sculptor made this," he commented. "I have never seen the like."

"They remind me of primitive Celtic sculpture," Watson murmured. "Or the rough hews of northern Africa."

"They are capsules of time, shaped within the aesthetics of a far distant school." Jerome smiled up at Anthony, impervious to the intimidating calm.

"Anthony is the saint of the lost and forgotten," Holmes muttered.

"Yes?"

"Nothing, good friar. I believe we are done for now."

"A moment, gentlemen," Watson blurted. "If I may have a word with Holmes?"

Lestrade and Jerome nodded and stepped back to the door, looking away to allow the other half of the group their privacy.

"Get used to that," the little detective whispered to his former comrade. "Watson's a sharp one, but he doesn't like to talk about his thoughts on the case so much in front of other people, just in case he might mis-direct the thinking. Very discreet."

"Good man," Jerome approved.

They heard Holmes chuckle. It rumbled like a very large bee in an even-larger hive.

"One last look at the carvings on the gospel side, gentlemen, and we shall bid you good-bye for the day."

Just in time, thought Lestrade, for he had been hearing Old Harry's nosy brush-brush of broom-bristles coming up behind them in the hall.

Part VI: The Saint Reveals the Lost

"I wonder that Saint Anthony is not the patron of the police, Lestrade."

"Why so?"

"He is the overseer of the lost and forgotten, the cast-out, the misplaced, is he not?"

"I'm afraid I don't follow your reasoning, Mr. Holmes. Yet again, I think . . . ."

Old Harry held to his broom, waiting ever-so-patiently for the interlopers to finish their clap and jow, to leave so he could sweep the Saints' floor! It was high time and they'd overstayed their welcome, and when they seemed to be making their home upstairs, the old fellow decided to hint upon their departure and made his way up the hallway, passing his broom and dust pan loudly upon the floor.

At long last, the unwelcome guests parted ways and filed singly past him: The priest (who at least belonged here), the detective, the doctor, and lastly the little policeman, fussily donning his gloves as he stepped over the threshold from the Holy Sanctum.

The hand!

It had been but a moment, but nothing escaped the sharp eyes of Old Harry! *The bird! That mark!*

The Sithcundman's brains fluttered and he reeled back, a lone breather before the treen council. He was alone in his awful awareness, but for the whispering buzz of a thousand imagined crimes battered his ears, magnified by the painted wooden eyes upon him. *Mr. Lestrade and the Tinker were the same!* The Tinker, snooping and poking in the Chapel! *A policeman in disguise!* And why would he be in disguise? *He was betrayed!*

The old man's confidence had crumbled, its dust scattered by a long, long lifetime of irrational fears and worse thoughts. The carefully-wrought world built by his willpower alone was revealed fragile as glass. His eyes swam and the eyes of wood, judging, met his from every angle. He imagined their censure, heard his own voice in his ears counseling against the dangers of charity and hospitality. Lestrade had *spied*. The Chapel would know he had *lied*. They would cast him out, and then what would happen to Axar? The boy must be protected at all costs. *But how?*

In his muddle, the old man latched to one thought, then another. Axar was being trained to succeed him. Brother Jerome had agreed it would be so. If his place were settled . . . .

Their gaze burned through him, aiming over the balcony where the Virgo Fortis hung suspended at altar. Was it a command, or freedom? In the glorious days, those of faith consigned themselves to miracles. They leapt and flew, saved by Heavenly hands, or found a swift death and eternal martyrdom. It was all up to the Divine – all one had to do was cosign their personal authority for the greater.

Oh, I am sorry!

With a sob in his throat, the Sithcundman spared one last look at the silent forest of faces before him before he clutched up the sill of the balcony and did just that.

It was a grey-faced league that awaited the verdict of Dr. Watson some hours later.

"He shall live. I fear for his state of mind more than his legs. He is not a man to be idle."

Jerome smiled sadly. "He was always a man of action."

"Where is Axar?"

"Taking a hot milk in the kitchen. He'll be tucked to bed by the inglenook. There's fewer places in London safer than the hawkish eye of Sister Sarai. I feel whatever is about to be said, is best said away from him."

Sherlock Holmes glanced at Inspector Lestrade. The little man had been wearing the same sick expression since finding Harry's broken body in the nave. It had been he that held the old man down during Watson's bone-setting and draughting, and he was every bit as tired as the doctor.

"I can't understand it," he whispered at last. "Did he believe himself a suspect?"

"Not precisely, Inspector. He thought we were hunting different game."

"I too do not understand, but, whatever it costs – " Father Jerome buried his face in his hands. " – I'll pay it. I must have answers."

"If we draw too close in our investigation, we may probe too deeply." Holmes smiled ruefully upon the world-worn Jerome. "My rates are fixed, my good Brother. I may be paid to solve a case, but that does not mean I will solve it to the client's satisfaction. You are worried about more than one person under the shelter of your responsibility."

"Yes. I am at that." Jerome closed his eyes.

The Sithcundman had shrunken in the world. Without his broom he was a frail, pitiable thing, small in his sickbed as a single pea in a pod.

"I'm ready to make my peace."

Sherlock Holmes bowed his head. "We would be honoured."

The old gentleman's rheumy eyes flitted from one man to the other in the quiet. "I used to clean the shop for Mr. Hansen. He paid and treated me well enough. No complaint I had, no, nowt. I swept and polished for my bread and board, and every month he gave me a whole shilling!" (Behind Sherlock Holmes, Lestrade flinched at such gratitude). "I hadn't any reason to spend my money, so I kep' it, put it aside . . . and one day there was a baby.

"I don't know how it got there, but it was there, and I was told to watch that it didn't crawl to the grate or anything like that. So, I did. There are powerful poisons in a silversmithy, and I worried at it being loose.

"One day, I forgot myself and asked where it had come from. I was told to take my wages and go." Old Harry gulped, and his eyes shone wet. "But I never forgot that baby."

"It would be a strange man who could forget his own nephew." Mr. Holmes said this without full regard for impact. Watson leaped to keep his patient from rearing up in bed.

"Oh, but how did you know?" Old Harry groaned.

"Do you recall when the lights were lit and you and young Axar sneezed?" Holmes smiled at Watson. "I have it on the finest of medical authority that the trait of sneezing in the sudden presence of light is passed down among family lines."

"It is true. Morgan and I – we were both the nephews of J. James Hansen, but campaigning in foreign parts ruint my body. I could not provide for myself and the shop was noble, but not wealthy. I earned my keep by keeping it clean, and in my shame, denied any relation to my family.

"Over time I saw the wickedness of money, sirs. What is silver, but just another metal? And yet for it, the customers would lie or cheat or steal . . . even murder or threaten to murder! And my cousin, he grew no better! His craft was all he cared for. His customers could do as they pleased!" The old man stopped for breath, his strength fading.

"Do not burden yourself," Holmes gently placed his hand upon the frail shoulder. "I can extrapolate. Somehow your cousin found himself inheriting an unwanted son, physically incapable of taking over the silverwork, and thus not worthy to acknowledge as his future investment for the shop. He was raised secret even from you, until you asked the wrong question."

"Yes."

"You found your place here at the Chapel, but you were worried for the child, and you watched all you could."

"There was a cupboard," Harry closed his eyes. "hid up inside another cupboard. I made it for Axar, so he would have a place to hide when my cousin had . . . He could get angry. He had rages. When I could, I would walk by at night, and I heard thrashing about . . . when . . . Oh, Heavens!"

Tears shivered in his eyes. "I called as quietly as I could, for when my cousin was in a rage, he must be spoken to softly. It felt like hours had passed, but then the door creaked open. Little Axar had opened it. He was pale as a ghost, and he didn't even know it was his own father lyin' dead on the floor."

"How did it happen?" Lestrade blurted, his whole body leaning forward.

"Axar heard him fall, as he did so many times when the rages took him. This time, he struck his head against the side of the stone. But the shop had not closed, and it didn't take long for someone to see the open door. Rascals took advantage of my cousin as he lay insensible, and clutched up what they could carry before running back out. I never saw them.

"Axar is so used to these terrible fits that he thinks my cousin is still alive and pattering away at his silver. I've kept him from knowing more."

"The coin, Harry? Was it his?"

"It was mine! When I had been a hale man, my uncle gave it to me before I went abroad as a soldier. I've never tried to sell it. It is my only legacy. When I brought Axar here, I gave it to him, for he ought to have something of his family besides wrack and ruin." Old Harry wiped at his eyes and sniffed.

"But . . . ." Lestrade was baffled. "If what you say is true, then this child will inherit the shop!"

"And its wickedness!" But spitting out too much truth took its toll. Harry fell back, gasping.

Dr. Watson stepped before his patient. "We should leave him to rest."

The party regrouped to the Saints. Lestrade was agitated. His hands played with his watch in a fruitless attempt to roll back time.

"The child was a blind alley. I have no idea what to say in my report."

"Be at peace, Lestrade. Answers were found, if not the expected ones." Holmes chuckled. "A man has fallen to ruin by his own hand, and thieves took opportunity of the situation."

"And a child is discovered, but still . . . unaccounted for. I'm not looking forward to writing about that."

"You might imply the child's identity was hidden for his own protection."

"Lying, is it?"

"Certainly not. It would be easy to point out that a frail child could be hidden in plain sight in the shop of a valuable silversmith.

"That is, close enough, to the truth. As for the silver thieves, they will emerge. Such a crime will not be kept forever in London. Patience is not

131

the forte of your superiors, but they may be satisfied that you have helped avert the criminals' attention upon a useless witness."

Lestrade only sighed again and leaned his head into his hands. "The Foreign Office is concerned with anything to do with silver and gold."

"In the meantime, Axar is the question." Watson looked at Brother Jerome. "What shall be done?"

"He will stay here. He is safe enough, and Harry will heal faster if he has purpose. I shall be the boy's protector and obfuscator." The priest buried his hands within his large sleeves and spoke to the wooden counselors, not his fleshly peers. "The matter of the lie is finished. It was for the greater good of things.

"And I was a policeman once, gentlemen. I will help you how I can, for blood was spilled and lives permanently changed. Come to me when you decide on your course of action."

He reached out, gently stroking his fingertips against the terrible, beautiful serenity of Anthony. "This will not be forgotten. That I promise."

His companions were unsure to whom he was speaking, they or the Large Eyed Saints, but they were mindful enough not to ask.

NOTE

For more information regarding Brother Jerome, and Galvin Dooley, Inspector Lestrade's disguise amongst the gipsies, see Marcia Wilson's *Sherlock Holmes and the Scotland Yarders* series.

*   The Ace of Diamonds, Irish slang for the lousiest card in the deck.

The Sharpshooter's Revenge
by P.C. Shumway

"I agree, Watson," stated Sherlock Holmes as he lounged upon the sofa and gazed at the ceiling. "The past decade has been a busy one and, contrary to the adage, time is *not* the healer of all wounds." The consulting detective was reclining amid the morning's discarded newspapers.

It was midway through a hot and humid July in the year 1890, and I was just a moment earlier thinking the ten-year anniversary of the Battle of Maiwand was approaching. I surmised my companion's deductive remarks were made, in part, from observing me massage my war-injured leg out of habit while I recalled a crude photograph on my desk at home of my old comrades from the Afghan field hospital. Three of the six men in the picture were killed when the Ghazis overtook our camp after I had left. Losing brethren on the battlefield were wounds that never heal.

I was also thinking of how quickly the past ten years seemed to pass by – mostly due, I supposed, to the number of extraordinary cases in which I had the pleasure of assisting Holmes. I was at a loss about how he deduced my thoughts along those lines, but I wasn't in the mood to humour him with my ignorance. Remembering my time as an assistant surgeon with the 66th Regiment of Foot during the Second Afghan War put me in a melancholy mood.

My wife Mary was away visiting her dear friend Mrs. Russell in Edinburgh for an extended stay. I took the opportunity to spend a short holiday from my practice in the company of my friend in his Baker Street rooms.

There was a ring at the front door, followed by the familiar crisp knock by Mrs. Hudson at our hall door. She stepped in with a telegram for Holmes. He stood up, shedding newspapers as he strode across the room, took the cable, and thanked the landlady. As soon as she had closed the door behind her, Holmes opened the dispatch and read it to himself. He tapped his forehead with the missive, knitted his brows, and paced around the room. He could sense he had my full attention and said, without looking at me, "It's from Edwin Farley."

"The name is unfamiliar to me."

"I imagine it would be. He is the director of schedules for the North British Railway. I haven't heard from him since the Forth Bridge over the Tay recently opened."

"Why on earth would a railroad executive contact you?"

Holmes looked at me with a mischievous smile.

"Farley is an informant. He is my closest link to Professor Moriarty."

Moriarty was, of course, the controlling brain of the underworld of crime in London and the greatest schemer of our time.

"The Professor," Holmes continued, "has gained a power over Farley, and uses a blackmailer's advantage to control rail shipments and schedules. When Moriarty needs a special at a moment's notice or the inspection of a rail shipment waived, Farley makes it happen. However, Farley has covertly established connections to Moriarty's inner circle and provides me with information when it is safe to do so. He is a more reliable link to the criminal mastermind than Porlock."

Porlock, employed by Professor Moriarty, had tipped us off to the tragedy in Birlstone in early 1888.

Holmes waved the dispatch over his head like a flag of war.

"Farley and Porlock never send telegrams. They always send handwritten notes by courier."

He handed me the dispatch, which read:

Noon at Branigans. Come alone.

Farley

"Surely he means Branigan's Pub in the East End," I suggested.

I handed the telegram back to Holmes. He walked across the room and tossed it upon his desk.

"I don't like it. But if the message is truly from Farley, then he must have urgent information and wasn't at liberty to write a note and hire a courier. If he didn't send it, then it is probable that Moriarty has discovered Farley's treason and sent the telegram himself – in which case, I will be walking into a trap."

"It's after eleven o'clock now."

Holmes slipped his revolver from his desk into his waistcoat, strode over to the door, and put on his coat and hat. He opened the door and said, "If I don't return, have Lestrade drag the Thames."

I was about to ask him if he was serious, but he was quickly out the door.

Holmes returned nearly four hours later. He tossed his hat on the stand, laid his revolver upon his desk, retrieved his clay pipe from the mantel, and began filling it.

"Farley is dead," he stated.

"Good Heavens!" I replied.

I set down the book I was reading. Holmes lit his pipe and flopped into his chair in the usual fashion.

"I had an informative meeting with Professor Moriarty in that wretched watering hole in Whitechapel," he said with an amused chuckle. "The pub, as to be expected in that neighborhood, was dimly lit, and reeked of mildew and stale beer. There was a bartender behind the counter wiping mugs, two rogues drinking at the bar, and a waitress tending to three shabby patrons at a table in the centre of the dining room. There was no sign of Farley, so I selected a booth on the left side of the room in the rear, near the back door, and sat facing the entrance. I took my revolver from my waistcoat and held it on my lap, hidden under the table. A few minutes later, Moriarty stepped into the room. There was no mistaking his lean frame, stooped shoulders, protruding forehead, and piercing eyes. He scanned the room with bird-like movements, walked over to my booth, and stood facing me."

"'You can put your revolver away, Mr. Holmes. There is no need for violence today,' he said with a snicker.

"I slid my revolver back into my waistcoat as he sat across from me. 'Where is Farley?' I asked.

"'I am afraid Mr. Farley met with an unfortunate accident two weeks ago at King's Cross. Train platforms can be dangerous places if one isn't careful. His death wasn't reported in any of the newspapers. It wouldn't be favorable for the North British Railway to have one of their executives found crushed upon one of their tracks.'"

Holmes re-lit his pipe before continuing his narrative.

"I threatened to sound an alarm.

"'You may make all the noise you care to make, Mr. Holmes,' Moriarty said. 'Everyone in this establishment, including the patrons, are under my employ. At the conclusion of our meeting, they will immediately exit the premises and change their identities. This building was leased to a fictitious investor, and this afternoon it will be on the market again. I have never met the owner, and he has never seen nor heard of me. I don't leave traces, Mr. Holmes.'"

Holmes took another draw on his pipe.

"Professor Moriarty had the upper hand. I inquired to the purpose of the meeting.

"He said, 'The life or death of Dr. John Watson.'"

Holmes grinned at my astonishment as I nearly fell out of my chair.

"I was as surprised as you, my good fellow. The Professor smiled at my raised brows and said, 'Your friend is in imminent danger, Mr. Holmes. A patient of his by the name of Miss Anderson passed away last week, and her bereaved brother, Carl, has vowed revenge. Carl Anderson was in my employ until I sent him word three days ago that his services were no longer needed. He had become mentally unstable, and I could no longer trust his judgement.'

"'What services did Mr. Anderson provide?' I asked.

"'He is the best long-range sharpshooter in all of England' the Professor stated. 'I suspect he was formally a rifleman in the British Army, but I have been unable to trace his past. Anderson is obviously an alias. He and his sister led private lives, residing in a flat in Blackwall. She passed away with no other known family, nor any known acquaintances. They didn't attend church and weren't members of any society clubs.'

"'A sharpshooter, you say.'

"'His weapon of choice is a Whitworth rifle. As you may know, the .451 caliber rifle is accurate to two-thousand yards.'

"'A testament to the hexagonal rifling design,' I replied. 'And you offer this information in hopes that I find him before he takes revenge upon you for terminating his services, I suppose.'

"'I will not insult your intelligence and deny my motives, Mr. Holmes,' he admitted. 'It is difficult to say what Anderson will do after he eliminates the doctor.'

"I must tell you, Watson, I never dreamed I would have Professor Moriarty as a client. I asked him for Anderson's description."

"'I never met him,' he replied. 'One of my operatives, Crowley, was my connection with the man. Crowley once described Anderson as being average in height, with black or dark-brown hair, slight in build, and with no distinguishing features. Anderson once told Crowley he could shoot a snow leopard from a mile away.'

"'Perhaps Mr. Crowley can identify Anderson from police photographs or military records,' I suggested.

"'Crowley was shot through the head from five-hundred yards away two days ago while walking through Hyde Park,' said Moriarty, without any sign of remorse. 'Anderson has vanished without a trace. His rooms in the Riverside Apartments building on the Blackwall Causeway are empty. The landlady had let the flat to Miss Anderson and couldn't describe the brother. None of the occupants in that loathsome tenement pay the slightest attention to each other.'

"'Apparently,' I noted, 'Anderson doesn't leave traces either.'

"'I have faith in your abilities, Mr. Holmes,' he said as he rose from the table and walked out the back door."

"Do you believe him? The Professor may be sending you on a wild goose chase for some nefarious reason. Is there any proof of this sharpshooter's existence?"

"I visited Scotland Yard after I left the tavern and talked to Lestrade. He pulled Edwin Farley's file for me. Farley apparently fell from the platform onto the tracks just as a train was entering the station. It was thought at first to be an accident or a suicide. The body was in poor shape after the train passed over it. However, the autopsy discovered this . . . ."

Holmes reached into his pocket and produced a hexagonal bullet.

"It was lodged in Farley's brain. There is only one rifle that uses a bullet with this shape."

"Yes, I am familiar with the Whitworth," I said. "I believe the Army considered replacing their Enfields with the Whitworth, but the rifle was tedious to load, so they chose the Martini-Henry cartridge rifle, though it has a shorter range."

"I then asked Lestrade about the man shot in Hyde Park two days ago. His name was Thomas Crowley, thirty-eight years of age and wanted for petty theft. He was shot with the same type of bullet that killed Farley. The police have kept the details of both murders out of the papers, as they wish to avoid public panic. They don't know what the connection is between the men. Lestrade was naturally interested in how I knew of the two shootings. I was less-than-forthcoming with him. However, I assured him I would keep him abreast of my investigations.

"I also visited Anderson's rooms in Blackwall. As Moriarty stated, they are completely barren and none of the other tenants remember seeing the brother's features. He's a phantom. What can you tell me about his sister?"

"Miss Anderson visited my practice without appointment two weeks ago. She was thirty-five years of age, but she appeared to be much older. From her symptoms, I surmised her kidneys and liver were failing. Her sunken, vacant eyes and severe jaundice told me she didn't have long to live. I gave her a blue bottle of laudanum and instructed her to take one teaspoon three times a day to ease her stomach pain. I sent her with a letter of reference to Dr. Wilson, who is a hepatologist at St. Mary's for tests and treatment."

"Can you describe her appearance, other than her medical state?"

"She had a plain, unassuming face, wore her dark-brown hair shoulder-length, and she was exceedingly thin. Nausea and loss of appetite are common with liver patients. She wasn't the brightest of women. She asked me if the purple potion I gave her was a cure. I informed her it was only to relieve the pain and tried to explain the serious nature of her ailments."

"What else can you remember about her?" Holmes asked.

"She wore a simple black dress with laced boots which were quite worn. Her pink bonnet didn't match her red shawl. I asked about her station, to which the frail woman replied she was unemployed and lived with her brother in a flat in Blackwall. I was surprised she hadn't consulted a physician closer to her residence. She explained her brother said I was the man to see. I didn't ask her how her brother had heard of me. I'm sorry, but I cannot recall any more than that."

My companion let out an exasperated sigh.

"I was quite busy at the time, so I'm afraid I didn't follow up with her care until four days later. I visited her at her apartment in Blackwall. Her brother wasn't at home. She hadn't seen Dr. Wilson, as her brother told her the laudanum was worthless, and it would be a waste of time to go to hospital. I read of her death three days later. I should have pressed the matter of hospital care."

"What can you remember about her apartment?" asked Holmes, ignoring my self-reproach.

"It was squalor and sparsely furnished. The green sofa clashed with the threadbare purple rug. We sat on mismatched chairs, and between us stood a small table with an oil reading lamp. The wallpaper, as you likely noticed, was a drab shade of grey and peeling in places, exposing the yellow plaster."

"We have little to go on. I will make some enquiries. In the meantime, I suggest you stay away from the windows and under no circumstance venture outside."

Though I disliked the idea of confining myself to the Baker Street rooms, I had no means by which to confront my adversary. Holmes was in and out during the next several days and reported little progress. He was kind enough to take walks with me at night for fresh air and exercise. We wore our hats low and our collars turned up like a couple of hoodlums, and avoided the light from street lamps.

On the fourth day, a letter arrived addressed to me from Major Clarke, who had been my commanding officer during my Afghan days. I had been transferred from the Fifth Northumberland Fusiliers to the 66th Berkshires field hospital under the Major's command. Clarke was a veteran of the Kabul campaign, a skilled surgeon, and a good friend. He was a stout fellow, six feet tall with red hair, and he sported bushy side-whiskers and a mustache.

The Berkshires had lost many men on the battlefield during the Battle of Maiwand, and afterwards during the retreat, and I'd nearly joined the number of the fallen when, during the recovery of my wounds, I contracted enteric fever. Major Clarke took a bullet in his hip, and was thereafter wheelchair bound.

The letter was an invitation to attend a reunion of our company's surviving commissioned and non-commissioned medical staff. When

Holmes returned that evening, he saw the letter on the table and asked how the Major was faring.

"He doesn't say. The letter is an invitation to a small reunion of some men from our company and their wives."

I thought it fortunate that Mary was in Scotland and out of the danger I was facing.

"The affair is scheduled for several days at a West Sussex inn. The Major says the place is managed by a retired Lieutenant Colonel from the Crimean War who is a disagreeable cuss, but his wife is pleasant enough, and the food is excellent. Under the current circumstances I don't see how I can attend."

"On the contrary, what safer place to be than amongst your fellow soldiers? If you take the precaution of traveling *incognito* during the nighttime, and stay indoors at the inn, I can think of no sounder course to take. While the sharpshooter is watching Baker Street, you will be making toasts and reminiscing about old times with comrades. I will remain in London and track down the assassin."

I couldn't argue with Holmes's logic. We made our arrangements, and I agreed to send a wire if I perceived any danger. Two nights later, we stole over to my Paddington digs. I packed two bags and caught a late-night train leaving from Victoria. Holmes made sure I was secured in a first-class compartment and bade me a safe trip.

The journey was uneventful. As the train traversed the South Downs, I could sense the rolling chalk grasslands, though I couldn't see them in the darkness. When I reached the station in Arundel, I was surprised to see my former orderly Murray standing on the platform. If it weren't for Murray's quick action and bravery, I would have surely perished in that God-forsaken country.

"Dr. Watson! I hardly recognized you."

I dropped my bags and shook his hand. Then, in a fit of emotion, I embraced my comrade.

"It is indeed good to see you, my friend," I said. "But please, just call me Watson."

"Watson it is. Can I carry your luggage?"

"Not on your life. You served me long enough," I said as I picked up my bags. He led me across the platform towards a carriage he had waiting. Murray had changed little. He was still lanky and boyish, with a perpetual smile on his smooth face. I noticed he avoided the lights on the platform and his carriage was parked under a dark tree. I wondered if Holmes had tipped off the Major to my situation.

"I suppose Holmes wired I was coming."

"Right you are. He sent a telegram to the Major, but it's difficult for him to get around, so I volunteered to greet you. It was kind of the Major to invite me. His orderly, Bennett, is here too. You remember him, don't you? He served the Major during your time. He and I shared quarters in the servant's tent."

"Yes, of course. Who else is expected to attend?"

"The Major said he invited the entire staff from the hospital tents, but most of them couldn't get away. He also invited his nephew, Lieutenant Percival Clarke, and the others of his squad who survived. They arrived this evening."

"The Berkshire Sharpshooters? They saved our skins during the retreat."

"They paid a heavy price in the end. Here's our carriage."

The ride to the inn was only a mile-and-a-half from the station. On the way, Murray said, "I'm sure you remember your colleague, Dr. Fielding. The two of you spent many hours up to your elbows in human tragedy. He and his wife, Ellen, arrived yesterday, just after I did. Fielding is as quiet as ever, but his wife is very talkative. She asked me a gaggle of questions about what my duties were as an orderly."

The lamps in and around the Kingfisher Inn were unlit. The dark stone building stood alone and loomed in the moonlight like one of the surrounding chalk hills. I was sure Holmes had warned my hosts of the peril I was in.

As we came to a stop, a stable boy appeared out of the darkness and took the reins. Murray walked me up the steps and opened the front door. Despite the late hour, I was greeted like a hero by Major Clarke, his wife Martha, Dr. Stephen Fielding, and an elderly woman introduced to me as our hostess, the Lieutenant Colonel's wife, Mrs. Bracken.

"Welcome to the Kingfisher Inn, Dr. Watson," she said. "The colonel is in bed. I'm afraid his failing health prevents him from keeping late hours."

A sleepy footman stepped into the entrance hall.

"Your room is on the first floor, Doctor. Saakaar here can help you with your bags up the stairs."

"Thank you, Madam."

The Major patted me on the back and said, "We'll see you in the morning, old chap."

I was led to my room and thanked Saakaar. The tall footman had a dark complexion, wore a turban, and had a surly disposition. Perhaps it was the late hour which discouraged any pleasantries. He set my bags on the floor, gave a nod of his head, and closed the door behind him. Being fatigued from the journey, I dressed in my nightshirt and crawled into bed.

140

The next morning, I awoke slightly past my usual hour. My room was on the northwest corner of the inn. I peered carefully out a window, looking westward. Below my window, a chalkstone storehouse attached to the rear of the inn. A grove of trees was visible two-hundred yards away, and a hedge row leading to a small sheep farm half-a-mile in the distance nestled in the low-hill grasslands. I repeated my reconnaissance out a north-facing window only to find more rolling grassland and the winding road leading to the inn from the station. Below the window was a small horse stable. I dressed and descended to the ground floor. Looking out a front window facing east towards the town of Arundel, I could see the tower turrets of the famous medieval castle peeking over the tree line, a mile in the distance.

I made my way to the spacious dining room, where several large round tables were set. The Major and his wife sat at one table and had just ordered breakfast. They invited me to sit with them. Across the table, Fielding and his wife, Ellen, were just finishing their rations. His wife was pouring seconds of coffee from a decanter while talking about the fine weather.

"Good Morning, Dr. Watson, "said she. "You simply must try the smoked kippers."

I sat in a chair next to the Major.

"Coffee this morning?" Mrs. Fielding asked.

"Yes, please. Thank you, Madam."

"Please call me Ellen, Doctor. We are an informal group."

"Quite so," agreed the Major, "although everyone insists on addressing me by rank."

"You will always be 'Major' to me," I replied. "No other title suits you."

Fielding chuckled at my remarks and said he had told the Major the same the day before.

I noticed seven men sitting at the table next to ours. I waved a hello to Murray. Next to him was Bennett, the Major's orderly during the campaign. He had changed some. His thick black hair was now thin and receding, making his narrow eyes appear shifty. He was talking intently to the others at the table, apparently eliciting their participation in some business speculation. The other five lads sitting at the table were smartly dressed, with alert expressions which I associate with infantry long-range riflemen. Upon closer examination, I thought the one red-headed man looked familiar. The Major noticed my glances and said, "You remember my nephew, Percival? You met in Kandahar before leaving for Maiwand."

At hearing his name, the attentive lad stood and bowed slightly. I call him a lad, but he was only about eight years my junior. He must have been about twenty when he was in Afghanistan.

"Dr. Watson. Nice to see you again. These four mugs and myself are what's left of the Berkshire Sharpshooters. The five of us were wounded and left for dead by the Ghazis. This here is Bertram Cooper, Leopold Taylor, Sanford Woodsworth, and Miles Robinson." The four men all nodded in my direction. I stood and gave them a slight bow.

"I am forever in your debt," I said. As I sat back down, Bennett resumed the discussion with his group. The sweet aroma of freshly baked bread and fried bacon followed the waitress as she entered the dining hall from the kitchen. I ordered the kippers and gave Ellen Fielding a nod.

"I'll have my usual, Suzie," boomed a voice from across the room. It was Colonel Bracken, with Saakaar the footman helping him with his walking sticks. The obstinate old Army veteran refused to use a wheelchair. Mrs. Bracken led them over to our table and they sat across from me. Save for his dark-blue dress cap, the colonel was in his red threadbare uniform which, as I was later told, was the only attire he wore in public. He had unkempt grey hair, a beak-like nose sporting spectacles, and an untrimmed grey mustache and beard.

"So, these are the medicos!" he exclaimed in his raspy voice. His wife ordered her breakfast and made our introductions as the colonel scowled at each of us in turn. The Major had warned me of our disagreeable host.

Mrs. Bracken sat next to her husband and said, "Please excuse my husband's brashness. He has never fully recovered from the Battle of Balaclava."

"Pshaw!" the colonel said with a wave of his hand.

Once the colonel was seated, Saakaar left the room.

"None of us have fully recovered from our time in battle," I said.

"Battle. What do doctors know of battle?"

"I know I was shot, as was the Major here."

"Yes, yes, the Battle of Maiwand, I hear. Second Afghan War. Nasty business. Outnumbered ten to one. Shame you lost your colours."

The Major wouldn't tolerate the colonel's impertinence and, with great effort, stood up from his wheelchair, bracing himself upon the table.

"The Berkshires fought bravely to the last man sir. And if you continue this offense, I will pack my bags and leave now."

Fielding, the five infantrymen, Murray, Bennett, and I followed the Major's lead and stood up as an act of solidarity.

"Come, come," the colonel said with more humility. "I meant no harm. Please sit. I am honored to have you as my guests."

142

It was a tense moment, and I was relieved when the Major sat down as his wife Martha held his arm. The rest of us took our seats.

"I am an old man," said the colonel. "I lost most of my regiment in the Crimean War. Dr. Watson here is correct. None of us ever fully recover from the battlefield."

Our breakfast was served and discussions became more civilized as Mrs. Fielding dominated the talk. She asked questions about the life in camps, the cooking conditions, and about the landscape of Afghanistan. The colonel ate quietly. I noticed his wife giving him an elbow every time he thought about describing his own harsh conditions fighting the Russians.

"Is it true they use camels over there?" Mrs. Fielding asked. "Stephen won't talk to me about the war."

"Watson and I shared a camel during out retreat," the Major remarked. Turning to me, he said, "You remember our time riding in the *kajawa*?"

"How could I ever forget?" I replied. "I recall every painful step that infernal beast made on that rocky terrain."

"Nasty animal, but it got us to Peshawar."

Mrs. Clarke sensed her husband wasn't enjoying recalling the suffering any more than I was. Out of the blue, she said, "We read your story about Mr. Sherlock Holmes and the Agra Treasure in *Lippincott's Monthly*. How exciting."

"Pshaw!" the colonel exclaimed. His wife gave him another nudge.

Mrs. Fielding loudly chimed in.

"Sherlock Holmes! The detective? We read a newspaper account of how Mr. Holmes shot that giant dog in Dartmoor."

"I was going to shoot the beast, but Holmes beat me to it."

Everyone at the table erupted in laughter. I think the colonel laughed the loudest.

The younger group at the next table became attentive at the mention of Sherlock Holmes and joined in the levity.

"What's he like?" asked Bertram Cooper. "Did he really leave you in Dartmoor to fend for yourself and then spy on you, as Sir Henry described in the newspaper? It seems underhanded to me."

"I was displeased that he kept me in the dark, as Sir Henry stated in the account, but Holmes often keeps his plans to himself. He has his methods."

"You should write about more of your adventures," suggested Mrs. Fielding.

"Perhaps you could recount some of your cases to us during your stay," Mrs. Bracken said.

"We've had some extraordinary cases this past year. Perhaps tonight after dinner, I can recite one of them."

We finished our breakfast, and Saakaar stepped back into the room to assist the colonel. Before the old soldier stood, he said, "Saakaar here was in the 130th in Maiwand."

"Jacob's Rifles?" the Major said. Turning to his wife, he added, "British Indian Army. Brave lads indeed."

The footman bowed slightly to the compliment.

"Saakaar was a long-range sharpshooter," said the colonel. "From what I hear, he was the best marksman in his regiment with a Whitworth rifle."

I nearly choked on my last sip of coffee at the mention of the Whitworth. I thought to myself, "*I'm surrounded by riflemen.*"

The Major's nephew, Percival, added from the other table. "We heard you shooting those rifles. The whistling rounds were quite distinctive."

Saakaar simply gave a mischievous smile before helping the colonel from the table and led him and his wife to their rooms. The five Berkshire Sharpshooters, along with Murray and Bennett, left to take a trip into town to see the Arundel Castle. I noticed Miles Robinson walked with a limp. The Major and I retired to a large drawing room. Two wide bay windows on either side of a set of French doors faced south, which opened to a veranda, and overlooked the grasslands leading to the River Arun. The trees along the river were barely discernable from where we sat, as it was almost a mile from the inn. The veranda was an open affair which ran the length of the south wall. It was constructed of grey Malmstone and sported no roof. It featured a low railing and steps leading to the gardens.

I noticed two copies of *The London Times* and *The Daily Telegraph* on the small table between our chairs in the drawing room.

"The inn has the newspapers delivered every morning by the milkman," Mrs. Clarke said in response to my glance. The Major's wife then left us alone to reminisce. Since we had few pleasant memories to recall, we read the papers and sat in silence for a time.

The footman, Saakaar, stepped into the room.

"Telegram, *Sahib*," he said, as he handed me the dispatch.

"It's from Holmes," I said as I read the missive:

Anderson left London three days ago. Be on guard.

SH

"No reply. Thank you, Saakaar."

144

The servant bowed and left us. We were, once again, alone in the drawing room.

As if he could read my expression, the Major said, "Mr. Holmes informed me of your situation with Anderson. Nasty business."

I handed him the dispatch.

After reading it, the Major asked, "You don't suppose the fiend could be outside watching the inn?"

"It is a possibility. He may even be someone staying here."

"Other than men from our regiment, there are no other guests at present. It is unthinkable to suspect one of our soldiers."

"Who else at the inn knows about Anderson?"

"Just Murray and our hostess, Mrs. Bracken. Mr. Holmes gave instructions that no one else be told. I didn't even tell my nephew."

We sat in silence for a minute before the Major asked, "What about your friend? Do you expect him?"

"It's hard to say. If he has threads to follow in London, he may forgo the trip."

"Fielding is quiet, but he's no fool. I think he suspects something is going on."

Our private talk came to a halt when the Fieldings and the Major's wife joined us in the sunny room.

"We are dropping Stephen off with you while Martha and I look for wildflowers," Mrs. Fielding said cheerfully, as she and Mrs. Clarke walked out the double glass doors with baskets in hand. We smoked and talked about our medical practices.

Luncheon was served after the ladies returned with their baskets full of wild orchids, cowslips, chamomile, and oxeye daisies. It was teatime before Murray, Bennet, and the five riflemen returned from the castle. Murray said they had a grand time spotting imaginary enemy targets from the tower's turrets. There was some dispute whether the Ghazi would advance using the riverbank, or a line of trees as cover.

I thought it interesting that none of the Berkshire Sharpshooters brought along their wives, and then I realized I didn't know if any of them were married. With the possibility of one of them being my adversary, I decided to acquaint myself with them and report my findings to Holmes.

Later, when I repaired to my room to dress for dinner, I ran into Murray in the hall. He was lodging in the room next to mine. I asked him to step into my room for a minute and showed him the telegram from Holmes. As I changed my costume, I questioned him as to what he knew of the men in his group.

"The Major's former orderly, Bennet, is married. He and his wife have no children and are in domestic service to Lord Blackstone. She

145

couldn't get leave from her duties to attend the reunion. Bennet is still the same loyal fellow you knew in Afghanistan. I don't suspect him to be Anderson, because I know for a fact he can't shoot worth a farthing."

"What about the Major's nephew?"

"Percival? All the fellows call him 'Percy' and tell him he's the teacher's pet because of the Major. Percy's father, the Major's brother, was killed during the Kabul Campaign. Percy told us he never married and takes care of his invalid mother in Worcestershire."

"What can you tell me about the others?"

"Leopold Taylor has never married and lives alone in a cottage in Hungerford. Percy contacted him using the Newbury post office box listed in the Army records. He has held odd jobs over the past ten years. He worked as a typesetter for three different newspapers, apprenticed with a blacksmith for a year, and drove a cab in London for a time."

"Bertram Cooper claims to be a widower. He prefers to not be addressed as 'Bert'. He still wears his wedding ring and said his wife and child died during childbirth a few years ago. I can ask Percy if he knew his wife. Bertram said he's employed at the gas works in Berkshire. He's a morose man. It's difficult to engage conversation with him."

"The men call Sanford Woodsworth 'Woody'. He told us he never married, and I suspect that is the truth. Sanford comes from a wealthy family. He exalts himself as a gifted writer, although he is unpublished and lives a privileged life at his family's estate in Norfolk."

"Miles Robinson wears a wedding band and talked about his wife and three children. He said his wife is home taking care of the 'little piggies'. Miles is the comic of the group. He can quickly make a witty comment about anything anyone says. However, I think there is a sadness beneath his humor. His limp is from injuries sustained at Maiwand. He's employed as a salesman for Hereford Brewers."

Murray took a breath before continuing.

"I don't believe any of them are killers. My money is on Saakaar. I caught him eavesdropping twice. I also saw him sneaking out of the Major's room when we returned from the castle."

"He is certainly a mysterious character," I said, as I finished dressing. Murray stood up and walked over to the door. He turned to me and said, "When all of us were looking west from the castle tower towards the inn, Bertram made the comment, 'If I had Saakaar's Whitworth, I could hit the flowerpot by the front door.' Sanford said he owns a Whitworth, but has only fired it a few times. It was a gift from his father. He said he also owns three Enfields, his Martini-Henry from the war, a Sharps, and a Snider. That led to a discussion comparing various rifles and a friendly argument about who among them was the best shot."

I asked Murray to take my place next to the Major at dinner so I could sit with the sharpshooters. Unfortunately, my attempts to elicit more information from the group failed miserably. They were polite and guarded in their responses to my prodding. Whether it was the half-a-generation in age difference, my station as a doctor, or perhaps my higher rank when we served, I couldn't tell, but they didn't regard me as a peer. Whenever Holmes visited a pub to mingle with the clientele for local gossip, he preferred to go *incognito*, dressed as a commoner, and spoke with a muddied vocabulary. He was a master at blending in.

After dinner, we all retired to the drawing room for drinks. Even the colonel and his wife joined us to hear an account of one of my adventures with Sherlock Holmes. I spied the waitress Suzie just outside the door to the dining hall, listening as I related the remarkable case from the previous summer of the disappearance of Neville St. Clair of Lee from an opium den on Upper Swandam Lane. Holmes revealed St. Clair had disguised himself as a hideous beggar before being arrested for his own disappearance. It took a master of logic and disguise to see through a masterful deception.

Everyone applauded at the conclusion except the colonel, who merely looked at his lap and shook his head. From the long faces of the Berkshire Sharpshooters, I gathered they wanted a story with a bloody murder, or at least a violent confrontation or an exciting chase through the streets of the city.

I excused myself after my narration to retire to my room to write a letter to Holmes about what little information I had concerning our suspects. As far as I knew, Anderson was watching the inn from a hilltop, waiting for me to step outside.

Sanford Woodsworth caught up with me in the hallway.

"Your story was a very interesting case, Doctor. Your friend kept you in the dark as usual."

"I am always grateful to be at his side. I trust Holmes to reveal his plans on his own terms."

"It seems to me his trust in you isn't as unconditional as yours is in him."

I looked the fellow in the eye.

"You aren't in the position to question my friend's loyalty, and I will not listen to any more of your impertinence."

I turned and entered my room, leaving the man sputtering an apology.

The next morning, on my way to breakfast, Woodsworth ambushed me again and offered another apology. I told him to forget it, considering his insolence to be a sign of a sheltered upbringing. We were met at the landing by Leopold Taylor, who was coming from the direction of the kitchen.

"Good morning, Dr. Watson. Woody."

"Morning, Leo. Checking on this morning's menu?" Woodsworth asked with a wry smile. Turning to me, he said, "Leo has his eye on that pretty waitress, Suzie."

I gave Taylor a raised brow as we walked into the dining hall.

Woodsworth added, "It's a good thing you fixed Leo's eyesight, Doctor. You remember when he had that eye infection in Afghanistan? His eyes were so red and swollen, he could barely see."

Miles Robinson, who was seated at his table next to Bertram Cooper, quipped, "I remember that. You were a sight for sore eyes, Leo. Ha!"

"Yet I could still outshoot you, Miles."

"I treated many soldiers for ophthalmia," I said to the group. "It was all that infernal dirt and disease over there." I turned to Taylor. "I'm sorry I didn't remember you. There were so many cases."

"Quite all right, Doctor," he said. "You fixed me up, and I was back at my post in less than a week."

Taylor and Woodsworth stepped over to their table, where the Brackens and the Clarkes were already seated at my table. As I sat next to the Major, he said, "Watson, my old friend, we enjoyed your story last night."

Mrs. Clarke cleared her throat and waved a finger dubiously at me. "I am surprised that Mrs. St. Clair didn't see through her husband's disguise when he dressed as a beggar. I think any woman would recognize her husband."

"It was the way the man twisted his lip into a perpetual snarl that contorted his features," I explained. "It was a face which averted, rather than invited scrutiny."

Percy, Murray, and Bennet came in from the drawing room, laughing about something and sat at their table. Fielding and his wife, Ellen, joined us at our table as Suzie came from the kitchen to take our orders. Taylor followed the waitress' movements with a predatory stare. All the young men at the other table watched the pretty girl. Suzie smiled and was polite with all of us, even the disagreeable colonel, yet I sensed she was uneasy. Perhaps she didn't welcome the attentions from the Berkshire Sharpshooters.

Mrs. Fielding asked if I would grace them again in the evening with another story about Sherlock Holmes. I replied I would think about it. In truth, I had no desire to be the nightly entertainment, especially if another story invited more skepticism and criticism.

The colonel complained his eggs weren't fresh, and there was no marmalade on the table. Mrs. Bracken leaned over to the other table and asked Bertram Cooper to pass the green jar of marmalade. As she spread the jam on the colonel's toast, she suggested to anyone looking for adventure that there was a path from the inn leading down to the river where they had a large rowboat tied to a tree. She also invited Mrs. Fielding and Mrs. Clarke on a trip into town to visit the shoppes. I handed her my letter addressed to Holmes and asked that she post it.

After breakfast, the colonel retired to his rooms. The Major, Stephen Fielding, and I found ourselves in the sunny drawing room once again. The room was ablaze with the aroma of the flowers picked the previous day by the ladies. Fielding remarked it was another beautiful morning and suggested that we repair outside to the veranda. Being unable to think of an excuse to stay inside, I told him of the peril I was in with Anderson. After reassuring the Major that Percy wasn't under suspicion, we talked about the other Berkshire Sharpshooters. I told them of my misgivings with Saakaar, and the possibility that Anderson was watching the inn.

We were joined by the colonel and his wife as we ate a light lunch in the drawing room, and laughed at the river explorers when they returned wet and covered in muck. They smelled of rotting fish as they tracked mud across the floor. After dinner, the colonel retired to his rooms while we smoked and talked in the drawing room. Mrs. Fielding invited me to orate another of my adventures with Sherlock Holmes. However, I feigned a sore throat and excused myself. As I was leaving the drawing room, Mrs. Bracken asked if I could step into their rooms for a minute.

As I entered their ground-floor rooms, Mrs. Bracken closed the door, and the colonel in his raspy voice said, "Have a seat, Doctor." Mrs. Bracken settled into a chair next to her husband. I wondered if they were going to ask for medical advice, or if they too had questions about the Neville St. Clair affair.

Mrs. Bracken said, "We enjoyed your narration last night, Doctor."

"Just one thing," the colonel interrupted.

"*Here goes,*" I thought to myself. I couldn't imagine what aspect of the story the old soldier was going to question me about.

The colonel smiled and said, "You forgot to mention my smoking an ounce of shag that night in Lee, Watson." It was the familiar voice of Sherlock Holmes that came from the colonel.

"Holmes!" I cried.

They both gave a chuckle as my friend stood up and put his hand upon my shoulder.

"Sorry for the deception. I'm afraid it was quite necessary."

My amazement quickly turned into embarrassment. How could I have been fooled so completely? I tried to gather my thoughts and control my resentment.

"And Mrs. Bracken?" I said, with more bitterness than I wanted to show.

"Let me introduce you to Miss Emily Compton. She is the finest stage actress of our time. You may remember her performance as Lady Macbeth at the Apollo."

I tried to smile in her direction, but I could only manage a nod. I turned to Holmes and said, "You have made a fool of me once again. It is unforgivable."

"You are a trusted friend and a valuable accomplice. There is no one I would rather have by my side in a tight spot. However, your honesty and good nature can give you away. Your admirable traits can be liabilities in the art of deception. I do apologize."

I wasn't consoled and asked who else was in on the deception.

"Just the staff. I sent the real colonel and his wife away, and it was necessary that the cook, the housekeeper, the maids, the stableboy, and the footman be included in the scheme."

"Saakaar? You trusted that surly Hindu, but – "

"I told you," interrupted Holmes, "it wasn't a matter of trust."

He waited a moment before continuing.

"The real Colonel Bracken and his wife are old family friends. In my youth, I knew them as Uncle and Aunt, although we aren't blood related. Almost ten years ago, their granddaughter Suzie was abducted from her bedroom in the middle of the night. From clues left at the scene, I tracked down the two blackguards and rescued Suzie. I suffered two broken ribs and a black eye in the process."

"Our waitress, Suzie?"

"Yes. She was a brave twelve-year-old then. She is nearly twenty-and-two now, and dreams of attending the London School of Medicine for Women to study psychiatry. Her wish is to help young women who have been abused."

Holmes reached for his pipe and relit it before continuing.

"Needless to say, the Brackens, who are kind and generous by nature, would do anything for me. When I told them I needed a place to gather the Berkshire Sharpshooters, to save the life of my closest friend, they offered the inn without hesitation. The entire staff volunteered to stay. I wanted to replace Suzie, but she refused to leave. Saakaar, who is an old and trusted friend of the colonel, said he would take a bullet for us."

I felt both honored and ashamed. Holmes took another draw on his pipe.

"I secured this inn and set my plans in motion after meeting with Professor Moriarty. I sent Major Clarke a letter by express messenger, explaining the threat and suggested he organize a reunion of your old comrades to keep you safe. His instructions were to confide only in Murray and Mrs. Bracken. The Major and Murray aren't aware of my presence here. I also asked that he invite his nephew and the surviving Berkshire Sharpshooters. To ensure their attendance, all their expenses were paid as gratitude for their service. I suspect one of them to be Anderson. He knows you. He sent his sister specifically to you. His reference to a snow leopard suggests a familiarity with South Asia. Where better could a long-range marksman know you professionally and personally other than in the field hospital in Afghanistan? I needed to study these men in person – thus the deception as the colonel."

I lit a cigarette and Mrs. Bracken – or Miss Compton, I should say – handed me an ashtray.

"We don't know for certain if any of them are Anderson," I said. "Murray and I suspected Saakaar, but of course, now I see we were completely mistaken. When you mentioned his prowess with a Whitworth rifle, I almost choked on my coffee."

"I mentioned the Whitworth to elicit an involuntary response from the other men at the other table."

Holmes produced the letter I wrote to him from his army coat.

"I read your notes about the five sharpshooters. All of Murray's information is firsthand. It is the least valuable of data since any or all of them could be lying. However, I read their military records and researched their status before I left London. Miles Robinson is indeed married and has three children. I have eliminated him from my list of suspects. I have also discounted the Major's nephew, Percival. His red hair makes him an unlikely suspect, and he is devoted to full-time daily care of his mother. She had a stroke after her husband's death and cannot care for herself. Percival hired a nurse to stay with her during this reunion."

"That leaves Leopold Taylor, Bertram Cooper, and Sanford Woodsworth," I said. "All three of them fit Anderson's description. They arrived at the inn before I did. Come to think of it, so did you. How did you manage that? You were at Charing Cross when I boarded the train."

"I rode the same train. I was dressed in an old frockcoat and holed up in a third-class car with two sheep farmers. When you arrived at the inn, Mrs. Bracken told you the colonel was asleep in his rooms, but in truth, I was following you from the station in a dogcart."

"An elaborate ruse," I said. "All done so that you could observe Taylor, Cooper, and Woodsworth while impersonating the colonel."

"Precisely. I have been observing them and testing their colour perception."

"Their colour perception?"

"I suspect Anderson is colour-blind, as was his sister. If you recall, she referred to the blue bottle of laudanum you gave her as a purple potion. Also, her apartment was furnished with clashing colours, and her pink bonnet didn't match her red shawl. If she was colour-blind, which is rare in women, then it is possible that her brother is as well. I am sure you are aware of John Dalton's study of colour perception which he published in 1803, and the further studies by David Brewster in 1844 and Hermann von Helmholtz in 1866. The Young-Helmholtz theory of trichromacy is regarded as scientific fact."

"And how have you been testing them?"

"Miss Compton here has been invaluable. She placed two jars of jam in front of Cooper, and a few minutes later, when I asked for marmalade, she asked him to pass the green jar. A green-weak deficiency is the most common form of colour-blindness. He didn't hesitate and reached around the tan jar to hand her the pale-green one. When they returned from the river, I asked Woodsworth to toss to me a blue shawl from several lying on the davenport in the drawing room. He reached past the light purple and dark purple ones to grab the blue one. Then I performed the same test on Leopold Taylor. Miss Compton as Mrs. Bracken called Woodsworth to the dining hall and asked Taylor to check on me in the drawing room. When I asked Taylor for the blue shawl, he hesitated for a full two seconds and then handed me the light purple one. The man is colour-blind."

"Being colour-blind doesn't make him a murderer," I said. "We need more proof than that."

"You treated him in Afghanistan for ophthalmia. He had a high opinion of your talents and sent his sister to you, hoping you would cure her as you did him. Now he blames you for her death. His only known address is a post office box in Newbury. He's a man who doesn't leave traces. It is also obvious he dyed his hair black and then back to brown within the past two months. I plan to expose Taylor tomorrow morning. Tuck your service revolver into your waistcoat before coming down to breakfast. And," he added with a smile, "don't forget to bring your contempt towards the colonel."

Breakfast the next morning was uneventful. As usual, Mrs. Fielding dominated the discussions at my table, and I heard the men at the other table talk of another trip into town. As we finished our meal, Mrs. Bracken announced Saakaar was going to give a demonstration of his skill with his Whitworth rifle and asked that we repair to the veranda. She asked

Leopold Taylor if he would be so kind to assist the colonel. Holmes, still in character, was disagreeable and struggled with his sticks. Then he insisted on retrieving his military cap from the stand by the front door before venturing outside. I assumed he was delaying Taylor for some reason. I was nervous about exposing myself to the outdoors, since I was still of the opinion that Anderson was out there waiting for me, but I knew I had to put my faith in Holmes.

We all made our way to the drawing room and through the French doors to the open veranda. Mrs. Bracken asked us all to sit and practically pushed everyone into the wicker chairs by the north wall to the right. I was assigned a chair a little distance from the others against the wall to the left of the doors. When Taylor and the colonel stepped onto the veranda, Mrs. Bracken took charge of the colonel and pointed Taylor to a chair at the southeast corner of the veranda, some distance from everyone else. Taylor had grabbed the morning newspapers from the sitting room on his way and handed a copy of *The Times* to me as he passed by before sitting. Mrs. Bracken and the colonel sat on a bench seat by the steps.

Saakaar wasn't present. Mrs. Bracken apologized for the delay and said he would join them shortly. I could see why the seating was choreographed the way it was done. If a confrontation with Taylor was about to occur, there would be no one behind me or behind our target. Taylor was looking at his newspaper, and I sensed Holmes was about to flush him out as he put his hand in his jacket.

Taylor suddenly stood up and said, "Did you see this article on the front page, Dr. Watson? Scotland Yard arrested a long-range marksman by the name of Carl Anderson for the murder of two men in London."

I glanced down at my paper and the article was there on the front page. A wave of relief swept over me as the constant threat of the sharpshooter's revenge was lifted. I looked at the colonel and said without thinking, "By Jove, Holmes!"

The game was up. Taylor drew a pistol and pointed it at Holmes. I went for my pistol, and Taylor shouted, "Don't move, Doctor, or your friend dies! Now place your hands on your head."

I did as I was told. I was furious with myself for exposing Holmes. Taylor never took his eyes off his target. "You too, Mr. Sherlock Holmes."

Murray and the Major were also stopped from producing their weapons.

Holmes cautiously withdrew his hand from his coat and placed his hands on his head. Then he slowly stood up and stepped away from Miss Compton. Her acting skills left her as a look of terror spread across her features.

"That's close enough, Holmes," said Taylor.

"Why the pistol?" I stated. "I thought you only shoot unaware and defenseless people from a mile away."

Taylor swung his pistol towards me. "Your blunder has forced my hand, Doctor." He pulled back the hammer of his revolver. "I sent my sister to you, and all you did was give her opium snake oil."

"She was beyond help," I said.

Holmes took another step away from Miss Compton. Taylor swung his pistol back towards Holmes.

"I said that was far enough, Mr. Holmes. If you move another inch, I will blow out your brains."

"You had that article placed in the newspaper so that Watson would lower his guard. I suppose you were planning a long-range shot during his return trip to the station."

"Correct, Mr. Holmes. It's the last deduction you will ever make."

"You are mistaken, Taylor. All I need to do is raise my cap."

Holmes lifted his cap, and two seconds later, Taylor's chest exploded and he collapsed to the floor. Death was immediate. At the same instant, we heard the shot made from Saakaar's rifle. He was positioned half-a-mile away on a grassy chalk hilltop with his Whitworth rifle.

We contacted the local police and gave our statements. Holmes testified that he fired the fatal shot in self-defense, and everyone present were witnesses. There was no mention of Saakaar or his Whitworth rifle to avoid suspicions that can arise when a foreigner is involved with shooting an Englishman.

It was late in the afternoon when the police left. We packed our bags to take our leave. I thanked everyone for their loyalty and commended their bravery. As I shook Saakaar's hand, I apologized for suspecting him of being Anderson. Suzie hugged both Holmes and me, and cried tears of joy.

We took the evening train back to London. Miss Compton shared our first-class compartment. She appeared to be twenty years younger without her makeup and grey wig. Not only did she give a splendid performance as Mrs. Bracken, but she showed great emotional strength withstanding the horrific shooting. We parted company at Victoria and I thanked her again. When we entered the Baker Street rooms, there was a large, unmarked envelope on the dining table containing two-hundred ten-pound notes.

Holmes chuckled and said, "It appears the Professor is satisfied with our results."

"I don't want any of his ill-gotten money," I replied.

"I agree, Watson. However, I believe I know a young waitress with a college education in her future."

The Indiscriminate Paragraph
by David Marcum

Paddington was quiet that Sunday morning when I stepped down from the hansom, threw up a wave of farewell, and stepped to my door. The brisk late-October air was bracing, and after being up all night it should have felt refreshing, but I felt a rawness in my throat that might be a new head-cold, or possibly just the need for a strong cup of coffee. It was far too early to rouse my wife or the maid, so I would make it myself. Truth be told, my former years of military service had given me great insight into the style of coffee-making that I most appreciated, and such a strong cup would be welcome.

I turned my key in the lock and was surprised when the door opened quickly, before I could make the effort myself and jerking the knob from my grip. But my surprise was even greater when I was confronted by the tall scowling Sikh, holding a gun . . . .

Less than twenty-four hours before, I had called upon my friend, Mr. Sherlock Holmes, not long after our recent trip to Vienna [1] and found him in deep conversation with an elderly gentleman displaying fiery red hair. Although it was a Saturday, it wasn't very unusual by then to find Holmes's services being sought on a daily basis, and weekends were no barrier to those in trouble. When I'd first began to share rooms with Holmes, nearly a decade before, his investigations consisted largely of consultations in our joint sitting room, wherein people of all walks and professions would climb the steps and take a seat, describing this or that situation. Holmes would listen, ask a few pointed questions, offer his opinion based on already-vast experience – "If you have all the details of a thousand at your finger ends," he would say, "it is odd if you can't unravel the thousand and first." – and pocket his fee.

Rarely in those early days did he have to get up and "move around", as he put it. Only in the last year or so, after meeting Holmes's older brother and seeing how he performed the same sort of armchair consultations on a much vaster scale, did I understand that when he was younger, Holmes was – perhaps without realizing it – trying to emulate the same format. But as his cases became more complex, and his fame more wide-spread, he often needed to personally examine the locations of crimes, or go out and question witnesses, or follow a person of interest, or don a disguise and insert himself into the narrative. And he much preferred movement around the web to sitting in the middle of it.

Such had been the requirement the previous day after Holmes's new client explained his difficulty: He had been lured to a run-down building for two months, paid a more-than-respectable fee by an odd organization for insignificant work, and then turned up that morning as usual to find the rooms locked and his employers vanished. Holmes's curiosity had been aroused, and after the client was shooed out of the sitting room – with a stern warning not to mention anything of his visit to engage Holmes's services – my friend and I set off for Aldersgate, and the client's small shop on the southeastern corner of adjacent Charterhouse Square. Although he didn't intimate so at the time, Holmes recognized the unusual clerk who was manning the business, marked by an acid splash and holes for earrings, as a significant agent of Professor Moriarty. This fellow's presence meant that something illegal was certainly going on, and Holmes soon established to his own satisfaction that a robbery on an ambitious scale of the nearby local branch of the City and Suburban Bank was afoot.

That night, we met late in Baker Street, crossed London to the bank, and hid ourselves in the dank lower vaults, sitting in darkness for a number of hours, constantly fearful that the gregarious and cranky bank officer who accompanied us would suddenly bawl out some question or lose patience and do something to alert robbers, whom Holmes was certain would make their play that night, leaving the rest of the weekend for their escape, undiscovered. But the hunt was successful, and soon we had the entire gang in custody – including the Professor's man, who claimed to have Royal blood in his veins. What followed were several more long hours at Scotland Yard as Holmes and I, along with Inspector Peter Jones (who had made the official arrest) and a number of other ever-increasing personalities carried out the man's interrogation.

Early morning had arrived, and with it enough of the wily criminal's story had been pulled from him to get a sense of the larger scheme. I could see that the young man, one John Clay (with no apparent connection to the Leen Valley mining magnate whose kidnapped sister Holmes had recovered), had started to realize that his arrogant bragging might have been just a little too forthright, possibly incommoding and inconveniencing his master, the Professor. We departed as he was shifting his tune from haughty demands to rather fearful suggestions that he be placed under protective guard, as his life might very well be in peril.

Outside, Holmes and I found a hansom – not unusual, even that early, as cabs are always to be found in the vicinity of the Yard, day or night – and set out to the northwest, first to drop me in Paddington, and then continuing with Holmes to Marylebone and Baker Street.

I was weary, and only half-responding to Holmes's conversation. He was quite alert, as often was the case after a particular success, but I knew that within a few hours he would display a certain marked exhaustion until the next affair to pique his imagination climbed the steps to his first-floor sitting room.

"He is the fourth-smartest man in London," Holmes repeated, having first said it the previous day after initially laying eyes on John Clay. I was mildly curious as to the identities of the first three, deciding that he certainly meant himself, his brother Mycroft, and Professor Moriarty. Holmes would place his brother above him in the hierarchy – had had no patience with false modesty – but I wondered just where the Professor fell. I hoped that Holmes didn't rank him at the top of that narrow pyramid, as I was certain that both of the Holmes Brothers placed higher than the Professor, and that with the two brothers working together, he would be no match for them. I thought about our last view of the prisoner, a glint of personal fear in his eyes as we departed the interrogation room. If John Clay was the fourth-smartest man in London, and presumably the second-smartest in the Professor's organization after the leader himiself, it boded well for the eventual defeat of the sinister academic.

The street was quiet when the hansom stopped, and I told Holmes that I would check in with him in a day or so. Then with a wave, I crossed the damp pavement to my own door, whereupon I encountered the threatening Sikh and his gun, looming large in the dim pre-dawn illumination of the nearby gas lamps.

"Dr. Watson," he said, with that curious accented English that had been so familiar during my long-ago days in India and Afghanistan. "It is good that you have returned. Your wife had no idea when to expect you, and my foster brother is becoming impatient. I must say that I, too, am more anxious that I'd like, here at the end, after waiting for so long. Come inside." And he stepped back into the shadowed hallway to allow me to enter.

When he mentioned Mary, I felt a flush of heat run all over me, and my initial thought was to charge the man, weapon be damned. Such had worked for me on more than one occasion, including the affair when I had overrun Desmond Wagenaar, [2] but I reined in my flaring emotions and stood my ground silently – possibly one of the most difficult things I've been forced to do.

I had no thought of turning to run away. When I had departed the previous evening, a little after nine-thirty to be in Baker Street by ten, I had kissed Mary good night and made sure that the door was locked behind me, leaving my wife and our maid secure – or so I thought. Now, nine or so hours later, I found that our defenses had been breached, and there were at least two intruders inside – this tall fierce man and his still-unseen foster brother.

And this one *was* fierce, there was no mistaking that. He was probably in his fifties, although I was uncertain. His already darkened features had been permanently burned by a lifetime spent in hot sun, and his skin was wrinkled and cured like very old and worn leather. The creases across his face were deep, and those around his eyes were particularly numerous – not from smiling, but rather from squinting, as if he had spent nearly all of his time outdoors in every sort of weather. The schlera of his eyes was a muddy yellow, offering further confirmation of his hard outdoor life.

In spite of his rugged appearance, he had contrived to garb himself in the required Sikh adornments. I observed the *kesh*, his untrimmed beard and unshorn hair, the latter of which was wrapped in a *pagari*, or turban, a wooden *kangha* or comb for his *kesh*, an iron bracelet called a *kara*, and a *kirpan*, a small curved iron knife tucked into the band wrapped round his waste. These were four of what was called "The Five *K*'s", and I was sure that the fifth, an undergarment called a *kachhera*, was beneath his outer clothing.

"Take off your coat and hat, Doctor Watson," said my captor, his voice a deep and damaged rasp. "We have much to discuss." I did so slowly, aware that my service revolver was resting in my right overcoat pocket that I was hanging it on the peg, abandoning in the front hallway. Clearly the older man hadn't seen it, and it didn't occur to him to search for it, but he would certainly be aware if I made any movement to retrieve it, either to raise it against him, or to slip it surreptitiously into my suit pocket. I placed my hat on an adjacent peg and, with an internal curse at being forced to do so, walked away from my weapon and toward the parlour, as directed by a wave of the Sikh's own outsized revolver.

It was a curious sensation to walk through my own modest home as a prisoner, directed at gunpoint and uncertain as to what I would find in the next room. This was a location where I ought to feel safe – and more importantly where my *wife* should expect to feel safe – with the world safely shut outside whenever we should choose to lock the doors. Instead, there were intruders here, and even the scents that I associated with home were masked by the odor of the armed stranger directing me deeper into the house.

And as we walked, I had time to identify the odor emanating from the man – that peculiar smell when someone is starving. I tried to remember what else I had noticed about him in the few seconds before he'd ordered me inside and moved behind me, out of sight, but I could recall very little – his height and weathered skin, his native clothing and accoutrements, and the menacing and brutal expression upon his angry features.

159

I was five paces from the back parlour, where the lamplight was spilling into the narrow hall. What would I find? My wife, also held at gunpoint by the unseen foster brother, her features constricted with terror. Or worse, would some violation have already been perpetrated against her? (I confess that for a moment, any consideration for our poor maid didn't cross my mind as I worried for Mary.) Would I find, instead of her fearful gaze meeting my own, her lifeless body, staring into eternity, her eyes already glazed with that flat sheen signifying death –

No! I cried to myself. I would not believe it. I would know in seconds – and should I find her so grievously taken from me, I swore that neither intruder would live, and that they would depart in agony, even if my own death – my very soul – was the price.

And then I entered the room –

– to find Mary sitting in her usual chair, a concerned and solicitous expression upon her face, while a man beside her in my customary seat, also dressed in quite-worn foreign costume, huddled and folded forward, grimacing as if in pain.

She glanced at me, betraying only mild annoyance, and then beyond and behind me to the doorway where the Sikh was holding the gun. "John," she said with no quaver in her voice, "this poor man is ill."

Even as she spoke, the man in the chair shuddered. He was focused on the floor a yard or so in front of his feet, and if he was supposed to be acting as Mary's guard, he had abandoned his post for internal contemplation of his illness. At a glance, I could see that he was also a visitor to our shores, likely the same place as the Sikh, and he appeared feverish. I could only hope that, sitting so close to my wife, he carried nothing contagious.

Beside Mary was our poor maid, Ivy, [3] sitting absolutely still, wide-eyed but calm, watching in every direction at once. I was proud of her – it took a special kind of brave girl to live in that house, which was often affected to varying levels by involvement with Sherlock Holmes.

Behind me, the Sikh whispered, "How long has he been like this?" I was puzzled – To whom was he speaking? Mary? She ignored the question, and then, to my surprise, a third man, whom I had not previously seen, stepped forward, behind me and at my left, replying in a harsh rasp.

"Five or ten minutes." His manner of speech, like the man holding the gun, was clearly from a foreign land, and I turned to my left, where I spotted the third intruder. "Just after you went to wait by the front door. He became dizzy and sat down."

The speaker was smaller than the other, his bones heavier and his stature wide at the shoulders. But like his companions, he was lean, as if something essential had been burned out of him long ago, leaving only tendons and gristle and sun-darkened leathery skin. He was also dressed as a Sikh, but seemed much more lax about the requirements. The second man, indifferent to our conversation as he tightened his ill grip upon himself, was simply dressed in foreign clothing, with no signs of apparent religious affectation.

At least the question was answered as to who had been guarding Mary while the man in the chair fell ill.

"John," Mary stated, more firmly this time, "can you do something for this poor man?"

My tone remained level as I turned to the Sikh who had met me at my own door with a gun. "Who are you, and why are you here? What do you want?"

"Ah, Doctor, we mean you no harm."

I nodded toward the weapon in his hand. "They why – ?

He glanced down as well, but did not lower the gun. "Perhaps I should say we don't wish to cause you any harm – but I cannot promise that we won't, if our questions are not answered satisfactorily. Killing is against our beliefs, but we have done it before, in pursuit of what we have bought with the years of our lives. Surely you have anticipated this moment – when we would arrive at your door. Feared it, perhaps? We knew that you would expect us. Any man who has the treasure, and knows its history, would surely know that someday we would come for it. It was inevitable. From what I've read of you – unless you have exaggerated your own qualities, and I do not think you are that sort of man – you would not be so innocent as to believe you were safe forever. Thus, we took the precaution of obtaining a weapon."

I shook my head. "I have no clue what you're raving about. Look around. This is a modest house and practice, and we're grateful for it, but if we had a treasure, would we be living in Paddington? Would we not be on a countryside estate, out of the smoke and fogs of London?"

The man to my left began to whisper rather harshly in his own tongue, and the first with the gun listened for a moment before waving his free hand, causing the other to fall silent.

"Mahomet Singh does not believe you. He reminds me that we have been lied to by British military officers before – and you were one of them once – and that you all lie very convincingly. Your wife's father lied to us. Major Sholto lied. It would be nothing for you to violate your supposed 'honor' and tell lies to protect the treasure. Men have killed for it. *We* have killed for it.

"From what we read," he continued, "you are not the type who would live an ostentatious life, flaunting the treasure. Rather, you are instead hoarding it for troubled times, taking from it only when necessary – a jewel here, a jewel here. Perhaps two when the house needs a repair or your lady wishes for a holiday. I cannot say that I blame you, Doctor Watson, for taking it when you had the chance. It was within your grasp, and you were canny enough to seize the opportunity. That is what we did, so many years ago. Perhaps you had to pay a share to the inspector who knew you had it, although as you have related the events, he never knew. You must have an excellent reputation for honesty, sir, to have pulled it off so neatly."

I was beginning to have a brighter idea to what he referred – and I was also starting to agree with Sherlock Holmes when he'd lamented that my tentative steps into publishing narratives of his adventures could only lead to trouble.

"Mahomet Singh," I said, glancing toward the second Sikh and repeating the name I'd just heard. The man took a deep breath and drew himself taller. Waves of hostility rolled from his angry features. I looked back at the Sikh with the gun. "Then you would be . . . Abdullah Khan?"

The man's eyes narrowed, and a smile pulled at the corner of his lips. He nodded, a glint in his eyes. "You *do* know us, then, Doctor. It was of never of any use to pretend otherwise."

I glanced toward the sick man in my chair. "And this would be your foster-brother, Dost Akbar."

"He is." The sick man chose that moment to give a small wet-sounding cough. "Unfortunately, his health suffered greatly during the long years of our unfortunate captivity, and his condition has only worsened by the London smoke and fogs you mentioned, and also the terrible cold."

"Captivity?" I said. "Is that how you define it to yourself? You were all jailed for murder. You were given penal servitude for life for the brutal death of the servant of a northern rajah, and the theft of the Agra treasure which had been entrusted to him. How is it that you are here – now, in my home?"

Khan smile widened – but there was no warmth in it. "Ah, Doctor, that is a tale, and after living it for so many years, I have no patience to sit here before your fire and relate it. Suffice it to say that, after many years, we escaped – together. Individually, we'd all had the chance many times over, but we waited until such time as all three of us could go. We had made a vow to one another, as you know. Such things mean something to men like us. We traveled – at first with urgency, and then, as the distance grew from our captivity, with greater confidence. Always we have kept to our vow that each will protect the interest of the others. Possibly a man such as yourself – another lying British officer – cannot understand such a thing as honor, where sworn obligations, sealed in blood, cannot be ignored."

162

"My husband is a man of honor," Mary interrupted. "As I've already told you, he does not lie, and we do not have the treasure. It lies on the bottom of the Thames, scattered for all time by your friend between Westminster Pier and the Plumstead Marshes."

The fierce Sikh shook his head. "You will forgive me, Miss Morstan – or should I say 'Mrs. Watson'? – if I choose to doubt you too. Your father lied to us, and you are married to a liar. You think to convince us with your charm, but it will not work, for you see, we have the doctor's own written account of what occurred and – as you British say – 'reading between the lines' reveals the truth.

With his free hand, he reached into his tunic and tugged forth a tattered periodical. Shifting his hand, he turned it so that I could see the cover. It was a copy of *Lippincott's Monthly Magazine*. Without leaning closer, I was certain that I knew which issue he held. Published the previous February, it contained a copy of my second written narrative describing one of Sherlock Holmes's investigations – and more specifically, a tale that included, in one way or another, every person there in that room, save Ivy the maid.

When the investigation recounted in the magazine had commenced, during those busy months in early September 1888, I had thought it no different than any other which regularly challenged Holmes. Little did I know what life-changing events were about to spiral from the initial visit to our Baker Street sitting room by a lovely orphaned governess, the recipient of six years' worth of particularly fine pearls – one every year, large and lustrous and with no explanation – and more recently a most-strange message requesting that she and two friends present themselves that night in front of the Lyceum Theatre.

The young lady was Miss Mary Morstan – now my wife for over a year. Her mother was long dead, and her father had been an officer in an Indian regiment who sent her home to Edinburgh when she was but a child. She remained there in a boarding establishment until she was seventeen, in 1878, when her father returned to England, requesting that Mary join him in London, at the Langham. She hurried south but just missed him, as he'd departed the night before on a mysterious errand from which he never returned, and no word was ever heard. A retired friend of her father's who had served in the same regiment, Major Sholto, was also living in London, and he could provide no information – though Holmes's investigation later established that Sholto had been involved in Morstan's death – possibly by accident, although I suspected a more intentional act on Sholto's part – and that he had subsequently hidden the body, the location of which ever after remained a mystery, even when the rest of the case was concluded.

Mary made do as best she could for the next four years, and just after obtaining a position as a governess in the spring of 1882, she answered a newspaper advertisement from someone trying to contact her. Upon replying, she received a single magnificent pearl, delivered anonymously and without explanation. Such had been the case on each of the subsequent five years. Finally, on that September night in 1888, she'd received another letter stating that she was a *"wronged woman"*, with an invitation for that night to *"have justice"*. From this curious beginning, Holmes and I had found ourselves involved in an *outrè* murder, a search across London to pick up some indication of a trail, and a desperate boat chase down the Thames, trying to catch the killers and recover the fabled Agra treasure.

Although we caught the surviving killer, a rough and dangerous man named Jonathan Small, the jewels were lost as he poured them over the side of the boat while being pursued down the Thames, vowing that if he and the other members of "The Four" couldn't have them, than no one would. But I found the actual treasure when Mary Morstan agreed to be my wife. [4] We married the following spring and settled into our Paddington house, with my practice taking up a portion of the ground floor. Then, the previous August, I had been invited to meet with an American publisher – Joseph Marshall Stoddart of the aforementioned *Lippincott's*, for dinner at the Langham.

I was unable to attend the small gathering – and frankly rather uninterested in allowing another of Holmes's adventures into print after the disappointing experience of late 1887 when *A Study in Scarlet* was published to resounding indifference, and with my name mistakenly left off the cover [5] – but at the last minute, I arranged for the some-time amateur literary agent who was connected with the first project to attend in my stead. He made a deal with Stoddart to publish another of Holmes's cases and, with my domestic joy still forefront in my mind, I chose to tell the story of how I met my wife, and the mysterious events related to the Sholto deaths, the elusive treasure, Jonathan Small and his curious companion who had perished during the Thames pursuit, and the band of killers who had given all that they had for the cursed jewels – Small and three others who had bonded themselves under the name "The Sign of the Four". Small was currently breaking rocks and digging ditches in Dartmoor, but the other three were now in my parlour, demanding the return of a treasure that was lost forever.

When Khan pulled out the magazine, I groaned to myself, although I didn't share any change of expression. I knew what he had read – for Sherlock Holmes had spotted the same thing when he looked over the manuscript and had commented upon my choice of description.

"This may cause you some Merry Hell," he'd commented after I urged him to read the publication.

"I cannot help it," was my reply. *"That's the way that events played out."*

He *tsk*'d twice and shook his head. *"You've left yourself open to some misinterpretation. Mark my words – this may come back to haunt you some day."*

And now it had.

Khan was flipping through the well-worn magazine until he found the page he sought. Holding it up to his eyes – and displaying a weakened vision that didn't need someone with Sherlock Holmes's gifts to observe – he read:

> *They landed me at Vauxhall, with my heavy iron box, and with a bluff, genial inspector as my companion. A quarter-of-an-hour's drive brought us to Mrs. Cecil Forrester's. The servant seemed surprised at so late a visitor. Mrs. Cecil Forrester was out for the evening, she explained, and likely to be very late. Miss Morstan, however, was in the drawing-room: so to the drawing-room I went, box in hand, leaving the obliging inspector in the cab.*

He lowered the magazine, looked at Mary with a knowing sneer – *"Your husband is a liar,"* he seemed to say without words – and then at me. *"'Leaving the obliging inspector in the cab.'* Really, Doctor – do you take us for fools? You recovered the chest from Jonathan Small, who swore along with us to protect the interests of The Four throughout the rest of our lives. You were sent with it *alone*, except for a police inspector, to Miss Morstan's house, and then you took it inside – *again, alone* – to where this lady waited – *alone* – and opened it to find that it was *empty?"*

His tone darkened. "Do you think we are *gullible dullards?"* he snarled. "The two of you, all alone and without witnesses, opened that chest and found the Agra treasure, and between the two of you, an arrangement was made to hide it – to *steal* it! I can only assume that you must really love the lady, Doctor, to have bothered to go all the way to see her and share anything with her at all. Or possibly you lied to the lady as well, and stopped to remove the treasure and hid it somewhere before you ever arrived at her lodgings to show her an empty chest."

"That is not true!" I said with heat. "There was an inspector with me – Youghal. He knows that I went straight from being put ashore in Vauxhall to the Forrester's house."

"If this inspector really exists," snapped Khan, "what does he really know? He didn't go inside with you. You carelessly revealed the events. *Alone* you carried in the chest. Only you and the lady were present when the box was opened. If this inspector exists, then all that he can confirm – *as based on your own narrative* – is that you carried the sealed chest inside, and then told everyone that the box was empty!"

I took a deep breath. "You are deliberately choosing to misunderstand. If you focus so sharply on those few words – that I had charge of the box and opened it with only Mary present – and if you give that statement such weight, why do you then ignore what is written just after that segment? I clearly describe about how Inspector Youghal and I took the empty box back to Baker Street and showed it to Athelney Jones, the officer in charge, and how we then questioned Jonathan Small, who confirmed to us that he had poured the jewels over the side of the boat during the chase along the Thames, preferring that no man should have it if you four couldn't."

"That is the final proof of your lie, Doctor, for Jonathan Small would have never simply thrown away the treasure. You kept the treasure and hid it – possibly in a bank vault, or more likely here in this house – and then you convinced the police that there was no treasure at all, adding the additional charge of putting it in the river on Small's already burdened back. You must have quite the reputation for honesty, Doctor, for them to have believed you so easily. Or more likely, you played upon the prejudice against Small, so that his denials were immediately taken to be lies. Then, when Small was safely tucked away in prison, you wrote your fictional account to further give weight to your version of what happened. History is always written by the winners. But you never expected that we three would cross the world to find you, and now you understand the mistake you made by writing the book – for if we hadn't found and read it after landing in London, on the trail of our old companion, we would have never known that you were the man who stole the treasure."

He took a step closer. "I have no wish to harm either you or your wife, or this little girl – but my friends and I traded our lives for that treasure, possibly before you were born, and we shall have it."

I had no idea how to respond to such dogmatic idiocy. When I'd arrived home, I had been weary from far too many hours without sleep, and the excitement of catching the men tunneling into the City and Suburban Bank. At that moment, I'd already been awake for slightly over twenty-four hours, and even though being taken prisoner at my own front door had given me a rush of excited energy, I could tell that my thinking was slow.

166

"John," said Mary, now holding out her hand to invite me over beside her, "I think that you should take care of this sick man, and then we can discuss the location of the treasure."

Her gaze held mine with extra emphasis, and as slow as my mind was, I could see that she was trying to relay something unsaid, if I was only able to grasp it. Apparently joining her was necessary, as she gave a small shake to her hand, finally setting me in motion toward her.

I took her hand and it was warm – not cold with fear as I might have expected. But then, my wife was no wilting flower. She might be small, and her body was not as strong as we would hope, but she had great strength. When she had been taken prisoner by the Rippers in the terrible autumn of '88, as leverage in an attempt to control Holmes's investigation, she had displayed none of the weaknesses that one might expect when found in such a situation. And it was her presence of mind that calmed me when we rescued her, and kept me from blotting my own soul with the righteous and surely-earned deaths then and there of her captors. They had deserved no mercy, but received it from me anyway, solely at the behest of my dear wife.

Reaching her, I looked into her eyes, again sensing that she was trying to tell me something. Not knowing what, but understanding that there was something to be learned, I gave a small nod and turned back to face Khan and Singh.

Together, they radiated menace. I hadn't realized from my brief glance just how wicked a figure was Mahomet Singh. His barely suppressed rage made Abdullah Khan seem almost avuncular by comparison.

But seeing the two of them together, one with a gun trained upon me and the other flexing his fingers as if he'd like to crush my throat, was suddenly irrelevant when I understood what Mary had been trying to tell me –

– For standing in the door behind the two killers, just barely visible as he leaned forward from the concealment of the dark hallway, and with a finger to his lips letting me know that I should betray no reaction to his presence, was Sherlock Holmes.

When he knew that I'd seen him, he nodded, gestured with a finger toward the darkened hallway behind him, and slipped silently back into the shadows. Before I could consider the implications of his presence, or how it might contribute to a plan to defeat the men who had invaded my home, Dost Akbar fell into a timely paroxysm of terribly racking coughs.

I glanced his way, noting that from where he was seated and the floorward angle of his gaze, he wouldn't have been able to observe Holmes in the hall. Ivy was to one side. Only Mary would have known that my friend was in the house. I didn't yet know how he'd entered, or what have given him to understand that his presence was necessary, but I was grateful.

"John . . ." Mary said, concern in her voice, and I nodded, suddenly understanding a way forward. I stepped to the sick man, raising my hand toward his head. He was bent forward, looking down and unaware of my approach. Singh growled behind me, but I continued, reaching forward and touching Akbar's forehead with the back of my hand. He was burning with fever. I turned and directed an accusatory look toward Khan.

"You say he's been like this since you arrived in London?" I asked. "When was that?"

"Three weeks ago," replied Khan. For such a cruel looking fellow, he looked momentarily abashed, as if confessing a sin. "We worked our passage from North Africa," he explained, "and were released at the West India Dock. We found help from an important Oriental man we were told to seek, in Limehouse. His name is not important, but his influence is great. We sought word of Jonathan Small, as we had in other ports across the world since regaining our freedom. We learned that our search was nearing completion – Small was in England, as we'd thought. But then our joy immediately turned to bitter ashes upon our tongues when we learned that he was in prison for murder. When we asked for further information, our local friend provided us with your account of Small's arrest. It was an easy matter to find where you live.

"By then, Dost Akbar had grown more and more ill, but we felt that we had no time to waste. Despite our attempts to be discreet, our interest in Small has generated speculation in certain quarters that we seek the lost treasure. It is unavoidable. As it becomes known that we are looking for you, others will follow. So we came here this morning, waiting until the hour when the house appeared to be awake. Then, believing that it was late enough for your office hours to begin, we knocked upon the door, planning to gain entry by seeking treatment for our sick friend's condition. We gained admittance, only to learn that you were away on a professional call. So we waited for you to return."

"And you've held my wife and poor Ivy hostage the entire time, while your foster brother becomes sicker by the minute," I said. "Before we discuss anything else, he must be treated." I looked at Singh. "You – bring him across to my consulting room."

I said it with authority, a combination of the stern gravitas cultivated by all physicians, and also as the military officer I'd been a decade earlier when speaking to fearful or recalcitrant patients who needed treatment in spite of their reluctance.

168

Singh looked back and forth from me to Khan, waiting for some confirmation. Finally, realizing that he still had the upper hand by way of his hostages, Khan nodded.

"Take him through to the consulting room. I will remain here with the ladies." He lifted the gun to remind me that he still held all the power. "I searched the consulting room when we arrived," he added, speaking to the more dangerous man beside him. "He has nothing there that can be used as a weapon." Singh grumbled something too low to understand, and Khan replied, "You won't need the gun. The doctor knows that while he's gone, it will be trained upon his wife. That will prevent him from doing anything foolish, and you are strong enough to prevent him from attempting to flee."

I stepped to Dost Akbar and touched him on the shoulder, telling him to come with me. He raised his rheumy eyes to me, displaying little comprehension of what was required.

"Does he understand English?" I asked. Khan shook his head.

"Not very well. Enough to follow simple commands – but he seems to have lost some of the ability since he became ill." Then he rattled off a string of syllables that I roughly thought to be, "Go with the doctor." The fellow rose and shakily found his balance. I gestured toward the hallway. Then I gave Mary a confident nod, smiled encouragingly at Ivy, and followed, Singh at my back.

I didn't know what to expect from Holmes, or even if I was doing the right thing. He had gestured toward the hallway. Did he mean that he would be out there and that I should join him? Mary had suggested treating Dost Akbar, and that served the purpose of separating the men – *Divide and conquer* – but had I misunderstood? *Was I doing something that would make things worse instead of better?*

There was no way that I could not be fearful at leaving my wife and our maid under the watch of a killer with a gun. I tried to tell myself that Khan didn't *want* to hurt us, and that as a Sikh, he was essentially a man of honor, believing in honesty, humility, hard work, and service. But this was the same man who had schemed with the others of "The Four" to murder a misled servant, brutally killed to steal his master's cursed jewels. Khan, Singh, Akbar, and Jonathan Small had all participated in the killing and subsequent hiding of the corpse, and then they had spent the next years – decades – in prison. Small had escaped by killing a prison guard – hitting him over the head with his wooden leg. He was complicit when his bizarre companion, Tonga the Andaman Islander, had killed Bartholomew Sholto. Who knew how many others Small and Tonga killed in their wanderings, and how many others had died at the hands of the rest of The Four during their escape and travels? Anything of the honorable man that might have

169

once lived in Khan was likely burned out ages ago, and such a one, obsessed with a treasure to the point that he would sacrifice his whole life to obtain it, would not care one jot about murdering two innocent women.

As I directed Dost Akbar into my consulting room, I hardened my heart for whatever must be done.

I'm not sure what I expected – for Sherlock Holmes to be waiting to one side, ready to affect a capture and arrest, perhaps, but there was no sign of him. The house was silent, and might have been empty save for the shuffling sound of Dost Akbar's shoes as he wearily dragged himself toward the treatment room. I considered quickly pivoting toward the front door to retrieve my gun, but it was never something I'd truly attempt. Vigilant Singh would cry out at my first movement, or attack me with the least provocation, and even if I managed to elude him and retrieve the gun, what would I do? Shoot both Singh and Akbar? Take them as my own hostages to trade for my wife and Ivy, whom Khan was still holding? It could only end badly. I would need to do something different, and no plan was springing to mind, other than to trust in the fact that Sherlock Holmes was somewhere nearby.

I directed Akbar to sit on the examining table, and then proceeded to give him a cursory medical examination. His fever was high, and if it climbed a few degrees more, he would likely pass out. With my stethoscope, I listened to his breathing, hearing the congestion that filled him. I poked and prodded, but he didn't have any unusual reactions. His heart was racing, but that was likely due to the fever and his impeded clogged breathing.

I continued my examination, aware that any minute my various maneuverings would be identified as simple attempts to waste time. All the while, Singh stood in the door, his back to the hall, watching carefully, tense and suspicious. I was becoming more uncertain as to what I might be able to accomplish.

During my movements around the patient, here and there, side to side, picking up the thermometer and then the stethoscope, I had shifted my reflex hammer where it could be easily grabbed – although I knew that finding just the right place to stand behind Singh and strike the narrow precise spot to knock him unconscious would likely be impossible. I had managed to palm a scalpel, slipping it into my pocket unseen, but I wasn't anywhere near the point where I'd consider brutally and preemptively killing Singh, slicing his throat before he could understand what had happened – although I had no doubt that he'd kill me at the slightest provocation.

170

Thinking of something else to delay further, I turned to a glass-fronted cabinet and pulled out a brownish bottle. Showing it to Singh, I said, "Medicine. To help him breathe."

I held out the bottle for him to examine. Likely the label meant nothing to him, and when he opened it, the bitter odor caused no suspicions. But then he shook his head. "No, no. *Poison.* You try to poison him."

I raised an eyebrow, looking as if I were talking to a child ranting nonsense. "It is medicine – to help him." I gestured toward a nearby tabletop, where a glass was sitting. "I'll take a sip first if you'd like."

In truth, I had no intention of doing any such thing. The bottle contained chloral hydrate, as my latest idea was to drug Dost Akbar – if Singh would let me get away with it – and then figure out what to do from there. My taking a drink, even a small one, would blunt my reactions. The various available drugs that I might have used to render either or both of them unconscious, despite the public perception to the contrary, were slow-acting, and useless in my situation. Chloral hydrate, chloroform, ether – all required several minutes to take effect. Various melodramas had convinced ignorant audiences that such drugs caused an instantaneous and long-lasting comatose state. In fact, I would have to soak a pad in chloroform and hold it over Singh's nose for several minutes until he finally dropped insensate at my feet – and as sick as Akbar was, he would certainly notice what was going on and rally himself to his comrade's defense.

I was aware that time was passing, and soon Khan would become suspicious. I was widely casting my mind, trying to see my next best option, when the matter became moot. Slipping behind Mahomet Singh was Sherlock Holmes. He made not a sound as he approached. As he was almost directly behind Singh, I made no inadvertent cutting of my eyes in a different direction, so there was nothing to betray Holmes's approach, his right arm raised. Just in case some indication might give away what was happening – the tiniest slip of shoe upon linoleum – I spoke anyway.

"Your friend is becoming more ill as we speak. If he isn't treated – " And then, Holmes's arm dropped quickly, the life preserver in his hand connecting surgically with the back of Singh's head. With nothing but a sigh, the villain dropped at my feet.

Holmes didn't wait, or bother to speak. He pivoted around me and the unconscious man to the examination table, where Akbar was just raising his glazed eyes toward us, little comprehension in them as everything he witnessed was certainly nothing but a fevered dream. Holmes, who had long before made a scientific study of such things, delivered another precise blow, this time to Akbar, and then eased the inert man to a reclining position.

Holmes held up the cosh, turned it to catch the light, and smiled. I recognized it – one of his favorite trophies, taken from Sir George Burnwell in early '88, when he was on the trail of some stolen Royal jewels.

He slipped the weapon into his pocket and raised a finger to his lips, stifling any of my questions. Then, to my puzzlement, he stepped to the window, opening the latch and raising it slowly and quietly.

To my astonishment, a pair of faces appeared at the window – young Peake, one of his Irregulars (as he called them), and Inspector Bradstreet of Scotland Yard. The latter had an inquiring look on his face, but he too exchanged no words. Holmes nodded, and then turned back toward me, gesturing with his head toward Singh.

"*Out the window,*" he whispered, in a tone so low as to barely be perceived.

Not bothering to question my orders, I took Singh's shoulders while Holmes grabbed his feet. We lifted him, and I was surprised to find him lighter than I'd expected. Underneath his filthy garments, he was more lean and bony than his frame suggested, and I suspected that, in spite of working his way to London, he'd been on a starvation diet more often than not.

Holmes and I shifted until Singh was passed out headfirst to the waiting policeman and street lad. Even as they were lowering him out of our sight, Holmes and I were retrieving Dost Akbar for similar disposal. When he was passed through, Bradstreet nodded and vanished out of sight. Holmes quietly lowered the window and turned back to me. "*Do you have your gun?*" he mouthed.

I shook my head. "*In my coat pocket,*" I similarly replied. "*By the front door.*"

"*Get it, and then go back with the others. Stand ready.*" Then he gestured toward the hallway. He followed me out, turning right, deeper into the house, while I quietly retrieved my weapon. Then, slipping it into my coat pocket, I took a deep breath, stretched and sighed, and returned with a false relaxed confidence to the sitting room, where Khan was standing between the two women and the parlour. The end of his gun was pressed against Mary's temple.

"Where is Dost Akbar?" Singh asked. "Where is Mahomet Singh?"

I clenched my fists, ready to charge the man, and yet fearful that he would have time to fire – or that the gun would accidentally discharge during my attempt.

"He's resting comfortably," I managed ot say, trying to sound as if I were simply reporting a patient's condition to a family member in the waiting room. "His fever is high, and he has an infection of the lungs, but with proper treatment. There is no need – "

"Singh?" he interrupted, looking past me toward the door. "Singh!" he called out, louder, and then he added something in Punjabi.

In a moment, from the depths of the house, there was a faint growling response. I couldn't understand it, but whatever was said, just a few terse words, seemed to slightly calm Khan. I knew that Holmes had some understanding of a number of languages. Apparently Punjabi was one of them.

Khan then turned back to me. "Now, Doctor, let us continue our discussion. You have our treasure, and we have paid heavily and then crossed the world to find it. If you want to avoid any injuries to your wife or this girl, you will tell me now where you've hidden it."

I was facing Khan and the women, and had no idea what happened. Apparently Holmes had returned, thinking that what had worked before would work again. He had approached the doorway and leaned just enough to see into the room. But this time he wasn't so lucky, as Ivy, finally surprised beyond restraint, gasped and cut her eyes in Holmes's direction. Khan immediately sensed that something was up, and with a snarl, he turned toward his gaze to the doorway – and Sherlock Holmes.

"So," Khan snarled. "More lies." He looked more closely at my friend, now fully entered into the room. "You would be Sherlock Holmes. I should not be surprised. I was warned, you see." Then he shifted the gun, pressing it more firmly against Mary's temple.

"I expect you have my friends in custody," he said, his voice low and menacing. "I only have this woman's life to trade for the treasure and my freedom, and such a bargain seems very unlikely to work out well for any of us. I will surrender – for in the end I must – but I have one demand before I do so."

"And what is that?" asked Holmes, a terrible expression of suppressed anger upon his face.

"I would speak with Jonathan Small."

Holmes was allowed to depart in order to make arrangements, and Khan let Ivy accompany him. With a grieved look back at her mistress, and assured by Mary's instructions for her to go, they departed, and I was left in the parlour with the weathered and wasted Sikh and his prisoner – my wife.

I found a seat across from them, and after a while, Khan lowered the gun, but he kept his wife by my side, and more importantly, he never seemed to lose focus on his purpose. From where they sat, he could see the door to the hall, so there would be no more unexpected observations. The house was deadly quiet, with only the usual noises drifting in from the street as the morning passed and more and more people moved about on their usual errands, unaware of the little drama that was being enacted so close, behind the plain door marked only by my professional plate.

It occurred to me that the police must have the area cordoned off, as there were no knocks at the door from patients. I attempted several times to engage Khan in conversation, possibly with some notion of lulling him into complacency. I asked questions about his time as a prisoner, and what else he had done during the Mutiny, and specifics of his travels to reach England, but he was having none of it, and while he didn't threaten either of us to make me be quiet, he did frown and express his disinterest by a complete refusal to engage with me.

Even as Khan never seemed to lose focus, neither did I. It was not my plan to find a way to charge him, or fight him for the gun, being unwilling to take any chances that Mary might be inadvertently injured. While Khan's companions had been rather wasted from their experiences, I couldn't say for certain whether my captor was in the same shape, and he might best me in combat. In any case, I was trusting that Sherlock Holmes was taking care of things beyond the walls of my house.

I don't how he did it, and he was never willing to provide specifics after the fact, but he used his influence to have Jonathan Small brought to London as fast as could be arranged. I did understand that upon departing, he and Bradstreet immediately arranged to have Small brought to the local station and put on a train – no small thing, this. Next, Holmes arranged for his brother Mycroft to pull all the strings required to clear the tracks so that the newly designated special train made a straight and flying trip to the capital. It was a journey of over two-hundred miles, and shortly after the time when I would have normally been eating my lunch before returning to my medical duties, there was a ring at the doorbell. The door opened and closed, and there were footsteps in the hall. Then, in walked Sherlock Holmes and beside him, in his prison uniform and chains, and still soiled from whatever labors he'd already begun that morning when yanked toward London, was Jonathan Small. I could see that his health was shattered after just a couple of years laboring in Dartmoor, and that he wasn't long for this world. (And after that morning, he died within a month.)

Khan rose, the gun hanging by his side. I think that just then, I could have walked to him and taken it, so surprised was his expression. He looked and looked at his old comrade, and Small met his gaze, but there was something broken about him, with none of the fierceness he'd displayed upon being arrested two years earlier.

"Khan," said the prisoner, his voice broken and weak. "It was an evil day when my path crossed yours. Curse you! I should have let you kill me."

The Sikh did not speak, though his mouth tightened.

"You told me that I must be with you, or that I must be silenced forever," continued Small. "I swore myself to you and the others, and little did I know just how that oath would bind me. I became a murderer – even if my only involvement was tripping that poor little man so that you could butcher him. I should have testified against you right then, but my damned honor held me to a promise that destroyed the rest of my life."

Small then looked toward Mary, who gazed upon him with a mixture of curiosity and pity and horror. "Apologies for the language, ma'am. You would be Major Moran's daughter, I expect. He treated us decent – as best he could. Not like that Sholto – may he be burning in Hell. I expect you feel the same, considering that he likely killed your father."

Mary's eyes widened. We'd both suspected as much, and talked about it before, but this was a bit more confirmation – although we'd never know for sure.

It was then that Khan decided to speak. "Moran was a liar, the same as Sholto. And now this doctor lies as well. He stole the treasure on the night he took it from you, Small, and he hid it, and then made everyone believe his story. They have all gone along with him and placed the blame upon you, but you know the truth – that you would never allow the treasure to be lost. That you would do all that you could preserve it for us – for The Four! You swore it!"

Small shook his head and gave a bitter laugh, saying something in Punjabi that made Khan growl. Then Small added, "I called him a fool, and something else that was worse. I did my best, Khan. I kept to my oath. When I escaped, I spent years working my way closer and closer to the treasure. Sholto had it, and I could find no way to get it back. Then he died, and I had to bide my time, watching while his fool sons searched for it. Then, they found it, and I managed to get it back – before these two – " He jerked his head toward Holmes and me. " – got on my trail. What you heard is the exact truth: I poured it over the side of the boat when I knew there was no escape. Better that none of them should have it than we four who wasted our lives over it.

"Until I met you, Khan, I'd never done an evil thing. I'd always tried my best to do what was right. But you gave me a choice, and I was weak. And having done one evil thing, others came more easily. I killed the guard to escape. I've killed since then – lives that should not have been taken.

Those men had done nothing to deserve death. Their only misfortune was crossing my path. And I can see that my path – every step of it – led back to that night outside the Great Fort at Agra and *you*. You're a devil, Khan, and two things I know: In spite of it all, I kept my oath, even though it wasted my life doing so, and also I'm glad – damned glad – that the loss of the treasure to Old Man Thames will make you grind your teeth in frustration and rage to the end of your days, and likely in your forgotten grave as well."

He turned to Holmes. "I've said my peace. Send me back to Dartmoor."

At that, Khan gave a cry that seemed to rip his soul, and he raised his gun toward the shackled and broken prisoner.

The single shot caused devastating damage, and the sound was deafening in the small room. I stepped forward, surprised at just how quickly it had occurred, even though the conclusion was inevitable.

The smell of smoke from the discharged gun was raw, and it caused a haze in the lamp-lit room. Before I could step forward or say anything, thundering footsteps clattered through the house, drawn by the gunshot. Inspector Bradstreet, followed by a pair of constables, appeared in the doorway, instantly perceiving what had occurred.

Abdullah Khan looked from the policeman to me, his expression was a mixture of shock, anger, and disappointment. His quest for the treasure had ended. As the policemen took him into custody, he glanced at the blood puddling at his feet, symbolizing all of the violence that had attached itself to the jewels over the centuries.

Then he slowly lowered his ruined hand, where my bullet had ripped a path when he had tried to fire at Jonathan Small. Meanwhile, Holmes stepped forward and picked up Khan's fallen weapon.

"I doubt that this would have even fired. It's in terrible condition." He looked at Khan. "Did you buy it from Evans, in the Commercial Road? As a newcomer to London, you wouldn't have known any better."

Khan started to nod before catching himself. Then he stumbled as he became dizzy, going into shock from blood loss. I had Bradstreet and the constables take him across the hallway to the consulting room, where I would fix him up before he was transported to Scotland Yard, where a police surgeon would carry on from there. But first, I went to my wife, who leaned into my embrace with a sigh of release.

Khan and Akbar received proper treatment, and were soon returned to the best possible health, although Khan's hand was permanently ruined. I was told that Khan continued to rage that I had stolen the treasure, even to Inspector Youghal, who made the pointless effort to meet with the prisoner and explain the true facts of the matter.

Small returned to Dartmoor, while the other members of The Four were each sent to different prisons, so that their association could never be rekindled, and I received no knowledge of them henceforth, except for the notifications when each one died of natural causes over the next three or four years.

After the prisoners were removed from my home and into police custody, Holmes and I settled into the consulting room, taking the first welcome sips of hot bitter coffee. Mary had put Ivy to work, realizing that the distraction of familiar tasks would calm her more than being allowed to dwell on their recent experience.

"How did you happen to be in the house?" I asked, and then, rephrasing to what I really wished to know, I added, "How did you know that we needed help?"

He paused for a moment, as if considering how to share his answer. "A mixture of chance and planning," he replied. "By merest chance, I happened to look back as the hansom drove away, and I had an instantaneous glimpse of what looked like a gun barrel projecting from your doorway, while you paused there, instead of stepping immediately inside. It was enough to alarm me, and on the next street I had the driver stop."

"And planning?" I asked. "How could you have planned for any of this?"

I thought that he would answer directly, but instead he played for time by taking a sip of coffee, and then another. That uneasy delay was rather unlike Sherlock Holmes, and my curiosity as to his answer was magnified. Finally, he sighed and answered the question.

"For some months, I've had your house watched."

That surprised me, and unexpectedly irritated me, but I held my tongue for an instant before immediately replying. Then, "You fear for our safety?"

Holmes sighed and nodded. "I do. My investigations into Professor Moriarty's affairs have been progressively more successful of late, with each crack giving me a finger-hold to open two others. He is aware, of course, and making counter-moves. And always he is seeking leverage to prevent my efforts."

"And Mary and I are that leverage," I added.

"I'm afraid so." He frowned. "Several years ago, the Professor was simply a consultant, happy to sit far back in the shadows, aware of each pluck and tug on the strands of his web, but willing to let his agents carry

177

out his public actions. But when he was first publicly exposed – the Lorait killing, and the trial where he contrived his alibi by manipulating the Royal Society, and then, when he was injured at The Tower while trying to steal the Crown Jewels, [6] he changed. He stopped trying to hide, and he became more vindictive. Dangerous. Unhinged."

"How long have you had us watched?"

"Since that flying trip to Germany and Switzerland last February, when we arranged for his assets to be seized, and simultaneously spoiled his attempt to disrupt the peace conference. [7] Upon our return, I knew that the danger had escalated exponentially."

"And when you returned this morning, you found your watchers and learned what was happening."

"I did. Peake was on duty, and was thrilled that I appeared so fortuitously. Just moments before, Khan and the others had knocked on the front door, ostensibly seeking treatment. Peake overheard as they were told you weren't home, and then he saw how they forced their way inside. He had just sent Mannering in one direction, to seek a constable, and Willett in the other, to notify me in Baker Street, when I arrived. I waited long enough for the constable to join us. Then I quickly briefed him, and had him summon an inspector. Then I picked the lock to enter your cellar, where I slipped through the house until I had a sense of what was going on, and who was involved.

"I was as surprised as you must have been when I figured out who the three men were – but at the same time, it wasn't entirely unexpected – nor should it be unexpected if something like this happens again. I recall warning you at the time I read your manuscript that your description of the order of events would doubtless lead some perspicacious but misguided reader to believe you'd had time to squirrel away the treasure during that period when you and Mary were out of official observation. One can only imagine what other clues and contradictions have appeared in your two published narratives that might lead to even-worse confusion. You'll recall the fiasco when we tracked down that supposed-woman who came calling for Jefferson Hope's wedding ring?"

I did recall, and I had to agree that he'd put his finger on the perfect example to make his point. That had turned into quite a farce – and the mess was revived upon the publication of that narrative in late '87. Yet I was not willing to concede that he was entirely correct.

"I really must advise you," Holmes continued, "yet again, not to put any more of my cases to paper."

"And I must disagree," I countered. "Let alone that my writing has served as a form of therapy for me. I have believed from the time I first understood your work that you should be publicly recognized, and that you should receive the proper credit for what you do." I kept my tone level, although the temptation was there to raise the discussion to a more heated level – as it had been on many past occasions when the same topic lay between us.

Holmes responded as expected. I contended upon a different but well-traveled track. Move and counter-move, the discussion continued through the rest of the coffee, now cold, my office hours fully neglected for the morning. Neither side had capitulated by the time lunch was served, and we tabled the discussion for more agreeable topics.

I had walked Holmes to the front door, conferring on when we would next meet, when there was a knock. Opening it, I found both Inspectors Lestrade and Gregson, uncharacteristically side-by-side, as they were noted rivals. Without explanation, Gregson held out a sheet of paper. Holmes studied it carefully, while I looked more quickly over his shoulder. Then I stepped inside to retrieve my hat and coat and tell Mary that I would send word when I knew what time I'd return. Then I joined Holmes and the inspectors in a waiting growler, headed to Hampstead at a fast trot. It would be many more hours before I obtained any sleep, but at the end of that new affair, another crack in Moriarty's edifice had been opened.

Looking back as we drove away, I was glad to see young Peake keeping watch nearby. He nodded, and I returned it, happy to know that my friend had taken precautions against whatever rising dangers were gathering around us.

NOTES

1. Research has indicated that the basic events of *The Seven-Per-Cent Solution* (as discovered by Nicholas Meyer in 1974) – Holmes's trip to Vienna to meet Dr. Sigmund Freud and attempt to master his cocaine addiction, and the mad chase across Europe – occurred in Autumn 1890 (and not the spring of 1891). However, Watson's original manuscript was horribly butchered by someone – likely a relative of the Moriarty family – in an attempt to rehabilitate the Professor's foul reputation by implying that he was simply an innocent academic, persecuted by a drug-crazed Holmes, and that The Great Hiatus never actually occurred, and was instead simply Holmes's journey about the Continent while his recovery continued. All nonsense, of course. Moriarty was evil, and the Hiatus – as described in The Canon and a number of other post-Canonical adventures – did occur.

2. For more about the encounter with Desmond Wagenaar, see "The Tracking and Arrest of a Cold-Blooded Soundrel" in *The Collected Papers of Sherock Holmes: Volume VII – Annals* and *The MX Book of New Sherlock Holmes Stories – Part XLII: Further Untold Cases (1894-1922)*

3. The identification of Ivy as the Watsons' maid during the Paddington years is attributed to Marcia Wilson, as explained in her *Sherlock Holmes and the Scotland Yarders* series – particularly in *A Sword for Defense.*

4. For more about what really happened to the Agra Treasure, see "An Actual Treasure" in *The Collected Papers of Sherock Holmes: Volume III – Accounts* and *The Strand Magazine* Issue LIII, 2017

5. See "The Unintended Offenses" in *The Collected Papers of Sherock Holmes: Volume VII – Annals* and *Steel True, Blade Straight* – 2022 Annual

6. Details of Professor Moriarty's disastrous attempt to steal the Crown Jewels were later somewhat fictionalized and presented in the 1939 film *The Adventures of Sherlock Holmes* starring Basil Rathbone.

7. Perhaps this trip to Switzerland served as the basis for the highly fictionalized events of *Sherlock Holmes: Game of Shadows* (2011), which unfortunately had a great deal of incorrect information (from the imagination of Hollywood film adapters) stacked on top of whatever real events were originally recorded in Watson's notes.

The Mystery of the
Caroline Crown
by Brett Fawcett

"Siger Holmes, with characteristic obstinacy, made one final attempt to pour his youngest son's mind into the mold of the engineer he still desired him to be. His method of effecting this was to employ, during the summer of 1872, a most extraordinary tutor[:] Professor James Moriarty . . . Between Sherlock Holmes and James Moriarty there flared up instant hatred. The professor could teach the boy nothing, and he soon left [the Holmes family farmstead in Yorkshire called] Mycroft to return to his academic calling . . . ."

– William S. Baring-Gould
Sherlock Holmes of Baker Street, pages 21-23, 26

"The element of most striking moment in [Moriarty's] philosophical concept [as discussed in *The Dynamics of an Asteroid*] is the relationship it adumbrates between the celestial and the atomic systematic structures . . . It would be going too far to say that Moriarty anticipated Albert Einstein in the construction of the formula $E = mc^2$, but, as bearing on upon the trend of his thinking along these revolutionary lines, deep significance must be attributed to the conclusions he reached with respect to the immanence of energy in the phenomenon of mass, and to the frequent introduction into some of his more abstruse calculations of a factor correlated with the speed of light . . . We cannot fail to recognize the magnificent vision Moriarty possessed of energy potential within the atom, and of the practicability of its release through fission."

– Edgar W. Smith
"Prolegomena to a Memoir of Professor Moriarty"
The Second Cab, pages 61-62

"As though seated on a royal throne, the sun governs the family of planets revolving around it."

– Nicolaus Copernicus
On the Revolutions of the Heavenly Spheres

"The vital dogma is not nationalism but royalism. For it is not a deification of the State, nor is it the idea of the sovereignty of the State machine; it is the reintroduction of loyalty to a king, who incarnates the idea of the Nation."

– T.S. Eliot
The Criterion, Vol. 8, page 689

"See if you can tell me, Watson," said Holmes, holding up a black rusty disk, "why this may be the most important clue in my entire career."

He was seated cross-legged on his bedroom floor, wearing his mouse coloured dressing gown and smoking a clay pipe. His large tin box sat open in front of him. Watson had entered the room carrying a rectangular package with markings indicating it had been mailed from Yorkshire and was addressed to Holmes. Before the doctor had a chance to say anything, Holmes had fished the coin out of the tin box and issued this bold challenge to him.

Watson was caught off guard, but decided to rise to the occasion. He leaned forward, took the disk from his seated friend, and squinted at it.

"It's an artefact of your investigation into the Musgrave Ritual, is it not? A coin from the reign of Charles the First. But, as I recall, it appeared at the conclusion of that case, rather than being a clue that figured into it."

"Astutely recounted! But– you can infer a whole world of information from this one tiny artefact."

Watson frowned. "I don't see how one press onwards could make so much out of such a small item."

"Tsk, Watson! Have you forgotten me telling you that one could infer the features of an entire ocean from the existence of a single drop? Nor am I the first to make such an observation. Thousands of years ago, Euclid began his *Elements* with the definition of a point. A single point, Watson! From there, he infers the existence of the thing called a line, which lies between two points. From the existence of the line, he infers the existence of shapes, and, from there, relying on pure deduction, Euclid draws out everything from the Pythagorean theorem to the Platonic solids to entire universe of geometry. Thirteen books worth of timeless insight, all inferred from a single dot. Surely you could do a bit better with a single coin!"

"Some geometers think there are better methods than Euclid's," grumbled Watson, as if in protest of having so much expected of him.

"But as my old instructor, Charles Dodgson, showed in his play on the topic, none of them hold a candle to the old Greek master."

Watson furrowed his brow. "Wait – I think I've seen this play. *Euclid and His Modern Rivals*. But that was written by – Lewis Carroll, no?" Watson's eyes widened with realisation. "Hold on, Holmes – did you know Lewis Carroll at college?"

Holmes smiled thoughtfully. "I assure you, he was hardly my most important geometry instructor."

He rose and took the package from Watson, slipping it into his robe pocket, then looked up at his untidy bookshelf. The very top row, which contained some boxes of papers, had only two books: *History and Heraldry of the Pre-Restoration Monarchy* by John Gilday and *The History of the Rebellion* by Lord Clarendon.

Those books had once sat on the shelves of the Holmes family estate, Mycroft, in Yorkshire. In his mind's eye, Holmes's wall at Baker Street softly transmuted into the wall at Mycroft. There, those two tomes sat above rows of books by English theologians beloved by Holmes's father, Siger, the squire of the estate. The shelves were filled with names like Richard Baxter, John Bunyan, Thomas Watson, and William Sherlock, Siger Holmes's favourite theologian and the one for whom Holmes (whose full name was William Sherlock Scott Holmes) had been named. On the wall next to the shelf hung a portrait of King Charles the First.

In Holmes's memory, a man stood in front of the bookshelf. He was extremely tall and thin, and, though he was only twenty-six years old, he was already balding, with a protruding forehead. He was clean-shaven, had sunken eyes, and his head seemed to float gently from side to side. There was something both authoritative and academic about his bearing, making him seem almost like a clergyman. His constantly oscillating face, which reminded Holmes of a grandfather clock's pendulum, made it seem as though he was perpetually in deep, contemplative thought, and suggested that his mind was as methodical and elaborate as clockwork. What hair he had was carefully combed, and he wore a sharp black suit with a matching waistcoat and a spotted grey breast pocket square.

This was the man Siger had hired to be Holmes's math tutor . . . .

1872

"Being an engineer," said James Moriarty, "is not so very different from being a detective."

The eighteen-year-old boy seated at the table before him raised an eyebrow.

"How did you know I want to become a detective?" asked Sherlock Holmes.

The two men studied each other closely, each trying to conceal that fact from the other.

"When your father told me he hoped for you to go into engineering," Moriarty answered, "he also mentioned that your desires lay in the direction of crime solving."

Holmes made a face. Moriarty's eyes narrowed.

"You look disappointed. Master Holmes."

"It isn't much of a deduction if my father told you about it. I assumed you determined it simply by looking at me."

Moriarty chuckled, but his look of concentration remained. "I do not put much stock in what one can tell about a person simply by looking at them. Looks can deceive. Take yourself. I am told you are an intelligent boy, but the phrenological sciences say that, in that case, your forehead should be larger. Perhaps you will exhibit more frontal development as you age. As it stands, I am dubious that one can deduce so much about a person simply from looking at them."

"Respectfully, sir," said Holmes, trying his hardest to sound respectful, "I disagree."

Moriarty folded his arms behind his back and raised his chin. "And what can you deduce just by looking at me?" he asked. It was a challenge, but not a defiant one – instead, it was a genuine invitation, fueled by real curiosity.

Holmes took a moment to wrestle with what to do, then looked over Moriarty from his balding head down to his gleaming shoes. He was about to say something, but stopped himself.

"I suppose I can't tell anything about you, either."

Moriarty brought his arms from around his back, pressed his palms together contemplatively, and looked at Holmes penetratingly.

"Yes, you can," he rebutted softly.

There was something complimentary about the tutor's contradiction, but, at the same time, Holmes felt somehow violated by how perceptive Moriarty was about him. He tried not to glare back at his instructor.

"I can tell," he said finally, "that you're rather disorganised. Your pocket square doesn't match your suit at all, and though your shoes are black, your shoelaces are dark brown. These are the characteristic oversights of the academic whose mind is occupied with more elevated concerns than personal appearance. I know it is impolite to point these things out, especially to one's superiors. But you insisted I do so."

Something unspoken and faintly dangerous hung in the silence that followed. Finally, Moriarty spoke.

"I am not merely obliging your father," he said, ignoring Holmes's remarks, "when I compare engineering to detection. In both cases, one is summoned to investigate a problem. One uses observation, inference, and scientific theory to identify what has happened, and, hopefully, one uses his knowledge, and a degree of creativity, to provide a solution to this problem."

"I would prefer," answered Holmes, "to use my intellect to solve the pressing problems of human life, not the technical problems of the physical sciences. Take yourself, Mr. Moriarty. I looked into you when

184

Father told me you would be coming to Mycroft, and I understand you were also something of a youthful prodigy. Back in 1867, at only 21 years of age, in addition to your work on the binomial theorem, you published some research on asteroids. Was understanding how rocks fly through the heavens the best use of your intellect? What relevance do the physics of asteroids have to any of the practical issues of society?"

"You'd be surprised how much they intersect, Master Holmes. Let me give you an example."

Moriarty gestured towards the painting of King Charles the First on the wall.

"I take it from this portrait that your parents are rather devoted to the Monarchy, no? Why is that?"

Once again, Holmes paused, deliberating how much to say to this man who already perceived so much, but whom he did not fully trust.

"My parents are rather religious, as I'm sure you gathered from my father's collection of theological texts. The Monarchy, for them, represents God's rule on earth. Father often says the only difference between organised crime and legitimate government is that government rules in accordance with God's will. The coronation shows that the monarch's authority comes from God, through the church. It is an anointing, not an appointment. It even comes down to us from a saint, King Edward the Confessor, whose crown was worn by every monarch after him – until Charles the First. Since the monarch's authority comes from God, then, in some sense, the Laws of England are the Laws of God."

"Is that why you want to be a detective?" asked Moriarty, with just a hint of derision. "Because you can enforce the Laws of God that way?"

Holmes shifted uncomfortably under Moriarty's gaze and ignored the question.

"St. Edward's Crown was lost when Charles was defeated by the Parliamentarians in the Civil War, and, when Charles the Second was installed on the throne in the Restoration, the crown could not be found. Some say it was destroyed and that the parts were used to build a new crown later on, though others think it may have simply been lost. Charles was killed, but he carried himself in such a noble and Christ-like way at his execution that some people view him as a kind of martyr – including my mother, whose French background gives her some rather Catholic proclivities towards saint veneration. Those are her books," Holmes added, nodding his head up at the texts by Clarendon and Gilday about the Caroline Era and Civil War on the highest shelf.

"For my parents," Holmes concluded, "Parliament represents the people, but the people become a mob – a chaos – without order. The Monarchy represents God's rational order."

185

Moriarty wore a strange smile, as if he were amused at a joke to which only he was privy.

"Would that the cosmos *were* rationally ordered," he mused. "This is where the physical sciences bear on the ordering of society, Master Holmes. The fact of the personal equation puts the lie to all that mystifying nonsense, and you'd know it if you'd studied astronomy."

Holmes was startled that Moriarty was so frank in describing his parents' perspectives this way, but he said nothing and let the professor continue.

"When observing the moment a planet crosses the meridian – its culmination, as they call it – one astronomer will be faster or slower in reacting to the event compared to another. Which is the correct measurement, Master Holmes? There *isn't* one – like beauty, truth is entirely in the eye of the beholder."

Moriarty leaned forward, his voice dropping to a confidential tone that was nearly a whisper.

"If there is no certainty about *physical* reality which we can measure and observe, Master Holmes, then how can there be any certainty about *spiritual* reality, which we cannot? How, indeed, can there be any certainty about . . . morality, about right and wrong at all? Different cultures have different moralities, you know. The Aztecs believed in human sacrifice until Spain came along. The Indians burned widows on their husbands' funeral pyres until we put a stop to it. There is no objective morality, only what is imposed by violence through weapons. Violence is the essence of all government. It isn't some heavenly mandate that gives a monarch authority. It is simply force."

The professor straightened and folded his arms behind his back again.

"There, too, my research has relevance. The principles of the solar system do not only apply to the heavens. You know of the recent work on the atoms, surely? The ancients and medievals rejected atomism because it seemed to mean the world was purely material – leaving no room for the gods to exist – but Dalton's investigations have shown that the world is made of atoms, after all.

"But he has not gone far enough. Despite what the Greek word 'atom' means, an atom is not indivisible. Laming is on the right track here: Each atom has a nucleus surrounded by electrified particles whirling about it. An atom is a kind of solar system. The macrocosm is made of infinite microcosms."

Moriarty's voice was beginning to rise with excitement.

"But unlike our solar system, the centre of an atom is not a single, round core around which the charges rotate. I believe it is a cluster of even smaller particles, not so much a single ball as a bundle of balls – which

186

means that those particles can be separated and the nucleus can be broken apart.

"And this is where the proofs in my book are important, Master Holmes – this is where observation of the solar system and the asteroids is so significant. Do you know how much power an asteroid carries? We saw something of it in 1795, when a meteorite struck the town of Wold Newton. The collision of one celestial being with another released forces that we still cannot fully comprehend. Consider how those principles could apply to the atomic solar system! If the nucleus – the 'sun' of the atom – could be ripped apart, how much power could be released? All governments are based on force, and one who wielded this kind of force could make the world bend to his will!"

He took a deep breath as if to temper his enthusiasm.

"In the past," he continued in a lower voice, "what stopped rulers from using force to its full potential were their moral codes. Now we have no reason to believe in any binding, objective morality. So what is stopping us from seeking all the power we can?

"Do you now see, Master Holmes, how studying the movements of the heavens has practical implications for society here on earth?"

As Moriarty said this, his eyes asked Holmes an additional unspoken question:

"And would you like to join me in obtaining this power?"

Holmes felt himself shaken by the invitation and neither said anything for a full minute.

"How's it going in there?" A boisterous voice blasted through the silence as a nearby door flung open.

Siger Holmes lumbered into the room, though his limp caused him to hobble a bit as he did so. He was an enormous, wide-shouldered, barrel-chested man with a bull-like head, a beard so black that it was almost blue, and eyes as grey and sharp as those of his son, whom he looked at suspiciously.

"I hope you're not finding Sherlock too resistant!" he nearly bellowed at Moriarty.

"On the contrary," smiled the professor, reaching for his hat on the table, "I'd say we just made a breakthrough, no?" And he smiled confidentially at Holmes, whose brow was furrowed and whose expression was solemn.

Siger looked pleased.

"Marvelous! You came highly recommended from the other noble families for whom you've tutored, Professor, and I'm glad to see I wasn't misled! We'll see you again tomorrow, eh? And be careful out there – Lord Wyndham disappeared a week ago and even the dogs can't find his scent.

Granted, he was dabbling in things he probably shouldn't have been, but, nevertheless, I'd avoid being out when the sun isn't."

"I am thankful for the warning," said Moriarty in a grateful tone.

"As for you, young man," Siger told his son, "it's nearly time for dinner!"

Moriarty bowed, put on his hat, and disappeared out the door, leaving Holmes with a mind full of alarming and confusing thoughts that swirled about like asteroids in the darkness.

Throughout dinner, Holmes was troubled. He could not look at his parents without being reminded of Moriarty's skeptical words. He especially found himself thinking about his confirmation, which had meant so much to them, particularly to his mother. Part of why his confirmation was significant was because he had perceived a kind of connection between that rite of passage and the Monarchy. The anointing oil that had touched his forehead somehow had a connection, through the church, to the oil that had consecrated Victoria as sovereign of England. It had been both a religious coming-of-age, as well as a deepening of his sense of being an Englishman. But had it all been nothing but legerdemain, as Moriarty had suggested?

Through the meal, the questions and answers of the catechism he had memorised for his confirmation kept haunting him:

> *What dost thou chiefly learn by these commandments?*
> "I learn two things: my duty towards God, and my duty towards my Neighbour."
> *What is thy duty towards God?*
> "My duty towards God is to believe in him, to fear him, and to love him . . . "
> *What is thy duty towards thy neighbour?*
> "My duty towards my Neighbour, is to love him as myself, and to do to all men as I would they should do unto me: To love, honour, and succour my father and mother: To honour and obey the Queen, and all that are put in authority under her: To submit myself to all my governors, teachers, and spiritual pastors . . . and to do my duty in that state of life unto which it shall please God to call me."

Holmes had felt called to the duty and state of life of a detective who worked for justice and combatted evil. But what was the point of devoting one's life to this when justice and evil might not even exist? Whom was he to follow here: His sense of calling? His father? Or his teacher?

Or should he follow his spiritual pastor?

As he left the dining room for his bedroom, he reflected on a conversation he had with the priest who had given him catechism lessons, Sabine Baring-Gould, who just so happened to have also been his godfather. * One of Baring-Gould's lessons had been on the concept of confirmation as a sacrament, which was the Latin word for "mystery". (This was why the proper name for these classes was "mystagogy", or initiation into a mystery.) The word "mystery", in turn, which shared a root with the word "mysticism", referred to a spiritual reality which could not be accessed by human reason alone. It could, however, be revealed by God through material means, such as the waters of baptism, the elements of Holy Communion, or the oil of confirmation, or coronation. Each of these were *mystical* rituals in the sense that they initiated a person into a *mystery*, and turned that mystery into a revelation.

Baring-Gould had used a particular illustration to make this point. As Holmes replayed that lesson and that particular illustration in his memory, his anxieties over his conversation with Moriarty melted away. Within minutes, he knew what he had to do.

He opened his window, climbed out of it, and headed off into the night towards a neighbouring pig farm.

"Trouble sleeping, Master Holmes?" asked Moriarty the lad at the table amiably.

Holmes certainly looked more dishevelled today than he had during yesterday's lesson, and had spots of dirt on his face and hands. However, while the previous day a dark cloud of resentment and confusion had hung over him, today he radiated a confident, triumphant glow.

"I was up late thinking about a couple of problems," Holmes answered with a grin. "One of them had to do with something my godfather shared with me in a confirmation class. Your remarks about the personal equation reminded me of it. It had to do with an old Asian story of blind men and an elephant."

"Ah, yes." Moriarty smiled in a way that was meant to look sagely. "Each blind man gets hold of a different part of the elephant. One holds the trunk and concludes the elephant is like a snake. Another grabs a leg and concludes it is like a tree. Still another finds its rump and concludes it is like a hill. Because of their blindness, each has their own understanding of reality, but none of them truly grasps it. The parable demonstrates my point that there is no objective truth exactly."

"And refutes it brilliantly."

Moriarty raised an eyebrow.

"The blind men themselves may not know the entire shape of the elephant," Holmes explained, "but this does not mean there is no elephant. The only reason each one can have his respective experience is precisely because there *is* an elephant, which does indeed possess each of the features that the blind men experience. The fact that they don't know the whole elephant does not prove there is no elephant, any more than the fact that some cultures are unaware of the Pythagorean Theorem refutes Euclid. 'The elephant may be mysterious, and even mystical, but it is not imaginary,' as my godfather put it, just as the only reason astronomers can measure the movements of the stars and planets differently is because there are stars and planets to measure in the first place. Disagreements over truth are only possible because truth exists.

"And, indeed, if the blind men investigated further, or simply shared their insights with each other, they would come to a better and more accurate conclusion. Combining each of their insights would give one a fairly good overall picture of the elephant. If we do the same with morality, comparing the laws of many nations, we shall find divergences, yes, but surely we will also find much in common. I suspect we will discover that they all agree that justice exists, and that we should use our talents to prevent and punish evil actions."

Holmes leaned forward across the table towards Moriarty.

"Evil actions like murder."

Moriarty's friendly disposition began to fade. Something more hostile began to take its place as his sunken eyes narrowed to slits. Holmes observed this, but kept speaking.

"I wasn't sure whether to trust you yesterday, so I wasn't fully honest with you. Now that I know *not* to trust you, I *can* be fully honest," Holmes smirked. "I said you were untidy, but of course you are not. Your suit and grooming are immaculate. So if that's the case, why the speckled grey breast pocket that clashes with your black suit? And why the mismatched shoelaces?

"This last point is especially key. Your shoes have been cleaned so recently that they are still practically shining. I suspect that is because something made them dirty enough to justify a thorough cleaning, something that got your shoelaces so dirty that they could not be cleaned and had to be hastily replaced. This must have occurred recently, or you would have had the opportunity to obtain a shoelace that matched the colour of your shoes. I posit that it occurred after you came to Yorkshire, which is why you haven't had access to your cobbler.

"Why this great urgency to get your shoes cleaned? Was this mere personal fastidiousness, or was it because you wished to remove evidence that might be carried in the dirt of your footwear?"

He leaned back in his chair, discoursing as though he were the teacher and Moriarty the pupil.

"The dirtiest place in the area is the nearby pig farm. Now, that is *very* interesting, since Lord Wyndham disappeared without a trace a week ago – around the time you would have arrived in Yorkshire – and pigs, as I have reason to believe you know, can consume almost an entire human body. Last night, upon remembering that good ought to be done and evil ought to be resisted, I paid a visit to swine and went digging around in their debris. My search yielded *this!*"

With a dramatic flourish, Holmes sprung to his feet and produced an ascot from his pocket. It was torn, muddy, and bloodstained, but beneath the dirt, it was grey and spotted and perfectly matched Moriarty's breast pocket. The professor's lip curled with contempt.

"I have three appendices to my previous deduction," announced Holmes. "One is that you murdered Lord Wyndham, who must have gotten entangled with you in some way, and fed him to the pigs, keeping his pocket square as a souvenir. From this, I draw two further conclusions. One is that you like to be reminded of your successes. You keep trophies from them and keep them close to you, perhaps to better enjoy them. The other is that you are an experienced criminal, since you handled this far too skillfully for it to be your first offence."

Practically beaming, Holmes held up the ascot as though displaying it to a crowd.

"I am obliged to you, Mr. Moriarty. You have taught me something very important already. Thanks to you, I am now absolutely certain I should become a detective instead of an engineer."

A moment passed in which Moriarty glared daggers at the youth. Then, in a flash, one hand had seized Holmes's outstretched wrist with a vice-like grip. Holmes gasped as sudden, sharp bolts of pain shot down his arm. Holmes had been trained in fencing and in boxing, but Moriarty's speed and strength had caught him off guard and he was powerless to wield him off. Moriarty twisted Holmes's wrist, causing him to cry out and drop the ascot. With his other hand, the professor snatched the ascot from the air and stuffed it into his pocket.

"I am disappointed in you, Master Holmes," he hissed.

He threw Holmes's arm down, seized his hat off the table, and stormed out of the room with a snarl.

"What's all this – ?" Holmes heard his father's voice boom from the hallway outside.

"I cannot teach him what he does not want to learn!" Moriarty's voice snapped back. A moment later, the front door of Mycroft slammed shut.

A moment later, Siger was standing in the doorway, his huge, hirsute, bull-shaped face red with fury. He opened his mouth, but before he could issue a stream of invectives, Holmes quietly but quickly said:

"He was uttering blasphemies, Father."

Siger stopped. His mouth hung open for a moment. His brows knit. Then his mouth closed in a look of resolution. He nodded in a sharp, military fashion.

"Very well, son."

Holmes bowed to his father, who nodded to him again and closed the door.

Alone in the room, Holmes felt a chill.

Part of this was simple deflation. He had found conclusive evidence to convict a killer, but his hubris and unchecked flair for the dramatic had undone it all, and he felt chastened and humbled.

But the other part of it was fear. He had just antagonised a man who did not hesitate to slay his enemies and feed their remains to pigs. What if Moriarty came back that night to do the same to him?

A vague feeling of dread flooded his consciousness. He had known this feeling before, when he had been deathly ill. *A person this young shouldn't have to fear death*, he thought, and yet he felt the looming shadow of death lie prickling against his back.

Turning from the door, his eyes fell upon a particular book on the shelf. It was one of the monographs authored by his namesake: *A Practical Discourse Concerning Death*, by William Sherlock. It was one of his father's favourite books.

Impulsively, Holmes pulled it down, sat at his table, and began to read it. Initially, the thought of Moriarty and the visions of bloodstained pigs' maws constantly distracted him, and he had to force himself to read it. Gradually, though, the book's counsel to trust in God as death drew near gave him some strange but genuine comfort.

The night passed uneventfully. It seemed that Holmes would have no further trouble with Moriarty.

For now.

For the most part, Holmes kept what he had learned about Moriarty to himself, not wishing to share what he had deduced in the absence of persuasive evidence. The only person with whom he shared this information was his older brother Mycroft, who had recently begun working for the British government.

He had learned two additional lessons from this incident.

One, which governed his choice of courses when he went to Oxford that October, was that not all information was valuable. Moriarty possessed a formidable amount of knowledge about the solar system, but that had not done him one whit of good towards making him more moral or even more reasonable. Heaping up information in one's mind was of no value unless it improved one personally, which also meant making individuals better equipped for their work – better equipped, as the catechism put it, "*to do my duty in that state of life unto which it shall please God to call me.*" For that reason, Holmes was very discriminating about only taking classes that dealt with the kind of chemistry and science he believed would be valuable to his work, and would even feign ignorance about the solar system later in life to try to make this point.

The other lesson he learned was that he needed to take up a form of self-defence that would better enable him to slip out of tight grips. If he ever had another physical encounter with Professor Moriarty, he did not want to be outmatched again. To that end, he took up *baritsu*.

At Oxford, he studied under Charles Dodgson, better known to the world as Lewis Carroll, and he met a fellow student named Reginald Musgrave of Hurlstone in West Sussex, a scion of one of the oldest families in England. Years later, when Holmes had set up his detective agency in Montague Street, Musgrave would call on him to solve a problem with roots as deep as the Musgrave family tree itself.

1879

The situation when Holmes went to Hurlstone to investigate was this: Musgrave had caught his butler, former schoolmaster Richard Brunton, rifling through the private Musgrave papers and examining a document containing "The Musgrave Ritual", a curious sequence of questions and answers passed down through the Musgrave lineage which no one fully understood. Musgrave promptly fired Brunton, who then disappeared. Shortly thereafter, Rachel Howells, the Hurlstone maid and Brunton's former fiancée, underwent a kind of mental breakdown and also disappeared. In searching for her, a linen bag full of black, rusted metal had been discovered in a nearby lake.

Holmes knew that understanding the cryptic ritual Brunton was studying would be essential to solving this case. He had Musgrave share it with him, and it went thusly:

Whose was it?
"His who is gone."
Who shall have it?

"He who will come."
What was the month?
"The sixth from the first."
Where was the sun?
"Over the oak."
Where was the shadow?
"Under the elm."
How was it stepped?
"North by ten and by ten, east by five and by five, south by
two and by two, west by one and by one, and so under."
What shall we give for it?
"All that is ours."
Why should we give it?
"For the sake of the trust."

Holmes immediately recognized this as a kind of strange catechism. It reminded him of the question-and-answer format he had experienced in his own mystagogy – his own initiation into a mystery. This made him suspect that something sacred, something mystical, was at the other end of this ritual, if only he could decode it. In other words, this catechism was also a *treasure map*.

To follow its directions, he would need to know the dimensions of the Hurlstone elm tree. Unfortunately, it had been destroyed by lightning a decade earlier.

"I suppose it is impossible to find out how high the elm was?" Holmes asked Musgrave.

"I can give you it at once," Musgrave answered. "It was sixty-four feet."

"How do you come to know it?" Holmes asked in surprise.

"When my old tutor used to give me an exercise in trigonometry, it always took the shape of measuring heights. When I was a lad I worked out every tree and building in the estate."

Using information like this, Holmes and Musgrave eventually pinpointed the location described by the ritual, which was in a cellar under the house sealed by a heavy flagstone. There, they found Brunton's corpse, along with a chest containing some rusty metal disks.

"These are coins of Charles the First," said Musgrave, holding up a lantern and peering at the chest's contents.

The moment he said this, a light flashed in Holmes's mind, a light powered by the memory of the knowledge of that era his parents had imparted to him. He had already determined that Brunton had correctly interpreted the ritual and gone after its treasure with Rachel Howells, whose heart he had previously broken. They found the treasure in this chest, and he would have passed it to her, but the flagstone must have then fallen and trapped him inside – or Rachel had caused the flagstone to fall in a jilted lover's act of revenge. (Perhaps, noted Holmes, it was safer to remain emotionally distant from women.) She had subsequently thrown the treasure into the lake and fled.

All that was left to determine now was exactly what this treasure was, and Musgrave had just given Holmes the insight he needed to answer this question.

"We may find something else of Charles the First!" he cried. "Let me see the contents of the bag which you fished from the mere."

They went up to Musgrave's study, and he laid out a mass of old rusted and discoloured metal and several dull-coloured pieces of pebble or glass before Holmes. The metalwork was in the form of a double ring, though it had been bent and twisted out of its original shape. When Holmes rubbed one of the dull pebbles on his sleeve, it glowed like a spark in the dark hollow of his hand.

"You must bear in mind,' said Holmes, drawing on his youthful reading of Clarendon's history, "that the Royal Party made head in England even after the death of the king, and that when they at last fled they probably left many of their most precious possessions buried behind them, with the intention of returning for them in more peaceful times."

"My ancestor, Sir Ralph Musgrave, was a prominent Cavalier and the right-hand man of Charles the Second in his wanderings," volunteered Musgrave.

"Ah, indeed!' said Holmes, his mind working rapidly. "Well now, I think that really should give us the last link that we wanted. I must congratulate you on coming into the possession, though in rather a tragic manner, of a relic which is of great intrinsic value, but of even greater importance as an historical curiosity."

"What is it, then?" Musgrave gasped in astonishment.

Holmes picked up the metalwork and looked at it closely, remembering the illustrations of coronations he had seen in Gilday's book as a boy.

"It is nothing less than the ancient crown of the kings of England," he said, casually handing it to his startled friend.

"The crown!"

"Precisely. Consider what the Ritual says: How does it run? *Whose was it?* 'His who is gone.' That was after the execution of Charles. Then: *Who shall have it?* 'He who will come.' That was Charles the Second, whose advent was already foreseen. There can, I think, be no doubt that this battered and shapeless diadem once encircled the brows of the Royal Stuarts."

Holmes picked up one of the rusty black metal disks that had once been a Caroline-era coin and looked at it contemplatively.

1890

Now, it was Watson's turn to examine this disk, having been told by Holmes that it may have been the most important clue of his whole career.

"Look at the coin carefully," urged Holmes, pointing at it with his clay pipe, "and tell me what you notice about it. Do not be afraid to begin with the obvious."

Watson looked down at the coin again and fingered it carefully. "Well, it's covered with black rust . . . "

"A-ha! As were the remnants of the crown. What does that tell you?"

"Very little, I'm afraid, beyond the obvious fact that being stored in a damp cellar meant it was exposed to moisture."

Holmes chuckled, putting the pipe in his mouth. "I remind myself that we pursued different disciplines at university. My calling was to become a detective, so I studied chemistry. Yours was to become a physician, so you studied medicine, and things that spring to my mind may crawl more sluggishly into yours. But, consider," he continued, his eyes twinkling, "a potato or an egg immersed in water will not rust. Why not?"

Watson felt a bit exasperated, but his curiosity was piqued. "Those aren't made of metal, of course."

"Is *that* the essential distinction? Does every metal rust?"

Something clicked in Watson's mind.

"No, Holmes – several metals don't. Brass, copper, aluminium, and – and the precious metals – "

His eyes widened as he finished his thought.

"Like gold."

Holmes clapped his hands in delight. "Bravo! We have inferred an ocean from our water drop!"

He leapt to his feet and pulled *History and Heraldry of the Pre-Restoration Monarchy* by John Gilday off its place of privilege on the top shelf of his bookshelf.

"I had this sent to me from my parents' estate to confirm that I was not misremembering it," said Holmes, opening it to a dog eared page. "Here is a contemporary description of the crown of St. Edward that Charles the First wore: It was a *'crowne of gould wyer worke sett with slight stones and two little bells'*."

196

He slammed the book shut dramatically and returned it to the high bookshelf.

"Gold does not rust, Watson, but pyrite – *Fool's Gold* – will. I immediately knew that the metalwork was made of pyrite from the simple fact of its being rusted, though I subsequently did a streak test to confirm this."

"What could this mean, Holmes?"

"It means that, at some point, someone decoded the ritual, got to the crown that Sir Ralph Musgrave had hidden, took it, and replaced it with a false crown, presumably so that anyone else who followed the ritual's instructions would not realise someone had beat them to it and subsequently come after them."

"Could it have been Brunton?"

Holmes shook his head. "Pyrite takes a decade to rust. The exchange must have occurred many years earlier. But I had reason to believe that, like Brunton, the guilty party was also a teacher."

"Oh?"

"Think, Watson! Who else would have the information necessary to follow the ritual's directions? Who else knew the height of the oak tree?"

Watson thought for a moment.

"I suppose Musgrave's geometry tutor would . . . "

"Very convenient that he assigned Musgrave that trigonometry exercise, no? I managed to casually ask him afterwards when this tutor had been at Hurlstone and learned that he had been there in 1866 – thirteen years before we saw the pyrite crown and ample time for it to have rusted."

"Did you learn the tutor's name?" asked Watson eagerly.

Holmes puffed at his pipe and reflected on what Siger had told the man he hired to teach his son geometry:

"You came highly recommended from the other noble families for whom you've tutored, Professor . . . !"

"I didn't need to," Holmes answered in a distant voice. "I already knew."

He puffed at his pipe, a melancholy mood coming over him as he remembered how it felt to know that, once again, he had identified a crime of Moriarty's, but had been unable to convict him for it. No wonder Moriarty had been so amused when the young Holmes had told him about his parents' devotion to Charles and his crown.

"I instantly knew that this metalwork could not have been the real crown, but I also determined that it would not promote the public welfare for it to become widely known that the crown of St. Edward was in a criminal's booty somewhere. All that would do is get the thief's defences up. Better to lull him into a false sense of security. The British Government agreed with me, and they allowed Musgrave to believe that what he had was the true lost crown of St. Edward and of Charles the First and to let him keep it at Hurlstone."

This had been achieved, Holmes neglected to add, through the machinations of Mycroft Holmes, who was already gaining influence in the back rooms of British governance.

"You must forgive me for also allowing you to believe this fiction, Watson – I knew you rather less well when I first recounted this story to you. Frankly, however, Musgrave and you ought to have known that there was no chance the government would allow public property like a historic crown to remain in a private citizen's possession."

"Fair enough, Holmes! After all, a crown being held by a private citizen for only a few hours almost ended in disaster in the case of the Beryl Coronet."

Behind the clouds of smoke emitting from his pipe, Holmes chuckled silently, for that case had been a sequel to that of the Musgrave ritual in a way that Watson did not realise.

February 1888

Just before the handsome man with the wound over his eye could swing his blackjack club at Sherlock Holmes, the detective had clapped a pistol to the man's head. The man froze and dropped the loaded stick onto the floor, his look of fury melting into an attempt at an ingratiating smile.

"Perhaps, Sir George," said Holmes, "we can now discuss business properly."

Holmes had been hired by Alexander Holder, a banker who had been entrusted with the jewelled crown known as the Beryl Coronet by a somewhat prodigal prince of the realm in exchange for fifty-thousand pounds. The prince had assured Holder that he would reclaim the crown in four days. Afraid of losing the coronet, Holder had brought it to his house, where he resided with his son, Arthur, who had been living a profligate life and incurring debts at his club, and his niece, Mary. That night, he had caught Arthur in the hallway with the crown, a corner of which was missing. Arthur refused to confess to stealing the coronet, but would not explain what had really happened. The next day, Holder had come to Holmes, who now had three days to recover the piece of the crown.

Holmes had deduced that Arthur's friend from the club, Sir George Burnwell, whom he would describe as "one of the most dangerous men in England – a ruined gambler, an absolutely desperate villain, a man without heart or conscience," had wooed Mary Holder into being his co-

conspirator in stealing the coronet. Arthur had caught them in the act and had successfully wrestled the crown back from Burnwell, cutting him over the eye in the process, but Burnwell was able to break off a piece of the crown and flee. Arthur had refused to explain what had happened to his father, even at great personal expense, in order to protect the honour of Mary, with whom he was deeply in love.

Having identified Burnwell as the thief and procured the evidence to indict him, Holmes confronted Burnwell to offer him three-thousand pounds to recover the stolen piece of the coronet. Burnwell initially denied everything and even tried to attack Holmes, but had become much more reasonable now that he had a gun at his head. It was too late, however. Burnwell had already sold the piece of the crown for six-hundred pounds, though he gave Holmes the name of the receiver who had bought it.

"Now there is only one other matter to discuss," said Holmes, pocketing his pistol. "That would be the question of how you came to know that the Beryl Coronet would be in Holder's house that evening."

"I was there that night to see Mary," Burnwell answered suavely, "and she happened to mention that her father had the coronet in his bureau. In that instant, I knew I had to have it, and told her she had to help me get it."

"Rubbish," snapped Holmes impatiently. "For someone so unsuccessful in gambling, it seems unlikely your luck would be so good as to place you at the precise place and time that one of the Empire's most prized and expensive possessions just so happened to be within arm's reach. Besides, you expect me to believe you were going to sell an imperial crown to a common fence? Common fences don't go in for that kind of trouble, and, anyhow, most couldn't afford the price the coronet would fetch. You and I both know this. It was no coincidence that you were at the Holder residence at the same time the coronet was, and you had someone in mind to whom you were going to sell this crown. Tell me the full truth, Sir George, or else I may reconsider involving the police and the prosecutors against you."

Burnwell tried to maintain his aloof and charming demeanour, but Holmes could see a flash of fear in his eyes – not fear of Holmes or the legal system, but at something – or someone – else. One of the most dangerous men in England had someone of whom he was frightened. Finally, he began to cautiously answer Holmes's question.

"I won't give you any names, Mr. Holmes, but I'll tell you a little more than I have. A few months ago, a member of my club, a colonel and rather a sharpshooter, introduced me to his employer. He told me that his employer would be interested in my particular – set of skills, shall we say?

As I'm always looking for a source of income to pay off my blasted gambling debts, I was happy enough to befriend a fellow rogue.

"As our acquaintance deepened, this potential employer invited me to his home to show me something he said I'd be very interested in seeing. Under his stairway was a door painted the same colour as the wall around it, so it was nearly invisible unless you were looking for it. He opened the door and brought me into a small room. It was windowless and rather barren with nothing in it but a couple of wooden chairs, a hat rack, and a table in the middle of the room. There was a lit lamp and a safe on the table. In front of the safe was something wrapped in a black velvet cloth. This chap – he gives me a curious smile and unwraps it. It's a *crown* – "

"A gold crown, with two small bells?" Holmes asked, quoting the description from Gilday's book.

Burnwell glared.

"You have your ways of finding these things out, I suppose. Anyhow, this employer nearly purrs to me, 'You see, Sir George, I am something of a collector of crowns, and one who can afford to pay what a crown is worth.

"'Now, I have made arrangements such that one of Her Majesty's sons will need money quickly, and I have reason to believe he will obtain it by depositing the Beryl Coronet with your friend, Mr. Holder, as a security. If, with your lovely Mary's help, you so *happen* to get the crown from Mr. Holder – the *whole* crown, mind you, not a jewel or two from it – I'd be able to reward you handsomely. Financially, of course, and perhaps by opening certain doors for you.'

"He had been friendly up until now, but it suddenly got very cold in that room. 'If you do obtain the coronet, don't try to negotiate with me, Sir George,' he adds, with ice in his voice. 'Give me the whole thing. Don't give me most of the crown but keep a beryl or two for yourself. I really *would not* do that.' And I knew he was serious, sir."

Once again, fear flashed in Burnwell's eyes. Perhaps, Holmes thought, Burnwell also knew what Moriarty did to those whom he disposed of. Perhaps he was also thinking of pigs with bloodstained mouths.

"With that, he wrapped up his crown and sent me on my way. Well, you know what I did. I got Mary to fetch the Beryl Coronet for me, but ended up only getting a chunk of it. I knew better than to even bother trying to sell what I had to the Prof – to this gentleman, so I figured I'd find a fence who might be less particular than he was to sell it to. And that's *all* you'll get from me," Burnwell concluded emphatically.

For the moment, it was all Holmes needed.

Holmes promptly went to the fence Burnwell had mentioned and purchased the corner of the coronet for three-thousand pounds. He returned it to Holder the following morning, just in time for him to return it to the prince the next day. Holder had shrieked with joy upon seeing the coronet piece, but internally, Holmes was even more excited than the banker. Thanks to the villainous George Burnwell, he now knew exactly where to look for the crown of St. Edward the Confessor and Charles the First.

March 1888

"Yes?" asked Professor Moriarty's butler flatly as he opened the front door. The butler was a hulking, muscular man who seemed to practically bulge out of his uniform. His stoic demeanour concealed his irritation, for he had been about to investigate some irritating noises coming from behind the house when he heard the doorbell.

A man with slicked back hair, a *pince-nez*, a military moustache, and a thick double breasted coat stood waiting on the doorstep.

"I come representing the King of Scandinavia," the visitor said with a pronounced European accent. "Professor Moriarty made a contribution to our international competition on celestial mechanics which I should like to discuss with him."

The butler wore a mask of impassiveness. "He's out right now, sir, and I don't know when he will be back."

This was, strictly speaking, true. At the time, Moriarty was in Europe managing his organisation, and he had not indicated to his local agents when he would return. Officially, however, Moriarty was supposed to be in London, which was his alibi in case authorities caught wind of his Continental crimes.

"Then perhaps I could wait just a few minutes?" suggested the visitor. "I would hate to miss him. And if you don't know when he will be back, it could be right away, no?"

The butler was not about to let this man call his bluff. He let the guest in, his face betraying none of his hesitation, and let him take a seat next to the hat rack by the door. The seat faced the house's main staircase.

A crashing sound, as if a glass bottle had been shattered by a cricket bat, broke out from the back of the house.

"If you will excuse me, sir," droned the butler, who turned on his heel and headed towards the noise. A moment passed after he left the visitor's sight.

"Well done, Irregulars," whispered Sherlock Holmes under his false moustache, and reminded himself to pay the street urchins an extra sovereign each for their help in this matter. He had warned them that, if the butler were to seriously threaten them, they were to flee instantly, for Holmes had reason to believe that the butler carried at least one sidearm and a blade in his shoe heel, and that he knew several ways to kill people with his bare hands. For those reasons, he knew that he would need to act quickly. He didn't want a run-in with this gentleman, either.

Holmes pulled a burglar kit out of his pocket and headed for the staircase. True enough, there was a camouflaged door underneath it. It did not take him long to pick its lock.

The room inside was exactly as Burnwell had described it. Holmes ignored the safe altogether. Burnwell had not seen Moriarty actually remove or replace the crown from the safe, and Holmes was certain that this was because the safe was not meant to contain the crown. Moriarty was too clever for that. He likely had this room built in order to show his operatives stolen or illegal goods under cover of privacy, but he would not be foolish enough to let them see where those goods were actually stored. The safe was likely a diversion in case any of Moriarty's agents got greedy and decided to come back and steal those goods for themselves. Holmes was sure the safe contained nothing but a deadly trap. That being said, the crown's true hiding place must be accessible from here.

Holmes went to the hat rack, the presence of which was inexplicable. No one who had made it that far into the house would still have a hat on – there was already a hat rack by the front door – so it must have had another purpose.

Holmes took hold of one of the rack's hooks and pulled it down. Part of the wall behind it swung open to reveal a narrow stairway. So this was Moriarty's design: Hide his valuables in another room, but, when called upon to display them to someone, bring them to this room and make it appear that they were stored in this safe. It was an ingenious way to fool fellow criminals.

Holmes mounted the steps. They ended with a wooden door with no handle. He pushed it open and found himself in Moriarty's study.

A momentary but powerful wave of discomfort passed through him. This was not his first time in Moriarty's study, but there was always something sickening about being here, in the belly of the beast. Of course, long ago, Moriarty had been in Holmes's home and had menaced him there. Perhaps it was only just that Holmes should now invade Moriarty's abode.

In any event, he now knew that this study was where the crown was stored. That should be no surprise, reflected Holmes. Moriarty had worn an artefact of a victim's body on his person. He liked to keep trophies from his crimes and he liked to keep them close, and an ancient British crown was the sort of trophy he would want near himself during work and leisure alike. Holmes may have seen this room before, but he now scanned it, not for general information, but specifically to look for a suitable hiding place for a crown.

There was a large bowl of dirt on the windowsill out of which grew an untamed chaos of plants and flowers. An oversized and elaborately built telescope sat next to the window. What appeared to be a diorama of the solar system sat on a table next to the telescope, but there were only three planets surrounding a smooth, round sun at the centre. Holmes soon realised what this was, as confirmed by the engraving beneath it: *The Moriarty Model of the Atom*. Next to this, in turn, was a peculiar suit of armour which Holmes did not recognize, one with strange geometric shapes and figures worked into its design and with curious angles around the arms and legs.

On the wall hung portraits of Democritus, Lucretius, and Cromwell. Next to the desk was a chalkboard on wheels. A bust of Napoleon sat on the desk next to a lamp, as did a smooth, shiny black statue of a falcon. A large round ottoman sat on the floor under the desk. Behind the desk hung Grueze's *Girl With a Gazelle*. Holmes pulled it aside, revealing a safe built into the wall. He quickly replaced the painting. On the bookshelf out of which Holmes had just emerged, alongside rows of books, there was a glass container. A label indicated that it was a piece of the famous Wold Newton asteroid. The glass case was sitting on a thick commentary on Leibniz's *Monadology*.

Holmes knew he wouldn't have time to search right now. His job was to figure out where the crown could be hiding and come back later to claim it. Scanning the room one last time, he hurried back down the secret passageway, into the private room, and out the door back to his seat just in time for the butler to return. The man's stoic visage had begun to crack with frustration. The Irregulars must have been giving him a hard time.

"I have other places to visit today," Holmes said in his affected accent, "so I'll be on my way. But let the Professor know I was here, eh?"

Before the butler could say anything, Holmes was out the door. It didn't matter if the butler's suspicions had been raised. Moriarty was too far away to do anything about it now, and by the time he *could* do anything about it, Holmes hoped to have already acted.

He hurried back to Baker Street. Watson was out that night playing billiards with his friend Thurston, so the flat was empty and quiet. Holmes stuck his clay pipe into the Persian slipper in which he stored his tobacco and dug out a mountain of it. Lighting it, he smoked his pipe intensely for some time as he pondered the Professor's study.

Based on the geography of the house, it did not appear that there could be any additional secret passageways to or from the study besides the one he had taken. The only other exit was through the study door, and the risk of bringing the crown out of the study into a relatively public hallway made it unlikely that Moriarty would have ever done so.

No – Holmes was certain the crown was stored in that room, and he would need to deduce where it was based on what he had seen. So he thought, and he smoked, until the sun began going down. Just as it became dark outside, Holmes's mind grew brighter than ever. The location of the crown had revealed itself to him, and he knew he would have it in a matter of hours.

Night had fallen. The false moustache and *pince-nez* had been replaced with a black silk mask. Now, along with a burglar's kit, Holmes carried a sack in his pockets as he returned to Moriarty's house in the darkness.

The front door and the door under the staircase had the same kind of lock, and Holmes was able to open them both. He went up the secret passage to the study and pushed open the bookshelf door.

Entering the study, he removed a long, thin knife from his burglar's kit and headed directly for the diorama of the atomic model.

The words Moriarty had said to him years ago came back to him:

"Unlike our solar system, the centre of an atom is not a single, round core around which the charges rotate. I believe it is a cluster of even smaller particles, not so much a single ball as a bundle of balls . . . ."

Yet a single, round, sun-like core was precisely what was at the centre of this display. This was not meant to represent Moriarty's theory of the atom. It had another purpose. The nucleus had that perfectly round shape for a very good reason: It had to contain something that was perfectly round.

Holmes stabbed the nucleus along its equator with the knife and pried off the top half. Once it popped up, he put the knife back in his kit, carefully removed the top of the nucleus, set it on the floor, and looked inside the bottom half.

There, on a velvet lining, sat the crown of St. Edward the Confessor, complete with two bells.

Moriarty had suggested that breaking open the core of an atom would release incomprehensible power. In a sense, that is exactly what had just happened. The sight of the Caroline Crown was like a blast of light to Holmes's soul. A lifetime of awareness of this lost treasure, this literal relic that had been worn by a saintly king, the mystique that comes from ancient mysticism and modern mystery, all washed over Holmes at once.

In that moment, looking upon this crown, he felt a sudden and only semi-rational urge to cross himself. He would later wonder whether that isn't precisely what he should have done.

Instead, he pulled out his sack and deposited the crown in it, carefully replaced the top of the nucleus, and quickly escaped out of the house.

He went directly to Pall Mall and gave the crown to Mycroft, who had been apprised of the situation and had waited up to receive the crown under cover of night. When he saw the crown, a beatific smile spread over his round face that it seldom ever bore. He, too, was thinking of his parents – and of the fact that his brother had scored his greatest victory to date against Moriarty. It was a smile that had been over a decade in the making. If only, thought Holmes, they could see Moriarty's reaction when he realised the crown was gone.

Of course, the revelation of the crown could not be made public – even Watson could not be informed about what had happened – which is why Holmes did not receive the knighthood he rightly deserved, and the somewhat illicit way it was recovered meant that Moriarty could not be charged with its theft. But the relic was now back with the Monarchy. Queen Victoria – *Victoria Regina* – was now once again in possession of that holy item that had given her throne legitimacy in the first place. In some sense, the cosmos had realigned.

Holmes arrived the next morning, marched past Mrs. Hudson, grabbed his revolver and a box of Boxer cartridges, flung himself into his armchair, loaded his gun, and, in a fervour of patriotism, excitement, and pride, shot the Queen's initials, *V.R.*, into the wall. Mrs. Hudson, with her Scottish nationalist proclivities, did not appreciate this English monarchist sentiment. But perhaps Holmes's parents would have.

1890

"I have not yet caught this elusive math tutor," Holmes said to Watson, returning the metal disk to the tin box, "but I continue to pursue him – and, I believe, he has begun to pursue me. You and I have had some close shaves with death, but I expect to have more as I tighten my net around him."

"Are you frightened?" asked Watson with concern.

Holmes smiled at his friend.

"I have my methods of dealing with that. Good night."

This answer did not fully reassure Watson, but he took the hint and left Holmes's room, closing the door behind him.

Holmes pulled the package from Yorkshire out of his dressing gown pocket. As he suspected, it was a delivery from his parents' estate, an item which he had requested sent to him. Holmes tore open the packaging and smiled at the book inside:

Practical Discourses on Death, by William Sherlock.

Once again, with the threat of murder by Professor Moriarty hanging over him, Sherlock Holmes read William Sherlock's book on preparing oneself spiritually for death.

And, once again, he found comfort in it.

NOTE

*.   This historical detail is included in Laurie R. King's *The Moor*.

The Case of the
Vanishing Adders
by Ian Ableson

Although I have faithfully written notes on nearly every case that Holmes and I have tackled together, the existence of thorough notation does not necessarily lead to the transcription of a story. Some tales are of too sensitive a nature to put to pen, particularly those of a political bent that intimately involve high-ranking individuals. With some of those, I will mask the individuals in question in a way I find sufficient, but in many the identities would be too immediately obvious to any who cared to deduce them. Most of these tales must sadly linger in my tin dispatch box, never to be fit for public writ, except perhaps by some adventurous storyteller who comes upon my notes many centuries hence. Then there are a few that feature an identifiable figure so prominently that I feel I can only put pen to paper with that person's permission.

While I do my best to anonymize the clients that grace our doorstep, some are simply too easy for even a casual reader to identify – and potentially harangue with questions or otherwise harass – if they so choose. Such is the case with the client of this particular tale, but due to the fact that he happens to be a personal friend, he happily agreed to the transcription of this particular story. Please note, however, that the names of any other colleagues of his that appear in the following narrative have been changed in order to maintain anonymity.

The man in question, Ferdinand Brandt, Curator of Herpetology for the Natural History Museum of London, has already played a role in one previous tale, in which his vast knowledge of all matters herpetological served to fill a key role in assisting Holmes and me with the identification and capture of a rather unique visitor to England. * It was a chilly winter morning not long before Christmas that found Brandt standing before the door of 221b Baker Street. Holmes and I had made plans to walk out to lunch, and so we nearly tripped over the man before us.

"Dr. Watson! Mr. Holmes!" said Brandt. He was tall and broad-shouldered, and he towered over Holmes and myself. One who had never met him could be forgiven for thinking that his stature more suited that of a construction worker or carpenter rather than a museum curator. The red beard sprouting from his chin showed just a few specks of grey. His continued presence on the island we called home had nearly erased the last traces of the German accent from his pronunciation, but he nevertheless still pronounced my name with a *V* at the beginning rather than a *W*. Given his otherwise perfect fluency in English, I had a feeling that he could likely correct this last little idiosyncrasy if he so chose, and did not mostly out of habit. He was one of the first friends I made after my return to England, and I had enjoyed meeting with him occasionally for lunch or a drink in the evenings. He and Holmes had met a handful of times, but were only acquaintances.

"Brandt!" I cried, startled, and shook his hand. "It's wonderful to see you. By now I expected you to be well on your way to Germany to spend the holidays with your family."

"And any other year you would be correct, my friend. But as you may recall, my wife gave birth just a few months ago, and we don't wish to subject the little one to the hardship of overseas travel just yet. My wife has an aunt over in Warwick who we haven't seen in some time. We will spend the holidays with her. Though I must apologize to both of you, as I have not come to you for a simple social visit."

"Dr. Brandt," said Holmes, shaking his hand warmly, "you have the look of a man with a problem that you would very much like solved before the holidays. Watson and I were just about to go for lunch. Join us, and let's see if we can help you."

"It's an unusual issue, Mr. Holmes," said Brandt as we picked at the last few leavings of our lunch at Simpson's, "One that would hardly rise to the merit of investigation, were it not for the repetition involved, and my fear that the issue will become exacerbated if I don't go about getting to the bottom of it. Over the past two months or so, several specimens have disappeared from the museum's herpetological collections."

Holmes's eyes gleamed as he polished off the final bite. "I think you may have undersold the urgency of the matter a little, Dr. Brandt. I would consider disappearances of valuable artifacts to be very worthy of my attention."

Brandt laughed. "Ha! As would I, Mr. Holmes, and if any items deserving of the title vanish, rest assured that calling on you will be my very first act. However, in this particular case, the objects in question are of such nominal value that I'm rather at a loss as to why anyone would want them at all. But they are reptiles, and as such do fall under my domain. You are familiar, perhaps, with the snakes of Britain?"

"Only in passing. It's rare that they factor into a case in any significant manner. As far as snakes are concerned, there was the rather unfortunate case that was brought to us by a young lady several years ago, but that involved a very venomous species from India. Given my inclination to keep myself abreast of the sordid world of poisons, I generally only concern myself with the more exotic individuals that produce such toxins."

Brandt chuckled. "Yes, I suppose that makes sense, although your reasons for such prioritization would undoubtedly alarm those who don't know you. Well, as with most of northern Europe, we have only a handful of species living in the British Isles. Undoubtedly there were more a few hundred years ago, but alas, we seem to have scared off all but the hardiest. Two – *Natrix helvetica* and *Coronella austiaca* – are completely harmless to humans, while the last – *Vipera berus*, more commonly referred to as the European Adder – is in possession of a mild venom. Oh certainly, a bite may cause some damage without treatment, but it is nothing compared to the lethality of many of its cousins in the south.

"Now, as you might imagine, these three species are among the most commonly donated specimens to the museum. Every ardent outdoorsman and farmer worth his salt has run into at least one of them, and more than a few think of the museum when they find or create a corpse of one. While I am always flattered by the generosity, sometimes I wish that we weren't so quickly considered. A snake corpse mailed from a farmer in Northumbria doesn't smell at its best by the time I open the box, you understand? And yet, I dutifully take care of all of them, noting the location of collection, date of receipt at the museum, my confirmation of identification, and the identity of the collector if they bothered to include such. The ones that are mostly still whole I preserve in alcohol or formaldehyde in jars, while those that are decayed beyond saving are delegated to the beetle box."

"The beetle box?" I asked, unsure whether I'd heard the man properly.

"Yes, the beetle box," said Brandt. He grinned widely at my perplexed expression. "Have I never mentioned the dermestid beetles to you before, Watson? Truly, they are among the hardest working members of our most noble institution. They are a unique species of flesh-eating beetle that devours everything we might wish to remove from a skeleton. I always pull the skeletons from the box before they get to the connective tissue so that the skeletons stay together, but everything else – skin, muscle, feathers, fur – all disappear into the little insects' voracious maws, leaving you nothing but bare bones."

"Rather macabre," I noted, my curiosity piqued. "Are they dangerous to the living?"

"Not in the slightest – until the flesh is dried they have no interest. And I grant you that they are perhaps not the cuddliest of the world's creatures, but without them I would be forced to clean each skeleton by hand, which I'm sure I need not point out would be tedious in the extreme.

But we are getting off-topic. Recently, the beetle-cleaned skeletons of one specific species have been disappearing from my collection. No other specimens have been taken, nor even moved."

"What species?" asked Holmes.

"That's the strangest part of it all, Mr. Holmes. Only skeletons belonging to the European Adder have vanished. They are, as I mentioned earlier, is one of the most commonly donated snakes to the museum. We have several specimens in the herpetological department that could be considered extremely valuable to the right buyer – massive sea turtle shells, preserved frogs that are new to science, countless crocodile and alligator teeth . . . And that's to say nothing of the value found in the mammalogy department! Furs and ivory aplenty, if one knows where to look. And then of course, there's the archaeological collections, which are in a different building, but of which I'm sure I need not emphasize the value. But no – our thief seems to have no interest in those – I even asked some of my colleagues if they'd been losing any specimens. Discreetly, of course, for at first I wasn't certain that an outside force was involved, and to raise an alarm only to later realized I'd somehow misplaced a dozen adder skeletons would be rather embarrassing."

"Of course. Assuming error rather than maliciousness so often avoids unnecessary unpleasantry. What led you to suspect thievery?"

"Quantity and specificity. It started small enough that I almost didn't notice. I'd put four adders in the beetle box for cleaning, and by the time I went to withdraw them only three skeletons were left. I may have thought it a simple error on my part, but my collection notes were very clear. Still, I mostly put it out of mind – there were plenty of innocent reasons that a colleague or an assistant might have removed a skeleton and forgotten to notify me. But then three adder specimens disappeared from the collections shelves. Then two more from the beetle box. I come to you now as a museum curator who has been robbed of no less than fifteen adder skeletons, and with no clues as to why, how, or by whom."

"An unusual tale," Holmes murmured. "Who has access to the collections room?"

"Well, the general herpetological collections are in a relatively large room in the basement that also hosts collections from various other disciplines. It isn't particularly well guarded. I imagine any member of the museum staff could access the room without raising eyebrows. Even guests have wandered down there accidentally, though we typically redirect them. Any artifacts that are oversized or of any substantial value are, of course, locked away in separate rooms."

"And the beetle box?"

"Equally easily accessible, though it is of course in a different room from any of the collections."

"Locked?"

"Generally."

"Are there any commonalities between the specimens that have disappeared?"

"Not as far as I can tell. I have examined the labels and field tags of all the specimens that have vanished. Certainly no pattern in terms of geographical location. Most of the missing bones are from England or Scotland, but there was also one from France, two from Norway, and one from Poland. Temporal range as well – some specimens originally collected a few decades ago, and others within the last year. All different collectors, of course. Otherwise, I might suspect some retired field worker of wishing to reclaim his collected specimens for himself."

"And the full specimens, those preserved in chemicals in jars – none of those have vanished?"

"Not a one. There are far fewer of those – formaldehyde is a brilliant method of preservation, but it has only become common practice relatively recently. With most of the older specimens especially, the skeleton is all that was ever saved."

"So our thief is after calcareous quarries alone. And is there any particular research study currently making use of the adder skeletons?"

"Not at the moment. We had a lad – a student – over from Cambridge for a few months who was plotting a distribution map of the museum's British collections, but that was last year. Promptly took a year off galivanting around the Continent when he was done, so we haven't even seen the map yet."

"Well, Dr. Brandt, you may consider me intrigued. At the very least, your question is puzzling enough that I fear I can offer no elucidation without a little fieldwork of my own. Shall we accompany you back to the museum?"

At this time, the most esteemed Natural History Museum was still a relatively new building. It had opened in 1881, and had finally settled into its place along the South Kensington skyline. Indeed, some of my first conversations with Brandt involved grumbling on his part about the arduous task of relocating all of the collections from the wing in the British Museum where they had originally been stored, a process that wasn't finished until two years later. The new building encouraged public visitation and study, and I was pleased to see a steady flow of people streaming in and out of its doors. Brandt, of course, affected an air of irritation at the crowds, but I knew that the museum's popularity was a source of pride for him.

The three of us stepped around a group of schoolchildren and their exasperated teacher and made our way towards an inconspicuous doorway. From there we descended a wide if stark staircase down to the basement where the collections were stored, and there the throng of people were of a decidedly different sort. Brandt kept up a running commentary for Holmes and me as we walked through the halls.

"That young fellow wearing the *pince-nez* is Dr. Shillingford, a new researcher in ornithology. Came to us from a fairly respectable family, and trying very hard to prove his worth. The man has more to say about parakeets than I have to say about anything at all. The lad over there with the red hair and the hopeful expression is one Mr. Dupont, here from Paris for some research for his doctorate. He needs to do a little comparative study on a few of the conch shells in our collections. Good luck to him, I say. Nothing demoralizes quite like a long evening spent squinting at shells as the sunlight fades to nothing."

Brandt nodded a respectful greeting to an older gentleman with a long white beard and weathered skin who rubbed his reddened hands together as he walked. "Dr. Bircham, our senior curator of paleontological studies. Specializes in dinosaurs of the late Triassic period. Been claiming for years that he's going to retire soon, but he recently returned from an excavation in China, so I find that to be somewhat dubious."

"Rather lively place for such a hallowed scientific institution," remarked Holmes.

"Science doesn't happen without people, Mr. Holmes. As much as some of us may wish that we could conduct our studies in a vacuum and communicate them to others via papers sent out the mail-slot, collective communication is key to true scientific progress. Here we are – the herpetological collections."

The room that we stepped into was adorned from wall to wall with specimens of all sorts. Massive shelves of wood and metal dominated the majority of the room. Some of these shelves held only boxes, but most were covered in mounted skeletons and jars of preserved specimens. Most of the shelves also had wide drawers in the bottom. Large labels on the shelves and drawers in a mixture of Latin and English categorized all of the specimens, typically by order, family, or *genera*, but occasionally by country of origin or some more esoteric grouping. One entire shelf was labeled *Unidentified Shells*, though some hopeful curator or researcher had penned the words *As Yet* in smaller type at the beginning of the label.

Some larger mounted specimens lurked in the corners of the room, covering a good deal of the little remaining floor space – a full Komodo

Dragon skeleton dominated the space near the doorway, while on the opposite wall an artful arrangement of labelled sea turtle shells immediately drew the eye. What little wall space that wasn't covered by shelves or specimens bore artwork depicting all sorts of colorful frogs, snakes, turtles, and salamanders – most in the scientific style, with each individual numbered and subsequently identified in the bottom corner of the piece, but a few appeared to be purely artistic renditions. Even on these, however someone (possibly Brandt) had written the Latin name of the species in ink in whatever blank part of the canvas they could find. The room was a shrine to all thing scaly and slimy, and it was a truly fascinating sight.

"Here we are," said Brandt, and he pulled open one of the larger drawers, labeled *Species of the British Isles*. "I have an entire drawer devoted to the few species of my domain that natively inhabit the British Isles – three snakes, three lizards, two frogs, two toads, three newts. Not the most impressive list, perhaps, but as I've mentioned I get plenty of donations of them nonetheless. Most of the other species I have arranged by their relation to each other, or at least morphological similarities, but I find it most convenient to keep our native species together. Well, except for the sea turtles, of course – they are difficult to fit in the drawer, you understand."

Brandt had neatly arranged the thirteen species by approximate size, with the frogs on the right side of the drawer and the snakes arranged on the left. Each skeleton had a little collections tag attached to the ankle or, in the case of the snakes and the common slow-worm, to the tail. The skeletons on the left side included dozens that were labeled as *Vipera berus*, our quarry for the day. A few obvious holes in the lines of skeletons clearly identified the stolen specimens. It seemed Brandt hadn't yet rearranged.

"An impressive collection, Dr. Brandt," murmured Holmes. He studied the skeletons for a few minutes, mostly looking at the adders, but occasionally casting a glance at the other two snake species. "Which of these specimens were prepared via the beetle box?"

"Oh, most, if not all of them, Mr. Holmes. Perhaps there are a few that were donated as skeletons to begin with, but most that are donated that way are incomplete. I keep those separate."

"Interesting. Tell me, is there any particular reason that the adder skeletons might be missing more rib bones than their fellow snakes? I imagine if they are placed in the beetle box while still contained within flesh, there is little chance of losing bones."

"Hmm?" said Brandt, seemingly taken aback by Holmes's question. "Let me see . . . ." He bent over the skeletons and examined them in turn,

213

occasionally picking them up gingerly and turning them about for further study. "Now, that is unusual! You are correct, Mr. Holmes. Several of these specimens have had ribs removed. If it were only one or two I could perhaps consider it mere coincidence, but I know for a fact that these two from near Glasgow were complete specimens just a few weeks ago."

"The mystery deepens," said Holmes. I could hear the cheerfulness in his tone. Though he took no pleasure in adding further bafflement to the already perplexed Brandt, it was clear that the extra complication had made the case much more intriguing in his eyes.

Holmes spent the next few minutes carefully examining the collections shelf and the immediate surrounding area, though I couldn't determine the exact object of his search. Eventually he asked Brandt for any records regarding the missing specimens, likely to doublecheck that there were truly no similarities between the missing specimens, and Brandt obliged. Being familiar enough with his methods to understand his need for concentration, I instead chose to chat with Brandt about a few mutual friends as we waited. Apparently satisfied that there was no more information to be gleaned from the physical examination, Holmes turned to us.

"Gentlemen, I believe the next piece of our inquiry must be to speak with those who spend the most time in this room. Dr. Brandt, apart from yourself, who is in here a significant amount of time?"

"Well, only my assistant curators and one research assistant. But I don't suspect any of them of theft – they're all good lads."

Holmes inclined his head. "Be that as it may, there is every chance that one or more of them saw something that escaped your notice. Between their recollections and your own, I would like to devise a list of those who have come and gone from this room between the date you first noticed the disappearances and now, that we might get a list of potential suspects."

We conducted the interviews in Brandt's office. I had visited the room a handful of times before, and the condition of the clutter had, if anything, worsened. Brandt's office was in a state of constant flux, piled high with boxes of bones, teeth, and shed skins to sort through and identify. His field equipment – including nets, snake handling sticks, and jars of all sorts – lingered in a corner, dripping mud on the floor and awaiting reuse. His desk was elegant enough for a man of his position, but was equally piled high with more specimens, as well a series of papers and a stack of sketches of various creatures, many half-colored and with margins filled with notes. We squeezed into the office as best we could, then Brandt went to fetch his first assistant curator.

The series of interviews took most of the afternoon, and by the end of them the list was lengthy and included curators, researchers, gaggles of students, visiting family members, maintenance and custodial staff, and the occasional lost museum patron, most of whom were listed only by identifying features rather than names.

Brandt leaned back in his chair. "Well, Mr. Holmes, you have your list. What do you suppose we do with it now? We cannot possibly conduct follow-up interviews with every person here. To do so would take much time, and that's just for the ones we could find again!"

Holmes was carefully studying the list before him, absorbing each name one by one, as well as whatever notes he'd taken on their reasons for visiting the herpetology collections. "That is true. However, I think that we can narrow it down considerably. There is the question of access, after all – many of these people will have only visited the room once or a handful of times. We can start some process of elimination."

"It still seems likely to leave us with a large number of suspects."

"A list of suspects, no matter how long, is the best head start anyone could ask for. However, I believe you are correct. Even after we've reduced the list, we'll likely need to pursue another method in order to determine the culprit. At the moment, I am thinking of some way to trap the skeletons and catch the thief when they inevitably return for another adder. Perhaps some sort of powder sprinkled on each remaining skeleton that will be visible on the thief's fingers . . . Or we could create a device that will make some sort of noise when the drawer is opened. Or perhaps something that will break."

Brandt blew air out of puffed cheeks and waved his hands in front of him in an exasperated gesture. "I suppose that makes sense. Though I must say, even for me it seems a lot of effort to go through for the sake of a few little vipers!"

This wasn't the first time I had seen an offhand comment create a shift in Holmes's perspective on a case, but it was certainly one of the more innocuous. His back stiffened, and he turned his attention away from the list to look at Brandt.

"Hold a moment, Dr. Brandt. You mean to say that our common adder is considered a viper?"

"Certainly, Mr. Holmes. Humble though it may be, we have reason to believe that it shares an ancestor with the more dangerous vipers of other parts of the world."

For the briefest of moments, I saw the shifting of the puzzle behind Holmes's eyes, and then the satisfied gleam as the last piece settled into place. He dropped the list carelessly on the table and stood. "*Vipera* . . . Of course. I should have realized at once. It would seem that evolutionary relations are amongst the gaps in my knowledge that rarely pertain to a case, but have somehow managed to do so now. Please, if you would kindly follow me, gentlemen, I will lead you to our thief."

As always, Holmes must have paid infinitely more attention to our surroundings than I had, for he unfalteringly led us straight to the paleontology collections, and there walked straight over to the older gentleman that Brandt had earlier introduced as Dr. Bircham, senior-most curator of paleontology. He was sitting at a small desk in the corner that appeared to have been hastily added to the room as an afterthought after the shelves had been designed to dominate all available space – for in this room, they were, if anything, even more numerous than the herpetology collections, and absolutely full to bursting with fossils of all shapes and sizes. Bircham was bent over what appeared to be a paper of some sort, occasionally crossing out a few words or making edits in the margins. A few fossils that appeared to be teeth of some sort were scattered across his desk, and these he referred to occasionally before returning to the pages and firmly crossing out a word or two.

"Dr. Bircham?" said Holmes pleasantly. "My name is Sherlock Holmes, and this is my associate, Dr. Watson. Would you kindly come with us to Dr. Brandt's office? We would like to have a few words in private."

The scientist glanced up at us, confusion written across his face. He seemed about to refuse, but Holmes quickly cut him off.

"We can speak out here, if you wish. But as we would like to discuss your rheumatism, and medical matters are generally of a relatively private nature, I thought it would be best if we spoke away from any potential prying ears." As Holmes made this fairly baffling statement, he cast a meaningful glance at Brandt. Dr. Bircham followed his gaze, and his expression changed. The confusion shifted to panic as the man paled and immediately dropped the pen he'd been using to edit onto the desk, forgotten. The panic then turned to a sort of quiet resignation. He rose as a man might when asked to make his way to the gallows.

"Ah. Well, as you would have it then. Please, lead the way, Dr. Brandt."

Together we returned to Brandt's office and arranged ourselves as best we could between the boxes of specimens and scattered field equipment. The moment the door closed, Brandt sputtered in disbelief.

"Dr. Bircham? Holmes, you believe Bircham to be the thief?"

Holmes nodded. "I do. I couldn't be completely sure until our interaction in the paleontology collections mere moments ago, but I think his demeanor now makes his guilt quite clear."

"I'll say. He's shaking like an autumn leaf in the wind. Bircham, what the devil are you playing at? Did I slight you in some way? I've always

216

thought you to be one of my more admirable colleagues! You will, of course, return the stolen adder skeletons at once."

"Have no fear, Brandt," said Holmes soothingly. "The incentive behind the thefts wasn't personal in nature. However, I'm afraid there is no way for Dr. Bircham to return your specimens. You see, he's ground their bones into powder in order to mix them into a traditional medicine for his rheumatism. It is a popular recipe for treating swelling of the joints via either rheumatism or arthritis. Indeed, viper oil is sold in many an apothecary here in Europe – although I imagine he began using this exact recipe, necessitating a powder created from viper bones, while on his recent expedition in China. It's been an exceptionally cold winter in England, and likely the symptoms of his rheumatism worsened significantly upon his return. Unable to find the ingredients required to make his cure, it occurred to Dr. Bircham that he had access to a rather large supply of viper bones right down the hall from his own office. He started small – just taking a few rib bones here and there. However, as he continued to grapple with the symptoms, he eventually resorted to taking whole skeletons."

"You have the right of it," said Dr. Bircham miserably. Now that I took a closer look at his hands, I saw the severe reddening and joint stiffness. He was trembling as well, though whether that was a further symptom or a result of anxiety at the reveal of his deception, I didn't know. "I'm sorry for the strife, Dr. Brandt, and please know that you have my full respect. But when I was in the depths of my discomfort with this damnable disease, I recalled you complaining earlier this year about the number of donations you receive of our native species, and I thought – Well, what harm would it be?

"I thought I would only need a few ribs to get me through the winter, but each one produces so little powder . . . and then I thought I would only take a skeleton or two, surely it would be marked up to a clerical error. I never should have . . . but . . . My hands, Brandt! Look at my hands! How can I be of any use at a dig now? You know I'm more of a man of the field than a desk, and I can't accept that holding a shovel may be beyond me. Even pens are problematic now! I thought that once the winter was over, I could send some students out to catch a few to replace those I stole, but now . . . ." He hung his head.

Brandt was still fuming, but his tone softened slightly at the sight of his obviously miserable colleague. "Out," he said sharply. "Please leave my office, Bircham. We will speak of this at length later. We are scientists, after all, and I fear that if I try to discuss it with you right now, my words will not be very objective in nature." Bircham scurried from the room, apparently eager to hide from Brandt's wrath.

Brandt breathed in and out through his nose a few times, eyes closed, as though sending cooling air through his lungs would cool the mind as well. Afterwards, he strode firmly to his desk, reached to a cupboard underneath, and took out a bottle of brandy and three glasses.

"Watson, Mr. Holmes, I hope I can impose upon the both of you to join me for a drink. I feel the need to stay sequestered in my office for a little longer before I go interact with others – elsewise, I may accidentally yell something about collegial backstabbing at an undeserving research assistant."

"I would be delighted to join you," I said.

"I will as well," said Holmes, his eyes twinkling. "For the sake of the research assistants."

When the glasses were nearly drained, Brandt and I asked Holmes to reveal to us the reasoning behind his deductions.

"One of the key clues to this case wasn't found in the skeletons that were missing, but rather in the ones that remained. The missing rib bones indicated that the thief desired the actual bones, for one reason or another, and not the complete specimen. In this way we could rule out the idea that some crazed collector, whether a member of the public or one of the museum staff, was simply trying to build as large a hoard of adder skeletons as possible. By my reasoning, the thief started with the rib bones so as to be as unnoticeable as possible – after all, snakes have so many ribs. Who would notice a handful missing from a few specimens? It's a reasoning that Dr. Bircham confirmed, as you just saw.

"The fact that only adder skeletons disappeared suggested that the perpetrator had some respect for the museum, or at least had no wish to cause more damage than required – a less-caring thief would have stolen the bones of more exotic beasts, or other species of vipers whose specimens are less-easily replenished. That they disappeared directly from the beetle box as well as the shelf suggested, once again, some knowledge of the museum's inner workings. A less-knowledgeable thief would almost certainly be hesitant to reach his hand in amongst the writhing mass of flesh-eating insects. And of course, there was the matter of access – Bircham's seniority meant that very few would question him spending time amongst collections that were not his own. Even if he were asked, he could undoubtedly regale his questioners with a falsified tale about some research he was conducting comparing adder skeletons to some prehistoric reptile."

"All so clear when you say it," grumbled Brandt. "Seems as though I should have figured it out myself."

I laughed. "I've been saying the same for years. But what of you, Brandt? What will you do regarding Bircham? Do you intend to inform the Board of Directors?"

Brandt made a noncommittal noise in response. "As difficult as it is to convince myself of the fact, I think not. To besmirch the career of such an esteemed colleague in the twilight of his years would be . . . satisfying, perhaps, but a punishment that I do not believe fits the crime. His reputation would be utterly ruined, and all the good work he's done for this museum through the years would bear the same mark as he. I think in this case, I must put my own feelings aside for the sake of the institution. However, I shall think of a suitable punishment. Perhaps I will make him accompany me on some field collection visits to replace the adders he stole, playing the role of my junior. That should be a humbling experience."

"You must encourage him to seek medical assistance regarding his condition, as well," said I. "I have little experience with his chosen medication, but there are certainly plenty of alternatives."

Brandt laughed. "Ever the medical professional, eh Watson? Be careful, or I'll send him straight to *you*." He drained the rest of his glass of brandy and set it on a miraculously clean part of his desk. "Well, I thank you both for taking the time to help me solve this little issue. I hope the tour of the museum's underbelly was worth the imposition."

"Of course," said Holmes graciously. "It's a suitably impressive place."

Brandt nodded. "That it is. Housing suitably impressive collections of all sorts, we hope. Who knows, eh Dr. Watson? Someday, perhaps your stories of Mr. Holmes here will line the walls of a similar institution."

"Hear, hear!" said Holmes. "One day, our fine Dr. Watson will be held in just as high of esteem as any of Britain's greatest literary talents."

"Come now, my friends!" I cried in protest. "Despite Holmes's prowess in the realm of deduction, my few published tales are mere trifles compared to true artifacts of literature, artistry, or science. I cannot imagine them ever proving significant enough for such an esteemed resting place."

"I think you underestimate yourself," said Holmes, the slightest smile curling at his lips. "I think your stories are valuable to a great many people indeed. More, perhaps, than either you or I will ever know."

NOTE

*   See "The Adventure of the Transatlantic Gila" in *The MX Book of New Sherlock Holmes Stories – Part XXII: Some More Untold Cases (1877-1887)*

The Case of the
Ghazi Genie
by Paula Hammond

It was March of 1891. The stately carriage of time had not yet delivered me to the watery abyss of Reichenbach Falls. Nor had I any inkling of the portentous events in which my dear friend, Sherlock Holmes, was then embroiled. All I knew was that he had been traveling for many weeks, and I didn't expect to see him.

Holmes had been never one to write where a telegram would do. Indeed, when circumstances compelled him to put pen to paper, his letters were so short as to verge on uncivil, so infrequent as to make them useless as a form of meaningful *communiqué*.

That morning, however, I'd received a letter which was so out of character that, incredulous, I'd read snippets of it aloud to Mary, over the breakfast table.

It was gregarious missive, with many references to past cases, and much good-humored small-talk. "Why John," my wife said in *faux* alarm, "I think you should call Scotland Yard, for I've no idea who this man is who claims such familiarity with you. He certainly isn't *our* Mr. Holmes."

"Indeed," I laughed. "He's almost civil!"

Despite the humor of the situation, I found myself re-reading the letter over coffee looking – I confess – for some hidden message. If there was one, I entirely failed to see it, but I was left with the nagging feeling that something was amiss.

That feeling only increased when, in place of my usual eleven o'clock appointment, Holmes himself materialised, looking like a man stretched thin.

"As your waiting room is empty, I thought I'd avail myself of a few moments of your time. That is, if you can squeeze me in?" he asked in a tone laced with exhaustion.

"By Jove, Holmes!" I cried, propelling him towards a chair, for he looked ready to drop. "Are you quite well?"

"A little tired. I've been using myself rather too freely of late."

"I thought you were in Europe?"

"I was. Unexpected events have brought me back to England. I will have to go away again, soon – for at least six weeks. Perhaps," he added darkly, "infinitely longer. I'm sorry to land at your door unannounced. I still have much to plan, many possibilities to consider . . . Yet I'm sorely

221

in need of my Watson. Why, do you know that it's ten years, this week, since we had our first adventure together?"

"So, that's what your letter was about!" I exclaimed, relieved that it was nostalgia, rather than anything more sinister that had prompted such a curious correspondence.

"Ah! I see – I've worried you?"

"No, no, not at all. Well, maybe a little. Mary's convinced you've been replaced by some nefarious *doppelgänger*. She's all set to bring in Lestrade to track down the real you!"

"Ha! Now, that I would like to see. The fellow couldn't find his own hat." For the first time since he'd arrived, I caught a glimpse of the Holmes I knew of old – glittering eyes, the whisper of a smile.

"I'm sorry to be the friend in need, Watson, but I'm sure my doctor would warn me that I cannot carry on as I have been – without any respite. What say you to a few days fishing? Perhaps Plymouth? We may have to make do with pollock or wrasse, but the weather has been mild of late. We may be lucky and bag ourselves some spring mackerel."

If I'd learned anything from Holmes during our long association, it was that often what someone doesn't say can be more significant than what they do. I couldn't have known that, even then, Professor Moriarty haunted his every step. I did know that my friend needed me – and I'd seen him wear himself weary with work too many times to refuse.

That day was Saturday the seventh. Sunday was a day of rest, giving me plenty of time to free my diary and arrange a *locum*. "If I clear my urgent appointments on Monday, I could be at Paddington for five o'clock, if that suits?"

"Excellent," Holmes said, suddenly jumping up. "I'll reserve a carriage on the 5:15. Now, I've intruded too much already. I'll arrange provisions. You bring the rods."

It was still an hour before sunset, but by the time I reached Paddington, the day had taken on a sombre aspect. The weather, which had been clear all week, had turned chilly and an untamed wind, tinged with the scent of snow, propelled me onto the platform.

It howled ominously across the station's great wrought-iron arches. Billows of steam, illuminated by electric light, formed a rippling aurora, turning Brunel's great monument into a cathedral of light.

I didn't know why, but there was something about the spectacle that put me in mind of my days in Afghanistan. Of a night-sky full of stars, of early morning mists, and the ruddy glow of guns guttering in the distance. I stood, trying to retrieve one particular memory for some minutes. Several times I thought I almost had it. Then, another gust quite blew it away.

I hurried on, shivering, thankful for my heavy Ulster and the carriage blanket, secured in my luggage. To think that I'd laughed at Mary for insisting I bring it, with spring just around the corner!

I've travelled a few times on the new City and South Electric-Traction Railway, and it may be that such modes of transport will soon be ubiquitous. Yet, for me, nothing beats the scents, sounds, and sensations of a steam train. The tang of coal-smoke in the air. The jubilant crow of the whistle. The heavy vibrations as the great iron beast gets up to speed. The rhythmic chug of the engine at full power.

I fought my way though the crowds, enjoying each and every sensation. My porter was less enamored of the spectacle, huffing like a miniature engine beside me, until he finally located our carriage. Holmes was already ensconced within, his pipe creating its own little steam-plumes.

I was relieved to see how relaxed he looked, and I mentally thanked Mrs. Hudson for the flush on his cheeks, which spoke of the benefits of good food and a well-turned-down bed.

As the train pulled out of the station, I noted that the weather had taken a turn for the worse. It was snowing in earnest now. Great globules battered the windows, and the wind veered so quickly from northeast to southeast that it quite obliterated the view.

The express can cover the two-hundred miles between London and Plymouth in less than four hours. Our more modest conveyance gave us five hours in which to sample the contents of Holmes's sizable hamper, which was packed with cheeses, potted meats, hearty cobs, shortbreads, Queen cakes, and, to my delight, small bottles of both port and brandy.

The windows were tightly shut, but the gale was such that, directly, we were compelled to close the ventilators and pack every crevice with wads of paper, torn from my notebook.

Soon, the temperature in the carriage had fallen so low that I was obliged to unpack my blanket. I was pleased to see that Holmes had brought his, and suitably immune to the chill, we settled down to enjoy the journey.

Our progress proved to be painfully slow. The rising winds and falling snow tested the train to its limits. It crawled along. At each station, we spent longer and longer lying in wait as, no doubt, the driver debated the prudence of pressing on.

Fortunately, our journey wasn't urgent. Indeed, we were merrily reminiscing over a pipe when, without warning, there was a deafening thud, like the sound of muffled ordinance booming in the distance. Immediately I had visions of Maiwand, of the guttering echo of nine-pounder guns, the leathery scent of black powder.

The vision quite stunned me. I sat, blinking, for some time, temporarily lost in the past. "Down, Watson!" Holmes cried, ducking low. There was another thud, followed by a strange, muted screech, as if metal claws were being raked along the side of the carriage. The curiousness of the sound shook me out of my reverie.

I quickly followed Holmes's advice, for it felt certain that we would be de-railed. Instead, the train teetered to one side, somehow righted itself, gave a great shuddering exhale, then stopped dead.

Holmes, still crouching low, edged open the blind, his keen eyes scanning the darkness outside with an air of nervous expectation.

"What is it?" I asked, looking at his taut features expectantly.

For some time, he said nothing then, eventually satisfied, he gave a great sigh of relief and unfolded his long, thin frame. "Forgive me, Watson, I'm jumpier than a cat. It would seem the weather has defeated us. We appear to be stuck fast in a bank of snow."

"Goodness, that came down quickly."

"And it shows no sign of abating" he said, still glancing out of the window, anxiously. I followed suit, but saw nothing but a blizzard of white, a pair of bobbing railway lanterns, and the echoing shouts of the driver to his fireman.

Soon, a third lantern joined the cabal. I watched their slow progression along the length of the train checking, I guessed, for damage. Then the little party headed back towards the engine, where I saw the glint of a coal shovel, accompanied in quick order by the dull grunts of the fireman getting to work on the drift that surrounded the train.

"It looks like they might try to dig us out. Where do you think we are?" I asked.

"Based on our rather pitiful speed, and the number of points we've passed, somewhere outside Exeter."

"Well, then, we've still plenty of time for a warmer. In the meantime, maybe you could put that brilliant mind of yours to work on a mystery that's puzzled me since my army days."

"Oh?" Holmes replied, suddenly rapt. "How is it that I've never heard of this mystery before now?"

"To be honest, I'd almost forgotten. There isn't a lot I do recall about Afghanistan. Perhaps I've tried to forget, for it's enough to feel the old wounds complain as winter closes in. I've no desire to pick at the scars. Still, there was something about that odd light-display at Paddington that set me thinking about the Khyber. Then, that noise we heard just before the train stopped – put me in mind artillery guns."

"It did sound rather explosive," Holmes commented, putting a strange emphasis on the last word. "Still, however long we're stranded, thanks to

224

the ever-dependable Mrs. Hudson, we'll be well fed. So, here, take that little warmer, and tell me your mystery."

I took a glass of port, feeling rather pleased to have something with which to regale Holmes while we waited out the storm. But where should I begin . . . ?

We'd struck camp near Ali Musjid Fort, looking towards Peshawar, at the end of November.

It's a place that lies heavy with the weight of history. Arid, narrow, bounded by precipitous cliffs of shale and limestone. Kipling called it "*a sword cut through the mountains*". In truth, it's so narrow in places that barely two camels can pass through, side-by-side.

The fort that guards the pinch-point of the Khyber Pass had only recently come under British control. The summits that surround it are less than four-thousand feet above sea level, but the cliff sides are near vertical. The result is a claustrophobic corridor where fast, low winds rise suddenly – just as the winds have done tonight. But it's only sand, not snow, that comes sweeping across your path.

We were a mixed bag: Baluchis, Gurkhas, Jats, Sikhs, Punjabi Muslims, Frontier Pathans, and a rag-tag collection of Brits.

Tensions were running high, for this was a spot where many young men had lost their lives. We'd neither seen nor heard the Ghazi, but that meant nothing. The hills were dotted with tunnels and caves, some natural, some cut by the Afghans to hide munitions and men.

It was in that mode – sensitive to the slightest sound or movement – that we made camp. The sappers set up our "Park" where we stored the ordinance, while we pitched our tents further along the old river bed.

If I'd had any say in the matter, we would have pressed on. I already had several patients wasting away with diarrhea, and one man had been tied to scaling-ladder and whipped so badly by his officer that I feared he'd die before we got to the Field Hospital at Lundi Kotal.

We'd been in Afghanistan long enough to be well-versed in the trick of making and breaking camp. We weren't, perhaps, quite the well-oiled machine of repute, but it wasn't long before the hospital tents were pitched.

I was busying myself readying the beds when I heard a commotion coming from the direction of the Park. Shortly after, one of the officers arrived to report that some of the levies had bolted.

That wasn't an unusual occurrence. The levies were fine fellows, individually, but had no particular interest in upholding British interests, at the expense of their own skin.

It wasn't exactly clear what had caused them to bolt, and soon all sorts of rumors started to circulate, as they tend to do in army camps. Finally, one of the boy drummers came running in.

Jimmy Johnson was an admirable young lad with whom I'd made an arrangement some months earlier: I was to supply him with slugs of chocolate, while he would ensure that I was kept abreast of camp news. "Those damn levies have cursed the whole bloomin' camp!" he chirruped, wide-eyed.

It's a curious thing that, despite the horrors of war, the young lads who took the Queen's shilling somehow still managed to be boys – with all the capacity for wonder and credulity of their kind. "Really, Johnson," I tutted, "what nonsense are you spouting now?"

"Honest, Doctor!" he replied, holding out a grubby hand for payment. "The sappers 'ave been digging up bones all morning. Fousands of 'em."

"Oh? Whose bones?"

"The levies say there's a shrine nearby – they're Holy Knights or summut. They say now we've disturbed their resting place, the genies will come to punish us. So off they scarpered."

"Genies! Good Lord, Johnson," I sighed, exasperated. "How many times do I have to tell you that you can't believe every little thing you hear?"

"God's honest truth, Doctor!" he protested, stuffing squares of chocolate into his mouth like a cocoa-addicted python.

"Pssh! The deal was news, not gossip! Now away with you – I have too much to do to be listening to fairy stories."

I thought little more of it until the next evening.

By then, the wind, had begun to rise again. Towards the Pass, I could see dust-devils gathering, sucking in debris as they whirrled and bobbed along. Abruptly, the wind started to shriek, until it reached to an ear-splitting crescendo.

An older, more circumspect Watson would have stayed in his tent. I wasn't that man.

I'd arranged to dine with chums in the Park, and was damned if I was going to let the weather deter me. So, with my cinder goggles firmly in place, I headed off.

Even with a lantern to guide me, it was tough going. Stumbling all the way, I weaved through the storm, head down, barely breathing, until my foot hit something hollow, and I tumbled into a dusty little oubliette.

In truth, it was little more than a scrape, over which someone had pulled a piece of tarpaulin. Yet the more I struggled, the more I became entangled. I would probably have remained there all evening, rolled up like over-sized caterpillar, if it hadn't been for Sergeant Kelly's mongrel, whose eager barks quickly brought the sentries running.

Thus, feeling rather bruised and foolish, I was delivered to Lieutenant Henn's tent, where Corporal Michael Brennan was already installed, glass in hand.

We were sitting and drinking milk punch when I asked Henn, who was with the Royal Engineers, if he'd heard about the levies.

"I should say so! Half-a-dozen of them gone. The Captain sent riders out to track them, but they've found nothing. His worry is, if the fools get themselves captured by the Ghazi, who knows what information the beggars will squeeze out of them before they kill them?"

"Do you know what set them off?"

"We seem to have stumbled onto some burial pit – Hazara most likely. Caused complete chaos. Aside from the necessity of finding the time to rebury the poor blighters, we had to relocate the whole Park. It isn't just the levies who are spooked, either. None of the lads want to spend the night camped on top of a graveyard. Mind you, bones or no, this is an eerie spot. Strange quality of light. Lots of echoes. Shapes that shouldn't be."

"Oh?" I said, sensing that Henn wasn't quite telling everything he knew.

"Oh, no! I'm not fool enough to tell the resident quack that I've been seeing and hearing things!"

"Ghosts?" I prompted, topping up his glass.

Henn sighed. "Well, you didn't hear it from me, but some of the men have reported lights, strange noises. I thought it was likely musket shot or rifle sights, glinting in the distance, so I headed out for a recce.

"I was outside the Park, looking up towards the Pass with my field glasses. Damn strange – there was a moment when the mountain itself seemed to move. Now, khaki is just the right color to blend in with the dust around here, so I started thinking that maybe our missing levies were hiding out in the hills. Some of those fellows are like mountain-goats, and they know this place like the back of their hand.

"I headed closer to get a better look. There are a few trackways hereabouts, used by goat-herders, but there were no foot-prints. No tracks of any kind. Yet here's the thing: I was just about to turn back towards the Park when I felt the air move. Then, clear as day, I heard a voice say '*Marg sta paa intizar di.*'

"I tell you, I came-about pretty sharpish. If there'd been anyone around, I'd have seen them. There was no one. But do you know what '*Marg sta paa intizar di*' means? '*Death awaits you*'. Put the bloody willies up me – and that's the truth!"

227

"Little Jimmy Johnson is blaming genies," I laughed. "Perhaps we'd better search the camp for magic lanterns!"

Brennan and Henn, both being Irish, had something of a literary streak. "Not genies. *Djinn*!" the one said. "Nothing like what you read about in fairy tales."

"Quite right!" the other chipped in. "Invisible spirits, the locals say. Capricious, like the fey folk. You don't want to get of their bad side. Who knows what devilry they'll get up to."

Henn looked to Brennan, a mischievous gleam in his eyes. "Half the sappers have stories. Noises. Things moving in the shadows. Kit going missing. Objects being moved. I believe you've met Bobby" he added, chuckling. "He's normally a perky chap, but he's been skulking around camp with his tail between his legs, growling at nothing all day. That is, until he had to go out and rescue some idiot doctor."

"Nonsense. He's probably upset that no one would give him a bone! Besides, there you've said it: The levies have stolen what they could, then hot-footed it to the nearest village to sell it. Wouldn't be the first time."

"Ah, the Captain's already thought of that. There's no sign of them along the usual routes. No way they could out-pace a horse on foot, either."

"They'll turn up eventually" I said.

"Maybe they will, maybe they won't. Or maybe the *djinn* have spirited them away!"

"You can't believe that."

"Our dear doctor's a sceptic," Henn nudged Brennan, conspiratorially.

"Only one cure for that," Brennan answered, grabbing a lantern. "Come on! The wind's dropped. Let's take a look over by the Pass. See if we can't whistle you up a genie or two!"

I was still a young man, with a reputation in the regiment as something of a hot-head. It didn't take much to goad me into doing something stupid – which, heading out into enemy territory with two drunken Irishmen to look for genies, undoubtedly was.

It was a clear night, bright, silent, with stars such as one only ever sees in truly wild places – the same stars, it occurred to me, beneath which Alexander the Great had marched forty-thousand men into India, two millennia earlier.

It was that cold, epic vista, I think, which began to unpick our bravado. It was easy to feel small and lost, beneath such a vast, timeless display. Soon, the gay chatter evaporated, to be replaced by cautious whispers.

By the time we'd reached Henn's goat-track, we'd all unholstered our weapons, suddenly sober, aware of the precariousness of our situation.

The path truly was a goat-track. It wove its way upwards, following the logic of an animal whose only concern was filling its stomach. It would veer, unexpectedly, towards this tasty shrub, or that patch of grass, with no concern for the steepness of the slope or the ease of passage.

Not being goats, we progressed fitfully, sending torrents of loose scree tumbling down with every tred.

Eventually the trail widened, straightening out towards what looked like a cave mouth. It was there that we found them. Six scattered corpses, surrounded by loot, their bodies positioned in such a way that they appeared to have died running from some unknown foe.

The Ghazi had a reputation for playing dead. I'd treated more than one solider with wounds inflicted by an apparently dead enemy, who'd miraculously returned to life to stab them the moment they'd walked past. Indeed, some soldiers had learned the habit of plunging a bayonet into any corpse they saw, just in case.

I wasn't about to follow suit. Besides, the levies may have been thieves, but we had no reason to suspect them of colluding with the enemy.

We inched towards the lonely clearing, revolvers at the ready, every step sounding like a pistol-shot, our breath echoing, thunderously. It seemed impossible that the enemy wouldn't hear us.

Still, we advanced. Still, the corpses in the clearing remained corpses – yet such corpses as I'd never seen before.

Symptoms of cerebral concussion showed themselves in their bloodshot eyes. There was blood, too, around their noses, indicating a rupture of the sinus and a fatal effusion. But there were no scalp wounds, no cuts, gunshot wounds, or lesions of any kind. If it hadn't been for their pallor, which looked so uncanny, paired with those crimson eyes, they might well have been asleep.

"How strange," Brennan said. "We haven't had any artillery drills."

It seemed an odd statement, for clearly none of the men had been hit by shot.

"Damn! Personally, I'd much rather have stumbled across a couple of *djinn* in these hills than this pitiful sight" sniffed Henn. "Come on – we can send a work party out later to collect the bodies but, discretion being the better part of valor, I suggest we make double-time back to camp. I think you'll agree, gentlemen, that one unpleasant encounter this evening is more than enough."

Two hours later, enlivened by a pot of strong coffee, I carried out what would be my first autopsy.

Every student doctor learns his craft in the dissecting room. In spite of that, my career thus far had been preoccupied with the often Herculean task of keeping frail humans alive. In times of war, it's a messy process, largely devoid of emotion – for the doctor who pauses to worry loses lives.

An autopsy is an entirely different affair. There's no sense of urgency. The spark that gives us life has been extinguished – yet one must still give the dead their dignity.

I knew nothing of the body before beyond a name, which time has now sadly erased from memory. Even so, I recall readying myself to make that first incision, aware that here lay – first and foremost – a man. I owed it to him to discover what had killed him and, if possible, ensure that those responsible were punished.

What I found puzzled me then, just as it puzzles me now. His internal organs showed signs of massive trauma. Indeed, his insides had almost been liquidized. Organs, blood vessels – exploded. His brain matter was little better.

Had the man come to me, fresh from the battlefield, I would have expected to see the outward signs of such inward injuries: A crushed skull, or broken ribs. He had neither.

I examined one of his companions, keen to ascertain if his injuries were unique. They were not.

I had no answers. I couldn't conceive of anything that could have caused such catastrophic damage without leaving any signs on the victims' bones or skin. Nor did I have the luxury of time to research the puzzle further.

The next day, we struck camp, heading for Lundi Khan. The next, we were for Basawal, then Barikab, then Kandahar, and on.

My life quickly became one long routine of route marches, making camp, striking camp, fire, fury, blood, bandages. Until, that is, the Battle of Maiwand . . . .

Holmes refreshed our glasses. For a moment he regarded me in silence. "My dear Watson . . ." he whispered.

"I know," I said. Further words were unnecessary.

He nodded. "Well then, let us see what we can make of you mystery." He closed his eyes, steeped his fingers, and began.

"We will never know if the levies were genuinely spooked by the discovery of the bones, or simply used it an opportunity to vanish through the Pass with British kit to sell. The events you relate do suggest a certain level of planning, sparked, no doubt, by the discovery of the burial pit.

"It would seem that the levies took advantage of the confusion in camp to steal what they could, hiding their loot in little dugouts around the

Park. It would have been a simple thing to wrap items in lengths of tarpaulin, dump them in a hole, and retrieve them later. It's likely that you yourself stumbled into such a hiding place.

"The levies couldn't risk carrying too many items at once – that would attract attention. No, they'd have to do it piecemeal, returning from their hiding place, after dark, to do so. That would also explain the strange shadows, noises, and 'moved objects' that the sappers reported.

"From your account, they took one of the little goat-tracks up into the hills, clearing their footprints, along with any other tracks, as they went – which is why Henn found none. They knew the territory. Knew the caves and hidden tunnels. Perhaps Henn even stood on top of one such tunnel, when one of the levies, hiding out below, made his rather ominous statement.

"As to what killed them? I believe I have a theory. Have you ever heard of 'wind of ball'?"

"Can't say I have."

"For as long as we've made war with black powder, there have been reports of men dying without any external injuries on their bodies. Sir Thomas Longmore devoted several pages to the phenomena in his rather interesting treatise on gunshot wounds. He described victims who had died without any marks of violence on their skin beyond symptoms of cerebral concussion. Despite this, their internal organs had become what he called 'viscus'.

"During the Napoleonic Wars, such deaths were observed by combatants on both sides. The same was reported during the American Civil War. It was long thought that the concussive power of the 'wind' created by the cannonball itself was the cause."

"So that's why Brennan remarked that there hadn't been any artillery practice!"

"Certainly. Did Brennan have family in the navy?"

"He did. But that still doesn't explain how the levies died."

"No, but I personally believe that Doctor Forbes, who was writing at the start of the century, had the truth of it. He suggested that the cause of such strange deaths wasn't a wind, but a *vacuum*, following in the wake of the cannonball. This would cause a sudden expansion and rupture of the fluids in the stomach, along with the blood in the blood vessels. The wind you mention, traveling low, and fast, trapped in a narrow pass, unable to escape the vertical cliffs, might create such a vacuum. Certainly, the epicenter of your dust-devil could.

"So that's it!" I cried, feeling, as I often did, foolish not to have seen the clues so clearly laid out before me.

"I believe so. Sadly, such a proposition leaves little room for *djinn*, I'm afraid."

"That's shame! I was rather hoping you might conjure up proof of a genie or two. Brennan and Henn would have enjoyed that."

"I assume . . . ?"

I shook my head. Brennan, Henn, and little Jimmy Johnson hadn't been as lucky as I.

"Well, then," Holmes said, raising his glass, "may I suggest a toast?"

"Of course."

"To absent – and present – friends."

"Here, here!"

Outside the window, I could see the fireman, stroking his chin, fresh snow falling into the hole he'd just cleared.

Once again my mind returned to Maiwand. To the wound I'd received there, which had put paid to my army career, and sent me, broken, back to England. It was a day which, for the longest time, I'd wished to forget, but which I now realized, had led me to London, to Baker Street, and to my Mary.

"Pass the port," I said to my dear friend and colleague. "It looks like it's going to be a long night. It wouldn't do to get a chill!"

NOTES

☐ Paddington Station was the London terminus of the Great Western Railway (GWR). Designed by Brunel, its glazed roof is supported by wrought-iron arches in three spans. The GWR first experimented with electric lighting in 1880, with Paddington Station being lit for Christmas that year. By 1886, the station was completely illuminated by electric light.

☐ The City and South London Railway began running trains on an electrified fourth rail in 1890. The route now forms part of the London Underground's Northern Line.

☐ The Express service that Watson refers to is likely The Cornishman, which began running between Paddington and Penzance, Cornwall, in 1890. The down train left Paddington at 10:15, and arrived at Plymouth at 13:50, making it the fastest west-coast service of the period. Today's travel times are little different.

☐ The Great Blizzard of 1891 was the worst storm Britain had experienced in generations. Snow and hurricane-force winds de-railed trains, sank ships, and brought the country to a halt. One train was derailed and buried in snow, only to be discovered thirty-six hours later, by a farmer looking for lost sheep.

☐ The Battle of Maiwand took place on 27 July, 1880. Named for the nearby village in Afghanistan, the battle was part of the wider Second Anglo-Afghan War, with the British campaigning to stop Russian influence in Afghanistan, which threatened British India and the vital trade route through the Khyber Pass.

☐ Ali Musjid Fort was captured by the British after the Battle of Ali Masjid, on 21 November, 1878.

☐ The make-up of British forces in this period reflects the complexity of the political situation in the region. Some native forces, such as the Sikhs, allied themselves with the British, as they believed it was the best way to keep their independence from India. Other forces felt threatened by Russian-backed Afghanistan.

☐ James H. Johnson was one of five drummers listed as casualties at the Battle of Maiwand. Although boy drummers were romanticized in fiction, they were often adult men. Fourteen year-olds could enlist with their family's consent – but in poorer families, boys did lie about their age to join the army. James enlisted in 1875. If he joined when he was fourteen, he would have been seventeen or eighteen at this point. Watson's description implies that he appears younger, which may have been the result of the privations of army life on a child.

☐ Ali Musjid Fort was named for Alī ibn Abī Ṭālib, the cousin of the Prophet Muhammad. There is indeed a shrine there, and the region is considered holy.

☐ Genie, *djinn*, or *jinn*, have long been a feature of pre-Islamic folklore.

☐ Lieutenant Thomas Rice Henn, Royal Engineers, and Corporal Michael Brennan (66th Regiment, 2nd Battalion Berkshires), were both killed at

Maiwand. During the battle, British forces were outnumbered ten-to-one and massively outgunned. It's reported that British ranks stood firm, their rifle barrels becoming so hot they had to wrap cartridge paper around their fingers to stop blistering.

Despite almost a thousand men from Watson's regiment falling in battle, eleven made such a brave stand covering their retreating comrades that the Afghans reported their sacrifice with great respect. Lieutenant Henn and a handful of his sappers, supported by native grenadiers, were amongst those eleven. They held the enemy at bay, fighting back-to-back until their ammunition was exhausted, before charging with bayonets. Every man was killed. In British military history, the action is known as "The Stand of the Last Eleven". The events are dramatized in Rudyard Kipling's poem "That Day". It was at Maiwand that Watson, positioned near the front, took a bullet which almost cost his life.

☐ Watson seems to have been ahead of the game here. Sir Garnet Wolseley, who in 1862 had been an observer of the American Civil War, had seen railway workers using "cinder goggles". When, in 1882, he was made Adjutant-General to the Forces in Egypt, he encouraged his troops to use cinder goggles to keep dust and sand out of their eyes.

☐ Bobbie was the regimental mascot dog. The mongrel, from Reading, was owned by Sergeant Kelly. Bobbie survived the final stand of the Eleven and escaped, wounded, to join the retreat to Kandahar. On his return to England, he was presented with the Afghan War Campaign Medal by Her Majesty Queen Victoria at Osborne House.

☐ The Hazara are a Shia Muslim minority who have long been the subject of persecution in the region. Between 1888 and 1893, over sixty-percent the Hazara population were slaughtered by the Afghan Army.

☐ "Put the willies up me". The origin of the phrase is said to come from the 1840's ballet *Giselle*, where the spirits of wronged lovers are led by the Queen of the Wilis to exact their vengeance.

☐ The book Holmes mentions is Sir Thomas Longmore's *A Treatise on Gunshot Wounds*, published in 1862. Longmore was Deputy Inspector-General of Hospitals and Professor of Military Surgery at Chatham. "Wind of ball" is also called "wind of the shot'", "*vent de boulet*", and "wind contusions".

☐ Doctor P. Forbes, writing in *The Edinburgh Medical Journal* of 1812, proposed that a vacuum, created by the passage of the cannonball, would suck air from the body and cause a sudden expansion of fluids in the body, rupturing organs and blood vessels.

☐ It's likely that Holmes is right and that the deaths were caused, not by the "wind", but by the vacuum the wind created. The phenomena has been noted in the modern day Khyber Pass by locals and travelers. It is notable for what's described as winds that reach an ear-splitting crescendo. The swirling sand then creates a low pressure area a couple-of-hundred meters above the surface which, in turn, creates a vacuum.

The Claws of Qift
by John Linwood Grant

In Qift, that antique town which the Ptolemys called Koptos, I saw a dead man step off a dhow one late afternoon. Some would say that this is the way of Egypt, where history and magic are drawn in with every breath.

That may be so. However, this particular man was neither priest nor pharaoh, but a fellow I had seen alive not two years before, on London's Strand, when my tutor Flinders Petrie had pointed him out a man who stood a few paces away from us, engaged in conversation with a cabbie.

"There," said Petrie, "is the mind which might have unravelled the mysteries of all Egypt for us, if only it had been harnessed in our field."

And I had noted at the time the hawkish profile, the slight sensitivity to the lips, and the deep set eyes. Those characteristics were no less impressive now, by the docks of Qift, as the dhows disgorged their mixtures of traders, minor officials, and workers.

My eyesight was excellent, and I found it hard to believe that I was mistaken. And yet . . . reports from the world's press would have it that this fellow died in Switzerland, only a few months after we had seen him in the capital. I abandoned my argument with a seller of pomegranates and stepped out towards the jetties before the newcomer disappeared. The Nile, high in this season, glistened in the morning sun, a fine backdrop for the tall figure who had paused to survey the town. He wore the robes of an Arab, and beneath, loose *shalvar* trousers – Persian, by the style.

I plucked up my courage and slipped to his side. "Ah, if only Dr. Watson were here as well," I murmured, "my day would be made."

He turned, and I thought for a moment I would receive a flood of uncomprehending Arabic or Farsi. Then he laughed, with what seemed genuine good humour.

"And what manner of detective do I have the pleasure of addressing?" he said.

"James Quibell, sir. It is an honour – and a shock, a delight, that stories of your demise were at fault. I am no detective, though. I saw you in London once."

He nodded his head. "Chance can always betray us."

I felt uncommonly pleased with myself.

"Sir, there is so much I would ask. Are you . . . Will you be in Qift long? I have a camp half-a-mile from the town, and would be delighted to extend hospitality to you, even for a night."

"I am bound for Alexandria – but I am not pressed. Very well, Mr. Quibell, I accept your kind offer." He looked me over. "Let us see if I still have my talent. A Shropshire lad by your burr, of modest means, with enthusiasm for his work and a readiness to 'muck in' with the workers. The worn knees of your trousers betray you. An Oxford man – the way your belt is tied. In Qift, in this season, and therefore an Egyptologist, most likely one of Petrie's students, left to examine the rubble while the master strides to yet another site."

"You are indeed Mr. Sherlock Holmes," I said. "But the reports of your – "

He waved me to stop.

"Mr. Quibell, I am Jabir al-Khadim, a wanderer of little importance, with a good command of English and some fluency in Farsi. If you can let the matter rest there, then we shall rub along splendidly."

"So be it. Al-Khadim, *effendi*."

I led him through the small town and to that sandy strip of land between the verdure of the Nile's banks and the arid eastern hills. There lay the tents of my camp, sheltered by the remnants of some un-named Graeco-Roman outpost.

"There are many such remains in the area," I said. "Men have cut quarries into the hills between here and the Red Sea for millennia. With Petrie gone elsewhere, there is little left to do here, but I am to make further notes and complete our catalogue of modest finds."

Holmes's tall, lean figure attracted brief interest from my *fellahin*. Fahim, my *gaffir* or foreman, salaamed and asked if I would have company for the evening meal, to which I said I would, and begged that he serve the last of the haunch of goat.

"It is not entirely fresh," I confessed to Holmes, "but the spices disguise it."

"When one has eaten sun-dried snake outside Medina, one does not argue with a plate of well-cooked goat. Tell me, what is your complement here?"

"Small, sir. I am, as you surmised, a student, very much a junior. A local French doctor occasionally potters with us – Jean Chavasse, an amateur Egyptologist only. Otherwise, I spread what little coin there is around Fahim: A camp boy and five or six *fellahin*. There was another Englishman, but – "

"The man whose body was found outside the town, two days ago."

I halted in mid-step.

"How – ?"

"I act as my own scout. In this case, I knew of a young Englishman's presence – though not that you would identify me so easily – and of other

236

relevant news. I do not generally wish my wanderings in Egypt and the Sudan to be noted."

"Well yes, that was the chap. Edward Bellingham. But come inside and have some tea. There are few Europeans in the area, other than the officials at Luxor and the occasional passing journalist or fellow Egyptologist."

I showed Holmes into the largest of the four tents, my own, and set a billycan of water to boil on the spirit stove. This had been Petrie's headquarter for the Koptos dig, and had a spare pallet under one sloping side. While I prepared our drinks, Holmes examined the pottery and broken carvings on the trestle table.

"Mostly late pieces, or Roman," I said. "Though there are some curious fragments from Pre-Dynastic times in the supplies tent."

We sat cross-legged on a rug, and as we sipped our tea, he explained that he had taken ship from the Arabian port of Jeddah to Suakin in the Sudan, and had even been to Khartoum. He would say nothing of his reported death, nor of his purpose since, only that his absence from England, and from public notice, had been expedient.

"But tell me of Bellingham." He slipped a tin of Turkish cigarettes from under his robes and offered me one. I was somewhat in awe of my guest as I recounted how the body had been discovered early one morning by one of my workers.

"I viewed the body *in situ*, Mr. Holmes, and by God, what a sight! He was a corpulent man, yet you might not have known that from what was left – the abdomen had been torn open, and most of the contents were missing. His corpse lay on its back, arms and legs straight, but the face so clawed that no expression could be discerned – "

He looked up. "It was definitely Bellingham?"

"No doubt about it being him – the upper portion of the head was unmarked, eyes staring through a cloud of flies."

"On the dhow, they said a lion was involved."

"It must be so, though it's a rum affair. Lions have been hunted almost to extinction in this area. There are striped hyenas, but they are smallish beasts, normally timid, and could not have inflicted the damage I saw – not given the dimensions of the slashes to the corpse."

"I commend your observational powers, Quibell. Do go on."

Emboldened, I decided to add a detail which I had not intended to mention.

"There was something else that was odd. There was no sign that the jackals had visited the scene – not a single scavenger had come during the night – and the town dogs would not approach Bellingham's corpse. They whined and slid away, which made folk talk."

"So much for his ending. What can you tell me of his life?"

"I'm not sure. In his early thirties, as at home in Egypt and the Sudan as any man I have known. He appeared about a month ago and asked if he could set up a tent in our vicinity. Said he had 'scholarly interests' in the area. Another Oxford man – Old College, he said – but a few years before me." I hesitated. "He had a manner . . . Well, he shifted between brusque and obsequious. I didn't like him, to be honest. There was something 'off' about him, despite his obvious learning. An Army officer passing through Qift had hinted at some scandal at the college, but would not be drawn."

Holmes lit another cigarette.

"Was there a medical report?"

"Barely. Qift is policed by a British sub-inspector from Luxor who is drunk much of the time, and a pair of local constables – natives. No one liked Bellingham, nor misses him, as far as I know, and so little effort was made. My friend Dr. Chavasse pronounced that the man had died during the previous night, either from shock or exsanguination due to his wounds. The body was crated up for tomorrow's steamer down river."

"A curiosity indeed. I admit to having a professional interest. I recall Watson once bringing me a patient of his who had been attacked by a tiger in India . . . ." He looked up, a wistful expression on his face. "Did your doctor take photographs?"

"He did – in case of further enquiry."

"Would it inconvenience you if I tarried at your camp a day or so?"

"Why, I would be delighted." I stood up, and reached out my hand, which he took. His grip was dry and firm.

"Welcome to Qift, Mr. Holmes."

My visitor slept with the dedication of the traveller who must rest whenever opportunity allows. After breaking our fast on bread and dates, I took him to see where Bellingham had been found, an isolated spot by a crumbling cistern. The nearest "modern" dwelling was more than fifty yards away. Holmes gave the scene a perfunctory examination, but was soon ready to be away, which suited me. I remembered too well the sight of a body sprawled on its back, the belly open to the morning sky . . . .

"As in London, so in Qift." said Holmes. "Too many people have been here, obscuring any useful evidence. Did you notice what is *not* here, Quibell?"

I thought back to those reports of Holmes and his methods which I had read in England.

"No bloodstains, sir. Neither on the cistern nor the soil. And we have had no rain, so they should still be – "

"Capital. Bellingham was clearly not killed here. Let us visit your friend. You know him well?"

"Well enough. Pleasant chap, here before I came. He collects various resins and concoctions used by the locals, always on the lookout for anything which might have genuine efficacy."

At Jean Chavasse's modest house in town, I introduced my visitor as an Anglo-Persian gentlemen known to me only through correspondence until now. After a few polite formalities, I let Holmes bring the subject round to Bellingham's death.

Chavasse gave a Gallic shrug. "Ah, *ce fou*. An interferer, a sly toad. He knew eight, nine languages, but in none of them did he inspire trust."

"You know why he was in Qift?" asked Holmes.

"*Mais oui*. He sought always papyri, the records rare of the oldest ways of *L'Egypte*. He pressed you, did he not, Quibell?"

"He did. I showed him a few transcriptions, but he pronounced them irrelevant. And his interests – I would have called him more an amateur occultist than an archaeologist, though he knew his stuff. 'The priests had secrets,' he said to me once. 'Secrets you would not comprehend, Quibell.' I told him to go pray to Isis."

"Here are the photographs, *M'sieur*. They are . . . not pleasant."

Holmes examined them – I had no need to see that scene again.

"Mr. Quibell tells me that the corpse is still here."

"Locked in a hut behind *ma maison*," said Chavasse. "The locals packed the abdomen with certain leaves, and it was doused with vinegar. Enough to keep it tolerable for passage to the British Consulate in Cairo."

"And it leaves with the afternoon steamboat?"

"*Oui*."

"Doctor Chavasse, will you indulge me? I have been many places, have knowledge of many practices. I would like to see the remains."

The doctor took us to a crude stone hut and undid the padlock on the door. Inside, we lost no time in opening the crate in the corner, exposing that awful sight once more. Despite the precautions that had been taken, the smell was none too pleasant – a mixture of vinegar, herbs, and decaying flesh.

"God, he looks worse than on the day." I covered my nose with my handkerchief.

"I once saw *un enfant* who had died and been found by the hyenas. *Bon Dieu!* It was far more dreadful than this."

Holmes circled the open crate, viewing the corpse from every angle. He teased aside the remains of Bellingham's jacket, using the spans of finger and thumb to measure the various long, deep slashes in the flesh.

He turned the ghastly head to one side, then another, with some difficulty, *rigor* having set in. Straightening up, he nodded.

"Yes. These do appear to be claw marks. Do either of you have a pencil you can spare?"

We looked at each other, and I took a serviceable HB from my jacket. "Thank you."

To our astonishment, Holmes then bent over the body and inserted the pencil up one of the torn, bloody nostrils, to almost its full length, twisting it.

"M'sieur, I do not think – " began Chavasse.

"I noticed a peculiar distension of the nostrils, and some tearing. Gentlemen, the brain has been removed – the bulk of it, anyway. The skull is almost empty."

"*Encroyable!*" The doctor rushed forward, and took the pencil from the other man, repeating the process. "*C'est vrai.*"

"What does that suggest to a student of Flinders Petrie?" asked Holmes. "The emptying of the abdomen, and the evacuation of the soft tissue within the skull . . . ."

I think my laugh was slightly hysterical.

"Why, a body prepared for mummification would undergo such indignities. But – "

"I would say that Edward Bellingham was 'prepared' in just such a manner. After death, I hope."

The crate was sealed once more, and we retired to Chavasse's kitchen, where he poured out brandy for two of us. "I assume, *M'sieur*, you are Mahometan?"

Receiving no reply – Holmes seemed deep in thought – we fortified ourselves. I tried to rally.

"If he was murdered, why the claw marks, and what caused them? If he was subject to some dreadful ritual, why was his body left out in the open to be found?"

"Fine questions," said Holmes. "I would agree the marks are too large for any common beast to have made them. But a lion could not remove a man's brain in such a manner."

"I am out of my depth, *mes amis*," Chavasse admitted. "I potter with Quibell on his site. I treat fever and dysentery in the town, or guess as to cause of heads which ache and joints which do not bend. I should inform *les gendarmes*."

"To what end?" I said. "They will only panic, and Carter will come from Luxor, half-cut, to bluster and tell us to stop being a bloody nuisance."

"What of the body?" The doctor toyed with the cigarette he had been offered.

"Let it be on its way when the riverboat comes," said Holmes. "It has told us all it can."

Fahim was drinking mint tea outside his tent, in front of a small fire. He had a family in a town downriver, but preferred to stay here – I think he feared his wife. He was a dry little man in is forties, with a heavy moustache and mournful eyes. Fluent as he was in English and Sai'idi Arabic, I would have struggled without him. My own Arabic was tolerable, but hardly outstanding.

We sat down with him, shook hands, and accepted glasses of tea. Holmes murmured a few lines in Farsi, and then again Arabic – poetry, I think. Fahim sighed.

"Allah blesses us with the gift of such words."

We sipped our teas, and then the *gaffir* scuffed one foot in the sand. "Quibell, *effendi*, they say your friend is a wise man, that he comes to avert the evil of Bellingham Pasha, who turned stones he should not have turned."

This was news to me.

"And do they talk of how the body came to be found only yards outside Qift?" asked Holmes. "In plain sight?"

"There are wanderers in the hills who move between the places where water can be found. Much like the *badawi*, the Bedu of the desert, but few in number. Perhaps he was taken by a lion on one of their routes, and they left the body for us, the *hadir* who live in towns, to deal with it . . . ."

"Nothing else?"

Fahim looked away. "When the fires are low, they say . . . they say that he was taken by the Children of Mehit and Apep, for he trod their lands, and had neither respect nor shame."

Holmes looked interested. "The Children of Mehit and Apep? A tribe?"

"Hardly," I interrupted. "Though I can show you what Fahim means."

I went to the collection tent, picked out a few sherds, and brought them back to the fire.

"Here."

In my outspread hands were fragments we had unearthed from a gorge which led off Wadi Hammamat, probably from offertory vases. In places a hieroglyph or two could be made out. More important were the beasts depicted – lionesses, but with enormously extended necks, serpentine from shoulder right up to the more traditional, leonine head.

"These are the so-called Children of Mehit and Apep. Mehit, you see, was the consort of Anhur, and she was commonly portrayed as a lioness. But there is an uncommon myth in these parts that she bore children by another deity – Apep, the Serpent God of Chaos. Lions with the necks of snakes, unpredictable and wild. There was even the skeleton of one displayed in Cairo, decades ago, but they say that the man who found it had added neck vertebrae from another great cat."

Holmes traced an outline with the tip of his finger.

"I find them unlikely murderers. Are these symbols common?"

"Not at all. A flash flood exposed an ancient road in the hills the other week. Bellingham was excited, and joined me on a trip up there, as did Chavasse. We found these fragments, and evidence of a few columns, but nothing more. Bellingham stayed out in the hills after we left. But I have no idea what he was seeking – or what he found, if anything."

"You have searched his tent since his death?"

"As I said, I didn't like the fellow. I left that to the police."

Fahim shuffled uneasily. "Even thieves would avoid that tent. It should be burned."

"Maybe so," said Holmes. "But first we must see what it holds."

So it was that the three of us entered Bellingham's tent – I with distaste, Fahim with evident trepidation, and Holmes with impatience. I felt I had let him down by not having been through Bellingham's belongings already.

One could stand inside, though it was a close thing for Holmes, who was taller than both of us. The inside was the usual affair – a spirit-burner, books, a table and a cane chair, along with a pallet bed. By the bed sat a travelling chest. I had not expected the disarray – someone had clearly rifled the dead man's belongings. The chair was on its side, books flung hither and thither, clothes tossed out of the chest and onto the dirt floor. If this was the work of the constables, they had been none-too-careful.

"Was he an intelligent man?" asked Holmes, reading the spine of a book. "Out of the ordinary, I mean."

"I would say so. And overly proud of it. He told me of his finds at Beni Hassan, downriver, some years ago when he barely had his majority, but he did so in a sneering way, as if I was below his intellectual league."

"A great mind without wisdom." Fahim folded a worn jacket and placed it on the bed. "Many in Qift welcomed him at first – he spoke like a native, and knew much of our past, but soon he angered or worried the elders among us."

"Indeed?"

Fahim's smile was wry. "Many British believe they are better than other peoples, but they are brash and open about this. Bellingham Pasha was cunning, sly, like a Turk."

Holmes nodded. "Much as the doctor said. Apart from comparing him to the Ottomans."

I reddened. "I say, Fahim, if I've ever – "

"You are a good man, Quibell *effendi*. Allah witnesses this."

Holmes was still investigating the dead man's belongings. "A clever man would leave nothing important in clear sight. Let me see . . . ." He opened the travelling chest, then ran long fingers around its edges, gauging its dimensions. "Nothing amiss here. Perhaps in the books . . . ."

He began to investigate the bindings of various texts.

"It is a very sturdy tent, al-Khadim *effendi*," said Fahim.

Holmes paused.

"Very sturdy," the Egytpian repeated, and pointed upwards.

"Fahim," said Holmes, beaming, "You are a *bey*, a veritable *pasha* amongst *gaffirs*."

"I don't see – " I began.

"Two poles, Quibell! Help me slide this along . . . ."

And then I saw what they meant. Alongside the main supporting pole which ran the length of the rectangular tent, another had been inserted through the canvas loop, shorter and of no obvious structural value. We slid it free, and Holmes removed a brass cap at one end, revealing the pole to be hollow. He soon had the end of a tightly rolled set of papers, which he extracted and spread out on the table.

The outermost was a modern map.

"That is Wadi Hammamat," said Fahim, pointing to the wandering route which heads east towards the Red Sea coast. "The marks to one side . . . that is where we searched after the rains, Quibell *effendi*."

"So it is." I saw that pencil lines marked the exposed road, and dots showed where the pillars stood. There was more, though. The lines seemed to indicate an extension of the road into a blocked ravine further north. We had gone no further – but perhaps Bellingham had.

Holmes drew out other papers. The outermost bore reproductions of very early hieroglyphs. Two delicate scrolls were wrapped more carefully in tissue, and I grew excited, until I realised that they were copies only, with Arabic notes. Fahim squinted at the faded writing and shuddered, pronouncing that the scrolls had to do with mummification – lists of herbs and methods of preservation.

The last sheet was a rubbing, charcoal on coarse paper.

"What are these, Quibell?"

243

I tried to read the symbols he showed me. "The cartouches are used for names. You would need a Petrie or an Amelia Edwards to make more sense of them. I can see the hieroglyphs for Mehit and for Apep. And this . . . ." I drew my finger back. "Is self-evident."

The rubbing had captured the impression of a prowling lion – or lioness, rather – with its paws upon a prone man, and her unnaturally long neck curving the head almost back to her tail.

Fahim tugged at my arm.

"*Effendi*, I did not wish to alarm you, but now that we have found these secret things . . . there have been desert shadows the last few days, around the camp. They are not known to me, these shadows."

I was not pleased. "Then are we in danger? Dash it, I'm only a student of Egyptology. What if these are Mahdists, or other fanatics? I know nothing of politics or territories, nor of whatever mysteries occupied Bellingham's odd mind."

Holmes placed the empty rod back into its loops. "I doubt the Khalifa has any interest in Qift. Tell me, Fahim: Are there tomb robbers in this area?"

"Not here, *effendi*. There are few tombs. East of our town is a land of mines and quarries only, for the stone."

"It's true," I agreed. "You can find the occasional half-finished stone sarcophagus in the hills, and blocks of basalt which have not yet been dressed. Plenty of rock carvings, as well."

"From which Bellingham no doubt made this rubbing. Perhaps he offended someone with his prying, and paid the price."

"But the claw marks, the lion . . . ."

"I cannot say, as yet."

The three of us repaired to my own tent, where Fahim and I fortified ourselves with some of the chocolate I had been sent from England.

"You may be in danger, Quibell," Holmes said at last. "What if the perpetrators decide that Bellingham shared his finds with you?"

"I don't even know what I'm not supposed to know!" I protested.

"Ignorance will not blunt a knife in the dark. I may stay a while longer, and see if I can unravel this matter. Or convince others of your innocence when it comes to Bellingham's affairs."

As the sun began to drop, colouring the eastern hills a dusty red, we went our separate ways – Fahim to pray, Holmes into town, and me to my journal, where I catalogued anything of interest among the finds.

My mind was more on recent events than the job, and my unease was amplified by a snuffling outside, amongst the ruins. Hyenas, probably. I pulled back the tent flap . . . .

The lantern in my tent gave enough light, or too much. A head, a bestial leonine head in the desert night, only yards from my tent, and no body to it, no form behind it!

I cried out, more in panic than anything. Instantly, Fahim tumbled from his own tent, an ancient Jezail in his hands. He lifted the long barrel – but there was nothing there.

"Don't shoot!" I cried, for in that instant I had a verse of Kipling in my mind, the way these things come to one in times of emotion:

A scrimmage in a Border Station
A canter down some dark defile
Two-thousand pounds of education
Drops to a ten-rupee Jezail.

The *gaffir* lowered his rifle, but summoned the camp boy, Younan, a wiry little Copt who cared nothing for myths and mysteries.

"*Yayay!*" shouted Younan, waving a stick around. "Is it dogs again, *effendi?*"

"Probably," I answered, my voice uneven. "Check if they have got into the supplies."

The low supply tent, where we kept carboys of water, grain, dried fruit, and tinned meat, was untouched. Glancing at Fahim, who strolled around with a lantern held high, I checked Bellingham's old quarters. The empty second tent pole had gone.

"Your friend al-Khadim, perhaps," said Fahim from the opening.

We scoured the surrounding land, Fahim and his Jezail always nearby, but we found nothing.

I did not sleep that night.

"I have had some interesting conversations," said Holmes.

He had reappeared at the camp an hour before noon, and from the look of him, he too had been awake most of the night. His tanned face was drawn, more angular than ever, and I wondered that I had recognised him that day at the Qift docks.

"During the night – "

"In a moment, Quibell." He arranged himself cross-legged on the sand. I bit back my impatience, and joined him, as did Fahim. I feared that my resourceful *gaffir* was handling these bizarre events far better than I.

Holmes drew in the hot, dry air. "You are not from Qift, Fahim?"

"No, *effendi*. Petrie Pasha hired me in Qena, where I have the misfortune to possess a large, expensive family. I live at the site."

245

Holmes smiled. "And so you are not party to all the stories which circulate in this town. I spent time on the hookah pipe, or *sheesha* as you call it here, late into the night and the hours before dawn. I found old men whose limbs had withered but whose minds were still in full fruit, and I told them of my travels – of Shiraz, Mecca, and Medina. In return for such tales, and a rumour or two of my own, I learned of a precedent to this case.

"In the time of Napoleon's occupation of Egypt, they say a man died, near Qift, in much the same manner as Bellingham: Clawed, and with his abdomen torn open. That body was found near the ruins of the Temple of Min. My informative hookah companion had heard this from his father's father, who had the tale from one who, as a young man, had witnessed the discovery."

Fahim frowned. "Almost a hundred years have passed since then."

"True. However, rather than being garrulous, the locals were reluctant to make any specific mention of such events, or of Bellingham's fate. My informant certainly believed what he told me, and the fact that it was the devil of a job to get the story out of him gives me pause."

"What are you suggesting?" I asked.

"I had entertained the theory that Bellingham had made an enemy in town, and that the bizarre manner of his death was down to someone's dark and twisted humour. Perhaps he had crossed some of the local elders, or cheated the wrong man. I can find, however, no evidence of that. And no one thought killing a European a wise move, in case it brought the authorities down on them . . . ."

I could hold my tongue no longer, and burst out with the events of the night – the hideous lion-like head, the absence of the hollow tent pole. He listened attentively, as if pleased.

"A game played for effect – which it achieved. A distraction while other purposes were served. Quibell, do you have those fragments which depict the serpent-lions?"

"Of course. I'll fetch them."

But when I slipped into the tent where our finds were kept, I made a further alarming discovery: All the sherds which bore serpent-lions were gone! I hastened back to the others. Holmes seemed unsurprised, but I expressed my alarm, at some length.

"It must have been done during the night. I'm not even sure if it is safe to be here," I ended. "Worse may be to come."

In truth, I was now all for taking a steamboat myself and finding some comfortable hotel in Cairo for a week or two.

Fahim scowled. "And what would we say to Petrie Pasha, if we left? I have given my word to be here when he returns."

"Good man," said Holmes. "Stiffen up, Quibell. Egyptology is all about mysteries. I believe that we shall solve this one."

"How?"

"By heading into the lion's jaws, rather than running from them. This case must concern the road in the hills, and something Bellingham found there."

I shifted awkwardly. "I would have thought we should 'not find' it as well, rather than make matters worse."

"A touch late for that," said Holmes. "I do not believe in mythical creatures roaming the hills. Tomorrow, we will make an expedition to your lost road, and take the map, scrolls, and the rubbings of the serpent-lion with us. We may discover the source of Bellingham's troubles – perhaps even find the men who left him at Qift. These Bedu, for example. They might tell us more."

Fahim looked uncertain. "The *badawi* would not do what you have told me – the piercing of the brain."

"No matter. If we find the right people, we shall offer them anonymity in return for the truth. Nothing more need be said once we are satisfied that Bellingham's death was an isolated incident."

"I suppose so," I sighed. "It sounds rather dangerous."

"Would you prefer another unwelcome night visit to your camp, after I am gone?"

That seemed a cheap shot at my nerves. "Very well. But may I ask Dr. Chavasse to accompany us? He hunts occasionally in the eastern hills, and knows them better than I do."

Holmes looked pleased. "I intended to suggest just that. We should leave, I think, at first light. Tonight we shall rest, keeping watch in turn."

We made our way the Chavasse's, where we found him examining various ochre powders.

"I know something of chemistry," said Holmes. "Perhaps I could assist you another day."

"It would be *un plaisir*." Chavasse put his work aside, and I explained Holmes's broad plan. The Frenchman was only too happy to accompany us.

Holmes shook his hand.

"Tell me, Doctor, have you ever heard of any similar deaths in the area. I understand you spend much time with the locals, and there is always gossip . . . ."

"*Non.* You have a theory, al-Khadim?"

"I am only a traveller, *M'sieur le Docteur,* merely seeking to be sure that Quibell *effendi* is in no danger."

"Then we share a common goal," agreed Chavasse. "Until the morning, *mes amis*."

Nothing of note occurred that night, except a brief visit to my tent from Holmes, in which he gave me a warning I had not expected.

"You and the doctor must keep your eye on Fahim tomorrow," he murmured.

"Fahim? He is as trustworthy as – "

"We shall see. There may be more to his involvement in this Bellingham affair than you realise."

His words filled me with additional trepidation. I loaded, emptied and reloaded my revolver, made up a travelling pack, and then took everything out once more, seeking solace at last in a bottle of brandy, which would no doubt cost me in the morning . . .

We prepared all we would need for a long day's journey – we did not expect to be out there at night. Holmes made a fuss of examining what we were taking – weapons, comestibles, and other equipment such a ropes. He admired the doctor's rifle, had a test shot with it at a prowling fox, and finally pronounced himself satisfied.

"An Ottoman Mauser – fine weapons, eh, *M'sieur le Docteur*?"

"*Mai oui*." Chavasse made some joke with Holmes about Fahim's Jezail, a comment I thought a little tasteless, though probably more accurate than the *gaffir*'s weapon.

Dark clouds hung over the hills as we made our way towards one of the northern branches of that great breach in the hills which runs as far as the coast. The doctor and I were in the lead, Chavasse with his weapon over the crook of his arm. Holmes and Fahim walked abreast a few paces behind, Younan following with a heavy pack.

"A storm coming," I said. "Brief but violent."

"Will that be a problem for us?"

"Oh, there are overhangs and elevated ledges, left by the quarrying. The downpour rarely lasts more than an hour or so, if it comes at all."

We hiked along narrow stretches of sand, gravel, and wiry tufts of grass which marked the paths of long-dead streams. Gone were the wiry acacias and the palms of Qift.

"A desolate place," I said, shivering. The view was dominated by the curious hills, which changed colour with the shifting of the sun, varying from a pale fawn to almost black. Atop one, far away, a Roman watchtower still stood guard over the route to the sea.

As we turned north off the main wadi, Fahim pointed out the plentiful carvings and *graffiti* on rock faces, which ranged from crude caricatures

248

to deeply cut hieroglyphs which recounted past endeavours here. Holmes was scanning the heights occasionally.

"Many fine places for sharpshooters," he said, when I asked what he was doing. "A glint from weapons or other equipment usually betrays them."

Chavasse saw my expression, and laughed. "Never have I seen such villains in these hills, *mon ami*. Those caravans to the coast are too well guarded."

The way was narrowing. After four or five miles, the winding beds of minor wadis passed through steeper hills. Occasionally an area opened out, where Egyptian, Greek, or Roman miners had encountered something of particular interest and delved more intensively.

"There is a dark green sandstone here, which was much sought for figurines and tombs," I called behind me, trying to take my mind off my worries. "And some fine-grained basalt which was used for larger statues."

I saw white flashes against the sky, between us and the heavy clouds to our east.

"Vultures are on the wing."

"A good omen," said Chavasse. "Protectors of the living. Devourers of the dead."

"They didn't devour Bellingham." I shivered again. "Damned beasts wouldn't go near his body." I let myself lag back so that I could watch Fahim. I had warned the doctor of Holmes's suspicions. The *gaffir* appeared on edge, his old Jezail over his shoulder. His commentary on the landscape had dried to only a rare word or two.

Around noon, sweating and ill at ease, I spotted the slightly wider, flat-bottomed gorge which we had entered with Bellingham weeks before, and within, the remains of pillars.

"A processional road, once. So Bellingham said. And see . . . ." I pointed out the crumbling outline raised on one side of a column, either a lion or leopard. The part beyond the forequarters had flaked away, so there was no telling as to the length of its neck.

"You stopped – where?"

"Before that rock-face at the end," said Chavasse. "But *peut être* there is a way beyond – we did not seek *l'aventure* at the time."

Holmes went forward with his long stride to examine a cliff of rough granite, many huge boulders at its foot.

"I believe . . . Ah, see here." For a moment his left arm appeared to have gone. "There is a fissure at an angle, wide enough for a man to slip into. It cannot be seen from where you stand."

We hurried to his side.

"Shall I go first?" asked Chavasse.

"Better I assess the way forward and report back, I think." Holmes slid halfway into the narrow crevice. "Bellingham would have found this more difficult, but not impossible." His voice had a strange echoing quality.

We had Younan dump his pack and head out past the entrance to the gorge, telling him to watch for the storm and run back if it seemed it was closer. With reluctance, I looked into the narrow opening Holmes had discovered, watching his robes disappear around a bend in the crevice.

I could not restrain myself. "For God's sake be careful, Mr. Holmes!" I called after him.

The doctor sighed. "Ah, the celebrated English detective. I knew there was something *inhabituel* – unusual – about your friend, Quibell."

I felt an utter fool. "I was not supposed to – "

"I will assume that no one else knows that this Holmes is in Qift."

"Oh, probably dozens of British officials," I said. "They'll be ready to look for him within a day, and . . . ."

"You are a terrible liar, *mon ami. Quel dommage.*" Chavasse raised his rifle, standing back to cover both myself and Fahim. "Follow him in, both of you. I have an eight-round magazine, and I am rather a fine shot. That muzzle-loader *très* antique will not serve you here."

My protests were met with a gun barrel directed at my head.

"*S'il tu plaît*, Quibell."

Somewhat shocked, I did as ordered, followed by Fahim. It seemed we had no choice but to take the same route as Holmes.

"I have my revolver," I whispered to Fahim, but my voice echoed, and I heard the doctor's laughter from the gorge. He knew how bad a shot I was, and evidently thought me no threat.

Our exit from the other end of the crevice, which was itself no more than ten feet long, brought us into a steep-sided valley of much the same dimensions as the one behind us, but separated from its predecessor by millennia. Here the columns stood tall and barely weathered on either side of us. Beneath our feet was a tiled road of smooth basalt slabs. The rock walls on either side, which rose steeply a good sixty feet or more above us, were richly marked with hieroglyphs and successions of deeply cut cartouches – and everywhere the serpent-lion ruled. These carvings referred not to pharaohs, but to priests and mason. I did notice the very spot from which Bellingham had taken his rubbing, though, low on one smooth section of the walls.

And at the end of the processional way lay a genuine temple, cut into the far cliff, before which lay one of those rare natural pools which I knew existed in the hills, but which I had never seen. Holmes stood examining a statue some three feet high and six long, the perfect depiction of a lioness with a sinuous, serpentine neck.

"Holmes, my God, Chavasse is involved in – "

"Of course." That hawk-nosed face was quite calm. "I deduced that he was, and that he had a darker purpose under his genial co-operation."

"Then why on earth did you let this go ahead?" I was torn between panic and wanting to shake him.

"Why, to discover the truth, Quibell. My entire career has been based on that single purpose."

I leaned against a pillar. "And now we are trapped here, hostages to a mad Frenchman."

"I am not mad, *mon ami*." Chavasse appeared from the crevice, his rifle aimed at us. "I have an arrangement with these people."

He indicated the three men who were emerging from the carved doorway of the temple. The were old and totally bald, their brown faces heavily wrinkled, and they wore simple tunics of white cotton, much as could be seen in Egyptian frescoes. All three carried long staffs . . . .

"That night at the camp!" I exclaimed. Each staff was crowned with a large carving in lacquered wood or metal – the head of a lioness, jaws open to bite. "That was what I saw."

"*Oui*." The doctor sighed. "I told them that I would deal with this matter myself, but they were alarmed and had to see if you had relics of theirs. You know a little too much, I fear."

"What are you going to do, Chavasse" I was furious at this betrayal, as I saw it. "Have us murdered, and left out like Bellingham?"

Holmes strolled over to us without evident alarm.

"Not quite like Bellingham, I imagine. That inquisitive fellow had entered the temple, unwelcome. What were his plans, I wonder?"

Before Chavasse could answer, the oldest of the three men came forward, rapping his staff on the paving stones. He fired a stream of strangely accented Arabic at Fahim.

The *gaffir* looked at me. "He says that Bellingham Pasha was a wicked man, a magician. He wanted certain secrets, *effendi*, the secrets of life and death. When discovered here, he knew . . . he knew things which he should not. The ways of hidden mysteries."

The priest – for surely that was what he was – spoke again, at length. Fahim shuddered.

"He says . . . there are few of the cult of Mehit and Apep left, barely more than you see before you. But they could not allow what Bellingham Pasha planned, and so – "

Holmes's penetrating stare was on Chavasse. "They showed him the way of death, but not of life. They took him and prepared him for mummification, but then discarded his body – an incomplete shell – and left it for the world outside to deal with.

"It was their doom upon his *ka* – his soul, as they saw it," agreed Chavasse.

"As happened to another man some ninety years ago, a French scholar. A relative, I assume, Doctor?"

"*Mon grand-père*, Thierry. He came with Napoleon and his scholars to catalogue the wonders of *L'Egypte*, and he found this place. He took the remains of a lioness from the temple – "

"*Stole*," said Holmes. The doctor ignored him.

"He sent the skeleton *très étrange* down the Nile to Cairo, but before he could follow, the priests came for him and had their vengeance. They missed his journals, however, which were sent home. My father thought them ravings. I found them as a child, and I alone believed."

"These gentlemen do not seem especially war-like," said Holmes. "How did they overwhelm Bellingham and your grandfather."

"They have a soporific which they use – they are immune, but outsiders become confused and incapable. You would have smelled the substance, Mr. Holmes, had the corpse been fresher."

"And had you not soaked it with vinegar. That seemed unusual. I considered that you might be masking whatever had deterred the scavengers."

"An additional precaution," Chavasse admitted. "I have experimented with some of their remarkable pharmacopeia – I am still a doctor, after all – and they have promised me more, in return for delivering you and all of Bellingham's materials. They will not make the same mistake twice."

"What in God's name do you get out of this, Chavasse?" I was angry, and in a funk at the same time.

"I followed *grand-père*'s notes. I told the priests I had left word with men beyond the wadi – I lied – but made it clear that I had no wish to expose them, only to know if the tales were true. And then I found out about the drugs. Our deal will erase *grand-père*'s folly, and make me wealthy. The priests know I have no interest in telling others of their location. Quite the opposite, in fact, if I leave here with substances unknown in France."

"And now?" asked Holmes.

"Now you will enter the temple, and be drugged into a final sleep. It causes less discomfort than dying of bullet wounds, and I have no wish to inflict unnecessary pain. There are Bedu in this area, men with whom the priests have an understanding. You and Fahim matter little, Mr. Holmes – who will miss a mere *gaffir* and a stranger called al-Khadim? Quibell's body here will be found elsewhere in Wadi Hammamat, the unfortunate victim of a dispute with the Bedu."

The doctor called something in Arabic to the priests, who nodded, though they did not seem enthusiastic.

"What about Younan, the boy?" I asked, my heart sinking.

"I will tell him you three have gone on to the old Roman quarry further east, and return with him to Qift, as if all is well."

"A capital plan," said Holmes. "Except for a few small points."

Chavasse narrowed his eyes. "There is no Scotland Yard out here, Mr. Holmes."

"No, only the working of a more orderly mind than yours. I took certain precautions, you see. Little Younan is even now on his way back to Qift, bearing a letter I prepared last night which outlines my suspicions, and our progress to this point. I left a copy with the most reliable of the native constables, as well, along with appropriate remuneration. You are named repeatedly within. One of them will pass everything to the authorities if we do not return by dawn. You may tell the priests that fact, Fahim."

The *gaffir* did so, causing the priests to break into agitated conversation with each other.

"And," Holmes continued, "you have a vexing decision to make, Chavasse. The magazine of your Mauser is empty. I saw to that earlier. As I know you have a round in the chamber, you have one shot for three men, and after that . . . ."

The doctor's face grew dark, and wheeled to face Holmes directly. "The others are nothing without you!" he snarled, and raised the rifle.

I was told later that a decent Jezail can be accurate to as much as two-hundred yards. At little more than four yards, Fahim's shot took the doctor in the side of the head, and dropped him where he stood.

Holmes nodded approvingly. "I asked Fahim to keep his weapon primed and loaded at all times."

"But . . . but . . . you said . . . ."

"You were my trusting Watson, Quibell. If you mentioned my supposed suspicions of your *gaffir*, it would put Chavasse at ease."

I could splutter, but hardly argue.

It is not easy to describe what followed. Holmes had many long and convoluted discussions with the alarmed priests, and all had to be in Arabic, causing the sweat to run from Fahim's brow as he struggled with Holmes's English and the archaic dialect of the three old men. I understood barely one word in ten. After more than two hours, Holmes turned to me.

"We may see inside the temple, if they have our oath never to speak of it to others – and to take nothing. Fahim has convinced them that I am a wise man from far away, a philosopher of the *sufi* persuasion. I have vouched for you – on my life."

"Oh. Yes. Of course."

While Fahim waited in the gorge, the two of us were led through a carved entrance wide enough to admit a pharaoh's chariot. It was clear that the entire place had been cut into the solid rock of the hillside. Inside, a single hall dominated. It was at least ninety feet long and almost the same wide, with a few shadowed doorways on either side, the main part lit by cunning slits cut into the ceiling, which let shafts of golden light pick out the details below. The air in here was cool, and bore a strange, elusive perfume which made my head swim slightly.

There are moments when fear will not do, when one encounters something which sweeps away all base emotion. Great carved columns, wider than three men stood before friezes of astonishing freshness, not left to flake and peel, forgotten, as were those in the temples of the dusty outside world. Here warrior-kings stood flanked by serpent-lions, their foes at their feet. Lotuses and lush palms were in proliferation, surrounding princesses in splendour.

And at the far end, a statue of the sacred beast of Mehit and Apep, twice the size of the one in the gorge. The entire beast had been fashioned from green sandstone, and its long neck was lowered, its head observing the length of the hall. Behind it stood a line of open sarcophagi, each one occupied by a perfectly preserved mummified figure with a lion staff in its linen-wrapped hands.

"First Dynasty," I whispered. "Or even before – a relic of the early Upper Kingdom. These are astonishing."

"Bellingham had an obsession with mummies, it seems, and these must be the finest in Upper or Lower Egypt, I imagine." Holmes bowed his head to the oldest priest. "Fahim, tell him that we are done here. There will be no record of our visit, no stories told. I would suggest they obscure that crevice with further boulders, and all being well. No more outsiders will come here for at least another century. Only an observation balloon would betray them now."

Once again Arabic sang between the *gaffir* and the priest, until at last the old man returned Holmes's bow, and the three defenders of an earlier age slipped away into the darkness.

"They will see to the body of the doctor," said Fahim. "His fate will be what was planned for you, left in some far-off wadi by the *badawi*. I think they are relieved – they find you far more worthy of trust than the Frenchman."

"As they should," said Holmes, displaying evident satisfaction. We left that holy place, leaving behind every scrap of what Bellingham had recorded. Walking by Chavasse's body, I kept my eyes averted – but I kicked it as I passed, all the same.

Beyond the fissure, Younan had left the pack he had borne. The three of us sat under a ledge, sheltered from the afternoon sun, sharing dates and water from the pack.

"We found lion spoor, and nothing else, on our trek," said Holmes at last. "No one else knows the truth, and they must not hear anything of the last few hours. And you, Quibell – if you wish to continue your career, you must be utterly silent as to the temple. Consider that your life might be at risk if you are not. The Bedu might be sent after you, if nothing worse."

"I understand. But the lions . . . ."

Holmes's face was impassive. "Do they exist, either as a few last beasts in this wasteland, or as lost creatures of Egyptian magic? My time in the East has taught me not to ask certain questions – not out here, at least. You did not notice, I imagine, certain tools – or weapons – in one dark corner of the temple. Rods some three feet long, each tipped with the likeness of a lion's paw in copper. Used to mutilate Bellingham's corpse, no doubt."

The journey back to Wadi Hammamat, and the route to Qift, was subdued. I marvelled – and was also shaken – that the last few days had seen two men killed, and brought another back from the dead, so to speak. Yet the promised storm had not broken over us, and the sky was clear.

"Allah, in His Mercy, keeps many secrets from men," said Fahim, and he pointed to where the last light of the day was falling on the eastern hills.

There, on a rose-tinted crag of bare rock, stood a lioness, unmistakable by her size and outline. The tufted tail was raised high, the head low, and that neck, that unbearably long neck . . . .

It was a trick of the light, I am sure.

The Devil's Bridge
by John Lawrence

Readers familiar with the accounts of my cases are aware that the author of these tales – which are occasionally embellished – has generally been my friend and companion of many years, Dr. John Watson. On two published occasions to date, "The Blanched Soldier" and "The Lion's Mane", I have served as the narrator, although I make no claim that my storytelling skills are equal to his.

In this case, I again take pen in hand to relate a hitherto undisclosed case in which Watson could not possibly have participated, for the simple reason that at the time of its occurrence, I was dead.

Or rather, I was *presumed* to have died following a *mano a mano* confrontation with the man I regarded as The Napoleon of Crime, Professor James Moriarty, at the Reichenbach Falls on 4 May, 1891. As readers of Watson's memoir "The Empty House" are already aware, I survived that battle and, over the course of the next three years, exploited the universal presumption of my death to disappear from the world and devote myself to planning the exposure and capture of the remnants of Moriarty's gang in London who would only emerge from the figurative rocks under which they lurked if they truly believed that Sherlock Holmes had perished, along with their benefactor.

Over two years after this sabbatical had begun, I found myself surrounded by rocks myself, visiting the desolate Territory of Arizona, a far-flung outpost of the American Empire inhabited predominantly, it seemed, by gold-seeking adventurers, Mexican banditos, and terrifying predators from tarantulas to rattlesnakes. I was surprised to discover that, as an Englishman, I was far from alone. For decades, many of my countrymen – a considerable number of them peers and other members of the aristocracy – had been infected by a desire to experience the wild, often uncivilized environs so foreign to the sophistication and culture of Whitehall and Fleet Street.

Influenced by Rousseau, titled countrymen and others sought to return to the simplicity of nature, unspoiled by modernity. For a half-century and more, they had transported their families, servants, and even pets across the Atlantic, stopping only briefly in the bustling coastal cities. Their goal was the distant, untamed region further West, some of which hadn't yet been admitted as states. There they would live under conditions that could only be described as crude and primitive, subjected to harsh winters and maddening isolation. In addition, one had to contend with violence from the indigenous populations, as well as those that the Americans refer to as "outlaws", but who are nothing more than habitual criminals. For many, the excitement of shooting bison and commiserating with painted, feather-wearing Indians proved exhilarating. Others, particular the women, found the experience isolating and rudimentary, and longed to return to their country estates in Sussex and the North Country.

My own interest in this desolate region had been aroused some years earlier during my introduction to members of the Church of Latter Day Saints in the Utah Territory in a case chronicled as *A Study in Scarlet*. During my Reichenbach sabbatical, it is now commonly known that I assumed the guise of a Norwegian named Sigerson and traveled widely, including to a remote outpost in Tibet where I had taken a liking to the physical challenge and mental clarity provided by climbing the majestic mountains of that isolated kingdom. It was during the ascent of a particularly picturesque Himalayan peak that I encountered several American alpinists who recommended that I try my mountaineering skills in the mountains of Colorado, Arizona, and other locales, in the American West.

It was in the fall of 1893 that I found myself in the tiny outpost of Oak Creek, Arizona, where a small cluster of cattle ranches and orchards struggled in that harsh picturesque territory. These dramatic cliffs, thick with the fossils of prehistoric creatures, provided me not only with rigorous physical challenges, but also with a most useful tutorial in the fields of geology and evolution. The spectacular isolation of the dusty village was a perfect refuge, thousands of miles from Baker Street, and living under an assumed identity, it was impossible for anyone to imagine that I was an English detective.

The village itself was little more than a cluster of buildings, including a number of homes, a sheriff's office and jail, a general store that sold farm product, and, this being the American West, a pub – or "saloon" – that seemed quite popular amongst the locals at almost any time of the day or night. There was a small hotel – or "hacienda" in the local dialect – in which I booked a room for the week I planned to explore the exceptional topography of this foreboding region. Operated by an innkeeper of Mexican origins by the name of José Camarilla, the building was constructed in the traditional mud brick and timber style known as *pueblo* that has been used for centuries by the local indigenous population. The heavy mud bricks known as *adobe* are covered with a thick, dun-coloured slathering of stucco whose components include mud, water, and several other ingredients too disgusting to mention.

Inside, there was a large parlour with a bar that was well-stocked with Mexican tequila, American whisky, and other strong spirits. A rough-hewn staircase led up to the story where a half-dozen rooms for visitors were located. On the walls, the preserved heads and stark white skulls of local animals were mounted, testament to the excellent hunting that brought many visitors to the area.

Other than the hotel's guests, the number of those in the village who manifested a command of the English language could easily be counted on the fingers on both hands. Those who, like myself, were primarily interested in the scenery were in the distinct minority. Many of my fellow guests seem to have been either the aforementioned hunters seeking hides and pelts, or fortune seekers mesmerized by the prospect of quick riches through discovery of gold, silver, and other valuable ores.

Whatever the appeal of the area might have been for a visitor, it mostly certainly was not culinary in nature. Each morning, a most rudimentary breakfast of hard rolls, coffee, and jam awaited the guests. Then, meagerly fortified, I would set out on the day's exploration of the magnificent mountains that rose up around Oak Creek. Unfortunately, reaching the trails required the one decided unpleasantry of my stay: Several miles of horseback riding. The size of the American horses and the rigidity of the saddles combined to strain ligaments in my thighs that were unchallenged by my daily exercise regimen and, at the end of the day, it required a half-hour and more for me to stretch my legs sufficiently to allow me to walk without what the ranch hands decried as the "dude's waddle".

During the course of the day, the scenery would undergo a remarkable transformation. Dull gray and often obscured by thick, low clouds, the mountains' hue would change dramatically as the sun rose and the clouds burned off. By mid-day, they were of a deep maroon colour, and by the time I returned to the hacienda in the later afternoon, the low sun illuminated them up as a deep red and a glowing orange, not unlike molten steel.

My walks also revealed the most astonishing diversity of plants and creatures, none of which I had ever encountered previously. What others might view as an unusual species or peculiar geologic formation, my brain instinctively perceives as offering a unique bit of evidence, even though crime was the further thing from my mind during these solitary strolls. Of particular interest were the cactus that came in innumerable sizes and shapes. Some had long, thin blades with needle-like tips that, if encountered accidentally, could easily penetrate even thick hiking boots. Others shed small balls of sharp-edged seeds that stuck with remarkable durability to any fabric with which they came into contact. Still others

258

grew enormous stalks, covered with tiny barbs, rising twenty feet from the squat plant and topped with outlandish flowers and leaves. In the still nights, I was often awakened by the plaintive lamentation of coyotes whose eerie cries mimicked a coven of witches stirring a bubbling cauldron!

With the chilly fall temperature replacing the scorching heat of the summer, a fire was crackling each evening in the fireplace that occupied the far corner of the parlour that served as a dining room. The dinner menu was based largely around the flat corn disks called *tortillas* and a variety of meats and vegetables one folded into them, topped off by the addition of cheese and a sauce made with fiery peppers (or "*chilés*") that appeared in every item the kitchen prepared.

The eclectic group of my fellow guests included a tall and lean Catholic clergyman, the Reverend Aloysius McSorley, who, despite his surname, was of Mexican background and spoke that country's language as well as English flawlessly, allowing him to communicate effortlessly with the hotel's owner. Traveling with him were with two abbesses more obviously of Mexican heritage, Sister Teresa and Sister Esquélla, who ate little and said nothing, but would look to the padre for instruction whenever a question was directed to one of them.

An ambiguous denizen of the hacienda's parlour was a desultory figure known only as "Slits", which I very much doubted was his given Christian name. He sat alone, sphynx-like, hour after hour at a small round table in a section of the room that received only a thin amount of light through a dusty pane during the day and was nearly dark after sundown. A glass of brownish liquid was never far from his hand as he remained oblivious to all human movement or conversation around him. Some thought him a veteran of the relentless battles with the indigenous tribal warriors in the Wyoming and Dakota territories. One rumor identified him as the only surviving member of General Custer's 7th Cavalry. His unconventional name, it was said, was attributed to his mastery with a large-bladed knife during hand-to-hand combat.

Several years earlier, a group of Mexican banditos burst into the parlour and attempted to rob the patrons. With a speed and grace one could no longer believe possible, Slits had sprung from the little table where he now brooded and employed his knife to dispatch three of the gunmen with remarkable speed and sanguinary results. The proprietor, Camarilla, was forever grateful and had awarded him permanent rights to the table at which he now sat, as well as a limitless supply of alcohol. In the days I stayed at the hacienda, I had never seen any guest approach him, nor observed him in conversation with anyone.

On my fourth day in Oak Creek, I found myself sitting at dinner with a young American couple that had arrived the prior evening. Carl and Pearl Wyndham of Chicago, Illinois explained that their trip was planned to celebrate their recent marriage, which had occurred only shortly after they met. The stylish cut and high quality of their clothing bespoke a considerable degree of affluence, which was confirmed in subsequent conversation.

Mrs. Wyndham was an attractive woman of perhaps twenty-three or twenty-four. Her bright red hair had clearly been dyed to achieve its remarkable colour, which contrasted markedly with her pale, almost translucent skin. She had been an entertainer who had made her living performing in one of Chicago's many music halls where she had encountered the man who was to become her husband. She was hardly the first of her profession who succeeded in winning the attention of a besotted member of the audience, particularly one who displayed significant wealth. Within weeks, they had married and spent the next two months buying furniture and moving into a large home he had purchased in a prestigious section of that city before embarking on their sojourn to the Southwest.

Carl Wyndham had been born a decade-and-a-half earlier than his wife and was raised on a cattle ranch in the small town of Durango, Colorado. The prospect of a lifetime of hard ranch labour held little appeal, he explained, and at his first opportunity, he had made his way to California to enroll at the new Leland Stanford Junior University near San Francisco, where he studied mining. Moving to the Southwest after receiving his diploma, he had become engaged in the mining industry in New Mexico and Arizona, resulting in considerable success before abandoning mining and relocating in Chicago, where he was invested in railroad construction.

Wyndham had clearly learned a great deal about geology at Stanford, and was eager to share information about the origins of the uniquely coloured mountains, the origins of the flat-topped mesas, and the peculiar stratification of the red rock cliffs around Oak Creek.

"This entire region was once under water, and not that long ago in geologic time," he declared. "As a result, these sedimentary and igneous formations create a pattern as though laid down by a mason with a trowel. If you dig in the right place, you can even find some of the bones of those terrifying dinosaurs that lived in this region tens of millions of years ago." It was a subject I knew a little about, having studied the discoveries of my countryman, Robert Plot who had uncovered a prehistoric femur near Cornwell in Oxfordshire in 1677. (Another British scholar, Robert Owen, had coined the term "dinosaur" a century later.)

During a dinner that consisted of a fiery pork and corn stew known locally as *"pozole"*, Wyndham regaled me with stories of his diggings earlier in the day that had yielded a promising bed of fossils from a mammoth, a sort of wooly elephant. I was intrigued and agreed to join him sometime when he returned to the fossil bed. Fatigued by those exertions, he and his wife had just excused themselves to retire for the evening when the hacienda's weathered door flew open and a burly stranger strode into the room, accompanied by a blast of chilled air.

The man was tall – certainly more than six feet – and broad shouldered, dressed in the ubiquitous heavy blue cotton trousers and rough cotton shirt that served as the uniform of the workmen of the region, His unshaved face and powerful hands had been darkened from long exposure to the brutal southwestern sun, and his palms revealed rough calluses that unmistakably indicated that he earned his living through hard, manual labour. His boots were heavy, not those typically worn by the cowhands, and were thoroughly scuffed and scratched. He limped noticeably, dragging his left leg, perhaps due to an injury or battle wound, a common affliction in the West. As he passed across the threshold, the unmistakable odour of the cattle pen wafted across the room.

He said nothing, but stood just inside the door and slowly examined each face in the room. In his eyes, I saw a sudden look of familiarity and then displeasure as he walked past me and several other guests to stand before Carl Wyndham. They stared hard into each other's eyes for what seemed an interminable moment before the new arrival spoke.

"Yeah, it's me, Rogers," he declared menacingly, taking a step closer to the man with whom I had been dining. Instinctively, Wyndham's wife grasped the arm of her husband.

Wyndham's eyes narrowed as he peered into the face of the stranger, and a look of recognition crossed his visage.

"Lewis?" Wyndham said with disbelief. "Lewis Castor? Why, it can't be you! I'd heard you were killed in San Francisco two years ago!"

"Can be, and is," the man called Lewis replied flatly. "That little problem in San Francisco gave me a nice scar on my leg and a limp in my step, but it's hardly slowed me down. And I haven't given up lookin' for you, old *friend*," he said derisively. "Lookin' for you. And now, what do you know? Here you are." His mouth broadened into a malevolent grin.

The silence in the room was broken by Mrs. Wyndham's question, one which we all shared.

"Carl, who is this man?" she demanded. "And why did he call you 'Rogers'?"

"I heard you'd got yourself a new name, didn't you, Carl?" Castor remarked. "I can't say as I'm too surprised at that! And got yourself a

261

pretty young lady, too!" He grasped her left hand and examined it. "A wedding ring! Why, Carl, have you been so fortunate as to marry?"

Wyndham pulled his wife's hand out of the man's grasp.

"Take your hands off my wife!" he said threateningly.

Castor sneered again.

"Your *wife*?" he repeated. "Isn't that a fortunate development for you, my old *friend*." He looked to Mrs. Wyndham. "Married my old partner, did you, young lady? Recently, I would think." Mrs. Wyndham nodded without speaking. "I thought so. And I wonder what he told you of his life before he met you." He looked at Carl Wyndham with curiosity. "What did you tell her, Carl? It doesn't sound like you told her your real name, now, does it?"

"This isn't the right place or time for this," Wyndham asserted. "It's late, and your unexpected appearance has understandably upset my wife."

"I'm sure it was unexpected, but we have so much to talk about!" Castor protested.

"We can talk in the morning," Wyndham declared. "Right here, over coffee, if you like."

Castor looked around the room at the astonished guests and then back at Wyndham, who had wrapped a protective arm around his wife.

"Yeah, sure!" he agreed. "Nine o'clock tomorrow morning. Right here."

"Why not earlier?" asked Wyndham. "Say eight?"

"I got my own schedule, Carl," he replied. "I can make it by nine. You just be here and I'm sure we can work this all out nice and respectable." He turned to José Camarilla. "You got coffee here in the morning, right? And maybe some ham, eggs, and beans?"

The hacienda owner nodded his head in the affirmative.

"*Si, Señor,*" he said. "*Café y heuvos* – in the morning."

"Nine o'clock," Wyndham repeated, and then turned with his wife to climb the stairs to their room. As he passed the two abbesses sitting with the Reverend McSorley, he leaned down behind his wife's back and whispered something in the ear of Miss Esquélla. Her eyes widened and followed Wyndham and his wife as they ascended the stairway.

"I'll be here, Carl," called out the intruder. "Be sure you are, too."

"I'll be here," Wyndham affirmed as the couple disappeared up the staircase.

The man named Castor sat down in the seat that Wyndham had recently occupied and called over Ebeneezer Magillicuddy, the lad of perhaps thirteen who helped out around the hacienda and served the food from the kitchen.

262

"Get me a steak, boy," he demanded. "A large one – and put it on my old friend Rogers' bill." He looked defiantly at the staring faces around the room. "And some whisky."

Ebeneezer rushed to the kitchen to comply with the demand, and I turned to face Castor. The boy brought a large glass of liquor of which Castor had downed half by the time I had sat down across from him at the table.

"Well, I congratulate you on a rather dramatic entrance," I remarked as I lit a cigarette.

"And who would you be?" he asked in a desultory tone.

"Sigerson," I replied, offering him a cigarette, which he took with a nod of appreciation.

"That's an odd accent for these parts," Castor asked. "I take it you're a visitor, too, just like my old partner?"

"Right you are," I replied brightly. "Norwegian. Here to try some climbing in these beautiful mountains."

"Mmm hmm, they are beautiful, aren't they?" he said, looking out the window at the deepening blackness. "And loaded with gold. Silver, too, and a dozen other minerals that could make a man very rich." He took a deep draw on the cigarette, whose end glowed orange. "Made *some* people very wealthy, at any rate."

"I am guessing those 'people' do not include you, Mr. Castor," I ventured.

"No, they don't, though I don't know why it's any of your business."

"I can't say it is," I agreed.

We smoked in silence until he ground out the small stub of his cigarette. His steak arrived from the kitchen and he cut off a large piece. As he chewed it, he regarded me carefully.

"Now, Carl Rogers, he's a different story," he resumed. "Carl and I, well, we go back quite a ways. All the way to college together at Leland Stanford. He was a good student – a hard worker. And a solid friend." He looked away. "Back then, anyways."

"I infer you had some sort of a falling out with Mr. Wyndham – or as you call him, Rogers?" I asked. "Over a woman?"

He laughed coarsely. "Over *money*, Mr. Sigerson. Women aren't worth fighting over, in my experience. They come and go as they like, and there's no laying claim to them, not even when you put a wedding ring on their finger." He paused in thought. "But a mining claim, well, that's something different. That's where Carl and I had our falling out."

"Yes, you mentioned he had been your partner."

"That's true. We graduated together and decided we would set off to find our fortune in the Southwest – New Mexico, Arizona, maybe Utah.

Wherever there was land worth claiming. I had a bit of family money we could use to put together some equipment. Carl didn't have two nickels to rub together, but he sure had the technical knowledge. After banging around together for a year or so without much luck, we found ourselves in a bar in Santa Fe where we got into a conversation with an old forty-niner."

"A 'forty-niner'?" I repeated.

"California prospector," he explained. "Had spent years up in the gold country north of Sacramento. Made and lost a few fortunes, and was down on his luck. Dry as a bone and itching to get back to Frisco." He laughed softly. "He couldn't even remember what had got him to Santa Fe. He wouldn't stop talking about Frisco, and how he never should have left in the first place.

"Well, we ran across the old man a few more times over the next couple of weeks, and each time we bought him a drink, he looked worse and worse. One night, after he had had too many glasses of whisky, he tells us he has a deed to some land that he's convinced is loaded with molybdenum."

"Valuable, if you can mine it successfully," I noted.

Castor looked at me incredulously. 'Don't tell me you know about molybdenum,' he says.

I quickly realized it had been unwise to appear overly knowledgeable about such a little-known element. I needed to provide some explanation, since not one person in ten-thousand, I would estimate, would even admit to having heard of the substance.

"Rather little, I must admit, except that I recall reading it is valuable in the manufacture of steel," I weakly explained.

"That's it!" he cried. "Carnegie pays a fortune for the stuff!" He had finished the steak and lit a cigarette. "Well, anyway, the old man tells us he's got title to a mine in a place called Cerrillos, just south of Santa Fe, but he doesn't have the money to buy the equipment he needs to do the mining.

"'If you could get someone who'd provide the capital, would you go in as partners?' Carl asked him. The old man shook his head.

"'No, this is for me and me alone,' says he. 'I don't want no partner. I figure I can earn a bit here during the winter and then do some digging sometime in the spring.'

"'Well, if you change your mind,' Carl answered, 'you let us know because we might just be able to get you the money you need for the equipment.'

"About a week later, about ten in the evening, I was in the room we shared in the hotel and Carl comes in.

"'Say, you know that old prospector we've been running into,' he said. 'Well, here's some news. He's dead!'

"'Dead?' I repeated. 'He hadn't been looking too well, but he didn't look like he was fixing to die!'

"'Well, looking like it or not, he's dead now,' Carl says. 'They fished him out of the river downtown about a half-hour ago, and I saw the body myself.'

"'The Santa Fe *River*!'" I repeated incredulously. 'Why, there isn't enough water in that river to drown a cat, let alone that old man!'"

"Carl looked at me hard.

"'Look here, Lew, we've run into a bit of good luck,' he said. 'I saw that old man earlier today and he remembered me saying we had some money. He said he'd changed his mind about having a partner and wondered if he could have a small loan to tie him over, just to pay for his room and eats. Well, I saw a chance for us to get in on his good side and so I said, 'Sure, we can help a bit, but we need some collateral so's we are sure you'll pay us back.' Sure enough, the old fool digs into his pocket and hands over a folded piece of yellow paper.' Wyndham reached into his trousers, pulled out a paper and handed it to me.

"'Why, this is that deed to that land he said was working in Cerrillos," I said. 'This is what he offered as collateral?' Wyndham nodded his head.

"'It sure is!' he said. 'The old man handed it over in return for twenty dollars I gave him to tide him over.'

"I don't suppose there is a contract or any other sort of written agreement attesting to the accuracy of Wyndham's account," I inquired. Castor shook his head.

"And the deed?" I asked.

"Rogers, or 'Wyndham,' as you call him, said it was ours now, and we should be off to Cerrillos to work the claim," Castor answered. "I didn't feel right about it though. It sure seemed awfully convenient that the old man had up and died so soon after first refusing our offer to go in together, and then turning around and giving Carl that deed for a twenty-dollar loan. I didn't like the smell of it, and told him I was thinking of heading back to Frisco as soon as he could give me back some of the money I had forked out for the mining supplies. He said he had almost none of it left, after having given the twenty to the old man, but he promised to send me half of whatever he got from the mine. 'We're equal partners, remember,' he said. I thought that was okay, seeing as I'd provided the money and he was going to be doing the digging. A couple of days later, I packed up and headed off to California, and he went south to Cerrillos to dig for molybdenum.

"Every now and then I'd get a letter, usually telling me the mine still was coming up empty, and sometimes asking for some more money. I sent a few thousand I inherited from my father, but then a letter arrived maybe a year ago saying he'd decided the mine was no good. He was packing it in and leaving. He had sold what remained of our equipment and promised to send me about twenty-five dollars. The rest was his share, he said, due to his 'backbreaking labour' while I was living comfortably in San Francisco. That was the last letter I received from him."

"Why didn't you come out to look for him?" I asked.

"I was planning to do just that, but I ran into a bit of a problem in Frisco with one of the Tang gangs – the Chinese, you know – and I got cut up pretty bad. Took a while to recuperate, but once I did, I lit out to Cerrillos with a bad limp and a genuine interest in reconnecting with my old colleague."

He took a deep gulp of smoke from his cigarette and blew out a large cloud of blue smoke. "Well, no surprise: By the time I got there, Rogers was gone. Some other miners at The Black Bird Saloon told me the mine got played out pretty fast and then he lit out, but before it did, Rogers took something like two-hundred-thousand dollars or more out of it."

"That is a considerable amount," I agreed.

"Yeah. And the way I see it, about half of it was mine. I checked with some people in Durango, thinking he might have gone back there, but they hadn't seen hide nor hair of him in years. Pretty soon, I was out of money and reduced to working at odd jobs here and there just to stay alive in this God-awful desert country.

"With what little I made, I hired myself a detective, but he came up as dry as Rogers claimed the molybdenum mine had been." A grim look crossed Castor's face. "I got on his track in Albuquerque a while back, but then I lost him. I heard he'd gone off to Dallas, so I tracked him there, but again, he was long gone. A few weeks ago in Flagstaff, a railroad man told me a well-heeled guy fitting Rogers' description had paseded through a few days earlier on his way down to the red rock canyons. He was sporting a pretty new wife and flashing a thick wad of bills, bragging about a rich strike he'd made in New Mexico a few years back. But his name wasn't 'Rogers', I was told. Now it was 'Wyndham'. Well, I was determined not to lose him again, and now I found him."

A determined, hard look had come over Castor's face. "I'll get my money," he declared, thumping a thick finger on the table "or I'll get *him*. One way or the other, I swear it." I had heard enough threats from cheated men in my life to recognize the Castor was deadly serious.

266

The following morning, I arose early for a brisk walk before returning to the hacienda for breakfast, where I seated myself at a table with the Reverend McSorley and his two abbesses, who spoke in Spanish quietly between themselves. The cleric prattled on to me about the many frustrations inherent in his mission converting the local indigenous Indian people to Christianity, a challenge that had resulted in the unexplained disappearance of several of his predecessors. That grim record didn't seem to diminish his enthusiasm for his assignment, which was evident as he recounted a myriad of stories of clerical survival on the hazardous Western prairie.

After several unsuccessful efforts to excuse myself, I finally escaped the Reverend's attention for several hours and set off again, clambering amid the jagged red mountains that encircled the little outpost. The exertions proved most worthwhile. The vistas were extraordinary, and as the sun rose and fell, the colour of the monoliths mutated from deeper reds and yellows to flaming orange. Despite the morning chill of the autumn air, I was grateful to have heeded the innkeeper's admonition to carry substantial quantities of water along for by mid-day, as the sun had risen with a torrid effect.

The sun had begun to approach the western peaks when I returned to the inn. No sooner had I set foot inside the door than a most frantic Mrs. Wyndham flew down the staircase and seized me by the hand.

"Oh, Mr. Sigerson!" she gasped, pulling me further into the foyer. Her voice was deeply distressed and her hands were cold. "You must help me!" she pleaded. "You *must!*" I could see the look of fear in her eyes, which were rimmed in a deep pink from hours evidently passed in worry. I guided the poor woman to a chair near an open window through which a dry, dusty breeze was blowing and signaled to Ebeneezer for some water. The distraught woman produced a large white handkerchief and blew her nose into it with a force that couldn't have been exceeded by an East End stevedore.

Two large glasses of water had appeared on the table between us, and I reached over again to grasp Mrs. Wyndham's trembling hand.

"What is it you need from me?" I asked as solicitously as possible. "Your husband? Is he about?"

"No! No!" she cried. "That's the problem. He's gone!"

"Gone where?" I insisted.

"Into the hills, I suppose." She motioned indeterminately towards several nearby hulking peaks. "I really don't know!"

"When did he depart?" I inquired.

267

"This morning," she answered. "Do you remember from last evening? He was to meet that horrid man who was so positively insulting to him."

"Hadn't you intended to go out together?" I asked, observing her heavy cotton trousers, thick flannel blouse and sturdy hiking boots.

"Yes," she said. "That was our plan once he returned from his meeting."

"And did you go out to look for him when he failed to return?" I asked.

She shook her red hair in the negative.

"To tell you the truth, I dislike traipsing through rugged countryside," she protested. "This wasn't my idea of a holiday. It was Carl's plan to wander about in the mountains where he had laboured as a miner. I prefer to remain here by a warm fire and read."

"Do you know if followed through on the plan to meet Mr. Castor?"

She looked disturbed by my mention of the man's name.

"I have no way of knowing," she replied. "I suppose he did. I know nothing about that man. Nothing whatsoever."

"Were you not curious about why he knew your husband under a different name than Wyndham?" I asked.

"My husband's name is Carl Wyndham," she insisted. "Not *Rogers*, or anything else! That man was obviously mistaken in identifying my husband as this man Rogers."

I found it implausible that she hadn't demanded, and received, a fuller explanation of Castor's accusation, but I chose to ignore her prevarication in the interest of gathering information about the far more urgent matter of her husband's unexplained absence.

"Here is the curious thing," she said. "When we awoke this morning, Carl found a curious note on the floor that apparently had been slipped underneath the door while we slept."

She reached into a pocket and withdrew a sheet of paper that had been folded in quarters. She handed it to me, and I opened it. In the thin afternoon light, I could read the message, scrawled crudely in pencil:

The Devils Brige at 10. I will see you alone.

I turned the message over, but nothing else was written on either side of the page.

"Was it in an envelope?" I asked.

The distraught woman shook her head in the negative.

"No," I agreed, turning the paper over. "I rather doubted it would be."

"Carl asked me if I knew anything about it, but of course, I'd never seen it before. He said he had a good idea who must have put it under the door and rushed out, telling me to stay in the hacienda and not to go outside. I was worried about him, but I resolved to follow his instructions."

The paper wasn't normal stationery, but of a cheap quality and with one ragged edge, indicating that it had been torn hastily from a book. The handwriting was firm and the impression forceful. Evidently whoever had written the note had simply seized upon any available material. I looked about the parlour and spotted a cluster of books piled near the hearth.

"Help me look through these books, Mrs. Wyndham," I said.

"What am I looking for?" she asked.

"This page was likely torn from a book," I declared. "Perhaps if we can discover which book, we might have a clue as to the particular interests of whomever tore it out and slipped the note under your door."

For several minutes, Mrs. Wyndham and I poured through a dozen books or more in hopes of finding the remnants of the torn page. There were cheap novels and guide books, two Bibles, several monographs on Medieval history, one Chinese book on the care and cultivation of water lilies, and a biography of the late president, Abraham Lincoln.

"Focus on the end of the book!" I suggested, "as that will be where you're likely to find blank pages."

"Here!" she cried, holding up a volume. "A missing page! See if this one fits the note!"

I took the book and fitted the mysterious note to the tear: The match was indisputable. I turned over the book to observe its cover and showed it to Mrs. Wyndham: *Rare Gems and Metals of the Southwest*, the title declared, by Overton B. Draymyer, Ph.D., a professor at the Colorado School of Mines.

"Do you think whoever wrote the note just picked up the book from this pile, ripped out a page, and wrote on the paper?" she asked.

I considered the book closely.

"No, whoever was reading this book very likely had a genuine interest in the subject of gemology," I declared. "This book wasn't randomly chosen in hopes there was a blank page suited for a note. I suspect the author of the note was reading this book when seized with the idea of writing such a note."

"How would you know that?" she inquired.

I could see the young woman was intrigued and a bit confused by my assertion.

"These books all had a fine layer of dust on them from having been placed close to the hearth where ash has settled on them," I noted, pointing to the small collection we had examined. "This book, however, had none, either on the cover or on the edges, which suggests it was not placed by the fire until *after* the paper had been removed for the purpose of writing the note. Therefore, it was likely done by the person who removed the page, who in all likelihood had picked up this book from somewhere else in the room, and only deposited it here near the fire after removing the blank page on which the note was composed."

I had reached this conclusion so effortlessly that I had neglected to consider how remarkable it might be to hear such analysis from a Norwegian trekker. I looked up cautiously and saw a puzzled look on Mrs. Wyndham's face.

"Well, what difference does that make?" she inquired.

"Perhaps one of the other guests saw someone with this book," I suggested, "or saw him place it hear the fire. That might well be the person who ripped out the page and wrote the note. We shall have to make inquiries."

"Say," she said with a hint of suspicion, "you speak more like a police inspector than a hiker."

'Oh, I assure you that I've never aspired to be a member of the constabulary!" I insisted breezily, which was an honest declaration. "But there are far more important matters to consider." I stuffed the paper into my pocket and guided the young woman to a chair, sitting down beside her.

"What does this note signify to you?" I inquired.

She seemed taken aback by my question.

"But I know nothing of this note at all!" she protested.

"What of the reference in the note to 'The Devil's Bridge'?" I pressed, removing the paper from my pocket and displaying the writing to her.

She shook her head. "I'm afraid I can be of no assistance to you," she insisted. "I have no idea what the messages refers to, except that it gives every appearance of being a threat against the life of my husband."

"Excuse me, sir," a thin voice interrupted. Turning to look behind me, I saw the man Slits, who had risen from the chair he occupied.

"Yes?" I inquired in response, as Mrs. Wyndham looked on with an irritated look on her attractive young face.

"I heared you say somethin' 'bout the Devil's Bridge, din't I?" he asked. I was surprised to hear the faint but unmistakable accent of East London in his voice.

"Yes, I did mention the Devil's Bridge," I acknowledged. "Do you know what that is?"

"Yeah, sure I do," he replied. "Up one of these canyons. Not too far from here. It's a big stone arch." He held his arms wide open to signify the breadth of the bridge. "Biggest 'round here, for sure."

"Excellent!" I cried, stuffing the note back into my pocket. "Can you take me there straightaway?"

"Certainly not," he insisted, motioning to the chair he typically occupied. "I stay here now. Too old to be clambering around in the mountains."

"But this could mean a man's life!" I protested. Slits had returned to his solitary table.

"Say, I could take you!" the boy Ebeneezer cried, reminding me very much of Wiggins and the other Irregulars whom I had left behind in London. The lads had proven most essential to me in any number of my cases over the years, and I felt a pang of regret at having deceived them, as well as everyone else (other than my brother Mycroft) about having survived the Reichenbach Falls.

"Excellent," I said. "Let us be off."

The boy looked dubiously over his shoulder at the window where the last rays of the sun were filtering through the grimy glass and thick drapery.

He shook his head. "Nope, not tonight, Mister," he exclaimed. "Too late. Will be getting' dark within a couple hours, and there's some treacherous rock climbing to get to the bridge – , not to mention the chances of runnin' into a cougar or some other critter lookin' for some supper at sundown."

"But my husband!" the woman cried in protest. "He could be hurt out there!"

I motioned the young man to come closer.

"There's a ten-dollar gold piece in it for you if you take me there tonight," I explained. The effect on the boy was dramatic.

"Ten dollars, you say?" he exclaimed. "Let me get some lanterns, and we can start off in five minutes!"

He disappeared into a room behind the hacienda's rudimentary reception desk and I turned to Mrs. Wyndham.

"I had little doubt a little gold would persuade him to change his mind," I explained.

In a few minutes, the young boy had returned with a pair of lanterns that he lit as we stood outside the hacienda's door.

"Now, you must try not to worry," I told her, although I was not confident of what we might discover. "I'm sure they will give you something to eat while we are off to examine the Devil's Bridge."

"You certainly don't think I'm going to sit here alone worrying about my husband while you're off traipsing about the mountains in the dark!" she declared.

271

"But it wouldn't be safe!" I protested. "You heard Ebeneezer's warnings."

"It's no less safe for me than for you, Mr. Sigerson," she declared. "I shall be perfectly fine." She spread her hands to display her attire. "Besides, my husband bought me these clothes to wear when the going got a bit primitive," she said with a small smile. "Now, I'm ready to accompany you to look for him!"

I despaired at her insistence on accompanying Ebeneezer and me on the rescue mission, not the least of which because with her lack of experience, she would most certainly slow us down, which we could ill-afford with sundown rapidly approaching.

"I cannot agree," I protested. "I've been out climbing in these mountains, and I assure you it's no place for a lady, particularly at this time of the day."

"Believe me, he's right," said a voice behind me. While we had been engaged in our disagreement, a young man with leathery skin and rugged clothing of the American cowboy had entered the doorway and listened in on our conversation. "Pardon me for listening in, ma'am, but if you ain't a pretty seasoned hiker, I wouldn't recommend you headin' out to the Bridge at dusk. A lot can go wrong out there at night, and there isn't much anybody can do about it if it does."

"And who might you be?" I inquired of the new arrival.

He grinned and held out his hand. "I'm Jasper Jennings," he declared as we shook hands. "I handle the cattle at Messina's ranch, a ways out of town. Everybody round here knows me."

He looked around the room and focused back on Mrs. Wyndham. "You're much too pretty to be riskin' your neck climbin' around big rocks this late in the day, wouldn't you say, José?" The innkeeper looked blankly at Jennings, who laughed roughly at his own inappropriate remarks, but I also saw noted the faintest hint of a smile on the face of the young woman.

"I know these hills around here as well as anyone," the newcomer said, turning back to me. "If you could find your way to makin' it worth my while, Mister – Well, I wouldn't say 'No' to one of those coins you're handin' out."

I hesitated, not certain what to make of this stranger who seemed terribly interested in heading out into the mountains at sunset, although I suspected his interest in the attractive young woman might help explain his enthusiasm for assisting me in the search.

"Look, I can you out there pretty fast, and frankly, I wouldn't recommend you're going with just with that young'un." He jabbed his thumb towards the direction Ebeneezer had disappeared. "Ben couldn't find his behind in a full moon with both hands." He turned to Mrs.

272

Wyndham. "And as I said, I wouldn't recommend your goin' at all, ma'am."

Mrs. Wyndham briefly protested, but then agreed to remain behind after we promised to locate her husband or provide her a full report upon our return. Satisfied with the compromise, we walked outside and Jennings disappeared behind the hacienda. He soon returned with Ebeneezer leading several substantial steeds. In a single, fluid motion, Jennings swung himself up and into the saddle of a large Appaloosa, and the boy did the same on a smaller pony.

"Okay," Jennings declared, motioning me to mount the remaining horse, "might as well move along as quickly as possible. This light ain't gonna last much longer."

I was somewhat chagrinned at the prospect of straddling the girth of one of these American behemoths, but there appeared no alternative if we hoped to reach our destination before nightfall. I grasped the thick mane of my horse – Beelzebub, by name – and launched myself up and onto the hard, odiferous saddle. The sun was sinking lower in the sky and the air was becoming decidedly chillier as Ben and I followed Jennings northward out of Oak Creek and towards the trail leading to the Devil's Bridge.

We hadn't ridden far into the canyons before I had become exceedingly uncomfortable. Americans, especially in these Western states, think nothing of clambering atop a two-thousand pound animal, sitting on a saddle that is as hard as a rock with nothing but a set of flimsy rawhide reins to control the stubborn creature. The experience made me decidedly nostalgic for London's hansom cabs, where both the discomfort and the smells are considerably less bothersome.

After twenty minutes of climbing up the mountain, we could look down upon the faint lights of the ranch houses strewn aimlessly around Oak Creek. Jennings pulled up his horse and swung himself down onto the trail. Before us, a wall of rock present a barrier to our proceeding any further on horseback. We all dismounted and gathered around Jennings.

"This is as far as we can go on horses," he knowingly said. He pointed to the obstacle blocking our way. "Here's where we do a bit of climbing." With Jennings in the lead, we ascended the cliff that was twenty feet in height, but, thanks to numerous outcroppings, not difficult to climb, and soon emerged onto a fairly narrow pathway.

"We can walk along here," Jennings said, "but be careful, especially in this light! You don't want to put a cactus thorn through your shoe or step on a rattler," which was his term for one of the poisonous snakes known to inhabit the region. We walked briskly for ten minutes, until the path opened onto a broad, flat area that sloped slightly away to our left.

Even in the thinning light, the view of the soaring dusky-colored mountains with their odd shapes and projections, was spectacular. Behind them, the sky was beginning to glow with an orange hue.

We followed Jennings around a bend, and then our destination suddenly came into view: *The Devil's Bridge*!

The Devil's Bridge

It was a stunning and yet terrifying sight: A massive stone arch of fifty or sixty feet in length that emerged as a thick protrusion from the cliff before narrowing towards its center, where it couldn't have been more than three feet in width and only slightly more in thickness. Deep vertical crevices cut their way through the stone all along its course, creating a distinct impression that, at any moment, the entire formation could crumble.

Beneath this archway was a harrowing void, and only when one ventured out onto the abutment could one look down to see the canyon floor two-hundred feet below. Recollections of the Reichenbach chasm were understandably acute in my memory as I contemplated venturing out to peer into the gorge.

274

"Here, let me go first," proposed Jennings, "I'm a lot more familiar with the path than any of you." He stepped onto the bridge and motioned for me to follow. "Be careful, Sigerson," he warned unnecessarily. "A foot placed in the wrong spot will loosen up some of these rocks and, well, I don't need to tell you that your chances of surviving a fall from up here aren't too good."

We ventured out on the bridge along the cracked and narrow path. We had nearly reached the terrifying halfway point when Jennings thrust his hand backward towards me.

"Sigerson, take a look down there!"

In the murky dusk, I followed Jennings' outstretched hand that pointed beneath the span of the Devil's Bridge. There, several hundred feet below, on the rocky plain, sprawled a crumpled figure. From its location, there could be little doubt that the victim had plunged from the height upon which we now stood.

The light was thin and the rock below in shadows. For a moment, I considered how Jennings was able to see the figure so quickly

There certainly was little question about the fate of the man lying prostrate beneath the arch. Even had Watson been with me, I instinctively knew there was little medical science could offer. We rushed back to the safety of the ledge from which the bridge projected and scurried down to the canyon floor where the body lay face down, his arms splayed out to his sides. The long plunge had resulted in the grotesque fracturing of the skull and a splattering of blood and brain tissue that was gruesome in the extreme.

Lighting an oil lamp we had brought with us, I knelt down beside the body. There was no question about the identity of the dead man. Even with his injuries, there was enough of his face to confirm he was the man with whom I had conversed only the evening before. His trouser pockets contained a billfold with a few American dollars, several coins, and a wallet. Whatever the explanation for the tragedy, robbery didn't seem to be a strong motive.

One couldn't rule out the possibility of an accidental plunge off the precipice. An inadvertent turn of an ankle, or unintentional stumble would send a hiker careening a into the void. And there were grimmer possibilities. The note Mrs. Wyndham had found in her room suggested Wyndham had come to this spot to meet someone. Perhaps that person, or someone else, had surprised him. I certainly couldn't rule out the likelihood that a confrontation had taken place leading to a tragic outcome, Could it have been Lewis Castor? Or might Jennings have played a role? I recalled his friendly exchange with Mrs. Wyndham back at the hacienda. Had they previously met, and had he already been out to the Devil's Bridge

275

earlier in the day? He certainly seemed as entranced by the attractive Mrs. Wyndham, as the lady's husband had been when he quickly married her, so soon after their meeting.

Ebeneezer Magillicuddy stood transfixed by the sight of the wretched corpse. "I ain't never seen no dead man afore," he croaked.

In the weakening light, I could identify nothing else in the vicinity that might prove informative about what had occurred. There was little but stone and ground vegetation. Not far from the body rested a three-foot segment of one of the long stalks that rise up out of the cactus plants, although none of those cacti were in the immediate vicinity.

Jennings looked at the crumpled figure on the ground.

"Well, Sigerson, it don't look to me like there's a whole lot to be done at all," he advised. "Man's dead. End of story." I couldn't help but note his lack of empathy.

"Perhaps," I mused. "Of course, we will have to determine how he ended up here."

"Not too difficult to figger that out," Jennings offered. "Slipped and fell, I would guess. Wouldn't be the first time."

"Or he was pushed," I added.

"Pushed?" he repeated.

There was little more to be done at the site of the tragedy, but the prospect of carrying the body down the mountain to the horses in the failing light seemed risky. I asked whether we might not wrap the corpse in a wool blanket Jennings had brought along and leave it overnight, returning in the morning to move the corpse back to Oak Creek.

"Not in these parts," Jennings said with a laugh. "Between the cougars and coyotes, there wouldn't much of him left by dawn."

We wrapped the body as best we could in the blanket.

"Better bring along that stalk as well," I advised, pointing to the caucus shoot."

"What you need that for?" Jennings questioned.

"Let's just bring it along," I suggested.

"Better use gloves, Ben," advised Jennings. "That thing is loaded with thorns and you'll be pickin' them out of your hands for a week."

Ebeneezer cautiously scrambled down the mountain with the cactus stalk to our horses while Jennings and I maneuvered our grisly cargo along the cliff and to the horses. We rode in silence with the shattered remains of Carl Wyndham, or Rogers, lashed unceremoniously onto the back of Jennings' Appaloosa. By the time we arrived back at the hacienda, the sky had grown dark.

The windows glowed orange in the moonless night, and an infinite number of stars such as no resident of London, or any other modern city, could imagine seeing sparkled in the heavens. We couldn't bring Wyndham's body, still rolled in the wool blanket, into the building, and decided it should remain in the chill of the ice house overnight. Jennings and I placed it in a large feedbox with a heavy, hinged cover where it would be protected from the coyotes and other scavengers of the desert. As Jennings went inside, I took the opportunity to use my glass to examine Wyndham's gruesome injuries in greater detail thanks to the illumination provided by a lantern.

As I entered the hacienda several minutes later, a fire blazed in the hearth and Señor Caramilla was serving the guests who had patiently awaited our return. Castor had returned and sat alone at the same table that he'd occupied the evening before. He was again drinking whisky from a tall glass and eyed me suspiciously as I entered the room. Ebeneezer, while but a boy, had secured a sizable glass of beer, as had the Reverend McSorley, who had several empty glasses arrayed in front of him. The abbesses had opted for tea, as did I, while Jennings stood by the bar with a glass of spirits. He reached into his pocket to remove a small leather bag that he opened and deftly poured some tobacco into a small rectangle of paper, which he rolled into something roughly approximating a cigarette. Unsurprisingly, Splits once again occupied his solitary seat in the shadows. On the far side of the room, a large man unfamiliar to me sat in another chair.

The murmur of conversation abated abruptly when Mrs. Wyndham emerged from her bedroom and descended the stairs to join the others. She was still wearing the hiking outfit she was wearing before we had left for the Devil's Bridge. She walked up to me and reached for my hand. The crackling of logs in the fireplace was the only discernible sound in the room.

"You haven't found my husband?" she demanded, anxiously surveying the room in search of the missing man.

"We found him, all right," Jennings disclosed. "Or maybe I should say, what's left of him."

José Camarilla was startled by the inelegant words and dropped a glass he was carrying, shattering it into a thousand slivers as it struck the stone floor. The unfamiliar man rose to his feet, but said nothing as Mrs. Wyndham gasped and brought a delicate hand to her mouth. As her knees began to buckle, I grasped her arm and eased her into a chair.

"Fell off the Bridge, he did," Ebeneezer exclaimed excitedly. "Cracked his head open like a gourd!"

"Silence!" McSorley rebuked. "Show some respect for the man."

Mrs. Wyndham's composure had dissolved utterly upon hearing this shocking news. Her large blue eyes filled with tears that ran down her powdered cheeks and onto her blouse.

"He couldn't have fallen!" she cried. "A more sure-footed climber there never was! He has spent years working in the mountains." She turned to me. "I must see my husband!" she declared. "Right now!"

"I don't think that's a very good idea," said Jennings. "I'm afraid it isn't a very pretty sight. He took quite a tumble."

She looked suspiciously at Jennings, and then to me. "Do you agree that he fell?"

"That's one possible explanation," I said, "although not the version I find especially compelling." I paused, and then asked, "Did your husband have enemies in this area?"

She shook her head in disagreement.

"None that I know of," she answered, before turning to glare at Castor, whose accusation the prior evening suddenly took on a new import. "I don't suppose you would be included among his close friends."

"I won't deny that your husband was no friend to me," declared Castor. "At least not any longer," "But I don't believe in killing everyone that I have a disagreement with! I had nothing to do with his death, I swear."

"Maybe he jumped!" offered Ebeneezer excitedly.

"God forbid!" invoked Father McSorley, shocked by the mention of suicide. Using his right hand, he fashioned a cross on his chest. "Is that possible?"

"No, it certainly is *not* possible!" Pearl Wyndham insisted. "Carl was very content with his life. We had made many plans together. There is no chance he would have done such a terrible thing."

"Mrs. Wyndham has a point," I noted. "A man need not travel several miles through difficult terrain, clamber up a dangerous cliff, and venture out on a thin, perilous archway in order to kill himself." A number of people in the room murmured in agreement. "Why go through all that trouble when there are many other opportunities much closer by? No, I cannot accept that explanation, regardless what pressures might have been incumbent upon him. The facts compel us to consider alternative explanations."

"You have an idea, then, as to what actually occurred?" asked Jennings.

"I have no such thing," I replied. "It's pointless to speculate when one lacks the facts."

"I couldn't agree more," declared the heavy-set, grim-faced man to whom I hadn't yet been introduced. As he stood and walked towards me,

I observed deep lines that streaked out from the corners of his eyes to his ears and several days of stubble covering his lower face. Wild tufts of gray-and-black hair were fighting to escape from underneath his wide-brimmed hat, and long gray hairs sprouted from his large ears. His tanned and weathered hands sported large knuckles that reflected years of hard work, and likely a number of poorly healed fractures.

He eyed me warily before turning to Mrs. Wyndham, who had resumed a quiet weeping, her head buried in a large white handkerchief that muffled her plaintive sobs. He next rested his eyes on Castor, whose belligerent countenance remained unaffected by the death of his one-time partner. He then gave Jennings a knowing nod and turned to face me.

"Who exactly did you say you are, Mister?" he asked me bluntly.

"The name is Sigerson," I replied, "and I wonder if I might not ask the same of you?"

The man looked annoyed by my innocent question and Jennings sniggered.

"My name's Fitzgibbon," the man repeated in a bored affect. "Pace Fitzgibbon. I happen to be the sheriff around here." He moved the lapel of his leather jacket to reveal a tarnished silver star pinned to the inside. "So I get to ask the questions, Mister," he declared, looking me over with a profoundly disapproving gaze. "You ain't from these parts, it's pretty clear. What's that accent you got?" His eyes narrowed. "You aren't some damned Frenchie are you? We don't need no damned Frenchies out here."

I struggled not to exhibit my disdain for his lack of linguistic diagnosis and decided to accentuate my practiced Norwegian accent.

"No, not French!" I assured him, "Norwegian." The sheriff looked puzzled by my explanation.

"Where's that?" he declared. His unfamiliarity with the map of Europe was not surprising, as I've found Americans to be quite insular in their knowledge of the continent from which most of their ancestors had departed.

"Quite near England," I responded, expecting the mention of a familiar nation would place the sheriff at ease, but he snorted and made a disapproving comment about "dandies" under his breath, drawing another guffaw from Jennings. "And now that we have had our geography lesson," I continued, "perhaps we could focus on the more important question before us: Who killed Carl Wyndham – or perhaps, as Mr. Castor would insist, Mr. Carl Rogers?"

My statement caused a great commotion to arise in the room, and even Mrs. Wyndham pulled her face out of the handkerchief.

"Killed?" Sheriff Fitzgibbon exclaimed. "Who said anything about him being killed? I thought he fell off the Devil's Bridge."

"I expect that is precisely what the murderer wanted you to believe," I replied. "After all, when you find someone under such circumstances, the first thought is likely to be that he tripped, or that a rock must have given way, causing him to fall."

"But you don't think so?" Jennings said suspiciously.

"No, I'm quite certain that he did not trip," I replied. "I'm persuaded that he fell to his death, thrown off balance after being struck with one of those impressive cactus shafts, most likely from behind."

"And why would you guess that's what happened?" asked the sheriff.

"Oh, it's a poor habit to guess," I assured him. "You must have the facts before you can speculate with any certainty about what might have occurred."

"What are you, some sort of a police inspector?" Sheriff Fitzgibbon asked, looking skeptically at me. "You seem to think like a lawman."

Immediately, I feared that my reflexive analysis had raised questions about my true identity. "Oh, no," I declared. "I just read those detective stories that appear in the penny weeklies."

"Well, how'd you figure Wyndham got hit in the head before he fell?" Fitzgibbon pressed. "You didn't read that in no detective story."

"I was very curious about the injuries on Mr. Wyndham's head," I explained.

"Pretty serious injuries," Jennings agreed, "but I don't see why you'd say he was hit with something. Seems to me the damage was done when he fell."

"The damage to his face was almost certainly due to the fall," I agreed. "But I was referring to an injury I found on the *back* of his head, one that was largely obscured by his hair and – " I looked apologetically towards the new widow. " – his other extensive injuries that commanded our attention."

"From that height, damage to the back of his head could have also been caused by the fall, don't ya think?" the sheriff hypothesized.

"Certainly that could be the case. But the large lump on the back of his head was the only indication of an injury on that side of his body."

"Could have been an older injury, right?" Castor inquired.

"I think not," I replied as I removed a cigarette from my case and lit it. "The blood was quite fresh, and any earlier bleeding likely would have coagulated quite quickly in this exceedingly dry climate. Moreover, I suspect the size of the inflammation would have been significantly less had the injury been inflicted much more than ten minutes before he fell. And then there is the matter of the organic material clearly embedded in the wound that is inconsistent with an injury caused by falling onto rock."

"Could have banged his head on a tree when he was hiking out to the bridge!" offered Ebeneezer.

"The wound was far too severe to have been caused by merely bumping his head on a branch," I answered. "No, I'm quite certain that he fell to his death after being struck from behind with that segment of cactus we found near his body. I didn't notice any plant of that type in the immediate area, so that stalk most likely had been carried to the vicinity and fallen or tossed down after it was used to strike Wyndham.

The sheriff was clearly intrigued by this observation and I immediately regretted blurting it out.

"Well, I didn't see no wound on the back of his head," Jennings protested.

"I'm not surprised," I responded. "Understandably, you were so transfixed by the terrible injuries to Wyndham's face that you neglected to examine the rest of his body. It's a little lesson I learned from the magazine detectives."

From a darkened corner of the room, a low whistle was emitted from the man known as Slits. Still, he said nothing and made no effort to join the conversation.

"But if someone wanted him dead, why send him all the way out to the Devil's Bridge?" Father McSorley interjected. "He could have just accosted Wyndham right here in town."

"Ah, but falling from the bridge would create an impression of an accidental death," I explained, "and the probability was that the murderer assumed the injury to the head would have gone undetected." Heads nodded in agreement at this comment. "It's always a mistake to assume anything," I added.

Sheriff Fitzgibbon looked quizzically at me again.

"You *sure* you ain't no copper?" he asked dubiously. "You sound an awful lot like a copper."

"I assure you," I said truthfully, "I'm no 'copper'!"

"Why didn't this other person just push Wyndham off the bridge?" Jennings asked. "Then there wouldn't a been no lump on the back of the head for you to discover?"

"An excellent question, Mr. Jennings, and the answer, I suspect, is quite instructive. Hitting Wyndham with a pole allowed the killer to avoid coming too close, where fisticuffs might have ensued with a very different outcome, especially if Wyndham might well have been the more powerful combatant. Hitting him from a distance of several feet, as Wyndham was facing the opposite direction, provided the murderer with a measure of personal security."

I could see that my analysis intrigued the sheriff.

"So," he summarized, "you think he was standing on the Devil's Bridge, maybe not even aware the other person was there, and that other person sneaked up on him quiet-like, hit him from behind with this stick or whatever, pitching him off the bridge onto the rocks below, and then tossed that stalk down after him?

I clapped my hands in approval. "I think that is an excellent summary of the facts," I said. "At least, it's quite consistent with the available facts, wouldn't you say?"

"Well, then who was the other person?" Fitzgibbon asked. "You seem to know everything else that happened on the bridge!"

"Oh, I don't think there is much doubt who that other person is, or that he's in this very room," I said, withdrawing a pipe from my jacket. I inspected the remaining plug in the bowl, and then struck a match to light it. "Rather an elementary matter, Sheriff Fitzgibbon, which we should be able to tie up relatively swiftly. In the meantime, I suggest that you instruct everyone to stay right where they are."

My comments caused each person there to cast probing eyes about the room. Another low whistle emerged from the darkened corner where Slits remained hunched over his whisky.

The sheriff coughed harshly and spit some foul excretion into a ceramic jar on the floor. Removing his hat, he scratched his balding head for a moment and replaced his hat.

"Yah, what this fellow says is what we'll do," he said thoughtfully. He moved close to me and, in *sotto voce*, questioned, "What *is* it you're thinkin' we should do?"

I hesitated for a moment, since assuming more of a leadership position in the inquiry could raise yet additional questions about my background. Were my true identity exposed, I had little doubt that word of Sherlock Holmes's presence in America would make its way back to Moriarty's remaining gang members in London and two years of diligent effort at concealment could be lost. I quickly determined, however, that my chances of exposure in this remote desert outpost were minute, so long as my true identity remained unknown. Moreover, from what I had seen of Fitzgibbon's investigative skills, my refusal to participate in the investigation would almost certainly result in allowing a clever murderer to escape justice, an outcome which I found intolerable.

"Well, any inquiry of this sort would have to begin by asking the very basic question of why any crime should be committed," I began. "The motive. *Cui bono* is the term the literary detectives use: *Who benefits?*"

"Well, I dare say it's pretty clear who in this room had a bone to pick with Wyndham," declared Jennings. He pointed his finger at the Castor, who rose, scowling in anger, and pointed back at his accuser.

282

"You watch what you say, you scoundrel!" he threatened. "I would advise you against making irresponsible accusations you cannot support. I can see it looks black against me because of that altercation with Rogers last night. Why, I'd wager half of you already can see me on the gallows. But there isn't a scintilla of evidence against me! You would do well to look elsewhere for your murderer."

"Or what?" Sheriff Fitzgibbon interrupted. Castor sat back down and continued to glower nervously. "That sounds a lot like a threat to me, fella, an' threats out here have a way of leading to trouble."

"I didn't do anything!" Castor again insisted, though from the disapproving looks of most people in the room, he seemed justified in believing that most of those in the room had already concluded the one-time partner of the dead man was the leading suspect.

"Well, where were you when Carl Wyndham got himself kilt?" Jennings pressed. "You wasn't here, that's for sure."

"I suppose I have no credible alibi," Castor lamented. "I haven't got much money, as you know, and I can't afford a room, not even in a modest hotel as this. I pitched a tent down the road a bit and was there all last night."

"Was you by yourself?" the sheriff pressed.

"Well, who do you think would be spending the night with me in a tent?" Castor answered with disdain. "Yes, by myself!"

"And this morning," I noted, "weren't you supposed to meet him right here at nine o'clock to talk out your dispute over the mine."

"That's right," he agreed. "I was here at nine, but Wyndham never showed. The innkeeper can confirm I waited about an hour, and then I took a walk of my own, but I didn't go anywhere near the Devil's Bridge." He paused to collect his thoughts. "Oh, I admit I was angry at Carl last night, real angry. The man cheated me out of all my money, and didn't want to share any of his earnings – the wealth *my* investment secured for him! That would make anyone angry."

"Angry enough to kill him?" I asked.

"Well, maybe," he admitted, "but killing him certainly isn't going to get me my money back, is it? I'd likely have had more luck suing him for embezzling my share. Judges out here aren't too sympathetic to people who jump claims and steal other peoples' investments."

"That's true enough – if you're thinkin' straight," Sheriff Fitzgibbon agreed. "But if you've gotten a snortful of mescal or tequila from José – " He pointed to the hacienda manager. "A man might *not* be thinking too straight. Wouldn't be the first time booze led a man to do somethin' he ordinarily wouldn't consider."

He turned to me and squinted. "How 'bout it, what's-yer-name? You think Castor here is the killer?"

"My name is Sigerson," I reminded him. "Possibly. But he might not be the only one with a motive."

I saw Castor nod at me in appreciation.

"Well, who else could it be?" inquired the Reverend McSorley. "If it was murder, there had to be a motive, right? You just said so yourself."

"Correct," I agreed. "Motives can be difficult to ascertain. Sometimes they're born of a long-term grievance, like that of Mr. Castor here against his former business partner. But a motive may arise over something recent that appears quite insignificant. For example, I couldn't help noticing that you were rather displeased last evening with the attention Mr. Wyndham here was paying to your travelling companion, Miss Esquélla." I motioned to the younger of the two abbesses to whom Wyndham had whispered indiscreetly the previous evening.

"I beg your pardon!" McSorley responded indignantly.

"And I might add, Reverend, I'm less-than-persuaded your companions are truly women of the cloth, as you profess."

The two women, supposedly capable only of speaking Spanish, looked at each other, but remained silent.

"As chaste as the day is long!" sputtered the surprised priest.

"The face powder on your jacket collar suggests something different," I pointed out.

Sheriff Fitzgibbon spit into the crockery again and leveled a gaze at McSorley, who looked at his collar and brushed away the incriminating powder. The two women seemed suddenly to understand their status had become a topic of conversation and drew back behind their protector.

"Now, that's curious, ain't it?" the sheriff asked. "Mebbe you ain't who *you* say you are?" (I presumed he meant "*maybe*".) "Sigerson has a point here. In my experience, a preacher don't travel around these parts with two women too often, let alone with women who are as attractive as these two." He squinted hard at the priest. "You got anything to prove you're a real preacher?"

McSorley stepped forward and thrust out his pointed chin.

"As a man of the Lord, I'm unaccustomed to being denigrated," he asserted.

"I dunno what that means," the sheriff responded, a look of irritation spreading over his leathery face, "but answer my question, if it ain't too difficult for you. You got any proof you're a genuine preacher?"

"No, I don't carry around proof certifying that I'm a man of the cloth!" McSorley asserted.

"Or that these two women are abbesses, I would imagine," I added.

284

The priest glared at me with a most un-Christian-like demeanor.

"Let's say, for the sake of argument, that Carl Wyndham discovered that you weren't a 'man of the cloth', but a charlatan, and that these women accompany you for less than, shall we say, Christian purposes." McSorley grew even redder in the face. "I think it's more than fair to say that his threat to expose such a charade would jeopardize the likelihood of your persuading innkeepers like Señor Caramilla to provide you and your abbesses with free lodging and nourishment. Such a threat might very well constitute a motive to confront Wyndham, mightn't it?"

"Why, you – !" McSorley exploded with a most unpriestly invective.

"I wondered if Wyndham's whispering a rather suggestive offer to one of these young ladies last evening – an offer I have no doubt she communicated to you – might not have inflamed what appears to be a most volatile temper! Perhaps a threat to expose your duplicity?"

McSorley's temper was, indeed, on the verge of erupting at gargantuan levels, leading the sheriff move protectively in my direction in hopes of shielding me from his wrath. For his part, Señor Caramilla appeared to have comprehended a sufficient amount of the conversation to appreciate the potential hucksters who had been taking advantage of his religiously inspired hospitality for the better part of a week.

"I'm going to need to see some credentials from you, Padre," the sheriff advised McSorley. "If you ain't who you say you are – Well, that there's charges of fraud and prob'ly somethin' a whole lot worse in your future."

"A secondary matter, I would venture," I interrupted. "There are other possibilities, of course. Mr. Jennings, you appeared at a rather opportune moment this evening."

The smile faded from Jennings' face and he stood up and squared his shoulders. "Wait a minute," he demanded. "I didn't even arrive until after this Wyndham had left. I didn't know the man or his wife. Why'd I go off and kill him?"

"One need not know someone to attack them," I refuted. "Perhaps you encountered him, offered to show him some local sites, and discovered he was a man of some affluence. You might well have arranged a little 'accident' out at the Devil's Bridge, taken most of his money, and then conveniently arrived here late this afternoon in time to lead us back to find his body."

"That's a lie!" he cried. "Why, you know there was money on him when we found him. I couldn't have robbed him!"

"There was *some* money on him," I agreed, "but there might well have been considerably more. Perhaps what remained was overlooked in your hurry to escape before others came across the scene."

Jennings glowered at me and emptied his pockets on a table.

"There, you dam'd Norwegian!" he cried. "Ain't none of his money on me!"

I shook my head in disbelief. "You know this countryside well," I corrected him. "Surely you would hide the money in a place where only you could find it, rather than risk having it found on you. You had hours to bury it before arriving at the hacienda and volunteering to serve as our guide."

My comments had succeeded in exciting considerable unease. In only a few short minutes, I had raised a rationale for no less than three of those in the room to have attacked Carl Wyndham, all for very disparate reasons.

"Of course, there is a most significant clue we haven't yet discussed: The handwritten note summoning Carl Wyndham, or Rogers, to the Devil's Bridge early this morning." I turned to the young widow who had been watching this interchange with a look of horror on her face.

"Have you any idea who might have put that note under your door?" I inquired. "Any idea at all?"

She shook her head slowly in the negative.

"I'm afraid I'm going to have to ask you a question in private, Mrs. Wyndham, with just the sheriff joining me" I advised. Fitzgibbon looked curious, but moved to join me in escorting the widow to a small alcove beyond the earshot of those in the parlour. "Again, my apologies, Mrs. Wyndham, but I most pose this to you."

"Go ahead, Mr. Sigerson," she said evenly. "What is it you wish to know?"

"Yes, what d'you wanna know?" the sheriff repeated with some irritation.

"The note. There is no question, I suppose, that it wasn't intended for your husband?"

"I just don't understand what you mean, Mr. Sigerson," she replied, a demure look in her eyes. The sheriff looked quizzically at me.

"Could the note have been intended for *you*?" I asked.

"For *me*? Why, I don't understand what you mean."

The sheriff was clearly losing his patience with my questioning.

"Yeah, what are you talkin' about, Sigerson?" he demanded.

"I make it a point to assume nothing," I explained, adding, "in my business dealings. The note supposedly was slipped under the door to your room."

"What d'you mean 'supposedly'?" Mrs. Wyndham sharply rebuked, her polished diction slipping inadvertently. "I told you Carl said he found it on the floor of our room this morning."

"Yes, that's what you said," I agreed. "But I must consider that it might not have been intended for your husband, but for *you*. And instead of slipping it under the door, might it instead have been given to you by someone last evening?"

Her eyes grew wide and her mouth set hard in a straight line.

"Say, what the heck are you suggestin'?" Fitzgibbon asked. "You think someone was schemin' to meet Mrs. Wyndham out at the Devil's Bridge, and her husband found out about it and went out to confront whoever it might a been trying to see his wife?"

I raised my palm towards both of them.

"I'm making no accusation. But the fact is that we know nothing whatsoever about the provenance of this note. It might have been a summons to Wyndham, which led him out to the Devil's Bridge for some reason we have yet to determine. But it might also have been an admirer's communication to this young lady suggesting an assignation in a remote location where her husband couldn't find them. If Carl Wyndham discovered the note and went to the Devil's Bridge to confront his would-be cuckolder, it wouldn't be difficult to imagine how a confrontation leading to Wyndham's death might have occurred."

Mrs. Wyndham looked at me with a gaze that I interpreted as more defiant than fearful.

"I resent your insinuation, Mr. Sigerson!" she responded. "There was no man trying to see me! And I wouldn't have accommodated him if there was! But I'll tell you this: If he'd a tried, yes, my husband would've knocked him in the head and dropped *him* off the Devil's Bridge! I assure you – no Lothario would've gotten the drop on Carl."

Sheriff Fitzgibbon could barely suppress a smile at the young woman's indignant words.

"Does that tell you what you want to know, Sigerson?" he asked.

I sheepishly nodded in the affirmative.

"I sincerely hope I didn't offend," I said. "As I've mentioned, my practice is to assume nothing, and I could therefore not presume such a plausible scenario did not occur."

The displeased young woman pushed past me as she walked in a huff back to the great room. We followed closely enough behind her to see her grasp the railing of the staircase and place her booted foot on the first step.

"Surely you aren't leaving now, before we've determined who bears responsibility for the death of your husband," I said.

"Let me tell you something, Mister," she responded. "My husband fell and kilt himself dead. I don't know why. I can't explain it, because he was all over these mountains for years afore he even knew me and he had feet like a mountain goat. But he fell, and that's that. And now," she stepped onto the staircase, "I'm goin' to bed, and tomorrow morning, making arrangements to take him home to Chicago on the next train I can book. And maybe you should head back to Norway or wherever you're from, Mr. Sigerson."

"It might take us a few days to sort out what's happened here," the sheriff corrected her.

"Perhaps I did not make myself clear," she responded. "I am leaving, and I am taking my husband with me. Whatever examinations or inquiries you need to make before then, you go right ahead and make. But as soon as I can arrange transportation to Flagstaff, neither you, nor Mr. Sigerson, nor anyone else is going to make me stay in this dreadful place."

It was clear that her plucky defiance had met with approval in the room. Her abrupt attitude reminded me of the British suffragists who were confrontationally demanding voting rights. Scowling, she moved several steps up the stairs before I called to her, "If you don't mind, Mrs. Wyndham, it would be most helpful to have you *here* for the denouement."

"The *what*?" said Sheriff Fitzgibbon. "Listen, Sigerson, I think she's got a point here. You're harassing her with all manner of inappropriateness. She has, after all, just lost her husband! Why don't you just tell us what you think really happened. You seem to have it all figgered out anyways."

Mrs. Wyndham was escorted back to her chair by a very attentive Jennings as I knocked the burnt ash from the bowl of my pipe, filled it with some shag, and put a match to tobacco.

"Yes, I suppose it's only right that I explain what transpired today," I said, "although the facts seem as clear to me as can be. I mentioned that most crimes can be explained by the principle of *Cui bono,* or *'Who benefits?'*" I reminded the group. "Well, let us examine the facts as we know them.

"Wyndham, then known as Rogers, and Castor were school chums at Stanford University." Castor nodded in agreement. "As we have learned, they soon became business partners in exploratory mining, with Castor putting up money from his family's accounts and Wyndham providing the expertise. Castor here returned to California while Rogers worked the mine, claiming to have found nothing, but in fact, becoming quite wealthy. And then he disappeared, leaving Castor with nothing."

I pointed to the chair where Sheriff Fitzgibbon was seated. "I presume you were quite relieved and surprised last evening to discover none other than Carl Rogers was here," I envisioned, "along with this young lady."

"Exactly right," Castor confirmed. "I didn't want to make a big deal about it in front of his wife, so I told him we needed to settle up the debt between us. I thought that was the plan for the meeting this morning that never happened."

"But you changed you mind about meeting here and slipped that note under his door suggesting a meeting at the Devil's Bridge," Jennings quickly interjected.

"Why would I do so?" Castor objected. "We had already set a meeting for nine o'clock right here. No, sir, I did not do that."

"Of course, you didn't," I said assertively.

"Well, now, how in the Hell did you known he didn't?" demanded the sheriff, who immediately apologised to Mrs. Wyndham for his use of profanity.

"Recall the note," I said, fishing then paper out of my pocket, unfolding it, smoothing it out and turning it so the assembled group could see it.

"Yeah, I see what it says!" declared the sheriff.

"But you do not observe what it shows!" I reprimanded. "Note how '*Devil's*' and '*bridge*' are spelled." Those in the room craned their necks to see the printing on the note:

The Devils Brige at 10. I will see you alone.

Sheriff Fitzgibbon shook his head in confusion. "Mister, I don't see your point at all."

"'*Devil's*' and '*bridge*'. The former word is missing the possessive apostrophe," I explained, pointing to the lettering, "and the latter word is misspelled."

"So, what of it?" asked Jennings in exasperation. "Any one of us could easily make them mistakes. We aren't much for *McGuffy's Reader* or spellin' lessons out here!"

"It's ironic that you should mention the work of William Holmes McGuffy, a second cousin of my father, twice removed," I noted, momentarily hesitating for fear of having inadvertently revealed my surname. But the confused look from all of the attendees convinced me there was little chance of any of them being genealogically curious under the circumstances. Only a grunt from the mysterious Slits was audible.

"With all due respect to all of you, I'm not surprised that you fail to identify the grammatical errors," I explained. "Anyone could easily make them, but it's unlikely a graduate of Leland Stanford Junior University would make such mistakes. Isn't that so, Mr. Castor?"

Castor looked at me through narrowed eyes.

"Yes, I know how to write simple possessives, if that is what you mean, Sigerson," Castor replied. "As I told you, I did not write that note, and I had never met Mrs. Wyndham before last night."

"I had no suspicion about your authorship of the note," I agreed. "Anyone who effortlessly uses the word 'scintilla' in conversation would doubtless know basic spelling. But you did have something that was very important to Mrs. Wyndham," I continued.

"What was that?" Castor demanded to know.

"A claim against Wyndham," I declared.

"I don't get you," interjected Jennings.

"If Castor could prove that he was a legitimate partner in what turned out to be a very profitable molybdenum mine, up to half of the fortune that had been taken from the mine might rightly belong to him."

"Well, then," insisted the sheriff, "Castor here had every reason to kill Wyndham."

"No, he did not," I corrected. "If Wyndham – or Rogers – were dead, the chances of Castor retrieving any of the money owed to him would be negligible, since it would be all-but-impossible to prove that the molybdenum mine was connected to his investment. No, Castor's best hope wasn't to kill Wyndham, but to assert a legal claim to Wyndham's banking records, take him to court, and attempt to recoup some of the money he was owed. It might take some time, but with enough effort, he could probably secure some restitution – either from a judge or maybe even from Wyndham."

"Then who wrote the note?" the sheriff asked, "and is that the same person who kilt Carl Wyndham?"

"Yes, it is. The author of that cryptic note, and the murderer of Carl Wyndham," I declared, turning to point at the defiant widow, "is none other than Pearl Wyndham,"

"What in tarnation?" Sheriff Fitzgibbon declared. "Will someone tell me what is happenin' here?"

"A clever plan," I said, "all the more so since it was devised on the spot."

"Is this true?" Fitzgibbon asked, looking to Mrs. Wyndham and them to me. "You're sayin' she kilt her own husband? But why?" He looked towards Jennings and then to the senoritas, who sat silently next to the man who might have been a priest, or perhaps was not.

Since the widow remained silent and defiant, I began to explain after first whispering a quick instruction to Ebeneezer.

"I will speculate," I said confidently, "which is uncharacteristic of me – and presume the issue was money – specifically Carl Wyndham's

290

money. The unexpected success of that molybdenum mine down in Cerrillos, New Mexico is the cause of this whole matter."

"How can you be so sure of that?" Jennings asked.

"Because it's the only explanation that logically makes sense, the only one in which all the links fit together into a durable. This is the progression of events as I anticipate they occurred:

"We know that the Wyndhams married recently after a brief courtship in Chicago, where Carl Rogers had settled under the assumed name of 'Wyndham', presumably to make it difficult for Mr. Castor or others from his earlier life to find him. As we now know, the molybdenum mine financed by Mr. Castor wasn't worthless, as Rogers had asserted, but fantastically productive. A year-and-a-half or so of hard labour had made him a wealthy man who had no intention of sharing his good fortune with the absent partner who had financed the mine's development.

"Mrs. Wyndham was an actress when her future husband met her – yes, I noted that Shakespearian reference to 'Lothario', which any actress worth her salt would know. But actresses merely learn lines, they rarely write them, and in my experience, they are beautiful and charming but hardly proficient at spelling and punctuation. A university-educated man like Mr. Castor was unlikely to mis-spell '*Devil's*' or '*bridge*', but a poorly educated actress very well might. That mis-spelling first raised my suspicion of Mrs. Wyndham. And then, naturally, one is always suspicious of the attractive young woman who quickly and conveniently falls head over heels for an affluent – but older and rather mediocre – specimen of man."

"Yeah, but any of us might have made them spellin' mistakes," protested Jennings. "Why do they point the finger of guilt at the lady?"

"Because while I doubted that she was the only person in the hacienda who might make a spelling error, she unquesionably stood to gain most from the death of Carl Wyndham," I explained. "None of you knew the man before his arrival in Oak Creek, and even if he had made intemperate asides to Miss Esquélla or threatened to expose the padre's masquerade, those were hardly reasons for murder."

The Reverend McSorley shifted uneasily in his chair but voiced no disagreement.

"There could have been something in their past that he'd come across," the sheriff protested.

"I admit to being somewhat curious about Mr. Slits over here, who seems very careful to keep his face hidden in the shadows whenever Mr. Wyndham was around. Perhaps they had some earlier unpleasantness between them."

Slits, in his seat in the shadows, made no motion in response to my comment. "But then agein, he behaved almost exactly the same way when Wyndham wasn't around, and so I deduced his predilection for solitude was likely unrelated to Wyndham and, as a result, that he had played no role in his death.

"What about Jennings?" Castor insisted. "He's been trying to catch Mrs. Wyndham's ever since he came in! And he knows the way out to the Devil's Bridge. He could'a lured Wyndham out there, killed him, and doubled back with you to 'find' the body. And that leaves Mrs. Wyndham a rich widow, which makes her even more attractive to him!"

Mrs. Wyndham winced at Castor's comment, and the expression on Jennings' face made it clear he did not appreciate the accusation either.

"What makes you think a filthy cowhand would hold the slightest appeal for me?" she responded.

"Precisely, Mrs. Wyndham!" I agreed. "Jennings might have had aspirations to win the affections of Mrs. Wyndham, but murdering her husband and hoping she would turn to him in her grief seems a bit far-fetched. No, I think the trail of facts leads directly back to Mrs. Wyndham." I turned to face the widow, who was listening intently to my remarks.

"I have no doubt that there was an altercation between her and her husband once back in the room about the nature of the dispute with Castor. Even if Wyndham refused to disclose the precise nature of their agreement or his reasons for adopting a new surname, Castor had already revealed enough for her to realize that his accusations placed her fortune potentially at risk."

"I'm afraid I don't follow you, Mr. Sigerson," said the young Ebeneezer.

"Under normal circumstances, a wife stands to inherit all of her husband's estate," I explained to the boy. "If he lived, Wyndham could have been ordered by a court to share half his fortune with Castor, who had financed the development of the mine that was responsible for Wyndham's wealth. It's even possible a court could have given the lion's share to Castor as the financier.

"Your courts, I note, are frequently sympathetic to those with the most capital resources. Either Castor or a law enforcement agent could also have pressed a criminal charges against Wyndham. And then there remains that matter of that old prospector who mysteriously died in the Santa Fe river after giving the deed to Wyndham for a mere twenty dollars. Perhaps that was not, on closer inspection, an accident. Any one of these actions might have cost Wyndham his fortune, his freedom, or both.

"That scenario was certainly not an appealing prospect for a young woman who had married a wealthy mine owner with expectations of a life of glamour and social standing in Chicago's high society. Now, because of this chance encounter in a remote hacienda in Oak Creek, Arizona, her entire privileged future seemed terribly at risk. Didn't it, Mrs. Wyndham."

I could see that everyone in the room was captivated by my account. Indeed, even the spectral Slits who, all had been hidden in the shadows, had turned in my direction.

I whispered instructions to young Ebeneezer, and as he slipped outside, I continued.

"Pearl Wyndham may not be educated," I said, with a nod of acknowledgement toward the young woman, "but she is clever. She knew that if her husband were to die before a claim could be made against him, she likely stood to inherit *all* of his money. Castor's chances for proving his claim, without Wyndham being available as a witness, would be slim."

Mrs. Wyndham had shrugged off the hand the sheriff had clasped around her arms and defiantly glared at me. Although I would never have dreamt of doing so in London, in this more primitive setting I decided to forgo niceties and offer her a cigarette, which she readily accepted. As I lit it for her and then one of my own, I continued my narrative.

"This morning, you arose before your husband, sneaked down to the parlour, and found the book from which you tore the page for your note. You chose a book on gemology to associate that field of study with whomever would be accused of writing the threatening note. Anyone who had been in this room, you knew, would have had access to that book and might have written the note, which meant a number of people would have become suspects.

"Returning to the room, you hastily wrote the extortion note and placed it on the floor where your husband would be certain to find it. Your husband understandably presumed the author was none other than Castor, who was providing a time and place for their meeting to resolve their financial disagreement. Once your husband departed for the Bridge, you dressed in the outdoor clothing you're wearing right now, making sure to conceal your very noticeable hair. The costume made you, from a distance, virtually indistinguishable from a man.

"I suppose you followed your husband out into the desert to the Bridge where you surprised him as he waited impatiently for Castor, who, of course, had played no part in arranging a rendezvous. If Wyndham saw you, he was doubtless most puzzled by your presence. More likely, you sneaked up behind him and hit him on the back of his head with the cactus stalk you'd found on the trail. The use of the stalk immediately suggested to me that a woman had delivered the blow that knocked him off the narrow bridge and to his death in the canyon below. A man likely would have pushed Wyndham, or perhaps struck him with a rock, but a woman wouldn't have dared to get so close to her victim.

"With all of the guests off hiking or relaxing, it would have been a simple matter for you to return to the hacienda undetected. You then spent the day pretending to wait for your husband to return for your outing. He never appeared of course, and when we returned to the hacienda in the afternoon, you summoned all of your theatrical training to raise the alarm, showing me the note that had supposedly been slipped under your door, and off we went to search for Mr. Wyndham."

"Well, what do you have to say for yourself?" the sheriff demanded of Pearl Wyndham.

A cactus stalk of the type used by Mrs. Wyndham
to strike her husband on the Devil's Bridge

"I say this to Mr. Sigerson," she said, a sneer appearing on her face. "You should write a few of those detective stories that we read in the magazines! What fantasy you spin! It's perfectly obvious that you've made this all up – for whatever reason I cannot say! I told you: I was here the entire day waiting for my husband to return. I even remained here when you went out to search for him. As you recall, you, specifically, refused to allow me to accompany you."

"That is true," I confessed, "and I clearly underestimated your skills as an actress! You quite convinced me of your interest in joining the search party."

"Where is your proof for these ridiculous accusations?" she demanded of me, her face turning angry. "You have none! You have a preposterous fabrication. You, not I, were out hiking when he was off to the Devil's Bridge. Why, *you yourself* might well have written wrote that note and lured my poor husband to his death!"

It was a bold, if pointless, accusation since I had no discernible reason for writing the note or harming a man I had just met. But I was just as unknown a person to those gathered in the parlour as was everyone else to each other, and I had no alibi for all of the time I had been alone hiking. For all they knew, I might well have had a considerable, if unknown, motive for wishing Mr. Wyndham dead.

Fitzgibbon turned to face me and shrugged.

"I hate to agree with her, Sigerson, but she does have a point. Is there any proof or is all this just a story?"

"I think I have more than enough evidence to establish that you have been lying about your whereabouts today," I declared. "For example, look at your shoes. They are covered with the red dust one picks up while walking along the rocky paths. It's quite characteristic of this area, particularly around the Devil's Bridge."

"Well, what of it?" she responded.

"You have told us that you haven't been outside today," I said, pointing to her boots. "But it's evident you have taken at least one lengthy hike, as evidenced by the thick red dust also clinging to your boots and the cuff of your trousers. Surely you would have cleaned off the dust from an earlier walk."

She looked down at her feet and involuntarily stomped hard on the wooden stairs to clear the dust.

"I'm afraid that isn't good enough, Mrs. Wyndham," I said. "Your effort may dislodge some trail dust, but not the burrs from the infernal local cactus and grasses that remain clinging to your trousers. It's so difficult to walk through this thick vegetation without the burrs affixing themselves. And I have no doubt that when Sheriff Fitzgibbon compares these particular burrs to those found in the vicinity of the Devil's Bridge, it will be manifestly evident that not only did you leave the hacienda, but that your hike took you to that very spot where your husband was assaulted."

"Dust and burrs!" she shrieked. "What nonsense! They prove nothing. You can barely walk outside the front door of this miserable hovel without being covered in dust and cactus burrs!"

"True, true," I agreed, "a most rugged landscape." A small smile of victory crept across her face.

"But there is the matter of that stalk from the Century cactus that you used to strike Carl Wyndham from behind, propelling him off the precipice."

From the doorway, the voice of my young friend Magillicuddy sang out.

"Here it is, Mr. Sigerson!" He triumphantly held up the three-foot piece of the stalk I had sent him to retrieve from the ice box containing Wyndham's corpse.

"I think this stalk will help clarify your involvement in your husband's death beyond any doubt."

"Nonsense!" she responded. "I never saw that before!"

"Be careful with that stalk, Ebeneezer! Use a cloth to protect your hands." I turned back to the widow. "You know it leaves tiny splinters and a distinct purple stain on the hand that is most difficult to wash off."

A look of alarm involuntarily crossed Mrs. Wyndham's face as she turned her hands to observe the palms. Her momentary panic quickly turned to satisfaction.

"There, you see, Mr. Sigerson," she proclaimed triumphantly, displaying her palms for the assembled group to observe. "There is no purple stain on my hands!"

"Of course there isn't, Mrs. Wyndham," I agreed. "The stalk of the *Agave americana* contains some small needles, but it leaves no purple stain." Mrs. Wyndham and the others looked at me in confusion. "But you didn't know that until I just mentioned it."

"I fail to see your point," she indignantly responded.

"I should think it obvious," I said. "Why were you momentarily so alarmed when I mentioned the possibility of your palms being stained if you had never handled the stalk? But your first instinct was to see if the telltale stain was present. I have no doubt that upon closer inspection, we will find the remnants of thorns from the *Agave* lodged under the skin of your palms."

The smile had faded from her face as she stood up and pushed her chair backward. With a fluid motion, she pulled a long-barreled pistol from her carpetbag. Despite its weight, she leveled the weapon at my heart.

"A Paterson revolver?" I said, recognizing the weapon.

"Your familiarity with American weaponry surprises me, Mr. Sigerson," she said. "Yes, my husband bought it from a Texan we encountered in the New Mexico territory last month. He felt that given his frequent absences, I should have the capacity to protect myself."

296

"A tricky weapon," I advised, pointing to the revolver. "Perhaps you are not aware that the trigger on that model can jam – "

"I know all about the trigger. And I assure you, I know how to use the weapon if need be. You aren't going to railroad me with such an absurd accusation!"

"Mrs. Wyndham! Is that necessary?" Jennings cried out. "This man obviously doesn't know what he's talking about."

"I wouldn't draw that conclusion from what he has already deduced," she replied, her voice rising to an eerie pitch. She aimed gun carefully in my direction and very likely would have fired but for the enigmatic Slits, who had silently emerged from the shadows and deflected her arm upward. She cried out in pain as he sharply twisted her wrist. The weapon tumbled harmlessly from her hand and Ebeneezer jumped on it and then held it out for me.

"Well done, Mr. Slits and Ebeneezer!" I declared. "I am deeply in your debt. The Paterson makes a rather definitive hole in the target."

Sheriff Fitzgibbon swiftly moved to Mrs. Wyndham's side and locked her hands in metal cuffs. Without saying another word, he walked her out the hacienda door and off to the local jail. Once she had departed, the room fairly exploded into astonished conversation. I moved to stand next to Ebeneezer and, having first wrapped my hands in a cloth, retrieved the cactus stalk.

"This is an important piece of evidence, young man," I said, "so I think it best that I keep it for the sheriff. But you performed your job with great expertise." I lowered my voice and added, "If you find yourself in London, I know a certain gentleman detective there who would be honoured to have you as one of his Irregulars!"

"Where's London?" the boy asked innocently.

Another grunt escaped the lips of the mysterious man known as "Slits", who had risen from his chair next to that recently occupied by Mrs. Wyndham. Catching my eye, he motioned for me to join him at the bar as the others milled about discussing the shocking denouement they had just witnessed. As I stood next to him, his weathered face surprisingly broke into a mass of creases and an easy grin that revealed a number of gaps among his yellowed teeth. When he spoke, my heart sank.

"'London', I heard the boy say. It's my old home, it is!" He took a sip of his drink. "Well now, that was a very nice piece of work you done there," he said, his voice now thick with the Cockney accent of East London. "Quite a little bit of 'trouble and strife', she is, eh?" The familiar phrase was the dialect's version of 'wife'. "I'd go so far as to say that was a very respectable bit of *deduction* work, I would." He sat quietly for a few moments, nodding his head and sipping his whisky while I waited impassively and silently.

"Y'know, there's just one man in the entire world, I would say, who could do what you just done here tonight," he continued "Take a bit of this and a lit'le bit of that and tie it all up in a great big story what nobody even knowed was a murder, let alone know who done it."

Again, I said nothing, hoping Slits had mistaken me for someone else. Slits leaned so close to me that I could smell his fetid breath.

"Mr. Holmes, ain't it?" He whispered so quietly that even I, whose ear was but an inch from his mouth, could barely hear him. "Sherlock Holmes! In the flesh! Here in Oak Creek, Arizona!" He let out a loud cackle that attracted the attention of the other patrons as he slapped the bar with glee. I grasped him by the shoulder.

"By all that is good, Slits, do not utter that name again!" I hissed. "You are assuredly mistaken." The man looked startled by my tone and drew back quickly. I laid several bills on the bar and signaled Camarilla to leave the whisky bottle in front of Slits, who had already consumed a prodigious quantity of spirits. "Here, my good man, is a bottle that you can enjoy all through this long and chilly evening. Why don't you take it with you when you retire?" I attempted to begin gathering him up to send him off to his room, but he pushed back and once again leaned close to me.

"Back in London, before I came to this godforsaken place to find my fortune, my nephew never stopped talkin' about you! He's one of them 'Irregulars' who helps you out from time to time! You know him? Desmond Waters?"

I shook my head in the negative.

"You have me confused with someone else, I assure you, Slits," I insisted. "Now, you go off to your bed and sleep off this impressive bout of inebriation." He stood up wobbly, and I gathered up his coat and the whisky bottle and moved him towards the door.

"You know where you're going?" I asked. He mumbled an incoherent reply, grasped the bottle, and shuffled out the door. From his state of intoxication, which undoubtedly would be compounded by the considerable volume of whisky remaining in the bottle, I was quite sure he would awaken the next morning with little recollection of anything that had transpired at the hacienda, and with a severe headache from his overindulgence. Even so, it was the closest I ever came during the three years of my sabbatical to having my true identity exposed. And to think, the revelation nearly came to pass in a rustic hacienda deep the Arizona desert.

Afterword

Years later, the lessons from this case would help in formulating my admonition to my friend, Dr. John Watson, in the case he recorded as "The Creeping Man". In that story, he quoted me as advising him on how to examine a perpetrator for evidence.

"Always look to the hands first," I told him, "then the cuffs, trouser knees, and boots." Indeed, upon examination, Mrs. Wyndham's hands showed the tell-tale splinters from grasping the cactus stalk, and the burrs on her cuffs were linked to grasses in proximity to the Devil's Bridge, all of which most certainly demonstrated that her story of remaining all day in the hacienda couldn't have been accurate.

That evidence was bound to be useful in prosecuting her for her role in the death of her husband. The outcome of the trial, needless to say, was no business of mine, although I admit I had feared that Sheriff Fitzgibbon would lack the expertise of Scotland Yard in presenting the case to the jury. I didn't remain to witness the outcome. Wishing to avoid any further risk of exposure, I quickly left the Arizona Territory without learning what fate had in store for a woman who, I admit, had proven more wily and willful than her unsophisticated background might have suggested.

I proceeded to Flagstaff, and thence on a three-day train journey to San Francisco. From there, I continued my anonymous sojourn with a trip into Central America where I studied the poisons of the Costa Rican orange tree frog. It was nearly spring when I crossed the Central American isthmus and boarded a tramp steamer at Limón bound for Portugal, where I immersed myself in the study of Moorish influences on the architecture of the Iberian Peninsula. One afternoon, just prior to returning to London, I found myself in a small library in Lisbon pouring through a backlog of American newspapers when a story nearly jolted me out of my chair.

Great Entertainment in Chicago!
"Bess of the West" Stars
Actress Pearl Wyndham

Theater-goers were enthralled with the performance of the actress Pearl Wyndham in the new play, "Bess of the West", a rollicking comedy she has written and in which she stars. The plot concerns a poor seamstress who marries the son of a financier who became wealthy when her husband disappears.

I could barely believe what I was reading, but the account became even more bizarre!

299

Miss Wyndham, of course, is herself the fabulously wealthy widow of a mining baron, the late Carl Wyndham of Chicago, who lost his life in a tragic fall while they were vacationing in Arizona last year. Remarkably, she was briefly accused of complicity in his death and put on trial for her life, facing the gallows if convicted.

Mrs. Wyndham was ably represented by the famed Chicago attorney Mr. Louis Chalmers, who skillfully persuaded the jury that her behaviour was attributable to the strange neurological condition "prairie fever". * This illness has afflicted numerous men and women who have abandoned their comfortable lives in Europe and the Eastern states for the rigors of life in the American West. As a result, she could not be held culpable for his death.

Mrs. Wyndham inherited three-million dollars from his estate and was required to fend off several claimants who insisted they were owed money by her late husband. Yet despite her great wealth, she was determined to return to the stage, where she made her debut last evening.

Despite the brutal nature of her crime, I couldn't suppress a chuckle at her audacity! To commit such a heinous act – and there remains no doubt in my mind that she did so with a clear mind and resolute intent – and yet persuade a jury to accept a patently ludicrous defense was remarkable. I tore the story from the newspaper and folded it into my coat pocket. It shall forever serve as a memento of the innovativeness of the American criminal mind and the incomprehensibility of that country's legal system.

NOTE

* Readers interested in this strange affliction might wish to read: Peter Pagnamenta, *Prairie Fever: British Aristocrats in the American West 1830-1890* (2013).

The Second *Strand*
by Tim Newton Anderson

I had climbed the steps to Holmes's former lodgings in Baker Street for what I thought would be the last time, to have a memorial lunch with Mrs. Hudson. My account of Holmes's last struggle with Moriarty and his death would be published in *The Strand* the following month, and it seemed an appropriate time to say goodbye to my best friend with the other person who knew him best.

"I'm surprised you have kept the room exactly the same as it was," I said to Mrs. Hudson as she poured me another cup of tea. "It is more than two-and-a-half years since he died."

"Mr. Holmes and yourself were special lodgers," she said, carving another slice of ham and placing it on my plate. "Perhaps you would like to move back in? It must be lonely for you at home since your wife passed."

I felt a stab of pain in my heart at Mrs. Hudson's words. The last few years had indeed been hard. First Holmes dying, and then my wife succumbing to a fatal illness. It had only been by throwing myself in to my medical practice that I had been able to cope. Tackling other people's problems had helped me forget my own.

"I'm not sure I would be able to live here comfortably without Holmes," I said. "Thank you for the offer, though. I will consider it carefully. I can see you miss him too. Perhaps moving back here would do us both good."

I looked around the room. Holmes's Persian slipper full of tobacco was still on the mantelpiece and there were still various items of scientific equipment laid out mid-experiment, as if he had just popped out for a moment and would soon return. I had avoided coming here, as each time I entered it reopened the wound left by his passing.

At that moment, there was a knock on the front door.

"I still get people coming to consult Mr. Holmes," said Mrs. Hudson. "How they don't know he is no longer with us, after all the obituaries in the newspapers, is a mystery even he couldn't have solved."

"I will go and inform them of the situation," I said, and walked down the stairs to open the door.

When I opened the door to the chill November mists, I saw our visitor was a woman in her thirties. Holmes would no doubt have been able to tell me everything about her from that first glance, but I could at least

301

speculate that she was moderately comfortable in her situation – her coat and shawl weren't expensive, but neither were they old and worn. Her face was smooth and pale enough to indicate that if she worked it was at some indoor trade – In a shop, or office, or at home. She wore a modest amount of make-up, and there was a thin gold band on the third finger of her left hand which showed she was married. I was surprised she wasn't wearing gloves, which the weather would have warranted, but she had a fur muff around her right hand which she had withdrawn the other from to knock on the door. Perhaps that suggested she was left handed.

"If you are here in the hope of seeing Mr. Holmes," I said, "I'm afraid you have had a wasted journey. My friend died over two years ago in Switzerland."

"I know," she said. "But I hoped I might see Dr. Watson here. I wanted to seek his help in persuading the police that something has happened to my husband. From the stories of Mr. Holmes's exploits in *The Strand*, I hoped Dr. Watson would know some people in the police force he could talk to, and be more persuasive than a poor shop girl."

My first instinct was to send her away with an apology, leaving Mrs. Hudson and me to our reminiscences, but her pain was so palpable, I decided to at least hear her out. Perhaps I could indeed intercede on her behalf with Lestrade or his colleagues.

"I am Dr. Watson," I said. "I cannot hope to emulate my friend's detective skills, but I may be able to be of some small assistance."

In truth, I missed not only my friend's companionship, but the excitement of the cases in which I had been involved. There had been precious little to look forward to in my life since both Holmes and Mary had passed.

Mrs. Hudson also seemed glad to have a visitor again, and quickly bustled off to get an additional tea-cup and saucer, and a plate for her cold collation. I invited our guest to sit in the seat I had recently vacated and sat in Holmes habitual chair by the fire. It seemed almost sacrilegious, but also appropriate.

"Please tell me everything," I said. "Don't leave out the smallest detail which may be of use in understanding your problem."

I took out my pipe and tobacco pouch and commenced to smoke.

"My name is Margaret Webster," she said. The agitation she had shown at the door seemed to subside and she started to relax as she told the tale. "My husband and I live in Camden in one of the terraced cottages in Reid's Place. My father, God rest his soul, was one of the original tenants and left the lease to me when he died. The rent is quite inexpensive, so we're able to live in relative comfort on Roger's wage as a typesetter, and the money I make in a local grocer's shop. It has been our home for

302

ten years now, and we'd hoped to raise a family there, but so far we haven't been blessed with children, and I fear we're now too old to hope for them. Still, we've been happy there and, despite Roger's lack of progression in his career, expected to live out the rest of our days there. We had even talked about the possibility of adopting, as there are many children in orphanages and workhouses that would welcome a loving home.

"Roger had been somewhat agitated for the last two or three weeks, but I believed this was due to rumours of the printers where he worked being sold to a new owner, as the current one is thinking of retiring. As I mentioned, Roger hasn't advanced since completing his apprenticeship eight years ago, and a new owner could either mean promotion, or dismissal, depending on what sort of impression he is able to make. To that end, he had been working longer hours in the hope the new owner would favour him.

"He was due to work late two nights ago, and I expected him home at nine in the evening. When he didn't appear, I assumed he was either working even longer, or had been persuaded by a colleague to visit a public house for a drink on the way home. I was tired, so I went to bed alone, expecting him to join me when he arrived home.

"When I awoke the next morning, he wasn't in bed with me, and his side didn't appear to have been slept in. I was upset, of course, but not unduly worried at that stage. He may have stayed with a friend on his way back from the print house in the East End because of the lateness of the hour and the desire not to disturb me. He would normally have taken sandwiches to work, so I made some up and went to drop them off at the printers before starting my own work. I was shocked when I arrived there to be told that Roger hadn't been seen by anyone since he left work at five o'clock the previous day.

"Fearing something had happened to him on his way home, I went to the police station in Whitechapel. As you will be aware, it isn't the safest part of London, and I was worried Roger had been attacked and robbed. The sergeant on duty told me there had been no reports of such incidents. He was kind enough to ring the nearest hospital – the London – and found there had been no admissions that fitted Roger's description. I asked them to look for him as a missing person, but I could tell they thought he had just left home for some reason and didn't take me seriously.

"It has now been two days since he failed to return and I visited the police again, but they said they were sure he would turn up eventually and I shouldn't worry. How can they expect me not to be concerned when something so out of character has occurred? Even if he did decide to leave, he wouldn't have done so without talking to me, and all of his belongings are still where he left them. There is even a set of proofs he brought home to check, still sitting on the kitchen table."

My first thought was that the police might be correct and her husband had simply decided that since his job wasn't going the way he hoped, he had decided to try his fortune elsewhere. However, her distress was so obvious that I said I would talk to my contacts at Scotland Yard and see if I could persuade them to allocate some resources to the search. This seemed to relieve her somewhat and, after writing down her address and a description of her husband's clothing, I arranged for a cab to take her home and left for Scotland Yard in Westminster. She had provided me with a photograph of her husband from their wedding. He was a short, slightly built man with a handlebar moustache and side-locks. According to Mrs. Webster, his swept-back hair was brown. One thing that seemed obvious from the look he and Margaret Webster were exchanging was that her statement about their mutual love was correct.

The staff on duty knew me well enough from visits with Holmes to usher me in to Inspector Lestrade's office. Although Holmes had often been dismissive of the policeman's skills I knew that he was a conscientious investigator, even if he lacked my late friend's deductive skills. As I entered, he stood up at his desk and walked round to greet me.

"I don't see you as much since Mr. Holmes died," he said. "I was afraid his death had deprived me of your friendship as well."

"I am sorry," I said. "Since he was killed, I haven't had the heart to maintain the links made on his investigations, however close those were. Tonight, however, I've come here on an errand from a lady in distress."

There was a black cloud over Lestrade as he resumed his seat. Despite their occasional clashes, he too felt Holmes's loss deeply. I told him what Mrs. Webster had told me and asked if he could persuade his colleagues to take the disappearance seriously. I drew the photograph from my pocket and laid it on the desk before him. He shook his head sadly.

"I'm afraid we will have to tell Mrs. Webster some bad news," he said. "I was called to the morgue this morning to view a body that had been retrieved from the Thames. The head had been hit several times with a blunt instrument – possibly a lead pipe – but there is no doubt it was Roger Webster."

"Do you know what had happened to him?" I asked.

"It seems he was the victim of an attack and his body was thrown into the river. The length of time it seemed he had spent in the river suggests he was killed two nights ago – when Mrs. Webster says he failed to come home."

"Was it a case of robbery?" I asked.

"I suspect not," he said. "There was no wallet on the body, which is why he hadn't been identified, but he had a purse in his trouser pocket with four guineas in it. The violence of the attack suggests there was some personal reason behind it."

Lestrade was kind enough to let me see the body in the morgue. It was either Webster or his twin brother. As the inspector had said, the head had been struck several times, cracking the skull and disfiguring the face, but not enough to prevent identification. The only thing I found unusual was that if it had been an attack, there was no bruising to the body. His killers seemed to have been determined to murder him rather than this being a brawl that had gone too far.

"Would you like us to inform Mrs. Webster?" he asked.

"I feel some responsibility," I said. "Perhaps we can do it together."

Lestrade and I took a hansom to Camden and walked down the short path to the Webster's home. A trellis with climbing roses hung on either side of the front door, which had been recently painted, and the dust from the street had been rigorously brushed from the entrance. It painted a picture consistent with Margaret Webster's assertion of a happy marriage.

Mrs. Webster greeted us with a smile of hope, which faded as soon as she saw the expression of sadness on our faces. Tears sprang to her eyes and she retreated back into her home, sobbing. Lestrade and I removed our hats and followed her into the neat living room.

"He is dead, isn't he?" she said from a face wet with crying.

"I'm afraid so," I said. "If it's of any comfort, he was probably on his way home to you when he was attacked."

Although I stated this as a certainty, the truth was that unless his attackers moved his body some considerable distance from the route he would have taken, he must have been in a different part of the city which wasn't on his way home.

I placed my hand on her shoulder to afford some comfort and steered her towards a chair in front of the fire. Lestrade took up the other armchair and I then brought a wooden one from the kitchen table.

"Do you know of anyone who would have cause to attack your husband?" Lestrade asked. "I'm afraid it doesn't look like a simple case of robbery, although we cannot rule out a random attack. He may have simply been in the wrong place at the wrong time."

"We kept ourselves to ourselves," Margaret Webster said. "I am sure Roger had no enemies. He always said he got on well with his colleagues at work, and we didn't know many other people, apart from our neighbours and a few friends from school who live nearby. Certainly there is no one who would have reason to attack him."

305

I felt I could contribute little to Lestrade's interview, and stood up to look round for clues. Sherlock Holmes would have taken in every detail of the house and immediately understood the full history of the family and the crime, but I had no such powers of observation, as he often reminded me. *"You see, Watson, but you don't observe,"* he would tell me.

I could see nothing that was exceptional in the room. The fire was part of a well-blacked range where Mrs. Webster placed a kettle when she had recovered enough to offer a tea to Lestrade and myself. A cup of sweet tea would do her good, I prescribed. On the mantel above was another copy of their wedding photograph, and a small vase with some of the roses from outside their door. The far side of the room had a dining table and two chairs – one of which I had commandeered – and a square butler sink and drainer with a single plate and cutlery on it. I was slightly surprised to recognise the knife and fork as one of Mappin and Webb's new designs.

"That cutlery is beautiful," I said.

"Roger bought me a set last week," Margaret Webster said. "He told me he had received a bonus for all of the extra hours he has been working, and felt I deserved a treat to celebrate our tenth anniversary."

I filed the information away in my mind. I knew how much such a set would cost.

I walked over to the kitchen table, and as she had said, there was a set of proofs there. I was surprised again, as they were for the forthcoming issue of *The Strand*, whose cover story was my account of Holmes's death – "The Final Problem". I couldn't help but glance through the sheets, even though I had been sent my own copy to check through.

"Is this what prompted you to visit me?" I asked, lifting them up.

"It is," said Mrs. Webster. "Roger's firm does all of the typesetting for *The Strand*. I've had the honour of reading all of your stories before the rest of the public. He would bring a copies home for me."

I started to read the page again.

"This must be an old version of the page," I said. "There are some mistakes here that don't occur in the pages I proofread last week."

"Roger said that was the latest version when he brought it home three days ago," she said. "Perhaps the mistakes have somehow crept back in since you saw it."

"Do you mind if I take these?" I asked. "I will pop into the printers on the way home and check."

Mrs. Webster said that would be all right. Lestrade said he had all the information he needed and would keep in touch with news of any progress. We left Mrs. Webster to mourn her loss.

On the way back to Whitehall, Lestrade and I exchanged notes. I mentioned the recent expensive purchase which he wrote down in his notebook. He hadn't managed to get any hints about why Roger Webster had been attacked from his interview with the widow. He was kind enough to get the cabby to charge Scotland Yard for the fare and asked the man to take me on to Whitechapel.

The print shop was one of a myriad of small businesses in the maze of alleys and courts that spidered back from the main thoroughfares in the East End. As I entered, the tang of the metal type assailed my nostrils, and I could hear the bangs of the typesetters tapping rows of letters into place in the page frames. I was greeted by a gnome-like man in a cloth cap and calico apron who beckoned me inside.

"Dr. Watson, I presume," he said. "I recognises you from Paget's pictures in the magazine. A good likeness."

As I got closer I realised he wasn't as short as I had first thought, just doubled over from hours spent closely checking pages for errors. He had blonde hair under his hat, and I noticed it didn't quite match the colour of his full beard. It was probably a wig. If so, it was a cheap one.

"What can I do you for?" he asked. "The next *Strand* isn't due out until next month. And anyways, we only make up the pages. The printing press is a few streets away."

"It's the proofs I've come to talk about," I said.

"Proofs, eh. Just the thing for a detective's assistant, methinks," he said. Given Holmes's death was still something that weighed on my heart, I didn't appreciate the joke.

"One of your employees had these in his home," I said, taking the sheets of paper from inside my coat where I had placed them to escape the damp autumn fog. "I had a quick look, and there are a number of mistakes in them."

"Mistakes, you say? We can't have that. Take a pride in our work, we do. No mistakes allowed, although I do have to say interpreting your handwriting ain't the easiest of tasks. Feel like if I took it to a chemist, he could have it made up in a prescription."

Again, I ignored his attempt at humour, as he unrolled the proofs on a metal table next to a wooden frame full of type. I was about to touch the page to indicate the error, but he held his arm out to prevent me. I remembered I had been warned before about the proscription on anyone other than a trained typesetter touching the table – the "stone" they called it.

"It was Roger Webster," I said. "Had you heard he was killed?"

The man – who had introduced himself as Billy Dolan – shook his head sadly.

"Terrible business," he said. "Heard as how he had his head bashed in. Wasn't the best worker – if he made some mistakes on this, I wouldn't be surprised – but he were a good man. Always on time, never slacked off. Don't know as how he had an enemy in the world. Certainly we all liked him."

I told him the story Mrs. Webster had told me and he nodded.

"As I said, he left here at the usual time," he said. "As for this overtime he was supposed to be doing, that don't match up either. He hadn't been leaving here late, so who knows where he had been going on his way home, like."

Dolan had taken a magnifying glass from the front pocket of his apron. I had a pang of nostalgia as he did so. How many times had I seen Holmes bend over a clue with a glass in his hand?

"Are you investigating how he died?" asked Dolan. "Helping the police with their inquiries, as it were? If so, we'd be glad to hear how you get on. As I said, popular man, Roger."

He continued to pore over the proof and the type as he talked. I admired his ability to read the set type – reversed of course for printing – as fast he could the printed paper.

"You're right, it's all wrong," he said as he reached the bottom of the page. "Well, not all wrong. Half-a-dozen or so words have been swapped for words of the same length. No reason we would do that unless the author or the magazine asked us to. Sometimes there's a mistake in the original, or someone thinks of a better word. These ones hardly make sense."

I looked closely at the page and the set type in its frame. My literary agent, Dr. Doyle, once told me that it was hard for a writer to check his own copy, as we remember what we *think* we have written, rather than what was *really* on the page. I had noticed the first mistake – replacing my "*two years*" with "*Wednesday*" – as it didn't fit with the rest of the sentence. As I examined the faulty proof, I spotted that "*Naval Treaty*" had also been changed for "*L. Nathanson*". I couldn't see any other mistakes, however, and told Dolan that.

"That's a couple of them," he said, "but there are two more. Look here, further down the page. The word "*three*" has been swapped for "*seven*" and the word "*engaged*" has been altered to "*armed*" with a couple of slugs put in to space the letters out."

"Could it be simply sloppy workmanship?" I asked.

"We doesn't do sloppy here," he said. "This here page has been checked by at least four people. First off, we goes through the original typed manuscript supplied to us by *The Strand*, and checks it against what you wrote. Secretaries can be sloppy, but *we* can't afford to be. Then, when the type is put together, we goes through it line-by-line against our corrected version of the typed story. Picks up any mistakes by the typesetter, see. Then when the type is originally placed in the frame, we reads it and also checks to make sure it is justified right. Sometimes the odd word gets dropped off if someone a bit slipshod is trying to make it fit in the frame. Then we draws off a paper proof and reads it the normal way round, again against the typewritten version. Only then do we send out copies to the magazine and they send them on to you and the other authors. If you makes any changes because you've messed it up or thought better of it, we does the whole thing again and sends out a second proof. This here page of type on the slate is a second proof version. It should be perfect, and it is."

"But Webster took his version home two nights ago," I said, "after you sent out the second proof."

"Then he, or someone else, has done the changes, pulled off a proof, and changed 'em back," the printer said.

"Why would they do that?" I asked.

"Look at what the different words are," he said. "'*Wednesday, L. Nathanson, Seven, Armed.*' Sounds to me like a message. Ain't Nathanson that posh jeweller in Bond Street? Sounds to me like a robbery."

I stood stiffly upright. The man was right.

"We must take this to Scotland Yard so you can explain to Inspector Lestrade," I said.

"Not me, chum," he said. "Who would believe a simple printer like me? The famous Dr. Watson on the other hand – the right-hand man of none other than the great detective, Sherlock Holmes. You take it to this Lestrade chappy and he'll believe it straight off."

I got Dolan to pull off a proof of the correct page and set off for Scotland Yard with that and the false version. If Dolan was right, and I believed he was, then Webster had probably been delivering the proofs with the message when he was supposed to be working extra hours. I could admire the cleverness of the plan. If he had been stopped taking the instructions 'round in letter form, the police would instantly have known of the plan and interrogated him to divulge the participants. However, if he was stopped carrying the proofs, the chances of the police spotting the message were extremely small.

I hastened to Scotland Yard to see Lestrade, and appraised him of my discoveries.

"There is no possibility of Webster being behind such an elaborate plot," he said. "By all accounts, he was basically honest, and there is certainly no record of him having been in trouble with the law."

"That is what you said when Holmes first accused Professor Moriarty," I said. "Perhaps if you had believed him, the confrontation at the Reichenbach Falls wouldn't have taken place."

His face was so crestfallen, I instantly regretted my accusation.

"If only he had been able to bring us proof rather than suppositions," he said. "We might have prevented that. It is one of the greatest regrets of my life that we did not. For all that Mr. Holmes and I clashed sometimes over cases, I held him in the greatest respect as a detective, and Scotland Yard is the poorer for his passing, as well as the world at large. Like you, I felt he was a friend as well as a colleague."

I smiled in sympathy, as I had become used to doing since Holmes's death. He had many mourners.

"If not Webster, then who?" I asked.

"If we didn't know Moriarty was dead, he would be at the top of my suspect list," Lestrade said. "This case has his style all over it. The person planning the theft has arranged matters so that those who will perpetrate it have no idea of their master's identity. No doubt the plan is to get them to exchange the loot for their payment at some secret location which has been revealed, along with the details of the theft, via other false proofs. I suspect Webster was killed because he knew too much about the mastermind behind this and may have been able to lead us to him."

"Do you have any suspicions as to who this new Napoleon of Crime is?"

"We were able to arrest many members of Moriarty's gang after their leader was killed by Mr. Holmes," Lestrade said. "He had left us copious notes, and we found more information at Moriarty's home. However, some of his lieutenants weren't traced. The closer we got to the top of the organisation, the more the members were shrouded in the same veil of secrecy as Moriarty. Like him, they were seldom directly involved in the commission of the many crimes that could be laid at the organisation's door. I suspect that one of those members of Moriarty's hierarchy has taken one of his plans and has recruited other crooks to bring it to fruition."

"I'm guessing you weren't able to find any clues at Webster's home or work to the names and addresses he was delivering to?"

"Unfortunately, no" Lestrade replied. "In a plan with such a great emphasis on secrecy, Webster was sure to have been ordered to destroy any paperwork. There is only one course of action open to us."

"You mean be present when the theft is due to take place and arrest the culprits in the act," I said.

"Precisely," said Lestrade. "I'll inspect the surroundings of Nathanson's and decide the best location for my men to conceal themselves. I'll tell the owners, of course, and have some of my men hidden on the premises."

"Would I be able to be there?" I said. "I've missed the excitement of being present at the *denouement* of a case."

310

"Of course," said Lestrade, "although I must insist you stay well back from the action. Unlike Mr. Holmes, I cannot risk a civilian rushing in with his old service revolver in hand in case it prejudices the operation. I trust you as much as Mr. Holmes did, but we have different responsibilities."

I was filled with nervous excitement all of the following day until I joined Lestrade at Scotland Yard in the afternoon and travelled with him in a cab to Bond Street. We took up position in a shop in Bruton Street which gave us an unobstructed view of Nathanson's Jewellers. Although I'm sure he didn't need to, Lestrade had asked my advice as a former Army officer on the deployment of his men. The only suggestion of mine he may not have thought of himself was to request the aid of some sharpshooters from the Army barracks at Hyde Park who were now stationed on the upper floor of the buildings on either side of the road. One thing we did know about the men who would be attempting the robbery was that they would be armed.

"Nathanson's were due a delivery of uncut diamonds this evening, which is the robbery's real target," said Lestrade. "Much easier to sell than identifiable pieces of jewellery. My men are manning the vehicle that was to make the delivery, as well as being behind the counter and in the back room of the shop. We have all of the approaches covered, and there will be a signal from the rooftop when the closed cab and the suspects are on their way. We don't know how many of them there will be, so we need every advantage we can get."

I nodded and settled back in my seat for the interminable wait until seven p.m.. I understood why we were in position so early, but felt the same tension that gripped my body when Holmes and I used to wait for the conclusion of an investigation.

After what seemed like a lifetime, but was only three hours, I saw Lestrade sit bolt upright on the seat beside me.

"My man on the roof has given the signal," he said. "The jewellery van is on its way, and he has spotted some likely suspects. Four of them so far."

I peered out through the curtain in the shop window and saw two men walking towards Bond Street, illuminated by the street lamps. Fortunately the thick fog of recent days had gone, and I could clearly see their approach.

"The one on the right is Brian Harris," said Lestrade. "Not long out of Newgate for armed robbery. Nasty swine – especially if he's cornered. The man next to him is Davey Swarbrick. Robbery isn't his usual occupation – he's more of a swindler – but he has a few more brains than Harris, who was probably recruited for his penchant for violence."

It was easy to tell who was who from their appearance. Harris was tall and heavily built and had the bristling walk of a boxer trying to intimidate his opponent. Swarbrick was slight and constantly looked around as if expecting to be challenged. The two men were in animated conversation. If we were correct and they were all brought into the plot separately, they would have a lot to talk about.

They stopped at the end of the street and stood in a doorway, with Swarbrick lighting a cigarette. Looking down Bond Street, I saw two other men approaching on opposite pavements.

"Dosser Hughes and Wendell Richards," Lestrade said. "Both suspected of involvement in high value heists, but we weren't able to get enough evidence to put them away. My superiors will be delighted to have them behind bars at last."

Hughes and Richards also stopped short of the entrance to Nathanson's and took up positions in shop doorways. Unlike their fellow conspirators, there was little to distinguish them from any other passers-by, and I had no idea which man was which. With their dark clothing, a pedestrian passing our end of the street would be unlikely to spot them, even with the street lamps soft glow.

They had only just taken up their positions when the fake jewellery delivery passed our shop window and swung into Bond Street. The thieves waited until it had stopped in front of the jewellers before they drew pistols from their coats and surrounded the vehicle. They were surprised as the coach driver and passengers pulled out rifles and more armed officers ran out of Nathanson's and adjoining shops. Hughes, Richards and Swarbrick dropped their guns immediately, but Harris took aim at the nearest policeman. He never got a chance to pull the trigger, as the army sniper on the roof shot him with military precision.

"All right, men," said Lestrade as he approached the scene. "Get the cuffs on them and take them to Scotland Yard. If we can find out where they were to take the diamonds, we may be able to nab more of the gang."

He was walking across to the scene when Swarbrick fell forward to the ground. I had also dismounted the cab and was crossing the road. As I reached the fallen criminal I saw he had been shot in the head by a narrow calibre bullet that had lodged inside his skull.

"I didn't hear a shot," said Lestrade. "Search the area, men! Find that shooter."

I bent over and looked at the fallen thief.

"I remember Holmes telling me he was worried about an attack by an air rifle before we left for the Continent on that fatal last case," I said. "Whoever masterminded this clearly wanted to leave no trace of his involvement. I would wager it was Swarbrick who was to hand over the loot, and the other two have no idea how to communicate with their boss."

Lestrade contacted me the following day and asked me to meet him that afternoon at Mrs. Webster's cottage in Camden. I assumed he planned to tell the widow the outcome of the investigation. My cab arrived simultaneously with the one which brought him to the Webster home.

"Well timed, Dr. Watson," he said. "Your guess was right about the weapon that killed Swarbrick, and the lack of useful intelligence from the other two."

Mrs. Webster invited us in at Lestrade's knock and bade us be seated by the range. I indicated she should take the best chair and brought one from the table for myself.

"We don't believe your husband was involved in anything more than creating some false proofs and delivering them to the would-be thieves," said Lestrade. "A foolish act, no doubt motivated by the desire to provide a more comfortable life for you. His greatest mistake was in failing to realise that as the person who knew all of the criminals and their addresses, the crook behind the plot couldn't afford to let him live."

Mrs. Webster took the news with a surprising degree of composure, but perhaps she had cried so much over the previous days she was no longer able to summon up tears. There was ample evidence for that in the redness of her eyes, and the dark shadows underneath them.

Lestrade drew forth an envelope from the inside pocket of his coat.

"I do have something that may be of small consolation," he said. "The jewel merchants whose goods were the target of the plan have provided a reward of three-hundred pounds, which I'm happy to give to you. If not for your persistence in trying to trace your husband and contacting Dr. Watson, we wouldn't have been able to foil the scheme."

I smiled at the news.

"That is a good result, Lestrade," I said. "Although I wonder if Billy Dolan should also be rewarded. It was he who managed to identify the full text of the message."

"I did try to track him down and thank him," said Lestrade. "He had left the company, it seems, not long after you met him. He'd only worked for them a few days."

"I never heard Roger talk of a Billy Dolan," said Mrs. Webster. "I knew at least the names of all of the people he worked with."

"Most mysterious," I said.

"There's another mystery," Margaret Webster said. "When I came down to breakfast this morning, there was knock on the door and a cabby

– John Clayton his name was – handed me an envelope which was addressed to you, Dr. Watson."

She reached down beside her chair and lifted up a brown foolscap envelope which she handed to me. Examining the outside, I saw my name had been printed rather than written upon it. I carefully slid a finger inside the flap and opened it.

"It's a proof of the first page of 'The Final Problem'," I said. "It has a Paget illustration of Holmes and myself in his study which wasn't used in either the correct version I received for checking, or the fake version that Williams had been delivering."

I confess I felt a tear try and surface in my eyes as I saw my friend and myself in our usual places. It was a scene I would never experience again and a lump came to my throat.

"Did you ask the cabby where it came from?" asked Lestrade.

"He said some man had left it at the cabmen's shelter with instructions that he should bring it to me," Mrs. Webster said. "The man left my address and the fare."

"I recall the cabman's name," I said to Lestrade. "He was involved slightly in the Baskerville affair."

Mrs. Webster offered us some tea, but Lestrade said he had to return to Scotland Yard to continue his interrogation of the robbers. I replaced the page in the envelope and tucked it under my arm.

"Thank you both," said Mrs. Webster. "Roger may have been taken from me, but at least I know what happened. I hope you will be able to find the culprit, Inspector."

"I will do my best, Madam," he said, as we left the widow's home.

"I've enjoyed working with you, Doctor," said Lestrade as we walked back to his vehicle. "It's a shame Mr. Holmes couldn't be with us on the case. We did a reasonable job, but I'm sure he would have been able to track down Webster's killer, the person who shot Harris, and the man behind the whole plan. He may no longer be with us, but he has changed both of our lives for the better, I think."

"And many more," I said. "I hope my stories about him and his investigations keep his memory fresh in the minds of the public he did so much to protect. His greatness deserves to live on in everyone's memory."

The Adventure of the Twice-Murdered Man

by Tracy J. Revels

"Mr. Holmes, you are my court of last appeal. No one will believe me. Inspector Willow thinks I am foolish and deluded, and the doctor has been resolute in his misguided opinion. They have forced me to bury my father without justice which – whatever his faults, however deep his madness – he surely deserved as an Englishman and loyal subject of the Queen. I have even made inquiry at Scotland Yard, but they scoffed at my pleas and gave me your name as a private agent. And so, sir, I throw myself upon your mercy and your wisdom. Only do not tell me my father wasn't murdered, for I know that he was!"

The young woman who delivered this most remarkable soliloquy was both lovely and strong-willed, clad in the simplest of walking dresses topped with the most modest of hats. Her voice was low and resolute, her gaze clear and her jaw firm. Some observers might have called her mannish, for her hair was cut severely short, yet there was a delicateness to her features not found in the common suffragist, or in the spinster behind a library desk. She was clearly a young person with some experience of the world, but one who had not been corrupted by it. She repeated herself, that she wouldn't leave until she had presented all her evidence and made her case for why her father's death should be investigated.

Sherlock Holmes, of course, was immune to all feminine charms – yet I could tell he was impressed with the lady's manner, which lacked any trace of hysterics or tears. My friend would always respond to the call for justice, and I sensed immediately his interest in her case.

"Your father was – ?"

"Mr. Silas Oakley, of Skye House, near the town of Lynhart. However, he was better known as 'The Great Oracle'."

I confess I almost dropped the notebook I had opened. "The Great Oracle? Then you are surely – "

"The Daughter of Heaven and Hell. I much prefer my given name, however, which is Mara."

Holmes looked between us with some confusion. "I confess I am in the dark. Watson, you have made the lady's acquaintance?"

"After a fashion," I said, in a rush, rising to pluck a yellow-backed pamphlet from the shelf. "I was handed this by a wild-eyed fellow on an omnibus. I had no idea that the story was true."

The lady sighed and took the item from my hand, elegantly gesturing to the picture on the cover. It showed a man, clad in some strange amalgamation of Oriental attire, preaching to a crowd. Beside him, wrapped in a diaphanous linen gown and wearing a sizeable Egyptian wig, was a beautiful young woman. She held out a platter, upon which serpents bared their fangs and hissed with menace at the overawed worshippers.

"Father was convinced this little book would draw people to his sermons."

"The story claimed he worked black magic and performed miracles."

Holmes looked bored. The lady shook her head.

"Father was a competent magician, having learned the art of legerdemain from the charlatans who worked the streets of Cairo. I can promise you, there was no true magic, only the kind managed with smoke and mirrors, a pair of trained birds, and a marvelously obedient poodle who sadly died last year. Khalil took some liberties by placing snakes in the scene. I am terrified of vipers."

Holmes now smiled. "Then you are a sensible woman. But how did you become the heroine of this tract, and how did your father perish?"

"My father inherited a comfortable country manor, but as a youth he had no taste for rural life. He attended Oxford, and at the university he developed a love of antiquity and a desire to travel. He carved out a career as a guide, leading many young English noblemen on adventures in the Mediterranean and in North Africa. He was forty-five when he married my mother, a Grecian lady. She also had no fondness for the British countryside, nor were the citizens of Lynhart – a sadly prejudiced lot, I have discovered – very welcoming to her. I was raised as a nomad, and by the time I was a mere schoolgirl, I was assisting my father in his enterprise, both as a storyteller, and as a playmate for children who travelled with their titled parents.

"Six years ago, when I was sixteen, Father led an excavation of a previously unknown tomb near Luxor. He found only a plague, which his diggers claimed was a curse leveled upon him by an ancient priest. Mother also fell ill. I remained strong, and nursed them both, but Mother succumbed after making me promise to protect and honor Father all the days of my life. Father's sickness raged – he wasn't even aware when we were forced to bury Mother – and when the fever at last departed, he was left in a state of madness. Father spoke of visions and dreams, claiming the gods of a world which had existed even before the Egyptians worshipped Ra had come to him, giving him directions. He proclaimed

316

himself 'The Great Oracle' and dubbed me 'The Daughter of Heaven and Hell'. He told me our mission was to return to Skye House and prepare worshippers for the return of the 'Desert Mother'. I felt I had no choice but to obey his whims."

"He never recovered his sanity?" I asked.

"No. Several times, prominent citizens offered to advocate for me and have Father committed, but I had promised my mother I would never betray him, and I could think of no greater betrayal than having him locked away in a lunatic asylum. And besides, his delusion was harmless. Father wore his strange robes and preached his nonsense about ancient gods, but once we settled into Skye House, he also made it his mission to aid the impoverished of the community. There was a meal provided at every service, and the poor folks who came first out of curiosity, or to laugh at him, were sent home with food and clothing. Father found jobs for young lads, provided modest dowries for several girls, and even invested money with the local mill owner so he might repair his machines and put more people to work. There are many residents of Lynhart who have good reason to mourn Father . . . yet surely it was one of them who killed him."

Holmes pressed his hands together, leaning back and slowly closing his eyes. "How did it happen?" he asked.

"Five days ago, Father was feeling poorly. He had contracted a cold, and his voice was weak and raspy. I sat in his bedroom, which is on the ground floor of Skye House, and read to him until almost midnight. Then I gathered up Amheh, put her on Father's chest, blew out the candle, and closed the door."

I looked up from my notetaking. "Who is Amheh?"

The girl gave a sigh. "Father's great black cat. The animal is totally devoted to Father, tolerates me, and despises everyone else."

"In other words," Holmes said, "a typical member of the feline species. Please continue."

"It was a wild, stormy night. My room just above Father's, and I must have been exhausted, for despite my initial thought that I shouldn't rest well with the wind and rain lashing the windows, I fell into a very deep sleep after I drank my usual small glass of wine. In fact, I didn't awaken until almost seven, which is late for me, and I might have slept longer had I not heard a yowling at my door. I opened it to find Amheh there – she cried and curled about my legs, clearly distressed. I rang for our housekeeper, Mrs. Conner, and asked her if she had delivered Father's morning cup of cocoa. She said she was just preparing it and hadn't yet tapped upon his door. We went down together, and I hurried to Father's chamber, Amheh at my heels.

"Father didn't respond when I knocked and then called to him. I opened the door and went inside, drawing aside the bed curtains. To my horror, Father was dead. I sent Mrs. Conner to fetch the doctor, who arrived an hour later. It was during that time, as I sat and mourned, that I also became convinced someone had entered the chamber and dispatched Father in his sleep."

Holmes now opened his eyes and leaned forward. "What did you observe?"

"Father looked peaceful. The bedclothes were neat, as if he had barely turned or twisted in the sleep that had preceded death. But three things gave me cause for alarm. First, I saw tiny drops of blood upon the white comforter that covered Father. These stains were so minute I might not have seen them, had I not been thinking of how Mrs. Conner and I had just washed and freshened the sheets the day before, as Father was most fastidious about cleanliness. The second was the small sheepskin rug by the window. I rose and paced, looking toward the road to see if Mrs. Conner was returning. When I did, my bare foot stepped into the thick wool. Mr. Holmes, it was sodden, almost as wet as if thrown into a river. It could only have gotten that way if the window had been open. Father never slept with his window ajar, and certainly wouldn't have raised it on such a wild night. But there was the evidence of the fleecy rug, so cold upon my toes – yet the window was latched from the inside, just as I had left it. There was one more thing – "

"The cat," Holmes said.

"Yes! Amheh slept beside Father, and every morning, when I came to wake Father, she would open her mouth and yawn, giving me a look of great contempt. Father would never have put her out of his room, yet she somehow appeared at my door in the morning. I had just begun to ponder this when the doctor arrived. His verdict was that Father died most peacefully, of old age and the lingering damage from his fever." The lady shook her head. "I made my objections to him, and later that day to Inspector Willow, but neither believed me, nor saw reason to investigate. I could do nothing except follow Father's instructions as to his burial, and afterward sally forth in search of a champion for him."

"Was any wound found upon your father's body?" Holmes asked.

"None, sir. Khalil and I prepared Father for eternity, and so I am certain. Father was thin, but there wasn't a scratch on his flesh."

"Khalil is a servant?"

"More of an acolyte," the young woman said. "He was a youthful digger for Father in Egypt, but Father saw great talent in him and paid for him to be sent to England for an education. He came to us when we returned home, and for two years helped Father establish his ministry.

318

Father bought him a cottage just down the lane from us, past Sir Nigel's house." The lady's voice warmed with pride. "Khalil is an author and an illustrator. He writes adventurous stories for children. It is he who produced the little tract."

"His age?"

"He is twenty-eight."

Holmes nodded. "Did your father have any enemies?"

"He had detractors, sir, and none more vigorous than the Reverend Jonas Stone, the vicar of St. Lucy's Church. He accused Father of leading St. Lucy's flock astray, and he wasn't pleased when Father said if he cared more for feeding his indigent parishioners than enlarging the vicarage, he would have more sheep. When we buried Father, the vicar interrupted the service, proclaiming Father had descended into Hell. His insult didn't please several of the young men, including Khalil, and they approached him in a body, prepared to teach him a lesson. Reverend Stone quickly leapt into his dogcart and sped away before any undignified punches were thrown. But as for actual enemies . . . No, sir, I don't see how anyone would hate Father so much as to murder him in his bed."

"Are there any other servants in the house?"

"No sir – only Mrs. Conner, who has been with me for three years, and is a faithful and gentle widow."

"Then I must pose one more question, Miss Oakley – and I will offer my apologies if it seems an indelicate one: Is there someone who might wish to cause *you* pain?"

"Sir . . . *No!* I have done nothing for five years except devote myself to Father and his strange ministries. I am certainly not a popular woman in the village – the respectable ladies do not call upon me or invite me for tea – but Father's poor followers have always been kind and dear to me."

"No suitors?"

The young woman's face turned red. "None."

"Madam," Holmes said gently. "I cannot aid you if you are not forthright with me."

Her blush deepened. "Mr. Holmes, no one has asked for my hand, and I am not active in society. Oh, I suppose you might say that Sir Nigel Marlow has tried to play the gallant, arriving at the house at odd hours and making a pest of himself, but he is a puffed-up old fool who has already buried two wives, and can talk of nothing but his collection of medieval antiquities! I presumed he was more interested in Father – for his historical knowledge – than in me. More than once I have dozed off in my chair while they harangued on Constantine and Charlamagne."

Holmes smiled at her spirited answer. "Did Sir Nigel attend the funeral?"

"No sir, but he sent condolences and a large spray of flowers. He has a most remarkable garden, which . . . ."

"Yes?" Holmes asked. The lady's sudden change of expression had betrayed a worrisome thought.

"I was just recalling how, a few weeks ago, there was a bit of a row when Sir Nigel accused Khalil of stealing blossoms. Khalil denied it at first, though later he confessed to me that he had clipped a few of the gentleman's roses to take home and study for an illustration he was working on. I insisted that he write Sir Nigel a letter of apology, and enclose two shillings as restitution – surely more than the flowers were worth." The lady shook her head. "Forgive me, sir. I didn't wish to stray from my story."

"Where was your father laid to rest?"

"In the ancient family mausoleum at Skye House. He was buried in a manner befitting a pharaoh, wrapped in linen sheets with his favorite ceremonial jewels and his solid silver magician's wand. We placed him inside an antique coffin that he had purchased in Egypt."

A knock on our door interrupted Holmes's next question. Mrs. Hudson came in with a card.

"A gentleman for you, sir. He is most insistent that you see him without delay."

Holmes frowned but quickly read the card and told Mrs. Hudson to show the visitor up. He turned to our guest.

"Miss Oakley, I apologize. It isn't generally my custom to admit one client into another's consultation. However – come in, Inspector Willow."

The gentleman who passed through our door was perhaps thirty years of age, neatly dressed, and holding his bowler hat in his hands. His soft round face flushed to the roots of his wavy blond hair when he spotted the feminine occupant of the room.

"Mara! What – how long have you been in London?"

She rose to her feet, glaring at the intruder. "I left home at seven yesterday morning. I spent yesterday and last night in London, with my great-aunt, before visiting Scotland Yard and then coming to see Mr. Holmes an hour ago – which would be just before one." She stiffened and tilted her head. "But I hardly see how this is any of your business."

The youthful inspector dropped his head and muttered an apology. Holmes stepped forward.

"Has some new evidence come forth, to bring you to my door?"

"I . . . in a certain way . . . This is most awkward. Mara – Excuse me . . . Miss Oakley. Please sit down. I have terrible news."

The lady warily perched on the edge of the sofa. "It cannot be worse than what I have already experienced."

320

"I fear that it is. Forgive me, but – your father's grave has been desecrated. His severed head was discovered this morning, and your friend Khalil Hassan has been arrested. However, there are certain aspects of the matter that I wished Mr. Holmes's expertise on and – *Mara!*"

The lady did not faint, but she slumped forward, giving way to a flood of tears and the strong emotions she had so bravely held in check. Holmes stepped close and whispered into my ear as the inspector moved to console our client.

"A twice-murdered man. This is proving to be a very interesting day."

Inspector Willow convinced Miss Oakley to return to her relative's abode, and Holmes promised to keep her informed as to his progress in the matter. We barely had time to catch the next train to the village, which was only a short distance from London. Holmes offered the inspector a draught from his flask, and he accepted gratefully.

"It has been a devil of a morning, sir. Thank you for coming with me."

"Why were you so dismissive of Miss Oakley's testimony about the night her father perished?" Holmes asked. "She didn't strike me as a hysterical witness."

"No, she was calm and collected. But the doctor was equally sure the old gentleman had died of natural causes, and when I came to the house, I found no evidence of a forced window in the dead man's room. The sheepskin was quite dry, and the spots of blood were very small, hardly more than one might have from a slight cut on a finger. The doctor told me Mr. Oakley likely coughed blood while *in extremis*, which would explain the stains."

"And the cat?" Holmes asked. The inspector shrugged.

"What of it? Perhaps the old gentleman grew tired of its yowling and pitched it through the door. Miserable beasts, cats – Give me a dog any day!"

"Very well. Tell us what happened earlier this morning."

"I was summoned to Sir Nigel's home at nine-fifteen. Sir Nigel and the vicar were waiting for me in the garden. The vicar's wife had returned to the dwelling, being in a very agitated state. Sir Nigel, you should know, is the most prominent gentleman in the neighborhood, and he complains frequently about 'crime' in the village, though there is very little of it.

"'Sir Nigel, what is wrong?' I asked. 'Your servant said there was a "bad business" that I must attend to.'

"'And there is!' he bellowed. 'Come and see what that black devil has done!'

321

"I crossed through the gate and into the garden, which is filled with peonies, lavender, and many varieties and shades of roses. There, on a gravel pathway, was a horrid sight – the severed head of the late Mr. Oakley. It was lying face down, with a few bandages still tight about the eyes and jaw. The flesh of the neck was ragged, as if someone had hacked the head free from its body with an ax."

"You are certain of the identification?"

"Yes – I recognized him immediately, and the gentleman had a distinctive tattoo upon his right cheek. Even in the head's gruesome state, this mark was visible."

Holmes nodded and signaled for him to continue.

"It seems that Sir Nigel had invited the vicar and his wife to take breakfast with him that morning. Before they sat down, he led them through his garden, as he gathered blossoms for the table. They were dining when Sir Nigel spotted the figure of Khalil Hassan hurrying down the path, with stolen cuttings in his hand. This, you must understand, has been a common problem. The man has confessed to thievery and trespass before. Sir Nigel was enraged and bid his guests come with him, to bear witness to whatever damage Hassan had caused. But as they approached, they saw something in the gravel – and belatedly recognized it for what it was. The vicar's lady fainted. Servants were summoned, and I was sent for."

Holmes lit a cigarette. "Causing, one presumes, quite a stirring of the gravel, and an obscuring of any helpful footprints. Please continue, Inspector."

"Sir Nigel was adamant he had witnessed the Egyptian running from the garden in a 'most furtive manner'. I sent Oakley's head to the village undertaker for safekeeping, then fetched my constable and drove out to the Hassan cottage, which is but a short distance from Sir Nigel's estate. We found Hassan seated at a large drawing table, sketching a bowl of rather wilted flowers.

"'I will need you to account for yourself this morning,' I told the man.

"'I walked to the village at seven-thirty, as is my custom every morning, to acquire my exercise,' he said, 'I purchased some bread, then returned, and have been here since. Is there a problem?'

"'Sir Nigel says you stole from his garden.' I pointed at the bouquet. 'How do you explain that arrangement?'

"'It was one that we used at The Great Oracle's funeral,' he said, with some sharpness. 'I confess I pilfered once from Sir Nigel, but I also made amends to him. These roses were given to me by Miss Oakley as a remembrance of her beloved father!'

"And here, Mr. Holmes, I tried to do as you might. Your friend's tales have made you famous among all of us in the official forces as an example to follow. I looked closely at Hassan's hands. They appeared to be dirty, stained with ink and charcoal from his art supplies. But would a grave robber's hands not also be filthy from his vile deed? Was this how he had hurried to hide his crime?"

Holmes winced. He started to speak, then stopped himself. The young man seemed to take this as encouragement.

"And then – I beheld proof of his despicable act!"

"What was that?" I asked, finding myself caught up in the breathless storytelling, despite Holmes's sour glance in my direction.

"His sketches! I saw the papers clearly on his table. One showed a man holding a severed head. Another, a pair of grotesque figures bending over a tomb. I spun about and accused Hassan of desecrating Oakley's grave. He at first denied it, then began to scream and wail in his foreign tongue. It took all we could do to bind him and bring him in."

Holmes frowned. "Have you been to the scene at Skye House?"

"It was my final stop. The housekeeper said her mistress had left home the day before. The servant didn't seem to know anything was amiss, so I quickly made up a pretense to gain access to the crypt. She took down a key from a peg, gave it to me, and went back to her chores."

"Is it the only key to the sepulcher?

"I didn't think to ask."

Holmes closed his eyes. I saw his jaw grow tense. "Pity. But describe what you found there."

"It is a great marble mausoleum that lies almost a quarter-mile from the house. The door was locked. There was no sign of damage, no hint that the portal had been forced open. The interior was grim and odiferous. A strangely shaped coffin was laid upon the floor, with its lid open, so the body was exposed. It was obvious the head was missing."

"But the remainder of the corpse wasn't disturbed?"

"No, it was still wrapped tightly and – " Here the Inspector shook his head. He looked at my friend with the weariness of a hound who has lost the scent of the fox. "Mr. Holmes, at that juncture, I suddenly realized I should seek you out."

"And what made you come to that conclusion?"

"Because as I stood there, with my handkerchief pressed to my face against the smell, I began to see flaws in my reasoning. Hassan might be a foreigner, but he had always been very devoted to the old man. I had heard a rumor that Oakley was buried in Egyptian finery, which might serve as a temptation to a fellow desperate for cash, as I presume Hassan must be, based on his very modest quarters. And indeed, there was a collar of gold and lapis atop his linen-bound chest, and a wand of solid silver laid at his side! It appeared that none of these expensive items had been touched by the thief."

"Why would Hassan take the head and leave the valuables behind?" I asked.

"And why would he toss the head into Sir Nigel's garden?" Holmes added. The inspector raked a hand through his blond curls.

"And that, Mr. Holmes, explains why my next action was to hurry to your address," Willow admitted. "I tried to work it through on the journey. Foreigners have queer beliefs – they thrive on superstitions. Perhaps by separating the head from the body and placing it on that property, Hassan felt he would place a curse on Sir Nigel, whom he despises. Some strange pagan practice may be to blame. But . . . I also fear I may have allowed my speculation to run ahead of my evidence."

"A common error," Holmes said dryly.

"You can help me?"

"I think so. However, you must be plain with me in return. What are your feelings toward Miss Oakley?"

A sudden fever sprang into the inspector's checks. "She is very beautiful. I admire her kindness to the poor. I pity her the loss of her father."

"And she is quite the heiress, I understand."

"Sir! As if that – !"

Holmes lifted a calming hand. "Do you know of fellows in the town whose intentions might be less than honorable?"

The inspector sighed. "Perhaps. More than one rough lad attended services to watch Mara in her linen gown, which was . . . *Ahem* . . . somewhat revealing. And Hassan . . . Well, he is too familiar with her for my comfort, though admittedly they have known each other since childhood."

"What of Sir Nigel?"

The inspector laughed. "Mr. Holmes, he is a pompous old humbug, almost the age of her father! He was once an instructor at a military academy, and his greatest passion, even beyond his flower garden, is a collection of antique weapons – canons, catapults, and the like – which he keeps just behind his house. To visit him is to risk getting dragged off for a lecture on crossbows, complete with a demonstration."

"Very well. Your tale has been most interesting. I shall muse on it for the remainder of our journey," Holmes said, pulling his cloth cap over his eyes. Inspector Willow shook his head.

"Can you at least tell me if my theory about Hassan is sound?"

"Frankly," Holmes said, "it is ridiculous beyond words. However, not all is lost. Let us speak again when we reach our destination."

Upon disembarking from the train, Holmes's first request was to view the severed head of the late Mr. Oakley. The much-humbled inspector led us to the village mortuary, where a sad-faced undertaker ushered us into a back room. Holmes placed the grisly artifact upon a cooling board.

"What do you make of it, Watson?"

I am a veteran of many hours in the dissection chamber and have witnessed more than my share of horrific casualties in Afghanistan, but somehow this relic tested my nerves. Decay had set in and the smell was unpleasant, but it was the indignity done to the poor mad fellow that made the relic most offensive.

"I agree the flesh was hacked at. Whoever did this was neither a doctor nor a butcher who would have known better where to cut."

"What about the face?" Holmes asked, turning the head around in his hands. My friend's coolness toward death, the way he viewed it as simply a piece of a larger puzzle, continued to amaze me.

"The nose appears to be broken."

"Indeed – but this is a *post mortem* injury, as Miss Oakley said her father's features were undisturbed at death."

"The villain tossed it into the garden," Inspector Willow offered, from his position in the furthest corner of the room. "Surely that is how the nose was damaged."

"Was the head found in a sack or bag?"

"No."

"I would like to meet the ghoul who would so blithely fling a severed head into a garden, in daylight, in full view on a public road," Holmes said. "There is no more to be learned here. A quick visit to the vicar is in order."

Our next stop was to a neat, ivy-covered cottage beside the ancient church. A maid showed us into a study, and we were joined by the Reverend Stone, a pinch-faced man of advanced years, bowed back, and strong opinions. He appeared unimpressed by the inspector's introduction of my friend.

"You've come at a poor time. I must write my sermon for Sunday. I intend to speak upon *Exodus* 22:18."

Holmes inclined his head. "And why that particular passage?"

"Is it not obvious? Severed heads, fiendish pagan ways? Old Oakley's soul is no doubt burning in the pit, and yet someone claims his skull to work devilish magic!" The vicar leaned close, putting one hand to his mouth, speaking in a stage whisper. "If you ask me, Oakley's slattern

325

daughter put the infidel up to it. Using her own father's corpse for her wicked ways! What has this world come to?"

Holmes drew back. Though his face was schooled to calmness, I could sense his utter revulsion. "Can you tell me what drew you and your good spouse to Sir Nigel's home this morning? Breakfast seems an unusual time for a pastoral visit."

"Why, he sent us an invitation the night before, saying he wished to discuss a donation to St. Lucy's – a very sizeable donation, one that would allow us to expand the vicarage kitchen and purchase a nice piano. Gertrude – that is my wife – would very much like a piano! Who are we to question the hour when such generosity is being offered?"

"And I understand that you three strolled about the garden before breakfast was served?"

"We did. Sir Nigel wished to show off his roses and clipped a fine bouquet as a little present for Gertrude. Do forgive her for not attending us, but she was quite shaken by the revelation of the severed head."

"Understandable," Holmes said. "What happened after you went into the house?"

"We sat down, and his maid brought out breakfast. A veritable feast it was. Bacon and sausages and eggs and tomatoes and sweet cakes with cream." The repulsive little man licked his lips. "Sir Nigel has a most excellent cook!"

"Did Sir Nigel leave you at any point?"

"Abandon us at the table? Of course not! He was a perfect host!"

Holmes frowned. "And at what point was the meal interrupted?"

"The maid had just cleared away the dishes, and the clock was striking nine when Sir Nigel spotted that nasty man running from his garden! 'See, there the rascal goes!' he cried. 'Come, let us try to catch him.'"

"And you ran outside?"

The vicar chuckled. "Well, Sir Nigel outpaced me – these legs are no longer those of a university sprinter."

"He was out of your sight?"

"What? No! I kept my gaze upon him, even when he went into the garden. I saw him slow down and then heard his cry. Gertrude had come out after us, and we walked up together and saw the horror."

"But you never spotted Hassan?"

The reverend sneered. "I did not – but would you call Sir Nigel a liar?"

"Very well. Thank you for your time. Might I suggest that *Matthew* 7:1-3 as a more appropriate scripture for this Sabbath's message."

Holmes turned on his heel and led the way out of the cottage. Much to our surprise, there was an elderly lady waiting at the door. She was crowned by a wreath of gray hair, and her face was deeply lined, but there was a gentleness, along with a hint of amusement, in her expression.

"Mr. Holmes, I came down the stairs just as you began to speak with my husband. I didn't wish to interrupt your conversation, for this is clearly a man's business, but I felt I must clarify one thing." She smiled at Inspector Willow, who had joined us at the threshold. "You know, Inspector, how forgetful my dear husband can be. Sir Nigel did leave us, just before our second cups of coffee were poured. He was gone for less than three or four minutes, and he came back quite flushed with exertion. He said he had run to his pantry to find some honey he wished us to sample – made, he claimed, by the bees in his own garden."

Holmes's smile was beatific. "Thank you, Madam. That does indeed clear up a very puzzling matter. Was Sir Nigel bearing this honey when he returned?"

"No, and that was what made it so amusing, for then he noticed that the pot was already on the table, and we all laughed about it."

"But what questions should I ask them?" Inspector Willow wailed as we drove out to Sir Nigel's estate. Sundown was nearing on this high summer day, and Holmes was anxious to bring our visit to a close before the evening train arrived. My friend's clipped words revealed he was nearly devoid of all patience with the young officer.

"Where they were last night and this morning? What are their routines? Have they seen any strange men lurking in the shadows? What is each person's favorite color? Surely, Willow, you can think of *something* to keep a master and his five servants occupied for an hour."

The inspector scratched his head. "Very well, but – why did you make me stop and buy that melon?"

Holmes tapped the basket on the floor of the carriage with his foot. "Because I am a great believer in experimentation. Now remember, it is essential you keep all of them together until I return – preferably in a sizeable chamber on an upper floor. Watson, I believe we shall disembark here."

The inspector halted the pair of horses, Holmes seized the basket, and we climbed down at a spot where Sir Nigel's house was just visible beyond some trees. Inspector Willow whistled to his pair and moved along. I pointed to a low brick fence that enclosed a large section of land.

"That must be the legendary garden."

"Indeed. I would estimate that it begins some fifty yards beyond the stately home. Quite a lovely bit of English landscaping, in the more antique style. We shall return to it presently, but let us smoke a cigarette or two and give our young friend time to assemble the servants and the master, so that our proverbial coast shall be clear."

"Holmes," I said as he struck a match on the sole of his boot, "I cannot shake a certain feeling."

"And that is?"

"No true grave robber would bother to separate the head from the body but leave valuable goods behind. Therefore, does it not stand to reason that Oakley's corpse was mutilated for another purpose?"

"It does indeed."

"But what could that be? The days of the resurrection men are past, and there is no value in a human head. Therefore . . . there must be some other motive in desecration."

"You scintillate."

"But – the only other motive I could think of is a desire to inflict some posthumous revenge. I do not wish to accuse a man of the cloth, yet – "

"The vicar concerns you?"

"Yes, because I know the text of *Exodus* 22:18 – *Thou shall not suffer a witch to live*. The old man is clearly fanatical, still enraged that a 'pagan' lured away his congregants. Would this not be a way to cause pain to Miss Oakley, or perhaps mark the start of a cruel attempt to drive her from the village?"

"Before she is burned at the stake?"

"Holmes!"

My friend held up a hand. "You are correct that the vicar is an unpleasant specimen of the Anglican faith. But how did our aged reverend get into the crypt? And how could he have placed the head in Sir Nigel's garden – or, better yet, *why* would he have placed it there? If he truly wished to terrorize Miss Oakley, putting the relic on her doorstep would have sufficed."

I nodded grimly. Holmes clapped a hand to my shoulder.

"Come – a simple exercise in history should resolve our quandary."

We made our way up the little hill to the fine, three-story brick house. As Holmes had instructed, the inspector had made certain the front door was unlocked, and we quickly glanced into the rooms on the ground floor. The breakfast chamber commanded a view of the garden, and a great study was filled with books on botany, as well as rows of historical tomes, all of them guarded by an elegant suit of arms bearing a fearsome mace in its gloved hands. Holmes wasted little time looking about, however, and rapidly led us to the rear of the building. We passed into a graveled yard, one filled – as the inspector had warned – with a vast array of ancient and medieval weaponry. Holmes hummed to himself as he walked about.

"What excellent pieces! Those crossbows on that rack behind you are completely authentic to the period. A battering ram, a miniature siege tower, swords – he must have stocked a veritable museum in his days as a schoolmaster. Ah . . . This is what I am looking for."

"It is a catapult," I noted, considering the strange device.

"Perhaps half the size of those used by the crusaders, but useful all the same," Holmes said. "Especially for replicating the crusaders' actions in flinging enemy heads over high walls."

Holmes took out the melon. He turned a crank, drawing tight a long rope and lowering the catapult's basket, laughing like a schoolboy as he worked. Before I could question the action, he placed the melon in the basket, grabbed one of the swords, and sliced through the rope, releasing the tension. The machine performed perfectly, and the melon went flying above the roof of the house.

"My God," I whispered. "So that was how it was made to appear in the garden after breakfast."

Holmes tossed the sword aside and slapped his hands together. "I couldn't put aside the fact that a minister and his wife were brought to this house so early – and even earlier were guided about the garden. I confess I despaired when the vicar said his host never left the table, but his wife's correction made it clear what had happened. The previous evening, Sir Nigel went to the Skye House crypt and removed the body's head. He hid it here in some secret place, and during breakfast raced into the yard to fling it into the garden, where it could be discovered in a spot it had not been an hour before. Sir Nigel was aware of Mr. Hassan's habits – that he went into the village and passed by the garden every morning. It gave Sir Nigel the perfect opportunity to pin the crime upon the immigrant."

"But why would he wish to do such a horrible thing?"

"Indeed, sir – *why?*"

I looked to my friend, whose eyes went wide. Slowly, we turned to look behind us, toward the speaker of the snarled question.

Sir Nigel had emerged from his home and seized one of the crossbows from the rack near the door. Having just witnessed a demonstration of his devices, I had no doubt that the chosen weapon would work as intended. In a twinkling, he could put an iron-tipped arrow through my heart, or Holmes's.

"Must I repeat myself?" the man demanded. He was gray-haired and bearded, but still agile and muscular, the only sign of weakness being a bandage wrapped around his right hand. "Why do you say these things?"

"Because they are true," Holmes replied.

"Ridiculous!"

"Allow me to explain myself. You will surely grant me this last request? You wanted the young lady, Miss Oakley. You killed her father to clear the path to her. I must compliment you, Sir Nigel. It is rare that I meet a villain with your capacity for planning such repugnant crimes."

The man ground his teeth together. "You have no proof."

"Shall I tell you how you did it?" Holmes asked, with such coolness that he might have been in Baker Street, puffing on his pipe, rather than standing helpless in a yard, with crossbow aimed at his chest. "You first found an accomplice in the lady's housekeeper. You need not look surprised. It is simple process of elimination – there was no other individual in the house who could both drug Miss Oakley's nightly glass of wine and open the window of Mr. Oakley's bedroom to admit you. Dripping wet, you climbed inside, leaving the window open for your rapid departure. You took up a pillow and held it to the old fellow's face, a tried-and-true method of assassinating the weak without leaving telltale marks. As a medieval scholar, you were perhaps inspired by the stories of the Princes in the Tower, whom many believe were killed in this manner. However, my friend will tell you that I disagree with common wisdom that the boys were slain by their wicked uncle – Will you not, Watson?"

I had tried to slowly ease myself closer to our captor, in hopes that I might grab at the crossbow. Sir Nigel swung back, growling as he leveled the arrow's vicious point in my direction. I froze. Holmes continued talking, reclaiming the villain's attention.

"The one thing you didn't count upon was the old man's faithful cat, which sprang upon you and scratched you viciously. Do not attempt to deny it, as you still wear the bandages about your hand. A cat's clawing can be notoriously hard to heal, even if it does not gush with blood. Either you or the housekeeper threw the beast out, so the murder of its master might be concluded. You departed as you had come, and she locked the window behind you, then closed the door. She forgot about the feline or, more likely, couldn't find it again. Neither of you noticed the bloodstains, and whatever dampness was on the sheets dried overnight, but the thicker sheepskin by the window did not. Miss Oakley noticed the wet rug, but the incompetent Inspector Willow was late in reaching the scene and found it dry – because your accomplice had, by the time of the inspector's arrival, exchanged the sheepskin for another while Miss Oakley was briefly removed from her father's chamber, perhaps dressing or swallowing a morsel of food.

"Though the old man was gone, there was still the foreigner to be eliminated. You knew the lady preferred the company of her childhood friend. Therefore, the grave-robbing and the amazing act of launching the head into the garden and blaming its placement on the man who passed by every morning, and with whom you had already quarreled. It was quite ingenious. You relied upon the stupidity of the inspector to arrest Hassan, and the prejudices of the villagers to convict him. Miss Oakley was a loving daughter – if convinced Hassan had committed such a despicable act against her father's corpse, she would reject him." Holmes folded his arms. "The most remarkable part of this plan is your conceit that the lady would love you after these gentlemen were removed from her life. That, Sir Nigel, is the one aspect of this tale that is almost beyond belief. Your arrogance is breathtaking."

"I could kill you," the man snapped. His face had turned red, and beads of sweat stood upon his brow.

"Certainly," Holmes said, with a hint of a shrug, as if his mortal existence meant little to him. "But surely by now, you have reasoned that Watson and I are standing too far apart to slay with one bolt. Therefore, you must decide which one of us is more satisfying to execute. Be assured that if you shoot me, my friend will waste no time in avenging my death. And if you kill him, I will dispatch you within seconds and leave your corpse to rot in your own garden."

The villain's eyes went wide. At the very next instant, a spike-studded mace – one which I hardly would have believed a woman could have lifted – crashed into his back. He lurched forward with an agonized cry. The crossbow bolt shoot uselessly into the gravel.

"I could not stay in London," Miss Oakley whispered as Holmes shouted into the house for the inspector, and I moved to aid the dazed and bleeding Sir Nigel. "They told me in the village you had gathered here. I saw his intentions, so I took a weapon from his study. I heard what Mr. Holmes said . . . and if Sir Nigel dies of his wounds, I will hang without protest. Father's justice is done."

Faithful readers of the sensational papers may recall the outcome of the events in the little town of Lynhart – how the housekeeper, Mrs. Conner, was arrested by Inspector Willow and quickly gave testimony against Sir Nigel. He had drawn her into the plot with promises of money, enough to pay off the debts of her two ne'er-do-well sons. She was sentenced to life in prison, but Sir Nigel danced at the end of a rope a year later.

Lesser known is the happier outcome of the case – how Miss Oakley abandoned her career as a pagan priestess but remained a patroness of the poor. When her year of mourning was done, she wed Mr. Khalil Hassan, who later achieved notable success as an illustrator and author of fantastic tales. His sketch entitled "The Lady Saves the Detective" was never publicly shown or printed, but remains framed upon the wall of Sherlock Holmes's bed-chamber to this day.

The Murano Musician
by Richard Gillman

It was, as I recall, a brilliant, sunny day in Baker Street on the eighth of August, 1894, that Holmes and I had finished breakfast and had retreated to our armchairs feeling replete.

Holmes had taken up his copy of *The Times* and appeared engrossed as plumes of blue smoke rose from behind the broadsheet, interspersed with the occasional grunt of displeasure. For my part, I picked up my August copy of *The Lancet*. Within it, I found a most informative article upon the subject of "On the Treatment of Tapeworm" by Leslie Ogilvie, and it was just as I began to read that a gentle knock at the door announced Mrs. Hudson.

Looking up, I saw her approach with arm outstretched, holding the silver tray upon which she brought our mail. The newspaper which hid Holmes from view didn't even twitch as he announced, "Be a good fellow, Watson, and take the mail from Mrs. Hudson." She paused for a moment and then approached, handing me a single letter from her tray. It was clear from her resigned look that Holmes was his usual self.

I smiled and nodded and then began to regard the envelope. Turning it over in my hands, I noticed that Holmes's name and our address had been written in a hand that I immediately recognised from a similar letter that he had received in February.

The envelope now had my full attention, and I sought to apply Holmes's methods. On holding it to my nose, the slight scent of cologne that I detected, and the flourish and the extraordinarily long serif on the figure "*1*" of our address, confirmed my suspicion.

Turning towards Holmes, I sought to tease him by saying, "it would appear that we have a letter from the Continent . . . Well, by way of Grosvenor Square."

Holmes slowly lowered the broadsheet, saying, "If you mean a letter from Count Ernesto Salvatore Emilio de Cagliari, the Italian ambassador, Watson, it was immediately obvious: The way you wafted the envelope around confirmed it."

I felt a little crestfallen and offered the envelope to Holmes who brusquely waved it away, saying, "No, no. You have begun, so pray continue."

Rising from my chair, I strode to Holmes's desk and took from it the fine Italian stiletto that had been a gift to Holmes from the Count and used it to slit open the envelope. Taking from it the single sheet of paper I opened it before reading it aloud.

My dear Holmes,

I trust this letter finds both you and Dr. Watson in good health. Once again, I am in a position where discretion dictates that I must solicit your services in preference, initially at least, to those of the Metropolitan police.

A member of my "external" staff, Señor Alphonso Breccia, was found dead this morning at his premises at No. 4 Mount Pleasant, Phoenix Place, Clerkenwell. The circumstances surrounding his death are most distressing.

I have dispatched Inspector Frosali from the embassy to meet you, and he has secured the address. I hope that you will agree, and are disposed, to meet him there this morning at ten a.m. Nothing has been touched since the discovery of the body, and I would greatly appreciate your observations and opinion before the embassy contacts Scotland Yard.

Yours most faithfully,

Ernesto

On hearing this, Holmes's face looked most troubled. "This is most unusual. I'm intrigued by the case, and particularly so by His Excellency's use of the term 'external' staff." Holmes frowned before rising to scribble a brief confirmation of our attendance to the Italian Embassy. He then returned to his chair and retired to that place in his mind where he considered all relevant possibilities.

We hailed a cab, with Holmes calling out the address to the driver before settling in for the brief ride to Clerkenwell. On arrival, I tossed the cabbie a sixpence and glanced around me as I strove to ascertain my bearings. Holmes raised his stick towards the impressive building before us which announced in bold, gold lettering, housed the Phoenix Brass Foundry. Looking more closely, I became intrigued by a stone plaque above the double doors which depicted cannon balls and gun barrels.

It was as I now looked left and right that I noticed a smartly dressed figure pacing on the pavement some ten yards from us. The fellow in question was undoubtedly Inspector Frosali, who appeared to be some forty years of age and dressed as a city gentleman, with a somewhat rounded body and similarly round face, topped with iron-grey hair. As we approached, it was plain that the ambassador had informed him of our appearance, as he greeted us saying, "Good morning, Mr. Holmes, Dr. Watson. I trust you are well, and that you are both blessed with a strong stomach." Frosali paused before continuing gravely, "What we will see here is . . . shall we say . . . not at all pleasant."

Holmes touched his hat in greeting and then nodded before replying, "Good morning, Inspector. I take it then, that this isn't a case of death by natural causes."

The inspector pursed his lips and then slowly shook his head, replying, "Indeed not, Mr. Holmes." Taking a large key from his pocket, he walked but a few paces towards a stout door to the left of the foundry entrance. Beside the door was a shop window which was covered with a strong, metal grille. This guarded an impressive display of colourful glass objects, clearly in the Murano style. These included large depictions of leaping fish, exotic birds, and glass tableware. I noted with interest that the grille hadn't protected the window from a large splash of red paint which had clearly been thrown at the shop.

On entering, I was immediately struck by the unmistakable stench akin to that of a charnel house. It took me a moment for my eyes to adjust to the gloom within, but we proceeded inside towards the shop counter, behind which stood shelves where more glassware rested. The inspector securely locked the shop door behind us and then turned towards us slightly before beckoning us towards a doorway at the back of the shop.

Once through the doorway, the smell of decay increased. The inspector took a silver match case from his waistcoat pocket and struck a vesta, which he used to light a pair of gas lights on the wall above the wooden workbench which ran the length of one side of the workshop.

As the gas lights hissed and spluttered into life, I could see by their meagre light a figure which I took to be Breccia. He was seated before the workbench, bound tightly to a chair with his head slumped against his chest at a strange angle. Before him on the bench was an assortment of tools. These, I noted included large scissors or shears, callipers, tongs and rounded iron bars . . . some of which were clearly bloodstained.

Holmes immediately took from his pocket his magnifying glass and began to closely examine the lifeless, bound figure. The inspector turned to me, holding out his hand towards the body while saying, "This was Alphonso Breccia. He was a very brave man, a credit to our nation, and he was my friend."

I gave a single nod and moved to observe Holmes as he examined the body. As I did so, my hand went to my mouth as I saw the extent of Breccia's injuries. Before me was a man of some thirty years who, before this cruel attack, had once been a handsome fellow, although his face was now badly beaten. Seated as he was, I noticed that both his wrists and forearms had been tied to the arms of the wooden chair, and that the first and third fingers on his left hand were missing.

Frosali peered over my shoulder and sighed. "His ring finger is gone. He always used to wear his father's wedding ring, in memory of him."

The light from within the room was indeed dim and, looking about me, I noticed a small side window that was covered by a dusty curtain. After asking and receiving the inspector's permission and a nod from Holmes, I opened the curtain to allow sunlight into the room. Holmes had now moved to examine the workbench and I moved forwards, taking my glass from my overcoat pocket to examine the body more thoroughly. From the amount of bruising and swelling, he had clearly suffered greatly before a savage wound to his throat had ended his ordeal. I then joined Holmes as he examined the items upon the workbench and its environs.

I noted that upon the bench was a Bunsen burner, beside which were a variety of hand tools which I assumed the victim had used to form the molten glass. Beside them stood a large rack which contained long, hollow pipes with a mouthpiece at one end. Also on the bench were some sketches, presumably of his ongoing work. However, the object that had drawn Holmes's attention was the most bloodied: A large pair of long-handled shears whose work I had already witnessed.

As Holmes continued his inspection, I began to look beneath the bench, where I found a series of cupboards and shelves which contained both colourless and vividly-coloured glass rods. To one side of this I noticed a large metal bucket which held some glass shards and curious blobs of waste glass. Beside this were two wooden cases which had previously held bottles of wine. Both had stencilled names and addresses printed upon them and appeared to have come from local wine merchants, one from *L. Fratelli* and the other from *C. Lombardi*.

Holmes now joined me and appeared to be intrigued by what was within the cases. Using a gloved finger, he gently moved some fragments of strangely drawn-out, thin, tubular glass. These had the appearance of dark green, handblown ampoules, and their delicacy was in sharp contrast to the heavy form of the rejected glass in the metal bucket.

His interest piqued, he took up an iron rod from the bench and began to poke around amongst the glass fragments. I saw him reach forward and withdraw a crumpled piece of paper from one of the wooden wine cases. Taking great care, he opened it. Upon the sheet, written in what appeared to be Italian, was a single sentence. Holmes handed it to the inspector who moved towards the light from the small window.

As I watched the inspector frowned, causing me to ask, "Is it of interest?"

Frosali pursed his lips before saying, "I believe so, gentlemen. The sentence reads, *'For the misery you have brought upon us, you will pay dearly.'* It is signed with a single letter *'A'*." Frosali would say no more, but I noticed him pocket the piece of paper and then peer at the wine boxes while scribbling something in his notebook.

Holmes had moved towards the far wall of the workshop and was now facing a closed door. He was seen to frown as he asked, "To where does that lead, Inspector?"

The inspector tilted his head slightly, saying, "It is direct access to the foundry next door, Mr. Holmes. Alphonso rented a small furnace from them for his glasswork. But do not concern yourself. The door was secured from the inside when I found the body."

Seeming satisfied, Holmes then asked a more serious question: "What was this man's role while working for the embassy?"

Frosali's brow furrowed as he seemed to hesitate for a moment before replying, "His Excellency, the ambassador, has instructed me to talk freely before you. Alphonso was an agent – a conduit, if you will, between political factions and families who are of interest to our government."

Holmes nodded slightly as Frosali continued, "Through his work making expensive glassware, he was able to have contact with the highest echelons of society but, at the same time, he could keep his roots here, within the Italian community. Earlier this year, he was the source of information that led to the arrest of an anarchist in Clerkenwell who was returning to his lodgings while carrying a bomb."

Frosali paused for a moment before continuing, "Alphonso had received some valuable information from a contact he only referred to as *'K'*." The inspector rubbed his brow, saying, "Yesterday, he was to meet me at a local coffee shop. I waited but he didn't appear. It had been arranged that if he was unable to pass on any intelligence in person, he would send it to us in a most secure fashion. What method he was going to use we do not know."

Reaching into his overcoat pocket, Frosali produced a crumpled telegram which he then passed to Holmes. "It seems that he could only send this to me at the embassy."

Non é il vino che è INVECCHIATO, chiedete ad Antonio S. il numero 294, ma solo in inglesi.

My face must have given away my incomprehension for the inspector gave a gentle laugh, saying, "Ah, Dr. Watson, allow me to translate. It says, *'It is not the wine that is aged –* ' Note that the word *'aged'* is fully capitalized. *' – ask Antonio S. for number 294, but only in English'*."

Holmes, I saw, had a pensive look upon his face while I shook my head as the inspector's translation still left me in a fog. "But what does it mean, Inspector, and why does it say, '*but only in English*'?"

The inspector gave a brief shrug, saying, "We do not know. He may have an English-speaking friend called Antonio, but we aren't sure, and now there is the note you found. Alphonso had a passion for Italian wines, and he had sent me a case from a local wine merchant on my birthday." Frosali turned slightly to Holmes and smiled sadly, saying, "It is a passion that we both shared, and a date for we both have the same birthday."

Frosali paused, took out his pocket watch and then continued. "The wine merchants are where I think you might go next, but I must return to the embassy to refresh my memory of Alphonso's military service and his time in Pisa. I'm aware that he took may of his meals at a nearby tavern. Might I suggest that you take luncheon and a little refreshment there? It is called The Apple Tree, and perhaps they can provide some information. In the meantime, I will send you Alphonso's file by messenger to your rooms this afternoon."

On hearing this, Holmes nodded in agreement. Frosali then smiled before saying, "Well, if we are finished here, let us be away from this place." We followed the inspector out into the street, and he firmly locked the door to Breccia's shop.

Holmes now stood on the pavement, his head slightly bowed and with a forefinger pressed firmly against his lips. Looking up, he asked, "I wonder, Inspector, if I might have a day to consider this matter further before informing Scotland Yard and letting loose the hounds? My brother Mycroft might, perhaps, ask this of His Excellency . . . and Mycroft undoubtedly has the ear of the Police Commissioner."

Frosali frowned and then nodded. "Yes, that may well be the best way forward, Mr. Holmes. I will suggest this to the ambassador upon my return to the embassy."

Leading the way, Frosali walked some small distance before pointing the way towards a tavern with the delightful name The Apple Tree before leaving with a wave.

As Holmes and I stood outside, there was a hint of ale from the open door . . . but also the air was filled with the aroma of roasting coffee. Entering the establishment, we made our way to the bar where a chalkboard listed the daily lunchtime menu. Across the top of the chalkboard were the two names, *William* and *Lucia*, together with a union flag intertwined with that of Italy. While this concern appeared to have its roots firmly set in English soil, it also seemed to embrace the charms of Italy. My mouth was already watering as I looked down the menu and I saw that day's dish, *La Cucina Casereccia*, was "*Tagliatelle* and Beef

Stew", which I knew to be a classic Neapolitan dish. My stomach rumbled as I suggested it to Holmes, and then ordered two portions for us, and of course two glasses of red wine.

After but a few minutes, a young waitress appeared with our steaming plates of pasta. She stood for a moment to see if we enjoyed our first forkful. I believe that my expression told her that I plainly did. Holmes too, I saw, was enjoying his meal and, with his fork poised for his second mouthful, he innocently asked, "Tell me, does Signor Breccia, the glassmaker, eat here often? I saw that his shop was closed."

The waitress thought for a moment. "Hmm . . . Not often, but he does, and always alone. He seems to be a lonely man, and I think some of the local boys make fun of him."

Holmes frowned slightly asking, "Why might that be?"

The girl thought for a moment before replying, "They see him in his shop and sometimes, when he is working, they will bang on the metal grille in front of the shop window . . . just to annoy him. I think he caught one of them a few days ago, just as I was passing by his shop. He shouted at the boy very angrily and the child looked terrified."

Holmes nodded and then pointed at the delicious food with his fork saying, "I mustn't let this get cold, thank you."

On finishing our first course, I sat back and drained the last of my red wine. Holmes must have read my mind, asking, "Surely not dessert?" My only thoughts now were on the possibility of some kind of sweet Italian dish. Making my way to the bar, I noticed that at the very bottom of the chalkboard's menu was a difficult-to-find favourite of mine, Placenta, a sweet, round cake made from a mixture of pecorino cheese and honey, layered between leaves of pastry made from wheat and spelt flour. I turned towards Holmes with a questioning look but he waved his finger to decline. Suffice it to say that I ordered, and then enjoyed, a large slice of this delight.

Paying the bill, we made our way outside. Holmes took out his pocket watch, noted that it was now a little before one p.m., and began to walk briskly. "We must make haste if we're to be at Baker Street and ready to receive the file from Frosali."

Stepping out smartly, we made our way towards the premises of Luigi Fratelli. As we approached, I could see a fine display of Italian wines displayed in a mullion-windowed shop front. On entering the shop, Holmes took the lead and approached the counter where a jolly-looking gentleman of middle years was standing. He was wearing working clothes and a large, brown, pocketed apron tied at the waist. Smiling he greeted Holmes in heavily accented English, saying "Good afternoon, sir."

In return, Holmes touched his hat and answered, "Good afternoon. I would like to speak with Antonio, please."

The wine merchant pursed his lips and looked a little confused, saying, "I'm sorry, sir . . . We don't have a person of that name working here."

Holmes frowned slightly, saying, "Apologies, My mistake. A friend of mine, Alphonso Breccia, was kind enough to send me a case of fine Barolo wine and I wanted to purchase another. He mentioned Antonio and No. 294. Is that a reference to a particular wine?"

The wine merchant frowned and shook his head. "No, I'm afraid it isn't, but strangely enough, you are the second person to have asked that question."

On hearing this, my eyes opened wide in surprise and Holmes took a step closer, asking most earnestly, "Do you remember that customer?"

"Why yes. It was late afternoon, yesterday, just before we closed the shop. He was quite tall and slim, perhaps forty years of age, and he wasn't Italian. He was, perhaps, German or Austrian. I remember him because he seemed quite annoyed when I told him that the number wasn't a reference to a bottle of our wines, and it meant nothing to me."

Holmes paused for a moment before asking, "Did he ask in Italian?"

The merchant shook his head. "No sir, he only spoke in English."

I looked towards Holmes as he asked, "I noticed as I walked past Signor Breccia's shop this morning that a large splash of red paint had been thrown across the shop window. Have you noticed this?"

Luigi Fratelli shook his head, saying, "No sir, but I have heard talk of it from my customers." The merchant lowered his voice slightly, asking, "You say you are a friend of Signor Breccia?" Holmes nodded as he continued, "Then you must tell him to be most careful. There is a family named Vicenza who seem to have some sort of quarrel with Signor Breccia." The merchant paused and looked around him before adding, "The head of the family, Arturo – he is a violent man. There have been rumours of . . . how shall we say . . . a 'meeting' between their daughter, Sophia, and Signor Breccia. Apparently, it didn't end well for either party." The wine merchant then raised an eyebrow, inclined his head, and then nodded slowly. I frowned as I understood the inference and digested this piece of information.

As the wine merchant had nothing further to say on the matter, and after Holmes placed an order for a case of the Barolo, he asked for the address of the Vicenza family. Once given, he then asked for the address and directions to Signor Lombardi's shop.

Upon Holmes asking for Lombardi's address, the merchant chuckled saying, "Carlo Lombardi is a good friend of mine. We are competitors but still friends, and he is a passionate Italian, you will see. His shop isn't far, but I think that he has been away on family business. I saw a note on his shop window which said that he was closed and that the shop would reopen tomorrow."

After shaking hands with Signor Fratelli, we left and walked around to Lombardi's shop. Indeed, a note confirmed he would be back the next day. We then hailed a cab back to Baker Street. Upon arriving, we saw that on the hall stand there was a small package, wrapped in brown paper and twine. It was addressed to Holmes, who eagerly snatched it up and galloped up the stairs to our sitting room. I was somewhat slower in my ascent and found that the package had already been unwrapped, and a slim folder had been placed upon the seat of my armchair. Holmes was sitting back, his briar already lit, and fingers interlaced across his chest. I knew then that my task would be to read the contents of the file from Frosali to him.

Taking up the folder, I noticed that there was a key within it, together with a brief note from Inspector Frosali and an address. The note informed us that we were at liberty to visit Breccia's house, as it was the property of the embassy. This was indeed unexpected, and I frowned as I sat back while informing Holmes. Then I turned to the pages which appeared to detail the years between Alphonso finishing his apprenticeship in glassmaking on the island of Murano and his joining the Italian army. Clearing my throat, I read aloud to Holmes, "It appears that Breccia had an interest in the physical sciences, particularly in the properties of glass, and had applied and been accepted as the student at the University of Pisa to study Physics." I paused for a moment as I read on. "There is a note here from Frosali where he states that Breccia was an excellent student while at Pisa, but Frosali knew that there was an artistic side to the fellow, for Breccia was also a very talented musician."

I looked towards Holmes as he sat with eyes closed, gently drawing upon his briar. The gentle wave of a single hand was a sign from him, encouraging me to continue. Turning the page in the file I was amused to find a small newspaper clipping from a local newspaper that had been attached to the file. The article reported on a gathering of staff and students at a local *trattoria* where Alphonso had combined his knowledge of the properties of glass with his love of music. He had, it seemed, entertained the group by playing the music to the *"Canto degli Italiani"*, using only wine glasses partly filled with water to different levels.

"It seems that at the end of his three years of study, Alphonso graduated from Pisa and went on to join the army . . . but there is little more than that mentioned here." Holmes nodded slowly and nothing more was said of the events of the day.

341

Soon after, Holmes left to carry out additional research, including finding out the Vincenzas' address, while I passed the rest of the day considering what we had learned. For my part, after reading the file and reflecting on the young man's achievements, it saddened me to then think of the poor creature that Holmes and I had seen in Clerkenwell.

After a sleepless and troubled night, we rose early and took a cab to Turnmill Street in Clerkenwell – a place, it would seem, that had in years past been named "Cut Throat Alley". As we left, Holmes slipped the key to Breccia's house into his pocket. Stepping down from the cab, Holmes tossed the cabbie a shilling and we watched as the hansom clattered away down the street. The terrace of houses before us were three-stories and made from ubiquitous red London brick. Each of the windows had a fan above it of contrasting yellow bricks. The front door led directly onto the pavement.

It took us but a few moments to locate No. 7, the address of the Vicenza family. Holmes knocked soundly upon the peeling, red-painted door with his cane and in less than half-a-minute, the door was roughly opened by a man who looked like a common pugilist. His head was shaven and he stood before us, something over six feet in height, dressed in a stained flannel vest and a pair of trousers that were tied at the waist with string.

He looked us both up and down and scowled before demanding coarsely "Yes? What do you want?"

Holmes touched his hat and proffered his card while saying, "Good morning, Signor Vicenza?"

The man before us gave but a single nod and glanced at Holmes's card. He took half a step towards us, asking, "And what business might a detective have with me?"

I had the impression that this was meant to intimidate us, but we stood our ground, and I saw Holmes's grasp on his cane tighten. "I understand that you know Alphonso Breccia. I would like to talk to you about your relationship with him."

The man glowered at us both, shouting, "Relationship! Ha! So . . . Breccia has involved a detective and his lackey. The coward!"

I couldn't hold back, my face grew stern as I replied, "The man has been murdered."

Holmes's cane rested lightly against my chest as he answered, "Perhaps, Signor Vicenza, you would like us to return to discuss your disagreement out on the street with a constable by our side?"

Vicenza poked his head outside his front door, spat on the pavement beside Holmes's foot, and then growled, "Come in, if you must." Then, as he strode down the passageway, he shouted, "Louisa! Shut the door!"

Arturo Vicenza led the way into the house and through a doorway into what I presumed was their poorly furnished sitting room. Upon the floor was a rug made from knotted rags, laid upon bare wooden floorboards. Ochre-stained wallpaper peeled at the edges, and the furniture was mismatched and tired-looking.

Vicenza pointed brusquely towards a pair of well-worn dining chairs before he swept a thin, tortoiseshell cat from another chair that was directly opposite ours. It was clear that none of the anger had gone from the man as he sneered, "How did he die . . . for I would have gladly fulfilled the task of dispatching him myself!"

I saw Holmes purse his lips before coldly replying, "He was beaten and tortured in his shop, and then his throat was cut."

The man before us seemed unmoved by this and simply shrugged. "That isn't my style. I would have taken him into an alley and beaten him senseless for what he did to Sophia." Vicenza was silent for a moment before adding, "I would have made him marry her, but then I found out from Sophia that he was already married."

I frowned and thought back to what Frosali had said in Breccia's shop before asking, "How do you know this? Did she ask him?"

Vicenza scowled and shook his head. "She told me that she had seen him in the street wearing a wedding ring, and she just ran away. She swore that she would never set eyes upon him again."

Saddened, I simply sighed. Holmes replied, quietly, "The ring that she saw was Breccia's father's. He wore it in his honour, as if it were his own." Holmes paused for a moment before asking, "Were you responsible for the red paint thrown against his shop window?"

Again, the man shook his head. "No. Breccia wasn't always a popular fellow in these parts. He seemed, on occasions, to be poking his nose into other people's affairs." Vicenza now seemed sullen, saying, "You must look elsewhere for your answers, Mr. Detective, I will say no more."

With a single nod and looking directly towards Vicenza, Holmes simply stated, "This business remains unresolved and answers will be found." Rising from our chairs and without a backward glance, we left the house.

Carlo Lombardi's wine shop should now be reopened, and that would be our next port-of-call. Having taken a cab to the address we had visited the previous day in Clerkenwell Road, we arrived at the shop just as it opened.

The premises were quite a grand affair. It was double-fronted and proudly presented its wares to the public. As we entered, our presence was announced by a small brass bell attached to the door. All around us were displays of bottles and a floor-to-ceiling wine rack which stretched across

343

one wall. As we approached the counter, I spied a bright young man stacking a shelf. The wooden case on the counter beside him proudly announced that the wine from that particular grower hailed from the region of Tuscany.

Holmes coughed discreetly to attract the man's attention. Then, he made the same request in English that he'd asked Signor Fratelli, "Good morning. I would like to speak with Antonio, please."

The young man smiled, replying in perfect English, "I am Antonio, sir. How can I be of service?"

Thinking that we had made progress, Holmes then asked for bottle No. 294. The young man slowly shook his head. "I'm sorry, sir. We sell our wines by variety or by a particular producer and also by vintage or by a specific region. Our bottles aren't individually numbered."

As I listened, I was indeed disappointed. I had expected us simply to have been presented with a specific bottle, but perhaps Alphonso's message had a more cryptic meaning.

Holmes held his forefinger to his lips before asking if he might speak to Signor Lombardi. The young man's expression lightened and he nodded. He then dashed off into the body of the shop while crying, "Signor Lombardi, there are two gentlemen to see you!"

Within moments, a large, florid, well-dressed figure appeared, mopping his brow. "Good morning, gentlemen. How may I help you?"

Holmes touched his hat, and proffered his card, saying, "Good morning, Signor Lombardi. My name is Sherlock Holmes, and this is my colleague, Dr. John Watson. Alphonso Breccia was a customer of yours, I believe?"

The wine merchant's face showed some confusion as he read Holmes's card before asking, "You say 'was a customer'. Has he moved? I personally delivered a case of wine to his premises two weeks ago, just before I closed the shop. I ordered a piece of his glassware . . . ." Seeing Holmes's serious expression, Lombardi faltered as the meaning of Holmes's words became clear. "No! He seemed so healthy . . . Was it an accident with his glass?"

Holmes shook his head. "He was beaten and tortured before being brutally murdered in his shop." On hearing this, Lombardi seemed to stagger a little and grasped the edge of the counter for support as Holmes continued. "I am discreetly investigating his death at the behest of His Excellency, the Italian Ambassador. Is there somewhere a little more private where we might talk?"

On hearing this, Lombardi turned and gestured for us to follow, saying, "*Si, si.* This way gentlemen."

344

He led us into a large, wood-panelled office, expensively furnished with fine, velvet-seated mahogany chairs and a large walnut desk. Motioning us to be seated, he moved to sit behind his desk and looked expectantly towards us.

Holmes began thus: "The embassy received a somewhat cryptic message from Signor Breccia. He had important information which he thought most valuable to Italy and it was, I believe, somehow related to a certain bottle of wine. The message contains the instruction to ask for Antonio, particularly in English, for No. 294. However, as your employee told me, your wine isn't numbered."

Lombardi nodded as I continued. "We visited your friend Luigi Fratelli, as he also supplied wines to Signor Breccia."

Lombardi's face brightened a little on hearing the name. "Ah, Luigi and I are good friends . . . from the old country."

Holmes now continued, "When we visited Signor Fratelli, he told me that his wines aren't numbered either. He also told me that someone else, perhaps a German or Austrian, had asked, in English, for a bottle numbered 294." Holmes paused for a moment before saying, most seriously, "I believe that the only other person who would ask for this bottle is the one who tortured Alphonso for this information."

On hearing this, Carlo Lombardi violently brought his fist down upon his desk, cursed most crudely in Italian, and then shouted, "This villain, he must be found!"

Holmes waited a moment for Lombardi to calm himself. "I believe, Signor Lombardi, that he will come to your shop, now that you have reopened, and ask for the bottle. He has only been prevented from doing so previously because of your absence, which caused your shop to be closed."

Lombardi then shouted, "Then we shall have him!"

Holmes held up his hand, palm first. "Unfortunately, we cannot as, I believe, this is a matter of State. If this man is a member of a foreign embassy, which is most likely, then he will have diplomatic immunity. He will be inviolate, untouchable in the eyes of the law . . . but his foul deed will not go unpunished."

Lombardi's furrowed brow indicated that he wasn't wholly satisfied with Holmes's response. He wanted something more. Leaning forward, Holmes addressed Lombardi saying, "I have a proposal. I would like, with your help, to set a trap for this man in such a way as to let him know that we are aware of his identity, and that retribution will follow."

Lombardi's expression changed, and I could see fire in his eyes as he eagerly asked, "How can I be of service?"

Holmes paused for a moment. "I need to prepare a bottle of red wine which will be our bait. Do you bottle some of your wine here, in the shop?"

Lombardi nodded, replying, "Why, yes! We import bottled wine by the case, but we also import it by the cask. Please come with me to our cellar."

Leaving his desk, Lombardi motioned us to follow him along a short passageway and then down a flight of stone steps. Here, beneath the shop, was a vast vaulted, brick cellar with wine racks stretching away into the distance and large, oak casks, lined up along one wall. Each cask had a small slate attached to it upon which the details of the wine and the year of production had been chalked.

Walking to one the racks, Lombardi picked up one of the bottles that lay in row upon row. "Here is a fine 1889 *Montepulciano d' Abruzzo*, a deep red wine which may serve your purpose." He passed Holmes the slightly dusty bottle with some reverence. Holmes then carefully held out the bottle towards one of the flickering gas jets that illuminated the cellar and seemed pleased to see that the wine made the bottle quite opaque.

Holmes gave a grim smile, saying, "Yes, a fine wine to serve the needs of an Italian Patriot." He fell silent for a moment, as though remembering Breccia's torment. "May I see a label for this wine? It needs to be quite dark, as I wish to write on the reverse and the writing to remain hidden while the bottle is full."

Lombardi thought for a moment before nodding and then adding, "Of course. This way." We followed as he led us to a part of the cellar to one side where there were piles of labels, large wooden crates of corks, and corking machines. Picking up a deep red label with a gilded edge and a white reverse, he passed it to Holmes, saying, "Your message cannot be read from the front with this one."

I was puzzled as Lombardi grimaced slightly and then shook his head. "It unsettles me that this isn't the correct label for this wine, but it will fulfil your purpose well."

Taking the label, Holmes plucked a small silver-cased pencil from his jacket pocket and then carefully wrote on the reverse of the label before passing it to Lombardi. Upon it I saw that he had written: "*Your identity is known. Breccia's death will be avenged.*" I noted that Lombardi glanced at the message and then gave a single, solemn nod. Taking up a small brush, he added a very thin layer of gum to the label before fixing it in place on the bottle.

Holmes looked around him and picked up a small fragment of the pale blue chalk used for marking the casks. This he used to write the No. 294 on the front of the bottle label.

346

Returning once more to Lombardi's office with the bottle of wine we sat for a moment before he asked, "How is this to be done, Mr. Holmes?"

Holmes pursed his lips together and held a finger aloft, saying, "I think that I may have to call upon Antonio . . . and any theatrical skills that he may have, Signor Lombardi."

At this, the proprietor shouted, "Antonio!" And then slapped the desk before crying, "Excellent!"

Within moments, Antonio appeared, and Holmes then explained to him what was to be his role. "Antonio, if a customer comes in and asks to speak to you, in English, and asks for bottle No. 294, you should then search beneath the counter to find this bottle." At this. Holmes held up the bottle that we had prepared.

Antonio then nodded as Holmes continued, "However, it is important that before you pass it to him, you should ask him for the name of the customer who had reserved that particular bottle. I believe that he will say Signor Breccia." Holmes now paused for a moment before saying, "Perhaps you might then turn away to look in an order book before confirming the name. Do you have such a book?"

Lombardi replied, "Yes, it is on the rear counter and we often refer to it when orders are collected."

I must admit, that I was pleased with Holmes's plan, and I felt that it wouldn't be long before Antonio would need to be on his mettle.

Returning to the body of the shop, I watched as Antonio carefully placed the bottle beneath the counter before busying himself with more stocking of the shelves. Looking around me, I continued to wonder at the delights on display and asked, "Signor Lombardi, Holmes and I are most grateful for your time. I wonder if I might trouble you further by asking you to suggest a wine that I may not have tried?"

Lombardi beamed, took my arm, and led me to the furthest corner of the shop. Here he opened a case and proudly presented me with a bottle saying, "Here you are, Doctor Watson. You must try this. It is an 1883 vintage, robust red wine that uses the Aglianico grape. It is quite a rare variety and can be found growing in the volcanic soils of Campania and Basilicata . . . ."

Lombardi's sentence went unfinished as the tinkling of the bell attached to the door of the shop drew our attention and we all turned instinctively towards it. Holmes, I saw, immediately turned his back to the door, an action that I thought most strange. For my part, I moved a little behind the rounded figure of Signor Lombardi from where I was able to observe more discreetly. As I watched, Antonio played his part to perfection. The customer's attention was fixed upon the bottle and I clearly heard from him the name "*Breccia*". I must confess that I shuddered as a wolfish grin was seen upon the face of the customer as he swiftly left the shop with his prize.

As the customer had now departed, I turned to Holmes and gave him a querying look. Holmes's face was grim. "The man who entered the shop was Hans Lange, and he has a chilling reputation as a member of the security staff at the German Embassy. Had I not turned away, I fear I would have been recognised and the game would have been up. He won't be hard to find when we're ready for him."

Holmes and I prepared to leave, Signor Lombardi would accept no payment for the fine bottle of wine that he had introduced me to. We wished Antonio and Signor Lombardi a good day, shaking hands with them both. We went in search of a cab to transport us to No. 3, St. John's Street, Clerkenwell, the home of Alphonso Breccia.

Arriving at the address, I tossed the cabbie a sixpence and walked the few steps to the front door. The house was one of a red bricked, three-storey terrace. We had been told by Frosali that the house didn't belong to Alphonso, but to the embassy, and had been ostensibly rented, to him by a property agent, although no money ever changed hands.

Holmes took from his waistcoat pocket the key that Frosali had sent and opened the front door. The house was tidy and in good repair, although it did bear the hallmarks of Alphonso's artistic nature. An outdoor coat had been tossed casually over the newel post at the bottom of the stairs, and the cushions on the red velvet sofa had been left at a jaunty angle.

Nothing appeared out of place. The bookcase was filled with books reflecting Breccia's interest in art and music, but there were two notable spaces where books had been removed.

Holmes moved to Alphonso's desk where a pair of books were present, these appeared to be the ones missing from his bookcase. These were, I saw, related to his interest in physics, and specifically to the resonance of glass. Holmes flicked through the pages of one volume and he appeared to be drawn to a picture and description of a mechanical musical instrument called a "glass harmonica", which had been manufactured in many places across Europe, including Murano. This instrument, it seemed, was played by placing moistened fingers upon revolving glass bowls of different sizes which produce notes of different pitch.

Beneath the books was a page of sheet music. Holmes picked this up, saying, "Ah, this is of interest. It is an adagio written in 1791 by W. A. Mozart, specifically for the glass instrument." Holmes attention now turned to a violin that rested on one side of the desk. I heard him sigh as he almost tenderly plucked the instrument from its case. "Magnificent. It could be a mirror-image of my own Stradivarius." I wondered then if

348

Alphonso had taken to playing the piece upon his violin . . . but we would never know.

Opening the top drawer of the desk, Holmes found Alphonso's diary with a single, red, silken ribbon as a bookmark. The ribbon had been placed to mark the page for the third of August. There were, it seems, two entries for that date. The first was simply a reminder to order more cigars from Carlins, the tobacconists, but the second was of more interest. It read, "*Meet with the K to discuss Herero.*' Unfortunately, the meaning of this entry eluded me, but Holmes muttered, "*Herero* . . . a link to Africa."

As we moved from room to room, it appeared as though Alphonso had simply left to go to work. Upon finding nothing amiss or of further interest, Holmes then re-locked the property and we made our way back to Baker Street.

As Holmes opened the front door, a further mystery was to reveal itself. On the table, I noticed a small rectangular parcel. This was again wrapped in brown paper and secured with stout hemp twine, with what appeared to be a glass seal on a metal clasp. Holmes now knocked gently upon the door of Mrs. Hudson's rooms.

After only a moment, she appeared. "Excuse me, Mrs. Hudson, but how was this package delivered, and by whom?"

She smiled, "It came this morning, Mr. Holmes, by messenger from the Italian Embassy. He also left this envelope for you."

Holmes smiled in return, taking the envelope from her and saying, "I'm most grateful, as always."

Holmes now bounded up the stairs clutching both the parcel and the envelope. When I entered our rooms, Holmes was to be seen with both items resting on his lap. "This is most puzzling, as the postmark on the package is the 9th of August, a date when we know that Alphonso Breccia was already dead . . . for this clearly comes from him."

Taking up the envelope, he carefully slit it with his stiletto and then removed the single sheet of notepaper from within it. "Ah, it is from Frosali. It appears that the parcel had been left on the oak chest in the hallway at St. John's Street ready to post, but had only been found and posted when the caretaker visited, after having been informed of Alphonso's death. It has been forwarded to us on the explicit instructions of the ambassador."

With the utmost care, Holmes now slit the twine and the brown paper of the package to reveal a wooden box which might have accommodated a single bottle of wine. Lifting the lid, he carefully removed the top layer of straw that the found within it. I moved to his side, curious to see what was within the box.

Lying on a further layer of straw, there wasn't one, but six complete, and most delicate, glass ampoules, identical to the fragments that we found beneath the bench in Alphonso's workshop. Each one of the ampoules was double-ended and had been formed from a tube of dark green glass. They all measured some four inches in length, but the glass walls of each one seemed to differ in thickness. Holmes then held them to the light, one by one, and it could be seen that each contained something – not a liquid . . . but perhaps, a tightly folded piece of paper.

Holmes now carefully put the box to one side before ringing the bell and asking Mrs. Hudson if we might be served with afternoon tea.

Taking out his favourite briar, Holmes now slowly filled it with tobacco from his Persian slipper. Striking a Vesta on the fender, he lit the pipe and then sat back with eyes closed as he steadily drew upon the pipe. He remained so for some minutes before taking it from his mouth and pointing the stem towards me, saying, "This has been an intriguing case, Watson . . . but I now believe we are at the point where we might bring it to a conclusion."

Holmes's brow furrowed slightly as he continued, "It is important, I believe, to look at the background of Alphonso Breccia as this is the key to all that followed. His apprenticeship in Murano gave him the tools necessary to pass on to Inspector Frosali the information that he thought most important but, not only that, it also gave him a legitimate purpose in Clerkenwell."

Turning to me, he asked, "What are your thoughts on our visit to Breccia's workshop, Watson?"

I pursed my lips slightly before replying, "Well, apart from it being most disturbing, it was clearly not the work of some common, casual thief. Breccia was most certainly tortured for information and, it seems, while he gave up some details, he did so, it seems, in such a way as to misdirect his assailant."

Holmes nodded, saying, "Quite so. The note that was found from Vicenza was something of a distraction. I don't believe that torture was an act of a person simply seeking retribution, but more an attempt to discover the identity of Breccia's contact that he only identified as '*K*'." Holmes drew strongly on his pipe and then continued, "Breccia was a most intelligent man. His telegram to Frosali revealed nothing of its true meaning to any casual reader. Indeed, it was intended to misdirect."

I thought for a moment, before asking, "Have you then discovered its secret?"

Holmes was silent for a few moments before answering. "Before I reveal it to you, it's important to consider how it was conceived. Breccia was a musician, and his knowledge of both the properties of glass and his

350

love of music are the key to discovering the contents of the mysterious glass ampoules that we've received. The details of the text in the message, particularly how it *must* be read in English, is the key."

I sat back and went over in my mind the English translation of the telegram. "If there is neither an Antonio S. at the wine merchants, nor a bottle numbered 294, what does it mean?"

Holmes chuckled, rose from his chair and returned with his violin. "The *Antonio S.* that you seek is very much older than any found at a wine merchant's. Perhaps, then, I might tune my violin and then play you a little music upon my own *Antonio S.*?"

The import of this struck me like a thunderbolt! "It's . . . it's a *Stradivari*, and your violin is tuned to *A*, *G*, *E*, and *D*!"

I looked towards Holmes, who was still smiling. "Bravo, Watson! Let us now consider the figure 294. If you recall the two books that we found on Alphonso's desk, they related to how glass could be made to vibrate to produce sound, notably, in the glass harmonica. Breccia had studied the physics of vibration, and particularly resonance in glass at the University of Pisa. With this in mind, how might we ask for 294? I believe that this relates to playing a musical note, specifically, a '*G*', where an oscillation of 294 times per second is achieved."

Waved the stem of his pipe at me once more. "So, how might this be used? It is my opinion that the fragments of glass ampoule that we found at Breccia's shop were the result of his experiments to find out which thickness of glass would vibrate – specifically at 294 times per second, and then break if the note were loud enough."

Holmes paused before continuing, "Breccia's diary revealed that he had a meeting with a person that he had given the codename '*K*'. Now that we have discovered the involvement of Lange, it appears that his informant is part of the German Embassy staff and has information relating to the German presence in Africa – specifically, to their involvement with the indigenous Herero people."

I frowned, asking, "How does this relate to Breccia referring to this person as '*the K*'?"

"Obviously, this is not the *King*, Watson. It might, perhaps, be that Breccia has chosen to give him the title '*Kaiser*', as this may indicate the senior status of his contact."

Nodding, I then asked, "Perhaps . . . and has this brought us any nearer to identifying the man?"

Holmes nodded slowly, saying, "I believe it does, for it is my opinion that only one of the ampoules that we received contains the name of his contact. Breccia was a most careful man. The package we received wasn't a single ampoule as, had that been intercepted, the contact would have been exposed." Holmes took his briar from his mouth and again pointed the stem at me, saying, "The six ampoules most likely contain the names of six senior members of the German Embassy staff, all of whose loyalty might then be questioned."

Holmes smiled, as he continued, "It is now my intention to contact Frosali and offer to take my Stradivarius to the embassy."

Postscript

Holmes was indeed invited to the embassy where he used his Stradivarius to good effect, breaking but a single ampoule, as Breccia had intended.

A little more than two weeks after Holmes's visit, an obituary appeared in *The Times* for a certain Hans Lange.

It would appear that Herr Lange was a creature of habit and always took the same route to the German Embassy. As he passed by a fruiterer's premises one morning, several crates of oranges fell from a barrow, forcing Herr Lange to leap into the road where he was fatally struck by a passing omnibus. The Italian owner of the fruiterers was most apologetic, and at the Coroner's Inquest, a verdict of death by misadventure was recorded.

A Yuletide Mystery
by Alan Dimes

Elsewhere in these memoirs, I have stated that of all the cases in which I acted as the companion and amanuensis of my distinguished friend, Mr. Sherlock Holmes, there were only two which I brought to his notice: That of Colonel Warburton's madness, and that of Victor Hatherley and his missing thumb. Since the publication of that story, however, I have had occasion to draw his attention to one other, which the newspapers at the time dubbed "The Yuletide Mystery", as it took place towards the end of a dark and snowbound December.

The King's Road, Chelsea, was crowded with shoppers on that winter afternoon, as I made my way determinedly through the thick snow towards a particular little shop that sold old, second-hand, and obscure books. I was warmly dressed in a thick coat over a tweed suit, a woolen muffler, stout boots, and leather gloves, with a cloth cap covering my head, but a chill, cutting wind was swirling the heavy snowflakes along the busy street, and I would be happy to be back in front of the fire in our rooms in Baker Street.

The bell rang as I stepped inside old Mr. Penfold's shop and pulled off my gloves. The interior felt pleasantly warm, and smelt reassuringly of leather-bound volumes and old ink. Mr. Penfold stepped out of his back room and gazed at me over his half-moon spectacles.

"Dr. Watson! Hello! I haven't seen you or Mr. Holmes in here for some time."

I smiled. With the fluffy little ring of whitening hair about the back of his head, his old-fashioned fingerless gloves, and his embroidered waistcoat, there was something distinctly Dickensian about the old bookseller. He might have stepped from the pages of *The Pickwick Papers* or *Martin Chuzzlewit*.

"I'm here to buy Mr. Holmes a Christmas present," I said. "Do you have any suggestions?"

"Well," said Mr. Penfold, "I've just had a delivery of a complete library. You know, relatives selling off the property of the deceased. I haven't had time to take them out and look at them. Perhaps you'd like to go through it with me, see if anything takes your fancy."

"I'd like that very much."

"Splendid! The crates are just inside the back door. The delivery man was in a hurry, so we just made sure they were out of the cold. Let me get the first one into the office."

"Let me do it, Mr. Penfold. They must be heavy."

"All right, let's do it together."

We pulled the crate next to the desk in the bookseller's office, where a coal fire was glowing in the hearth. Mr. Penfold sat in his wooden chair, leaving me to occupy the rather more comfortable armchair opposite. I took off my hat and coat and sat down.

"Right," he said. "I suggest I take them out first and hand them to you. If it isn't clear what a volume is, I have a better chance of identifying it than you. Oh, while I think of it, would you like a cup of tea? Sorting through books can be dry work."

"I'll do it. That will give you a chance to start going through them."

"Very well. The kitchen is just through there. You can see where everything is."

I was pouring boiling water into a big brown ceramic teapot when Mr. Penfold cried, "Ah, I think I've found something Mr. Holmes would like."

"Oh, what's that?"

"*The Course of Positive Philosophy*, by Auguste Comte."

I put the pot, two cups, the milk jug and the sugar bowl on a tin tray and carried them into the little office.

"I'm afraid he already has it," I said as I laid the tray on the table. I had made a thorough survey of Holmes's bookshelf before coming out.

"Harrison Ainsworth – *The Tower of London* and *Rookwood* and *The Lancashire Witches*. Sir Walter Scott's *Kenilworth*, *Peveril of the Peak*, *Rob Roy*, and *Redgauntlet*. Old Mr. Greville seems to have had quite a taste for historicals. Ah, what about this? *The Mystery of a Hansom Cab*, by Fergus Hume. "

I couldn't help smiling.

"Mr. Holmes has very little patience with the detectives of fiction. None of them seem to come up to his intellectual standards."

"Well, it was quite a big seller a few years ago, I seem to recall."

"That would cut no ice with him. 'What does the general public know?' he'd say. 'They cannot even tell a shoemaker by the state of his trousers or a journalist by the condition of his second finger, so how can they be trusted when it comes to evaluating the plausibility of an invented crime investigation?'"

Just then the bell rang. As Mr. Penfold rose to go into the shop, he said. "Carry on looking. I shouldn't be too long."

There was nothing Holmes would have cared to read in the rest of that crate, so I went to the back door, made a pile of about twelve books from the second crate and carried them into the office. I put the pile on the floor next to the armchair and picked up the first volume. It was a copy of Kipling's first collection of short stories, *Plain Tales from the Hills*. Now, the reader might imagine that given my experiences in our Eastern possessions, the wounds I had sustained during the Afghan campaign, and my subsequent bout with enteric fever, I would have no desire to revisit those dark days, even via the medium of fiction. It is a curious fact, but with the passage of time, what remained with me was the memory, not of my pains, but of the stout fellows I had met and befriended, and of the courage and self-sacrifice they had shown. I set the Kipling volume to one side for myself.

The next two books in the pile were distinctly promising – a collection of the poems of Francois Villon in French – Holmes disdained translations if he had a grasp of the original language – and a book on fingerprints by Sir Francis Galton.

I could hear Mr. Penfold finishing up with his latest customer.

"Right, sir. So, the complete Galland *Thousand and One Nights*, Sir Richard Burton's *The Gold Mines of Midian*, and *The Episodes of Vathek* by William Beckford. Not many of that last one about. Nice edition, too. That'll be twenty-five pounds, thank you sir. And a good Christmas to you too, sir."

I placed my empty cup in its saucer, put on my cap and coat, and went out into the shop, handed Mr. Penfold the little pile and reached into my pocket for my wallet.

"I've found three things I'd like. How much is that?"

"Six pounds, please."

I pulled out the exact amount and Mr. Penfold wrote me a receipt.

"Would you like these delivered?"

"No, I'll take them now."

"Oh, in that case I'll wrap them up and put them in a bag for you. Don't want the snow getting at them, do we? Now, where did I put that brown paper?"

He turned to a shelf behind him.

The bell rang, and there was a brief gust of cold air as the door was opened and closed. Mr. Penfold turned around. The shop was empty.

Sherlock Holmes took a sip from his hot toddy and leaned forward eagerly in his armchair.

355

"Ah, at last, Watson, you come to the nub of the matter! Why did you leave old Mr. Penfold's shop in so precipitous a manner? You had seen something, I take it, but what?"

"I saw a murder, Holmes. What made me glance through the window of the bookshop at precisely that moment I cannot say. It was already dark and snowy, but there was a streetlamp nearby. The victim was leaning up against the lamppost, and the other man – the killer – was very close, right in front of him. I saw something glitter in his hand, and then he thrust upward, up through the ribcage into the heart. The victim must have died instantaneously. Then the murderer pulled the knife out, put it in his pocket and left his victim propped against the post."

"And no else saw the killing take place?"

"Apparently not. As I said, it was dark, and snowing heavily. After a second's hesitation I decided that I had to pursue the killer, as there was nothing I could do for the victim. At that moment, a tram pulled up at a nearby stop, and the culprit jumped on board. As it pulled away, I was forced to run after it, fearing all the time that I would lose my footing and tumble forward onto the icy road. But I managed to reach it and pull myself up onto the platform."

"Well done. That was no small feat for a middle-aged man with a damaged *tendo Achillis*."

"I was in time to see him climbing the stairs to the upper deck, so I took a seat on the lower deck and waited for him to come down. When the conductor asked me for my fare, I had to buy a ticket for the terminus at Highbury, as I had no idea where my quarry would be getting off. Eventually he descended at The Angel, Islington. His face, as before, was half-obscured by a woolen scarf, but I had no doubt as to his identity. I had also seen that the collar of his overcoat had a distinctive red trimming."

"Excellent, old friend! Your powers of observation certainly seem to be improving. What happened then?"

"He crossed the road and I followed him, at a distance, through a maze of very similar streets, until he entered a house. Number 43. I went to the end of the road and made a note of its name, Allingham Street. As you know, I do not have your encyclopedic knowledge of the metropolis, so I found myself wandering those near-identical streets, trying to find a way back to the Pentonville Road."

"Where you knew there was a police station, from one of our previous exploits in that area."

"Quite so. I was lucky enough to encounter a beat officer who escorted me to the station, where I made a full statement of what I had seen and how I had followed the fellow to his house. I don't doubt that I will be called upon to testify when the case comes to trial."

"A fine afternoon's work, dear doctor. And now, I am sure you are more than ready for one of Mrs. Hudson's splendid suppers."

The following morning, the papers were full of the King's Road murder. The condition of the victim, whose identity remained as yet unknown, was not discovered until a passerby bumped into him, and his corpse was knocked to the snowy ground, where it left conspicuous red stains. As of the next day, the Metropolitan Police stated they were confident that an early arrest would be made, as they had already received vital evidence from an eye witness, whose name they declined to reveal in the interests of that individual's personal security.

I imagined that the matter was settled, and that there was no more to be done until I was summoned to appear before the court. When the early edition of *The Evening Standard* arrived, however, it told a different story. The Christmas murder, as they were calling it, the 25th being only a few days away, was still unsolved. The suspect, when questioned by the police, pointed out by the still-unnamed eye-witness had an unshakeable alibi, having been with his sister and brother at the time in question.

"Hardly what I'd call unshakeable," said Holmes after I had drawn the article to his attention. "I'm sure the Scotland Yard files are bursting with cases where a spouse or a sibling, or a parent, has lied to support a murderer. Does it mention anywhere who is in charge of the investigation? I can't imagine Bradstreet, or Gregson, or even Lestrade making such a cardinal mistake."

I glanced further down the article until I reached the name.

"Inspector Drayton."

"No, I don't know him. He must be a recent addition, or elevation, to the ranks of the detective division."

"Holmes, it's always possible that I followed the wrong man. That is the conclusion most people would come to. It was dark, and the snow was heavy."

"If I had to cite every instance of 'the conclusion most people would come to' being utterly and demonstrably wrong, we'd be here 'til tomorrow morning."

My old friend reached forward and patted me reassuringly on the arm.

"As so often, your characteristic modesty leads you to underestimate your own abilities. I have no doubt that the man you pursued was the culprit, as I am sure our investigations will confirm."

"Our investigations? You intend to look into the matter?"

"I can hardly see how I could do otherwise, so let us begin. You said the killer put the murder weapon straight in his pocket?"

"Yes."

357

"So, Inspector Drayton should have had the pockets examined for bloodstains. On the basis of what we know so far, that gentleman doesn't seem fated to rise any higher in the force."

"Perhaps not, but what should we do?"

"We find out the name of the man, and as much as we can about him. It would help if we can discover the identity of the victim, too. It's unusual for someone to have no form of identification on him at all, not even a wallet."

"Should we call on Inspector Drayton and ask him about the suspect?"

"As far as Scotland Yard is concerned the fellow's been cleared, so he will not be permitted to give us that information. But we have the man's address, so it will only require a visit to the Town Clerk for Islington and an examination of the electoral roll to provide us with his name. No, stay where you are, Watson, and remain by the fire. This task only requires one of us."

He stood, took his heavy coat from its hanger, and went to the door.

The Islington electoral register revealed that the inhabitants of 43 Allingham Street (or at least, those eligible to vote) were two men, Jonathan and Christopher Morton.

"Our next move," said Holmes, "must be to ascertain what employment the man has, if any. We will keep the house under surveillance, and when he comes out, I will follow him, while you continue to watch the house. That will mean getting there early in the morning, before most people are up, so I suggest that you get a good night's sleep."

"Holmes, the fellow is a murderer. Should we not both follow him? What if he should turn on you?"

"Your concern is touching, Watson, but a little misplaced. However bulky and formidable the man may be, I have my knowledge of the Eastern martial arts, and I am confident that I can hold my own in any confrontation."

"Nevertheless, he may be armed. I will take my revolver, and I urge you to do the same."

"Very well, if it will ease your mind."

Perhaps my awareness of the importance and potential danger of our task was colouring my perceptions, but my memory of the following morning is that it was the darkest and coldest of the year. Even as we made our way through the pre-dawn streets in a hansom cab which Holmes had ordered the previous evening, the snow was descending in great sheets which were then scattered and dispersed by the icy swirling winds.

Looking through the cab window, it was almost as if we were inside one of those glass snow globes, and in my imagination a giant hand might at any moment shake the globe and plunge us into a hazy white chaos where up was down and back was front.

At last we arrived at No. 43 Allingham Street. Holmes paid the cab fare, and I wished the driver a Merry Christmas. Then we alighted and began to look around for a suitable location from which we might observe the door of the murderer's dwelling. By great good fortune, a house which was almost opposite No. 43 was derelict and unoccupied. Holmes glanced briefly around to make sure that we were unobserved, then plied his lock-pick, and within moments we were inside. Through the windows of the front parlour, we had a clear view of the killer's door.

We didn't have long to wait. At about half-past-six, the man himself came out of the house.

"That's him," I whispered.

"You're sure?"

"Same height, same coat, same hat."

Holmes waited a few seconds, then made for the front door. I followed, and gripped his arm for a second.

"Be careful."

Holmes said nothing, but smiled at me, and then he was gone.

He returned to the empty house at about half-past-two in the afternoon. We walked to Pentonville Road, where we found a cab to take us home. On the journey back to Baker Street, we said little. I was waiting to return to the warmth and comfort of our rooms before sharing my experience, while Holmes appeared to be contemplating what he had seen and sifting through it for what was relevant and what might be discarded. A fire was blazing in the sitting room grate when we arrived at No. 221b, and as we took our seats, our landlady brought in a plate piled high with sandwiches and laid it on the table between us.

"You went out early without any breakfast," she said, "so I thought you might be hungry. I didn't make anything hot, because I didn't know what time you'd be back."

"And you lit the fire too," I said, reaching for a cheese-and-tomato sandwich. "Mrs. Hudson, you are an absolute angel."

"Well, I don't know about that. Would you like some coffee?"

"An excellent idea," said Holmes. "Just the antidote to a short night's sleep and several long hours spent out in the cold."

When most of the sandwiches had been consumed and the coffee cups were empty, I looked across at Holmes.

"I have little doubt that your morning was more interesting than mine," I said, "so I'm eager to hear about it."

Holmes reached into the coal scuttle for his cigars and we each took one from the box. When they were both lit and drawing well, he began.

"Our friend caught a tram from the Angel, and I just managed to get on it. He alighted at Bank Station and walked to what I imagine must be his place of work, a law firm called Stringer and Cunliffe in Mercer's Lane. Judging from where he lives, he cannot be a solicitor, so he must be something like a clerk. If he was a messenger, he would have gone out, and I would have seen him, as I was seated on a little bench opposite the building. Anyway, he left at about quarter-past-twelve, and I followed him to a cafe where I assume he was having his lunch, and I came back to you. When exactly did you see him outside the shop?"

"At about half-past four."

"He started work at seven-thirty, so I wouldn't have thought he'd be out until four at the earliest. Bank to King's Road, Chelsea. That's an eleven tram. With the traffic at that time, in this sort of weather, it's unlikely he'd be there by half-past four."

"He might have had the afternoon off. Some companies do that at Christmas so their employees can go shopping for presents. Or perhaps he doesn't start at the same time every day."

"Possibly, though neither of those things usually apply to law firms. What did you see?"

"The only person who called, at a quarter-to-ten, was a tradesman of some sort, and I caught a glimpse of a wife, or sister or whatever she might be, when she answered the door to him. I didn't see anyone else."

Holmes stood up.

"I have to go out again."

"Whatever for?"

"I have to buy an overcoat."

"I can't see that there's anything wrong with the one you have."

"Nor is there. I should be back in time for dinner."

When he returned at about half-past-six, he was carrying a parcel wrapped in brown paper which I assumed contained his new overcoat. As we ate our evening meal, he made it clear that he didn't wish to discuss the case. After our long association, I was used to this reticence on his part, nor did it come as any surprise to me when, the following morning, he steered our conversation over breakfast onto trivial and commonplace lines. I knew that when he saw fit, he would give me a full account of his doings, whatever they might be. He left at about half-past-eleven, wearing his new purchase, and returned at about two. After taking a light lunch, he lit a cigarette and embarked on an explanation.

"Human beings, as you know, are creatures of habit, so my purchase of an overcoat similar to that of Mr. Morton was predicated on the belief that he would lunch at the same cafe as he had the previous day. When a man finds an establishment to his liking within a few minutes' walk of his place of work, he is likely to return to it. And so it proved. The cafe, which was in South Place, E.C., was fairly crowded, but fortunately there were one or two empty places. I watched through the front window as he hung up his coat. He then went over to the counter to order his lunch and sat down opposite another diner to wait for the arrival of his food. I went in, took off my coat and hung it on the hook next to his. I ordered and paid for a cup of tea and found a sear near the window. When my tea arrived, I drank it at a leisurely pace, after which I left, making sure to lift Morton's overcoat from its hook instead of my own."

"You wished to examine it, and using this subterfuge, you could claim that you had taken it by mistake if he challenged you on it."

"Exactly. A swift glance in his direction as I went through the door told me that he was only halfway through his meal. I went a few yards down the street and turned a corner. Then I took off the coat and looked at the pockets, where I found his wallet, which identified him as *Jonathan*, rather than *Christopher* Morton. Fortunately that style of overcoat has pockets you can pull out and examine. In the other there was a distinct bloodstain, which by its colour seemed to be fairly recent. When I returned to the cafe Morton was just finishing his first course and was about to start on a bowl of apple pie and cream. I put his coat back on the hook, donned my own, and made my exit. Then I went to Scotland Yard to tell them what I'd found. There was a little bit of a stink – Drayton was in charge of the case, but Gregson was there too, and as the senior man, he had some harsh words for Drayton for not having had Morton's clothing examined the first time they brought him in. Anyway, speaking of coats, get yours."

"Why?"

"They're bringing Morton in, and Gregson convinced Drayton that we should be there."

By the time we arrived at the station, there had been fresh developments. The corpse had been identified as Michael Byrne of 22 Arlington Road, Peckham.

"You took the afternoon off from Stringer and Cunliffe because you said there was a family emergency and you needed to get back to Islington," Drayton, a big young man with a head of frizzy red hair, was saying to Morton as we came into the interrogation room with Inspector Gregson. "What was the nature of this 'family emergency'?"

"None of your damn business."

"Since your presence at 43 Allingham Road constitutes your alibi, I'd say it's very much 'our business'. You weren't at Allingham Road, were you? You were in King's Road, Chelsea, at approximately four-thirty, stabbing Michael Byrne to death. Then you went back to Islington and convinced your brother and sister to tell us you'd been there since you got back from work. Isn't that what really happened?"

There was a knock at the door. It was opened to reveal the station sergeant, accompanied by a young man, who, to judge from the similarity of their features and their blond hair, could only be Morton's brother.

"This is Mr. Christopher Morton," said the sergeant, "and he says he has information vital to this case."

The other brother half rose from his seat and cried, "No, Chris, no!" before he was pushed back into his chair by Drayton.

"I'm sorry, Jon, but the truth must be told. This business has gone far enough."

"What about what we swore to mother? What about the lambs?"

"Curse the bloody lambs! You've given up the best years of your life, and for what? So that this could happen?"

"Why are you here, Chris? And what have you done with her?"

"I gave her a pill and locked her in her room. She'll be out for hours."

"I think it would help," said Gregson. "If you could tell us what this is all about . . . ."

"On the morning of the murder, Jonathan thought the weather was going to be a little warmer, so he left his heavier topcoat at home and put on a lighter one – "

"Chris, don't do this!"

"Our sister Alice is Jon's twin. They're the same height, and Alice is quite broad-shouldered for a woman. Alice has had mental problems for quite a long time – "

"Oh God!" said Jonathan, and covered his face with his hands.

"But when mother was dying, Jon promised that he'd always look after her – that we'd both always look after her. And as long as one of us was there, she was usually all right. Jon is better with her than I am, but we needed money, and as he is also a better earner than I am, he worked and I stayed home with Alice. But lately, she's been getting more difficult to handle, and we started giving her drugs. I suppose whatever they did to her, she blamed it on me. I was about to give her that morning's medication. I turned my back on her for one moment, and the next thing I knew, she hit me on the back of my head with something, and I came around at about two. She'd taken Jonathan's overcoat, one of my hats, and a sharp knife we use for cutting vegetables. I got one of the boys on our street to take a message to Jon to summon him home. When he arrived, there was nothing we could do but wait. Alice came in and we feared the worst. We knew she could be violent because – because – "

"No, Chris, no. Please."

"We knew she could be violent because my mother died because Alice stabbed her. Our doctor was an old family friend. He falsified the death certificate to say she died of heart failure."

"You should have put her in an institution," said Drayton. "They would have known how to deal with her there."

Jonathan turned to the inspector, his eyes blazing with anger.

"Have you ever seen the inside of one of those places? Well, have you? If you had, you'd never, ever think of putting someone you loved in there."

"I'm afraid the price paid for your reluctance to do so was the life of an innocent man," said Holmes, "killed at random by the sound of it."

Christopher resumed his narrative.

"She came home at about six, in a state of exhaustion, not knowing where she'd been, or what she'd been doing. We put her to bed, and I found the bloody knife in one pocket and this in the other."

He tossed a brown leather wallet on the table. The letters "*MB*" were embossed on one corner.

"That doesn't tell in her favour," said Gregson. "It makes it look as if a robbery was a motive. But from what you have told us, she may well be found irresponsible due to insanity. As for you gentlemen, I'm afraid the penalties for being accessories after the fact can be severe, whatever the judge decides about your sister's culpability. We must arrest you. Take them to the cells, Sergeant, and then arrange for their sister to be brought here."

"We weren't like the lambs after all, were we?" said Jonathan.

"No, we weren't," his brother replied.

After the Morton brothers had been taken to the cells. Drayton said, "So what the Hell was all that business about '*lambs*'? What have bloody sheep got to do with any of it?"

"It wasn't '*lambs*' with a small '*l*'," said Holmes. "It was '*Lambs*' – the name – with a capital '*L*'. Charles and Mary Lamb. They were part of a literary circle that included William Hazlitt and Samuel Taylor Coleridge, and wrote a book for children together called *Tales from Shakespeare*."

"I'm no wiser," said Drayton.

"Well, they were brother and sister. In 1796, Mary suffered a mental breakdown and stabbed her mother to death. She was put in an asylum, but in 1799, Charles took sole charge of her and they began living together in London. As long as she was with Charles, she was balanced and sane. Charles devoted the rest of his life to her and they both died unmarried. Do you understand it now?"

"Pardon me," said Drayton. "I didn't have the benefit of a university education."

"I doubt that the Mortons did either," I said. "Some families read, some don't."

"A sad story all round," I remarked to Holmes the following evening. "Poor Michael Byrne killed, Alice Morton likely to spend the rest of her life in an institution, separated from her brothers, and the pair of them doomed to serve whatever term in prison the judge deems fit."

"We cannot always hope for a happy ending, Watson, as you well know, and I'm sure you will agree that it is better for all concerned that there should be no chance of Miss Morton roaming the streets with murderous intent, even if she cannot be held responsible. As for her brothers, they may come before a sympathetic judge."

"Or they may not."

"Come, old friend, tomorrow is Christmas, one of your favourite times of the year, and I happen to know that Mrs. Hudson has made a special effort this Yuletide. I don't believe I've ever seen so large and plump a goose."

Christmas! In all the flurry and activity of the previous few days, I had completely forgotten the books I had purchased at Mr. Penfold's shop.

There was a ring at the door. Mrs. Hudson answered and a few moments later a dapper elderly man appeared on our threshold bearing a brown paper parcel. I failed to recognise him at first, but then I knew him.

"Mr. Penfold!"

"I'll only stay a moment. I'm just bringing these around."

He handed over the parcel.

"I'm sorry I didn't bring them earlier, but you know, I close quite late, and I live in the opposite direction. Tonight I'm on my way to spend Christmas with my daughter Susan and her family in Camden Town, so you're on my route,"

"We were just about to have some mulled wine," said Holmes. "Stay and have one with us. Something to warm you up before you go back out into the cold."

"Oh, don't mind if I do. Just the one, though."

"Thank you again, Mr. Penfold," I said, "and Happy Christmas to you."

"And to you, gentlemen. And to you."

The Case of the Covent Garden Medium
by Paula Hammond

We never talk about Mary.

I didn't know how much Holmes had gleaned about the circumstances surrounding my bereavement – nor had I asked. It was enough that he did know, and had shown his concern in those little ways that friends do. I understood that he would never press me for details – and I gave none, for while loss is something that every man must bear, how he bears it is for him, alone, to decide.

It may seem proof of some deep personal failing that the woman with whom I had shared so many wonderful years was an enigma to those closest to me. Outside of the social niceties, I rarely spoke of her. What we had seemed so precious that we felt no need to share it with the world. Together, we were complete.

The day that I had stood, peering down at the black rocks of Reichenbach Falls, listening to the dull echo of my own voice reverberating off the cliffs, I believed I would never again feel such emptiness. But that was as nothing compared to the loss of my Mary. My dear, sweet wife, Mary, who had made my life richer than I had ever hoped, and who had left me so suddenly, I felt I could not endure it.

I had held her hand, and breathed in her last breath as a kiss. I had draped our door handle with black crepe, and tied it with a ribbon. I had watched her small coffin being lowered into the earth. I had endured the million-and-one things society requires of the grieving husband, before returning to our empty home to endure the ticking of the clock, and the passage of the hours, alone.

For months, I had found myself setting the table for two, pulling up her chair near the fire every evening. I knew that it was mere grief, working its loathsome tricks upon me, but sometimes, as I sat reading in silence, I would have sworn that I'd heard the sound of her laugh, felt the brush of her fingers on my shoulder, as she walked past to take her seat in the easy-chair beside mine.

Then, without warning, the friend who had been lost to me was found. Inexplicably, extraordinarily, alive, and as vital and as real as I remembered. The joy of that moment was as a panacea to my grief, which was so new that I still wore my mourning weeds.

Now, our lives have returned to their old, familiar pattern at Baker Street and I find myself wondering: *What of Mary?* I'm not so far gone as to hope for the impossible, but I have good reason to wonder about the permanency of death.

Such thoughts had been my companion for some time, until the day I was approached with a proposition that threw my mind and spirit into turmoil.

"Calamity" Smith [1] is my publisher at *The Strand* magazine. He's a tall, lean, no-nonsense chap, with a penchant for tobacco and word-puzzles. It was he who had been instrumental in putting Holmes's adventures before the wider public. Since then, we've met socially many times, and I've come to think of him as a friend.

Smith's usual lunch venue was The Albion. [2] Close to both the British Museum's reading rooms and Fleet Street, it's usually packed with academics, actors, and authors. The air is Bohemian and unpretentious, with a quaint dining room partitioned into booths to afford privacy, and a smoking room which is one of the most pleasant of its kind in London.

One day, in late July of 1895, I determined that a stint at the Albion was exactly what I needed to shake off my funk. Holmes was busy and, in need of good food and convivial conversation, I'd called at Smith's offices, timing my arrival so that I might tempt him out to lunch.

The Strand is a delightful thoroughfare, whose eastern end is home to many of the nation's most popular publications. This includes *The Strand* magazine, which perversely stands in Southampton Street, in a handsome building with a triple entrance bounded by large plate-glass windows. One enters by the left door, where a spacious room, decorated in pale tints of salmon, green, and cream is given a more sober appearance by the addition of heavy mahogany doors and partitions. It's a building designed to impress, lined with bookshelves, and wired throughout for electric lights and telephones.

Smith's airy offices boast large windows overlooking the street, and even though padded chairs are provided for visitors, it's still very much a work room – and one piled with manuscripts and India-paper proofs.

The publisher is almost my age, with a pair of fine mustaches and a *pince-nez* that he balances on his nose in such as way that, when he looks directly at you, it gives one the impression of being thoroughly examined.

"Ah, Watson!' he said, as I entered, "just the man I wanted to see!"

Benjamin Franklin noted that time is money, and I've found that newspaper men take that aphorism very much to heart. Before I'd even had time to broach the topic of lunch, Smith had waved me to a chair and launched into a conversation which he declared "would be of great interest to both of us".

"What do you know of spiritualism?" he asked. [3]

"Lord!" I said, stunned to be asked about a topic which had been so much in my thoughts. "Not a lot."

"'Do you *believe?*'" he queried, looking directly at me over his eyeglasses.

His question gave me pause. "I cannot say," I answered truthfully. "Oh, I'm sure that some of these people are in deadly earnest, but what I read of table-tilting and levitating seems like pure showmanship. Why, if the dead want to speak to us, I'm sure they could do so without ringing bells in shuttered rooms."

Smith nodded soberly. "*The Strand*, so far, has tip-toed around the topic. Indeed, spiritualism, while hugely popular, is a thorny issue. There are many who do believe – and whatever we write, we must respect those beliefs. At the same time, we aren't the sort of publication who indulges in cheap sensationalism."

"Do *you* believe?" I asked.

"The magazine's official position – which accords with my own – is that ghosts *may* be scientifically possible, but we will publish nothing without proof."

"And how would one obtain proof?"

"Why, we must see for ourselves. That is, if you're willing? I already have a medium in mind who's impressed a number of colleagues [4] – and with your investigative skills, it should be a simple task to put her to the test."

"But why me?" I answered, half-alarmed, half-intrigued.

Smith isn't a man overly fond of emotion. "If you'll forgive me for being blunt," he said, "it seems that, if the dead are to speak, then they should speak to those who knew them best."

His words startled me, and I found myself struggling to keep my tone steady, my eyes fixed on his. "The medium is a *she*?" I replied, feeling I ought to say *something*.

"Yes, a delightful young woman by the name of Christine Burkins. I'll get my secretary to send over her address and some clippings from our files. She's making quite a splash."

"Shall I invite Holmes?"

"That's for you to decide. However, Miss Burkins' father is very protective. Should Holmes accompany you, then he may require additional assurances before he allows the séance to proceed."

"Additional?"

"Why, of course. What you report will greatly affect Miss Burkins' reputation. I have guaranteed that you will not interfere with the séance in any way and that, should you perceive anything amiss, Miss Burkins will be given the chance to respond, directly, before anything is published."

"In that case," I announced, in a hot rush, "let it be two weeks today."

We shook hands there and then and – all thoughts of lunch quite gone – I headed back out, into the heart of the city.

I was certain Holmes would dismiss the whole thing as tommyrot. Yet, since Mary's death, I'd frequently wondered whether we leave this world entirely once our spark has been extinguished, or whether some part of us remains to offer whispered reassurances in times of need. I'd considered what, if anything, would happen should I find myself sat, in a circle, calling out her name. I'd never had the nerve to do it, but I wasn't sure if I was afraid that there *was* something in it, or that there wasn't.

I walked in a desultory fashion, so occupied by my thoughts that I quite lost my way. Finally, finding myself in a warren of dark, claustrophobic alleys, I was gripped by a sudden, irrational fear. I recalled how, in *The Book of Samuel*, [5] King Saul, desperate for guidance from the dead Samuel, conducts a séance – something God has strictly forbidden. And while he does indeed speak to Samuel, he's later condemned to death for his transgression.

Holmes had once said to me "work is the best antidote to sorrow," and I realized that work was exactly what I needed. Over the next week-and-a-half, I threw myself into my work in a way that I hadn't since Mary died.

It was Monday. The séance was in two days. Outside our window, autumn was putting on its best show. The day was warm and bright, with not a cloud to obscure a sky of cerulean blue. Yet, nothing – not even exhaustion – seemed to shake my mood.

"Out with it, my dear fellow!" Holmes suddenly said, seeming, as he so often did, to know my thoughts before I'd voiced them.

I was grateful for the prompt, but reluctant to admit my folly. "Oh, it's nothing. Nothing at all."

"Watson, I'd be a poor friend indeed if I hadn't noticed your mood. Why, for almost a fortnight, I've seen you reach for your pocket watch a dozen times a day, but never look at it – and Mary's likeness lying within. I've watched you smile at some remembrance, then seen your eyes mist over, and heard the smallest of sighs escape your lips. Come, Watson, on this week of all weeks, let us shake off this gloom. Out with it!"

"I'm afraid you'll think me rather foolish, Holmes" I replied.

"So, Smith persuaded you to go to Covent Garden then?"

"Why! How did you – ?"

"You returned from *The Strand's* offices in rather a brown study. As you hadn't eaten, I assumed Smith had given you the brush off, but it was soon clear that you had something more compelling than a missed rump-steak pudding on your mind. Immediately you returned, you pulled your old family Bible off the shelf and started pouring over something in the *Samuels*. You left the ribbon bookmark in place, so it was easy to find the exact passage you'd been so interested in. Given your recent loss, it's no great feat to put two-and-two together and naturally come to four."

"But Covent Garden? There must be a hundred mediums in London. How could you possibly know Smith wants me to visit one in Covent Garden?"

"Ah!" Holmes said, with a small smile. "*Mea culpa.* I glanced at the papers that Smith had delivered to you, as you read them over breakfast. Upside-down reading is one of the detective's oldest and most reliable tricks. Sorry, but you've been out on your rounds at all hours, buried in those journals of yours, and in between hardly eating or sleeping. Come: The cat's out of the bag. Let me refresh your coffee while you tell me all about it."

Holmes pulled up his chair beside the fireplace and began reading. He sat, pulling on his pipe for some time, checking and re-checking the clippings that Smith had provided, until he was thoroughly satisfied.

"Automatic writing, secrets revealed, materializations, mysterious knocking . . . It's all very compelling, isn't it?"

"I expected you to dismiss the whole thing out of hand!"

"I said it was compelling. I'm far from persuaded. Indeed, should you put me in a darkened room, I would immediately ask why is the room dark? For darkness has the potential to hide all manner of deceptions."

"Here – " Holmes jabbed his finger at one of the clippings in the manila folder and began reading: *". . . the medium was removed to the bedroom, her head covered in a shawl to keep out the light and thus aid her in maintaining her trance. Shortly after, her spirit guide appeared and walked amongst us."* I would ask what proofs are there that the medium remained in the room? Why does her head, not simply her eyes, need to be covered? Is it to hide the fact that she is, in fact, this wandering spirit?"

"And here – " Holmes pulled out another clipping. "We have an account of objects apparating – but they always fall from *above*. I would ask: Could they have been tethered to the ceiling? Could they have been thrown by an accomplice?"

"I do not say that trickery is involved. I remain, as ever, open-minded. But with reports such as these, much depends on what those present choose to see – or not see. None of these journalists question the events that took place. They're *watchers*, not *observers*."

"You'll come then?"

"If the father will have me. He seems to be quite the bulldog. What is it says here: ". . . *manages his daughter's career and protects her reputation as only a father can.*" I'd be curious to know exactly what that means. It sounds rather ominous.

"The real question, my dear chap, is: Are you certain *you* want to go through with it?" Holmes looked at me, his face the picture of concern, and I felt a great calm descend upon me.

"I confess, I find the idea unsettling, but I think I need to do it."

Holmes lent forward, regarding me with those singular eyes of his. "Well, then it's decided. On Wednesday, we will see what Miss Burkins has to show us."

I immediately telegrammed Mr. Burkins to inform him that both Holmes and I would be attending Wednesday's séance. Much to my amazement, I received a reply within the hour to the effect that, "*Sherlock Holmes and Dr. Watson will most welcome.*"

"So much for the bulldog!" I glanced across at Holmes, feeling a warm certainty that, whatever surprises Wednesday held, I would not have to endure them alone.

"Excellent," he said. "In that case, I think a little reconnoiter might be in order."

"What do you have in mind?"

"Let us learn what we can of Miss Burkins and her father."

"You want to speak to the neighbors? Discover if anyone has seen accomplices rapping on the walls, or howling down the chimney?" I said, lightly.

Holmes chuckled appreciatively. "Stranger things have happened. But I suspect we'll learn a lot more about the young lady and her father from neighborhood heresy than from a folder full of yellow journalism."

Thus decided, we set out for Covent Garden.

Christine Burkins lived in a modest home above F.W. Collins and Sons, the ironmonger in Earlham Street. [6] The Doric sundial which once stood at the intersection of the streets that meet at Seven Dials [7] is long gone, but many of the houses in this area still date from the Stuart period.

The street is overshadowed by the Woodyard Brewery whose sights and sounds dominate – from the scent of hops roasting, to the noise of horse-drays clattering across the cobbles.

A hundred years earlier, this area was known as a place of dissent and political agitation, where the poor and desperate were crowded into unsanitary lodgings and left to rot. Today, the poverty is still there, disguised with a fresh coat of whitewash and an air of industrious purpose. Indeed, the streets that form Covent Garden's distinctive triangular plots are full of dark and narrow passages, an endless intracity of courts and yards, with taverns, boarding houses, and workshops at street level, and homes above. Even during the day, it's a dangerous place. Or so we were to discover.

Holmes and I were making good progress, working our way along the street, chatting to passers-by, making enquiries about the Burkins family, without seeming to be too interested.

"I hear this place has its very own Oracle," Holmes said to a saw-toothed man who was setting up his barrow, and had paused to pull out his pipe.

"Stuff and nonsense!" the man said good-humoredly. "Such a sweet a girl too – How her pa managed to persuade her to be part of his flim-flam, I'll never understand."

"A bad lot?" Holmes prompted, offering the man some tobacco from his pouch.

The man sniffed at it experimentally and, clearly finding it superior to his own, began enthusiastically packing his pipe. "Ha! David Burkins is the man who gives the bad lot a bad name," he spat. "And he makes a very good living from fleecing fools too!"

"What's this, Pete? Playing that tune again?" A red-faced man, possessed of prodigious eyebrows, suddenly materialised. "Don't you pay no attention to Pete, here," he said, eying-up Holmes's tobacco pouch hungrily. "Him and Burkins have bad blood between 'em. Not saying he's a good man, mind. But that girl of his has the gift, right enough."

Holmes gave a little nod and, thus encouraged, Eyebrows helped himself to a fistful of tobacco. Soon, Pete and Henry – as the newcomer revealed himself to be – were batting it back and forth – their energetic debate punctuated by plumes of smoke, like steam engines taking a breath between underground stations. [8]

"You said he makes a good living . . . ?" Holmes interjected.

"Ah, Pete don't know what he's on about. Why, if he does make money off the girl, you wouldn't know it. Both of 'em only have one decent set of clothes. Still, what if they do a little bit of the old flim-flam, as Pete says? Worse ways for a young girl without a muvver to make a living." Henry sniffed.

"So Burkins has no other work?"

372

"Laboring, hauling and shifting, casual, like a lot of us round here. He's brains enough. 'Book smarts', they say, before the drink got him."

"A drunk?" Holmes nodded encouragingly.

"A drunken brawler!" The man named Pete grumbled.

"Ah, life's took more than it's given of late, for poor old Burkins. So what, if he takes a drink? And so what, if sometimes he takes a drink too many, and talks too loud, and throws the odd punch at folk like Pete, here? He's always been a hot head, but since he lost his missus, it sometimes seems he's lost what sense he had too."

Exhausted by tobacco – and gossip – the two men finally returned to their work, leaving Holmes and me to continue our stroll.

We were just about to turn into passageway which afforded a better view of the Burkins' top-floor flat when Holmes grabbed my hand. "Watch out," he said. "Looks like company."

Ahead, I could see a short, brute of a man, holding a heavy stick, striding towards us with ominous purpose. I glanced over my shoulder to discover our way back now blocked by a rangy youth, wide-shouldered, with the build of one attuned to physical work.

"Gristle or fat?" Holmes whispered, his eyes fairly gleaming.

I nodded towards the stocky man. "Fat," I said. "Gives me something to swing at."

I've been in enough tough spots to know how to handle big, slow fellows like the neckless beast now roaring towards me. I steadied myself, and with my good ash stick raised, I prepared for his charge.

He was less than a foot away when I hit him. It had been many years since I'd played at single-stick, [9] but I was delighted to find that the skills I'd learned at school, and polished in the army, hadn't deserted me.

True "gamesters", as they're called, keep their left elbow up, and advance with the right hand above and in front of the head, holding the stick across, so that the whole head is completely guarded. However, I had no time for such formalities. The aim of the game was to rattle your opponent's brains, and I went at him with all the dexterity the narrow passageway could afford.

"Why, I'll break you, an' that's the truth!" he bellowed.

Ho! I thought. *So you say! But I know this game better than you!* He came at me, trying to break my guard by virtue of strength alone. But single-stick is as much about speed and skill as it is strength. I caught every blow and returned it, like for like.

He was bigger than me, but shorter, and I used that to my advantage, reigning down blows on his knuckles and wrists until finally, with a curse, he dropped his cudgel. I caught him a smart blow on the chin, and another in the ribs.

373

He let out a wheezing groan and lunged for his lost weapon. *Too slow!* He backed away, winning himself another blow to chin, before he finally turned on his heels and ran.

Beside me, Holmes was doing steady work. Gristle was almost as tall as he was, with a reach the equal of his own. But compared to Holmes he was a poor pugilist. He telegraphed his punches so clearly that Holmes merely had to step aside to avoid them. Indeed, while I was too busy with my own entertainment to see much of Holmes's match, the proof of my friend's efficiency could be clearly heard in the echoes of blows landing.

With my own opponent finally disposed of, I turned to discover Gristle, red-faced and bloody-nosed, backing away down the passage way. I caught his eye and, seeing that it was now two to one, he let out a dog-like yelp and bolted. Holmes lunged at him, catching him by the coattails. The fellow let out another whimper, gave a curious shudder and, shedding his coat like a reptile sheds its skin, he vanished into the maze of Covent Garden.

There's nothing like seeing off ruffians half your age to put one in high spirits. Indeed, Holmes declared himself "quite delighted with the morning's exertions."

As for myself, although my muscles had already begun to protest, I found Holmes's mood infectious.

We decamped to the Café Royal, [10] where we sat on red-plush banquettes and ate like warriors of old, our meal punctuated by tales of blows landed and blows dodged. It was only as we were taking our leave of Madam Nicols, who sits – French style – in her little glass-walled desk taking the money, that I wondered if our assailants had anything to do with the infamous David Burkins.

"It is a dangerous part of town. They could simply have been thieves. But if Burkins put them on to us, for what purpose?" I pondered.

"Indeed. If he intended to have us beaten enough to prevent our attendance at the séance – or to scare us away – then he'll going to be sorely disappointed. Still, it adds a little extra *frisson* to upcoming events, don't you think?"

I wasn't sure what to think, but I was content to enjoy a full belly, with the comfort of a pipe in front of the fire at Baker Street still to come.

Holmes spent the next day in the British Library's reading rooms, pouring through back issues of publications with titles such as *The Spiritualist* and *Borderland* in order to "get a feel for the common tricks mediums use."

He returned, early evening, clearly eager to share his findings.

"There's more to this business than I'd imagined" he said, stretching his back in a way that suggested many hours hunched over a table. "These publications treat spiritualism as some sort of new science, to be studied and tested. Why, there were just as many articles exposing frauds as there were extolling the virtues of some new, mystic prodigy."

"Oh? Learn anything useful?"

"I did," he replied, and began pulling a collection of assorted objects from his pockets: Several pairs of surgeon's rubber gloves, a pair of dark glasses, a yardstick, folded in the middle, some fishing line, and a set of pastel chalks.

"I picked these up at Harrods," he pointed to the gloves. "Apparently many mediums use their legs and feet to raise tables, tip chairs, and create rapping and scratching noises. So skilled are they that they can do so with the merest twitch and stretch – and yet their upper bodies remain static. Tomorrow, I will make a pair of rubber tourniquets from the gloves, and tie them around both legs, beneath the knee. I believe two hours should be sufficient for my legs to begin to swell. I will endeavor to sit next to the lady and, with my skin sufficiently tenderized, I should detect the slightest movement – no matter how skillfully done." [11]

"Or you'll give yourself a thrombosis!" I protested.

"Fortunately, I know a fine medical fellow who will ensure I don't do myself any permanent damage!" he answered, laughing.

"Delighted to hear it. And the other items?"

"I shall wear the glasses tomorrow to accustom my eyes to the gloom of the séance room. The twine will be almost invisible in the dark – and will make a terrible trip hazard should anyone, unknown to us, attempt to enter the apartments after the séance has started. As to the other items, I cannot tell until we're actually there. We may assume that, if there is some trickery, Burkins will be working with his daughter. If so, there may be moments when I'll need you distract both of them. So when I wish to get to work, I will do one of three things: Sneeze, cough, or make some comment about the temperature in the room."

Holmes liked nothing better than a challenge, and a thrill ran through me as I recognized my friend of old – the Holmes I'd thought lost. Yet, almost as quickly, came the aching reminder of the loss that remained.

Sunset was half-past seven, and by the time we arrived at Miss Burkins' apartments, the gas-lighters were already on their rounds.

We found the street door open and wound our way, three flights, up a perilously steep staircase, at the top of which was another door.

Before we'd a chance to knock, the portal opened and a whiskered man, wearing a shiny suit, much worn about the cuffs and collars, appeared.

David Burkins was nothing like the man whose reputation had preceded him. He was tall and wide, with a strong handshake and a clear eye. Yet, I could see a tremor shake his muscular frame, and as he greeted Holmes, his voice broke. *Lord,* I wondered, *is it the drink or nerves?*

There was no hallway. The door opened directly into a small parlor whose shuttered window was covered in heavy drapes. The only illumination in the room came from a gas lamp in the centre of a large, round table – and the gas was turned so low I practically had to feel my way into the room. Holmes, I noted, moved with considerably more ease, having already adapted his eyes to the dark.

"Glad you could make it" Burkins said in a tone that suggested otherwise.

"We very nearly didn't," Holmes replied, "for we were in the area just a few days ago and were set upon by a pair of ruffians."

Our host raised his eyebrows, looking genuinely shocked. "*Crikey!* I'd heard some gents had a spot of bother. Thieves, was it?"

"They didn't say," Holmes replied cooly, giving the man one of his appraising stares. One thing was for sure: If Burkins had been involved in Monday's *contretemps,* Holmes would know, and he'd have every reason to feel uneasy.

A young lady was already seated at the table. I saw her rise to greet us, and a high timorous voice said, "I'm Christine. Please, make yourself comfortable. We have two more guests tonight but, hopefully, we will not make the spirits wait too long."

She'd barely finished speaking when I saw Burkins move to open the door again. Holmes seemed to take Burkins' movement as his cue, for he said, pointedly, "I find it abominably close in here, if you don't mind I'll take the opportunity to remove my jacket before we begin."

Holmes busied himself looking for somewhere to place for his jacket, while I did my best to keep Miss Christine busy with small talk.

In the corner of my eye, I could see Burkins at the door, speaking with two young women, both dressed expensively and fashionably in rainy daisies [12] and close-fitting jackets.

They spoke quickly and breathlessly, introducing themselves as "the Miss Clevertons".

The ladies had the attitude of children undertaking a dare who, as soon as their object is at hand, quite lose their nerve. For as soon as they had entered the little salon, their cheery chatter evaporated and they stood, hand in hand – all set, it seemed, to bolt at the slightest sniff of a spook or spirt.

Much to Burkins' chagrín, Holmes had already installed himself in the seat beside Miss Christine. "Come, sit beside me, Watson. That way, the ladies Clevertons will have the comfort of each other during the proceedings."

"Surely, Mr. Holmes, Doctor Watson, the ladies would prefer to have a gentlemen between them in case of distress?" Burkins protested.

"Oh, I think there's nothing like the reassuring hand of a sister in times like this," Holmes responded.

"You're so right!" the ladies chorused, gratefully.

However Burkins seemed determined to rearrange the seating, and there followed a verbal tug-o-war, with Holmes smoothly countering every objection.

It was Miss Burkins herself who put pay to the debate. "Don't make a fuss, Pa," she said. "The spirits don't care who sits where. Now, if we're ready, I'll dim the lamp. Please don't be concerned. I will not leave you completely in the dark. Pa, if you'll light the candle – the spirits much prefer it – then we will take each other's hands."

As the gas was extinguished, I heard Burkins, who still stood, sentinel-like, near the door strike a match but, wherever the candle was, it cast such poor light as to make little difference to the gloom.

Almost immediately, Miss Burkins began her invocations, inviting the spirits to join us. "Miss Cleverton," she said, "who is it you wish to speak to?"

"Our Aunt Agatha" they replied in unison.

"Mr. Holmes, who is it you wish to speak to?"

"My grandmother," he said, much to my surprise. [13]

"And Doctor, who is it you wish to speak to?"

"Mary," I answered. No sooner had I given my reply, then I had a sudden revelation, which was so shocking it made me cry out.

"Why, Mary is here!" Christine said – and indeed she was, for I could smell her perfume!

"She will answer your questions if you ask," Miss Burkins said.

My mind was in such a riot that I barely knew what to say. "My dearest? Is it really you?"

I heard a voice, then, whispering in my ear. It sounded faint, muffled, as though someone was speaking from far, far away. "*Yes . . .*" came the answer.

"Does today mean anything to you?" I asked, barely able to keep my voice steady.

"*Sad . . .*" came the reply.

That day – the day I'd deliberately chosen for the séance – was my birthday. [14] It was a day that Mary and I always celebrated with friends and much laughter. Why would she think it "*sad*"? Her reply made no sense! But I must understand!

I attempted to calm myself and think. *Was she sad that she could no longer share it with me? Or was death the cause of her sadness?* I had been so wrapped-up in my own pain, it hadn't occurred to me that the dead, too, may feel grief! I was about to ask more when I realized that I could no longer feel Holmes's cool, reassuring hand resting on mine. I felt a movement, beside me, fast and sudden, followed the sound of a hollow slap, and a clattering noise as of something falling.

The ladies Cleverton gave terrified little yelp.

"Don't be afraid," Christine said by way of explanation. "The spirits are with us, and you may hear and see things tonight that cannot be easily explained."

I could still smell Mary's perfume, but it seemed that she was unable to answer any further questions. I tried several more, until finally, Miss Burkins told me what I feared – that the veil between us was too heavy – that she could not break through.

"Don't be disheartened, Doctor. It sometimes takes time for a loved one to learn how to speak to us" she explained. "Let us try Agatha. Come, Agatha, will you not speak with us? Anna and Jane are here."

"Yes, yes," came the voices of the ladies Cleverton, "are you there, Aunt?"

For a moment all was silent. Then, without warning, there came a dull thud from above.

The ladies gave a delighted squeal, for apparently the spirts choose to communicate in many ways, and tonight Agatha was making her presence known with taps and raps on the ceiling.

"Oh, my dear, how we've missed you!" the ladies chimed. "We've come for your advice. Anna has had an offer of marriage. Should she accept? It's from dear James Mathers!"

Another dull thud followed, which the ladies took as a vote of confidence for the intended. More questions quickly followed – Should Anna wear the silk or the satin? Should she invite her hated cousins to the wedding? Should she choose a spring or a summer date? – until it seemed that the ladies' entire future was to be determined thus: One rap for yes, two for no.

Once again, I noticed that Holmes had released his grip from mine, and once again I felt a movement, beside me, fast and sudden, followed the sound of a hollow slap. Then another, and another.

The ladies seemed oblivious to the noise, but the loquacious aunt – perhaps chastised by some spirit, impatient to speak – suddenly fell silent.

Despite there still being "a million questions we have to ask," Anna and Jane professed themselves delighted with their evening – apologizing profusely for, as they said "monopolizing the spirts" and insisting that "dear Mr. Holmes must have a go."

It was at this point that Mr. Burkins appeared beside the table. He whispered something to his daughter and, with her apparent acquiescence, he leaned across to relight the gas.

I noticed, as he did so, there was a strange red dust on his hands and around his lips. I glanced at Holmes, whose hand was now back in mine, and saw the whisper of a smile cross his face. Of course!

Now that I knew – or at least guessed the trick – I felt a bolt of anger. By God! Smith would have his article, and Burkins and his child would never again be able to play on the misery of others.

Still, the evening wasn't over, and despite my ire, I determined to say nothing until the final proofs had been gathered.

"It's been suggested," Miss Christine said, "that, in order to contact Mr. Holmes's grandmother, we attempt automatic writing. I confess this is something I've rarely tried. One clears the mind and writes the first words that come to mind – guided by the spirit's hand. It isn't exact, but we will try it."

Burkins placed a sheet of paper and some ink on the table. The gas lamp was turned to full, and for the first time that evening I was finally able to see exactly what sort of person Christine was. Like her father, one wouldn't have known by looking at her that she was a liar and a fraud. She was young, fair-faced, with a wide-eyed look that, had I not known better, I would have taken for honesty.

"I'm ready," she said, closing her eyes, pen in hand. "Mr. Holmes, ask your questions."

"I only have one and it is this: *Si tu es là, grand-mère, s'il te plaît, écris ton nom sur le papier.*"

The silence that followed Holmes's unexpected question was priceless! We sat there for many minutes, Christine's hand poised over the paper, but no matter how many times she entreated the spirts, Holmes's grandmother didn't write her name on the paper as requested.

The ladies Cleverton had taken their leave, and Miss Christine had retired to her room to rest, leaving just Holmes and me with Burkins in the little parlor.

379

With the ceiling gas jets lit it was difficult to imagine anything supernatural could ever have happened within these very drab, very ordinary walls.

I knew Holmes had much to reveal, and I was just as keen to hear what he had to say, as I was to give Burkins a piece of my mind. Yet what he said next took me completely by surprise.

"I must apologize, Mr. Burkins," Holmes began matter-of-factly. "I had no intention of interfering with tonight's performance. Ghostly chatter about fiancés and weddings was enough to test the most patient man – and I'm not that! – but I'm afraid I quite saw red at seeing my friend so sorely abused. '*Sad*' was a good guess, for many people visit mediums on the anniversary of their loved one's death. It was not, I suspect, the answer the Good Doctor expected, and his distress as he attempted to make sense of it was palpable." He materialized the foldable yardstick from his sleeve and, with a snap of his wrist, flicked it open. "I do hope I haven't done you any serious injury?"

Burkins looked like a man lost at sea. "I knew I was taking a risk letting you come, Mr. Holmes. But things are getting out of hand, and I'd rather be exposed by a gent like you than some Fleet Street hack. If I've gotten a few raps across the knuckles tonight – well, it's no more than I deserved. But what the Hell is this red stuff?"

"Just a little pastel chalk, Mr. Burkins. I had the occasion to examine the room while you were greeting the Miss Clevertons. There were two things that struck me as out of place in a parlor used for best: A broom, and a three-foot spool tube of the type used inside rolls of cloth. Both were suggestive, so, I marked them with chalk, if case anyone should touch them, knowing the red wouldn't be visible in the dark.

"I must say, it was well done. The violet scented candle was a nice touch. Violet is one of the most popular ladies' fragrances – and most will know someone who uses that scent. I only have one question: *Why?* It's clear your daughter knows nothing of the deception, for it would have been much simpler to have her tap on the table with her knees. She could have had the tube between her knees, too, and moved it with her feet into a position where she could speak into it by merely lowering her head. Yet, she did neither. Indeed, she barely moved at all.

"Switching to automatic writing was a good gamble, too. The skilled medium quite naturally picks up clues about her sitters during the course of an evening, and guided by her subconscious, may write things that seem insightful or prescient. If not, no matter, for the willing participants of a séance will find truths in the merest scribble. Yet, Miss Christine made no attempt to fake a reply to my question.

"No – I know the *how*, but I cannot fathom the *why*. You aren't even making any great profit from the exorcise, despite the interest of the press and society ladies like the Clevertons."

Burkins let out a long, slow breath. "Lord! I never meant any harm. It was me – all me. I felt so lost after my Paulette died, and someone said that Mrs. Williams over in Soho had the gift. So we went along – me and Chrissy. And, well, Mrs. Williams said all the right things. Said Chrissy had the gift too. And so Chrissy starts up with the Ouija board and the cards. And she got so distressed that her Ma wasn't speaking to her, so I sort of helped things along . . . And that just made things worse . . . ."

"And people heard about it?"

Burkins nodded sadly. "What could we do? Chrissy was so happy. And we made a bit of money – like you said, not much, for Chrissy doesn't like to profit from the spirits' good will. And one thing led to another, and me having to find more and more ways to keep the illusion working, like . . . But I guess now you'll write your article, Doctor, and me and Chrissy will be branded frauds and thieves. Lord!" he cried, tugging at his beard distractedly. "What if they put us away?! What if they set the law on us?"

As Burkins spoke, I felt my anger ebb away. Here was a man who had lost his love and lost his way. It didn't seem fair to press more losses upon him. "Don't worry, Mr. Burkins, I'll give my editor my apologies. Tell him I changed my mind and won't be writing the article after all. But it would be best if you discontinue before, as you say, some hack writes what I will not. How will you manage it? What will you tell Christine?"

Burkins looked from myself to Holmes before shaking his head determinedly. "I'll think of something. Tell her it's time to let the spirits rest, maybe."

"I think," Holmes said, "that's a fine idea." I saw Holmes, once again, quietly appraising the man before adding, "Now, if you will excuse us, while it isn't yet nine o'clock, given the Garden's reputation – and our recent tussles – we'd rather not linger."

It wasn't until we were on the street that I asked, "Burkins didn't set Fat and Gristle on us, then?"

"I think not."

"So what now?"

"Well, given that it's your birthday, I was about to suggest The Albion. And I think, if you're willing, we might speak of Mary?"

"I think" I said, linking Holmes's arm in that way that friends do, "I would like that. I would like that very much."

NOTES

1. "Calamity" Smith was the pen name of Herbert Greenhough Smith, editor of *The Strand* magazine, 1891-1930.
2. The Albion tavern, at 26 Russell Street, opened in 1829 and was demolished in the 1920's to make way for the Fortune Theatre. According to Charles Eyre Pascoe, writing in 1892, it provided its customers *"with a thoroughly home-like English dinner, which costs, with a moderate quantity of light wine or ale, from three shillings to five shillings"*. Like many public houses of the period, he notes that the "dining-room is never honored with the presence of ladies".
3. The hugely-popular Spiritualism movement has its origins in the United States in the 1840's. It was based on the belief that the spirits of the dead can communicate with the living – and offer them insights into the human condition. As the Victorians viewed themselves as living in a progressive and scientific era, many spiritualists sought to cast ghosts and spirits in terms of scientific possibility, rather than something mystic and unknowable.
4. "Colleagues" may include Watson's editor, Sir Arthur Conan Doyle, who is known to have attended séances in his youth and would later become a notable champion of the Spiritualist movement.
5. In 1 *Samuel* 28:3-25, King Saul approaches a medium for advice from the dead Samuel, in direct opposition to God's prohibition. According to 1 *Chronicles* 10:13, Saul later died because he *"was unfaithful to the Lord"*.
6. F.W. Collins and Sons were a legendary London ironmonger. The business was at 14 Earlham Street from 1835-2008.
7. The Seven Dials area of London features seven streets which today meet at a roundabout with a sun dial in its centre. The dial only has six faces, with column itself acting as the seventh dial. The current sun dial was put in place in 1989 replacing the original, which was removed in 1773 and (despite London council's attempts to repatriate it) is still kept by Weybridge Council.
8. To avoid asphyxiating passengers, early steam-powered underground trains had to "hold their breath" between stations, and were provided with regular "breathing holes" along their routes.
9. Single-sticking was a popular martial arts, which began as a way of training soldiers and marines in the use of swords in the 1700's. It last appeared as an official Olympic sport in 1904.
10. The Café Royal, at 68 Regent's Street, was established by French wine-merchant, Daniel Nicols, in 1865. By 1895, it was being run by his widow, Célestine. It was widely considered to have the best wine menu in London.
11. Rubber surgeon's gloves were invented in 1889-1890 and used to protect doctors' hands from abrasive detergent. Interestingly, Harry Houdini used the exact same tourniquet trick in 1924, as described in his "Margery" Pamphlet. In it, he details his attempts to debunk a spirit medium known as Mina Crandon, who was a contender for the $2,500 prize offered by Scientific American magazine to any medium who could produce

"*conclusive psychic manifestations*". As Sir Arthur Conan Doyle and Houdini were friends, it's likely he learned of the technique from Doyle.

12. Rainy daisies were style of walking skirt popular with sporty young ladies in the 1890's.

13. In "The Adventure of the Greek Interpreter", Holmes mentions that his grandmother was "a sister of Vernet, the French artist". Although he never specifies which of the artistic Vernet brothers, given the resemblance between Horace Vernet and Holmes, it's likely that his grandmother was Camille Françoise Josephine Vernet (later Camille Le Comte).

14. Watson was born on 7 August, 1852. This, in 1895, would have been his forth-third birthday.

The Adventure of the
Tattooed Men
by Arthur Hall

The adventures which I was privileged to share with my friend, the consulting detective Mr. Sherlock Holmes, took many forms. Some faded from my memory in time – indeed, there were some that I could hardly have brought to mind were it not for my notes – while others were deeply ingrained upon my consciousness. Murder, robbery, and other heinous crimes were part of his everyday existence, and he conducted himself admirably in bringing about the conclusion of them all, even the curious and grotesque situations which occasionally confronted us.

I recall the early autumn evening when Holmes and I had not long settled ourselves to enjoy a glass of excellent port after dinner. We sat comfortably on either side of the fireplace, its contents unlit since the weather had lately been unseasonably warm. Our day had been spent in the final unravelling of the case which I hope one day to publish as "The Adventure of the Double Ace of Spades", but at my friend's insistence this must be delayed until the participant's families have departed from this world.

The procedure had been tiring, and had told visibly upon us both. I was considering retiring early, and I'm certain that this was in Holmes's mind also, when all thoughts of it were banished by the sudden ringing of the doorbell.

We listened as our landlady answered the summons. After a brief discussion we heard footfalls upon the stairs.

"It is a man, at any rate." Holmes commented.

"Mr. Silas Franklin to see Mr. Holmes," she announced after being bidden to enter. Holmes thanked her as she withdrew, leaving a young man of about twenty-and-five years, dressed in a solemn fashion, before us. I knew at once that he had some previous acquaintance with my friend, since he had no difficulty in recognising which of us he sought.

"Good evening, gentlemen," he began. Then, looking away from me, "Thank you for seeing me at this late hour, Mr. Holmes, I doubt if you remember me, but . . . ."

"It was during a visit to Whitehall to see my brother," my friend interrupted. "I recall that you had delivered some documents and were about to leave."

Mr. Franklin nodded. "I am surprised that you recall such a slight

384

encounter. I should mention that I'm here with the full knowledge and approval of Mr. Mycroft Holmes, who recommended that you should be consulted."

"Very well, Mr. Franklin. Pray take the basket chair, and we will discuss the situation." He saw the doubt on our visitor's face and hastily reassured him. "This is my friend and colleague, Doctor John Watson. Doubtless, Mycroft would have mentioned that he can be trusted absolutely."

His expression became one of relief. "Of course."

"Before we begin, shall I call for tea?"

"Thank you, no."

"Or something stronger?"

Mr. Franklin shook his head. "I would prefer to begin the explanation for my presence."

"Then let us take our seats."

When we were settled, our visitor let his eyes roam around our sitting room before he began. I took this to be a sign of slight nervousness, and concluded that he hadn't often been selected for such errands.

He raised a hand and brushed back a stray lock of black hair. "My position now is that of second secretary to Sir Albert Hatton, the Minister for Interior Affairs. As you will know from his frequent comments in the newspapers, he is very, ah, definite in his views. You may also have thought it curious that his comments have been absent lately."

Holmes nodded. "A recent report stated that he had taken a long sea voyage, due to sudden ill health."

"Quite so, but that was to cover the actual truth. He has left his house in Mayfair in the charge of his servants, and currently resides in temporary accommodation in Warwickshire. Sir Albert is an unmarried man with few relatives, so it wasn't difficult to secretly install him there without family disturbance. There can no question of his returning to his post until the difficulty that he presently faces is resolved."

"The nature of which you have yet to make clear," Holmes pointed out. "I am curious as to the necessity for secrecy here. If, as you have implied, all news of his indisposition is false, then what is it that has caused these precautions to be taken? Does he no longer maintain contact with his colleagues in the government?"

"I can tell you," Mr. Franklin said hesitantly, "that only I, since his first secretary is away on another matter, and his personal physician are permitted to see him. As for your other question, I have been instructed to request that you journey to Warwickshire with me to hear the answer from Sir Albert directly and to assure you, sir, that the urgency is great. May I take it that you will be with me on the early train tomorrow?"

Holmes stared at him steadily. "Are you quite certain that his doctor, or perhaps a more qualified practitioner or a priest wouldn't be of more assistance? Also, does this summons come from Sir Albert himself, or from another?"

"Mr. Holmes, the instruction was given to me from Sir Albert's own lips, to implore you to attend, if that is possible. Between us, he is a desperate man."

"But he has forbidden you to elaborate?"

"He has, but I can say that, even if you aid him in this, it is unlikely that he will be able to continue his career. His main intention is that no other will suffer his misfortune."

"His concern for others is consistent with the impression one gains from the articles in the dailies," I remarked.

Holmes seemed to consider all that we had been told. There were a few moments of silence in the room, while snatches of the conversations of passers-by in Baker Street reached us through the half-open window.

"It appears then, that I am obliged to visit Warwickshire if I wish to satisfy both Sir Albert and my curiosity." He turned to me briefly. "Watson, are you able to be with us?"

"I'm free until the end of the week."

"Then, Mr. Franklin, we will come with you and see what can be done."

The journey to Warwickshire the following morning, to the outskirts of Shakespearean Stratford-upon-Avon, was largely uneventful. Holmes had telegraphed to make rapid arrangements to procure for us a smoker, and to our mutual satisfaction we had a compartment to ourselves. Mr. Franklin, however, proved to have a slight aversion to tobacco, and therefore experienced some discomfort until I opened wide the window. His bleary eyes quickly cleared, and he appeared fully restored as he led us to a waiting cab the moment we arrived at the little station.

I estimated the drive to be less than a mile. Along a quiet road, we alighted at a long, whitewashed house with black beams and a thatched roof. We entered into a large room with warming pans decorating the walls and polished brass much in evidence. It smelled faintly of cooking and brandy. At the far end was an area shrouded in shadow. I could barely make out a figure sitting in an upright chair, facing us silently.

"Good morning, Sir Albert," Mr. Franklin said as he closed the door behind us. "As you see, I was successful."

"Thank you, Franklin." The voice from the unseen person was kindly with a slight tremble to it, I thought. It echoed against the solid walls. "You have performed your duties admirably."

Introductions then took place, but Sir Albert made no effort to emerge from the gloom to shake hands.

"I apologize, gentlemen, for my apparent lack of courtesy," he explained then. "But all will become clear to you presently. For now, and before I tell you why I have requested your presence today, I suggest we all partake of a brandy which will act as a restorative after your journey."

I thought it a little early and knew that Holmes would feel likewise, but Mr. Franklin passed round crystal glasses of the harsh spirit. The three of us drank sparingly, but I heard our host place his empty glass down almost immediately.

"When you are ready, Sir Albert," Holmes said then, "you have my undivided attention."

After a slight pause, our host began. "I have recently suffered a . . . misfortune, which may force me to retire from the government prematurely. It was inflicted upon me by an unknown person, who I beg you to trace and bring to justice. It isn't only for myself that I ask this, for two of my fellow ministers have recently failed to appear consistently and I fear they have met the same fate."

Again he paused, and Holmes took the opportunity to interrupt.

"Watson and myself are distressed to hear of this, Sir Albert, and we will of course assist in any way that we can. First, will you enlighten us as to the nature of what has happened to you?"

"Very well," came the reply. "Gentlemen, you must prepare yourselves for something of a shock."

At that he rose and emerged from the shadows. As I had imagined, he was, a stocky man with strong distinctive features, and I saw why he had felt it necessary to conceal his appearance. His pallor resembled that of a corpse, as if he had suffered much under great strain, but the reason for his anguish was at once apparent: The word *LIAR* had been tattooed prominently across his forehead in capital letters of a scarlet hue.

Even Franklin, who I assumed had seen Sir Albert like this before, was unable to prevent a sharp intake of breath as the politician became visible to us. I stifled my own response and saw that Holmes's expression remained unchanged.

"You see now," Sir Albert said, "why I sought refuge in this retreat."

"And you have no knowledge of how this came to occur," I asked, "or by whom?"

He shook his head sadly.

"It would be best, I think, if you were to tell us all from what appears to you as the beginning," Holmes suggested. "We can then arrive at a starting point for our investigation. Pray omit no detail, however irrelevant it may seem to you."

Our host led us to a small table in a far corner, surrounded by four armchairs in which we settled ourselves. He held up a full carafe of what appeared to be the brandy we had already sampled, but he alone drank.

"It was after a meeting in the House," he recalled as he again replaced his empty glass. "We had discussed for hours the proposed new rail link for the north of England and, with little accomplished, I left for home a very weary man. While settled in my carriage, I had the strange feeling that I was being followed, which I dismissed at first. I looked back often, and despite the gathering dusk, it was apparent that my fear was well-founded, so I instructed my driver to take several turns into roads that deviated needlessly from my usual route.

"The pursuing hansom remained, and curiosity replaced my anxiety. It even occurred to me that it might be occupied by an old friend who had noticed my conveyance and wished to renew our acquaintance. Consequently, as we passed a tavern that I knew from my student days, I alighted and told my driver to collect me in an hour. I entered the building and took a table near a window from which I could observe the road. The cab that had followed me came to rest, allowing a man who was quite unfamiliar to me to dismiss it before approaching the inn. Moments later the stranger came directly to my table and sat down opposite me without as much as a by-your-leave."

"The tavern," Holmes said with his eyes half-closed in concentration. "Pray be specific."

"It was the Admiral Verney, in Piccadilly."

"Thank you. Please continue."

"As I mentioned, this man was unknown to me. I anticipate that you will require me to describe him, Mr. Holmes, so I will do so to the best of my recollection. His hair was longer than is usual and had turned to silver, despite his not having reached an advanced age. He had a moustache and beard so contrasting in colour that I formed the impression that it was probably a disguise. For a moment there was silence between us. Then he signalled to the innkeeper who brought a bottle of wine and glasses."

"Did this man introduce himself?"

"His name, he said, is William Black."

Holmes made no reply, and our host continued.

"He then apologized for the intrusion, but explained that he represented a charitable organisation that seeks to better the lives of children in the north of England. He seemed aware of my recent involvement in bringing improved transport to that area, and also of my donations to various causes there. After at first being outraged at his effrontery, I felt it prudent to listen to him. On reflection, he was a master of persuasion, for after only a short while I found myself sharing the wine

388

with him and agreeing to use my influence on his behalf with the minister who could comply with his requests which were, after all, quite modest. By this time, I had long since decided that I had been unnecessarily alarmed, and there was nothing sinister or threatening about him."

"How, then, did the situation alter?"

"I cannot say," Sir Albert's expression was that of one who is completely mystified. "I didn't see it, but I suppose he must have put something in my drink. I have a dim recollection of my driver, much astonished, bundling me into my carriage and mumbling something about blood before I found myself in my own bed with my physician leaning over me and my housekeeper in a state of panic. I imagine Mr. Black somehow conveyed me to a convenient place where he could inflict this upon me – " He gestured at his forehead. " – or to some accomplice who waited in readiness."

Holmes nodded. "Clearly, this was all arranged previously. Have you any explanation for this yourself, or of the reason for such an outrage?"

The answer came as a hopeless shake of the head. "As far as I'm aware, I have no enemies. I see no profit in this, so it must be an act of vengeance, but as to why or by whom I cannot speculate."

"And yet, since this man Black was informed as to your affairs, he must have the confidence of someone familiar to you."

"I had thought as much, but much can be reasoned from the speculations in the newspapers."

"Quite." Holmes fell silent, staring at the black beams above us.

"Do you think there is anything that can be done, Mr. Holmes?" Mr. Franklin asked presently.

"I will be able to tell when I have all the facts at my disposal. Are you quite sure, Sir Albert, that there is nothing more you can tell me?"

Our host appeared to have suddenly remembered something important. "Gentlemen, forgive me. I was so concerned with this . . . misfortune, that I neglected to explain my notion that I'm not alone in it. I suspect that two other members of the House have suffered the same experience recently. The newspapers have published totally misleading accounts of the reasons for their sudden absence from public life."

I looked up from scribbling my notes. "If you would name them, Sir Albert?"

He hesitated, as if he felt he was betraying a confidence, but only for a moment. "The victims are Sir Jacob Currie, the Minister for Finance, and the Right Honorable Roland Chance, the Minister for Colonial Development."

"Apart from sharing your vocations, are you aware of any fact or experience that connects these gentlemen and yourself?" Holmes asked at once.

"I'm not well acquainted with either, since we have barely exchanged a few words in the House, but other than our attendance there, I know of no such similarity."

Holmes continued his questioning for almost another hour. He declined the offer of luncheon, much to my disappointment, and I was denied sustenance until I discovered that the return train to London boasted a dining coach. To him this was a troublesome distraction, for he contented himself with a pot of strong coffee, and his mind was clearly elsewhere while I ate.

"Why would anyone do such a thing to Sir Albert?" I asked him to interrupt his reverie when we had returned to our smoker. Silas Franklin had remained with Sir Albert.

"An act of revenge," he said absently. "An old grudge – none of which he is evidently aware." He took out his old briar and lit it, surrounding himself with a cloud of fragrant smoke. "You may wish to spend the afternoon reducing the pile of accumulated medical journals in our sitting room, Watson. As for me, I shall consult my index. There is surely a link between Sir Albert and the other two victims which may set us on the right track."

I produced my own pipe and we smoked contentedly, silent except for his occasional observations of the passing scenes until we reached our destination. We procured a hansom without difficulty and found ourselves back in Baker Street by late afternoon.

Holmes's expression made it clear that he had discovered little by the time Mrs. Hudson served dinner. He barely ate any of the Dover sole and none of the dessert. Afterwards, we repaired to our armchairs as was our custom, but it was easy to see that his mind was still much occupied with the predicament of our client and his colleagues.

Our conversation was sparse. By nine o'clock he had entered into one of his long silences, and I had become tired of reading. I was about to retire early when the chimes of the doorbell disturbed our silence. I heard our landlady answer the door briefly, and then her footfalls upon the stairs.

"A telegram," Holmes mused.

He was indeed correct. As soon as Mrs. Hudson withdrew he tore open the envelope. His eyes scanned the contents and he looked up at me instantly.

"It is from Sir Albert," he said. "One of the other victims, Sir Jacob Currie, has taken his own life."

"Good Heavens!"

"He had an unblemished reputation," Holmes continued. "I cannot imagine what drove him to such lengths, unless some hitherto undiscovered scandal has come to light."

"Do you believe it was because he suffered the same experience as Sir Albert?"

He nodded. "The word '*Cheat*' was tattooed across his forehead."

We didn't linger over breakfast. Holmes had the air of a runner at the starting post about him. I had hardly pushed away my empty coffee cup when he thrust my hat and coat into my hands and put on his own.

"We are to visit Sir Jacob Currie's house?" I ventured.

"Dead men can tell me nothing. The Right Honorable Roland Chance may be more helpful."

Within a half-hour, we stood knocking at the politician's door. The grim-faced butler who answered was determined that his master shouldn't be disturbed, until Holmes insisted that we were there on a matter of the greatest urgency. The door was closed then, rather rudely I thought, only to be opened a second time a moment later. The butler bade us follow him into a spacious drawing room, where a short man in a grey morning suit stood gazing through a tall window into a luxuriant garden.

He turned to face us the moment his servant left. A bandage across his forehead hid most of his hair, resting above sour features. His moustache bristled like the fur of an angry terrier.

"I have heard of you, Mr. Sherlock Holmes," he began in a tone that was devoid of greeting, "but I fail to see what you could possibly want with me. If this is anything connected to Jacob Currie's death, there can be no urgency about it. Well, man, speak up. What has brought you here?"

Holmes's answer was calm and polite, though I sensed both his anger at being addressed in this manner, and his instant dislike of the man.

"I'm here to enquire if I can assist you, Mr. Chance, in discovering who disfigured you. Your colleague, Sir Albert Hatton, has suffered a similar assault and so, I believe, did the late Sir Jacob Currie. It struck me that you might be able to furnish some item of information that would enable me to identify the assailant before he continues his assaults with other members of the House."

Mr. Chance's expression didn't change, nor did his tone. "I hardly knew either of those gentlemen. I suppose I may have argued with one or other of them in the course of a debate in the House, but that would be all. They have no connection with me otherwise."

"There can be no common acquaintance, then? For example, with friends of yourself or your wife?"

The response was a look more unfriendly still. "My wife died four years ago, sir. And about my friends and acquaintances I am most particular."

"You didn't recognize the man who rendered the tattoo?"

"Would I not have taken that information to the official police, if I had it? The fellow must have approached from behind and clubbed me, but I have a thick skull and soon came to myself. I never laid eyes on him."

"Yet he had sufficient time to do his work before you regained consciousness. He must have considerable skill."

"Would you allow me to examine what has been done to you?" I interrupted. "I am a doctor."

Mr. Chance stared at me sharply. "That, sir, would be an impertinence."

He peered through the window again to see a swan alight upon a pool that was thick with lilies.

"Perhaps he has some experience," he said, ignoring me but replying to Holmes. "On awakening, my forehead seemed stiff, but it was only after making my way here that I realized what had been done to me." He took a gold pocket watch from his waistcoat and consulted it briefly. "But now I see that I have an appointment very soon. Gilders will show you out."

"Not a very helpful fellow," I remarked as we sought a hansom. "Quite rude, I thought."

"Indeed," Holmes smiled faintly, "but also considerably embarrassed, I think, by his unfortunate experience."

He raised his stick, and a cab came to a halt beside us.

"We learned nothing from Mr. Roland Chance," I said when we were on our way back to Baker Street. "How do we proceed now?"

"To the contrary, we have at least established that he hardly knew the other victims, and that he also is mystified as to the identity of his assailant." He paused, glancing out at the passing scene. "Yet there must be a common factor of some kind here. Only a man completely deranged would select victims at random for such a bizarre assault."

On our return to our lodgings, Mrs. Hudson served a luncheon of poached salmon, but again Holmes consumed little. When that good lady had cleared away the plates and utensils, I expected that we would repair to our armchairs where my friend would give the matter his further consideration, but as it was, I sat down alone.

"I regret having to leave you," he said as he seized his outer garments, "but I need a more substantial source of reference. The London Library may hold the key to this enquiry, so a visit to St. James Square will be time well spent. I expect to be back before dinner."

With that he was gone, and from the window I saw him hail a passing cab. Once more I resorted to my pile of back-numbers of *The Lancet* and other periodicals, but before long I sank into a dreamless sleep.

I was awakened by Holmes's footfalls upon the stairs. He entered with a flourish, and I was shocked by his unkempt appearance. His hair stuck out from his head, and I saw at once the bloodstain upon his coat.

"Holmes! What has happened to you?"

"There is no need for alarm," he said breathlessly. "I observed someone following me as I left the library, but he got the better of me at first by placing a sack over my head from behind. I struck out in the direction of his voice, however, and knocked him down. As I removed the sack he attacked me with a knife, which I was able to turn against him. His wounds appeared substantial. He wasn't a very successful assailant."

"You're bleeding."

"Not at all. The blood isn't mine, and will doubtless yield to rubbing with a wet cloth. I am unharmed."

"Did you recognize your attacker?"

"He was unknown to me, but Sir Albert would surely know him."

"The man with silver hair?"

"Precisely. At one point I gripped it, so it seems that it is genuine and not a disguise as our client surmised. He is aware of our pursuit of him and is likely to strike again. In that event, we must do what we can to accommodate him."

"He escaped then?"

Holmes nodded. "I chased him, but he had a cab waiting. It's number was conveniently obscured."

Three weeks passed without a further incident. Holmes made enquiries at several hospitals, since he believed his attacker was cut rather badly, but none had treated a patient conforming to his description.

With due modesty, I must record that it was I, myself, who discovered the clue that eventually led us to the final stages of this enquiry.

Holmes hadn't referred to the matter for several days, having transferred his attention to the rather brief affair that I will one day set down as "The Adventure of the Chinese Symbol". I recall that we had seated ourselves one morning after breakfast when I saw that it was a beautiful day. I resolved to suggest a walk in Hyde Park. Holmes was busily conducting a chemical experiment, but assured me that it would shortly be complete. He indicated that I would have no more than ten minutes to wait, so I took up the early edition of *The Standard* to scan the first few pages. I had scarcely read past the headlines when I saw a photograph that caused me to sit up straight in my chair.

"Holmes!"

He extinguished his Bunsen burner and looked up. "What is it?"

"You must see this."

He left his completed work and came over. I held out the newspaper and pointed to the photograph.

"This is a picture of the funeral of Lady Firthford, which took place yesterday," I began. "There, among the mourners is, unless I'm much mistaken . . . ."

"Yes, I see," he said before I could finish. "Mr. Roland Chance."

"Indeed. And could the man in the background be he who attacked you, the man with silver hair?"

He drew the page closer. "I am uncertain, for the picture isn't a clear one, but it is possible."

"Then could it be that he is following Mr. Chance, with the intention of attacking him again?"

"Perhaps, and apparently without being recognized. It is certain that our Right Honorable Member didn't remain at the service for long."

"How did you deduce that?" I asked, puzzled.

"You can see that he wears a top hat, appropriate to the circumstance, but pulled down low over his forehead so as to hide the tattoo. If he had remained, perhaps repaired to Lord Firthford's London house to offer his condolences, he would have been required to remove the hat. Remembering his understandable embarrassment, I believe he would have avoided such an encounter."

"And the silver-haired man?"

"We now have the means to find him."

I looked at the picture again. "Who was Lady Firthford? I confess to never having heard of her."

Holmes, all thoughts of his experiment and our excursion to Hyde Park apparently forgotten, sank into his armchair. I resumed my seat opposite.

"Until about a year ago, she was Eleanor Quiltham, a notorious courtesan. Her scandalous conduct, involving at various times the Dukes of Weltham, Orbury, Bordingham, and the Frenchman who claimed to be of the family of the Marquis of Delagne, has been the subject of countless newspaper articles, despite her efforts to avoid a public display of her exploits. She finally married Lord Firthford, who must now be almost seventy years of age – no doubt with the intention of outliving him and inheriting his estate, but it appears that events have prevented that."

"She appears to have been a hard-hearted woman."

"Indeed. She has proved herself capable of great deception over the years. As her youthfulness faded she sought security, but her past overtook her. An illness, probably resulting from her previous adventures, ended her life before her husband's decline."

"Not a woman I would have cared to know."

"You would have done well to haven't known her. In any case, she

394

was attracted only by wealth."

"How is it we can now find the silver-haired man?" I referred to his earlier remark, to change the subject.

"We now have a connection between him and Roland Chance, and Sir Albert mentioned his assailant, William Black, as having silver hair also. In addition, the introduction of Lady Firthford into our investigation suggests to me his identity. If you would care to accompany me on a further visit to Sir Albert, I will be ready to depart in ten minutes."

He then returned immediately to his index, furiously turning pages and scanning texts before moving on to others. Less than the time he had allotted himself had passed before he turned away from the bookshelf with a triumphant smile upon his face.

"As I expected," he said as we left. "Confirmation from Sir Albert will complete my case."

The politician seemed mildly surprised when we arrived at his Mayfair house, an old Tudor building surrounded by a sprawling lawn and garden. We had learned from the dailies of his return from Warwickshire, apparently much improved.

"Mr. Holmes and Doctor Watson!" he exclaimed as we were shown into a tastefully appointed sitting room. "It is good to see you again."

"We are pleased to see you in such fine spirits," my friend replied.

We were bidden to be seated and were offered sherry, which we accepted. As the butler withdrew, our host joined us.

"I see that you are wondering about the freshly bloodstained bandage around my head, Mr. Holmes. Doctor Astaire, who has been my physician for many years as well as a personal friend, has treated those infernal marks as best he can, and we are hopeful that most of the scarring will fade in time. It is a matter of cultivating patience, he informs me."

"I'm glad to see that your disposition has improved also."

Sir Albert drank before putting his glass aside. "The prospect of hiding my face from the world for the remainder of my life brought on melancholia," he reflected, "but now I have hope. Tell me, gentlemen, have your endeavours been at all fruitful?"

"Allow me to show you where our investigation has led us." Holmes passed him the photograph from the newspaper.

There was a moment of silence, and Sir Albert's expression deepened.

"So she has died," he said gravely. "I did not know."

"You were once engaged to her, I understand."

"That was many years ago. Being much younger, I was easily seduced. She could be very persuasive, when she had a mind to."

"But what happened?" I asked, puzzled by Holmes's revelation.

395

Sir Albert shook his head slowly. "Whispers began among my friends. I received curious glances at my club. Of her past I was entirely ignorant, until I received an anonymous communication that explained all. I rejected the accusations, but made enquiries. Soon I discovered that my unknown informer had furnished me with accurate, but incomplete truths, and the weight of the scandal appalled me. I ended our association at once, of course, and she left for abroad soon after. Since then, I have tried my utmost to erase her from my memory."

"It appears," Holmes explained, "that she became involved with Roland Chance and Sir Jacob Currie also, at various times. Apparently the three of you were unaware of each other. At last, we have our common factor. Can you now tell me, Sir Albert, of the most likely identity of your attacker?"

Our host looked again at the photograph. His genial mood now gone, he said in a quiet voice. "Yes, it is obvious now. The man at the graveside is Eleanor's demented brother, Barnabas Quiltham. His hair was red when I knew him, but it is the same man. I'm surprised that he has been freed."

"He was released some months ago," confirmed Holmes, "from the asylum where he has been confined for years. It was assumed that he is cured, but the news wasn't widely circulated. Pray, tell us what you know of him."

Sir Albert leaned forward in his chair and rested his head in his hands before raising himself mournfully to meet our eyes.

"He was obsessed with his sister. Their parents were absent for much of their childhood, and they were left in the care of servants and others. Naturally they grew close, because they had only each other, but as they matured, Barnabas treated her almost as his intended bride. I cannot speak for his attitude to the other suitors that admired her later, but his treatment of me was insolent and bordering on insulting."

"You were about to take her from him," I explained.

"Indeed. He worshipped her. When she left our shores, he drifted in and out of many professions, and acted with increasing strangeness. He began to erupt into violence at the slightest provocation."

"At some time," Holmes said, "he evidently acquired some knowledge of the tattooists' art."

Sir Albert touched his bandage with feeling. "Also of altering his appearance, for he was unfamiliar to me."

"Clearly, he must be apprehended, before more of his late sister's former . . . companions are assaulted."

"Barnabas bitterly resented the closeness of their association, yet resented even more those who eventually abandoned her. I recall vividly his furious conduct when I announced that our engagement was to end."

"The reasoning of an unsound mind," I commented.

"Precisely." Holmes got to his feet. "Sir Albert, we will take our leave of you now. I think a visit to Mr. Barnabas Quiltham is called for."

"I believe he now resides in Whitechapel," our host murmured as we left.

We first returned to Baker Street. During our short wait for Mrs. Hudson to serve luncheon, Holmes riffled through some papers which he had secured, as was his custom, with a jack-knife to the mantlepiece.

"As I thought," he murmured as he read a crumpled sheet. "I made a note when Lestrade informed me that he would be in Liverpool this week, but I was rather preoccupied at the time. Ah well, it will have to be Gregson, or whoever is available."

"We are to visit Scotland Yard?"

He nodded. "How else will we trace Barnabas Quiltham? With his history, he is sure to be known to them."

Our landlady then appeared, bearing plates of succulent roast beef. Holmes consumed a portion of his thoughtfully, saying little.

"I see that you are impatient for us to depart," I said as I finished my apple pie. "I will delay no more than another few moments."

"Bring your service revolver."

"I have it with me."

"Also your medical bag. Barnabas Quiltham sustained injuries during our recent encounter. I have no way to ascertain their extent, or if he has received treatment."

"That was weeks ago."

He replaced his coffee cup. "Nevertheless."

We arrived at Scotland Yard in the early afternoon to discover that Inspector Lestrade was indeed absent. After a short while, we were granted an interview with the flaxen-haired Gregson, who agreed to consult the records on our behalf.

"You have been of use to the Yard from time to time, Mr. Holmes," the inspector acknowledged. "I see no reason why we should not assist you in this matter." He then summoned a constable to fetch the appropriate file from the archives. Shortly afterwards, Holmes expressed his thanks and we left.

About an hour later we found ourselves in Slaughterhouse Lane, an old and neglected part of Whitechapel.

"This is the address that Gregson gave us," Holmes said as we approached a dilapidated house near the end of the street. He rapped upon the door with his stick twice, but without response.

I peered through the grimy window, but could see nothing but shadows. "The place appears to be empty."

"Perhaps, but this gate at its side undoubtedly leads to the rear of the house."

He lifted the latch and we entered a short path strewn with foul-smelling rubbish. We trod carefully and with distaste. The large window that looked out upon the unswept yard revealed nothing. Holmes ducked beneath a clothes line laden with washing to adopt a different view.

"Someone is in there," he said, rattling the door and knocking, but receiving no answer. "Probably a woman who is short-sighted and deaf. We will return to the front of the house and try again to attract some attention."

"How do you know this?" I asked. "I saw no one."

"Nor did I, but the garments hanging there are still damp, indicating that they were placed recently. Who but a housekeeper or landlady would have that duty?"

I nodded as we retreated. "But you specified that you expect her to be short-sighted and deaf."

We reached the end of the path, and I closed the gate.

"Deaf she must be, not to have heard our noisy summons to both front and rear doors. Almost certainly she is elderly."

"But that doesn't necessarily signify poor sight."

He turned to me a little impatiently, I thought, as he made to strike the door again. "I was able to see a candle through the rear window. The wick was smoking, revealing that it had been snuffed out only moments before. Ask yourself: Who but a short-sighted person would need a candle on a bright afternoon such as this?"

He was, of course, correct as usual. A moment later the door was flung open to reveal a wizened woman enclosed in a tattered shawl. She blinked at us and thrust her head forward to see us more clearly."

"What do you gentlemen want here?" she asked without introduction.

"We would like to speak to your tenant, Mr. Barnabas Quiltham," Holmes began in his most charming manner.

"What did you say?" She inclined an ear towards us and advanced further still.

"Mr. Barnabas Quiltham!" I said loudly, in the hope that she would hear.

She appeared to consider for a moment. "Mr. Quiltham, you say? He ain't here. He's gone out."

"Can you tell us where?" Holmes enquired pleasantly.

"I can, but you won't understand any more than I did. He said he was going to see his sister, but he only had one. I could have sworn that he told me she'd died, and is buried in Highgate Cemetery."

Holmes and I exchanged glances.

"Our thanks, Madam," he said as we turned away to retrace our steps in search of a cab.

It proved difficult, probably because of the district, but we eventually procured a hansom, and were on our way.

"Highgate Cemetery?" I questioned after hearing him direct the driver. "Do you believe he will be there?"

"We know of the obsession of Barnabas Quiltham regarding his sister. After her demise, where else would he go to be near her?"

In truth, I could think of no alternative. After the cab had left us, we walked along wide gravel paths between stone crosses and weathered angels. Many of the headstones were centuries old, and their epitaphs no longer readable. All around us was a sea of vaults and tombs, some neglected as the families passed into history.

"It will not be easy to find Mr. Quiltham," I observed. "There are thousands of burial places here."

"True," Holmes answered. "But our task is made somewhat easier because we are searching for a grave attended by a man, and because the burial is recent – too much so for a headstone to be erected."

We continued our systematic hunt for over an hour. As we searched from path to path, Holmes scrutinized and dismissed small gatherings of mourners time after time, and I found myself ready to tactfully suggest that his presumption had been in error, when he began to walk more slowly.

"Over there, near the vault of grey stone. Do you see, Watson?"

I glanced in the direction that he had indicated. Five newly dug graves awaited their occupants, while a sixth had evidently received recent attention. Garlands of flowers in various states of decline rested upon the pile of earth, with new blossoms placed by the man who stood over them. His attitude was as mournful as one would expect, a picture of grief.

He didn't turn or look up as we approached.

"Good afternoon, Mr. Barnabas Quiltham," Holmes said as we drew near. "I fear that our previous encounter was too brief for us to become acquainted."

The man turned sharply towards us. His silver hair was unkempt and his face unshaven. I saw that his clothes were in dire need of pressing, and also why Holmes had insisted that I bring my medical bag since, among other minor wounds, this man's shirt was soaked with dried blood. His eyes held the look of someone utterly lost and, despite myself, I felt pity for him.

"Holmes, this man is ill."

"Nevertheless, he cannot be allowed to continue his activities. I don't wish to harm him, but to ensure that he is confined and receives treatment."

Mr. Quiltham studied us for an instant, then drew a long knife from his coat.

"You are the man who protects my sister's tormentors," he snarled. "I saw you as I watched Hatton's house, and that of Chance. I hadn't finished with them, you see. They had not fully paid the price."

"Put away your weapon," I advised. "Nothing will be gained with it."

"You do not understand, sir," he said tonelessly. "My sister was a goddess. She was always the only woman in my life. Men, powerful figures, took up with her, and it was hard for me to bear, but when she was cast aside I could stand it no longer. I knew I had to avenge her, first by leaving my mark of shame upon them, and then by ending their miserable lives. My work is not finished." His expression changed, and I realised that he was preparing to strike. "You should not have interfered."

He raised the knife and slashed at Holmes with astonishing speed. My friend evaded the assault narrowly, and I drew my service revolver.

"If you continue, I have no choice but to shoot."

Abruptly he became still, as if considering a further attack, and I wondered if he could be held responsible for his actions. I saw the fire of madness in his eyes, as he reversed his weapon and raised his arm to throw it."

"Watson!"

Holmes shouted a warning, and I aimed at our adversary's chest, but before I could fire a loud report reached our ears. Mr. Quiltham staggered, and the knife clattered to the ground as he sank to his knees. Blood stained the arm of his crumpled coat, and he moaned in agony.

I turned to see Inspector Gregson and two constables, avoiding graves and headstones as they raced towards us. The inspector arrived breathlessly.

"Are you harmed, gentlemen?"

"Thanks to your timely intervention, we are unscathed," Holmes replied.

"I knew there was something behind that earlier visit you made to the Yard," Gregson said as he put away his revolver and the constables seized their prisoner. "I saw the old lady in Slaughterhouse Lane, and she told me of your conversation. From her remarks, it wasn't difficult to work out where you had likely gone from there."

"You progress constantly, Gregson. But this poor fellow is bleeding. See what you can do for him, Watson."

His urging was unnecessary, for I was already in attendance. Mr. Quiltham was now babbling incomprehensibly, as I cleaned the wound.

"His arm will be of little use to him for a few weeks," I announced, "but he will heal if infection is prevented."

"Perhaps they will ensure that," Gregson said without sympathy, " in the asylum."

"Do what you can to make it easier for him, Gregson," Holmes asked.

The Scotland Yard detective regarded my friend curiously. "But Mr. Holmes, he was about to kill you or Doctor Watson."

"He was unaware of his actions, Inspector," I told him. "We know so little of illnesses of the mind, it is sometimes hard to determine fault or intent."

"I'll explain that to the magistrate," he promised reluctantly.

"Thank you," Holmes said as Mr. Quiltham was led away. "Are you returning to the Yard now?"

"I am," agreed Inspector Gregson. "Indeed, I wouldn't be anywhere else today, for I will enjoy watching Lestrade's face when he returns this evening as I relate to him my adventure of this afternoon."

The Adventure of the
Tallowed Cadavers
by I.A. Watson

"There is a second city beneath London, Watson," Holmes lectured me, as he had before on the subject. "As with any old habitation on suitable geology, our capital is riddled with cellars and tunnels, with forgotten chambers and abandoned passages as far back as the time of the Romans."

"And then there are the underground courses of the Lost Rivers," I added, to prove that I had been paying attention last time.

"The Lost Rivers," Holmes agreed. "The Walbook, Fleet, and Tyburn, Counters Creek, Stamford Brook – "

"Not to mention the various railway tunnels and the new construction of the deep-level line at King William Street," [1] I mentioned.

"All adding to the world beneath our feet, Doctor," Holmes agreed.

We strode on through the clinging fog towards the work-site where three constables with lamps directed traffic away from an uncovered pit. A flood had welled from the burst manhole and covered the street. The pavements about were rank with damp effluent.

"And then there is Bazalgette," I noted, knowing where next Holmes's enthusiasms on the hidden *subterrania* of his home city would go. "His intercepting sewer systems ended a cholera epidemic and made London the world's first truly modern capital."

"Sir Joseph Bazalgette was the genius behind one of the greatest engineering feats or our age," my friend responded enthusiastically. "His works constructed one-thousand-one-hundred miles of brick-lined street sewers, feeding into eighty-two miles of intercepting sewers, and they now connect four-hundred-and-fifty miles of main sewer and thirteen-thousand miles of lesser sewers, all in a gravity-based system that – "

Holmes stopped short and turned to me. "Watson, you are humouring me. Or twitting me."

I raised my brows innocently.

My friend snorted. "You are perhaps due some revenge. On occasion, I can wax too effusively about the underground wonders of our metropolis. You indulge me by listening often to my *encomia*."

"Holmes, I can assure you that of the many briefings you are moved to deliver regarding your studies *du jour*, your comments and descriptions of the hidden terrain beneath our feet are always of interest."

"Whereas other topics are not," Holmes snorted. "I recall a diatribe that had you almost cataleptic, upon the catadromous eel and the remarkable findings of Lady Colin Campbell regarding the efficacy of hanging loosely plaited grass ladders over the barriers of their fisheries to enable elvers to ascend the river more easily. [2] My comments on the developments of the analysis of wood ash since the time of Emil Wolff caused your eyes to glaze as if Old Sherman had stuffed you. [3] And of course, my recent researches on the motets of Lassus [4] must have tried your patience, old friend. You are a kind companion to endure such torments."

I privately thought that Holmes's garrulity and his repetition of previous data were likely signs of the return of that restlessness of intellect which so afflicted him when he lacked challenge. Holmes had already been up and dressed at his chemical research workbench at two-ten in the morning when a messenger had knocked up our household with an urgent summons to attend Inspector Lestrade at London Wall.

"I am always pleased to expand my knowledge of the world," I told Holmes now, assuring him that his eccentric discourses did not offend.

"You are a man with a curious nature, Watson. It is one of our commonalties. Let us now satisfy our interests in the reason for Lestrade's urgent summons."

The pinch-faced, dark-eyed detective-inspector awaited us in the shadow of the last remnants of London's old Roman Wall, in the alley off Aldersgate that is the last sad remains of the long road that once lined the interior of the city's defensive curtain. [5] The fog-hazed street-lamps made the Scotland Yard man look even more sallow than usual. Lestrade was watching for us, and gestured for a sergeant to open a trestle barrier to admit us to the investigation.

"Good of you to come at this ungodly hour," he acknowledged. Big Ben had sounded five a.m., not ten minutes earlier. "I'd have waited for morning, except that last time you complained about not seeing the evidence at the scene while it was fresh. And, well . . . the evidence probably won't be there later."

"Quite correct," Holmes agreed. His eyes darted about, taking in the scene: The flood-filthied alley were the recent rainstorms had caused the sewers to back up, the manhole lids pushed from their places and washed free from their inspection pits, the scattered detritus of effluence that now stank up the whole area, the lacing of frost laid down over everything by the Thames night-fog, and most of all the canvas work-hut that covered one particular access point where an unfortunate uniformed officer stood sentry despite the overwhelming stench.

"You said there had been an accident and a discovery in the sewer," I prompted the inspector.

"That's right," Lestrade confirmed. "Evidently the recent rains were causing the waters below to run too high. The Council [6] suspected that there was some blockage impeding the passage of effluent close to this point, but no man could be sent down to discover it due to the perils."

"The sewers may carry dangerous and deadly currents when the rains run," Holmes knew. "For that reason, when work is done in the main tunnels there is always a spotter left up top to rap upon the manhole covers if the weather turns for the worse, so that maintenance workers can flee the sewers before the levels rise. Our recent atmospheric conditions have been especially inclement."

He looked down at the sewer mud that had accumulated and part-frozen on the old cobbles. "I perceive that the Council's concerns about this blockage were such that during the lull in rain around ten-thirty or so last night, they decided to send two men down to conduct an emergency inspection. A third man stood up top, sheltering in the lee of the old wall there, smoking Ship's tobacco. The sewer explorers lifted this cover and descended the ladder, bearing those storm lanterns now discarded beside the tent. The explorers were forced back to the surface soon after, not by rainfall or flooding, but because of the dangerous gases they countered. One assisted the other up the rungs. The younger and taller of the two workers was scarcely conscious. He vomited his supper into the gutter there, as you can see. Both of them were sufficiently ill that the third man summoned aid and had them transported to hospital."

Lestrade blinked in surprise to have his narrative usurped. I snorted in amusement. "Come, Inspector, you know Holmes's methods. He has read the better part of your story in the tread marks about this manhole."

"I could describe the height and age of both men and much of their habits," my companion agreed. "I shall refrain from doing so since the conclusions are elementary. Better that we turn our attention to what Lestrade can reveal that cannot be so easily read in dirty footprints."

Lestrade nodded his agreement. He set aside shock and chagrin and added to our investigation. "Well, you've lucked into the right facts about the sewer-men. They went down about half-past-ten and only lasted for twenty minutes before they had to pull out. But in that time, they discovered the blockage, a short way west from here, which is evidently downstream in those pipes. And in that blockage, they discovered human remains. Perhaps more than one fellow."

"That must be ascertained," insisted Holmes.

"The tapper – that's the fellow who waits up top and bangs on lid-covers to warn of rain – helped his comrades out and summoned assistance

404

from a constable, who whistled for an ambulance. The beat bobby wasn't keen on going down the hole to look for bodies – and I don't blame him – so he sent back to his station for instructions. That's as well, for soon after there was another surge and a second flood rose down the street there. That's when I was roused from my sleep, for my sins."

Holmes nodded as if all of that merely confirmed conclusions that he had already reached.

"And you thought of us," I observed wryly to the Scotland Yard man.

"One or more unidentified corpses, all rotted and scattered – that's when I call upon Mr. Sherlock Holmes," he accepted.

Holmes frowned. "Watson, my apologies as one with whom you share digs, but I must descend and view the evidence."

"Mrs. Hudson may as well complain about both of us as one," I responded. "Is it safe for us to re-enter the sewer?"

Hovering nervously, as if guarding the workman's hut beside the constable, was a junior official of the London Corporation, hastily roused from his bed to represent the administration of the city's sewers. He consulted with the tapper, a humbler man dressed in workman's overalls who squatted out of the drizzle enjoying a pipe of Ship's as Holmes had predicted. These two between them opined that the most recent flood-blast that had lifted the sewer covers would have flushed out the worst of the toxic gases. It might be safe to venture the tunnels again as long as the rain did not intensify.

"The blockage where them bones is will be about there," the watchman in work-clothes estimated, indicating a spot some forty paces down the alley, close to its termination. "That's why the first flood welled up all along the street, leaving the mess you c'n see – and smell. That must 'ave unblocked part of the plug, so as a second torrent came up a bit further along and flooded the next bit of alley."

"That's why there are still frozen footmarks about this entry for Holmes to read," I realised. "The second inundation didn't wash this part of the thoroughfare again."

Holmes calculated weather conditions. "The glass is falling. Air over the city will be cooling during the night. Pressure from the east will be pushing up the Thames Valley. The temperature is already less than thirty-two degrees, [7] and will drop further below freezing point before morning. I estimate heavier precipitation within the hour. As Lestrade suggested, renewed flooding may wash away any remains lodged in the tunnel, making further investigation impossible. It is now or never."

"You are going down there?" Lestrade asked Holmes anxiously. "I could send in some constables . . . ."

405

"It may become necessary to drag a corpse or corpses out before the flood returns," Holmes noted. "If that is so, we may require ropes and men to haul them, so have them standing ready. First, it is essential that I review the scene while it is still intact. Watson, you need not come . . . ."

"But I may offer some small assistance, if only as a foil for your observations," I owned. "Also, I am given to understand that it is common practice to enter these tunnels in pairs for safety reasons, as the two men who ventured down earlier illustrated."

There was no point in further debate. Holmes and I doffed our long-coats in exchange for workmen's sack coats, [8] acquired waist-deep waders from the workmen's tent, rekindled the miners' lanterns that had been especially designed not to ignite flammable gases underground, and descended the embedded metal rungs that formed a ladder down to the connecting sewer.

"Portland cement," Holmes told me as we ventured into the tunnel. "Quarried at the Isle of Portland in Dorset, named and patented by Joseph Aspdin in 1824, perfected by his son in the eighteen-forties. It hardens as it reacts with water. It is now the most common form of cement used around the globe, but it was innovative back when Bazalgette built these tunnels. It is the reason why these sewers will remain viable for a century to come!" [9]

I was well aware of Holmes's regard for the civil engineer. Had Holmes not been overseas in March of '91 pursuing his final campaign against Professor Moriarty, I am certain that he would have attended Bazalgette's funeral. [10] At the moment however, I was more concerned with other details of the dark pungent sewers.

The waters that had lately welled to fill the entire tubular tunnel were now fallen again to calf height. They flowed with an urgency that I found disquieting, pressing us forward as if we waded in an insistent tide. The malodour was nigh unbearable even through our scarf face-wrappings. The flickering lantern-light added to the sinister atmosphere, causing slithering shadows across the dripping walls.

Several main sewer outlets emptied into our tunnel, teardrop-shaped passages three feet in diameter that voided filthy streams into the channel under our feet. Along with the expected human waste were all manner of odd items, from rags, newspapers, and broken glass to discarded books and children's toys. All the outlets were coated with thick layers of grease where cooking fat had been emptied into the drains. Tiny bite marks in the accumulations showed that the fat had become a staple treat for the countless rodents that occupied the sewer.

"We should use haste tempered with caution," Holmes called to me. His voice seemed strangely distant above the thrum of moving waters because of multiple echoes. "We will not have very long."

As the river of freezing effluent sluiced about us, Holmes and I fought our way downstream to where a clog of debris blocked more than half the tunnel, creating a formidable dam.

"More fat, I'll warrant," I called over the splashing of the sewage. "It's as big as a boulder!" [11]

Holmes moved closer to inspect the tangle. The large lump was plastered with rags, rubbish, dead rats, and all the unspeakable and unwanted things that are flushed into our public sewers. The stench was, if anything, worse than before. I held back, eyes watering, and tried to shield Holmes from the pipe's tow with my body.

Even from my position I could see that there were disarticulated bones embedded in the sticky lump, and that many of them were human. I recognised several of the longer bones – humerus, radius, femur, two fibulae, and some ribs – but there were fragments of other remains too that were difficult to identify in that grotesque morass.

My detective companion didn't immediately examine them but instead poked his cane into the barrier itself. "This is not made from regular fat and grease," he reported to me. "There is a surface covering of those substances, making the object glutinous, but there is a harder material beneath. I would say that it is tallow."

"Tallow? As in candlewax?"

"Exactly as in the sort of thing one finds in the cheaper kind of candles."

"Then there is a tanner or waxworks nearby who stints on having his refuse carted away and abandons it to the drains."

"Most likely, and judging from the many layers of wax here, he has made it a common practice for several years. The City of London Council may wish to have words with the fellow who has blocked their drain and caused these floods."

"The remains are trapped in wax?"

"Quite so," Holmes agreed. "And that is helpful to us, for the . . . I am counting at least three cadavers here, all caught in this blockage rather than being washed into an intercepting main drain and sluiced out into the Thames at Barking." [12]

"Three?" I echoed, then saw what Holmes had already observed, the differing lengths of the two fibulae and the relative size of the humerus, which must have belonged to an adolescent or child. This wasn't one set of human remains, but several!

"You believe that the bodies were dumped into the sewers as a means of disposal?"

"It is a common enough method. The shifting flow that moves the remains, its passage through contaminated water, the predations of rodents and insects in the tunnels, and the indeterminate period until it emerges at the river to be discovered all help to obfuscate time and location of death, and even the cause of the victim's demise."

"This is a grisly business, Holmes. It cannot be so common." And yet I recalled the Thames Torso Murders of 1887 to 1889, those four young women's remains discovered in the river from Rainham to Whitehall. Had Holmes been called to consult on that case, the murderer might have been discovered. [13]

Holmes mentioned that on average, one body a week was discovered in the Thames, [14] and that smaller remains were likely most often washed out to sea and never recovered. To further cheer me, he indicated the clear marks of hatchet and saw that proved these particular corpses hadn't been separated by the natural processes of the sewer's flow. A deliberate hand had sliced up and discarded the decayed body parts that the wax-plug had preserved for us.

I regarded the sad remains lodged in the foetid heap. I didn't relish the job of picking them over to search for clues.

Holmes seemed more enthusiastic. "We have been offered a wealth of evidence," he told me over the rush of the water. "Now we must gather what data we might before time catches us out!"

He began to separate the tangle of detritus to reveal what lay beneath. It was possible to wrench free some of the bones we had seen, and Holmes was additionally able to retrieve some skull parts, a portion of pelvis, a patella, and three phalanges.

When I dutifully enquired whether I could render assistance, he invited me to bag up a brace of the dead rats that were stuck in close to the bodies.

"May I ask why?" I ventured, worrying already about attempting rat autopsies to recover devoured human flesh.

"I need to determine what poisoned them," Holmes replied. "Come, Watson, even your powers of deduction must be sufficient to see that there are a good many examples of *Rattus norvegicus* dead in close proximity to these human body parts. If these people were poisoned, then the vermin who came to devour them would likewise succumb. Since we cannot detect venom in these defleshed victims, then we might discover it in the predators who feasted on them."

I saw the sense of that and picked out some useful-looking well-preserved specimens from the dead rat collection before us.

"Now that you are engaging your critical faculties, what else do you see?" Holmes challenged me.

"The smallest corpse was female and rather young," I judged from the pelvic inlets and the lack of granulation on the pubic bone. "These other remains came from adults not older than middle age. The bones are not too healthy, suggesting that the victims didn't have a good diet. The remaining teeth in that skull-part were in poor condition, without a dentist's attention."

Holmes nodded as if I had passed some school test, albeit scraping by with a minimal grade. He went on to supply the other answers. "The three of them were deposited into the sewer at different times. The depth to which they are embedded in the wax is different, as is the exposure discolouration of the skeletons. The same tools were used to dissect each of them. The body parts were fleshed when they were cast into the drain, sufficient to attract the attention of the rotted rodents we now see entombed about them."

The water flowing past us and breaking across the wax barrier swelled visibly. A tapping from the street above warned us that our time was short.

"It has begun to rain again," I knew.

"We don't have time to secure the whole evidence," Holmes recognised with some frustration. "Bring what we have. We shall also dig out the skulls and hand-bones from this mess, Watson, and then retreat to a place that is dryer and less pungent to continue our deliberations." He dug deeper into the tallow mound. "Help me to drag this arm free of its wax encasement. It was protected from predators by the tallow and still contains some flesh. Hurry!"

The water which had come to our middle thighs began to rise higher as the storm-drains and sewer grates did their jobs. Another more-urgent tapping came from above, reminding us of our peril.

Holmes and I worked quickly, securing three skulls-parts into our sacks and then struggling to free what other fragments we could from the sinister mound. By the time we had finished, the chilly water was verging up to our hips, threatening to inundate our waders.

"We must go," I insisted to Holmes. "We cannot solve this case if we are washed away in the sewers like the corpses that are tossed here."

Holmes reluctantly recognised the wisdom of my plea and abandoned his inspection. We turned back to brave the icy current and return to the ladder where we had entered.

It soon became clear that the rain-swollen waters were now too powerful for us to overcome their push.

We saw the lanterns shining down where we should have emerged. I fancied that I heard Lestrade's worried voice shouting to us, but couldn't discern what he called over the rising flood's thunder.

"We must go the other way," Holmes told me. "Come, climb through the gap in the wax plug where the last flood broke some part away. Make haste! We shall go with the water's flow until we find the next manhole access."

Holmes heaved me up and over the festering pile of tallow and debris. I squirmed through the gap and dropped right into the liquid on the other side. My friend slithered through behind me, almost shot from the gap by the building pressure behind him.

Our disturbed lanterns guttered, striking me with fear that we might be left lightless in this enclosed, flooded nightmare of a place, but at last one of the miners' lamps survived our hasty climb and continued to show us our way.

In the lee of the wax blockage, we had a moment to catch our breaths, to blink acrid sewer-water from our eyes and spit it from our mouths. I worried about cholera or any of the myriad diseases we might contract from our exposure, but our more immediate concern was the sewer channel's intensified flow.

We waded downstream. Motion was no longer the difficulty, but rather controlling our passage so as not to be swept from our feet by the current and washed away. The chilly waters numbed our limbs, making every step a struggle. The heavy bags containing Holmes's vital evidence actually helped to anchor us as we staggered along the straight dark pipe.

It could only have been a hundred yards at most, but it felt like miles and hours before we apprehended the metal rungs of the next access point. I almost wept when I saw that the hole had already been opened for us. The tapper had anticipated our strategy and had run ahead.

It was still a struggle to haul ourselves up the ladder, hand out our satchels, and then climb in our sopping gear to emerge gasping into the foggy night.

Lestrade hastened along when he realised that we had escaped through a different opening. "I thought you might have been goners that time," he admitted to us, wiping his forehead with his handkerchief to signify his relief.

Holmes had no time for sentiment. "A brisk wash and change of clothes is all we have time for," he told the Inspector. "We cannot stop now that the hunt has begun. Make haste!"

We hosed ourselves off at a public baths in Liverpool Street, and then I administered Epsom salts as a purgative so that we choked up as much fluid from our stomachs as possible. By the time we had cleansed ourselves sufficiently to rejoin human society, it was six o' clock and our house-boy had arrived bearing fresh-pressed garments dispatched from Baker Street, and some chemicals and test tubes that Holmes had specified.

Another man might have been willing to leave off his investigations for the night, but Holmes seemed to feel that time was pressing. "While we dawdle in luxury," he objected, "a murderer may escape."

Since the public baths had been commandeered by Scotland Yard for our ablutions, Holmes made further use of the facilities to wash down and examine the remains we had retrieved. He ruthlessly occupied the steam sauna to prepare his collection of bones. When I enquired what the proprietors of the establishment might think of this unusual application of their premises, Holmes invited me to speculate upon what our landlady might say or do if we attempted such forensic procedures in our flat.

Lestrade ventured into the steam room, where the fumes were as thick as the fog outside but were considerably hotter. His scrawny whiskers sagged even more in the heat, adding to his miserable appearance. "I suppose that you have solved the case by now," he said sourly.

"Not yet," my friend told him good naturedly, from which I concluded that Holmes was enjoying the puzzle. He might even have found our foray into the sewers of interest. He seemed to have forgotten his earlier dour atrabiliousness. "I can only tell you the descriptions, trades, and likely history of the dead man and two girls, and a little about the circumstances of their demises."

Inspector Lestrade flinched. His enquiry had been mocking. Who could solve a trio of murders from broken skulls, random bones, and dead rats?

Holmes and I had sorted the collection we had retrieved by discolouration, size, and position in the wax wall to identify three people. "This was the earliest victim," he announced, indicating an assemblage of bones that included a partial skull with cranium, sphenoid, and zygomatic still intact. The part-fleshed arm belonged to this cadaver. "Female, aged between fifteen and twenty-five, five-foot four or thereabouts, slender, pale-skinned. She had occasional employment in a match-factory. The residue of white phosphorous in her skin in a clear tell-tale. [15]

"Of course," Lestrade responded, as if that had been his conclusion also.

"The second girl was perhaps twelve or so," Holmes continued. "She may have been related to the other. There isn't sufficient of her skull to make any definitive deduction. She suffered from malnutrition. Her finger-tips were worn and calloused, probably from picking oakum in a workhouse for some time." [16] He showed Lestrade the child's humerus, indicating signs of an old untended greenstick fracture that might have left the girl with a slight limp and kept her from harder labour.

"And the other?" Lestrade asked, disguising the natural sentiment that any man might feel at the ending of so young a life, a poorhouse child with a halt leg.

"A man of middle age," Holmes told him. "He stood some five-feet-ten and was broad shouldered, though he had a slight stoop from long years of hauling heavy objects. His face would have been broad with a prominent nose. I might venture that he was a veteran, since his radius betrays a nick most likely caused by a bullet-wound in his youth. It had long-since healed up, but it may have caused him to have been pensioned-out of military service, perhaps fifteen or twenty years since. He was still strong and hale at the time of his death, but he must have been feeling the years creep in. He wouldn't have been able to continue in his manual work for even another decade."

Lestrade had that look he gets when Holmes rattles off his findings. I decided to add to his troubles. "And there's this," I mentioned, showing him the one bone that didn't fit any of our three collections. "This is part of the mandible – that is the jawbone – of someone else entirely. From its rounding and size, it is probably from a girl also, but different from either of the others."

"A *fourth* corpse?" the inspector asked, dismayed.

"It may be that our murderer has been using that sewer to discard his kills for longer than that tallow-wedge has been there," Holmes pointed out. "It is now impossible to tell how many other severed parts have gone unnoticed into the Thames."

"We'll need to find out when that tallow-wall formed," I proposed practically. "When was that sewer last inspected? That'll give us the earliest date for the first murder."

"It is murder for certain, then?" Lestrade checked, although he must have been almost sure before he had even summoned us from Baker Street.

Holmes indicated our assemblages of remains. "It is very likely," he admitted. "It is certain that a soporific drug was administered before death. Those rat carcasses tell us that some sedative was administered to these victims *pre-mortem*. A dose of poppy-juice enough to knock out a man would prove quite lethal to a small rodent."

"Opium? Smoked or ingested?" Lestrade asked. Both methods were popular and easy to come by. I often prescribed it for multifactorial pain, cough, dysentery, diarrhoea, and suchlike. Any respectable person could purchase a range of hashish pastes or obtain morphine with a complementary injection kit.

"I shall need to review the rodent remains more closely," Holmes allowed. "There isn't much in the literature about the absorption rates of opium or morphine into the body by vapour, pill, powder, or liquid – regrettable lapses – and of course there is no study on the secondary ingestion of opioid-laced human flesh by *Rattus norvegicus*. [17] But time presses. Such experiments must be postponed until other elements of our investigation receive attention."

"Such as finding how those bodies were introduced to the sewer tunnel," I suggested.

"There are thousands of adjoining sluices," Lestrade objected. "And they are too small for a man to crawl up them to check."

"Nor will it be safe to re-enter the waterways for some time now that the rains have recommenced," I added.

Holmes was, as I mentioned, a keen student of Bazalgette. "I have sent the boy to procure me a set of engineer's plans for this section of the sewer system. The drawings are meticulously maintained and will help us to trace the probable route of larger body parts such as we discovered. The smaller and more friable sections of corpse will have been swept away already, or else pulled apart by vermin, but since we can estimate the fleshed weight and mass of the remnants, we have recovered we might be able to calculate some hydraulic flow pattern. But all of that may be circumvented by a stroll along London Wall."

"A stroll?" Lestrade objected. It was still a freezing cold and rainy pre-dawn.

I comprehended Holmes's strategy. "You wish to discover where the candlewax was introduced into the sewer. And that is likely a simple matter of backtracking along the channel's route until you find a suitable shop or manufactory."

"A conduit that could sluice that amount of tallow could also serve to dispose of corpses," my friend pointed out. "I don't maintain that it was the place, but it is a suggestive enough possibility to warrant early attention."

"We shall wish to interview the fellow who caused two floods at Aldersgate anyhow," Lestrade admitted. "You feel that there is a need for urgency about these murders? The bodies have surely been in place for several weeks at least?"

"Do not underestimate the depredations of hungry rats and insects, Inspector! These most recent remains, the adult male, might be as recent as this week. See the scratches on the bones. The meat hasn't rotted away but been devoured. And now the floods have brought a good deal of police attention to the area. Word will spread quickly that bodies have been found. A killer who felt that he had perfectly disposed of his victims again

413

will soon learn that his deeds are discovered. He may endeavour to expunge evidence that might prove his guilt or else seek to flee the city."

"We have only until the time that London awakes to make our enquiries," I recognised.

Holmes agreed. He pulled on his coat and swept out of the bath-house, leaving strict instructions to the dismay of the attendant that the body parts in the steam room shouldn't be disturbed for any reason whatsoever.

Lestrade and I trailed Holmes along the ramshackle row of shops and houses behind Roman Wall. Holmes was preoccupied staring up at the eccentric collection of frontages and merchant signs, and at the occasional empty property that was boarded against occupation, so Lestrade addressed his concerns to me.

"This matter must be resolved, and quickly, Doctor. It's one thing to haul a suicide out of the river, but this sort of murder will command the headlines and outrage public opinion. The broadsheets well know that a string of murders will sell copies, especially when the victims are young and female. I shall have the Commissioner, the Council, and the Lord Mayor himself on my heels!" The inspector took a breath and then added sheepishly, "Also, three lives at least have been taken. We have a duty to the dead."

Holmes paused at a frost-rimed manhole cover, crouching to examine the heavy metal lid. He produced a pocket-knife to test how embedded the grate might be.

"I doubt that the bodies were introduced to the sewer from here," observed Lestrade. "One could hardly drop bits of human into this drain in plain view of the street. Even now, at this dismal hour, there are noses twitching behind curtains in some of those windows, and occasional night-walkers on their way home."

"I am merely eliminating the possibility," Holmes replied. He showed us the dirt and gravel on his knife-blade where he had passed it around the rim of the manhole. "See, the sediment includes rotting wads of dandelion and groundsel seeds, from the waste patches of the verge there. Those are September-flowering plants, which betrays the last time this lid was lifted as around six weeks to two months ago. There will be a Council record of the inspection which will verify it was an official event. I am convinced that the most recent remains were discarded since then."

We continued to trace the route of the sewer. Only another thirty paces took us to the narrow frontage of a chandler's shop.

"A candle-maker's store!" Lestrade exclaimed excitedly. "And look in the window – it still sells bundles of the old-fashioned tallow candles. And soap!"

I looked into the dingy window display. This wasn't one of the prestige chandlers of the West End, with hand-crafted candles of beeswax or spermaceti to delight the Christmas crowds, [18] and scented soaps for fine ablution. Tallow candles such as this shop offered, made from animal fat, smoky and dim, were for the restricted budget of poorer households. Likewise, the coarse tallow-and-lye slabs of scrubbing soap that this emporium offered for sale wouldn't have passed from the soapers who created clear or scented cakes from coconut, olive, or palm oils.

"This looks like the sort of cheap place that might dump its remnants into the sewers rather than pay for them to be hauled away," Lestrade suspected. His whiskers twitched at the prospect of fining an offender.

"The place isn't yet open for the day," I pointed out. "Shall we knock the proprietor up?"

Holmes examined the none-too-scrubbed doorstep into the establishment and the frozen ground outside. "We shall check the rear yard," he decided.

A five-foot-wide covered passage led to a shared space I couldn't dignify with the term courtyard. It was no more than eight paces across, formed by back walls of several premises. All the ground floor windows had been boarded or bricked up, though some few filthy casements overlooked the dark narrow space.

Holmes was content to discover a drain grill, indicating that he was still on the course of the sewer below.

A back service entrance to the chandler's premises showed no external lock, surely being reinforced by bolts and bars in this unchancy neighbourhood.

Holmes's attention was on the cobbles of the yard. "This is a working candle-maker's," he reported to Lestrade and me. "Observe these wheel-ruts in the frozen mud, betraying the visit of two-wheeled barrow carts within the last few days. Some of the imprints in the mud are deeper coming up to that back door than they are leaving. Vendors brought the necessary materials for the chandler's business – the fatty remains to render into tallow, the lye-drums for soap manufacture, and so on. However, this set here, of a poorly-maintained handcart with an axel span of four-feet-two and a tread width of three inches, was heaver leaving than coming. That vehicle was taking stock away from the shop for sale elsewhere, and it is the most regular of the visitors to the rear exit. Its track alone indicates that it was taken inside the premises through this double-door."

"Possibly a sales-barrow," I ventured. The streets were full of such trader's handcarts travelling along with their wares. This was the season when householders might come out and purchase a bundle of cheap candles from such an itinerant merchant.

Another thought occurred to me. "A small cart like that could easily be pushed along by a young woman or a girl." Candle-girls, match-girls, and soap-girls are common sights in London, along with all the other vendors of foodstuffs hot and cold, flowers, and gimcracks. Ours is a city of commerce, great and small.

Holmes nodded soberly, evidently ahead of me as usual. "This barrow was most often used by a girl in worn-down often-patched square-toed boots with a nick on the left heel. The same treads are visible on the front step, going into the premises but not coming out, the last person to enter that way. She is around five-feet tall and weighs about seven-stone-three. We might infer that she is an employee of the premises whose task is to vend its products in the locality. I cannot tell more since the rain and frost have rather marred the traces that might have informed me."

"Might she be one of the dead girls?" Lestrade wanted to know.

Holmes shook his head. "These tracks are very recent, else they wouldn't have been preserved. The ground here can tell us nothing past the last four or five days. But if you examine the pattern of wheel-prints, observing which tracks and footprints cross on top of others, you will note that the girl's treads, commonest in the older signs, are absent from the most recent. I would venture that she didn't attend to her work yesterday – but she did visit the premises via the shop entrance sometime after the business closed."

"And there is no sign of her coming out," I realised. "Holmes – !"

"This is quite concerning," considered Lestrade. "Is it your judgement – your professional judgement, Mr. Holmes – that there is proper cause to effect an entry and search the premises if the owner doesn't respond to my call?"

"I would say so, Inspector," Holmes agreed. "I shall back you if there is any question of judgement from your superiors."

I wished that we had time to find revolvers, but Holmes and I had canes and Lestrade carried a night-truncheon. He used that heavy wood and rubber stave now to beat a stern tattoo on the shop door. "Open in the name of the Police!"

There was no reply at the first, second, or third challenges, although neighbouring windows were thrown open by those whom the noise had roused.

"Who lives here?" I demanded of the curious onlookers.

"That's Skerrowclough's [19] place," someone called down to me.

416

"Where is he?" Lestrade demanded, but the neighbours were reticent to speak of the chandler. He evidently didn't have a good local reputation. No one had heard that he wouldn't be in the flat above his shop, or if they had, they didn't tell us.

"We must break the door in, or smash a window," Lestrade decided.

Holmes snorted. He was already at work on the shop's front door-lock using a pair of strange tools he had extracted from a velvet roll in his pocket. I was well aware of his training and facility with tumblers.

The lock yielded. Holmes pushed the door open cautiously, lifting a hand to suppress the bell that hung above the threshold to alert when a customer entered.

The chandler's shop was narrow and gloomy. Even without the pre-dawn mist and darkness, this would have been a bleak and miserable place. A counter ran along one side-wall, facing a set of shelves containing the cheap merchandise that Skerrowclough sold. I noted that he must do a good trade in "brothel candles", the seven-minute timing candles that were given to habitués of cheap bawdy houses to signify the duration of the services they had bought.

An archway led to the rear portion of the premises, where a clunky cast-iron candle-making press and an ill-cleaned soap-cutter sat beside barrel-sized mixing tubs and frames festooned with skeins of plaited wick. Barrels of tallow and lard [20] and a bottle of lye [21] stood ready for use. Pushed against the rear wall was the very barrow that Holmes had postulated, a shabby rickety two-wheeler packed with boxes of the cheapest candles and soaps.

Lestrade fixed upon the open staircase to the upper floor. "Skerrowclough!" he bellowed. "This is the law! Come down!"

When there was no answer again, he bulled upstairs to seek his man.

Holmes still prowled the shop, finding a small door into an adjacent storeroom. Although two walls of that space were stacked with crates of candles, a third contained a table and water basin with a tea set and caddies. A threadbare twin couch and box-filled bookcase were the only furniture, a high thin barred window the only means of light and ventilation.

We lit a couple of the candle stubs on the trestle. Holmes shined his bullseye lantern along the storage shelves and then upon the sofa. He bent in close to the couch's worn fabric cover to examine it with his lens, then sniffed it.

"What have you found?" I was obliged to ask.

"Evidence of intimate relations," he told me. "One end of this sofa drops down to make a day bed. It has been employed as such."

I remembered Holmes's description of a barrow-girl who had taken out the candle cart. It was far too common for unscrupulous employers to

417

demand advantage of their desperate staff. But then again, Skerrowclough was a man who sold brothel candles and might well offer "special discounts" to his customers in exchange for "considerations". Either way, my opinion of the man diminished further. I said as much.

"Your view of Skerrowclough may fall yet lower, Watson," Holmes warned me. He sniffed the cheap brown teapot next to a paraffin tripod [22] beside the sink, then touched the side of the pot and indicated that Lestrade and I should do the same.

"Still slightly warm," Inspector Lestrade noted. "He can't have been gone long."

Holmes lifted the pot lid and dipped a cautious finger into the remaining contents. He smelled and then tasted the drop of lukewarm tea, and regarded two cheap pottery cups discarded unwashed into the sink's crockery bowl.

"Poppy tea," my friend determined. "Very strong stuff, too, with a much greater dose of *Papaver somniferum* than one might except in a domestic blend."

"Opium poppy," I translated for Lestrade. "The drink is sometimes prescribed as a sedative or analgesic."

"And often in opium dens," the inspector objected. "Skerrowclough is an addict?"

"It may be worse than that," I suggested, appalled at my suspicion. The experience of three separate continents had left me well aware of the follies and vices that men perpetrate – and of the innocents upon who they are too often perpetrated. "There are two cups on the side rack. One has been emptied out down the sink's sluice, you can see the dregs. Skerrowclough prepared a beverage for a guest – a drugged drink that might quickly render its imbiber insensible, or at least unable to defend herself. It is a simple matter for a fellow to feign sipping from his own cup while his guest swallows down the narcotic she has been given and it takes effect."

Holmes nodded approval at my summary of the sordid practice. Lestrade immediately understood the implications and used a rough but appropriate word to describe the chandler who had prepared such a pot of tea.

The Scotland Yard Officer frowned at the presented scene. The discarded cups, the lukewarm pot of strong opium-juice, the soiled truckle-bed, the proximity of those gristly remains in the sewer below . . . .

"Am I to understand that Skerrowclough arranged for his delivery girl to attend his premises last night – perhaps to receive her wages for her previous days' labour – only to be sedated to compliance by a vile and practiced seducer?" he demanded. He kept his temper well in check, for

G. Lestrade was a methodical and dogged villain-catcher, able to subordinate his feelings into implacable resolution, but I knew he was affected by the implications of what we deduced. "And that this girl was somehow murdered, butchered, and due for disposal as others have before?"

"There is insufficient data to yet attach Skerrowclough to the corpses in the wax," Holmes responded magisterially. "Watson's hypothesis regarding the teacups and the day bed fit the available evidence and may be a likely deduction, although there are other possibilities. This candle-maker's establishment is almost certainly the source of the tallow build-up in the drains below. Whether this unpleasant Lothario is also the source of three or more murders is yet to be discovered."

"But the likelihood – " I objected.

"We deal in evidence, Watson! And there is more that this place can tell us."

Lestrade was impatient. "If Skerrowclough is our man, then he cannot have left long ago. We must put out word for a watch, a hunt. He might take ship or train to avoid arrest and disappear forever!"

"And where is the girl with whom he had tea with last night?" I worried. "Is she also now severed parts hurled into the torrenting waters of the now-unblocked sewer? If so, then she may never be found."

"Haste is important," Holmes agreed, "but not at the cost of sloppiness. I require some few minutes more before I can recommend a course of action."

He looked about the back room, those sharp eyes darting from corner to corner, seeing everything. He found a day ledger on the shabby bookcase and flicked through the recent entries.

"One '*Effie P.*' is recorded here, receiving variable daily payments for the last three weeks," he noted. "These are the last items on each day, proportionally correlating to larger income entries for sales, suggesting that Effie was the most recent barrow-girl who took his candles to the streets, and who received a meagre commission based on her efforts. There is no payment to her for yesterday or the day before."

"But she, or some girl, entered the shop last night," Lestrade reminded us. He pondered the problem further. "Suppose that Skerrowclough made improper advances towards her, unwelcome suggestions and offers, until she at last fled in disgust. That would be the night before last. She didn't remain to collect her wages. She came again last night to demand what she was owed. Even the small sums of commission that the chandler paid her would be significant for a girl in her position."

"Skerrowclough apologies to her, and sits her down with a cup of tea while he calculates her due," I continued postulating. "But the poppy tea is a trap, rendering her helpless to his lusts."

Holmes ignored our speculations, flicking back in the accounts. "Before '*Effie P.*' came '*Florrie J.*'," he reported to us. "She received payments for just under four weeks. Before that was '*Annie S.*', who remained in employment just two scant days and was preceded by '*Dorrie A.*'" He looked up from his study. "You should locate this 'Annie S.', Inspector. It's likely that she spurned her employer's desires and quit her position without ever returning for her last day's wages. She may confirm your theory about Skerrowclough's predatory habits."

"And the other girls?" I asked gloomily.

"Those . . . we may have found," Holmes allowed.

"But the man's bones . . ." Lestrade objected.

"An angry father or other male relative of a missing girl," I offered. "He comes to the chandler's looking for her, perhaps making threats against the proprietor. Skerrowclough calms him down, makes denials, gives him tea as they discuss the problem, and then – "

"Murders and dissects him also!" Lestrade concluded. He caught Holmes's expression, "But there is no proof of it."

Holmes regarded us with mild pity, as one who cannot comprehend how limited are the capacities of those around him. "My dear fellows, there may yet be the proof you hope. It is all a matter of proportion."

"Then what?" I enquired, mildly ruffled by my friend's dismay.

"A matter of *proportion*," Holmes replied, as if that would clarify everything.

"You must speak plainer, Mr. Holmes," Lestrade admitted with a sigh.

Holmes emitted a defeated breath. "If Skerrowclough is a murderer, then where is the evidence of his slaughter? Where and with what were the bodies cut up? The soap-making vat might help deflesh them with lye, but there are no butchery instruments suitable for dissevering limbs."

"So it isn't Skerrowclough?" I ventured, though certain that Holmes had more to reveal.

The detective winced. "Watson, you have missed the obvious omission in what we have seen. Did we not agree that this shop must have been the source of the waxen wall in the sewer? That the unscrupulous and cheap Skerrowclough had deposited his unused stale tallow down there? Then how did he introduce that molten fat into the tunnels? The small drain outside had no waxy residue. Where did he pour his discard away?"

"There is . . . some place in these premises that we haven't yet seen," I recognised. "A cellar! Where is the cellar?"

"A trapdoor!" Lestrade barked out. "But there are no rugs or linoleum to conceal such a thing."

"Proportion!" I worked out at last. "As you said, Holmes. You paced this room. You paced the shop outside. This chamber is shorter than it should be. That means a staircase behind a wall – that wall there, where the package-filled bookcase stands. A door behind the bookcase?"

Holmes granted me a look of mild relief, as a man might offer to a congenitally ill patient who shows slight promise of recovery. "I suspect we will find that the entire bookcase hinges. You will note that it is hung off the wall, not stood on the floor. There is a half-inch gap beneath. If I read these signs aright, there should be a catch to release it just . . . *here*!"

Holmes pivoted the shelves outwards, showing that the whole cheap case had been affixed to a low cellar door. A narrow brick stairway descended into darkness. The vile pungency of the sewers welled up to choke us.

A rough voice shouted from below. "Don't come down! I 'as the girl, and I'll do for 'er if you try it!"

"Skerrowclough!" Lestrade exploded. "When he heard us seeking entry, he took refuge in his hidden slaughterhouse. He dragged drugged young Effie downstairs with him as captive and hostage!"

"That awful smell!" I protested, trying not to gag. "Of course! The same flood that inundated Roman Wall must have backed up all the pipes and passages that usually feed into the main drains. Skerrowclough's refuge is now knee-deep in sewer detritus. Even if the villain has body parts down there to dispose of, he cannot now cram them into those flooded drain-holes. Not until the backwash has subsided."

A girl's scream came from the cellar, proof from her captor that she was still alive as a bargaining piece.

"Holmes – !" I called to my friend. Bad enough that Effie had fallen prey to Skerrowclough's abuse. Was she now to become the bounder's last murder?

"Give it up, Skerrowclough!" Lestrade called down to the monster. "The game's up! There's no escape for you now from the gallows tree!"

"If you don't let me loose, then I'll cut up this little minx, just like the others!" came the reply from the darkness.

"So you confess to your crimes!" the inspector noted. "You killed those girls and that man!"

"More than you'll ever prove!" gloated Skerrowclough. "And I'll add one more if you don't agree to my going free."

"You're going nowhere," the Scotland Yard man insisted. "We have you now."

"He will kill his captive," I objected. "We can't let him go, but – "

"We can't promise he'll escape the rope," Lestrade told me, "because he won't. The public wouldn't allow it. Nor would it be justice. Problem is, he knows we have nothing to bargain with for the lass' life."

"True," Holmes purred like a tiger waiting for prey in the long grass. "A moment."

He ducked back into the chandler's shop and returned wrestling a demijohn [23] glass jar labelled as lye.

"Mr. Skerrowclough," he addressed the murderer down the cellar steps. "This is Sherlock Holmes speaking. I am not a member of the London constabulary and am not constrained by their Judges' Rules of Conduct. You believe that no worse fate can befall you now than the courts and the hangman. I am here to promise you differently."

That won a grudging, "What d'you mean?" from the villain.

"I mean that I am holding your entire bottle of lye in my hands, ready to toss it down the stairs," Holmes threatened. "You know how lye deliquesces, don't you? You work with it every day, understand just how caustic it can be in strong doses on unprotected skin? What do you think would happen if I spilled this entire container into the floodwater in which you stand?"

"You wouldn't," Skerrowclough denied. "Effie is 'ere with me . . . ."

"The girl is already lost," Holmes dismissed him. "My interest is in making you suffer for it, Skerrowclough. I can give you an end worse than hanging, right here and now in your sewage-swamped cellar. It will make for an interesting monograph – published anonymously, of course."

"Holmes!" I objected, before I recognised my friend's calculated bluff. As Sherlock Holmes had declared, he was not a policeman under policeman's regulations.

"Mr. Holmes, you must allow me to arrest him," Lestrade played his part. "Put down that jar."

"I fancy not," Holmes replied mercilessly. "Local questioning will identify those girls who have gone missing after working at this shop or on its barrow. We will discover why Mr. Skellowclough has such a poor reputation with his neighbours. We shall doubtless learn the identities of those mentioned in the ledger, and of a male relative or friend who showed concern about a disappearance and then likewise vanished. But before that, Skellowclough will have already paid for his crimes."

"It's murder, Holmes," I protested. "I admit, it isn't one that could ever be proven in law except if Lestrade and I testified against you . . . ."

"I am not sure that I would," the Scotland Yard man answered, catching on. "Perhaps its best to save the nation a length of hemp."

"You wouldn't do it!" the actual murderer protested. "You aren't – "

"I am Sherlock Holmes!" my friend announced. "If any man in Britain could kill a man and get away with it, then it is surely I. Nor should you count upon Dr. Watson or Inspector Lestrade to stay my hand. They have pieced together your depravities, both figuratively and literally. Your chances for mercy grow smaller every moment."

"Give up, man!" I urged Skellowclough. "Holmes is a man of logic and resolution. If he determines that the world is best served by your gristly demise here and now, no argument of mine or fear of consequences will stay him!"

"Quite right, Doctor. The severed corpses of this man's victims cry out for vengeance. Poppy tea cannot now quieten them. They may not be severed up and washed away and forgotten. The soap-maker's lies must be cleansed with lye. It will be a fitting end, much slower and more painful than a hangman's drop."

So vehement, so amoral did my friend sound that for a moment I wondered if he might really tip the lye into the foetid waters below, condemning murderer and hostage alike to a horrible caustic end. Lestrade must have entertained similar doubts. But then I recalled Holmes's remarkable thespian talents and calmed my fears.

Skellowclough, that murky denizen of the demi-monde of Aldersgate, must know of Sherlock Holmes only as the bogeyman whose nigh-supernatural powers had brought so many felons to their doom, the downfall of James Moriarty, Albert Stevens, [24] Culverton Smith, John Clay, and so many others. How could he not believe that so terrible a scourge of criminals might not resort to the cruelty he threatened?

"I . . . I shall give myself up to the law," the villain finally answered in a small voice. "To the law!"

Lestrade bade the chandler to emerge from the cellar, leaving Effie restrained for rescue once Skellowclough was cuffed. When the vile and sewage-encrusted murderer was safely if none-too-gently removed, I hastened down to retrieve the battered barrow-girl from her chains. She was fortunately still drowsy from her poppy juice and had therefore survived her ordeal. Skellowclough preferred his victims to regain full sensibility before he inflicted his tortures.

I can assure that proper care was taken to ensure the young woman's recovery and future.

Little remained for Holmes to do. He replaced the lye bottle on its shelf, signified the key evidences that Counsel of the Prosecution might require to convey Skellowclough to the gallows, and withdrew as soon as the closing investigation might allow.

"There is a second city beneath London," my friend repeated, "but for now it is the city above that I require. It has been a long chilly night, and I want some tea that hasn't been infused with anything but good old tannin. Come, Watson, let us put sewers and sadists aside and retire to the comforts of Mrs. Hudson's breakfast table!"

Holmes is a man of logic and resolution. If he determines that we are best served with a hot drink and a full morning platter, then no argument of mine or fear of consequences will stay him.

So we went home.

NOTES

1. The world's first underground railway opened in January 1863 between Paddington and Farringdon, using gas-lit wooden carriages hauled by steam locomotives. It transported 38,000 passengers on its opening day, borrowing trains from other railways to supplement the service. By 1884, both the District and Circle lines were in operation.

   Watson refers here to the world's first dedicated deep-level underground "tube" railway, opened in 1890 by the City and South London Railway Company, using then-innovative electric traction to propel trains between six stations along two tunnels running 3.2 miles from the City to Stockwell, passing under the Thames. The line was later extended to cover 13.5 miles with 22 stations. The carriages were restricted in size by the tunnels' small diameters, earning the rolling stock the nickname of "padded cells". Since London's underground trains were taken into public ownership in 1933, these tunnels and stations have formed the Bank Branch of the Northern line from Camden Town to Kennington and the southern leg of the line from Kennington to Morden.

   There were no other deep-level lines until the Waterloo and City Railway in 1898, and the Central London Railway's "tuppenny tube" in 1900.

   The first underground station at Baker Street, at its junction with Marylebone Road, was amongst those opened in 1863, with an additional northbound platform completed in 1868. In 1906, it became the terminus of the new Baker Street and Waterloo ("Bakerloo") Railway.

2. *A Book of the Running Brook: And of Still Waters* (1886) by Gertrude Elizabeth Blood Campbell may be found online at *https://archive.org/details/abookrunningbro00campgoog*

3. *Aschen-analysen von landwirthschaftlichen producten* (1871) by Emil Theodor von Wolff established comprehensive analyses of wood ash composition from many tree species. The original German text is online at: *https://archive.org/details/aschenanalysenv01wolfgoog.*

   Holmesians may recall Old Sherman as the taxidermist master of Toby the scent-dog in *The Sign of Four* (1890).

4. Late Renaissance composer Orlando di Lasso (c.1532–1594, a.k.a. *Lassus*) wrote over two-thousand works in Latin, French, Italian, and German vocal genres, including five-hundred-thirty motets (Latin religious choral compositions or secular compositions for soloist(s) in any language with instrumental accompaniment, with or without a choir).

   Watson records in "The Bruce-Partington Plans" (*His Last Bow*, 1908) that Holmes authored a monograph on the motets which has "*since been printed for private circulation, and is said by experts to be the last word upon the subject.*" However, Watson's report of Holmes mentioning "*polyphonic motets*" has been criticised by music aficionados since *all* motets are polyphonic by definition, demonstrating the Good Doctor's imperfect recounting of Holmes's expert comments.

5. Roman Wall is a surviving remnant of the route originally taken by the northern Roman and medieval wall that protected London. Before developments in 1957 and 1976, London Wall – the street, not the Roman ruin – ran behind the line of the City Wall for its original entire length, from Wormwood Street to Wood Street. Considerably more of the old curtain wall and its bastions existed in Holmes and Watson's time than has been preserved to the modern day, though the "ghost" of the wall can still be traced on present-day street plans.

6. This would be London County Council, which took over responsibility for the city's sewers from the Metropolitan Board of Works in 1889.

7. 32^0 Fahrenheit is $0°$ Celsius.

8. The sack coat was a forerunner of the labourer's donkey jacket introduced by draper George Key in 1888 that eventually became standard work-wear for manual labourers and later of trade unionists, members of the political left, Teddy boys, Rockabillys, and skinheads. The sack coat and its donkey jacket successor were both waist-length hard-wearing thick wool garments, offering protection from the elements and able to survive rough usage. The sack coat lacked the leather shoulder-panels of the donkey jacket. They often included capacious side-pockets and sometimes in interior "poacher's pocket".

A postcard photograph in the George Eastman House Collection of Sergeant Boston Corbett "*16th N.Y. Cav. Who shot J. Wilkes Booth, April 26, 1865*" shows him dressed in such a sack coat:

9. Bazalgette's tunnels, laid from 1859-1865, continue to form the backbone of London's modern sewerage system, despite now coping with a population more than four times greater than that in Bazalgette's time. He famously calculated capacity needs by using the densest population figures, declared, *"We're only going to do this once and there's always the unforeseen,"* and doubled the diameter of the pipes he wanted built. Sewers he designed to cope with up to four-million users now service nine-million London residents.

    London's population is estimated to rise to sixteen million by 2160, which will certainly overwhelm the Victorian system at last.

10. Watson refers to Holmes's overseas absence over the winter of 1890-1891 in "The Final Problem" (1893, collected in *The Memoirs of Sherlock Holmes,* 1894), writing, *"During the winter of that year and the early spring of 1891, I saw in the papers that he had been engaged by the French government upon a matter of supreme importance, and I received two notes from Holmes, dated from Narbonne and from Nimes, from which I gathered that his stay in France was likely to be a long one. It was with some surprise, therefore, that I saw him walk into my consulting-room upon the evening of April 24th."* That this work was preliminary to his ultimate encounter with Professor Moriarty is posited in W.S. Baring-Gould's *Sherlock Holmes: A Biography* (1962).

11. The term "fatburg" was coined in 2008 to describe the rock-like mass of waste matter in a sewer system formed by the combination of flushed non-biodegradable solids, fat, oil, and grease deposit, although the phenomenon dates back to the Victorian era.

    Modern disposal of sanitary napkins, wet wipes, cotton buds, needles, condoms, and food waste have exacerbated the problem. Thames Water now spends more than eighteen-million-pounds-per-year on treating such blockages. In 2017, a two-hundred-fifty-metre long fatberg weighing one-hundred-thirty tonnes blocked the Victorian-era sewer in Whitechapel. It was subsequently displayed at the Museum of London and eventually converted into biodiesel. In 2021, a fatburg *"with the same weight as a small bungalow"* was removed from Canary Wharf, and a three-hundred-tonne specimen was found in the Hodge Hill area of Birmingham, England.

12. The northern part of Bazalgette's sewer system deposited its load at Beckton in the East London Borough of Newham, where it was originally released raw to be washed away by the Thames tide. The first of a series of treatment systems was installed to moderate future pollution after six-hundred casualties in the 1878 *"Princess Alice* disaster", Britain's worst inshore shipping tragedy, where a ship of that name crashed and passengers and crew drowned in the sewage released from Beckton. The Beckton Sewage Treatment Works is now the biggest in Europe, covering 100 hectares (250 acres).

13. These four atrocities, the "Rainham Mystery", the "Whitehall Mystery", the murder of Elizabeth Jackson (the only identified victim), and the "Pinchin Street Torso Murder" were first attributed to a returned Jack the Ripper but

were later considered to be the work of a different mass-murderer since they lacked the genital mutilation of the Ripper's victims and included the bodies being cut to pieces. At least three earlier London cases have since been tentatively identified as part of the same set of crimes, as well as an 1886 Paris case and the 1902 discovery of a woman's torso in Lambeth.

14. Around fifty bodies a year are still recovered from the Thames, most of them accounted as suicides.

15. Up to the end of the nineteenth century, most matches were tipped with white phosphorous, which caused severe health issues for the "matchgirls" who worked in the manufactories, including the necrosis "phossy jaw" that made the affected bones glow greenish-white in the dark. The London Matchgirls Strike of 1888 at the Bryant and May factories, and negative publicity that it provoked, led to eventual changes being made to limit the effects of inhalation of white phosphorus and the eventual adoption of the red phosphorous matches most common today.

16. The Victorian homeless were often compulsorily placed in "workhouses", dormitory accommodation where inmates were obliged to undertake manual labour to pay for their upkeep. The elderly infirm and the young who were not suited to heavier manual labour were set to unpicking tarred ropes for reclamation of the fibres as oakum, used for caulking of timber vessels or as sealing for cast iron pipes. In earlier times, oakum was also used as a kind of bandaging on open wounds.

   There was a stigma attached to being "forced into the workhouse". As late as 1973, "Granny" Murgatroyd, a stubborn elderly resident of Leeds, Yorkshire, declined treatment in Leeds General Infirmary since it occupied buildings that had once been the civic workhouse, personally telling young neighbour I.A. Watson that she "refused to die in the workhouse".

17. The brown or grey *Rattus norvegicus* is the possibly most common rat in Europe, growing up to eleven inches (28 cm) and weighing up to eighteen ounces (500 g). The Norwegian Rat did not originate in Norway, but gained the binominal misclassification in English naturalist John Berkenhout's *Outlines of the Natural History of Great Britain* (1769), replacing its earlier eighteenth-century description as the "Hanover Rat" by propagandists that wanted to link problems in England with the Royal House of Hanover. It is also known as the *Sewer Rat*.

18. One of the earliest traditions to accrete into what would become our "modern" Christmas was the use of special candles for celebratory purposes at home. In 1848, *The Illustrated London News* featured a drawing of the Royal Family surrounded by a Christmas tree adorned with candles, sweets, fruit, homemade decorations, and gifts.

19. Pronounced "*ske-ROW-cluff*" to rhyme with "*meh-SLOW-puff*".

20. Technically, tallow is beef or mutton suet, recovered from the hard raw fat around the animal's loins and kidneys. Lard is the equivalent product from pigs. Shmaltz is the equivalent from chicken fat.

21. Lye usually refers to sodium hydroxide (NaOH), but historically also to potassium hydroxide (KOH), both powerful highly soluble alkalis. They are

the traditional ingredients of soap, an old method of curing food, and a popular grease-remover, but are dangerous to handle without precautions. Nineteenth-century corpses were sometimes packed in lye to quickly degrade and dissolve the remains as a deterrent to graverobbing for medical cadavers.

22. This was a metal tripod to heat liquids over a paraffin-fuelled lamp-flame, a common Victorian arrangement in houses without cooking fireplaces. It was generally held to be an inferior "Bohemian" way to brew tea, since Victorian etiquette required that the whole teapot should be gently warmed over the stove before the boiling water and tea-leaves were introduced to it.

23. A demijohn, carboy, or lady jeanne is any large bottle with a narrow neck, generally with a capacity of between one and sixteen gallons (sixty litres). Demijohns are perhaps now best recognised as the large bottles atop office water coolers.

24. *"Bert Stevens, the terrible murderer"* is mentioned *en passant* in "The Adventure of the Norwood Builder" (1903, collected in *The Return of Sherlock Holmes*).

The Incident of the Poisoned Shipping Magnate
by Sean M. Wright and DeForeest B. Wright, III

With special thanks to Lourdes Brent, Don Yanan, and Karen Teliha

In his treatise upon tragic poetry, Aristotle observed that the pleasure derived therefrom is paradoxical. Roused though it is by the consideration of terrible persons and events, *"the most ignoble beasts and dead bodies"*, these are not properly the objects of pleasure in themselves, for they are rather objects both of pity and of fear.

The philosopher resolves his paradox with the proposition that *catharsis*, the pleasure and the aim of tragic poetry, derives from the *contemplation* of the objects, *not* from the objects themselves. The love of tragedy finds its root in the love of imitation or play, which is itself the love of learning.

Such philosophy as this, it seems, is wasted on our modern moralists and critics, at least in England and her former colonies. Even as his works are dismissed in this country and his own as mere sensation-literature, across the Channel, Mr. Edgar Allan Poe is oft esteemed as the greatest tragedian of our age.

Whether his stormy powers came in spite of being an American or in reaction to the especial, sometimes cloying, optimism of that people, I shall not venture to guess, but it seems most certain that his works appeal to all or most, excepting those who earn their daily bread by their reproof of the popular taste.

I beg the reader's pardon if this introduction to my narrative seems roundabout, or even abstruse. I felt the need to introduce such matters as my brother and I discussed and agreed upon at the outset of this tale.

Brother Sherlock is among Poe's critics. As a professional detective-consultant, however, he is not repulsed, as are lesser critics, by the morbid fancies of that writer. He is instead critical of Le Chevalier Auguste Dupin, the detective-hero of Mr. Poe's few masterworks of mystery *sans* madness.

Even as a youth, Sherlock expressed mixed feelings in regard to Monsieur Dupin, [1] admiring his love of logic, yet dismissing him as a second-rate intellect given to brash and superficial displays of deduction.

I recall coming to Dupin's defense. Le Chevalier had scoured the newspaper accounts of the titular crimes in "The Murders in the Rue Morgue". Noticing the witnesses could not agree upon the language of the killer's frenzied cries, he reasoned they could scarce be made by human speech at all. Yet they were so similar that they deceived all auditors. So strange a set of cries as that could therefore only be the cries of a lesser primate. I was pleased by this pretty piece of *ratiocination*, as the character refers to his method. My brother stood fast.

I wearily joked to Sherlock that, since my early days working in the Foreign Office, I have heard more than my share of maddened ululations in uncanny tongues – perhaps none so mad as those of England's native primates at York and Canterbury. My brother smiled slightly but, as is his wont, stood fast.

While I labored in the Foreign Office and my brother was immersed in his chemical experiments at Saint Bartholomew's Hospital, I chanced upon another tale featuring Dupin. Once again, the detective and his friend, the nameless narrator, compared accounts from the daily news to resolve the mystery.

The story struck me as unique in that there is no action save the characters' recitation of the accounts reported in the press. All the drama, all romance, is relegated to the off-stage, so that the austere lustre of the thinker's chain of inferences might glisten brighter for the limelight. Readers of Dr. Watson's narratives will be reminded how, in *The Sign of Four,* he recounted my brother's annoyed remonstration that his chronicler should dwell upon the science of detection without "*inserting a love-story or an elopement into the Fifth Proposition of Euclid*".

I sent Brother Sherlock a copy of "The Mystery of Marie Rogêt" for his approval, sure that he would find it up to his standards.

Sherlock remained unimpressed. His note of thanks included his review, in which he extolled the virtues of empiricism. This did not rankle me until my brother, waxing wry in self-assent – a habit he developed at the age of eight or nine – compared me to Dupin by way of temperament.

"*Surely,*" he wrote, "*you would be the greatest detective in all London, as Dupin might be in Paris, if inquiry began and ended in the velvet confines of an armchair.*" As a man who disliked altering his daily habits, Sherlock teased, I was thus a natural admirer of Mr. Poe's reclusive reader of the dailies.

In this he had a point, no doubt, but it is the office of an elder brother, indeed a profound filial obligation, to remind the younger, when necessary, of the error of false pride. It is a delicate task, and one to be undertaken with tact and sensitivity. I resolved therefore to prove to Sherlock the efficacy of Dupin's method.

431

In later years I have even brought cases to my brother's attention so he might hire himself out to investigate problems during slow periods, or when I thought he might wish to turn his mind to look at a problem. I confess to finding amusement in keeping him on his toes, as it were. [2] Other older siblings will understand, I'm sure. But alas, I am getting ahead of my tale.

At sundry times thereafter, I betook myself to scour the pages of *The Evening News*, *The Echo*, *The Morning Post*, *The Daily Mail*, *The Globe*, *The Morning Chronicle*, *The Daily Telegraph*, *The Illustrated London News*, and even *The Times*, among others, for accounts of varied criminal enterprises. This I undertook, as a casual amusement to be had over breakfast.

Attempting to fit together such details could prove trying at times. Press accounts are, in some cases, poorly assembled, or they exhibit no great interest, the transgressions described lacking any features of significance. Nonetheless, every so often an incident caught my eye and I would send the clipping 'round to Sherlock for his perusal.

In this way, I daresay I have had occasion to wade through veritable rills of printer's ink spilt more on tragedies staged in Whitechapel rather than the statecraft in Whitehall. My father's dictum, "*Fallacies are common. Logic is rare*," [3] was ever present in my mind as I dissevered matters of fact from those of opinion.

It was as sunny a Monday morning as ever we see in London on the fourth of May in the Year of Grace 1896. I surveyed the newspaper over one of Mrs. Crosse's hearty breakfasts of beans, bacon, mushrooms, scrambled eggs, and French toast, topped by her own plum jelly.

The early edition of *The Times* carried the headline, "*Mysterious Death of a Shipping Magnate*", and I read of how Nathanael Burgess, dubbed the "*Sheik of Shipping*" by the American press, had died the night before. The wealthy financier had passed away shortly after hosting a dinner party at his mansion in the West End.

The Burgess name was familiar to persons staffing several departments within the Foreign Office. Beyond issuing the usual memoranda of permissions and certifications, I knew nothing more about him. His fleet of merchant vessels, famed for delivering goods to ports all over the world, would no doubt fall to his next of kin according to some, to his firm's board of directors according to others, or to one of the directors according to yet others. At present, the cause of death was unknown. The reporter concluded that the market was likely to hold steady.

The Daily Mail told the same story, bearing a brief statement from Doctor Anthony Abercrombie, physician to the deceased, who said that Mr. Burgess' death was due to an as yet undiagnosed stomach disorder.

Nathanael Burgess proved a personage of enough importance to generate feature stories throughout the day. All mirrored the piece appearing in *The Times*, although *The Morning Chronicle* added that twelve guests had been invited for dinner, including Burgess' twenty-four year-old, daughter, Karen, his only child, and that she was accompanied by her fiancé, thirty-year-old Donald Yananson. Burgess, a widower, had excused himself a short time after dinner was concluded – dying soon after. Doctor Abercrombie, the family physician, had been sent for and was present at Mr. Burgess' death. It was he who notified the coroner.

Despite the butler's resolute refusal to speak about his employer, the names of the diners, all of whom were long-time friends of the deceased, were found within the pages of *The Echo*. They included Mr. and Mrs. Nicholas Barksworth, the president of Crosby's Bank who, with Burgess, had begun his career as a runner at the 'Change. [4] Sir Kenneth Huntington, the sportsman, was present with his wife, as were Mr. and Mrs. Abner McKillop, the gentleman being a member of the board of directors for Burgess Shipping. Also in attendance were Mr. and Mrs. Gregor Yananson, the parents of Mr. Donald Yananson, to whom Miss Burgess was affianced, and finally, Mr. Reginald Kincaid, accompanied by a Miss Jennifer Owens, both members of the acting profession, friends of the young Mr. Yananson. They were appearing in a current production of a play entitled *The Shadow of Death*.

The Daily Telegraph's reporter, seeking a statement, had tracked Donald Yananson to his club. His family's name was known to me as it was to many in England those many years ago. His father's manufactory was celebrated for the beauty and craftsmanship of cabinets, beds, tables, and chairs sold here and abroad. Burgess Shipping took them to South Africa, Canada, the United States, and Brazil.

Yananson told the correspondent that, upon the doctor's arrival, the other guests, out of deference to Miss Burgess' loss, departed the premises while, in company with his mother and father, he had stayed with the young lady, comforting her until, exhausted with grief, she retired for the evening.

"*Mr. Burgess thought highly of my parents. He was pleased when I told him I'd convince them to arrive a little early for the dinner party so Miss Burgess and I might have a short time together before the others arrived.*

"*And he was always very kind to me,*" the young man continued. "*Last night was one instance. After first expressing a desire to court Karen four* months ago, he took the time to learn more about me. Discovering how much we both enjoyed those marzipan candies shaped and colored to look like tiny pieces of fruit, he would order them served after dinner whenever I was invited to dine with him and Karen. He was wonderfully considerate. I shall miss him very much."

After expressing sorrow for the loss of his friend, the Scotch huntsman and marksman, Sir Kenneth Huntington, told *The Evening Standard* that Burgess was the only man to ever best him in a shooting match. Known for his prowess deerstalking in Scotland and hunting lions in Africa on the Veldt, Huntington described the great care he and his wife, Marigold, had taken on their way home. Sir Kenneth confided to the reporter that he had been sure a catastrophe would follow since there were thirteen seated at table.

"*Nothing good ever follows a meal shared by thirteen diners, you know,*" he stated solemnly.

The next morning, Tuesday, fifth of May, a representative from *The Pall Mall Gazette,* having sent a letter to Miss Burgess requesting a brief interview, explained that her father had meant so much to the world that it was important to know more about his life. The young lady wrote back with her acquiescence. I later learned that Miss Burgess did this on Doctor Abercrombie's advice. Aware of the public's curiosity, he suggested she speak to the press then, rather than be hounded by journalists later.

Upon arrival, the reporter found her in company with Donald Yananson, "*composed yet supremely grief-stricken, her dark hair falling in ringlets about her face, fighting back tears.*" Yananson thought it rather cheeky to intrude on Miss Burgess' privacy, but the young lady put the journalist at ease, saying that she really wanted to share what details she could about her family life.

"*Father was an American, a self-made man who did all he could to make life comfortable for Mother and me,*" the young woman said. "*He was kind to those who worked for him, from stevedores to captains, and he labored as hard as any of them in order to make his shipping company the best in the world.*

"*Even on the day before he died, I was with him at the docks. He was checking shipping invoices as one of his ships was being loaded. A line parted and he removed his jacket to aid in hoisting a heavy crate. He also helped load a fifty-pound bag of grain onto a pallet. Everyone who worked for Father knew of his abiding belief in the dignity of honourable work, and they respected him for it.*

"*Mother died when I was ten. Father and I lived moved to England afterward, living for a time in Sussex. Father was a dedicated birdwatcher. During the summer he would sometimes waken me before daybreak so I might join him, laughing and singing, as we tramped through the nearby woods, recording whatever species of birds we found. He enjoyed this a great deal. In fact, for many years Father kept up correspondence with the late Mr. James Fyfe, the noted author of* Fyfe's Ornithological Cyclopedia."

Asked about his recent health, Miss Burgess said that her father was quite active. Indeed, he was just returned from a business trip to the firm's Scotch shipping adjunct in Port Glasgow, on the Firth of Clyde. Her father had been in good spirits during the meal and after, looking forward to munching the little marzipan candies he had always served when Donald was invited to dinner.

The young woman thought it odd that, after only some fifteen or twenty minutes, he excused himself and, stopping by the parlor, quietly told her he was feeling nauseous and was going to bed. Excusing himself to the ladies, he left the room.

"*A few minutes later,*" Miss Burgess continued with a sob, "*Janet, one of our maids, hurried into the room to tell me that father had simply crumpled on the stairs. Wallace the butler and Terence the valet carried him to his bedroom. Dorset the groom was sent to bring round Doctor Abercrombie.*"

Miss Burgess told the reporter that everyone asked to stay with her to be of whatever help they could be but, after thanking them for their kindness, she thought it best they leave.

The young woman concluded the interview by thanking her fiancé for his love and thoughtfulness in her hour of great sorrow. It seemed likely that Miss Burgess' statement would conclude the matter in the public prints, but no.

The Globe recounted that after dinner, the gentlemen had retired to the library for brandy and cigars, while the ladies gathered in the parlor for sherry. Burgess had left the library, and incidentally his cigar, to bid his daughter a good night, and retired early to his bedchamber. Upon his retiring, just before the doctor was called to his bedside, one of the maids, Janet MacKinzie, had found her employer collapsed on the main staircase of his mansion

"Och, *I called the butler when I saw Mr. Burgess fallen on the stairs,*" she was quoted as saying. "*As he and the valet carried the master to his bed, I sent the groom around for the doctor.*

"*Whatever came on him must have come sudden. He'd eaten only a few of the marzipan candies he enjoyed so much. I also found the master's cheroot sitting in an ashtray near his chair, still in its mouthpiece, smoked only half-way. The master was very particular about removing the end of his cigar, then giving the mouthpiece a wipe with his handkerchief before putting it away in its little case into his pocket.*"

On Wednesday, 6th May, it was reported in *The Morning Telegraph* that, due to the suddenness of Mr. Burgess' death, the Board of Directors at Burgess Shipping had asked the Metropolitan Police to make a routine investigation. On the same day, reported *The Daily Mail*, Doctor Abercrombie certified Nathanael Burgess' death as being caused by cancer of the pancreas.

On Thursday morning, the seventh of May edition of *The Times* said Scotland Yard Inspector Stanley Hopkins had taken charge of the investigation of the Burgess death. The afternoon edition stated that a thorough search had turned up nothing.

In the afternoon *Globe*, an enterprising reporter revealed, while chemical analysis at the Yard found no poison in the marzipan, traces of prussic acid had been found in the dead man's cigar mouthpiece, richly formed from amber and meerschaum. As I read this data sitting at the Diogenes Club, I recall the nutty aroma of my own cigar's Cameroon wrapper souring slightly.

So now here was a mystery: *Who has poisoned Nathanael Burgess?* The doctor declined to give further details. An autopsy was ordered.

All the guests and household staff were questioned by the police. I considered possible culprits for motive and opportunity.

Burgess had approved of his daughter's engagement. She was eager to speak well of him, and so vigorous a father could only be expected to improve the value of her fortune. In ordinary circumstances, Miss Burgess would have made a likely murderess but, when taken on the whole, the facts made this suspicion most improbable.

Miss Burgess was now an heiress. Were the young Mr. Yananson to marry her, he could take over Burgess Shipping, a boon to his own family's business. Without the marriage finalized, however, it made no sense for him or for his parents to kill Nathanael Burgess. Murder for such a reason would be much too precipitate. Both Barksworth of Crosby's Bank and McKillop of the Board of Directors as men of means had no motive that I could see. But greed has been known to override good sense and friendship. The two actors were complete strangers to the Burgess family.

Could it be that Sir Kenneth resented Burgess for being the only man to outshoot him? Such a mixture of hubris and bitterness had driven persons to murder before. If that were his motive, how did he apply the poison, as the cigar mouthpiece was always in Burgess' pocket? The same lack of opportunity seemed true for the other guests.

436

Suspicion briefly fell on the cook staff when it was hypothesized that the cyanide in the cigar holder might have been ingested by Burgess prior to smoking, conveyed from his mouth to the mouthpiece rather than *vice versa*. The marzipan pieces would have been apt, as marzipan is made from almond paste, and would thus cover the notorious taste of bitter almonds said to attend that poison. This vague conception dissolved when the marzipan was subjected to the Prussian blue test, yielding nothing unusual. The staff affirmed that none but they had access to the kitchens, save the master and the butler, Terence.

Only Terence, who was both butler and valet to Mr. Burgess, had access to his master's clothing and to the cigar mouthpiece on the rare occasions when it was not on his master's person – while he slept or during his toilette. This revelation settled my mind on the matter.

Friday, the following morning, now certain of the culprit's identity, I laid out my inferences and sent them to Sherlock. These I presented together with suggestions on how to proceed. Should he present himself to Miss Karen Burgess, an offer to render his services regarding the death of her father might bring him a fee. Among other points, I impressed upon Sherlock the need to find the handkerchief carried by Burgess at the dinner party, which would be found in the breast pocket of his dinner jacket.

I sent my letter by second post. Sherlock's reply was immediate, admitting gratitude for a source of easy cash and a certain joy at the elegance of my solution to the mystery. For the very fact that the butler and the valet were the same person, and he the only man besides the victim with access to the cigar holder, put Terence beyond suspicion. It was absurd to think a murderer would choose the one implement that would finger him on the spot when, having access to the kitchens as the staff had said, he might have poisoned the marzipan and put a great multitude of suspects between himself and the official police.

Stimulating detective work had been sparse that spring, my brother's missive continued. "*There is little to do unless one succumbs to chasing after either wayward puppy dogs or wayward spouses,*" he wrote in exasperation.

Receiving my brother's telegram, Miss Burgess proved amenable to his offer. He was already on his way to the Burgess home in Knightsbridge, a multi-storeyed, Queen Anne-style mansion adjacent to Cadogan Square Gardens.

The following afternoon, Saturday, 9th May, I received word from my brother regarding the Burgess matter:

My dear Brother Mycroft, [he wrote]

Following your suggestions, I arrived at the Burgess home to find Hopkins had made a capable investigation, save for, as you supposed, taking Burgess' handkerchief to the Yard for analysis. With his daughter's permission I removed the cloth from the dinner jacket's breast pocket and returned to Baker Street with it.

Subjecting the cloth to the usual chemical examination, it became obvious that cyanide, in the form of prussic acid, had permeated nearly one-quarter of the cloth. It was certainly the instrument used to apply the poison to the cigar-holder.

I next called upon Dr. Anthony Abercrombie as you suggested – a tall, spare, balding man. I explained that I was acting for Miss Burgess and sought to speak to him about her father's death. He hesitated until I told him that my testimony given in confidence to Inspector Hopkins now would forestall inquiries into the doctor being an accomplice to suicide, and any disciplinary action which may be contemplated by his medical board in future.

"In January," the doctor told me, "Nathanael Burgess came to me to be examined for occasional pains he was experiencing in his abdominal area. After a number of tests proved indeterminate, I suggested he visit the Glasgow Royal Infirmary where my friend, Doctor John Macintyre, had recently opened a department for the use of what is being called 'X-radiation'. So Burgess traveled to Glasgow under the pretense of visiting his company's Scotch affiliate.

Mycroft, this X-radiation – so-called by its discoverer, a German doctor named Roentgen, originally at a loss to explain its properties – can pass through solid bodies of wood, metal, and flesh as if they were transparent, leaving images of their interiors on a screen for study. This amazing invention showed doctors at the Royal Infirmary that Burgess had cancerous growths affecting his pancreas, signaling certain death. The results were sent Dr. Abercrombie.

Returning in late April, Burgess asked the doctor what his chances were. His friend frankly advised him to put his house in order.

"He thanked me for being straight with him," said Doctor Abercrombie. "We said nothing more. I knew

Nathanael Burgess well. He was not a coward, but he loved his daughter greatly and wished to save her the prolonged agony of watching him die."

So Mycroft, I am determined I shall not break faith with the father's wish, deplorable as I find his action. [5] *Nor shall I leave Miss Burgess in uncertainty. I will, as I have done on occasion, compound a felony and explain to the young lady that her father's death was by misadventure. He had come in contact with prussic acid at work and, wiping it from the counter, allowed it to dry. Without thinking, he wiped his cigar-holder with it. I shall say, "Nathanael Burgess died by accident, but already had received a death sentence." That solution should hold for the Yard as well.*

Many thanks, Brother, for presenting me a case with some interesting features, although I feel a slight regret that it was solved so easily.

Gratified, I replied that he was welcome, but observed that his thanks were hardly mine alone. Itt was Mr. Edgar Poe's Dupin who had inspired me and, without that inspiration I would not have found the mystery, let alone its solution.

The next post brought his letter lightly admitting that Monsieur Dupin was not without some genius. This was accompanied by a commission cheque which would keep me in Madeira and Maduros for some time. I have not heard him criticize Dupin of late but, soon after the curious incidents recounted here, I received a box of marzipan. This I gave to Mrs. Crosse, for Marzipan is not among my favorite sweets, as Sherlock is aware.

NOTES

1. Doctor Watson quotes Sherlock Holmes's dismissal of Dupin in similar language in *A Study in Scarlet.*
2. Mycroft also alludes to this genial, big-brotherly twitting in "The Greek Interpreter" regarding The Manor House Case.
3. This would appear to be the source of Sherlock's advice to Dr. Watson, *"Crime is common. Logic is rare. Therefore it is upon the logic rather than upon the crime that you should dwell,"* as noted in "The Copper Beeches".
4. Mycroft familiar reference to the London Stock Exchange was in common during the Victorian era. Readers of Dickens' *A Christmas Carol* will recognize its use: *"And Scrooge's name was good upon 'Change, for anything he chose to put his hand to."*
5. A case came later in 1896 to Sherlock Holmes, again featuring prussic acid, "The Adventure of the Veiled Lodger". Watson showed how compassionate his friend could be by setting down a conversation between him and the horribly disfigured Eugenia Ronder:

    We had risen to go, but there was something in the woman's voice which arrested Holmes's attention. He turned swiftly upon her.

    "Your life is not your own," he said. "Keep your hands off it."
    "What use is it to anyone?"
    "How can you tell? The example of patient suffering is in itself the most precious of all lessons to an impatient world."

The Adventure of the
Black Diamonds
by Ashley Williford

The year was 1896, and while most of London's citizens were happy to let their vision be obscured by twinkling holiday lights, my friend Sherlock Holmes was never one to be buoyed by anything as ordinary as Christmas spirit.

Though it had only been a month since the conclusion of matter of the Sussex vampire, I recognized the symptoms of Holmes's dangerous boredom and had caught him eyeing the sinister Moroccan case containing his hypodermic syringe more than once over the past few days.

We sat in our study in 221b Baker Street, Holmes picking morosely at his violin while I failed spectacularly in my attempts to induce holiday cheer into my friend. I'd had precious little to celebrate in the Christmases of late, and I was determined to make merry as a result. I hung our stockings on the mantel, having already filled Holmes's with his customary shag tobacco and a new pipe that I had noticed him examining on our last visit to the tobacconist. Frustrated as I was with his complete disregard of my efforts, I remonstrated with him over his refusal to come down and partake in the small concert given by some carolers who had visited the previous evening.

"You might at least have come to the door. It would ease Mrs. Hudson's mind significantly to see you participating in some Christmas activities. She does fret so over your health."

"I refuse to put on a show for anyone's sake. Mrs. Hudson knows my ways and would never truly expect such an absurd occurrence as my attendance in listening to the racket those carolers were making. I quite nearly sent for Lestrade to arrest them for disturbing the peace."

I sighed heavily, knowing the battle was lost. For he was right: The singers had been far from harmonious.

"Well, for that matter, you might take a little more care in the tune you choose to strum on that absurd fiddle in the early hours of the morning. I can't say it is a pleasant alarm when you – "

Holmes suddenly ceased his playing and began to laugh, interrupting my complaints as if he had not been listening to a word I had said.

"Well, well, Watson! Just as I began to despair of another dull Christmas, for people do tend to turn a blind eye to wrongdoing in favor of holiday cheer and alleged goodwill, it appears we have a visitor. Other

441

than the fact that he is a member of the aristocracy and the father of twin girls, likely under the age of ten, I can tell nothing of him as yet.

"Holmes, you astonish me! How could you possibly know he has twin daughters, much less their age?"

He tutted. "Well, given your limited view of the carriage, I suppose you can be forgiven this particular lack of observation. There were two dolls, dressed similarly, sitting side-by-side in the carriage from which he alighted. They appeared to be new, and with Christmas quickly approaching, it is reasonable to deduce that they are meant to be given as gifts. No one would give one child two of the same gift, and children of different ages would hardly wish for the same toy. Therefore, they are twins. As for their age, dolls are popular gift choices for younger children, not girls approaching adolescence."

Before I had a chance to respond, a rap sounded on our door. Mrs. Hudson entered, followed by a tall, middle-aged gentleman in obvious distress. Holmes made no move other than to turn a bored gaze upon our visitor.

"Have a seat, my Lord. I am Sherlock Holmes, and this is my good friend, Dr. Watson. We'll be glad to listen to your problem and happy to assist if we can."

The visitor appeared surprised. "You know who I am, Mr. Holmes? You shock me, as I didn't have an appointment or take the time to send up a calling card."

"Sir, if I had missed your distinct crest on your carriage, I wouldn't be worthy of my friend Watson's effusive, though frequently exaggerated, praise of my deductive skills."

"Ah, but of course, although it does seem very obvious now that you mention my crest. Have you been able to gain anything else through my appearance?"

Holmes smiled. "It was, as you say, quite obvious. I confess that I have gained little else." Our visitor appeared quite smug at this. "Now," Holmes continued, "as your little problem no doubt requires a near instant solution, let us waste no time in hearing the details."

Our client sat and gave us his account of his case.

"Before I begin, Mr. Holmes, I must first insist on a guarantee of your discretion, and that of Dr. Watson. Can I depend on your complete silence in this matter?"

"I can promise you nothing without hearing the facts. I can, however, tell you the same thing I tell all my clients: As I do not work for the police, I am under no obligation to report my findings. I can allow my own conscience to prevail in most matters. If there has been no violent crime committed, I can foresee no reason why you shouldn't rely on our discretion. Do you agree, Watson?"

I nodded. This promise has led me to omit and alter names in the recording of this case.

"Well, that is fine then. As far as I know, this is a simple case of burglary. However, I will start from the beginning and let you form your own opinion.

"Around six months ago, my wife became aware of a small indiscretion of mine. The specifics on this aren't important. Suffice it to say that she was extremely angry and threatened to leave me. This would have broken my heart."

Holmes gave an inpatient snort. "My Lord, I must stop you there. If you refuse to tell me the truth – the whole truth, mind, I will be forced to refuse your case. So far you have sailed over several important facts. First, the 'small indiscretion' you mentioned was in fact an extramarital affair with a much younger woman, and nearly bankrupt you in keeping up with her expensive tastes. The gossip columns have been positively gushing on the subject. Second, although your heart is undoubtedly your own business, your primary reason in preserving your marriage to Isabella DelRico is the retention of her sizable dowry. Now, complete honesty if you please. Otherwise, good day to you."

The client appeared angry, but gained control of his emotions more quickly than I would have given him credit for. This was clearly not a man who was accustomed to submitting to the demands of others.

"Very well, Mr. Holmes. All you say is true. Isabella, who is as quick-tempered as her Spanish blood would suggest, learned of my affair. She flew into a violent frenzy, threatening life and limb, but also divorce and financial ruin. I have spent every moment of the past six months trying desperately to smooth her ruffled feathers, for quite aside from the reasons you listed, I do love her. You must believe that I do love her more than any woman in the world." He quickly continued, as if to prevent Holmes from having a chance to rebuke this claim.

"One of her complaints is that, while generous in my gifts to her, I have never been as thoughtful as she would like. So this Christmas I wanted to surprise her with a gift that I knew she truly desired – something that I would only know she wanted if I had truly listened to her over the years.

"As it happens, a few times in the past she has remarked to me how much she adored a pair of black diamond earrings that belonged to her mother when Isabella was only a child. These earrings were stolen from her family long ago, and they have a notorious history that includes theft, murder, and some rumors of a curse, though I'm not familiar with the specifics of this, as I am a sensible man and don't believe in such nonsense.

"I spared no expense. I secretly hired the best jewel experts and eventually tracked down the earrings. I was able to purchase them anonymously through an agent. The cost was exorbitant, but seeing her joy and surprise would have been worth every penny.

"Given the violent history surrounding the earrings, I took no chances on having them disappear before Christmas. Very few people knew of their purchase, and not a soul in my house knew anything of the search for them or their acquisition. I wrapped them myself, another effort to show my affection, and have kept them in my private safe for weeks. A few days ago, I pulled out the package and placed it carefully in the branches of the Christmas tree, for the presents underneath it were growing in number, and I didn't want her to feel as if I hadn't gotten her a gift or that I had waited until last minute to do my shopping. Again, no one in the house knew what the package contained, and there were many other packages that should have attracted a burglar's attention before this plain, amateurly wrapped little gift.

"One question," Holmes interrupted. "What was written on the tag?"

Our client appeared a little surprised and thought for a moment before replying, "I had only written her name: *Isabella.*"

Holmes nodded, "Thank you. Please carry on."

He cleared his throat and continued. "Following my breakfast this morning, I happened to pass the tree. I stopped in my tracks when I noticed the package wasn't in the tree where I had placed it. Naturally, I assumed it had fallen and began to search. I took every gift out from under the tree, Mr. Holmes. It had vanished.

"My wife found me underneath the tree, frantically rustling through the branches. She must have thought me quite mad, for as soon as I ascertained their disappearance, I ran straight out to the carriage, calling to her that I must go into London post-haste. And here I am, Mr. Holmes. That is my full account."

"There are just a few points I should like to clear up. You say no one in the house knew of the purchase of the earrings? Surely your man, the housekeeper, or someone must have known."

The client shook his head emphatically. "No. I assure you that not a soul knew of their existence in the house. I know how the servants gossip, and I knew that if a whisper reached my wife's maid, all hope of genuine surprise was lost, for she is very devoted to my wife and has no secrets from her."

"Very good. And there was nothing else missing? Can you be certain?"

444

"I admit that I didn't make a very thorough search of the house. In my haste to reach London, I neglected to inquire if anyone else had noticed missing valuables, but when I started my search, all the gifts under the tree seemed to be where they were the night before."

"Very well. One more question and I think we will get started. You don't mind if we ride with you in your carriage? The snow is falling rapidly, and I fear that if we delay much longer, none of us will be able to return to your estate."

"I would be most grateful for you and Dr. Watson to accompany me. You would, of course, be welcome to spend Christmas as my personal guests. But you mentioned another question?"

"Yes. What were your daughters doing when you left for London?"

Our client appeared nonplussed. "My daughters? Well, hmm, let's see." He appeared to think for a moment. "I remember seeing them last night, I do tuck them in every night, of course. But this morning . . . Ah! Yes, as the carriage was pulling down the drive, I noticed them playing in the snow. But that is extraordinary. How did you know I had daughters? And in what way are there movements important to this case?"

Holmes stood. "It is of no matter. Well, Watson, what do you say to a country Christmas? Would you be so good as to accompany me to the estate? Yes? Excellent. Let us pack our bags and be off."

We arrived at the estate a few hours later. The journey took much longer than it normally would have with the snow now falling in sheets, and Holmes had left the small talk during the journey to me and our client, only participating in conversation when asked a direct question. I was well used to his moods, and was happy to give him time to ponder of the necessary aspects of the case.

We had evidently arrived in the nick of time – not an hour later, the drive was invisible.

A footman took our coats, hats, scarves, and gloves before the butler ushered us into a supremely cozy library complete with a roaring fire and comfortable arm chairs. A young maid soon entered with a tea tray, and a more welcome sight would be hard to imagine. Holmes, of course, showed no interest in the refreshment. I briefly considered pressing a cup into his hands, but knew my efforts would be wasted. He was all energy now that the game was afoot. I've been on the receiving end of his scorn more times than I cared to recall regarding his need for nourishment, and knew better than to insist.

His attention was focused on the tree, magnifying glass in hand, all efforts at conversation ignored or waved away. The maid appeared quite startled at this eccentric behavior, especially as no one in the house had any idea as to our identities or the purpose of our presence.

The butler, however, showed all the discipline expected in one employed by a member of the British aristocracy. He cleared his throat and addressed his master. "Will there be anything else, my Lord?"

"No, no, Hopkins. That will do."

He bowed and exited without a second glance at Holmes, who was now completely underneath the tree, only his long legs visible.

He extracted himself more gracefully than I would have thought possible. "It is as you say: The gift isn't here. It does just as well to be sure, however, before launching a full scale investigation. Now, you say there have been no strangers or visitors to the house over the past day?"

"No, I'm quite sure there has been no one."

We were interrupted by a flurry of skirts, inhabited by one of the most beautiful women I have ever seen, despite her evident fury at her husband.

"Charles! How dare you run out without an explanation on the day before Christmas Eve! You know we have guests coming and I quite doubted you would be able to make it to London and back in this weather. And who is this, then?" she asked, turning to us. "You must excuse me, gentlemen. My husband has behaved insanely and caused me a great deal of worry."

Our client appeared abashed.

"Bella, dear, please accept my apologies. I assure you, I wouldn't have acted so rashly unless the matter was quite urgent. Please allow me to introduce you to Mr. Holmes and his friend, Dr. Watson."

"Sherlock Holmes, the detective? But Charles, whatever could be the reason for fetching a detective so urgently? I'm not aware of any reason why we should need one. Not that you normally bother to keep me informed of your business." She appeared hurt and bewildered, and I hated the necessity of deceiving her.

Holmes rose to his feet and took her hand, bowing slightly. "My Lady, I apologize for interrupting your Christmas celebrations. The fact is, I wrote to your husband requesting an urgent consultation regarding a very delicate matter brought to me by Scotland Yard. It is a matter of national importance, and I greatly appreciate your husband's immediate response. Indeed, the country will very soon owe your husband and yourself a great debt, although you understand, the facts may never come to public light. Your husband very kindly invited Dr. Watson and myself to spend the Christmas holiday with you and your family, as we would have been in great danger had we remained in London until Scotland Yard has acted upon the information supplied by your husband."

He had evidently struck the right note, for the lady gazed astonished at Holmes, and then her husband with a look I felt confident she hadn't bestowed upon him for quite some time, judging by his reaction of surprised pleasure.

"Oh, Charles, I . . . I apologize. I did not know. I shouldn't have assumed . . . ."

"Bella, don't be sorry. I should have given some word of my goal, but confess I was all anxiety to get to London and back as quickly as possible with the weather. I wouldn't miss the opportunity to spend Christmas with you and the girls for anything."

Her eyes were shining. "Well, please don't let me interrupt you, darling. You must have much to discuss with these gentleman. I will let Cook know that two more will join us for dinner. I hope that you will both feel welcome in staying until at least after Boxing Day, and indeed as long as you wish."

She left the room, and our client turned to Holmes. "Mr. Holmes, I cannot thank you enough for your explanation to Isabella. I confess that I have been so distraught over the theft that I gave no thought as to how I would explain your presence in the house. You have saved me from certain disaster."

Holmes looked the man over. "I do hope you will prove to be as valiant a husband and man in the future as I have portrayed you to be."

"You have my word, Mr. Holmes. I shall not do anything to dim the new light with which my wife now views me. Even without the diamonds, you have no doubt saved my marriage from ruins."

Holmes returned to the matter at hand. "I wish to ask you about the footprints on the front porch. The snow has obscured any that might have been gained in the grounds, but there appears to have been quite the crowd standing under your covered front porch sometime since the first snowfall yesterday, as there are at least twenty different shoe prints and all of the same relative depth. Are you quite certain you have had no visitors?"

Our client was visibly shocked. A minute later, his face cleared and he offered a sheepish explanation. "Why, I have proven to be a very poor witness, Mr. Holmes! I had completely put the carolers of last night completely from my mind. Yes, there was a group of carolers who visited yesterday evening."

Holmes was impatient. "Yes, my Lord, I had gathered as much. Carolers! Watson, you observe how these self-appointed merry-makers may have caused even more grief than their poor attempts at singing alone." He sighed as he turned back to the client. "I take it that you didn't join in the revelry?"

The man appeared confused, but dared not inquire into Holmes's reasoning. "No, I did not. I had important business to attend to and stayed in my study during the caroling."

"Quite. Had you attended, no doubt you would have remembered the visitors more readily. They do tend to leave one's ears ringing for days following the experience. However, this is certainly concerning. We have now added numerous suspects to our list, and have little chance of following any of the leads with the storm outside preventing passage into the village." Holmes sat silent for a while. After a few moments he turned abruptly to our client. "Well, I do believe I have finished with my questions for now. Pray, do not let us keep you from your duties. Watson and I will stay here by this delightful fire and enjoy a cigar before going up to our rooms to change for dinner. We'll ring for the butler when we're ready for assistance."

If our client was surprised at being dismissed from his own sitting room, he didn't show it. He stood gracefully. "Very well, Mr. Holmes. Should you have any further questions, don't hesitate to send for me. Otherwise, I shall see you at dinner."

Holmes turned to me as the door closed behind him. "Well, Watson, this is quite a pretty little problem we have here. You noticed, I trust, the importance of my elaborate explanation to the lady of the house?"

"I confess that I was impressed at how delicately you were able to sooth her feelings and reignite some of her lost respect for her husband – although it does feel a shame that we should deceive her."

"Quite. However, we would have no chance of succeeding in this case without the lady as an ally. You have noticed, no doubt, how removed our client is from the goings-on of the house. The servants are no doubt loyal to their mistress, and we'll have a much easier time of gaining vital information from the staff with her trust than would we would if we were an element of suspicion. My explanation of a national threat will allow us to ask unusual questions without the expectation of an explanation. Allowing the maid so spot me underneath the tree will aid us as well, as no doubt rumor of my eccentric behavior is even now spreading throughout the staff, and any further strangeness will be attributed to my unusual habits rather than suspicious activity."

"I was a bit shocked myself to turn and find you under the tree with a magnifying glass at the ready."

He smiled. "Yes, I saw your surprise even through the thick branches. You have rather a way of expressing your emotions most vividly."

He stood. "Well, night approaches quickly and I have a few more observations to make before that time. I shall see you at dinner."

He was off like a flash, leaving me to ring the bell. The butler appeared almost instantly. "Does your friend wish to be shown to his room as well, Doctor?" I explained that Holmes kept his own schedule and would no doubt ring soon for assistance. Again, the well-trained servant hid his emotions expertly and bowed. "Very good, sir. Right this way."

I followed him upstairs and through corridors, my mind racing with possibilities about the diamonds' whereabouts. I didn't see how Holmes could hope to solve the case and recover the black diamonds before Christmas if the culprit was indeed one of the carolers or some other outside thief. It seemed to me our only hope in restoring them to our client in time was if the thief was a member of the household.

Even with Holmes's story of national security, I was puzzled as to how we would be able to discreetly question the staff about seemingly routine household matters without raising a few eyebrows. However, I trusted his judgement implicitly and resolved to follow his lead in every matter, regardless of how trivial or odd that judgement might seem to me.

The dinner gong sounded some time later, and I was surprised to meet Holmes in the hall outside my room, now changed into a fresh suit and looking as energetic as he always did when caught in the grip of a perplexing case.

"When did you come upstairs?" I asked. "The butler has a heavy tread, and I haven't heard anyone in the corridor since he showed me up. Did another servant bring you?"

Holmes laughed. "Well, I'm happy to hear that your observational skills are improving! But I should be a poor detective indeed if I couldn't even find my room without assistance. No, I showed myself up soon after you arrived to your own room."

I laughed, thinking of the confusion Holmes was bound to cause the servants during our stay. I felt sure they were unused to such an independent guest.

"Well, what have you found? Any clues?"

His eyes sparkled as we strolled down the hall. "Oh yes, I have found clues. I daresay some may even prove important. However, there is nothing further to be done at present. Let us enjoy ourselves and what will certainly prove to be an excellent dinner."

I took this as a sign that the investigation was indeed going well, for Holmes rarely accepts refreshment until a case is all but solved, maintaining that the brain operates better when the body is wanting for nourishment.

Holmes proved to be quite a jovial guest, much to the lady's delight. He was charm itself – another great sign that the events were proceeding to his satisfaction.

His mood was infectious, and soon even our client's worries seemed to fade and he was joining in the merry conversation, his wife frequently smiling in his direction, her eyes holding a look of a woman in love. I recognized it with a pang. It was the same look my Mary had always bestowed upon me.

After dinner, we retired to the billiards room for after-dinner drinks. Our client excused himself in order to say goodnight to his daughters, and I noted a very peculiar smile upon Holmes's lips. After our client had exited, I asked him quietly, "What is it? You have a very odd expression. Do you expect a new development?"

He laughed quietly, "I was just wondering whether our client's observational powers will fail him yet again while tucking in his little daughters. But I have no doubt that they shall do so. He doesn't strike me as an overly attentive father."

Though true, it seemed to me that this assessment of our client's character had little to do with the disappearance of the priceless diamonds, and I wondered what it was Holmes expected him to overlook in his daughters' room. However, I was no stranger to the miracles he could achieve with the barest scraps of information, and resolved to pay close attention to the little girls and their movements the next day.

Before I could respond, the butler appeared to prepare our postprandial drinks. We fell silent and accepted our cocktails appreciatively. Our client returned after a short time with a large smile. "Mr. Holmes, I must thank you once again. The girls asked for a bedtime story, which my wife and I read them together, each acting out different parts. We haven't laughed so much in each other's company in years. Though I fervently hope you will be able to find the diamonds, their purchase and loss have been worth it as these events led me to seek your assistance."

We spent the rest of the evening in light conversation. Our client and I played a game of billiards, with him being the victor. We all three went off to bed, and no one seeing us would have guessed that such depressing circumstances had brought us together only a few hours previously.

The next morning, I knocked on Holmes's door across the hall before proceeding to breakfast alone. Upon descending the stairs, I found our client staring out the window with such a look of astonishment on his face that I hurried to him, convinced there had been some new development in the case overnight.

"My Lord, what is the trouble?"

He turned slowly to me and asked, "Dr. Watson, is your friend quite mad? I have heard of his strange ways, but playing in the snow with the children while there is a case to solve – ? I would never have believed him a man to shirk duty in order to build snowmen and participate in snowball fights!"

Naturally, I thought our client had taken all leave of his senses. Surely the stresses and emotions of the last twenty-four hours had taken their toll upon this poor man. *Holmes – playing? With children?* I had never heard anything more unlikely.

I moved to stand beside our client at the window, and my heart quite nearly stopped when I saw Holmes, just as the client said, playing with two small girls in the snow.

We shared a look and rang the bell for the butler, who brought our hats and coats. We trudged out to meet Holmes and the girls. As we were approaching, Holmes called the girl's attention to our presence. "Isabella, Olivia, it appears your father and Dr. Watson have come to join in our little games."

The children squealed with delight at seeing their father. "Daddy, Daddy! Come look at our snowman!"

While obviously wishing to avoid dampening his newfound popularity with his family, our client clearly felt he must speak to Holmes at once regarding his behavior.

"Go ahead, girls. Have a race to the snowman. I will be right along." The girls took off at breakneck speed with the abandon only possessed by children.

Once the girls were out of earshot, our client continued. "Sir, I must admit that I'm extremely puzzled at your choice of morning activities – especially as Christmas draws ever nearer and you have yet to find the diamonds you were hired to locate. While my sentiments of yesterday still stand, I'm grateful to you with or without the diamonds, I would much prefer you to continue efforts to find them prior to engaging in such frivolous activities as snowball fights with a pair of eight-year-old children.

Holmes replied in his usual superior fashion. "I assure you, I don't require your assistance in deciding how to run an investigation. You need have no further fear about your diamonds, however. They are quite safe."

Our client sputtered, "Wh-what? You cannot mean to say you have found them! Why, man, where are they? You must give them to me at once!"

"But your daughters are waiting. See how excited they are to play with you? I insist that we satisfy this wish before carrying on with the business of the diamonds. They are, as I have said, quite safe."

What choice did he have but to comply? The girls jumped up and down eagerly as we started in their direction.

We spent the better part of an hour playing with the girls before their father finally insisted they had been out in the cold long enough and must return to the house to have tea.

Holmes smiled. "Before we go, I insist you take one more look at the snowman."

I turned my gaze to the snowman's face and stopped in my tracks when I realized what Holmes was alluding to. Our client took a bit longer to catch on, but exclaimed in disbelief when he realized what he was seeing. There, right in front of us, was a snowman staring at us with two beautiful, black-diamond eyes.

"The diamonds!" He rushed forward to pluck them and examine them. "But this is extraordinary! How could they possibly have ended up as eyes on a snowman?" He turned toward his daughters, one of which was giggling uncontrollably. The other appeared a little ashamed and was gazing at the ground.

"Isabella, was this your doing? How on earth did you come to be in possession of these earrings?"

Holmes cleared his throat. "I believe I can explain the chain of events for you, my Lord. When you explained that the tag on the gift read 'Isabella', it crossed my mind that your daughter, who of course was named for your wife, may have assumed the package was for her. Especially if, as you mentioned, you weren't previously in the habit of wrapping gifts for your wife."

Isabella had stopped giggling and appeared surprised. "You mean the earrings weren't meant for me, but for Mummy?"

Our client bent down to hold her hands. "Yes, darling, but rest assured you also have a great number of special gifts for Christmas. But I don't understand: Why did you open the gift, even if you believed it was for you? You know you aren't to open presents before Christmas."

Isabella flashed an impish grin. "But Daddy, Mummy only said we couldn't open any of the gifts *underneath* the tree. But this one wasn't underneath it – it was *in* the tree. Wasn't it, Livy?"

At once, all three adults began to laugh. What a mischievous child this was!

After securing the earrings in his pocket, the father took the hand of each girl and began their walk back to the house. Holmes and I followed at some distance behind. "I must confess that I'm astonished," I said. "However did you guess that the earrings were the eyes of the snowman?"

"My dear Watson, you wound me. You know that I do not guess, I deduce based on facts. Prior to the knowledge that carolers had visited, our client had insisted that no one had visited the house. Therefore, the most likely culprit was in residence. His insistence that no one in the house knew of the diamonds purchase was vehement, and I was inclined to believe how closely he had guarded his secret. What would induce a servant to take that package over all the others present under the tree? It would have been a terrible coincidence. Therefore, who was most likely to disturb packages under the tree? Why, children of course. No child can resist examining their presents before Christmas. When I learned that the daughter shared a name with her mother, I knew our inquiries had to begin in that direction. Before dressing for dinner, I made a quick examination of the girls' room. Having just spied them in the yard with their governess, I knew the room would be empty. And what do you think I found?"

"Why, I have no idea. Weren't the diamonds already serving as eyes for the snowman?"

"Indeed. But there, pushed under one of the beds, was the paper and tag with which they had been wrapped."

"Then that accounts for your good mood at dinner last night."

"Indeed, Watson. Although I hadn't yet located the jewels, I was certain they hadn't been stolen and were somewhere on the grounds to the house. I determined to watch the girls closely, knowing they would lead me to the earrings. You must have thought me mad when you observed me making a snow angel with two children."

I laughed, shaking my head. "Never mad. Peculiar. Singular. Unique . . . but never mad."

The next morning, the elder Isabella was reduced to tears when presented with her precious gift. She embraced her husband with such love, and I was inevitably reminded of my Mary once again. This was my fourth Christmas as a widower, and though I doubted the pain would ever fully subside, I stole a glance at my friend and felt that I was indeed a lucky man to have such companionship in my life.

We returned to London a few days later, leaving a very satisfied client in our wake.

"Well," asked Holmes and his admired his new pipe and packed it with his shag tobacco, "did our merry little Christmas live up to your festive standards?"

I sat, replaying in my mind the scenes of the last few days. "It certainly did, Holmes. It certainly did."

About the Contributors

The following contributors appear in this volume:
The MX Book of New Sherlock Holmes Stories
Part L: The True Sherlock Mr. Holmes –
England's Greatest Hero (1889-1896)

Ian Ableson is an ecologist by training and a writer by choice. When not reading or writing, he can reliably be found scowling at a clipboard while ankle-deep in a marsh somewhere in Michigan. His love for the stories of Arthur Conan Doyle started when his grandfather gave him a copy of *The Original Illustrated Sherlock Holmes* when he was in high school, and he's proud to have been able to contribute to the continuation of the tales of Sherlock Holmes and Dr. Watson.

Mike Adamson holds a Doctoral degree from Flinders University of South Australia. After early aspirations in art and writing, Mike secured qualifications in both marine biology and archaeology. Mike has been a university educator since 2006, has worked in the replication of convincing ancient fossils, is a passionate photographer, master-level hobbyist, and journalist for international magazines. Short fiction sales include to *Metastellar, Strand Magazine, Little Blue Marble, Abyss*, and *Apex, Daily Science Fiction, Compelling Science Fiction*, and *Nature Futures*. Mike has placed some two-hundred stories to date, totaling over a million words. Mike has completed his first Sherlock Holmes novel with Belanger Books, and will be appearing in translation in European magazines. You can catch up with his journey at his blog "The View From the Keyboard":
http://mike-adamson.blogspot.com

Tim Newton Anderson is a former senior daily newspaper journalist and PR manager who has recently started writing fiction. In the past six months, he has placed fourteen stories in publications including *Parsec Magazine, Tales of the Shadowmen, SF Writers Guild, Zoetic Press, Dark Lane Books, Dark Horses Magazine, Emanations*, and *Planet Bizarro*.

Brian Belanger, PSI, is a publisher, narrator, graphic designer, editor, and actor. In 2015 he co-founded Belanger Books publishing company along with his brother, author Derrick Belanger. His illustrations have appeared in *The Essential Sherlock Holmes* series, the *MacDougall Twins with Sherlock Holmes* series, and *Scones and Bones on Baker Street*. Brian has published a number of Sherlock Holmes anthologies and novels through Belanger Books, as well as new editions of August Derleth's classic Solar Pons mysteries. Brian continues to design all of the covers for Belanger Books, and from 2016–2023 he designed the majority of book covers for MX Publishing. In 2019, Brian received his investiture in the PSI as "Sir Ronald Duveen". More recently, he created the logo for the *ACD Society* and designed *The Great Game of Sherlock Holmes* card game. In July 2022, he played Sherlock Holmes onstage in "Yes, Virginia, There is a Sherlock Holmes" and "Sherlock Holmes Goes West". Brian has been narrating Belanger Books audio releases since April 2023.
www.belangerbooks.com and
www.redbubble.com/people/zhahadun and
zhahadun.wixsite.com/221b

Alan Dimes was born in Northwest London and graduated from Sussex University with a BA in English Literature. He has spent most of his working life teaching English. Living in the Czech Republic since 2003, he is now semi-retired and divides his time between Prague and his country cottage. He has also written some fifty stories of horror and fantasy and thirty stories about his husband-and-wife detectives, Peter and Deirdre Creighton, set in the 1930's.

Sir Arthur Conan Doyle (1859-1930) *Holmes Chronicler Emeritus*. If not for him, this anthology would not exist. Author, physician, patriot, sportsman, spiritualist, husband and father, and advocate for the oppressed. He is remembered and honored for the purposes of this collection by being the man who introduced Sherlock Holmes to the world. Through fifty-six Holmes short stories, four novels, and additional Apocryphal entries, Doyle revolutionized mystery stories and also greatly influenced and improved police forensic methods and techniques for the betterment of all. *Steel True Blade Straight.*

Steve Emecz's main field is technology, in which he has been working for about thirty years. Steve is a regular speaker at trade shows, and his tech career has taken him to more than seventy countries. In 2008, MX published its first Sherlock Holmes book, and MX has gone on to become the largest specialist Holmes publisher in the world with over 600 books. MX is a social enterprise and supports three main causes. The first is Undershaw, Sir Arthur Conan Doyle's former home, which is a school for children with special educational needs (SEN) that MX has been partnered with for a dozen or so years and raised over $135,000 for. Steve has been a mentor and Advisory Council member for the World Food Programme's Innovation Accelerator (based in Munich) for several years, and was part of the Nobel Peace Prize winning team in 2020. The third is Happy Life, a children's rescue project in Nairobi, Kenya, where he and his wife, Sharon, spent every Christmas at the rescue centre in Kasarani for a decade. They have written two editions of a short book about the project, *The Happy Life Story.*

Brett Fawcett is a humanities and Latin teacher at the Chesterton Academy of St. Isidore in Sherwood Park, Alberta. He lives with his wife and son in Edmonton, where he is a member of The Wisteria Lodgers (The Sherlock Holmes Society of Edmonton). He vividly remembers the first time he finished reading the Sherlock Holmes stories in Grade 6, and has been a student of Holmesian literature and scholarship since then. He is also a frequent author of columns and articles on topics like theology, education, and mental health, as well as the occasional mystery story.

Mark A. Gagen BSI is co-founder of Wessex Press, sponsor of the popular *From Gillette to Brett* conferences, and publisher of *The Sherlock Holmes Reference Library* and many other fine Sherlockian titles. A life-long Holmes enthusiast, he is a member of *The Baker Street Irregulars* and *The Illustrious Clients of Indianapolis*. A graphic artist by profession, his work is often seen on the covers of *The Baker Street Journal* and various BSI books.

Dick Gillman is an English writer and acrylic artist living in Brittany, France with his wife Alex, Truffle, their Black Labrador, and Jean-Claude, their Breton cat. During his retirement from teaching, he has written over twenty Sherlock Holmes short stories which are published as both e-books and paperbacks. His initial contribution to the superb MX Sherlock Holmes collection, published in October 2015, was entitled "The Man on Westminster Bridge" and had the privilege of being chosen as the anchor story in *The MX Book of New Sherlock Holmes Stories – Part II (1890-1895).*

John Linwood Grant is a writer and editor who lives in Yorkshire with a pack of lurchers and a beard. He may also have a family. He focuses particularly on dark Victorian and

Edwardian fiction, such as his recent novella *A Study in Grey*, which also features Holmes. Current projects include his *Tales of the Last Edwardian* series, about psychic and psychiatric mysteries, and curating a collection of new stories based on the darker side of the British Empire. He has been published in a number of anthologies and magazines, with stories range from madness in early Virginia to questions about the monsters we ourselves might be. He is also co-editor of *Occult Detective Quarterly*. His website *greydogtales.com* explores weird fiction, especially period ones, weird art, and even weirder lurchers.

John Atkinson Grimshaw (1836-1893) was born in Leeds, England. His amazing paintings, usually featuring twilight or night scenes illuminated by gas-lamps or moonlight, are easily recognizable, and are often used on the covers of books about The Great Detective to set the mood, as shadowy figures move in the distance through misty mysterious settings and over rain-slicked streets.

Arthur Hall was born in Aston, Birmingham, UK, in 1944. He discovered his interest in writing during his schooldays, along with a love of fictional adventure and suspense. His first novel, *Sole Contact*, was an espionage story about an ultra-secret government department known as "Sector Three", and was followed, to date, by three sequels. Other works include seven Sherlock Holmes novels, *The Demon of the Dusk, The One Hundred Percent Society, The Secret Assassin, The Phantom Killer, In Pursuit of the Dead, The Justice Master,* and *The Experience Club* as well as three collections of Holmes *Further Little-Known Cases of Sherlock Holmes, Tales from the Annals of Sherlock* Holmes, *The Additional Investigations of Sherlock Holmes* and *The Hidden Enquiries of Sherlock Holmes.* He has also written other short stories and a modern detective novel. He lives in the West Midlands, United Kingdom.

Paula Hammond has written over sixty fiction and non-fiction books, as well as short stories, comics, poetry, and scripts for educational DVD's. When not glued to the keyboard, she can usually be found prowling round second-hand books shops or hunkered down in a hide, soaking up the joys of the natural world.

James R. Hawkins, BSI writes: "I discovered Sherlock Holmes on my fortieth birthday, in Norman, OK. In high school, in Texas, I mainly read Ernest Hemingway and true-life stories set in exotic locations, like Alaska. I was inordinately interested in Eskimos.
I was born in Jacksboro, Texas, in 1944, the only son of Leon and Ruth Hawkins, owners of Hawkins Funeral Home, and little brother to Linda (1939) and Jane Hawkins (1940). My Dad wanted me to take over the funeral home, but I chose a life in music education, which took me to Oklahoma Baptist University in Shawnee, OK, and to the Eastman School of Music in Rochester, NY. With my vocal chops, I landed a place in The US Army Chorus in Washington, DC, during the Vietnam war, (1969-1973). Married in 1966, my wife and I struck out for Los Angeles to work on a doctorate in music at the University of So. California. From there, we moved to Norman, OK, where I was the music director at 1st Baptist Church in Norman before becoming the Youth, Adult, and Senior Adult Music Consultant for the Southern Baptist Convention in Nashville, TN (1985-1992). In 2001, I switched from music to aviation and joined that highly successful company, Southwest Airlines, where I held various positions, settling into the Flight Attendant job, retiring some sixteen years later in 2017. Since then, my life has revolved around Sherlock Holmes and the men and women who are Sherlockians, devotees of the detective *"who never lived, and so, could never die"*. In 2018, I wrote about the man who influenced the most in my Holmes and Watson journey, John Bennett Shaw. The website I built for him caught the attention of many of The Baker Street Irregulars, who honored me with membership in their august

body and shared with me the same investiture given to Shaw back in 1965, *The Hans Sloane of My Age*."

Roger Johnson, BSI ("The Pall Mall Gazette"), ASH, PSI, etc, is a member of more Holmesian Societies than he can remember, thanks to his eighteen years as editor of *The Sherlock Holmes Journal* - a responsibility he has recently and gratefully passed over to Dr. Mark Jones. Roger founded and for thirty-two years edited *The Sherlock Holmes Society of London*'s newsletter, *The District Messenger*. For six years, it was edited by his wife Jean Upton, ASH, BSI, and is now in the safe hands of Holly Turner. At its 2025 Annual Dinner, Roger was awarded Honorary Membership of *The Sherlock Holmes Society of London*.

John Lawrence served for thirty-eight years on personal, committee, and leadership staffs in the U.S. House of Representatives. A visiting professor at the University of California's Washington Center since 2013, he is the author of *The Class of '74: Congress After Watergate and the Roots of Partisanship* (Johns-Hopkins, 2018) and *Arc of Power: Inside the Pelosi Speakership 2005-2010* (Kansas, 2022). His collected "history mystery" Sherlock Holmes pastiches have been published in *The Undiscovered Archives of Sherlock Holmes, The Further Undiscovered Archives of Sherlock Holmes*, in numerous volumes of *The MX Book of New Sherlock Holmes Stories*, and in Belanger Books' *After the East Wind Blows*. His novel, *Sherlock Holmes: The Affair at Mayerling Lodge* was published in 2023. He blogs at DOMEocracy (johnalawrence.wordpress.com). He is a graduate of Oberlin College and has a Ph.D. in history from the University of California (Berkeley).

Bonnie MacBird, BSI is the author of six critically acclaimed Sherlock Holmes novels for HarperCollins. They have been translated into fourteen languages and have been praised by *The London Times, Washington Post* , and *The Wall Street Journal*. MacBird read her first Sherlock Holmes story at age ten, and has been a fan since then. She's had a forty-year career in entertainment as a studio story editor, a screenwriter, a multiple Emmy winning documentary film producer, and a screenwriting teacher. She's also acted professionally and directs theatre. She lives in London with her husband, computer scientist Alan Kay, where she continues to write, as well as work in theatre.

David Marcum plays *The Game* with deadly seriousness. He first discovered Sherlock Holmes in 1975 at the age of ten, and since that time, he has collected, read, and chronologicized literally thousands of traditional Holmes pastiches in the form of novels, short stories, radio and television episodes, movies and scripts, comics, fan-fiction, and unpublished manuscripts. He is the author of over one-hundred-thirty Sherlockian pastiches, some published in anthologies and magazines such as *The Best Mystery Stories of the Year 2021* and *The Strand*, and others collected in his own books, *The Papers of Sherlock Holmes, Sherlock Holmes and A Quantity of Debt, Sherlock Holmes – Tangled Skeins, Sherlock Holmes and The Eye of Heka*, and *The Collected Papers of Sherlock Holmes* – seven volumes and more to come. He has won back-to-back first place fiction awards from *The Arthur Conan Doyle Society* (2023 and 2024) and from the Nero Wolfe *Wolfe Pack*. He has edited over 1,200 Holmes adventures and one-hundred books, including dozens of traditional Sherlockian anthologies, such as the ongoing series *The MX Book of New Sherlock Holmes Stories*, which he created in 2015 to promote traditional Canonical Holmes. This collection is now finishing at fifty-two volumes. He was responsible for bringing back August Derleth's Solar Pons for a new generation with his collections of authorized Pons stories, *The Papers of Solar Pons* and *The Further Papers of Solar Pons*. Pons's return was further assisted by his editing of the reissued authorized versions of the original Pons books, and then several volumes of new Pons adventures. He has done the same for the adventures of Dr. Thorndyke, and has plans for similar projects in the future. He has contributed numerous essays to various publications, and is a member of a number of Sherlockian groups and Scions, as well as *The Mystery Writers of America*. His irregular Sherlockian blog, *A Seventeen Step Program*, addresses various topics related to his favorite *Book Friends* (as his son used to call them when he was small), and can be found at *http://17stepprogram.blogspot.com/* He is a licensed Civil Engineer, living in Tennessee with his wife and son. Since the age of nineteen, he has worn a deerstalker as his regular-and-only hat. In 2013, he and his deerstalker were finally able make his first trip-of-a-lifetime Holmes Pilgrimage to England, with return Pilgrimages in 2015, 2016, and 2024, where you may have spotted him. Another Pilgrimage is planned in mid-2025. If you ever run into him and his deerstalker out and about, feel free to say hello!

Sidney Paget (1860-1908), a few of whose illustrations are used within this anthology, was born in London, and like his two older brothers, became a famed illustrator and painter. He completed over three-hundred-and-fifty drawings for the Sherlock Holmes stories that were first published in *The Strand* magazine, defining Holmes's image forever after in the public mind.

Tracy J. Revels, BSI, a Sherlockian from the age of eleven, is a professor of history at Wofford College in Spartanburg, South Carolina. She is a member of *The Survivors of the Gloria Scott* and *The Studious Scarlets Society*, and is a past recipient of the Beacon Society Award. Almost every semester, she teaches a class that covers The Canon, either to college students or to senior citizens. She is also the author of three supernatural Sherlockian pastiches with MX (*Shadowfall*, *Shadowblood*, and *Shadowwraith*), and most recently, the three-volume pastiche set, *Tales of Light*, *Tales of Shadow*, and *Tales of Darkness*. She is a regular contributor to her scion's newsletter. She also has some notoriety as an author of very silly skits: For proof, see "The Adventure of the Adversarial Adventuress" and "Occupy Baker Street" on YouTube. When not studying Sherlock, she can be found researching the history of her native state, and has written books on Florida in the Civil War and on the development of Florida's tourism industry.

Peter Shumway is a retired computer professional residing in Pennsylvania with his wife, Patty. They have been married forty-one years and have two daughters and four grandchildren. In the early 1970's, Peter performed magic with Bill Baker's World of Magic, John Bundy's Magic Concert, and traded secrets with David Copperfield when they were teenagers. Peter read the original Sherlock Holmes stories while in college in 1979, and has enjoyed rereading them many times since. He published his pastiche *Sherlock Holmes and The Kiss of Death* in 2005 and *Gullible's Journey* in 2023. When he was offered the opportunity to write a short story for the MX Series, he picked up his pen yet again.

I.A. Watson has written over fifty Sherlock Holmes stories, and is always surprised that there are still new things for The Great Detective to do, which is a real testament to the genius behind Doyle's most famous creations. His most recent Holmes activities though were in providing extensive notes for a talk about the character in a New York public library, which was quite a different creative challenge. In addition to the novel *Holmes and Houdini*, the anthology *The Incunabulum of Sherlock Holmes*, and the forthcoming *The Paralipomena of Sherlock Holmes*, I.A. Watson has provided entries to all twenty of the *Sherlock Holmes Consulting Detective* books, to about the same number of MX volumes, and another dozen or more in other eccentric places. In his spare time he produces other novels such as *The Death of Persephone*, *The Labours of Hercules*, *The Legend of Robin Hood*, *Women of Myth*, *The Transdimensional Transport Company*, and *Vinnie de Soth, Jobbing Occultist*. It is perhaps not traditional to use an "About the Author" paragraph to offer thanks, but I.A. Watson would like to dedicate this "About the Author" piece to Mr. David Marcum for his astonishing accomplishment with the MX Holmes series, and his tireless enthusiasm as one of the stoutest Holmesians. A full list of I.A. Watson's publications is available at:

http://www.chillwater.org.uk/writing/iawatsonhome.htm

Emma West joined Undershaw in April 2021 as the Director of Education with a brief to ensure that qualifications formed the bedrock of our provision, whilst facilitating a positive balance between academia, pastoral care, and well-being. She quickly took on the role of Acting Headteacher from early summer 2021. Under her leadership, Undershaw has embraced its new name, new vision, and consequently we have seen an exponential increase in demand for places. There is a buzz in the air as we invite prospective students and families through the doors. Emma has overseen a strategic review, re-cemented relationships with Local Authorities, and positioned Undershaw at the helm of SEND education in Surrey and beyond. Undershaw has a wide appeal: Our students present to us with mild to moderate learning needs and therefore may have some very recent memories of poor experiences in their previous schools. Emma's background as a senior leader within the independent school sector has meant she is well-versed in brokering relationships between the key stakeholders, our many interdependences, local businesses, families, and staff, and all this while ensuring Undershaw remains relentlessly child-centric in its approach. Emma's energetic smile and boundless enthusiasm for Undershaw is inspiring.

Ashley Williford writes: "This is my first Sherlockian publication. I am a devoted Sherlockian and Ravenclaw and a member of my local Sherlockian scion society. *The Giant Rats of Sumatra* in Memphis, Tennessee. I have a hilarious three-year-old boy, Williford "Will" Roney, as well as two goldendoodles, Albus Percival Wulfric Brian Dumbledoodle (eight) and Merlin Aberforth Dumbledoodle (six). I am an Adult-Gerontological Acute Care Nurse Practitioner with a Doctorate in Nursing Practice, and I specialize in critical care. My favorite of my many hobbies include writing Sherlock adventures, hand embroidery, puzzles, games, reading, starting flowers from seeds only to abandon them after sprouting, and listening to absolutely everything Steven Fry narrates."

Marcia Wilson is a freelance researcher and illustrator who likes to work in a style compatible for the color blind and visually impaired. She is Canon-centric, and has written many acclaimed stories about Sherlock Holmes and the Scotland Yard inspectors who knew and worked with him. Long unavailable, nine of these novels will be released by MX Publishing in Spring 2025, with more in preparation.

DeForeest Wright III has a day job as a baker for Ralphs grocery stores. It helps support his love for books. A long-time lover of literature, especially of the Sherlock Holmes tales, he spends his time away from the oven hunched over novels, poetry, anthologies, or any tome on philosophy, mathematics, science, or martial arts he can find, sipping an espresso if one is to hand. He writes prose and poetry in his off hours and currently hosts "The Sunless Sea Open-Mic: Spoken Word and Poetry Show" at the Unurban Coffee House in Santa Monica. He was glad to team up writing with his father.

Sean Wright, BSI makes his home in Santa Clarita, a charming city at the entrance of the high desert in Southern California. For sixteen years, features and articles under his byline appeared in *The Tidings* – now *The Angelus News*, publications of the Roman Catholic Archdiocese of Los Angeles. Continuing his education in 2007, Mr. Wright graduated from Grand Canyon University, attaining a Bachelor of Arts degree in Christian Studies with a *summa cum laude*. He then attained a Master of Arts degree, also in Christian Studies. Once active in the entertainment industry, and in an abortive attempt to revive dramatic radio in 1976 with his beloved mentor, the late Daws Butler, directing, Mr. Wright co-produced and wrote the syndicated *New Radio Adventures of Sherlock Holmes*, starring the late Edward Mulhare as the Great Detective. Mr. Wright has written for several television quiz shows and remains proud of his work for *The Quiz Kid's Challenge* and the popular TV quiz show *Jeopardy!* for which the Academy of Television Arts and Sciences honored him in 1985 with an Emmy nomination in the field of writing. Honored with membership in The Baker Street Irregulars as "The Manor House Case" after founding The Non-Canonical Calabashes, the Sherlock Holmes Society of Los Angeles in 1970, Mr. Wright has written for *The Baker Street Journal* and *Mystery Magazine*. Since 1971, he has conducted lectures on Sherlock Holmes's influence on literature and cinema for libraries, colleges, and private organizations, including MENSA. Mr. Wright's whimsical *Sherlock Holmes Cookbook* (Drake), created with John Farrell, BSI, was published in 1976, and a mystery novel, *Enter the Lion: a Posthumous Memoir of Mycroft Holmes* (Hawthorne), "edited" with Michael Hodel, BSI, followed in 1979. As director general of The Plot Thickens Mystery Company, Mr. Wright originated hosting "mystery parties" in homes, restaurants, and offices, as well as producing and directing the very first "Mystery Train" tours on Amtrak, beginning in 1982.

The following contributors appear
in the companion volumes:
The True Sherlock Mr. Holmes –
England's Greatest Hero
Part XLIX – (1880-1888)
Part LI – (1897-1901)
Part LII – (1902-1923)

Mike Adamson *also has a story in Part LI*

Tim Newton Anderson *also has a story in Part LII*

Hugh Ashton was born in the U.K., and moved to Japan in 1988, where he remained until 2016, living with his wife Yoshiko in the historic city of Kamakura, a little to the south of Yokohama. He and Yoshiko have now moved to Lichfield, a small cathedral city in the Midlands of the U.K., the birthplace of Samuel Johnson, and one-time home of Erasmus Darwin. In the past, he has worked in the technology and financial services industries, which have provided him with material for some of his books set in the 21st century. He currently works as a writer: Novelist, freelance editor, and copywriter, (his work for large Japanese corporations has appeared in international business journals), and journalist, as well as producing industry reports on various aspects of the financial services industry. However, his lifelong interest in Sherlock Holmes has developed into an acclaimed series of adventures featuring the world's most famous detective, written in the style of the originals. In addition to these, he has also published historical and alternate historical novels, short stories, and thrillers. Together with artist Andy Boerger, he has produced the *Sherlock Ferret* series of stories for children, featuring the world's cutest detective.

461

Deanna Baran lives in a remote part of Texas where cowboys may still be seen in their natural habitat. A librarian and former museum curator, she writes in between cups of tea, playing *Go*, and trading postcards with people around the world.

Donald I. Baxter has practiced medicine for over forty years. He resides in Erie Pennsylvania with his wife and their dog. His family and his friends are for the most part lawyers who have given him the ability to make stuff up just as they do.

Derrick Belanger, BSI ("The Board Schools"), PSI ("Albert, the Dove") is an award-winning author, publisher, and educator most noted for his books and lectures on Sherlock Holmes and Sir Arthur Conan Doyle. Derrick is co-owner of the publishing company Belanger Books, which published the first eBook editions of the original Solar Pons books by August Derleth. Derrick's work has been published in *The Baker Street Journal*, *The Sherlock Holmes Journal*, *The Strand Magazine*, and in *The Mysterious Bookshop Presents the Best Mystery Stories of the Year (2023)*. Derrick is a board member of Dr. Watson's Neglected Patients, the Denver-based Scion Society. In January 2020, Mr. Belanger was awarded the Susan Z. Diamond Award in recognition of outstanding efforts to introduce young people to Sherlock Holmes, and in 2024, he won the Arthur Conan Doyle Society Doylean award in fiction for his short story, "The Joyce-Armstrong Confession". Derrick currently resides in Broomfield, Colorado. Find him at: *www.belangerbooks.com*

Mike Chinn's first ever Sherlock Holmes fiction was a steampunk mashup of *The Valley of Fear*, entitled *Vallis Timoris* (Fringeworks 2015). Since then he has written about Holmes' archenemy in *The Mammoth Book of the Adventures of Moriarty* (Robinson 2015), appeared in several volumes of *The MX Book of New Sherlock Holmes Stories*, and confronted the retired detective with cross-dimensional magic in the second volume of *Sherlock Holmes and the Occult Detectives* (Belanger Books 2020). He also had a non-Holmes story published in the Lovecraftian anthology *Sherlock & Friends: Eldritch Investigations* (Tule Fog Press, 2024).

Martin Daley was born in Carlisle, Cumbria in 1964. His thirty-year writing career has seen over twenty books and numerous short stories published. Inevitably, Holmes and Watson remain his favourite literary characters, and they continue to inspire his own detective writing. In 2010, Martin created Inspector Cornelius Armstrong, who carries out his police work against the backdrop of Edwardian Carlisle. With the publication of the first *Inspector Armstrong Casebook* (published by MX Publishing), Martin became a member of the Crime Writers' Association. Most recently, he published *The Selected Cases of Sherlock Holmes.* He lives with his wife Wendy, in Kirkcudbrightshire, in Southwest.

Alan Dimes *also has a story in Part LI*

Stuart Douglas is an author, editor, and publisher, and the creator of the Lowe and Le Breton Mysteries. He has written four Sherlock Holmes novels for Titan Books, and contributed stories to the anthologies *Encounters of Sherlock Holmes*, *Further Associates of Sherlock Holmes*, and *The MX Book of New Sherlock Holmes Stories*. He runs Obverse Books and lives in Edinburgh with his wife, three children, a dog named after Dusty Springfield and cat named after David Bowie.
Follow him on Bluesky: *@stuartdouglas.bsky.social*
and on Instagram: *@stuartamdouglas*

Arianna Fox is a triple-published and bestselling author, keynote speaker, actress, professional voiceover talent, award winner, book editor, and public figure whose passion is to motivate, educate, and entertain others through her work. From stories that connect with a modern audience to classically inspired works of literature, one of Arianna's foremost passions has always been writing. An avid Sherlockian and lover of all things Victorian, Arianna disliked reading for years until she read the first few paragraphs of *The Return of Sherlock Holmes* in a bookstore and immediately fell in love with classic literature and the intricate themes woven into its messages. As a whole, Arianna's ultimate goal is to empower others to achieve maximum success and keep their brain-attics well stocked.

Mike Fox is a CEO, entrepreneur, multi-award-winning filmmaker, director, producer, writer, designer, actor, voiceover talent, and all-around versatile creative professional. His professional work is known across the U.S. and has received numerous accolades and awards. As a filmmaker and director, Mike has produced three full-feature films, with over twenty-five Film Festival Awards, including several shorts and many commercials. With a unique flair for suspenseful storytelling, he derives much inspiration from the Sherlock Holmes universe, both of The Canon and adaptations. He was named Alignable's "Business Person of the Year" four years in a row, and has been featured in several news and media outlets, along with a myriad of interviews on podcasts and more. Mike's goal is to impact, empower, and inspire through various forms of media. His professional work is known across the U.S., including having received numerous accolades and awards, including receiving the prestigious Delaware Press Association (DPA) several years in a row. He continues to speak, write, film, and direct to bring quality content to audiences.

Paul D. Gilbert was born in 1954 and has lived in and around London all of his life. His wife Jackie is a Holmes expert who keeps him on the straight and narrow! He has two sons, one of whom now lives in Spain. His interests include literature, ancient history, all religions, most sports, and movies. He is currently employed full-time as a funeral director. His books so far include *The Lost Files of Sherlock Holmes* (2007), *The Chronicles of Sherlock Holmes* (2008), *Sherlock Holmes and the Giant Rat of Sumatra* (2010), *The Annals of Sherlock Holmes* (2012), *Sherlock Holmes and the Unholy Trinity* (2015), *Sherlock Holmes: The Four Handed Game* (2017), *The Illumination of Sherlock Holmes* (2019), *The Treasure of the Poison King* (2021), and *Sherlock Holmes: Tales of Darkness* (2023).

Arthur Hall *also has stories in Part LI*

Paula Hammond *also has stories in Part LI*

Stephen Herczeg is an IT Geek, writer, actor, and film-maker based in Canberra Australia. He has been writing for over twenty years and has completed a couple of dodgy novels, sixteen feature-length screenplays, and numerous short stories and scripts. Stephen was very successful in 2017's International Horror Hotel screenplay competition, with his scripts *TITAN* winning the Sci-Fi category and *Dark are the Woods* placing second in the horror category. His collection, *The Curious Cases of Sherlock Holmes*, is now at four volumes. His work has featured in *Sproutlings – A Compendium of Little Fictions* from Hunter Anthologies, the *Hells Bells* Christmas horror anthology published by the Australasian Horror Writers Association, and the *Below the Stairs*, *Trickster's Treats*, *Shades of Santa*, *Behind the Mask*, and *Beyond the Infinite* anthologies from OzHorror.Com, *The Body Horror Book*, *Anemone Enemy*, and *Petrified Punks* from

Oscillate Wildly Press, and *Sherlock Holmes In the Realms of H.G. Wells* and *Sherlock Holmes: Adventures Beyond the Canon* from Belanger Books.

Liz Hedgecock grew up in London, England (a train and a tube ride away from Baker Street), did an English degree, and then took forever to start writing. Now Liz travels between the nineteenth and twenty-first centuries, murdering people. To be fair, she does usually clean up after herself. Liz's reimaginings of Sherlock Holmes and her Victorian and contemporary mystery series are available in eBook and paperback. Liz lives in Cheshire with her husband and two sons, and when she's not writing you can usually find her reading, messing about on social media, or cooing over stuff in museums and art galleries. That's her story, anyway, and she's sticking to it.

Paul Hiscock is an author of crime, fantasy, horror, and science fiction tales. His short stories have appeared in a variety of anthologies, and include a seventeenth-century whodunnit, a science fiction western, a clockpunk fairytale, and numerous Sherlock Holmes pastiches. He lives with his family in Kent (England) and spends his days taking care of his two children. You can find out more about Paul's writing at: *www.detectivesanddragons.uk*.

Christopher James was born in 1975 in Paisley, Scotland. Educated at Newcastle and UEA, he was a winner of the UK's National Poetry Competition in 2008. He has written three full-length Sherlock Holmes novels, *The Adventure of the Ruby Elephant*, *The Jeweller of Florence*, and *The Adventure of the Beer Barons*, all published by MX.

In the year 1998 **Craig Janacek** took his degree of Doctor of Medicine at Vanderbilt University, and proceeded to Stanford to go through the training prescribed for pediatricians in practice. Having completed his studies there, he was duly attached to the University of California, San Francisco as a Professor. The author of over two-hundred medical monographs upon a variety of obscure lesions, his travel-worn and battered tin dispatch-box is crammed with papers, most of which are records of his fictional works. These include several collections of *The Further Adventures of Sherlock Holmes*: *Light in the Darkness*, *The Gathering Gloom*, *The Treasury of Sherlock Holmes*, *The Travels of Sherlock Holmes*, *The Chronicles of Sherlock Holmes*, *The Histories of Sherlock Holmes*, *The Acts of Sherlock Holmes*, and *The Assassination of Sherlock Holmes* – as well as two Dr. Watson novels (*The Isle of Devils* and *The Gate of Gold*), the complete and expanded *Adventures* and *Exploits of Brigadier Gerard* (*Set Europe Shaking* and *A Mighty Shadow*), and two non-Holmes novels (*The Oxford Deception* and *The Anger of Achilles Peterson*). His short stories have been published in several editions of *The MX Book of New Sherlock Holmes Stories, Part I: 1881-1889* (2015), *Part IV: 2016 Annual* (2016), *Part VI: 2017 Annual* (2017), *Part VIII: Eliminate the Impossible* (2017), *Part XI: Some Untold Cases* (2018), *Part XVIII: Whatever Remains Must be the Truth* (2019), *Part XXIII: Some More Untold Cases* (2020), *Part XXV: 2021 Annual* (2021), *Part XXXII: 2022 Annual* (2022), *Part XXXVI: However Improbable . . . .* (2022), and *Part XXXVIII: 2023 Annual* (2023). Other stories have appeared in *Holmes Away From Home: Tales of the Great Hiatus* (2016), *Tales from the Stranger's Room 3* (2017), *Sherlock Holmes: Adventures Beyond the Canon* (2018), *Sherlock Holmes, A Year of Mysteries – 1881* (2021), and *Sherlock Holmes: Stranger than Fiction* (2021). He lives near San Francisco, California with his wife and two children, where he is at work on his next story. Craig Janacek is a *nom-de-plume*.

Steven Philip Jones has written fiction novels for adults and young adults, comic books, graphic novels, radio scripts, non-fiction, and advertising pieces. His Sherlock Holmes pastiches include the novel *The Adventure of the Coal-Tar Derivative* from MX Publishing and the radio dramas "The Adventure of the Petty Curses" and "A Case of Unfinished Business" for Jim French Productions' *Imagination Theatre*. He currently makes his home with his family in northern Utah.

Naching T. Kassa is a wife, mother, and writer. She's created short stories, novellas, poems, and co-created three children. She resides in Eastern Washington State with her husband, Dan Kassa. Naching is a member of *The Horror Writers Association, Mystery Writers of America, The Sound of the Baskervilles, The ACD Society, The Crew of the Barque Lone Star*, and *The Sherlock Holmes Society of London*. She works in Talent Relations at Crystal Lake Publishing and was a recipient of the 2022 HWA Diversity Grant. You can find her work on Amazon.
https://www.amazon.com/Naching-T-Kassa/e/B005ZGHTI0

Susan Knight's newest Mrs. Hudson novel is *Death in the Harem* (October 2024, MX publishing), in which Sherlock Holmes and Dr. Watson enlist their landlady's help in solving a series of murders at the court of the Sultan of Turkey. Susan has written four previous Mrs. Hudson books, starting with a collection of short stories, *Mrs. Hudson Investigates* (2019). This was followed by the novels, *Mrs. Hudson Goes to Ireland* (2020), *Mrs. Hudson Goes to Paris* (2022) and *Death in the Garden of England* (2023). She has also contributed to many recent MX anthologies of new Sherlock Holmes short stories and enjoys writing as Dr. Watson as much as Mrs. Hudson. Nine of these stories have been included in *The Strange Case of the Pale Boy and Other Mysteries* (MX, 2023), and another story, *The Case of the Reluctant Footman*, has been released on Kindle Unlimited as Volume 7 of its *Discoveries* series (2025). She is the author of two other non-Sherlockian story collections, as well as three novels, a book of non-fiction, and several plays, and has won several prizes for her writing. She lives in Dublin, Ireland.

Gordon Linzner is founder and former editor of *Space and Time Magazine*, and author of four published novels and dozens of short stories in *F&SF, Twilight Zone, Sherlock Holmes Mystery Magazine*, and numerous other magazines and anthologies. He is a full member of the *Horror Writers Association* and a lifetime member of *Science Fiction and Fantasy Writers Association*.

Steve Lockley is responsible for around 100 short stories and 20 novels, though not all under his own name, including contributions to a couple of Doctor Who anthologies and a novel based on the TV series *Ghost Whisperer*. He has also written several Sherlock Holmes stories, including an appearance in *Encounters of Sherlock Holmes* (Titan Books), and another due to appear in a future issue of *Sherlock Holmes Mystery Magazine*. Steve's work as both writer and editor has been shortlisted several times for British Fantasy Awards. He lives in Swansea and hates writing about himself in the third person.

David MacGregor is a playwright, screenwriter, and novelist. His plays have been performed from New York to Tasmania, and his work has been published by Dramatic Publishing, Playscripts, and Theatrical Rights Worldwide (TRW). He adapted his dark comedy, *Vino Veritas*, into a feature film, and several of his short plays have also been adapted into films. He is the author of three Sherlock Holmes plays: *Sherlock Holmes and the Adventure of the Elusive Ear, Sherlock Holmes and the Adventure of the Fallen Soufflé*, and *Sherlock Holmes and the Adventure of the Ghost Machine*. He adapted all three plays into novels for Orange Pip Books, and the novels have also been translated into Italian by Mondadori Publishing. In addition, he wrote the two-volume nonfiction *Sherlock Holmes: The Hero with a Thousand Faces*, which traces the evolution of the character over three centuries. He teaches writing at Wayne State University in Detroit. His website is: *david-macgregor.com*

David Marcum *also has stories in Parts XLIX, LI, and LII*

J. Lawrence Matthews has contributed fiction to *The New York Times* and *NPR*'s *All Things Considered* and is the author of *One Must Tell the Bees: Abraham Lincoln and the Final Education of Sherlock Holmes* (East Dean Press, 2021). The first novel to bring Sherlock Holmes together with Abraham Lincoln during the American Civil War, *One Must Tell the Bees* was called "*beautifully written and immediately engaging*" in the summer journal of *The Sherlock Holmes Society of London*. Matthews is at work on the sequel, which takes Sherlock Holmes to Tibet in 1891 for Holmes's encounter with the 13th Dalai Lama. He resides in Naples, FL, where his favorite breaks from writing are travel, book club meetings with his readers, visits from children and grandchildren, and, when the house gets a little too quiet, playing the drums.

John McNabb is a Welshman and an archaeologist, and a proud member of *The Sherlock Holmes Society of London*. He has published academic analysis of aspects of Conan Doyle's work, as well as its broader context. Mac also has a long-standing interest in Victorian and Edwardian scientific romances and the portrayal of human origins in early science fiction.

Paul Metcalfe has been a librarian for twenty-eight years, starting in public libraries, but is now the librarian at a technical college in rural Western Australia. He has been a lifelong Holmes fan since reading the original stories aged twelve, and now enjoys many of the later pastiches and Holmesian nonfiction as well. In 2005, he made the semifinals of the ABC television quiz show *The Einstein Factor* with the Sherlock Holmes stories by ACD as his special subject. He thinks Jeremy Brett is the television Holmes *nonpareil*, he collects old books and antiques, and is a strong advocate of the use of graphic novels to encourage reading. This is his first work of fiction.

Adrian Middleton is a Staffordshire-born independent publisher. The son of a real-world detective, he is a former civil servant and policy adviser who now writes and edits science fiction, fantasy, and a popular series of steampunked Sherlock Holmes stories.

Mark Mower is a long-standing member of the *Crime Writers' Association*, *The Sherlock Holmes Society of London*, and *The Solar Pons Society of London*. His pastiche collections include *Sherlock Holmes: The Baker Street Case-Files*, *Sherlock Holmes: The Baker Street Legacy*, *Sherlock Holmes: The Baker Street Epilogue*, and *Sherlock Holmes: The Baker Street Archive* (all with MX Publishing). His non-fiction works include the bestselling book *Zeppelin Over Suffolk: The Final Raid of the L48* (Pen & Sword Books). Alongside his writing, Mark maintains a sizeable collection of pastiches, and never tires of discovering new stories about Sherlock Holmes and Dr. Watson.

Will Murray is the author of some 75 novels, including some 20 posthumous Doc Savage collaborations with Lester Dent, and 40 books in the long-running Destroyer series. Other Murray novels star the Executioner, Tarzan of the Apes, The Spider, Pat Savage and the Mars Attacks characters. His book, *Nick Fury, Agent of S.H.I.E.L.D.: Empyre* (2000) foreshadowed the 9/11 terrorist attacks. Murray has penned nearly sixty Sherlock Holmes short stories. Murray's Holmes short stories have been collected as *The Wild Adventures of Sherlock Holmes*, Volumes 1 through 4. His novelette, "The Adventure of the Vengeful Viscount", in which Tarzan of the Apes, otherwise Lord Greystoke, hires Sherlock Holmes to solve a mystery, was approved by both the Estate of Sir Arthur Conan Doyle and Edgar Rice Burroughs, Inc. Murray is the author of the non-fiction book, *Master of Mystery: The Rise of The Shadow*, which is an exploration of the famous radio and magazine character, and a sequel, *Dark Avenger: The Strange Saga of The Shadow. The Wild Adventures of Cthulhu* Vols 1 & 2 collect Murray's Lovecraftian short stories. For Marvel Comics, Murray created the Unbeatable Squirrel Girl with legendary artist Steve Ditko. Website: *www.adventuresinbronze.com*

Paul W. Nash is a librarian, bibliographer, and printing historian. He has worked at the Royal Institute of British Architect's Library in London and the Bodleian Library in Oxford, and is currently editor of *The Journal of the Printing Historical Society*. He writes fiction and composes music as a relaxation.

Orlando Pearson is an accountant. He commutes into London by day and communes with the spirits of Baker Street by night. He was born a short rather than a long shot away from 221b. He is the creator of the series, *The Redacted Sherlock Holmes*, which runs to eight collections of short works, two novels, and a book of plays. A new collection of short works is appearing later this year and a Mycroftian novel will come out in 2026. These accounts of real events were redacted one-hundred or so years ago at the time The Canon was being published. The liberality of modern times means we can now read of Holmes's exposure of the rigging of the home-insurance market, his identification of an alternative claimant for the British throne, and his investigation into someone even better known than himself who rose from the dead. Orlando's profile can be found at:
https://www.amazon.co.uk/Orlando-Pearson/e/B07DWP857S/ref=dp_byline_cont_book_1

Tracy Revels *also has stories in Parts XLIX and LI*

A professional author since 2007, **Josh Reynolds** has over thirty novels to his name, as well as numerous short stories, novellas, and audio scripts. Born and raised in South Carolina, he now resides in Sheffield with his wife and daughter, as well as a highly excitable dog and something he hopes is a cat. A complete list of his work can be found at *https://joshuamreynolds.co.uk/*

Roger Riccard's family history has Scottish roots, which trace his lineage back to Highland Scotland. This ancestry encouraged his interest in the writings of Sir Arthur Conan Doyle. He has authored the novels, *Sherlock Holmes & The Case of the Poisoned Lilly*, and *Sherlock Holmes & The Case of the Twain Papers*, which was featured at the Museum of London Sherlock Holmes Exhibit in 2015. In addition, he has produced dozens of short stories, and has now joined the Sherlock Holmes 60+ Club, having exceeded Sir Arthur Conan Doyle's number of original Sherlock Holmes stories. All of his books have been published by Baker Street Studios and can be found at his website: *www.sherlockriccard.com* He credits his success to the encouragement of his wife/editor/inspiration and Sherlock Holmes fan, Rosilyn. She passed in 2021, and it is in her memory that he continues to contribute to the legacy of the *"man who never lived and will never die"*.

Dan Rowley practiced law for over forty years in private practice and with a large international corporation. He is retired and lives in Erie, Pennsylvania, with his wife Judy, who puts her artistic eye to his transcription of Watson's manuscripts. He inherited his writing ability and creativity from his children, Jim and Katy, and his love of mysteries from his parents, Jim and Ruth.

Jane Rubino is the author of *A Jersey Shore* mystery series, featuring a Jane Austen-loving amateur sleuth and a Sherlock Holmes-quoting detective, *Knight Errant, Lady Vernon and Her Daughter*, (a novel-length adaptation of Jane Austen's novella *Lady Susan*, co-authored with her daughter Caitlen Rubino-Bradway, *What Would Austen Do?*, also co-authored with her daughter, a short story in the anthology *Jane Austen Made Me Do It, The Rucastles' Pawn, The Copper Beeches from Violet Turner's POV*, and, of course, there's the Sherlockian novel *Hidden Fires*. Jane lives on a barrier island at the New Jersey shore.

Andrew Salmon has won several awards for his Sherlock Holmes stories and has been nominated for the Ellis, Pulp Ark, Pulp Factory and New Pulp Awards. He lives and writes in Vancouver, BC. His novels include: *Fight Card Sherlock Holmes: Work Capitol, Blood to the Bone*, and *A Congression of Pallbearers* (collected in the *Fight Card Sherlock Holmes Omnibus) The Dark Land, The Light Of Men*, and *Ghost Squad: Rise of the Black Legion* (with Ron Fortier) and his first children's book, *Wandering Webber*. His work has also appeared in numerous anthologies covering multiple genres. His tales from the award winning *Sherlock Holmes Consulting Detective* series were collected in *Sherlock Holmes Investigates. Ace of Devils*, the second novel in the Eby Stokes series featuring the female pugilist turned Special Branch agent, is out now and he's working on the third book, as well as a myriad of other projects. To learn more about his work check out: *amazon.com/Andrew-Salmon/e/B002NS5KR0*

Geri Schear is a novelist and short story writer. Her work has been published in literary journals in the U.S. and Ireland. Her first novel, *A Biased Judgement: The Diaries of Sherlock Holmes 1897* was released to critical acclaim in 2014. The sequel, *Sherlock Holmes and the Other Woman* was published in 2015, and *Return to Reichenbach* in 2016. *Great Warrior* was published in 2024. She lives in Kells, Ireland.

Brenda Seabrooke's stories have appeared in thirty-eight literary magazines, mystery anthologies, and magazines. Twenty books for young readers were published, and then two Sherlock's Dog books. She discovered that she liked writing about the world's greatest consulting detective and mysteries. Two collections of Sherlock Holmes stories were published by MX UK, and her stories have been included in "4 Best Mysteries of New England" (Level Best Books). She has received a grant from the NEA, a fellowship from Emerson College, and is an MWA runner-up. She has twice judged and once chaired Edgar mystery categories. Brenda is the former president of the Children's Book Guild of DC, a member of AG. *Viva* Holmes and Watson!

Shane Simmons is the author of the occult detective novels *necropolis* and *Epitaph*, and the crime collection *Raw and Other Stories*. An award-winning screenwriter and graphic novelist, his work has appeared in international film festivals, museums, and lectures about design and structure. He was born in Lachine, a suburb of Montreal best known for being massacred in 1689 and having a joke name. Visit Shane's homepage at *eyestrainproductions.com* for more information.

Robert V. Stapleton was born and brought up in Leeds, Yorkshire, England, and studied at Durham University. After working in various parts of the country as an Anglican parish priest, he is now retired and lives with his wife in North Yorkshire. As a member of his local writing group, he now has time to develop his other life as a writer of adventure stories. He has published a number of short stories, and he is hoping to have a couple of completed novels published at some time in the future.

Award winning poet and author **Joseph W. Svec III** enjoys writing, poetry, and stories, and creating new adventures for Holmes and Watson that take them into the worlds of famous literary authors and scientists. His *Missing Authors* trilogy introduced Holmes to Lewis Carroll, Jules Verne, H.G. Wells, and Alfred Lord Tennyson, as well as many of their characters. His transitional story *Sherlock Holmes and the Mystery of the First Unicorn* involved several historical figures, besides a Unicorn or two. He has also written the rhymed and metered Sherlock Holmes Christmas adventure, *The Night Before Christmas in 221b*, sure to be a delight for Sherlock Holmes enthusiasts of all ages. 2024 saw the publication of *Sherlock Holmes for Letter or Verse*. Joseph won the Amador Arts Council 2021 Original Poetry Contest, with his Rhymed and metered story poem, "The Homecoming". Joseph has presented a literary paper on Sherlock Holmes/Alice in Wonderland crossover literature to the Lewis Carroll Society of North America, as well as given several presentations to the Amador County Holmes Hounds, Sherlockian Society. He is currently working on his first book in the Missing Scientist Trilogy, *Sherlock Holmes and the Adventure of the Demonstrative Dinosaur*, in which Sherlock meets Professor George Edward Challenger. Joseph has Masters Degrees in Systems Engineering and Human Organization Management, and has written numerous technical papers on Aerospace Testing. In addition to writing, Joseph enjoys creating miniature dioramas based on music, literature, and history from many different eras. His dioramas have been featured in magazine articles and many different blogs, including the North American Jules Verne society newsletter. He currently has fifty-seven dioramas set up in his display area, and has written a reference book on toy castles and knights from around the world. An avid tea enthusiast, his tea cabinet contains over five-hundred different varieties, and he delights in sharing afternoon tea with his childhood sweetheart and wonderful wife, who has inspired and coauthored several books with him.

Kevin Thornton has, by his own count - and remember he's a writer, not an arithmetician – been in seventeen of these volumes, including this one. That's not a bad record, neither near the top nor the bottom, metaphor for his life mayhap. A middling student of English in South Africa, he was taught by two Nobel Literature Laureates to little noticeable effect, and has since been a soldier in Africa, a military contractor in Afghanistan, a forklift driver in Ontario, a bartender everywhere, and a logistician in Northern Alberta, which is, naturally, why he now works as a Communications Consultant for an Indigenous Nation of Cree, Denesuline, and Metis people. It has evolved into a good life, improved immeasurably by a tolerant, beautiful, and loving wife, two sons who smarter than they let on, and a Belgian Malinois with all of the energy of that breed and none of the intelligence. He lives in Northern Alberta, not quite in the North Pole, Santa Claus neighbourhood, but near enough for it to be a local telephone call. He is content.

William Todd has been a Holmes fan his entire life, and credits *The Hound of the Baskervilles* as the impetus for his love of both reading and writing. He began to delve into fan fiction a few years ago when he decided to take a break from writing his usual Victorian/Gothic horror stories. He was surprised how well-received they were, and has tried to put out a couple of Holmes stories a year since then. When not writing, Mr. Todd is a pathology supervisor at a local hospital in Northwestern Pennsylvania. He is the husband of a terrific lady and father to two great kids, one with special needs, so the benefactor of these anthologies is close to his heart.

A Sherlock Holmes fan since reading *The Hound of the Baskervilles* at about age twelve, **Tom Turley** has been writing pastiches since 2006. Most have appeared in previous volumes of *The MX Book of New Sherlock Holmes Stories*. All except the latest three have been collected in two books available from MX Publishing and Amazon. *Sherlock Holmes and the Crowned Heads of Europe* (2021) is a collection of four historical novellas that involve Holmes and Watson in the events leading up to World War I. The four stories are also available individually on Audible. As its title indicates, *Watson's Wives and Other Tales of Sherlock Holmes* (2023) focuses primarily on the Doctor's marriages. It likewise will soon be available on Audible. Currently, Tom is at work on a Sherlockian novel. A retired historian and archivist, he resides with his wife Paula in Montgomery, Alabama.

DJ Tyrer is the person behind Atlantean Publishing and has had fiction featuring Sherlock Holmes published in volumes from MX Publishing and Belanger Books, and an issue of *Awesome Tales*, and has a forthcoming story in *Sherlock Holmes Mystery Magazine*. DJ's non-Sherlockian mysteries can be found in anthologies such as *Mardi Gras Mysteries* (Mystery and Horror LLC) and *The Trench Coat Chronicles* (Celestial Echo Press), and on *Mystery Tribune*.
DJ Tyrer's website is at *https://djtyrer.blogspot.co.uk/*
DJ's Facebook page is at *https://www.facebook.com/DJTyrerwriter/*
The Atlantean Publishing website is at *https://atlanteanpublishing.wordpress.com/*

Peter Coe Verbica lives in the redwoods of Northern California. He grew up on Rancho San Felipe, a cattle ranch, where he learned the value of a strong work ethic. He obtained a BA from Santa Clara University, a JD from Santa Clara University School of Law and an MS from the Massachusetts Institute of Technology. Readers can find ten of his short stories in *The MX Book of New Sherlock Holmes Stories* anthologies, edited by David Marcum. These include "The Disfigured Hand", "The Magic Bullet", "The Adventure of the Matched Set", "The Musician Who Spoke from the Grave", "The Dutch Imposters", "A Ghost in the Mirror", "The Deceased Priest", "The King of Spades", "The Hyde Park Blackmailer", and, most recently, "The Ambassador's Dilemma". An additional seven stories, including "The Lucky Strike", "The Mystery of the Five Keys", "The Man Who Didn't Smoke", "The Noble Heart", "The Curious Case of the Bald Prince", "The Lost Uncle", and "Death at Hampton Court" can be found in *The Missing Tales of Sherlock Holmes*. Mr. Verbica is the author of non-fiction articles as well, including "Rise of the Rothschilds: A Legacy of Lessons", featured in *Opportunity Now Silicon Valley*, "We are thinking about . . . Artificial intelligence and trading platforms" featured by Silicon Private Wealth, and "The Divine Leaven of Self-Sacrifice (written in honor of Lenah Sutcliff Higbee)" presented at the Mast Stepping Ceremony of *USS Lenah Sutcliff Higbee* (DDG-123). His free verse works, such as "Small Mound of Stones", "A Visit with Quentin", "Dreams of a Burning Man", "The Locusts", "Visitor 231", "A Thanksgiving Lesson", "Small Miracles", "Brazil", Gold", "Fear of Long Words", "Speak Easy", "Heaven", "The Home Which Dreams", and scores of other pieces appear in various anthologies and books across the globe. The author has also served as moderator and host of a popular speaker series, featuring the former CTO of the US Space Force; Deputy Director of the National Intelligence Agency on cybersecurity; the former US Ambassador to Ukraine on Eurasian security issues; the former US Ambassador to Thailand on US-China relations; a former USN Rear Admiral on the importance of civility in society; an expert on US tax law

regarding proposed changes, and other speakers of merit, including the preeminent publisher of Sherlock Holmes-based fiction. Mr. Verbica currently serves as a Managing Director and Principal of Silicon Private Wealth, a Registered Investment Advisor where he helps "clients achieve their dreams through prudent and personalized investment planning." He won a top-two slot in the primary election for Board of Equalization in the State of California. He has served as President, Vice-President, and Chair for numerous non-profit local and statewide non-profit and political organizations' boards. For more information, please visit:
www.peterverbica.com

I.A. Watson *also has a story in Part LII*

Marcia Wilson *also has stories in Parts XLIX and LI*

The MX Book of New Sherlock Holmes Stories
Edited by David Marcum
(MX Publishing, 2015-2025)

"This is the finest volume of Sherlockian fiction I have ever read, and I have read, literally, thousands." – Philip K. Jones

"Beyond Impressive . . . This is a splendid venture for a great cause!"
– Roger Johnson, Editor, *The Sherlock Holmes Journal,*
The Sherlock Holmes Society of London

Part I: 1881-1889; Part II: 1890-1895; Part III: 1896-1929

Part IV: 2016 Annual

Part V: Christmas Adventures

Part VI: 2017 Annual

Eliminate the Impossible
Part VII: (1880-1891); Part VIII: (1892-1905)

2018 Annual
Part IX: (1879-1895); Part X: (1896-1916)

Some Untold Cases
Part XI: (1880-1891); Part XII: (1894-1902)

2019 Annual
Part XIII: (1881-1890); Part XIV: (1891-1897); Part XV: (1898-1917)

Whatever Remains . . . Must be the Truth
Part XVI: (1881-1890); Part XVII: (1891-1898); Part XVIII: (1898-1925)

2020 Annual
Part XIX: (1882-1890); Part XX: (1891-1897); Part XXI: (1898-1923)·

Some More Untold Cases
Part XXII: (1877-1887); Part XXIII: (1888-1894); Part XXIV: (1895-1903)

2021 Annual
Part XXV: (1881-1888); Part XXVI: (1889-1897); Part XXVII: (1898-1928)

More Christmas Adventures
Part XXVIII: (1869-1888); Part XXIX: (1889-1896); Part XXX: (1897-1928)

2022 Annual
Part XXXI: (1875-1887); Part XXXII: (1888-1895); Part XXXIII: (1896-1919)

"However Improbable . . . ."
Part XXXIV: (1878-1888); Part XXXV: (1889-1896); Part XXXVI: (1897-1919)

2023 Annual
Parts XXXVII (1875-1889), XXXVIII (1889-1896), and XXXIX (1897-1923)

Further Untold Cases
Part XL: (1879-1886), Part XLI: (1887-1892) and Part XLII: (1894-1922)

2024 Annual
Parts XLIII (1874-1888), XLIV (1889-1897), and XLV (1898-1917)

Occupants of the Canonical Realm
Parts XLVI (1861-1889), XLVII (1890-1898), and XLVIII (1899-1924)

The True Mr. Holmes: England's Greatest Hero
Parts XLIX and L (18XX-18XX) and (18XX-19XX)

473

The MX Book of New Sherlock Holmes Stories
Edited by David Marcum
(MX Publishing, 2015-2025)

475

An Investees' Anthology
Edited by David Marcum
(MX Publishing, 2022)

Selected Contributions to
The MX Book of New Sherlock Holmes Stories
by Members of
The Baker Street Irregulars

*All royalties from this collection are being donated
for the benefit of the preservation of Undershaw,
a school for special needs students located at
one of the former homes of Sir Arthur Conan Doyle*

Stories, Forewords, and Poems in this volume
have previously appeared in Parts I – XXXVI of
The MX Book of New Sherlock Holmes Stories

Featuring Contributions by:

Mark Alberstat, Marino C. Alvarez, Peter Calamai, Catherine Cooke, Carla Coupe, David Stuart Davies, John Farrell, Lyndsay Faye, Sonia Fetherston, Jayantika Ganguly, Jeffrey Hatcher, Roger Johnson, Leslie S. Klinger, Ann Margaret Lewis, Bonnie MacBird, Stephen Mason, Julie McKuras Nicholas Meyer, Jacquelynn Morris, Otto Penzler, Christopher Redmond, Tracy J. Revels, Steven Rothman, Nancy Holder, Mark Levy (and Arlene Mantin Levy), Nicholas Utechin, and Sean M. Wright (and DeForeest B. Wright, III)

478

MX Publishing

MX Publishing is the world's largest specialist Sherlock Holmes publisher, with over six-hundred titles and over two-hundred authors creating the latest in Sherlock Holmes fiction and non-fiction

The catalogue includes several award winning books, and over four-hundred-and-fifty have been converted into audio.

MX Publishing also has one of the largest communities of Holmes fans on Facebook, with regular contributions from dozens of authors.

www.mxpublishing.com

@mxpublishing on Facebook, Twitter, and Instagram